D0713267

# THE ESSENTIAL HAL CLEMENT

## Volume 1

## TRIO FOR SLIDE RULE AND TYPEWRITER

MN YA SF CLEMENT, H.

# THE ESSENTIAL HAL CLEMENT

## Volume 1
### TRIO FOR SLIDE RULE AND TYPEWRITER

## Hal Clement

edited by Mark L. Olson and Anthony R. Lewis

MESA PUBLIC LIBRARY

0738847113

The NESFA Press
Post Office Box 809
Framingham, MA 01701
1999

Copyright 1999 by Hal Clement

"Introduction"
Copyright 1999 by Poul Anderson

Dust jacket illustration
Copyright 1999 by "George Richard" (Hal Clement)

ALL RIGHTS RESERVED. NO PART OF THIS BOOK MAY BE RE-
PRODUCED IN ANY FORM OR BY ANY ELECTRONIC, MAGICAL
OR MECHANICAL MEANS INCLUDING INFORMATION STORAGE
AND RETRIEVAL WITHOUT PERMISSION IN WRITING FROM
THE PUBLISHER, EXCEPT BY A REVIEWER, WHO MAY QUOTE
BRIEF PASSAGES IN A REVIEW.

FIRST EDITION, February 1999

International Standard Book Number:
1-886778-06-X

# Acknowledgments

The introduction is original to this volume

*Needle* first appeared in *Astounding Science Fiction,* May–June 1949
*Iceworld* first appeared in *Astounding Science Fiction,* October–December 1951
*Close to Critical* first appeared in *Astounding Schence Fiction,* May–July 1958

All three novels appear by permission of the author.

The Author and Editors dedicate this book to
Monty Wells
who might have been the model of Sallman Ken
—without the tentacles, of course.

# Contents

# INTRODUCTION

by Poul Anderson

From time to time over the years, the honor and pleasure have fallen to me of writing an introduction to a book by someone else—L. Sprague de Camp, Gordon R. Dickson, Fritz Leiber, Clifford D. Simak, Jack Vance—and, once before now, Hal Clement, for the Gregg Press edition of his *Mission of Gravity.*

Honor indeed. I've asked myself, "What the dickens am *I* doing presenting *him?*" Usually the best answer seems to be that this is work reprinted after lapses of a decade or longer. Young readers, who have always made up the majority of the science fiction audience, will probably be unfamiliar with it. Given the annual avalanche of new books in the field these days, some may actually not recognize the author's name. My business has been to tell them, and everybody, that here is great stuff, which they are sure to enjoy and, in fact, get more out of than simply amusement.

As for pleasure, I have reread the stories, seeing how well they stand up, still fresh and lively (as if I ever doubted it), and often discovering aspects of them that I missed earlier. When they first appeared, they were inspirations to every other writer. Whether or not he or she did similar things—science fiction covers a mighty wide range, after all—these were shining, stimulating examples of how marvelously a concept could be developed and a theme handled. They remain wellsprings to which each of us can and should return

Therefore it is noble undertaking for the New England Science Fiction Association to issue three volumes of Hal Clement's tales, and I am delighted to offer a few words. For well over half a century, he has been a towering, even decisive figure in our special literature. A modest and soft-spoken man, he has never to my knowledge made any such claim himself, but it's true. He deserves to be properly appreciated.

Some background is in order. Intelligent nonhumans have been imagined for a long time, and a number were extraordinary; but they occurred in myth, folklore, or fantasy: gods, angels, demons, ghosts, elves, trolls, and whatever else. Several became cultural icons, such as the Minotaur. Vivid modern characters cover a spectrum from Tolkien's Ents to Mr. O'Malley, the ineffectual fairy godfather in the lamented comic strip *Barnaby,* and there is no dearth of laudable creations nowadays. However, they all belong to a different class from fictional "real-life" figures— Romeo and Juliet, say, or Oliver Twist or, for that matter, the dog Buck in Jack London's *The Call of the Wild.* Living things that we have never encountered but that might possibly, or at least conceivably, exist in the same way we do, subject to the same laws of nature as us, are a rather recent literary phenomenon. First humans had to gain some scientific understanding of the universe,

Then the aliens started to spring forth—for instance, the "sky-blue man with seven heads and only one leg" that Mark Twain's Captain Stormfield spied on his way to Heaven. Truly *science* fictional examples are hard to find before H. G. Wells; and he doesn't go into much detail about his Martians or his dwellers in the oceanic abyss, while his Selenites are meant satirically. Nevertheless, and understandably, they were enormously influential on later writers.

A while afterward, extraterrestrials were proliferating in pulp science fiction and in not a few books, some of the latter seriously intended (notably those of Olaf Stapledon). But hardly any were the slightest bit convincing. Many were human, with occasional variations such as pointy ears, green skin, or four arms. Nearly all the rest were no more believable, and generally far less interesting: chimeras that could never have evolved or survived anywhere, more often than not senselessly hostile to Earthlings.

In 1934 Stanley Weinbaum started a revolution with his "A Martian Odyssey." Here were creatures truly strange, yet entirely plausible in their unearthly environment. The sapient individual, unforgettable long-beaked Tweel, was eager to make friends and reach mutual understanding with the human explorers. This was far from easy, because the mentalities were as unlike as the bodies, a dazzling glimpse into the wonder and mystery of the cosmos. Weinbaum went on to other worlds of the Solar System, trying to stay within the bounds of what science knew or conjectured about them. That has completely changed, of course, but the stories are still grand reading.

A tragically premature death cut his career short. Had he lived, science fiction would have grown up faster than it did. As was, his work affected such writers as John W. Campbell and E. E. Smith, themselves seminal but nothing comparable to his imagination, both bold and disciplined, came along for a number of years.

Then in June 1942 we got a short story, "Proof," by somebody called Hal Clement.

I don't know to what extent it derived from the visions of Stapledon, if at all, and that makes no difference. To take a colleague's idea and carry it further, or in a new direction, has always been a legitimate and vitalizing practice, not only in science fiction but throughout literature. As brilliant as the stars themselves, "Proof" showed sentient beings living in them, even traveling among them, to whom solid matter was unknown. When one spacefarer ran into one insignificant object, namely Earth, not only did he never comprehend what had happened, afterward his story was never believed.

Granted, the basic concept was far-fetched, although modern research into plasmoids and magnetohydrodynamics has made it somewhat less so, but Clement developed it with rigorous logic in a tale that was hugely entertaining to boot.

The aliens in "Impediment," August 1942, were of organic material, as most Clement life forms have been, but telepathic. This was the single fantastic assumption he allowed himself, aside from faster-than-light spaceships. otherwise the voyagers were scientifically credible, including their nonhumanness. And the inherent limitations of the telepathy were the theme, a completely original suggestion.

The author's real name was Harry C. Stubbs. At the time he was majoring in astronomy at Harvard. He used a pseudonym because he didn't want his professors looking on him as a nut. Later he found out that one of the most distinguished had also been trying, but failing, to publish science fiction under a pen name,

Shortly afterward he went off to war, serving in the then Army Air Corps. He is among the few men who have flown a heavy bomber on a rooftop mission. Only two or three more Clement stories appeared before the end of hostilities, unique, thoughtful, and beguiling. Back again in civilian life, he had more time to spare for writing. It was, though, a sideline. He became a science teacher at a prestigious prep school, active in civic affairs and a regular blood donor. He was in the Air Force Reserve until he retired with the rank of colonel. He got married and continues to be a dedicated family man, who today will gladly show you pictures of his grandchild. He took up painting as a hobby, mainly of astronomical scenes, and has exhibited his work in art shows, under another alias so that it would be judged on its own merits. He has often attended science fiction conventions, where his genial personality makes him doubly welcome.

Somehow he has also managed to produce a comparatively small but important body of novels and shorter fiction. Now that he's likewise retired from teaching, perhaps we can hope for more. Certainly the years have not diminished his talents.

His most famous work is doubtless *Mission of Gravity*, in which he created a totally unearthlike world and its inhabitants in breathtaking detail. Later scientific discoveries have upset some of the assumptions he made, but this is the common fate of science fiction, especially the "hard" sort. It has nothing to do with the impact of the tale, its deep and abiding influence, or its sheer readability.

But he has given us others that are fully comparable. Here are three short novels, far too long out of print. Each of them broke new ground a and provoked new thought. Each of them is not just imaginative yet solidly timbered, it's fun.

Let's glance at them in chronological order.

John Campbell, who went from writing to editing and led the development of modern science fiction, once declared that a mystery story within this field was impossible. He meant the classic kind, where the reader is given all the clues and has a chance to solve the puzzle before the detective does. How can this be done when an author is free to pull anything out of the hat? He probably intended the remark as a challenge, and Hal Clement was very likely the first to rise to it. *Needle* (1949) was the result.

In it, an extraterrestrial police officer is pursuing a criminal of his race across interstellar space. Both are wrecked on Earth. The bad one escapes, and the good one sets out to find him before he can do worse harm. Both are wholly foreign to humans, small jellylike globs with a viruslike rather than a cellular structure, who can infiltrate and interact with animals more nearly similar to us, including us. Clement explores and explains this concept so well that a reader may readily decide something of the kind must exist somewhere in the galaxy. The Hunter's task looks hopeless. He goes into symbiotic partnership with a human, but his quarry could be hiding inside anybody else. Clement lays the clues in front of you, skillfully and fairly.

Needle's chief terrestrial character is young but intelligent, brave, and resourceful. This is the case in several Clement books. Perhaps his service as a counsellor to the Boy Scouts has had something to do with this. Moreover, he was among the first writers in the field to show females with the same strengths.

Nearly all his stories share certain qualities. The people in them, human and nonhuman, are generally well-intentioned and cooperative. When they become antagonists, it is usually out of necessity, or what they perceive as necessity, and the conflict stays within moral bounds. Even the few out-and-out villains are seldom monstrously evil, as too many real-life humans have been. Characters are apt to talk quite a lot, but it is excellent conversation, interesting and to the point. The narrative builds up to an exciting denouement and then ends where it ought to end, with no dragged-out anticlimax.

As I observed before, scientific and technological obsolescence is inevitable in science fiction. (The overtaking of imagined social events by actual history is too.) Hence in this volume you'll see occasional things like slide rules aboard starships, and computers are not much in evidence. So what? Nobody this side of God can foresee everything. If somehow he or she could, and wrote it today, the text would be incomprehensible to us. That spectacles are mentioned in *King Lear* and cannon in *King John* doesn't detract from Shakespeare's achievements. We must take literature on its own terms, in its own context.

As a matter of fact, *Needle* gets ahead of its setting. It describes biological production of oil as a going industry. To date, we merely wish that this will come to pass before it is too late.

Faster-than-light travel commonly figures in Clement's work, as in that of many of his fellows. It's necessary when characters are to get from star to star in a reasonable time, but has seemed an impossibility. Probably most physicists still think so. However, recent work on the frontiers of general relativity suggests that it may somehow, someday be attainable. In that case, Clement's reputation for scientific fidelity will gain even more stature.

Almost thirty years after *Needle,* he wrote a sequel, *Through the Eye of a Needle.* Unlike most sequels, it's just as fine as the original.

Meanwhile, in 1953, *Iceworld* had come out. It also involves a police operation, though in that respect it's a straight crime story rather than a mystery. Otherwise everything it presents is new. The gloomy, lethally cold iceworld is our Earth, seen by the natives of a planet where normal temperatures are in the hundreds of degrees. Again the physics and chemistry are worked out with loving care.

This novel is clearly a bit dated—which of course, doesn't lessen its interest. Astrophysicists now believe A-type stars have too short a residence time on the main sequence for much, if anything, in the way of life to develop on any planets they may have. (But Sallman Ken's home sun may be a late type A, longer-lived, and evolution may have proceeded very fast under its fierce radiation.) The planets of our Solar System have turned out to be different from what was supposed forty-odd years ago; and we already have better techniques for investigating them than these visitors from afar do. (But the excitement of exploring them has never been better evoked than it is here.) once again, none of this really matters to the story.

The vile drug the alien crook is obtaining from Earth is tobacco. Clement's a lifelong nonsmoker. still, in view of current attitudes toward the habit, we may perhaps consider this a piece of foresight.

*Close to Critical* (1958) shows us yet another weird planet, and now we get to see it on the ground through native and human eyes. Tenebra is more massive than Earth, not enough so to be a gas giant but with thrice the surface gravity and a vast atmosphere. Conditions of temperature and pressure are such that between night and day, water changes from the liquid to the gaseous state. The consequences for geology, biology, and sapience are fascinating. The story itself is as rattling good as its companions. The outsiders who descend by accident and badly need rescue are two children, human and nonhuman. The former is a little girl, whose intelligence and indomitability recall several of Robert Heinlein's characters.

Hal Clement, though, is very much his own man, in writing as in everyday life. There's nobody like him. He's been a tremendous force in science fiction, receiving honors for it but not nearly enough. Here are three examples. Read, learn, think, and, above all, enjoy.

# NEEDLE

# I. Castaway

Even on the Earth shadows are frequently good places to hide. They may show up, of course, against lighted surroundings, but if there is not too much light from the side, one can step into a shadow and become remarkably hard to see.

Beyond the Earth, where there is no air to scatter light, they should be even better. The Earth's own shadow, for example, is a million-mile-long cone of darkness pointing away from the sun, invisible itself in the surrounding dark and bearing the seeds of still more perfect invisibility—for the only illumination that enters that cone is starlight and the feeble rays bent into its blackness by the Earth's thin envelope of air.

The Hunter knew he was in a planet's shadow though he had never heard of the earth; he had known it ever since he had dropped below the speed of light and seen the scarlet-rimmed disk of black squarely ahead of him; and so he took it for granted that the fugitive vessel would be detectable only by instruments. When he suddenly realized that the other ship was visible to the naked eye, the faint alarm that had been nibbling at the outskirts of his mind promptly rocketed into the foreground.

He had been unable to understand why the fugitive should go below the speed of light at all, unless in the vague hope that the pursuer would overrun him sufficiently to be out of detection range; and when that failed, the Hunter had expected a renewed burst of speed. Instead, the deceleration continued. The fleeing ship had kept between his own and the looming world ahead, making it dangerous to overhaul too rapidly; and the Hunter was coming to the conclusion that a break back on the direction they had come was to be expected when a spark of red light visible to the naked eye showed that the other had actually entered an atmosphere. The planet was smaller and closer than the Hunter had believed.

The sight of that spark was enough for the pursuer. He flung every erg his generators could handle into a drive straight away from the planet, at the same time pouring the rest of his body into the control room to serve as a gelatinous cushion to protect the *perit* from the savage deceleration; and he saw instantly that it would not be sufficient. He had just time to wonder that the creature ahead of him should be willing to risk ship and host in what would certainly be a nasty crash before the outer fringes of the world's air envelope added their resistance to his plunging flight and set the metal plates of his hull glowing a brilliant orange from heat.

Since the ships had dived straight down the shadow cone, they were going to strike on the night side, of course; and once the hulls cooled, the fugitive would again be invisible. With an effort, therefore, the Hunter kept his eyes glued to the instruments that would betray the other's whereabouts as long as he was in range; and it was well that he did so, for the glowing cylinder vanished abruptly from sight into a vast cloud of water vapor that veiled the planet's dark surface. A split second later the Hunter's ship plunged into the same mass, and as it did so there was a twisting lurch, and the right-line deceleration changed to a sickening spinning motion. The pilot knew that one of the drive plates had gone, probably cracked off by undistributed heat, but there was simply no time to do a thing about it. The other vessel, he noted, had stopped as though it had run into a brick wall; now it was settling again, but far more slowly, and he realized that he himself could only be split seconds from the same obstacle, assuming it to be horizontal.

It was. The Hunter's ship, still spinning wildly although he had shut off the remaining drive plates at the last moment, struck almost flat on water and at the impact split open from end to end along both sides as though it had been an eggshell stepped on by a giant. Almost all its kinetic energy was absorbed by that blow, but it did not stop altogether. It continued to settle, comparatively gently now, with a motion like a falling leaf, and the Hunter felt its shattered hull come to a rest on what he realized must be the bottom of a lake or sea a few seconds later.

At least, he told himself as his wits began slowly to clear, his quarry must be in the same predicament. The abrupt stoppage and subsequent slow descent of the other machine was now explained—even if it had struck head on instead of horizontally, there would have been no perceptible difference in the result of a collision with a water surface at their speed. It was almost certainly unusable, though perhaps not quite so badly damaged as the Hunter's ship.

That idea brought the train of thought back to his own predicament. He felt cautiously around him and found he was no longer entirely in the control room—in fact, there was no longer room for all of him inside it.

What had been a cylindrical chamber some twenty inches in diameter and two feet long was now simply the space between two badly dented sheets of inch-thick metal which had been the hull. The seams had parted on either side, or, rather, seams had been created and forced apart, for the hull was originally a single piece of metal drawn into tubular shape. The top and bottom sections thus separated had been flattened out and were now only an inch or two apart on the average. The bulkheads at either end of the room had crumpled and cracked—even that tough alloy had its limitations. The *perit* was very dead. Not only had it been crushed by the collapsing wall, but the Hunter's semiliquid body had transmitted the shock of impact to its individual cells much as it is transmitted to the sides of a water-filled tin can by the impact of a rifle bullet, and most of its interior organs had ruptured. The Hunter, slowly realizing this, withdrew from around and within the little creature. He did not attempt to eject its mangled remains from the ship; it might be necessary to use them as food later on, though the idea was unpleasant. The Hunter's attitude toward the animal resembled that of a man toward a favorite dog, though the *perit*, with its delicate hands which it had learned to use at his direction much as an elephant uses its trunk at the behest of man, was more useful than any dog.

He extended his exploration a little, reaching out with a slender pseudopod of jellylike flesh through one of the rents in the hull. He already knew that the wreck was lying in salt water, but he had no idea of the depth other than the fact that it was not excessive. On his home world he could have judged it quite accurately from the pressure; but pressure depends on the weight of a given quantity of water as well as its depth, and he had not obtained a reading of this planet's gravity before the crash.

It was dark outside the hull. When he molded an eye from his own tissue—those of the *perit* had been ruptured—it told him absolutely nothing of his surroundings. Suddenly, however, he realized that the pressure around him was not constant; it was increasing and decreasing by a rather noticeable amount with something like regularity; and the water was transmitting to his sensitive flesh the higher-frequency pressure waves which he interpreted as sound. Listening intently, he finally decided that he must be fairly close to the surface of a body of water large enough to develop waves a good many feet in height, and that a storm of considerable violence was in progress. He had not noticed any disturbance in the air during his catastrophic descent, but that meant nothing—he had spent too little time in the atmosphere to be affected by any reasonable wind.

Poking into the mud around the wreck with other pseudopods, he found to his relief that the planet was not lifeless—he had already been pretty sure of that fact. There was enough oxygen dissolved in the water to meet his needs, provided he did not exert himself greatly, and there must, consequently, be free oxygen in the atmosphere above. It was just as well, though, to have actual proof that life was present rather than merely possible, and he was well satisfied to locate in the mud a number of small bivalve mollusks which, upon trial, proved quite edible.

Realizing that it was night on this part of the planet, he decided to postpone further outside investigation until there was more light, and turned his attention back to the remains of his ship. He had not expected the examination to turn up anything encouraging, but he got a certain glum feeling of accomplishment as he realized the completeness of the destruction. Solid metal parts in the engine room had changed shape under the stresses to which they had been subjected. The nearly solid conversion chamber of the main drive unit was flattened and twisted. There was no trace whatever of certain quartz-shelled gas tubes; they had evidently been pulverized by the shock and washed away by the water. No living creature handicapped by a definite shape and solid parts could have hoped to come through such a crash alive, no matter how well protected. The thought was some comfort; he had done his best for the perit even though that had not been sufficient.

Once satisfied that nothing usable remained in his ship, the Hunter decided no more could be done at the moment. He could not undertake really active work until he had a better supply of oxygen, which meant until he reached open air; and the lack of light was also a severe handicap. He relaxed, therefore, in the questionable shelter of the ruined hull and waited for the storm to end and the day to come. With light and calm water he felt that he could reach shore without assistance; the wave noise suggested breakers, which implied a beach at no great distance.

He lay there for several hours, and it occurred to him once that he might be on a planet which always kept the same hemisphere toward its sun; but he realized that in such a case the dark side would almost certainly be too cold for water to exist as a liquid. It seemed more probable that storm clouds were shutting out the daylight.

Ever since the ship had finally settled into the mud it had remained motionless. The disturbances overhead were reflected in currents and back-washes along the bottom which the Hunter could feel but which were quite unable to shift the half-buried mass of metal. Certain as he was that the hull was now solidly fixed in place, the castaway was suddenly startled when his shelter quivered as though to a heavy blow and changed position slightly.

Instantly he sent out an inquiring tentacle. He molded an eye at its tip, but the darkness was still intense, and he returned to strictly tactile exploration. Vibrations suggestive of a very rough skin scraping along the metal were coming to him, and abruptly something living ran into the extended limb. It demonstrated its sentient quality by promptly seizing the appendage in a mouth that seemed amazingly well furnished with saw-edged teeth.

The Hunter reacted normally, for him—that is, he allowed the portion of himself in direct contact with those unpleasant edges to relax into a semiliquid condition, and at the same moment he sent more of his body flowing into the arm toward the strange creature. He was a being of quick decisions, and the evident size of the intruder had impelled him to a somewhat foolhardy act. He left the wrecked space ship entirely and sent his whole four pounds of jellylike flesh toward what he hoped would prove a more useful conveyance.

The shark—it was an eight-foot hammerhead—may have been surprised and was probably irritated, but in common with all its kind it lacked the brains to be afraid. Its ugly jaws snapped hungrily at what at first seemed like satisfyingly solid flesh, only to have it give way before them like so much water. The Hunter made no attempt to avoid the teeth, since mechanical damage of that nature held no terrors for him, but he strenuously resisted the efforts of the fish to swallow that portion of his body already in its mouth. He had no intention of exposing himself to gastric juices, since he had no skin to resist their action even temporarily.

As the shark's activities grew more and more frantically vicious, he sent exploring pseudopods over the ugly rough-skinned form, and within a few moments discovered the five gill slits on each side of the creature's neck. That was enough. He no longer investigated; he acted, with a skill and precision born of long experience.

The Hunter was a metazoon—a many-celled creature, like a bird or a man—in spite of his apparent lack of structure. The individual cells of his body, however, were far smaller than those of most earthly creatures, comparing in size with the largest protein molecules. It was possible for him to construct from his tissues a limb, complete with muscles and sensory nerves, the whole structure fine enough to probe through the capillaries of a more orthodox creature without interfering seriously with its blood circulation. He had, therefore, no difficulty in insinuating himself into the shark's relatively huge body.

He avoided nerves and blood vessels for the moment and poured himself into such muscular and visceral interstices as he could locate. The shark calmed down at once after the thing in its mouth and on its body ceased sending tactile messages to its minute brain; its memory, to all intents and purposes, was nonexistent. For the Hunter, however, successful interstition was only the beginning of a period of complicated activity.

First and most important, oxygen. There was enough of the precious element absorbed on the surfaces of his body cells for a few minutes of life at the most, but it could always be obtained in the body of a creature that also consumed oxygen; and the Hunter rapidly sent submicroscopic appendages between the cells that formed the walls of blood vessels and began robbing the blood cells of their precious load. He needed but little, and on his home world he had lived in this manner for years within the body of an intelligent oxygen-breather, with the other's full knowledge and consent. He had more than paid for his keep.

The second need was vision. His host presumably possessed eyes, and with his oxygen supply assured the Hunter began to search for them. He could, of course, have sent enough of his own body out through the shark's skin to construct an organ of vision, but he might not have been able to avoid disturbing the creature by such an act. Besides, ready-made lenses were usually better than those he could make himself.

His search was interrupted before it had gone very far. The crash had, as he had deduced, occurred rather close to land; the encounter with the shark had taken place in quite shallow water. Sharks are not particularly fond of disturbance; it is hard to understand why this one had been so close to the surf. During the monster's struggle with the Hunter it had partly drifted and partly swum closer to the beach; and with its attention no longer taken up by the intruder, it tried to get back into deep water. The shark's continued frenzied activity, *after* the oxygen-theft system had been established, started a chain of events which caught the alien's attention.

The breathing system of a fish operates under a considerable disadvantage. The oxygen dissolved in water is never at a very high concentration, and a water-breathing creature, though it may be powerful and active, never has a really large reserve of the gas. The Hunter was not taking very much to keep alive, but he was trying to build up a reserve of his own as well; and with the shark working at its maximum energy output, the result was that its oxygen consumption was exceeding its intake. That, of course, had two effects: the monster's physical strength began to decline and the oxygen content of its blood to decrease. With the latter occurrence the Hunter almost unconsciously increased his drain on the system, thereby starting a vicious circle that could have only one ending.

The Hunter realized what was happening long before the shark actually died but did nothing about it, though he could have reduced his oxygen consumption without actually killing himself. He could also have left the shark, but he had no intention of drifting around in comparative helplessness in the open sea, at the mercy of the first creature large and quick enough to swallow him whole. He remained, and kept on absorbing the life-bearing gas, for he had realized that so much effort would be needed only if the fish were fighting the waves—striving to bear him away from the shore he wanted to reach. He had judged perfectly by this time the shark's place in the evolutionary scale and had no more compunction about killing it than would a human being.

The monster took a long time to die, though it became helpless quite rapidly. Once it ceased to struggle, the Hunter continued the search for its eyes, and eventually found them. He deposited a film of himself between and around their retinal cells, in anticipation of the time when there would be enough light for him to see. Also, since the now-quiescent shark was showing a distressing tendency to sink, the alien began extending other appendages to trap any air bubbles which might be brought near by the storm. These, together with the carbon dioxide he produced himself, he gradually accumulated in the fish's abdominal cavity to give buoyancy. He needed very little gas for this purpose, but it took him a long time to collect it, since he was too small to produce large volumes of carbon dioxide very rapidly.

The breakers were sounding much more loudly by the time he was able to take his attention from these jobs, and he realized that his assumption of a shoreward drift was justified. The waves were imparting a sickening up-and-down motion to his unusual raft, which neither bothered nor pleased him; it was horizontal motion he wanted, and that was comparatively slow until the water became quite shallow.

He waited for a long time after his conveyance stopped moving, expecting each moment to be floated and dragged back into deep water again, but nothing happened, and gradually the sound of waves began to decrease slightly and the amount of spray falling on him to diminish. The Hunter suspected that the storm was dying out. Actually, the tide had turned; but the result was the same as far as he was concerned.

By the time the combination of approaching dawn and thinning storm clouds provided enough light for his surroundings to be visible, his late host was well above the reach of the heaviest waves. The shark's eyes would not focus on their own retinas out of water, but the Hunter found that the new focal surface was inside the eyeball and built a retina of his own in the appropriate place. The lenses also turned out to be a little less than perfect, but he modified their curvature with some of his own body substance and eventually found himself able to see his surroundings without exposing himself to the view of others.

There were rifts in the storm clouds now through which a few of the brightest stars were still visible against the gray background of approaching dawn. Slowly these breaks grew larger, and by the time the sun rose the sky was almost clear, though the wind still blew fiercely.

His vantage point was not ideal, but he was able to make out a good deal of his surroundings. In one direction the beach extended a short distance to a line of tall, slender trees crowned with feathery tufts of leaves. He could not see beyond these, his point of observation being too low, though they were not themselves set thickly enough to obstruct the view. In the opposite direction was more debris-strewn beach, with the roar of the still-heavy surf sounding beyond it. The Hunter could not actually see the ocean, but its direction was obvious. To the right was a body of water which, he realized, must be a small pool, filled by the storm and now emptying back into the sea through an opening too small or too steep for the surf to enter. This was probably the only reason the shark had stranded at all—it had been washed into this pool and left there by the receding tide.

Several times he heard raucous screeching sounds and saw birds overhead. This pleased him greatly; evidently there were higher forms of life than fishes on the planet, and there was some hope of obtaining a more suitable host. An intelligent one would be best, since an intelligent creature is ordinarily best able to protect itself. It would also be more likely to travel widely, thus facilitating the now-necessary search for the pilot of the other ship. It was very likely, however, as the Hunter fully realized, that there would be serious difficulty in obtaining access to the body of an intelligent creature who was not accustomed to the idea of symbiosis.

All that, however, would have to wait on chance. Even if there were intelligent beings on this planet, they might never come to this spot; and even if they did, he might not recognize them for what they were in time to get any good out of the situation. It would be best to wait, several days if need be, to observe just what forms of life frequented this locality; after that he could make plans to invade the one best suited to his needs. Time was probably not vital; it was as certain as anything could be that his quarry was no more able to leave the planet than was the Hunter himself, and while he remained on it the search would be decidedly tedious. Time spent in careful preparation would undoubtedly pay dividends.

He waited, therefore, while the sun rose higher and the wind gradually died down to a mild breeze. It became quite warm; and he was aware before long of chemical changes going on in the flesh of the shark. They were changes which made it certain that, if a sense of smell were common to many of the creatures of this world, he was bound to have visitors before too long. The Hunter could have halted the process of decay by the simple expedient of consuming the bacteria that caused it, but he was not particularly hungry and certainly had no objection to visitors. On the contrary!

# II. Shelter

The first visitors were gulls. One by one they descended, attracted by sight and smell, and began tearing at the carcass of the shark. The Hunter withdrew to the lower parts of the body and made no attempt to drive them off, even when they pounced upon the eyes of the great fish and speedily deprived him of visual contact with the outside world. If other life forms came he would know it anyway; if they didn't, it was just as well to have the gulls there.

The greedy birds remained undisturbed until midafternoon. They did not make too much progress in disposing of the shark—the tough skin defied their beaks in most places. They were persistent, however, and when they suddenly took wing and departed in a body, it was evident to the Hunter that there must be something of interest in the neighborhood. He hastily extruded enough tissue from one of the gill slits to make an eye and looked cautiously about him.

He saw why the gulls had left. From the direction of the trees a number of much larger creatures were coming. They were bipeds, and the Hunter estimated with the ease of long practice that the largest weighed fully a hundred and twenty pounds, which, in an air-breather, meant that the addition of his own mass and oxygen consumption was unlikely to prove a serious burden. Much closer to him was a smaller four-legged creature running rapidly toward the dead shark and uttering an apparently endless string of sharp yelping sounds. The Hunter placed it at about fifty pounds and filed the information mentally for future use.

The four bipeds were also running, but not nearly so rapidly as the smaller animal. As they approached, the hidden watcher examined them carefully, and the more he saw the more pleased he was. They could travel with fair speed; their skulls were of a size that gave promise of considerable intelligence, if one could safely assume that this race kept its brain there; their skins seemed almost entirely unprotected, giving promise of easy access through the pores. As they slowed up and stopped beside the hammerhead's body, they gave another indication of intelligence by exchanging articulate sounds which unquestionably represented speech. The Hunter, to put it mildly, was delighted. He had not dared hope for such an ideal host to appear so quickly.

Of course there were problems still to be solved. It was a fairly safe bet that the creatures were not accustomed to the idea of symbiosis, at least as the Hunter's race practiced it. The alien was sure he had never seen members of this race before, and was equally sure he knew all those with whom his people normally associated. Therefore, if these beings actually saw him approaching, they would almost certainly go to considerable lengths to avoid contact; and even if this proved futile, forcible entry on the Hunter's part would create an attitude highly unlikely to lead to future co-operation. It seemed, therefore, that subtlety would have to be employed.

The four bipeds remained looking down at the shark and conversing for only a few minutes, then they walked off a short distance up the beach. Somehow the Hunter got a vague impression from their attitudes that they found the neighborhood unpleasant. The quadruped remained a little longer, examining the carcass closely; but it apparently failed to notice the rather oddly placed eye which was following its movements. A call from one of the other creatures finally attracted its attention, and as the Hunter watched it bounded off in the direction they had taken. He saw with some surprise that they had entered the water and were swimming around with considerable facility. He marked down the fact as another point in their favor; he had seen no trace of gills in his rather careful examination of their bodies, and as air-breathers they must have had a considerable margin between their ability to absorb oxygen and their actual need for it to remain under water as long as he saw one of them do. Then he realized that there was another good point: he could probably approach them much more easily in the water.

It was evident from their behavior that they could not see very well, if at all, under water—they invariably raised their heads above the surface to orient themselves, and did this with considerable frequency. The quadruped was even less likely to see him approaching, as it kept its head above water at all times.

The thought led to instant action. A threadlike pseudopod began groping rapidly toward the pool an inch or two under the sand. The eye was kept in operation until most of the jelly-like body had crossed the four-yard gap, then another was formed at the water's edge, and the Hunter drew the rest of his body into a compact mass just below it. The operation had taken several minutes; winding among sand grains had been an annoyingly devious mode of travel.

The water was quite clear, so it was not necessary to keep an eye above the surface to direct the stalk. The mass of jelly quickly molded itself into an elongated, fishlike shape with an eye in front, and the Hunter swam toward the boys as rapidly as he could. In one way, he reflected, it was really easier to see under water. He could use a concave lens of air, held in shape by a film of his own flesh, which was far more transparent than an optical system composed entirely of the latter substance.

He had intended to swim right up to one of the boys, hoping his approach would not be noticed and his efforts at contact marked by swirling water or his subject's friends—they were indulging in acts of considerable violence as they swam and plunged. However, it speedily became evident that only luck would bring him in contact with one of the creatures, since they swam much more rapidly than the Hunter could; and, realizing this, he found what seemed to be an excellent means of making an undercover approach. He suddenly noticed beside him a large jelly-fish, bobbing rather aimlessly along after the manner of its kind; and with his attention thus diverted, he saw that there were quite a number of the things in the vicinity. Evidently the bipeds did not consider them dangerous or they would not be swimming here.

Accordingly, the Hunter altered his form and method of locomotion to agree with those of the medusae and approached more slowly the area in which the boys were playing. His color was slightly different from that of any of the other jellyfish but these, in turn, differed among themselves, and he felt that shape must be a more important criterion than shade. He may have been right, for he got almost up to one of the bipeds without apparently causing any alarm. They were fairly close together at the moment, and he had high hopes of making contact—he did, in fact, with a cautiously extended tentacle, discover that the varicolored integument covering a portion of their bodies was an artificial fabric—but before he could do any more, the subject of his investigation slid to one side and moved several feet away. He gave no sign of alarm, however, and the Hunter tried again. The approach ended in precisely the same fashion, except that this time he did not get so close.

He tried each of the other boys in turn, with the same annoying near-success. Then, puzzled by a phenomenon which seemed to be exceeding the generous limits of the law of chance, he drifted a short distance away and watched, trying to learn the reason for it. Within five minutes he realized that, while these creatures seemed to have no actual fear of jellyfish, they sedulously avoided physical contact with them. He had chosen an unfortunate camouflage.

Robert Kinnaird avoided jellyfish almost without conscious thought. He had learned to swim at the age of five, and in that and each of the nine subsequent years of his life he had enough first-hand experience with their stinging tentacles to assure his avoiding their company. He had been fully occupied in ducking one of his companions when the Hunter had first touched him, and even though he had dodged hastily on noticing the lump of jelly in the water beside him he had not really thought about the matter—if he did, it was merely a brief reflection that he was lucky not to have been stung. He forgot the incident promptly, but his attention had been sufficiently diffused by it to prevent the thing's again approaching so closely.

About the time the Hunter realized what was wrong, the boys grew tired of swimming and retired to the beach. He watched them go in mounting annoyance, and continued to watch as they ran back and forth on the sand playing some obscure game. Were the mad creatures never still? How in the Galaxy could he ever come in contact with such infernally active beings? He could only watch, and ponder.

Ashore, once the salt had dried on their sun-browned hides, the boys did finally begin to quiet down and cast expectant glances toward the grove of coconut palms between them and the center of the island. One of them seated himself, facing the ocean, and suddenly spoke.

"Bob, when are your folks coming with the grub?"

Robert Kinnaird flung himself face downward in the sun before replying. "'Bout four or half-past, Mother said. Don't you ever think of anything but eating?"

The redheaded questioner mumbled an inarticulate reply and subsided flat on his back, gazing up into the now cloudless blue sky. Another of the boys took up the conversational ball.

"It's tough, you having to go tomorrow," he said. "I kind of wish I was going with you, though. I haven't been in the States since my folks came out here. I was only a kid then," he added serenely,

"It's not so bad," returned Bob slowly. "There are a lot of good fellows at the school, and there's skating and skiing in the winter that you don't get here. Anyway, I'll be back next summer."

The talk died down and the boys basked in the hot sunshine as they waited for Mrs. Kinnaird and the food for the farewell picnic. Bob was closest to the water, lying stretched in full sunlight; the others had sought the rather inadequate shade of the palms. He was already well tanned but wanted to get the last possible benefit out of the tropical sun, which he would miss for the next ten months. It was hot, and he had just spent an active half hour, and there was nothing at all to keep him awake. . .

The Hunter was still watching, eagerly now. Were the peripatetic things really settling down at last? It looked as though they were. The four bipeds were sprawled on the sand in various positions which they presumably found comfortable; the other animal settled down beside one of them, letting its head rest on its forelegs. The conversation, which had been almost incessant up to this point, died down, and the amorphous watcher decided to take a chance. He moved rapidly to the edge of the pool.

The nearest of the boys was about ten yards from the water. It would not be possible to maintain a watch from the Hunter's present position and at the same time send himself under the sand to a point below the now motionless body of his intended host. He must, however, keep the other in sight. Once more camouflage seemed indicated, and once more the ever-present jellyfish seemed to fill the need. There were a number of them lying on the sand motionless; perhaps if he moved slowly and emulated their shape the Hunter could escape notice until he was close enough for an underground attack.

He may have been excessively cautious, since none of the creatures was facing his way and all were nearly if not entirely asleep, but caution is never really wasted, and the Hunter did not regret the twenty minutes he took getting from the water's edge to a point some three yards from Robert Kinnaird. It was uncomfortable, of course, since his skinless body had even less protection from the hot sun than the jellyfish it was imitating; but he stood it, and eventually reached a point which his earlier experience suggested was close enough.

Had anyone been watching the large medusa lying apparently helpless a few feet from the boy at that moment he might have noticed a peculiar diminution in its size. The shrinking itself was not remarkable—it is the inevitable fate of a jellyfish on a hot beach—but the more orthodox members of the tribe merely grow thinner until only a cobwebby skeleton remains. This specimen dwindled not only in thickness but in diameter, and there were no remains whatsoever. Until it was almost completely gone, of course, there was an odd little lump in the center which preserved its size and shape while the body vanished around it; but this at last went, too, and no trace remained except a shallow depression in the sand—a depression which that careful observer might have noticed extended all the way from the water's edge.

The Hunter kept the eye in use during most of the underground search. His questing appendage at last reached sand that was more closely compacted than usual and, advancing very cautiously now, finally encountered what could only be living flesh. Robert's toes were buried in the sand, since he was lying on his stomach, and the Hunter found that he could operate without emerging at all to the surface. With that fact established, he dissolved the eye and drew the last of his mass out of sight below the sand—with considerable relief as the sunlight was cut off.

He did not attempt to penetrate until his whole body had been drawn through the sand and was wrapped about the half-buried foot. He surrounded the limb with extreme care, bringing himself into contact with the skin over several square inches. Then and only then did he commence interstition, letting the ultra-microscopic cells of his flesh slide through pores, between skin cells, under toenails—into the thousands of openings that lay unguarded in this, to his way of thinking, singularly coarse organism.

The boy was sound asleep, and remained so; but the Hunter worked as fast as possible nevertheless, for it would have been extremely awkward to have the foot move while he was only partly inside. Therefore, as swiftly as was compatible with extreme caution, the alien organism flowed smoothly along the bones and tendons in foot and ankle; up within the muscle sheaths of calf and thigh; along the outer wall of the femoral artery and through the tubelets within the structure of the thigh bone; around joints, and through still other blood vessels. It filtered through the peritoneum without causing sensation or damage; and finally the whole four pounds of unearthly life was gathered together in the abdominal cavity, not only without harming the boy in the least but without even disturbing his slumber. And there, for a time, the Hunter rested.

He had a bigger oxygen reserve this time, having entered from air rather than water. It would be some time before he needed to draw on his host for more. He was hoping, if it were possible, to remain exactly where he was for an entire day, so that he could observe and memorize the cycle of physiological processes which this host undoubtedly performed differently from any he had known before. At the moment, of course, the creature was asleep, but that would probably not be for long. These beings seemed pretty active.

Bob was aroused, like the other boys, by the sound of his mother's voice. She had come silently, spread a blanket in the shade, and arranged the food on it before speaking; and her first words were the ancient "Come and get it!" She would not stay to help them eat it, though cordially and sincerely pressed to do so by the boys, but went back through the palm grove to the road that led to their home.

"Try to be back by sundown," she called to Bob over her shoulder as she reached the trees. "You still have to pack, and you'll have to be up early in the morning." Bob nodded, with his mouth full, and turned back to the food-laden blanket.

After disposing of the meal, the boys sat, talked, and dozed for the standard hour after eating; then they returned to the water, where they indulged further in games of violence; and at last, realizing that the abrupt tropical night would soon be upon them, they gathered up the blanket and started for the road and their respective dwellings. They were rather silent now, with the awkwardness natural to their ages when faced by a situation which adults would treat either emotionally or with studied casualness. The farewells, as they passed their respective dwellings, were brief and accompanied by reiterated and reciprocated promises to "write as soon as you can."

Bob, proceeding at last alone to his own house, felt the mixture of regret and pleasurable anticipation which he had come to associate with these occasions. By the time he reached home, though, the latter feeling had gained the ascendant, and he was looking forward with considerable eagerness to meeting again the school friends he had not seen for more than two months. He was whistling cheerfully as he entered the house.

The packing, done with the tactful assistance of his mother, was quickly completed, and by nine o'clock he was in bed and asleep. He himself considered the hour rather early, but he had learned the value of obedience at certain times very early in life.

The Hunter was able to remain quiescent, as he had hoped, for some hours—till well after Bob was asleep, in fact. He could not, however, last an entire day; for no matter how quiet he remained, the mere fact of living used up some energy and consequently some oxygen. Eventually he realized his store was growing low, and he knew it would be necessary to establish a supply before the need became desperate.

He knew, of course, that his host was asleep, but this in no way decreased his caution. He remained for the time being below the diaphragm, not wishing to disturb in any way the heart he could feel beating just above it; but he was able to find without effort a large artery in the abdomen which offered no more resistance to penetration than had any other part of the human organism thus far. He discovered, to his intense satisfaction, that he could draw enough oxygen from the red cells (he did not think of them by color, since he had not yet seen them) to supply his needs without seriously diminishing the quantity that passed through the vessel. He checked this fact very carefully. His whole attitude in the present exploration was utterly different from that which had directed his actions within the body of the shark, for he had come to look upon Robert in the light of a permanent companion during his stay on the earth, and his present actions were ruled by a law of his kind so ancient and so rigid as to assume almost the proportions of an instinct.

*Do nothing that can harm your host!*

# III. Out of Play

*Do nothing that can harm your host!* For the majority of the Hunter's kind even the desire to break that law never existed, since they lived on terms of the warmest friendship with the beings whose bodies harbored theirs. The few individuals who proved to be exceptions were regarded with the liveliest horror and detestation by their fellows. It was one of these whom the Hunter had been pursuing at the time of his crash on the earth; and that being, he well knew, must still be found—if only to protect this native race from the inroads of the irresponsible creature,

*Do nothing that can harm your host!* From the moment of the Hunter's arrival the swarming white cells in the boy's healthy blood had been aroused. He had avoided the most serious contacts with them up to now by keeping clear of the interiors of blood vessels, though there were enough of them wandering free in the lymphatics and connective tissue to be a nuisance. His body cells were not naturally immune to their powers of absorption, and only by constant evasive action had he been able to avoid serious damage to himself. He knew this could not go on indefinitely; for one thing, he must occasionally direct his attention to other matters, and, for another, the continuation of such a misunderstanding, whether he persevered in evasive action or began to fight back, would mean an increase in the number of white cells and probably some sort of illness to his host. Therefore, the leucocytes must be pacified. His race had, of course, worked out long since a general technique for solving this problem, but care still had to be taken in individual cases —particularly unfamiliar ones. By a trial-and-error process carried out with as much speed as was practical, the Hunter determined the nature of the chemical clue by which the white cells differentiated invading organisms from legitimate members of the human body; and after prolonged and still extremely careful effort he exposed every one of his cells to sources of the appropriate chemicals in his host's blood stream. A few molecules of the desired substance were absorbed on the surface of each cell, and this, to his relief, proved to be sufficient. The leucocytes ceased to bother him, and he could use the larger blood vessels safely as avenues of exploration for his questing pseudopoda.

*Do nothing that can harm your host!* He needed food as well as oxygen. He could have consumed with relish and satisfaction any of the various forms of tissue surrounding him, but the law made selection necessary. There were certainly intruding organisms in this body—besides himself—and they were the logical food source, for by consuming them he would be eliminating their menace to his host and thereby helping to earn his keep. Identifying them would be easy; anything a leucocyte attacked would be legitimate prey for the Hunter. Probably the local microbes would not keep him fed for long, small as his needs were, and it would also be necessary to tap the digestive tract at some point; but that need not cause damage, unless a slightly increased appetite on the part of the host came under that heading.

For many hours the cautious exploration and adjustment continued. The Hunter felt his host awaken and resume activity, but he made no effort to look outside. He had one problem which must be carefully and accurately solved; and, although his dodging the attentions of thousands of leucocytes at once, as he had done for a time, may seem evidence to the contrary, his power of attention was limited. That had simply been an automatic action roughly comparable to a man's carrying on a conversation while he climbs stairs.

Filaments of the Hunter's flesh, far finer than human neurons, gradually formed an all-inclusive network throughout Bob's body from head to toe; and through those threads the Hunter came gradually to know the purpose and customary uses of every muscle, gland, and sense organ in that body. Throughout this period most of his mass remained in the abdominal cavity, and it was more than seventy-two hours after his first intrusion that he felt secure enough in his position to pay attention once more to outside affairs.

As he had done with the shark, he began to fill the spaces between the boy's retinal cells with his own body substance. He was actually able to make better use of Bob's eyes than their proper owner could, for the human eyes see in maximum detail only those objects whose images fall within an area of retina less than a millimeter across. The Hunter could use the whole area on which the lens focused with reasonable sharpness, which was decidedly larger. In consequence, he could examine with Bob's eyes objects at which the boy was not looking directly. This was likely to be a help, since many of the things in which the hidden watcher was most interested would be too commonplace to the human being to attract his direct gaze.

The Hunter could hear dimly even within the human body, but he found it helpful to establish direct physical contact with the bones of the middle ear. Thus, hearing as well as seeing better than his host, he felt ready to investigate the planet on which chance had marooned him and his quarry. There was no further reason—he thought—for delay in searching for and destroying the criminal of his own race now free on the world. He began to look and listen.

The search itself he had never regarded as more than a routine job. He had had similar problems before. He had expected to look around from the vantage point of Bob's body until he found the other, leave, and eliminate his opponent by standard means—regardless of the fact that all his equipment was at the bottom of the sea. He had had, in short, a viewpoint which is excusable in a space navigator but not in a detective: he had been regarding a planet as a small object and thinking his search was practically over when he had narrowed it down to one world.

He was rudely jolted out of this attitude as he took his first look around since meeting Bob Kinnaird. The picture that fell on their common retinas was that of the interior of a cylindrical object vaguely suggestive of his own space ship. It was filled with several rows of seats, most of them occupied by human beings. Beside the watcher was a window through which Bob was looking at the moment; and the suspicion that had entered the Hunter's mind was instantly confirmed by the view through that window. They were on board an aircraft, traveling at a considerable altitude with a speed and in a direction which the alien was in no position to estimate. Start looking for his quarry? He must first look for the right continent!

The flight lasted for several hours and had probably already consumed several. The Hunter quickly gave up the attempt to memorize landmarks over which they passed. One or two of them did stick in his mind and might give a clue to direction if he could ever identify them later; but he put little trust in this possibility. He must keep track of time rather than position, and when he was more familiar with human ways find out where his host had been at the time of his own intrusion.

The view itself, though, was interesting, even if the landmarks were lacking. It was a beautiful planet, from his alien viewpoint; mountains and plains, rivers and lakes, forests and prairies were all visible at various times, now clearly through miles of crystal atmosphere and now in glimpses between billowing clouds of water vapor. The machine he rode was also worthy of attention; from Robert's window he could not see very much of it, but that little told him a great deal. A portion of a metal wing was visible, bearing attachments which evidently contained engines, as rapidly rotating air foils were visible ahead of them. Since the craft was presumably symmetrical, the Hunter decided there must be at least four of these engines. He could not tell with accuracy how much of their energy was wasted in heat and sound—for one thing, he suspected that the cabin in which he rode was quite effectively sound-proofed. The machine as a whole, however, suggested that this race had evidently attained a considerable degree of mechanical advancement, and a new idea blossomed from that: might he not attempt to enter into communication with this being which was his host and secure its active co-operation in his search? It was a point well worth considering.

There was plenty of time for thought before the airplane gradually began to descend. The Hunter could not see directly ahead, and it happened that they entered a solid cloud layer almost immediately, so he was unable to get any idea of their destination until just before the landing. He chalked up another point for the race: they either had senses he lacked, or were very competent and ingenious instrument makers, for the descent through the clouds was as smooth as any other part of the flight.

After some time spent letting down through the gray murk, the machine broke out into clear air. As it banked into a wide turn the Hunter saw a large city built around a great, crowded harbor; then the faint drone of the engines increased in pitch, a large double wheel appeared below one of the nacelles, and the craft glided easily downward to contact with a faint jar a broad, hard-surfaced runway located on a point of land across the harbor from the largest buildings.

As Robert disembarked he glanced back at the airplane, so the Hunter was better able to form an estimate of its size and construction details. He had no idea of the power developed by the four bulky engines, and could not, therefore, guess at the speed; but he could see the quivering in the air above the huge nacelles that told of hot metal within and knew at least that they were not the phoenix converters used by his race and its allies. Whatever they were, though, it had already become evident that the machine could put a very respectable fraction of the planet's circumference behind it without having to descend for fuel.

After alighting from the airplane the boy went through the usual formalities incident to reclaiming his baggage, took a bus around the harbor to the city, walked about for a while, and visited a movie. This the Hunter also enjoyed; his vision persistence involved about the same time lapse as the human eye, so he saw the show as a movie rather than a set of separate pictures. It was still daylight when they emerged and walked back to the bus station, where Bob reclaimed the luggage he had checked, then they boarded another bus.

This turned out to be quite a long ride; the vehicle took them far outside the city and through several smaller towns, and the sun was almost down when it finally left them by the roadside.

A smaller side road, with broad, well-kept lawns on either side, led off up a gentle slope, and at the top of this slope was a large, sprawling building, or group of buildings—the Hunter was not sure which from his viewpoint. Robert picked up his bags and walked up the hill toward this structure, and the alien began to hope that the journey had ended, for the time being at least. He was far enough from his quarry already. As it turned out, his hopes for once were fulfilled.

To the boy the return to school, assignment to a room, and meeting with old acquaintances were by now familiar, but to the Hunter every activity and everything he saw and heard were of absorbing interest. He had no intention, even yet, of making a really detailed study of the human race, but some subconscious guide was beginning to warn him that his mission was not to be quite the routine job he had expected and that he might possibly have use for all the earthly knowledge he could get. He didn't know it yet, but he had come to the best possible place for knowledge.

He looked and listened almost feverishly as Bob went to his room, unpacked, and then wandered about the dormitory meeting friends from former terms. He found himself trying almost constantly to connect the flood of spoken words with their meanings; but it was difficult, since most of the conversation concerned events of the vacation just past, and the words usually lacked visible referents. He did learn the personal names of some of the beings, however, among them that of his host.

He decided, after an hour or two, that it would be best to turn his full attention to the language problem. There was nothing whatever at the moment that he could do about his own mission, and if he understood the speech around him he might be able to learn when his host was to return to the place where they had met. Until he did return, the Hunter was simply out of play—he could do nothing at all toward locating and eliminating his quarry.

With this idea finally settled upon, he spent Robert's sleeping hours organizing the few words he had learned, trying to deduce some grammatical rules, and developing a definite campaign for learning more as quickly as possible. It may seem odd that one who was so completely unable to control his own comings and goings should dream of planning anything, but the extra effective width of his vision angle must be remembered. He was to some extent able to determine what he saw and therefore felt that he should decide what to look for.

It would have been far simpler, if he could only control his host's movements in some way or other, or interpret and influence the multitudinous reactions that went on in his nervous system. He had controlled the *perit*, of course, but not directly; the little creature had been trained to respond to twinges administered directly to its muscles, as a horse is trained to respond to the pressure of the reins. The Hunter's people used the *perits* to perform actions which their own semiliquid bodies lacked the strength to do, and which were too delicate for their intelligent hosts to perform—or which had to be performed in places those hosts could not reach, such as the interior of the tiny racer which had brought the Hunter to Earth.

Unfortunately for this line of thought, Robert Kinnaird was not a *perit* and could not be treated as one. There was no hope, at present, of influencing his actions at all, and any such hope in the future must rest on appeals to the boy's reason rather than on force. At the moment the Hunter was rather in the position of a movie spectator who wants to change the plot of the film he is seeing.

Classes began the day after their arrival. Their purpose was at once obvious to the unlisted pupil though the subjects were frequently obscure. The boy's course included, among other subjects, English, physics, Latin, and French; and of those four, oddly enough, physics proved most helpful in teaching the Hunter the English language. The reason is not too difficult to understand.

While the Hunter was not a scientist, he knew something of science —one can hardly operate a machine like a space ship without having some notion of what makes it work. The elementary principles of the physical sciences are the same anywhere, and while the drawing conventions accepted by the authors of Bob's textbooks differed from those of the Hunter's people, the diagrams were still understandable. Since the diagrams were usually accompanied by written explanations, they were clues to the meanings of a great many words.

The connection between spoken and written English was also cleared up one day in a physics class, when the instructor used a heavily lettered diagram to explain a problem in mechanics. The unseen watcher suddenly understood the connection between letter and sound and within a few days was able to visualize the written form of any new word he heard— allowing, of course, for the spelling irregularities that are the curse of the English language.

The learning process was one which automatically increased its speed as time went on, for the more words the Hunter knew, the more he could guess at from the context in which he met them. By the beginning of November, two months after the opening of school, the alien's vocabulary had the size, though not the precise content, of an intelligent ten-year-old's. He had a rather excessive store of scientific terms and many blanks where less specialized words should have been. Also, the meanings he attached to many terms were the strictly scientific ones—for example, he thought work meant "force times distance," and only that.

By this time, however, he had reached a point where tenth-grade English had some meaning to him, and the opportunities to judge word meanings from context became very frequent indeed, ignorant as the Hunter was of human customs.

About the beginning of December, when the strange little being had almost forgotten everything in the pleasure of learning, an interruption occurred in his education. It occurred, the Hunter felt, through his own negligence and restored him to a better sense of duty. Robert Kinnaird had been a member of the school football team during the fall. The Hunter, with his intense interest in the health of his host, somewhat disapproved of this, though he understood the need of any muscled animal for exercise. The final game of the school season was played on Thanksgiving Day, and when the Hunter realized it *was* the final one, no one gave more thanks than he. However, he rejoiced too soon.

Bob, reconstructing one of the more exciting moments of the game to prove his point in an argument, slipped and twisted an ankle severely enough to put him to bed for several days. The Hunter felt guilty about it because, had he realized the danger even two or three seconds in advance, he would have "tightened up" the net of his tissue that existed around the boy's joints and tendons. Of course, his physical strength being what it was, this would not actually have been much help, but he regretted not trying. Now that the damage had actually been done, there was nothing whatever he could do—the danger of infection was already nil without his help, since the skin had not been broken.

The incident, at any rate, recalled him to not only his duties to his host but also those he had as a police agent; and once again he started thinking over what he had learned that could bear on his police problem. To his astonishment and chagrin this turned out to be nothing at all; he did not even know where the boy had been at the time of his own arrival.

He did learn, from a chance remark passed between Bob and one of his friends, that the place was an island, which was one of the few bright spots in the picture—his quarry, if it had landed at the same place, must either still be there or have left by some traceable means. The Hunter remembered too vividly his own experience with the shark to believe that the other could escape successfully in a fish, and he had never heard of a warm-blooded air-breather that lived in the water. Seals and whales had not come up in Bob's conversation or reading, at least not since the Hunter had been able to understand it.

If the other were in a human being, that person could leave the island only in some sort of craft, and that should mean that his movements would be traceable. It was a comforting thought, and one of the few the Hunter was to have for some time to come.

It remained to learn the location of the island, as a preliminary step to getting back to it. Bob received frequent letters from his parents, but for some time the Hunter did not recognize these as clues, partly because he had a good deal of trouble reading script and partly because he did not know the relationship of the boy to the senders of the letters. He had no particular scruples about reading the boy's mail, of course; he simply found it difficult. Robert did write to his parents as well, at somewhat irregular intervals, but they were not his only correspondents, and it was not until nearly the end of January that the Hunter found that by far the greater number of the boy's letters were going to and coming from one particular address.

The discovery was helped by the youngster's receipt of a typewriter as a Christmas present. Whether his parents meant this as a gentle hint is hard to say, but at least it greatly facilitated the Hunter's reading of the outgoing mail, and he quickly learned that most letters went to Mr. and Mrs. Arthur Kinnaird. He already knew, from his reading, the custom of family names descending from father to offspring, and the salutations removed any doubt there might have been about their identity. The deduction seemed defensible that the boy would spend the summer with his parents, and if that were the case, then the Hunter had the name of the island from the address an the letters.

He still did not know where it was, or how to get there; he could only be sure, from the duration of his airplane ride, that it was a long way from his present location. Bob would presumably be going back at the time of the next vacation, but that gave the fugitive another five months to get under cover—as if the five he had already enjoyed were not enough.

There was a large globular map of the planet in the school library and almost a plethora of flat maps and charts on the walls and in the various books in the school. Robert's persistent failure to bestow more than a passing glance at any of them promised quickly to drive the Hunter mad; and the alien, as time went on, was tempted more and more strongly to attempt to overcome the comparatively tiny muscles controlling the direction of his host's eyes. It was a bad and dangerous idea, but being intelligent does not mean that one's emotions are any the less powerful, as many men have demonstrated.

He controlled himself, therefore—partially. At least he controlled his actions; but as his patience wore ever thinner he began to look more and more favorably on what had at first seemed a mad notion—that of actually getting into communication with his host and enlisting the human being's aid. After all, the Hunter told himself, he might ride around seeing the world from Bob's eyes for the rest of the boy's life, which would probably be a long one with the alien to fight disease, without either getting a clue to his quarry's whereabouts or a chance to do anything even if the other were located. As things now stood, the other could appear in public and perform the amoeboid equivalent of thumbing his nose at the Hunter without any risk to itself. What could the little detective do about it?

With the beings who normally served the Hunter's kind as hosts, communication eventually reached a high level of speed and comprehensiveness. The union took place with the host's full knowledge and consent; it was understood that the larger being furnished food, mobility, and muscular strength, while the other protected him from disease and injury as far as possible. Both brought highly intelligent minds into the partnership, and the relationship was one of extreme friendliness and close companionship in nearly all cases. With this understood by both parties, literally anything the symbiote did to affect his host's sensory organs could be utilized as a means of speech; and as a rule, over a period of years, multitudes of signals imperceptible to anyone else but perfectly clear to the two companions would develop to bring their speed of conversation to almost telepathic levels. The symbiote could administer twinges to any and all muscles, build shadow images directly on the retina of his host's eye, move the fur with which the other race was thickly covered—there was no limit to the various means of signaling.

Of course Bob did not have this background, but it was still possible to affect his senses. The Hunter dimly realized that there might be some emotional disturbance when the boy first learned of his presence, but he was sure he could minimize that. His own race had practiced symbiosis for so long that they had practically forgotten the problems incident to establishing the relationship with a being *not* accustomed to the idea. All that the Hunter really thought about, once he had made up his mind to communicate, was the apparent fact that circumstances were playing into his hands.

There was the "protective" net he had constructed over Bob's muscles; and there was the typewriter. The net could be contracted, like the muscles it covered, though with far less power. If a time arrived when Bob was sitting at the typewriter without particular plans of his own, it might be possible for the Hunter to strike a few keys in his own interest. The chances of success for the experiment depended largely on the boy's reaction when he found his fingers moving without orders; the Hunter managed to make himself feel optimistic about that.

# IV. Signal

Two nights after the Hunter made his decision to act, the opportunity occurred. It was a Saturday evening, and the school had won a hockey game that afternoon. Bob had come through it without injury, to the Hunter's surprise and relief, and had managed to cover himself with a certain amount of glory, and the combination of institutional and personal triumph proved sufficient stimulus to cause the boy to write to his parents. He went to his room immediately after supper—the other occupant was not in at the time—and pounded off a description of the day's events with very fair speed and accuracy. At no time did he relax sufficiently to give an opportunity for control, in the alien's opinion; but with the letter finished and sealed, Robert suddenly remembered a composition which his English teacher had decreed should be turned in the following Monday. It was as foreign to his nature as to that of most other schoolboys to get his work done so early, but the typewriter was out, and the hockey game offered itself as a subject which he could treat with some enthusiasm. He inserted a fresh piece of paper in the machine, typed the standard heading of title, pupil's name, and date, and then paused to think.

The alien wasted no time whatever. He had long since decided on the wording of the first message. Its first letter lay directly under the boy's left middle finger, and the net of unhuman flesh about the appropriate muscle promptly tugged as hard as it could on the tendon controlling that finger. The finger bent downward obediently and contacted the desired key, which descended—halfway. The pull was not powerful enough to lift the type bar from its felt rest. The Hunter knew he was weak compared to human muscles but had not realized he was that weak; Bob's manipulation of the keys had seemed so completely effortless. He sent more of his flesh flowing into the net which was trying to do the work of a small muscle and tried again—and again and again. The result was the same: the key descended far enough to take up the slack in its linkage, and stopped.

All this had attracted Bob's attention. He had, of course, experienced the quivering of muscles abruptly released from a heavy load, but there had been no load here. He pulled the offending hand away from the keyboard, and the suddenly frantic Hunter promptly transferred his attention to the other. As with a human being his control, poor enough in the beginning, grew worse with haste and strain, and the fingers of Robert's right hand twitched in a most unnerving fashion. The boy stared at them, literally terrified. He was more or less hardened to the prospect of physical injury at any time, as anyone who plays hockey and football must be, but there was something about nervous disorder that undermined his morale.

He clenched both fists tightly, and the quivering stopped, to his intense relief; the Hunter knew he could never overcome muscles opposed to his own attempts. However, when the fists cautiously relaxed after a few moments, the detective made another try—this time on the arm and chest muscles—in an effort to bring the hands back to the typewriter. Bob, with a gasp of dismay, leaped to his feet, knocking the chair back against his roommate's bed. The Hunter was able to deposit a much heavier net of his flesh about these larger muscles, and the unwilled tug had been quite perceptible to the boy. He stood motionless, now badly frightened, and tried to decide between two courses of action.

There was, of course, a stringent rule that all injuries and illnesses must be reported promptly to the school infirmary. Had Bob suffered damage such as a cut or bruise he would have had no hesitation in complying with this order, but somehow the idea of owning to a nervous disorder seemed rather shameful, and the thought of reporting his trouble was repugnant. He finally decided tentatively to put it off, in the hope that matters would be improved by morning. He put the typewriter away, took out a book, and settled down to read. At first he felt decidedly uneasy, but as the minutes passed without further misbehavior on the part of his muscular system he gradually calmed down and became more absorbed in the reading matter. The increasing peace of mind was not, however, shared by his unsuspected companion.

The Hunter had relaxed in disgust as soon as the writing machine had been put away, but he had no intention of giving up. The knowledge that he *could* impress himself on the boy's awareness without doing him physical damage was something gained; and even though interference with the youngster's muscles produced such a marked disturbance, there were other methods which suggested themselves to the alien. Perhaps they would prove less disconcerting, and he knew they could be equally effective as means of communication. The Hunter may have had a smattering of the psychology peculiar to the races he knew, but he was certainly failing to analyze properly the cause of his host's disturbance.

His race had lived with others for so many hundreds of generations that the problems of starting the relationship had been forgotten much as man has forgotten the details surrounding his mastery of fire. Nowadays children of the other race grew up expecting to find a companion of the Hunter's kind before they passed adolescence, and the Hunter failed completely to realize how a person not brought up with that conditioning might be expected to react.

He put down Bob's disturbance to the particular method he had employed, rather than to the very fact that he had interfered. He did, in consequence, the worst thing he could possibly do: he waited until his host seemed to be over the shock of the first attempt, and then promptly tried again.

This time he worked on Bob's vocal cords. These were similar in structure to those he had known, and the Hunter could alter their tension mechanically in the same way he had pulled at muscles. He did not, of course, expect to form words; that would have required control of diaphragm, tongue, jaw, and lips, as well as the vocal cords, and the symbiote was perfectly aware of the fact; but if he did his pulling while the host was exhaling air, he could at least produce sound. He could control it only in an off-and-on fashion, so he could hardly send an articulate message that way; but he had an idea in mind for proving that the disturbance was being produced deliberately.

He could use bursts of sound to represent numbers and transmit series—one and its square, two and its square, and so on. No one, surely, hearing such a pattern of sound, could suppose it originated naturally. And now the boy was calmed down again reading, fully absorbed, and breathing slowly and evenly.

The alien got further than any human being, knowing the facts, would have believed possible, principally because Bob was just finishing a yawn as the interruption started and was not able to control his own breathing right away. The Hunter was busily engaged in producing a set of four rather sickly croaks, having completed two and paused, when the boy caught his breath and an expression of undiluted terror spread across his face. He tried to let out his breath slowly and carefully, but the Hunter, completely absorbed in his work, continued his unnerving operation regardless of the fact that he had been interrupted. It took him some seconds to realize that the emotional disturbance of his host had reappeared in full force.

His own emotional control relaxed at this realization, for, recognizing clearly that he had failed again, knowing perfectly that his young host was almost frantic with terror that robbed him of most of his control, the alien nevertheless not only failed to desist from his attempts but started still another system of "communication." His third method involved cutting off the light from his host's retinas in patterns corresponding to letters of the English alphabet—in utter disregard of the fact that by this time Robert Kinnaird was rushing down the hallway outside his room, bound for the dispensary, and that a rather poorly lighted stairway lay ahead.

The inevitable results of interference with his host's eyesight under such circumstances did not impress themselves upon the Hunter's mind until Bob actually missed a step and lunged forward, grasping futilely for the rail.

The alien recovered his sense of duty rapidly enough. Before the hurtling body touched a single obstacle he had tightened around every joint and tendon with his utmost strength to save Robert a serious sprain. Moreover, as a sharp, upturned comer of one of the metal cleats which held the rubber treads on the stairs opened the boy's arm from wrist to elbow, the Hunter was on the job so fast that practically no blood escaped. Bob felt the pain, looked at the injury which was being held closed under an almost invisible film of unhuman flesh, and actually thought it was a scratch that had barely penetrated the skin. He turned the comer of the cleat down with his heel and proceeded to the dispensary at a more moderate pace. He was calmer when he got there, since the Hunter had been sobered into discontinuing his efforts to make himself known.

The school did not have a resident doctor, but did keep a nurse on constant duty at the dispensary. She could make little of Robert's description of his nervous troubles, and advised him to return the next day at the hour when one of the local doctors normally visited the school. She did examine the cut on his arm, however.

"It's clotted over now," she told the boy. "You should have come here with it sooner, though I probably wouldn't have done much to it."

"It happened less than five minutes ago," was the answer. "I fell on the stairs coming down to see you about the other business; I couldn't have brought it to you any faster. If it's already closed, though, I guess it doesn't matter."

Miss Rand raised her eyebrows a trifle. She had been a school nurse for fifteen years and was pretty sure she had encountered all the more common tales of malingerers. What puzzled her now was that there seemed no reason for the boy to prevaricate; she decided, against her professional knowledge, that he was probably telling the truth.

Of course some people's blood *does* clot with remarkable speed, she knew. She looked at the forearm again, more closely. Yes, the clot was extremely fresh—the shiny, dark red of newly congealed blood. She brushed it lightly with a fingertip, and felt, not the dry, smooth surface she had expected, or even the faint stickiness of nearly dry blood, but a definite and unpleasant *sliminess*.

The Hunter was not a mind reader and had not foreseen such a move. Even if he had, he could not have withdrawn his flesh from the surface of Robert's skin; it would be many hours, more probably a day or two, before the edges of that gash could be trusted to hold themselves together under normal usage of the arm. He had to stay, whether he betrayed himself or not.

He watched through his host's eyes with some uneasiness as Miss Rand drew her hand away sharply and leaned over to look still more closely at the injured arm. This time she saw the transparent, almost invisible film that covered the cut, and leaped to a perfectly natural but completely erroneous conclusion. She decided the injury was not so fresh as Robert had claimed, that he had "treated" it himself with the first substance he had found handy—possibly model airplane dope—and had not wanted the fact to come out since it constituted a violation of the school rules.

She was doing a serious injustice to the boy's common sense, but she had no means of knowing that. She was wise enough to make no accusations, however, and without saying anything more took a small bottle of alcohol, moistened a swab with it, and began to clean away the foreign matter.

Once again only his lack of vocal cords kept the Hunter silent. Had he possessed the equipment, he would have emitted a howl of anguish. He had no true skin, and the body cells overlying the cut on his host's arm were unprotected from the dehydrating action of the alcohol. Direct sunlight had been bad enough; alcohol felt to him as concentrated sulfuric acid feels to a human being—and for the same reason. Those outer cells were killed almost instantly, desiccated to a brownish powder that could have been blown away, and would undoubtedly have interested the nurse greatly had she had a chance to examine it.

There was no time for that, however. In the shock of the sudden pain the Hunter relaxed all of the "muscular" control he was exerting in that region to keep the wound closed; and the nurse suddenly saw a long, clean slash some eight inches from end to end and half an inch deep in the middle, which started to bleed freely. She was almost as startled as Robert, but her training showed its value; she quickly applied compresses and bandages, though she was surprised also at the ease with which she managed to stop the bleeding. With that accomplished she reached for the telephone.

Robert Kinnaird was late getting to bed that night.

# V. Answer

The boy was tired, but he had trouble in getting to sleep. The local anesthetic the doctor had used while sewing up the gash was beginning to wear off, and he was becoming progressively more aware of the wound as the night wore on. He had almost forgotten the original purpose of his visit to the dispensary in the subsequent excitement; now, separated by a reasonable time from the initial fright, he was able to view the matter more clearly. There had been no recurrence of the trouble; maybe he could let it go. Besides, if nothing more were going to happen, how could he show anything to the doctor?

The Hunter also had had time to alter his viewpoint. He had left the arm entirely when the anesthetic was injected and busied himself with his own problem. He had finally realized that *any* disturbance of a sense organ or other function of his host was going to result in emotional trouble, and he was beginning to have a shrewd suspicion that the mere knowledge of his own presence might be as bad, even though he did not actually make himself felt. Equally bad, nothing originating in the boy's own body was ever going to be interpreted by him as an attempt at communication. The idea of symbiosis between two intelligent life forms was completely foreign to this race, and the Hunter was slowly coming to realize just what that meant in terms of mental attitudes. In his own mind he was berating himself for not recognizing the situation much earlier.

He had been blinded to any idea save that of communication from within by at least two factors: lifelong habit, and a reluctance to leave his present host. Even now he found himself trying to evolve a plan which would not involve his departure from Robert's body. He had realized from the beginning what his chance of return would be if the boy saw him coming; and the thought of being barred from the home to which he had become so well adjusted, of sneaking about as an almost helpless lump of jelly in an alien and unfriendly world, seeking host after host as he worked his way stepwise back toward the island where he had landed, seeking unaided for traces of a fugitive almost certainly as well hidden as was the Hunter himself right now—it was a picture he put from his mind.

Yet communicate he must, and he had demonstrated to his own satisfaction the futility of trying it from within. Therefore he must—what? How could he get into intelligent conversation with Robert Kinnaird, or any other human being, from outside? He could not talk, he had no vocal apparatus, and even his control over his own shape would be overstrained by an attempt to construct a replica of the human speech apparatus from lung to lip. He could write, if the pencil were not too heavy; but what chance would he get? What human being, seeing a four-pound lump of gelatinous material trying to handle writing materials, would wait around for legible results—or would believe, if he stayed to read?

Yet there might be a way, at that. Every danger he had envisioned was a provisional one: he could not get back into the boy's body *if* Bob saw him coming; no human being would take his senses seriously *if* he saw the Hunter writing; no human being would believe a message written by the Hunter without seeing him—*if* the Hunter could not furnish substantial evidence of his existence and nature. Although the last two difficulties seemed to possess mutually exclusive solutions, the puzzled detective suddenly perceived an answer.

He could leave Bob's body while the boy slept, compose a written message, and return before he awakened. It seemed too simple all at once. No one would see him in the darkness; and as for the authenticity of the note—Robert Kinnaird, of all people on the planet, would be the one to have to take such a message seriously. To him alone, as things were at the moment, was the Hunter in a position to prove both his existence and, if desirable, his whereabouts. If he did decide to tell where he was, at least the boy need not *see* him, and the knowledge might not have such an emotional impact.

The idea seemed excellent, though admittedly there were a few risks. A good policeman is seldom too reluctant to take chances, however, and the Hunter had little difficulty in deciding to adopt the plan. With a course of action thus firmly in mind, he once more began paying attention to his surroundings.

He could still see. The boy had his eyes open then, and must still be awake. That meant delay and still more strain on the Hunter's patience. It was annoying, this night of all nights, that Bob should take so long to go to sleep—annoying, even though the alien could guess the cause and hold himself at least partly responsible. It was nearly midnight, and the Hunter was having trouble holding his temper in check, by the time respiration and heartbeat gave definite proof that his host was asleep and he dared begin his planned actions. He left Bob's body as he had entered, through the pores of the skin in his feet—he was well enough acquainted with the boy's sleeping habits to know that these were least likely to be moved during the process. The maneuver was accomplished successfully, and without delay the detective flowed downward through sheet and mattress and reached the floor under the bed.

Although the window was open and the shade up, it was too dark to see very well; there was no moon and no bright light at all close to the dormitory building. He could, however, make out the outlines of the study table, and on that table there were, he knew, always writing materials. He moved toward it in a smooth, amoeboid flow, and a few moments later was among the books and papers that littered the table top.

Clean paper was easy to find; a scratch pad was lying by itself at the edge of the table in front of one of the chairs. There were pencils and pens as well; but after a few minutes of experimentation the Hunter found them unmanageable because of their weight and length. He found a remedy, however. One of the pencils was a cheap variety of the mechanical type, which the Hunter had previously seen refilled, and he was able to work the lead out of it with a few minutes of prying. He found himself with a thin, easily manageable stick of the usual clay-graphite writing compound, soft enough to make a visible mark even with the feeble pressure the Hunter could apply.

He set to work on the scratch pad. He printed slowly but neatly. The fact that he could barely see what he was doing made no difference, since he had disposed his body over the whole sheet and could feel perfectly well the position of the pencil point and the shallow groove it left behind it. He had spent considerable time planning just what the note was to say, but was aware that it might not be too convincing.

"Bob," the note began—the Hunter did not yet realize that certain occasions call for more formal means of address—"these words are to apologize for the disturbance I caused you last night. I must speak to you; the twitching of your muscles and the catching of your voice were my attempts. I have not space here to tell you who and where I am, but I can always hear you speak. If you are willing for me to try again, just say so. I will use the method you request; I can, if you relax, work your muscles as I did last night, or if you will look steadily at some evenly illuminated object I can make shadow pictures in your own eyes. I will do anything else within my power to prove my words to you, but you must make the suggestions for such proofs. This is terribly important to both of us. Please let me try again."

The Hunter wanted to sign the note but could think of no way to do so. He had no personal name, actually; "Hunter" was a nickname arising from his profession. In the minds of the friends of his former host he was simply the companion of Jenver the Second of Police; and he judged that to use such a title in the present instance would be unwise. He left the message unsigned, therefore, and turned his attention to the problem of where to leave it. He did not want Bob's roommate to see it, at least until after his host had done so; therefore, it seemed best to carry the paper back to the bed and place it on, or under, the covers.

This the Hunter started to do, after he had succeeded in working the sheet loose from the pad to which it had been attached. Getting a better idea on the way across the room, however, he left it in one of the boy's shoes, and returned successfully to the interior of his body, where he proceeded to relax and wait for morning. He did not have to sleep in that environment—Bob's circulatory system was amply capable of taking care of the visitor's metabolic wastes as fast as they were formed. For the first time the Hunter found himself regretting this fact; sleep would have been a good way to pass the hours which would have to elapse before Bob read the note. As it was, he simply waited.

When the reveille buzzer sounded in the corridor outside—the mere fact that it was Sunday was not considered an excuse for remaining in bed—Bob slowly opened his eyes and sat up. For a moment his actions were sluggish; then, remembering that it was his turn, he sprang barefooted across the floor, slammed down the window, and leaped back to the bed where, more leisurely, he began to dress. His roommate, who had enjoyed his privilege of remaining under the covers until the window was closed, also emerged and began groping for articles of clothing. He was not looking at Robert, so he did not see the momentary expression of surprise that flickered across Kinnaird's face as he saw the sheet of paper loosely rolled up and thrust into one of his shoes.

He pulled out the note, scanned it quickly, and thrust it into a pocket. His immediate thought was that someone—probably his roommate—was up to some sort of trick; and it was in his nature immediately to decide to deny the perpetrator the satisfaction of the expected reaction. For half the morning he drove the Hunter nearly mad by his indifference but he had not forgotten the note.

Bob had simply been waiting until he was alone and could count on being so for a while. In his room, with the other boy away, he took out the note and read it again carefully. His initial opinion remained unchanged for a moment, then a question occurred to him. Who would have known about his troubles the night before?

Of course he had told the nurse; but neither she nor the doctor, it seemed to him, would indulge in a practical joke of this nature—nor would they tell anyone who might. There might be other explanations—

there probably were, but the easiest to check at the moment was that which took the note at face value. He looked outside the door, in the closet, and under the bed, being normal enough not to wish to be caught falling for a practical joke; then he seated himself on one of the beds, looked at the blank wall opposite the window, and said aloud, "All right, let's see your shadow pictures."

The Hunter obliged.

There is a peculiar pleasure in producing cataclysmic results with negligible effort. The Hunter felt it now; his only work was in thickening by a fraction of a millimeter some of the semitransparent body material already surrounding the rods and cones in his host's eyeball so as to cover those sensitive nerve endings and cut off some of the incoming light in a definite pattern. Accustomed as he was to the maneuver, it was almost completely effortless, but it produced results of a very satisfying magnitude. Bob started to his feet, staring; he blinked repeatedly, and rubbed his eyes, but persistence of vision carried the rather foggy word "thanks," which had apparently been projected on the wall, until he opened them again. The word tended to "crawl" a little as he watched. Not all the letters were on the fovea—the tiny spot of clearest vision on the human retina—and when he turned his eyes to see them better, they moved too. He was reminded of the color spots he sometimes saw in the dark, on which he could never turn his eyes property.

"Wh—who are you? And where are you? And how—?" His voice died out as questions flooded into his mind faster than he could utter them.

"Sit quietly and watch, and I will try to explain." The words flowed across his field of vision. The Hunter had used this method before, with many other written languages, and in a few minutes managed to find Bob's normal reading speed. He held the rate of letter change at that value, since if he either speeded up or slowed down the boy's eyes started to wander.

"As I said in my note, it is hard to explain who I am. My job corresponds to that of one of your police agents. I have no name in the sense that you people have, so you had best think of me as the Detective, or the Hunter. I am not a native of this world, but came here in pursuit of a criminal of my own people. I am still seeking him. Both his ship and mine were wrecked when we arrived, but circumstances made me leave the scene of the landing before I could begin an orderly search. That fugitive represents a menace to your people as well as mine, and for that reason I ask your help in locating him."

"But where do you come from? What sort of person are you? And how do you make these letters in front of my eyes?"

"All in good time." The Hunter's limited English reading had made him rather fond of clichés. "We come from a planet of a star which I could point out to you but whose name I do not know in your language. I am not a person like yourself. I fear you do not know enough biology to permit a good explanation, but perhaps you know some of the differences between a protozoan and a virus. Just as the big, nucleated cells which make up your body evolved from protozoan-type creatures, so did my kind evolve from the far smaller life forms you call viruses. You have read about such things, or I would not know your words for them; but perhaps you do not remember."

"I think I do," Bob replied aloud. "But I thought viruses were supposed to be practically liquid."

"At that size, the distinction is minor. As a matter of fact, my body has no definite shape—you would think of one of your amoebae if you were to see me. Also, I am very small by your standards, although my body contains thousands of times as many cells as yours."

"Why not let me see you? Where are you, anyway?"

The Hunter dodged the question.

"Since we are so small and flimsy in structure, we frequently find it awkward and sometimes dangerous to travel and work by ourselves, and we have formed the habit of riding larger creatures—not in the sense you probably take that word, but living inside their bodies. We are also able to do that without harming them, since we can adjust our shapes to the available space and can even make ourselves useful by destroying disease germs and other unwelcome organisms, so the animal enjoys better health than it otherwise might."

"That sounds interesting. You found it possible to do the same with an animal of this planet? I should think it would have been too different for you. What kind are you using?"

That brought the question about as close to home as it could get. The Hunter tried to postpone the evil hour by answering first questions first. "The organism was not too different from—" He got no further, for Bob's memory had started to function.

"Wait a minute! Wait—a—minute!" The boy sprang to his feet again. "I think I see what you've been leading up to. You don't mean you *ride* other animals, you go into partnership with them. And that trouble last night— So that's what held that cut closed! What made you let go?"

The Hunter told him, filled with relief. The boy had realized the truth sooner than the alien had really wanted, but he seemed to be reacting well—he was more interested than shocked. At his request the symbiote repeated the muscle-pulling effects that had caused so much disturbance the previous evening, but he refused to show himself. He was too relieved by the present state of affairs to want to take any chances with Bob's feelings.

Actually, he had made an incredibly lucky choice of hosts. A much younger or less well-educated child could not have begun to understand the situation and would have been frightened out of its senses; an adult would probably have headed at top speed for the nearest psychiatrist's office. Bob was old enough to understand at least some of what the Hunter had told him and young enough not to blame the whole thing on subjective phenomena.

At any rate he listened—or rather, watched—steadily and soberly as the Hunter unfolded the series of events which had brought him first to earth and then halfway around it, to a Massachusetts boarding school. The alien explained the problem which lay before him and the reason why Bob should interest himself in it. The boy understood that clearly enough: he could easily envision the mischief of which his guest would be capable in his present location if he did not possess a strong moral sense, and the thought of a similar organism running loose among the human race uninhibited by any such restriction made him shudder.

# VI. Problem One

Bob turned to practical considerations even before the Hunter started to bring them up. "I suppose," he said thoughtfully, "that you want to get back to the place where you found me and start scouting among the islands for your friend. How can you be sure he got ashore at all?"

"I can't, until I find traces of him," was the answer. "Did you say islands? I was hoping there would be only one within reasonable distance. How many are there in that region?"

"I don't know; it's quite a large group. The nearest to my own that I know of is about thirty-five miles to the northeast. It's a smaller one, but they have a power station there too."

The Hunter pondered. He had been almost exactly in the line of flight of the other ship up to the time he had gone out of control; as nearly as he could remember, they had both come nearly straight "down," so that even after his ship began spinning he should not have left that line by far. It had been his close-range screen that showed the other sinking after it had struck water; their points of landing could not be more than two or three miles apart. He explained this to Bob.

"Then if he got ashore at all, it's most likely on my island. That gives us about a hundred and sixty people to check, if he's still there. Are you sure he'll use a human body, or do we have to check everything alive?"

"Any creature large enough to spare the food and oxygen we use will serve. For a warm-blooded air-breather like yourself I should guess that the animal that was with you the day we met was about the smallest likely. However, I should expect him to use a human being, eventually if not at first. You represent, as far as I know, the only intelligent race on this world; and it has long been recognized by my people that an intelligent creature is the most satisfactory host. Even though this creature will not be seek-

63

ing companionship, the fact that a man is probably the safest host available will guide him, I am sure."

"That is, if he is ashore yet. All right, we'll devote most of our attention to people. It's just as well, I guess; we have a needle in a haystack as it is." The Hunter was familiar with Bob's expression from his reading.

"That describes it well, except that the needle is camouflaged as a wisp of hay," was his answering comment.

They were interrupted at this point by Bob's roommate, returning to prepare for dinner, and there was no further chance for conversation that day. Bob saw the doctor about his arm during the afternoon, and, since the Hunter possessed no miraculous healing powers, the doctor considered its progress normal. It was pleasantly free from all signs of infection, "in spite," the doctor remarked, "of that silly trick of yours. What did you try to close it with, anyway?"

"I did nothing to it," replied the boy. "It happened when I was on my way to the dispensary, anyway, and I thought it was just a scratch until the nurse started cleaning it and everything let go." He saw the doctor did not believe him, and decided there was little use pursuing the argument. Nothing had actually been said between him and his guest about keeping the latter's presence a secret, but it had occurred to the boy that if knowledge of the alien spread too far—assuming his story were believed, of course—it might have a serious effect on their chances of success, so he let the doctor finish his lecture on first aid and left as soon as he could.

Shortly after the evening meal he found an opportunity to get off by himself, and at once put a question to the Hunter.

"What do you plan to do about getting back to the island? Normally, I won't be going until the middle of June, nearly six months from now. Your fugitive has already had about that much time to get under cover, or out of the way. Do you plan to wait and let him bury himself deeper, or have you thought of some means of getting us there sooner?" The Hunter had been expecting the question and had an answer ready—one designed to teach him more about the boy's personality than he had been able to guess.

"My motions, from now on, are wholly dependent on yours. To leave you would be to waste much of the work of the last five months; true, I know your language, which would help me anywhere, but I suspect that securing the co-operation of anyone else would be a lengthy job. You are the only human being on whom I can count for understanding help. At the same time, it is true that the sooner I get back to the island the better it will be, so it seems best that you should come as well. I know that you are not completely free to control your own actions, but if you could devise some means of getting us back there, it would be a great help. I can be of little assistance in the matter; you have grown up in this environment and can judge more accurately the chances of any given plan. All I am qualified to do is advise about the actions and nature of our quarry and what to do when we really start looking for him. What valid reason could you offer your people for returning immediately to the island?"

Bob did not answer at once. The idea of taking such a matter into his own hands was rather new to him; but inevitably it grew more attractive as he thought about it. Of course he would miss a lot of school, but that could be made up later. If the Hunter were telling the truth, this matter was much more important; and Robert could see no reason why his guest should deceive him. The alien, then, was right: he must solve the problem of getting home at once.

Simply disappearing was not to be thought of. Apart from the purely practical difficulties of crossing the continent and a good part of the Pacific without assistance, he had no desire to cause his parents anxiety if it could be avoided. That meant that a *good* excuse for the journey must be found, so that it could be undertaken with official approval.

The more he thought about it, the clearer it seemed that only illness or physical injury would serve. Homesickness had been known to produce results in one or two cases, but Robert remembered what he had thought of the individuals involved and decided he didn't want that reputation. It would be nice to acquire an injury in some manner which would reflect credit on himself—through a heroic rescue or some similar adventure—but he had sense enough to realize that the opportunity was small and the actual merit of the idea nil. Of course the hockey season was still on; anything might happen of its own accord.

As for illness, that could not very well be acquired at will. He could perhaps imitate something well enough to fool friends and teachers, but he did not for an instant deceive himself into thinking he could fool a doctor for any length of time. Faking seemed out, therefore. The usual run of ideas, such as false telegrams requesting his presence, pretense of bad news from home, and all their variations ran through his mind, for he had read his share of the more melodramatic literature; but none of them satisfied the objections which his sound common sense at once raised. He found himself in a complete quandary, and told the Hunter so after many minutes of thought.

"This is the first time I have regretted choosing such a young host," answered the alien. "You lack the freedom of travel that an adult would take for granted. However, I am sure you have not exhausted your fund of ideas. Continue to think, and let me know if I can help in any of your plans." That terminated the conversation for the time. Bob left the room moodily.

He brightened up presently, however, shelved his worries for the moment, and presently was engaged in a game of ping-pong with one of his classmates in the recreation room next to the gym. The relaxation allowed his subconscious mind to work on the problem, and in the middle of the first game he had another idea—as luck would have it, at a time when he could neither tell the Hunter nor secure his views on the matter. He became so preoccupied with the plan that the game, which had been going well for him up to this point, deteriorated almost to a slaughter. He managed to pull himself together for the next game only by reminding himself that it was certain to be some time before he could get in touch with his guest, even if he stopped playing. Also, this early he was developing an exaggerated fear of doing anything abnormal lest his secret should be suspected; and there was nothing normal about his being beaten so thoroughly as he had just been.

It was indeed quite a time before he managed another talk with the Hunter. When he returned to his room, the other occupant was already there, and his presence prevented conversation not only until "lights out" but throughout the night, as Bob was not sure how much disturbance it would take to wake the fellow. Anyway, he could not very well see the Hunter's answers in the dark. The next day was Monday, with classes, and he was not alone until after supper, when, in near desperation, he took some books and went in search of an empty classroom. There, talking in a low tone to escape notice from anyone passing the door, he finally managed to unbottle the repressed questions. He started, however, with a point other than his idea.

"Something will have to be done about this," he said. "You can talk to me whenever I'm not actually doing something else, but I can't say anything to you when anyone's around without having them think I'm crazy. I've had an idea since last night and have been wondering when I could tell you."

"The conversation problem should not be difficult," answered the Hunter. "If you simply talk in an inaudible whisper—even keep your lips closed if you wish—I think I can learn quite easily to interpret the motions of your vocal cords and tongue. I should have thought of it long ago but gave no particular attention to the need for secrecy with which we are faced. I shall start practice at once. It should not be hard; I understand many of your people become quite adept at lip reading, and I have more than lips to go by. What was the idea that was worrying you so?"

"I can see no way of getting to the island, except through feigning sickness and being ordered to take an early vacation. I can't possibly fake an illness well enough to fool a doctor, but you are in a position to give me all sorts of symptoms—enough to drive them crazy. How about it?"

The Hunter was hesitant in his answer.

"It is certainly a possibility, but there are objections. You, of course, cannot realize how deeply bred into us is the repugnance to the idea of doing anything that can harm our hosts. In an emergency, with a being whose physical make-up I knew completely, I might carry out your plan as a last resort; in your case I could not be sure that no permanent harm was going to result from my actions. Do you see?"

"You have lived in my body for more than five months, you say. I should think you must know me as well as you ever will," Bob objected.

"I know your structure but not your tolerances. You represent a completely new species to me, of which I have data on only one individual. I do not know how long given cells can do without food or oxygen; what constitutes the limiting concentration of fatigue acids in your blood; what interference your nervous and circulatory systems can stand. Those things obviously I could not test without harming and possibly killing you. There are, I suppose, a few things I might do in the line you suggest, but I certainly would not like it; and, in any case, how do you know that you would be sent home in case of illness? Would they not be more likely to hospitalize you here?"

The question silenced Bob for several seconds; that possibility had not occurred to him.

"I don't know," he said at last. "We'll have to find something that calls for a rest cure, I guess." His features wrinkled in repugnance at the idea. "I still think you could do something about it without having a nervous breakdown."

The Hunter was willing to concede that point but was still reluctant to interfere with his host's vital processes. He said he would "think it over," and advised the boy to do the same—also to produce another idea, if possible.

This Robert agreed to do, though he felt the chances of success were small. The Hunter was not sanguine, either. Little as he knew of human psychology, he was pretty sure that Bob could not really work on another plan until his present one was proved impossible rather than merely undesirable. The boy still liked the plan and had no real conception of the way it affected the Hunter's feelings.

Consequently, the only real progress made in the next few days was in communication. As the detective had expected and hoped, he was able quickly to interpret the motions of the boy's vocal cords and tongue, even when he kept his lips nearly closed and spoke in a whisper audible to no one but himself. Answering was easy, provided Bob's current occupation left him free to turn his eyes on some relatively blank space. Also, a few mutually understood abbreviations began to creep in, so that their exchange of ideas speeded up noticeably. Neither, however, produced another idea for getting the boy away from school.

An observer during those few days, familiar with the course of events not only between Bob and his guest but in the offices of the school officials, would have been amused. On the one hand, the Hunter and his host were concentrating on trying to find an excuse for leaving; on the other, the headmaster and his staff were wondering volubly about the cause of the boy's suddenly developed inattention, listlessness, and general failure to measure up to his earlier standards; more than one of them remarked that it might be well to get the youngster back to his parents' hands for a time. The Hunter's mere presence—or rather, Bob's knowledge of it—was producing conditions bound in the end to lead to the very situation they wanted. He was, of course, doing the boy no physical damage, but the preoccupation with the current problem and a number of too-public conversations with the concealed alien constituted a behavior pattern only too noticeable to those responsible for Bob's well-being.

The doctor was eventually consulted on the matter. He reported the boy's health sheet clean, with no illness whatever this term and only two minor injuries. He examined the still-healing arm again, on the chance that an unsuspected infection might be responsible, but of course found nothing. His report left the masters mystified. Bob had changed from a normally pleasant and gregarious youngster to a solitary and at times almost sullen individual. At their request the doctor had a private interview with Robert.

He learned nothing concrete this time, either, but he gained the impression that Bob had a problem on his mind which he did not wish to share with anyone. Being a doctor, he formed a perfectly justified but quite erroneous theory on the nature of the problem, and recommended that the boy be returned to the care of his parents for a few months. It was as simple as that!

The headmaster wrote a letter to Mr. Kinnaird, explaining the situation as the doctor saw it, and stating that, if there were no objections, he planned to send Robert home immediately until the opening of the fall term.

Bob's father rather doubted the doctor's theories. He knew his son well, considering the relatively small amount he had seen of him in recent years; but he concurred with Mr. Raylance's suggestion. After all, if the kid were not doing well at school it was a waste of time to have him there whatever the reason for the trouble. There was a perfectly good doctor and—though Mrs. Kinnaird had her doubts—a perfectly good school on the island, and it would be easy to fill the gap in his education while a more careful study of the situation was being made. Also, quite apart from these reasons, Mr. Kinnaird would be glad of the chance to see more of his son. He cabled the school authorizing Bob's return, and prepared for his arrival.

To say that Robert and the Hunter were surprised at the news is a distinct understatement. The boy stared wordlessly at Mr. Raylance, who had called him into his office to inform him of the imminent journey, while the Hunter strove unsuccessfully to read a few papers which were exposed on the headmaster's desk.

Eventually Bob recovered the use of his voice. "But what is the reason, sir? Has anything happened at home?"

"No, everything is all right. We felt that you might be better off there for a few months, that's all. You haven't been hitting your usual mark lately, have you?"

To the Hunter, this remark explained the situation with crystal clarity, and he metaphorically kicked himself for not having foreseen it; to Bob, understanding came more slowly.

"You mean—I'm being kicked out of school? I didn't think it was that bad—and it's only been a few days."

"No, no, nothing of the sort." The headmaster missed the implications of Bob's last remark. "We notice that you seemed to be having trouble, and the doctor thought you needed a little time off. We'll be glad to have you back next fall. If you like, we can send along a study outline with you, and the teacher on the island can help you keep up with it. You can spread that work through the whole summer and will probably be able to stay with your class when you come back. Is that all right? Or"—he smiled—"is it just that you don't want to go home?"

Bob returned the smile rather lamely. "Oh, I'll be glad enough to go, all right. I mean—" He paused, rather embarrassed as he realized another possible construction of his words.

Mr. Raylance laughed aloud. "All right, Bob. Don't worry—I understand what you mean. You'd better get packed and say good-by to your friends; I'll try to get you a reservation for tomorrow on the usual air route. I'm sorry you're going; the hockey team will certainly miss you. However, the season is nearly over, and you'll be back in time for football. Good luck."

They shook hands, and Bob dazedly went to his room and began to pack. He said nothing to the Hunter; it was not necessary. He had long since given up taking the statements of his elders at face value simply because they were his elders, but try as he might he could find no ulterior motive lurking behind the words and actions of the headmaster. He decided, for the time being, to take his luck without question and leave the next step to the Hunter.

That individual had ceased to worry from the time he had realized the import of Mr. Raylance's words. The removal of a source of anxiety affected him just as it frequently does a human being—he tended to feel, for a time, as though troubles were a thing of the past. It might be too much to say that he felt his job was as good as done; but there would have been some excuse if he had felt that way. He was a good detective. He had, of course, some failures against his record, but not one of them had occurred while he had the advantage of an intelligent and co-operative host to supply the physical powers his own body lacked. Bob was not Jenver, but he had come to feel strongly attached to the youngster.

This atmosphere of self-congratulation continued during Bob's packing and even through part of the trip. Mr. Raylance was successful in obtaining the reservation, and the next day Bob took the bus to Boston and caught the noon plane to Seattle, where they were to change to the TPA plane. During the ride and flight the boy talked with his guest whenever possible, but the conversation was purely about the events and scenes of the trip. They did not turn to business until they were over the Pacific, for Bob always accepted without any particular thought the Hunter's ability to take care of things once they reached the scene of action.

"Say, Hunter, just how are you going to find this friend of yours? And what will you do to him then? Have you some means of getting at him without hurting his host?"

It was a shock. For once the Hunter was glad that his method of speech was less easily used than Bob's. Had it been otherwise, he would almost certainly have started talking before he realized he had nothing to say. In the next five seconds he wondered whether he might not have left behind somewhere the mass of tissue that normally served him for a brain.

Of course his quarry had long since hidden—must by now be established in another body, just as the Hunter himself was. That was nothing unusual. Normally, however, such a being—undetectable by sight, sound, smell, or touch—was detected by chemical, physical, and biological tests, with or without the co-operation of the being acting as host. He knew all those tests; he could administer them, in some cases, so rapidly that while merely brushing against a suspected organism he could tell if one of his own people were present, and even make a good guess at his identity. There were something like a hundred and sixty people on the island, Bob had said. They could be covered in a few days' testing—*but he could not make the tests!*

All of his equipment and supplies had gone with his ship. Even with the fantastic assumption that he could find the hulk again, it would be folly to suppose that instruments had remained unbroken and chemical containers sealed through the crash and the five subsequent months under salt water.

He was on his own, as few policemen had ever been before; hopelessly isolated from the laboratories of his own world, and the multitudinous varieties of assistance his own people could have given him. They did not even know where he was, and with a hundred billion suns in the Milky Way system. . .

He remembered, wryly, that Bob had actually brought up the question days before and the cavalier manner in which he had disposed of it. Now it was bitterly clear that the summary they had made of the situation on that occasion had been glaringly accurate. They *were* looking for a needle in a haystack—a haystack whose human straws numbered more than two billion; and that deadly, poisoned needle had thoughtfully crawled inside one of them!

Bob got no answer to his question.

# VII. Stage. . .

The great plane bore them from Seattle to Honolulu; from there to Apia; in a smaller machine they flew from Apia to Tahiti; and at Papeete, twenty-five hours after leaving Boston, Bob was able to point out to the Hunter the tanker which made the rounds of the power islands and on which they would make the last lap of their trip. It was a fairly typical vessel of its class and far from new, though the Hunter could not see many details as they passed overhead. That opportunity came a couple of hours later, when Bob had made sure that all his luggage was still with him and was being transferred to the harbor.

Baggage and boy—Robert was the only listed passenger—eventually found their way onto a small lighter, which chugged its way out into the harbor to deposit them on the ship that they had seen from the air.

Even the Hunter could see that she was designed for cargo rather than speed. She was very broad for her length, and the entire midship section was occupied by tanks, which rose only a few feet above the water line. Bow and stern were much higher, and were connected by catwalks crossing above the tanks. From these, ladders dropped at frequent intervals, giving access to the valve and pump machinery; and the tall, brown-skinned mate who saw Bob climbing the companionway glanced at these and groaned inaudibly. He knew from past experience the impossibility of keeping the boy off the oil-slick rungs, and lived in fearful anticipation of the day he would have to deliver a collection of compound fractures to the elder Kinnaird.

"Hi, Mr. Teroa!" Bob yelled as he reached the level of the bridge. "Think you can stand me for a day or so?"

The mate smiled. "I guess so. It seems you're not the worst possible nuisance, after all." Bob opened his eyes wide, in mock astonishment, and shifted to the hodgepodge of French and Polynesian dialects used among the islands.

"You mean someone has turned up who causes more trouble? You must introduce me to this genius."

"You know him—or rather them. My Charlie and young Hay sneaked aboard a couple of months ago and managed to stay out of sight until it was too late to put 'em off. I had quite a lot of explaining to do."

"What were they after—just the trip? They must have seen everything on your run long ago."

"It was more than that. Charlie had some idea of proving he could be useful, and getting a steady job. Hay said he wanted to visit the Marine Museum in Papeete without a lot of older folks telling him what to look at. I was kind of sorry to have to keep him on board until we got home."

"I didn't know Norman was a natural-history bug. This must be something new; I'll have to see what he's up to. I've been gone five months, so I suppose he could have got started on anything."

"That's right, you have. Come to think of it, I wasn't expecting you back this soon, either. What's the story? Get heaved out of school?" The suggestion was made with a grin which removed offense.

Bob grimaced. He had not worked out a story in any detail, but judged correctly that if he himself could not understand the school doctor's motive there would be nothing odd in his being unable to explain it.

"The doc at school said I'd do better at home for a while," he replied. "He didn't tell me why. I'm O.K. as far as I know. Did Charlie get the job he wanted?" Bob thought he knew the answer, but wanted the subject changed if at all possible.

"Strangely enough, he's getting it, though you needn't tell him just yet," the mate answered. "He's a pretty good seaman already, and I figured if he was going to pull stunts like that I'd better have him in sight, so I applied for him, and I think it's going through. Don't you get the idea that you can do the same by stowing away, though!" and Teroa gave the boy a friendly push toward the catwalk that led aft to the limited passenger accommodations

Bob went, his mind for the moment completely away from his main problem. He was absorbed in memories of his friends and speculations about what they had done during his absence (as usual, there had been very few letters exchanged while he was at school). The island itself he regarded as "home," though he spent so little time there; and for the moment his thoughts were those of any moderately homesick fifteen-year-old.

The Hunter's question—projected against the blue of the harbor as Bob leaned over the stern rail—could hardly have been better timed to fit in with the boy's mood. The alien had been thinking hard. He had come to one conclusion, about his own intelligence, but that was not really constructive; and he realized that much more data were going to be needed before he could trace his enemy. His host could certainly furnish some of that information.

"Bob, could you tell me more about the island—its size, and shape, and where people live? I am thinking that our job will be one of reconstructing the actions of our friend rather than locating him directly. Once I know more about the scene of action, we can decide where he is most likely to have left a trail."

"Sure, Hunter." Bob was more than willing. "I'll draw you a map; that will be better than words. I think there's some paper with my things." He turned from the rail, for the first time in many trips ignoring the vibration that swelled from below as the great diesels pounded into action. His "cabin" was a small room in the sterncastle containing a bunk and his pile of luggage—the ship was definitely not designed for passengers. After some search Bob found a piece of paper large enough for his purpose, and, spreading this out on a suitcase, he began to draw, explaining as he went.

The island, as it took shape under the boy's pencil, was shaped rather like a capital L, with the harbor formed by the interior angle facing north. The reef that surrounded it was more nearly circular, so that the enclosed lagoon was very broad on the north side. There were two main openings, apparently, in the reef; Bob, pointing at the more westerly, said that it was the regular entry, as it had been deepened by blasting away the coral until the tanker could enter at any time.

"We still have to knock brain corals out of the channel every so often. The other way we don't bother with—small boats can go through, but you have to be careful. The lagoon is shallow, not more than about fifteen feet, and the water is always warm. That's why the tanks were built there." He indicated a number of small squares penciled on the area of the lagoon. The Hunter thought of asking just what the tanks were for, but decided to wait until Bob finished.

"In here"—the boy pointed to the bend of the L—"most of the people live. It's the lowest part of the island—the only part where you can see from one side to the other. There're about thirty houses sort of scattered there, with big gardens around them so they're not very close together—nothing like the towns you've seen."

"Do you live in that area?"

"No." The pencil sketched a narrow double line almost the whole length of the island, close to the lagoon side. "That is a road that goes from Norm Hay's house near the northwest end down to the storage sheds in the middle of the other leg. Both branches have a row of hills—the low place where the houses are is a sort of saddle in the row—and several families live on the north slope up here. Hay is at the end, as I said; and coming back down the road you pass Hugh Colby's house, Shorty Malmstrom's, Ken Rice's, and then mine. Actually, that whole end of the island isn't used much, and is grown over except right around the houses. The ground is all cut up and hard to mow, so they grow the stuff for the tanks at the other end, where it's a lot smoother. We practically live in jungle— you can't even see the road from my house and it's the closest of the five. If your friend has decided to pass up his chances at a human host and simply hide in there, I don't know how we'd ever find him."

"About how large is the island? There is no scale on your map."

"The northwest branch is about three and a half miles long, the other about two. This causeway out to the dock in the middle of the lagoon is about a quarter mile or a little more—maybe nearly half. It's about the same from the shore end of it to the road—that's another paved one, leading from the causeway to the main road—reaches it practically in the middle of the village. It's a mile and a half from the junction to my house, and about as far from there to the end, where Norm lives." The pencil traveled somewhat erratically around the chart as Bob spoke and as his enthusiasm ran further and further ahead of his sense of order.

The Hunter followed the racing point with interest, and decided it was time to seek an explanation of the tanks to which the boy had referred more than once. He put the question.

"They call 'em culture tanks. They have bugs—germs—growing in them; germs that eat pretty near anything, and produce oil as a waste product. That's the purpose of the whole business. We dump everything that's waste into the tanks, pump oil off the top, and every so often clean the sludge out of the bottom—that's a nasty job, believe me. People were howling for years about the danger of the oil wells giving out, when any good encyclopedia would tell 'em that the lights they saw in marshes were caused by the burning of gases produced from things rotting under the swamp. Someone finally got bright enough to connect the ideas, and the biologists bred special bugs that would produce heavier oils instead of marsh gas. The island waste isn't enough to keep the five big tanks going, so the northeast end of the island is always getting the vegetation shaved off it to feed them. The sludge goes back to the same ground to serve as fertilizer. That's another reason, besides the smoothness of the ground, that we use only that end of the island for that—it's downwind from the settled part, and the sludge is awfully smelly when it's fresh. There are pipelines connecting the big tanks to the loading dock, so we don't have to cart the oil around the island, but there's a special fertilizer barge."

"Does no one live on the south side of the hills?"

"No. On our leg of the island that's the windy side, and every so often that means a lot. Maybe you'll see a real hurricane before you're
through. On the other leg it's usually in fertilizer, and I can't see anyone
wanting to live there."

The Hunter made no comment on this, and after a moment the tour
went on. He got a good idea—better than Bob had, owing to his much
greater knowledge of biology—about the workings of the island's principal industry, though he was not sure how useful the knowledge would
be. He learned, from Bob's eager descriptions of past excursions, to know
the outer reef and its intricacies almost well enough to find his way around
it himself. He learned, in short, about all anyone could without actually
journeying personally over the patch of rock, earth, and coral that was
Bob's home.

When they came on deck again Tahiti's central peak alone was visible
behind them. Bob wasted little time looking at it; he headed for the nearest hatch and descended to the engine room. There was only one man on
duty, who reached for the phone switch as though to call assistance when
he saw the boy, and then desisted, laughing.

"You back again? Keep off the plates in those shoes—I don't want to
have to unwrap you from the shaft. Haven't you seen all you want of my
engines yet?"

"Nope. Never will." Bob obeyed the injunction to stay on the catwalks, but his eyes roved eagerly over the dials in front of the engineer.
He could interpret some of them, and the engineer explained others; their
power to attract faded with their mystery, and presently the boy began
prowling again. Another crewman had come in and was making a standard inspection round, looking and listening for oil leaks, faulty bearings, and any of the troubles which plague power plants with and without warning. Bob tagged along, watching carefully. He knew enough to
make himself useful before he was considered a nuisance, and ran several
errands during the trip; so presently he found himself, unrebuked, down
by the shaft well while his companion worked on a bearing. It was not a
safe neighborhood.

The Hunter did not fully realize the danger, strangely enough. He
was used to less bulky machines whose moving parts—when they had
any—were very securely cased while in operation. He saw the nearly unguarded shaft and gears, but it somehow never struck him that they might
be dangerous until a stream of rather lurid language erupted from under
the shaft housing. At the same instant Bob jerked his hand back sharply,
and the Hunter felt as well as his host the abrupt pain as a dollop of hot
oil struck the boy's skin. The man had reached in a little too far in the

semidarkness and allowed his oil gun to touch the shaft. The abrupt jerk had caused him to tighten on the trigger, releasing an excessive amount of lubricant onto the bearing he was checking. It had needed the oil, running hot as it was, but had flung off the excess, with rather painful results.

The crewman backed out of his cramped position, still giving vent to his feelings. He had been scalded in several places by the oil, but when he saw Bob another thought took precedence. "Did you get hurt, kid?" he asked anxiously. He knew what was likely to happen if Bob *were* injured in his company—there were stringent orders from the bridge dealing with the things the boy was and was not to be allowed to do.

Bob had equally good reasons for not wanting to get in trouble where he was, so he held the scorched hand as naturally as possible and replied, "No, I'm O.K. What happened to you? Can I help?"

"You can get some burn ointment from the kit. These ain't bad, but I can sure feel 'em. I'll slap it on here; no sense in bothering anyone else."

Bob grinned understandingly and went for the ointment. On his way back with it he started to put a little of the stuff surreptitiously on his own burn; but a thought struck him, and he refrained.

The idea bothered him while he was helping the crewman apply the ointment; and as soon thereafter as he could, he left the engine room and made his way back to his quarters. He had a question to ask, which grew more urgent as the pain in his hand grew more intense.

"Hunter!" He spoke as soon as he was sure no one was around to distract his attention from the answer. "I thought you were able to protect me from injury of this sort! Look what you did to that cut." He indicated the nearly healed slash on his arm.

"All I did there was prevent bleeding and destroy dangerous bacteria," replied the Hunter. "Stopping pain would demand that I cut nerves in this case—burns are not cuts."

"Well, why not cut 'em? This hurts!"

"I have already told you that I will not willingly do anything to harm you. Nerve cells regenerate slowly, if at all, and you need a sense of touch. Pain is a natural warning."

"But what do I need it for if you can fix up ordinary injuries?"

"To keep you from getting such injuries. I don't fix them—I simply prevent infection and blood loss, as I said. I have no magical powers, whatever you may have thought. I kept this burn from blistering by blocking the leakage of plasma, and the same act is making it much less painful than it would otherwise be, but I can do no more. I would not stop the pain if I could; you need something to keep you from getting careless. I expect trouble enough, since blocking minor cuts stops most of the pain, as you have found out. I have not mentioned this before, as I hoped the occasion would not arise, but I must insist that you be as careful in your everyday activities *as though I were not here;* otherwise you would be like a person who ignores all traffic rules because someone has guaranteed him free garage service. I cannot put that too strongly!"

There was one other thing the Hunter had done, which he did not mention. A burn, of all injuries, is one of the most likely to produce shock—the condition in which the great abdominal blood vessels relax, dropping the blood pressure so that the sufferer turns pale, loses his temperature control, and may become unconscious. The Hunter, feeling this condition start almost immediately after the accident, had tightened around the blood vessels as he had before around Bob's muscles, save that this time he administered the pressure intermittently—timing the squeezes to synchronize with the beating of Bob's heart; and his host had never even felt the nausea which is of the first warnings of shock. This job was done at the same time as the Hunter was sealing the burned tissue against plasma leakage with more of his own flesh, but he did not mention it.

It was the first time there had been anything like strong words between the symbiote and his host. Fortunately Bob had sense enough to see the reason behind the Hunter's statements and sufficient self-control to hide the slight annoyance he could not help feeling at the Hunter's refusal to relieve his pain. At least, he told himself, shaking the throbbing hand, nothing dangerous could come of it.

But he had to revise his idea of life with the Hunter. He had been visualizing the period during the search as a sort of Paradise—not that he ever was bothered seriously by minor injuries, colds, and the like, but it would have been nice not to have to consider them. Mosquitoes and sand flies, for example—he had wanted to ask the Hunter what he could do about pests like those, but now he felt rather uncomfortable at the thought. He would have to wait and see.

The night which finally closed in on them was calm. Bob, making the most of his lack of supervision, stayed late on the bridge, sometimes silently watching the sea and sometimes talking with the man at the wheel. Around midnight he left the bridge and made his way aft. For a little while he leaned over the stern railing, watching the luminous wake of the tanker and thinking of the resemblance between the trackless breadth of the ocean and the planet which the Hunter might have to search. Finally he sought his bunk.

The wind picked up during the night, and when Bob arose in the morning the sea was rather high. The Hunter had opportunity for research into the causes and nature of seasickness, eventually reaching the conclusion that he could do nothing about it without doing permanent damage to his host's sense of balance. Fortunately for Bob the wind died down after a few hours, and the waves subsided almost as speedily; the tanker had barely touched the edge of the storm area.

He quickly forgot his annoyance once he could associate with the crew again, however, for, as he knew from previous experience, his home island should become visible shortly after noon. For the latter half of the morning he practically vibrated between bow and bridge, gazing eagerly ahead over the long swells toward family, friends, and—danger, though he did not fully appreciate the last.

# VIII. Setting. . .

Though the island was "high" in the local terminology—that is, the submarine mountain which formed its base actually projected above the surface of the sea, rather than merely approaching it closely enough to serve as foundation for a coral superstructure—its highest point was only about ninety feet above sea level; so the tanker was comparatively close before Bob could point out anything to his invisible guest. The Hunter, finally seeing his hunting ground actually before him, thought it was time to call the meeting to order.

"Bob," he projected, "I know you enjoy this, but we really cannot see much as yet, and we will be ashore in a couple of hours. If you don't mind, I should like to see your map again."

Although the alien had no means of expressing emotion in his writing, Bob caught the undercurrent of seriousness in his words. "All right, Hunter," he answered, and went aft to the cabin where he had left the map. When the sheet was spread out in front of them, the detective went right to the point.

"Bob, have you thought about how we are going to catch this being? I never answered your question before."

"I was wondering, when you didn't. You people are so queer—to me, that is—that I decided you must be able to smell him out or something. You certainly can't see him, if he's like you. Do you have some sort of gadget that will find him for you?"

"Don't rub it in." The Hunter did not explain his phrase. "I have no apparatus whatever. This is your planet; how would *you* go about it?"

Bob pondered for a few moments. "If you actually go into a body, I suppose you can tell if there's another of your people there." This was more a statement than a question, but the Hunter made the brief sign which Bob had come to accept as an affirmative. "How long would such

81

a search take? Could you get through the skin far enough while I was shaking hands with someone, say?"

"No. It takes many minutes to enter a body like yours without giving warning. The openings in your skin are large, but my body is much larger. If you let go of the other person's hand while I was still partly in both bodies, it would be very embarrassing for all concerned. If I left you entirely and worked at night while people were asleep, I suppose I could cover the whole island eventually; but I would be very much restricted in speed, and would be in an extremely awkward position when I found him. I will undoubtedly have to make the final check that way, but I should very much like to be pretty sure of my ground before testing anyone. I still want your ideas."

"I don't know any of your standard methods," Bob said slowly. "And I can't, right now, think of means for checking people for company; but we might try to trace his course from the time he landed, and find what people he *might* have got at. Could that be done?"

"With the addition of one word, yes. We can trace his *possible* course. There is likely to be little or no evidence about his actual path, but I can judge, I think, with considerable accuracy what he would do in any given situation. Of course I'll have to know a lot about the situation: all you can tell me, and all I can see for myself."

"I can see that," answered Bob. "All right, we'll have to start with the time he reached the island—if he did. Any ideas?"

"We'll have to start sooner than that. Before we can guess where he landed, we must judge where he crashed. Will you point out on your map the place where I found you?"

Bob nodded, and his finger indicated a point on the paper. At the northwest tip of the island—the end of the longer branch of the L—the land tapered to a blunt point; and from this point the reef extended, first northward and then curving to the east and back to the south to enclose the lagoon. Bob was indicating the west side of this point.

"This," he said, "is the only real sea beach on the island. It's the only part of the shore not protected by the reef. You see south of the tip there's a few hundred yards before the reef starts again and keeps the breakers from the whole south shore. It's the place the fellows and I like best, and it's where we were swimming the day you arrived. I remember that shark."

"Very well." The Hunter took up the conversation. "Up until shortly before we reached the earth's atmosphere I was tracking him on automatic control, so that I was within a few feet of his line of flight. When I realized how close we were to the planet I went on manual and tried to drive straight away, but it was along the same line. Even allowing for the disturbance your atmosphere caused on our lines of flight, I don't think we could have struck the water more than a mile or two apart. I can check that; I was watching him on the bow scanner, which has only a ten-degree field of vision.

"Also, I could not have crashed far offshore. Do you know how rapidly the water deepens off the island?"

"Not in feet. I know it's steep, though; large ships can come quite close to the reef."

"That's what I thought; and I was in shallow water. We crashed, we will say, within a two-mile radius of this point." The Hunter momentarily shaded, on Bob's retina, a point a little way off the shore from the beach. "And much of that can be eliminated. He certainly did not crash on shore; my instruments showed him sinking after the initial check. I am equally sure he did not land in the lagoon, since you say it is very shallow, and he must have struck hard enough to reach its bottom instantly—at a guess, he must have had over fifty feet of water; I certainly did, though not much over, I should say.

"We can, then, act on the assumption that he landed in the two-mile semicircle to the west of the island, centered just offshore from your beach. I admit that is not an absolute certainty, and it may be hard to prove, but it gives us something to start on. Have you any other ideas?"

"Just questions. How long would it have taken him to get ashore?"

"Your guess is as good as mine. If he had the luck I did, a few hours. If he was in very deep water, with even less oxygen than I, and a stronger sense of caution, he might have spent days or weeks crawling along the bottom to shore. I myself would never have attacked that shark, or ventured to swim out of touch with the bottom, unless I had been very sure I was near shore."

"How would he have known the right direction? Maybe he's still crawling around down there."

"Maybe. However, with the storm that night he could have determined the direction of the breakers as easily as I did; and if the bottom slopes as steeply as you think, it would have furnished another clue for him. I don't think that problem would have been serious. Of course he is known to be a coward; that may have kept him with the wreckage of his ship for quite a while."

"Then in order to go any farther we'll have to explore the reef for a mile or so each way from the beach, to see if he left any traces. Is that right? And if he has, what do you suppose he will have done after landing—same as you?"

"Your first guess is right. As for the question, that depends. He would certainly want to find a host as soon as possible; but whether he simply waited for one where he landed, or went in search of something suitable, is hard to say. If he landed at a spot where any artificial structures are visible, he would probably have made his way to them, on the theory that intelligent beings were bound to come to them sooner or later. It's something that can't be predicted exactly, that's why I said I would have to know *all* the circumstances to guess his actions."

Bob nodded slowly, digesting this. Finally he asked, "What sort of traces are you likely to find at his place of landing? And if you don't find any, what will we do?"

"I don't know." There was no indication which question was being answered; and Bob finally grew tired of waiting for further explanation. It bothered him, for even he could see that the methods they had just outlined were not very promising. He thought intently for a time, half hoping his guest would come out with some supplementary technique from his own science. Suddenly an idea struck him.

"Hunter! I just thought of something! Remember the only time you could get to me, that day on the beach, was when I fell asleep?" The alien expressed assent. "Well, won't the same be true of this other fellow? He couldn't catch a person, or at least couldn't do it without being seen. You said yourself that it would take several minutes to get right inside; and even if this fellow doesn't care about the feelings or health of his host, he still wouldn't want to be seen. So it ought to narrow things down a bit if I found out who had been sleeping near the water in the last few months. There aren't any houses near the sea—Norm Hay's is the closest, and there shouldn't be too many people who made picnics the way we did that day. How about it?"

"You may have a point there. It is certainly worth trying; but remember, there is no part of the island that he could not reach given time enough, and everybody sleeps at some time or other—though he mightn't know that, come to think of it. Certainly anyone who has slept near the shore is, as you say, suspect."

A change in the rhythm of the engines interrupted the thoughtful silence that followed this remark, and Bob went back on deck, to find that the tanker had slowed and was turning to line up for the entrance to the western passage through the reef. A hasty trip along the catwalks took them to the bow, from which an unobstructed view could be had of the north reef and lagoon.

The reef, it seemed to the Hunter, was not too encouraging a field of search. Certainly no human being could have hidden there for long; and while his quarry could undoubtedly remain concealed, life in such a place would not be pleasant. Long sections of the barrier were barely visible above water, their position betrayed mostly by the breakers. Some portions were higher and had accumulated enough soil to support sparse vegetation—even coconut palms in one or two places. As the tanker nosed into the narrow passage, he realized that, in spite of this, searching the reef for clues might not be easy; it was never possible for a person to travel more than a few rods on foot, as he could see from the broken-up nature of the barrier; and on the outer side at least boating would be extremely dangerous—the endless breakers crashing through the openings in the coral created fierce and unpredictable currents and eddies almost certain to sweep any small craft against the rock-hard roughness of the reef. Even the tanker, big as she was and with plenty of steerage way, kept to the center of the marked channel while Bob and the Hunter watched the coral slip by on either side.

Even inside the lagoon they stayed carefully between the buoys, the Hunter noticed; and he recalled what Bob had said about the shallowness of the water here. On either side of them, scattered over the several square miles between reef and island proper, were angular concrete bulks that the Hunter assumed to be the culture tanks. These were from two to three hundred feet on a side, but their walls did not extend more than five or six feet above the water. The nearest was too far away for small details to be made out, but the Hunter was pretty sure it was covered by a roof consisting mostly of glass panes, while small square superstructures at various points were connected by catwalks to each other and to a diminutive landing stage on the side toward the channel.

Ahead of them was a larger structure, rather different in detail, and as they approached its purpose became evident. Like the tanks, it was rectangular in shape, but it rose much higher out of the water—almost as high as the tanker's bridge for the central portions. The "deck" level was lower but still considerably above that of the culture tanks. This surface was covered with various structures, some obviously storage tanks and pumps, others more obscure in nature. On the side toward the approaching vessel were great mooring cables and even bigger hoses, with twenty or thirty men visible working around them. The structure obviously was the dock to which Bob had referred and which was used to store and transfer the fuel oils which were the chief product of the island.

Both watchers looked through Bob's eyes with interest as the tanker glided in to the dock and settled against the fenders. More lines snaked across and were pulled aboard, drawing the hoses after them; and in a remarkably short time the thudding of pumps showed that the last eight days' production was flowing into the tanker. It took a hail from the bridge to distract them from the process.

"Bob! You'll need some help with your stuff, getting it ashore, won't you?" Teroa was calling down to the boy.

"Yes, thanks," Bob called back. "I'll be right there." He took one more quick look around, and his grin broadened at something he saw; then he was speeding over the catwalks to the stem. Partly visible around the comer of the dock from where he had been standing was the long causeway that connected the structure with the shore; and along that causeway he had seen a jeep driving furiously. He knew who the driver of that vehicle would be.

The baggage was tumbled out onto the dock in record time, but the jeep had squealed around the corner and come to a halt beside the hoses some minutes before Bob and the mate came down the plank with the last piece between them. Bob dropped his end of the foot locker and ran to meet the man standing beside the little car. The Hunter watched with interest and some sympathy.

Even he was sufficiently familiar with human faces by now to detect the resemblance between father and son. Bob still had six or seven inches of height to pick up, but there was the same dark hair and blue eyes, the same straight nose and broad, easily smiling mouth, and the same chin.

Bob's greeting had the exuberance natural to his age; his father, while equally delighted, maintained an undercurrent of gravity that went unnoticed by the boy but which was both seen and understood by the Hunter. The alien realized he had one other job—it was going to be necessary to convince Mr. Kinnaird that there was nothing actually wrong with his son, or the latter's freedom of action might be seriously curtailed. He filed that thought for the moment, however, and listened with interest to the conversation. Bob was overwhelming his father with a flood of questions that threatened to involve the doings of the entire population of the island. At first the Hunter was minded to criticize his host's action in starting the investigation so early; but he presently realized that the search was far from the boy's mind. He was simply trying to fill a five-month gap. The detective stopped worrying and listened carefully to Mr. Kinnard's answers in the hope of finding some useful information; and he was human enough to be disappointed when the man cut off the flood of questions with a laugh.

"Bob boy! I don't know what *everyone's* been up to since you left; you'll have to ask them. I'm going to have to be here until they finish loading; you'd better take the jeep up to the house with your luggage—I expect your mother could stand seeing you, if you can spare the time. Your friends won't be out of school yet, anyway. Just a minute." He rifled through the jeep's toolbox recklessly, finally extracting a well-cased set of calipers from the collection of center punches, cold chisels, and wrenches.

"Oh, my gosh, that's right; I'll have to see about school myself, won't I? I'd forgotten I wasn't coming back for vacation this time." He looked so sober for a moment that his father laughed again, not realizing the cause of his son's sudden thoughtfulness. Bob recovered quickly, however, and looked up again. "Okay, Dad, I'll get the stuff home. See you at supper?"

"Yes, provided you get that jeep back here as soon as you've finished with it. And no remarks about my needing exercise!"

Bob grinned, good humor completely restored. "Not until I'm dressed to go swimming," he replied.

The loading was quickly accomplished, and Bob, sliding under the wheel, sent the little vehicle rapidly along the causeway to the shore. From here, as he had told the Hunter, a paved road led straight inland for a quarter of a mile, where it joined the main thoroughfare of the island at right angles. There was a large cluster of corrugated-iron storage sheds flanking the short road, and when they reached the turn the Hunter could see that these extended to the left, up the shorter arm of the island. He could also see the white concrete of at least one more culture tank peering around the corner of the hill in that direction, and resolved to ask Bob at the first opportunity why these were not built in the water like the others.

Just at the turning where the two roads met, the dwelling houses started to replace the storage sheds. Most of the former were on the shoreward side of the main road, but one, surrounded by a large garden, lay on their right just before the turning. A tall, brown-skinned youth was busy in the garden. Bob, seeing him, braked the jeep quickly and emitted an ear-hurting whistle through his front teeth. The gardener looked up, straightened, and ran over to the road.

"Bob! Didn't know you were coming back so early. What have you been doing, kid?" Charles Teroa was only three years older than Bob, but he had finished school and was apt to use a condescending tone to his juniors who had not. Bob had given up resenting it; besides, he now had ammunition if there was to be a contest of repartee.

"Not as much as you have," he answered, "from what your father tells me."

The younger Teroa grimaced. "Pop would tell. Well, it was fun, even if that friend of yours did back out."

"Did you really expect them to give work to someone who spends half his days sleeping?" Bob gibed, mindful of the order to keep the job a secret for the present.

Teroa was properly indignant. "What do you mean? I never sleep when there's work to do." He glanced at a patch of grass in the shade of a large tree which grew beside the house. "Just look; best place in the world for a nap, and you found me working. I'm even going back to school."

"How come?"

"I'm taking navigation from Mr. Dennis. Figured it would help next time I tried."

Bob raised his eyebrows. "Next time? You're hard to discourage. When will that be?"

"Don't know yet. I'll tell you when I think I'm ready. Want to come along?"

"I dunno. I don't want a job on a ship, that's certain. We'll see how I feel when you make up your mind. I've got to get this stuff home, and get the jeep back to Dad, and get to the school before the fellows get out; I'd better be going."

Teroa nodded and stepped back from the side of the jeep. "Too bad you're not one of those things we learned about in school, that splits in two every so often. I was wishing I was a little while ago, then part of me might have gotten away with that stunt."

Bob, on occasion, was a quick thinker. This time, at least, he managed to conceal the jolt Charles's words had given him; he repeated the farewells, started the vehicle, swung around the corner to the right, and stepped on the gas. For the half mile the road ran among the houses and gardens he said nothing, except at the very end, when he pointed out a long, low building on their left as the school. A short distance beyond this, however, he pulled to the side of the road and stopped. They were out of sight of the rest of the island, having driven with startling suddenness into the densely overgrown section Bob had mentioned.

"Hunter," the boy said tensely as soon as they were stopped, "I never thought of it, but Charlie reminded me. You folks are like amoebae, you said. Are you entirely like them? I mean—is there any chance of—of our having more than one of your people to catch?"

The Hunter had not understood the boy's hesitance and did not understand the question until he had digested it a moment.

"You mean, might our friend have split in two, as your amoebae do?" he asked. "Not in the sense you mean—we are slightly more complicated beings. It would be possible for him to bud off an offspring—separate a portion of his flesh to make a new individual—but that one would be at least one of your years reaching full size. He could, of course, release it at any time, but I don't think he would, for a very good reason.

"If he tried it while in the body of a host, the new symbiote would have no more knowledge than a newborn child of your own race; it would certainly kill the host in its blind search for food, or simply while moving around in ignorance of its surroundings. While it is true we know more biology than your race, we are not with the knowledge; learning to live with a host takes time and is one of the chief phases of our education.

"Therefore, if our quarry does reproduce at all, he will do it from purely selfish motives—to create a being which will almost certainly be quickly caught and destroyed, so that the pursuers he expects will think he himself has been killed. It was a good point, of course—I had not con-sidered the possibility myself—but it is true that a creature such as we are pursuing would probably not hesitate to do such a thing—if he thinks of it. Of course his first care will be to find a hiding place; and if that turns out to be a satisfactory host, I doubt whether he would take the chance of leaving for the purpose you suggested."

"That's some relief." Bob sighed. "For a few minutes there I was think-ing that the last five months might have given us a whole tribe to chase down."

He restarted the jeep and drove the short remaining distance to his home without interruption. The house lay some distance up the hill from the road, at the end of a drive completely roofed in by trees. It was a fairly large, two-storied dwelling in the midst of the jungle—the heavy growths had been cleared away for only a few yards around it, so that the first-floor windows were shaded most of the time. In front, where the drive emerged, an extra amount of labor had made a sun porch possible, though even this Mrs. Kinnaird had found better to shade with flowering creep-ers. The temperature of the island was not excessively high, because of the surrounding water, but the sun was frequently intense and shade some-thing to be ardently sought.

She was waiting on the porch. She had known of the ship's arrival, and had heard the jeep coming up the drive. Bob's greeting was affection-ate, though less boisterous than the one on the dock, but Mrs. Kinnard could find nothing wrong with either her son's appearance or his behav-ior. He did not stay long, but she did not expect that; she simply listened happily to his almost endless talk as he unloaded the jeep, dragged the luggage up to his room, changed out of his traveling clothes, found his bicycle and loaded it into the car, and departed. She was fond of her son and would have liked to see more of him, but she knew that he would not enjoy sitting around talking to her for any length of time; and she was wise enough not to regret the fact particularly. As a matter of fact, if he had gone so much out of character as to do some such thing she would have been worried; as it was, the load that the school communication had put on her mind was partly lifted as she watched and listened. She was able to turn to her housework with a lighter heart, when the jeep bounced back down the drive on its way to the dock.

Bob met no one and stopped for nothing on this trip. He parked the jeep in its accustomed place beside one of the tanks, unloaded his bi-cycle, and started to mount. There was a slight delay, caused by his hav-ing forgotten to check the tires before leaving home, then he was pedal-ing back along the causeway. There was excitement and anticipation writ-ten large on his face, not merely because he was to rejoin his friends after a long absence, but because an exciting play was, from his point of view, about to start. He was ready. He knew the stage—the island on which he had been born, and whose every square yard he was sure he knew. The Hunter knew the setting—the habits and capabilities of the murderous being they sought, and only the characters were left. A trace of grimness tinged the excitement on Bob's face as he thought of that; he was far from stupid, and had long since realized that, of all the people on the island, the most likely ones to have afforded refuge to his quarry were those who spent the most time near the shore and in the water—in short, his best friends.

# IX. The Players

Bob timed his arrival well; the school was dismissed only a minute or two after he reached it, and he was immediately surrounded by a riotous crowd of acquaintances. The school-age population of the island was a rather large fraction of the total. When the station had been established some eighteen years before, only young married couples were accepted for positions there. Consequently there was a great deal of chatter, hand-shaking, and mutual inquiry before the group finally broke up and left Bob surrounded by a few of his closest friends.

Only one of these could the Hunter recognize as a member of the group who had been swimming together the day he met Bob. He had not, at the time, been very familiar with the distinguishing criteria of human features, but Kenny Rice's mop of flame-colored hair was hard to forget. The alien quickly learned from the conversation which of the others had belonged to the swimming party: they were boys named Norman Hay and Hugh Colby—presumably the ones to whom Bob had already referred in describing the layout of the island. The other one he had mentioned, Kenneth Malmstrom, was the only other member of the present group; he was a blond fifteen-year-old approximately six feet tall who had come by his nickname in the usual manner—he was distinguished by the inevitable sobriquet of "Shorty." These four, together with Bob, had been companions ever since they were old enough to go out of sight of their neighboring houses. It was more than coincidence that the alien had found most of them swimming at the point where he first came ashore; any islander, knowing the point where he had landed, would have been perfectly willing to bet that the Hunter would make one of the five his first host. They were born beachcombers. None of them, therefore, thought it strange when Bob quickly brought the conversation around to such matters.

91

"Has anyone been poking around the reef lately?"

"*We* haven't," replied Rice. "Hugh stepped through the bottom of the boat about six weeks ago, and we haven't been able to find a plank that would fix it so far."

"That bottom had been promising to go for months!" Colby, ordinarily an extremely quiet and retiring youngster—he was the youngest of the five—came stoutly to his own defense. Nobody saw fit to dispute his statement.

"Anyway, we've got to go the long way around to the south shore now if we take a boat," added Rice. "There was a lallapalooza of a storm in December, and it shifted a brain coral bigger than the boat into the gate. Dad has been promising to dynamite it ever since for us, but he hasn't got around to it yet."

"Can't you persuade him to let us do it even yet?" asked Bob. "One stick would be enough, and we all know how to handle caps."

"Try to convince him of that. His only answer has been, 'When you're older,' ever since I was old enough to pronounce the word."

"Well, how about the beach, then?" asked Bob. There were many beaches on the island, but the word had only one meaning to this group. "We could walk part of the south shore and grab a swim as we went around. I haven't been in salt water since I left last fall." The others agreed, and dispersed to collect the bicycles which were leaning against the school building.

The Hunter made good use of Bob's ears and eyes during the ride. He learned little from the conversation, but he did clarify considerably his mental picture of the island. Bob had not mentioned the small creek which wound down to the lagoon a couple of hundred yards from the school, and he had not noticed it himself on the trip to the boy's house; but this time the well-made wooden bridge which carried them over it caught his attention. Almost immediately after they passed the spot where Bob had stopped the jeep, then, three quarters of a mile from the school, the other boys stopped and waited while Bob pedaled up the drive to get his bathing suit. A quarter of a mile farther Rice did the same; then there was another small creek, this time carried under the road through a concrete culvert. The Hunter gathered from several remarks made at this point that the boat to which Rice had referred was kept at the mouth of this watercourse.

Malmstrom and Colby in turn deposited their books and collected swimming trunks; and finally the group reached the Hay residence, at the end of the paved road and somewhat more than two miles from the school. Here the bicycles were left, and the group headed westward on foot around the end of the ridgelike hill which formed the backbone of the island and on which all their houses were built.

Half a mile of traveling, partly along a trail through the jungle-thick growth of the ridge and partly through a relatively open grove of coconut palms, brought them to the beach; and the Hunter at last found a spot on Earth that he recognized. The pool in which his shark had stranded was gone—storm and tide had done their usual work on the sandbanks—but the palm grove and the beach were the same. He had reached the spot where he had met Bob—the spot from which his search for the fugitive should have started had it not been for some incredibly bad luck; and the spot from which, without further argument, it *would* start.

Detectives and crime were far from the minds of the group of boys, however. They had wasted no time in getting into swimming costume, and Bob was already dashing toward the surf, ahead of the rest, his winter-bleached skin gleaming in odd contrast to the well-tanned hides of his young friends.

The beach, though largely composed of fine sand, contained many fragments of sharp coral, and in his haste the boy stepped hard on several of these before he could bring himself to a stop. The Hunter was doing his duty, so Bob saw no evidence of actual damage when he inspected the soles of his feet; he decided that he was simply oversensitive from several months in shoes, and resumed his dash for the water. Naturally he could not show that he had gone soft before his friends. The Hunter was pardonably annoyed—wasn't one lecture enough?—and administered the muscular twinges he had been accustomed to give his former host as a signal that he was going too far; but Bob was too tensed up to feel the signal and would not have known its meaning in any case. He churned into an incoming breaker, the others at his heels. The Hunter gave up his attempts at signaling, held the cuts closed, and seethed quietly. Granting that his host was young, he still should have better self-control, and should not throw the entire burden of maintaining his health on the Hunter. Something would have to be done.

The swim was short; as Bob had said, this was the only part of the island unprotected by the reef, and the surf was heavy. The boys decided in a few minutes that they had had enough. They emerged from the water, bundled their clothes into their shirts, and set off southward down the beach carrying the garments. Before they had gone very far the Hunter took advantage of Bob's gazing momentarily out to sea to advise him in strong terms to don his shoes. The boy allowed his common sense to override minor considerations of vanity and did so.

After the first few hundred yards the reef appeared again at the shore line and gradually drew farther away, so the amount of jetsam on the beach naturally decreased; but in spite of this they had one piece of good fortune—a twelve-foot plank, fourteen inches wide and perfectly sound, had somehow found its way through the barrier and been cast up on the sand (the boys carefully refrained from considering the possibility that it might have been washed around from the construction work on the other end of the island). With the damaged boat foremost in their minds, they delightedly dragged the treasure above high-water mark, and Malmstrom wrote his name in the sand beside it. They left it there, to pick up on their return.

Aside from this the "south shore"—the nearly straight stretch of beach that extended for some three miles along the southwest side of the island's longer branch—yielded little of interest or value to any of the youthful beachcombers. Near the farthest point of their walk they encountered a stranded skate, and Bob, remembering how the Hunter had come ashore, examined it closely. He was joined by Hay; but neither got much for his trouble. The creature had evidently been there for some time, and the process of examination was not too pleasant.

"A good way to waste time, as far as we are concerned," the Hunter remarked as Bob straightened up. For once he had correctly guessed the boy's thoughts. Bob almost agreed aloud before he remembered that they were not alone.

Bob returned to his home late for supper. The plank had been borne, by their united efforts, to the mouth of the creek where the boat was kept, so the only concrete souvenir of the afternoon's activities that he brought home with him was the beginning glow of a very complete sunburn. Even the Hunter had failed to appreciate the danger or detect the symptoms early enough to get the boy back into his clothes before the damage had been done.

The alien, unlike Bob, was able to see one good point in the incident. It might be more effective than lectures in curing the boy's unfortunate increasing tendency to leave the care of his body to the Hunter. He said nothing this time, and let the sufferer do his own thinking as he lay awake that night trying to keep as much of himself as possible out of contact with the sheets. Bob was, as a matter of fact, decidedly annoyed with himself; he had not been so careless for years, and the only excuse he could find for himself was the fact that he had come home at such an odd time. Even he could see that this was not a very good one, which made it more annoying.

The several square feet of bright red skin that descended to breakfast the next morning enclosed an exceedingly disgruntled youth. He was angry with himself, somewhat annoyed at the Hunter, and not too pleased with the rest of the world. His father, looking at him, was not sure whether it would be safe to smile, and decided not to. He spoke with some sympathy instead.

"Bob, I was going to suggest that you go down to school today to get straightened out on enrollment, but maybe you'd better cool off first. I don't imagine it will hurt to leave it till Monday."

Bob nodded, though not exactly in relief—he had completely forgotten school. "I guess you're right," he answered. "I wouldn't get much from school this week anyhow; it's Thursday already. Anyway, I want to look over the place for a while."

His father glanced at him sideways. "I'd think twice before going outdoors with that hide of yours," he remarked.

"He won't, though," cut in Mrs. Kinnaird. "Even if he is your son." The head of the family made no reply, but turned back to Bob,

"Be sure you keep yourself covered, anyway, and if you must explore, it might be a good idea to concentrate on the woods. At least it's shady there."

"It's just a case of having him carved or cooked, if you ask me," Mrs. Kinnaird said. "If he's cooked, at least his clothes are all right; usually after a session in the woods both his hide and his clothes are a lot the worse for thorns." The smile on her face belied the heartless implication in her words, and Bob grinned across the table at her.

"O.K., Mother, I'll try to hit a happy medium."

He went back up to his room after breakfast and donned an old long-sleeved khaki shirt of his father's instead of the T-shirt he had originally worn, came back and helped his mother with the dishes—his father had already driven off—spent a while fighting the ropy jungle growth which persistently threatened to overwhelm the house, and finally put away clippers and hormone spray and vanished into the tangle south of the dwelling.

His course carried him gradually farther from the road and distinctly uphill. He traveled as though with a definite purpose in mind, and the Hunter forbore to question him—the background of jungle was not very suitable for his method of communication anyway. Shortly after leaving the house they crossed a brook, which the detective correctly judged to be the same watercourse that was bridged by the road a little lower down. A fallen tree, whose upper surface bore signs of frequent use, crossed it here.

Mrs. Kinnaird had not exaggerated the nature of the jungle. Few of the trees were extremely tall, but the ground between them was literally choked with smaller growths, many of them, as she had said, viciously thorned. Bob threaded his way around these with a speed and skill that suggested long experience. A botanist might have been puzzled by many of the plants; the island bore a botanical and bacteriological laboratory in which work was constantly in progress to improve the oil-making bacteria and to breed better plants to feed the tanks. Since what was desired was very rapid growth with a minimum of demand on the mineral content of the soil, the test plants occasionally got out of hand.

The place Bob intended to go was barely eight hundred yards from the house, but the journey took more than half an hour. Eventually they reached the edge of the jungle and the top of the hill, and found themselves looking down toward the settled portion of the island. Where the jungle had been stopped by hormone sprays to make room for the gardens was a tree, taller than any they had seen in the jungle itself, though not so high as the coconut palms near the shore. Its lower branches were gone, but the trunk was ringed with creepers that made a very satisfactory ladder, and Bob went up without difficulty.

In the upper branches was a rough platform that indicated to the Hunter that the boys had used the place before; and from here, well above the general level of the jungle, practically the entire island was visible. Bob let his eye rove slowly around the full circle, to give the Hunter every chance to fill in details that had been lacking on the map.

As the Hunter had thought from his glimpse up the road the day before, there were some tanks on shore on the northeast end of the island as well. These, Bob said when questioned, housed bacteria which worked so much better at high temperature that it was worth while to have them up in the sunlight and accept the fact that their activity would stop at night.

"There seem to be more of them than there used to be," he added. "But, then, they're always doing work of one kind or another. It's hard to be sure—most of them are on the far slope of the northeast hill, which is about the only part of the place we can't see very well from here."

"Except objects in and near the edge of this jungle," remarked the Hunter.

"Of course. Well, we couldn't expect to find our friend from a distance, anyway; I came up here to give you a better idea of the layout. We'll have to do a good deal of our searching in the next three days; I certainly can't put off school longer than Monday." He nodded at the long building down the hill. "We could go looking over the reef now if the boat were in shape."

"Are there no other boats on the island?"

"Sure. I suppose we could borrow one, though it's not too smart to poke around the reef alone. If anything happens to the boat, or a person bashes himself falling on the coral, it's apt to be too bad. We usually go in boatloads."

"We might at least look over some of the safer portions, if you can get a boat. If not, can any parts near your beach be reached on foot?"

"No, though it wouldn't take much of a swim to get to the nearest part. I'm not going to swim today, though, unless you can do a good deal more about sunburn than you have done."

He paused a moment, and went on, "How about the other fellows? Did you see anything about them yesterday that might make it worth while to try firsthand testing?"

"No. What would you expect me to see?'

Bob had no answer to that, and after a moment's thought slowly descended the tree. He hesitated for a moment more at the bottom, as though undecided between two courses of action, then he headed downhill, threading his way between garden patches and slanting gradually toward the road. He explained his hesitancy with: "Guess it isn't worth the trouble to get the bike."

They reached the road about two hundred yards east of the school and kept going in that direction, Bob glancing at the houses they passed as though estimating his chances of borrowing such a thing as a boat from the occupants. Presently he reached the road which led down to the dock, with the Teroa house at the corner, and Bob quickened his steps.

He walked around to the shoreward side of the dwelling, rather expecting to find Charles working in the garden, but the only people there were the two girls of the Teroa family, who said that their brother was inside. As Bob turned toward the house the door was flung open and Charles burst out.

"Bob! You doubting Thomas! I've got it!" Bob looked slightly bewildered and glanced around at the girls, both of whom were grinning widely.

"Got what?"

"The job, fathead! What were we talking about yesterday? A radiogram came this morning. I didn't even know there was an application in it—I thought I'd have to try all over."

"I knew." Bob grinned. "Your father told me."

"And you didn't tell me?" Teroa reached out for him and Bob moved back hastily.

"He said not to—you weren't supposed to know. Anyway isn't this better than sweating it out?"

Teroa relaxed, laughing. "I suppose so. Anyway, that red-headed friend of yours will be mad—it's what he gets for backing out!"

"Redhead? Ken? What has he to do with it? I thought it was Norman went with you."

"It was, but it was Rice's idea, and he was supposed to come along. He got cold feet or something and never showed up. Can I razz him now!" He turned suddenly serious. "Don't you tell him about this job. I want to!" He started to walk toward the dock, then turned back. "I'm going out to Four to collect something Ray borrowed a while back. Want to come along?"

Bob looked at the sky, but the Hunter expressed no opinion, and he had to make up his own mind. "I don't think so," he said. "The barge is a little ripe for my taste." He watched as the brown-skinned eighteen-year-old disappeared among the storage sheds, then turned slowly back up the road.

"That was our only real chance for a boat," he said to the Hunter. "We'll have to wait until the fellows get out of school. As a group, we stand a better chance of borrowing one—or maybe it won't take long to fix our own. I didn't have time to look at it very closely when we took the plank down yesterday."

"Was that boy going to use his own boat?"

"Yes. You heard him say he was going out to Four—that's Tank Four—to get something. The person he mentioned works on the barge they use for carrying the tank wastes. Charlie wants to collect from him before he leaves the island."

The Hunter was instantly alert. "Leaves the island? You mean the bargeman?"

"No—Charlie. Didn't you hear what he was saying?"

"I heard him talk about a job, but that was all. Is it taking him away?"

"Of course! Charlie's the son of the mate of that ship—the one who stowed away, hoping to get a job on her! Don't you remember—his father told us the first night, on the ship!"

"I remember your talking to an officer on the tanker," the Hunter replied, "but I did not and do not know what you said. You were not talking English." Bob stopped short and whistled.

"I forgot all about that!" He paused a moment to marshal his thoughts, and told the story as briefly and clearly as he could. The Hunter thought for a time after he had finished.

"Then this Charles Teroa has left the island once since my arrival and is shortly to leave it again. Your friend Norman Hay has also left once. For Heaven's sake, if there are any others you've heard about, tell me!"

"There aren't, unless you want to count Charlie's father, and I don't suppose he's been ashore here much. What does it matter about the other trip? They never got ashore, you know, and I'm sure they didn't sleep in port, so if our friend was with them he couldn't have left except at sea."

"You may be right, but that will no longer be true for this one you just saw. He must be examined before he leaves! Start thinking, please."

For the first time that day Bob completely forgot his sunburn as he walked back up the road.

# X. Medical Report

Bob managed to hide his concern at lunch; his mother had thought of something during the morning to take his mind off the new problem. She had been wondering how to persuade her son to have a checkup by the island doctor, and had realized just after he disappeared what a splendid excuse the sunburn provided. She had no opportunity to discuss it with her husband, since Bob had arrived home first, but he would probably have agreed with her anyway. She brought up the subject as they finished the meal.

She did not really expect to win without argument; she knew Bob was ashamed of having acquired the sunburn and did not want more people than were strictly necessary to know about it. She was therefore somewhat astonished when her son agreed without a murmur to the suggestion that he drop into the doctor's office that afternoon, though she had the control and presence of mind not to show it.

The fact of the matter was that Bob had been thinking about the Hunter's failure to answer certain of his questions, particularly those which dealt with the details of how he was to recognize his quarry and still more, what he was to do after the creature was found. If the Hunter knew, well and good; but the suspicion that his invisible guest did not know was growing. It followed that Bob must get some ideas of his own; and for such ideas to be any use, he must learn more about the Hunter's species. The alien had said he resembled a virus. Very well. Bob would find out about viruses, and the logical place to do that was in a doctor's office. He had known it would be somewhat out of character for him to make the suggestion himself, but it did not occur to him to wonder that his mother should have done so; he simply accepted it as a piece of luck.

Dr. Seever knew Bob very well—as he knew every other person born on the island. He had read the communication from the school doctor, and agreed with Mr. Kinnaird's opinion of it; but he was glad of the chance to see the boy himself. Even he, however, was a little startled when he saw the color of Bob's skin.

"Good heavens! You really celebrated getting back here, didn't you?"

"Don't rub it in, Doc. I really know better."

"I should think so. Well, we'll tan your hide for you—not the way it ought to be done, but you'll be more comfortable." The doctor set briskly to work, talking steadily the while. "You certainly aren't the fellow you used to be. I can remember when you were one of the most thoughtful and careful people here. Have you been sick lately at that school of yours?" Bob had not expected the question so soon or in just this form, but he had made plans for putting it to his own use when it came.

"Certainly not. You can look me over all day and won't find any germs at work."

Dr. Seever looked over his glasses at the boy. "That's certainly possible, I know, but is hardly assurance that nothing is wrong. It was not germs that caused that sunburn, you know."

"Well, I sprained an ankle and had a cut or two, but they don't count. You were talking about *sickness,* and you could find out about that with your microscope, couldn't you?"

The doctor smiled, conceiving that he knew what the boy was driving at. "It's nice to find someone with such touching faith in medical science," he said, "but I'm afraid I couldn't. Just a minute and I'll show you why." He finished applying the sunburn material, put the container away, and brought an excellent microscope out of its cabinet. Some searching among rather dusty slide files found what he wanted, and he began slipping the bits of glass onto the stage one after another as he talked.

"This one we can see, and recognize, easily. It's protozoan—an amoeba, of the type that causes a disease called dysentery. It's big, as disease-causing organisms run."

"I've seen them in bio class at school," Bob admitted, "but I didn't know they caused disease."

"Most of them don't. Now this"—the doctor slipped another slide under the objective—"is a good deal smaller. The other wasn't really a germ at all. This causes typhoid fever when it gets a chance, though we haven't had a case in a long time. The next is smaller still and is the cause of cholera."

"It looks like a sausage with the string still on one end," Bob remarked as he raised his head from the instrument.

"You can see it better with the high-powered objective in place," Dr. Seever remarked, turning the turret at the lower end of the instrument and sinking back into his chair while Bob looked once more.

"That's about as far as this gadget can go. There are many smaller bacteria—some of them harmless, some not. There is a class of things called Rickettsia which are smaller still and may not be bacteria at all, and there are viruses."

Bob turned from the microscope and attempted the difficult feat of looking interested without showing that the conversation had finally reached the point he wished.

"Then you can't show me a virus?" he asked, knowing the answer perfectly well.

"That's what I'm getting at. A few of them have been photographed with the aid of the electron microscope—they seem to look a little like that cholera bug I showed you—but that's all. As a matter of fact, the word 'virus' was simply a confession of ignorance for a long time; doctors were blaming diseases which seemed to be life-caused for one reason or another, but for which they could find no causative organism such as I've shown you, on what they called 'filterable viruses'—so named because no matter how fine a filter you squeezed the juice from a diseased creature through, the cause seemed to go through with it. They even found ways to separate the virus stuff chemically and crystallize it; it would still cause the same disease when the crystals were dissolved in water again. They devised a lot of very pretty experiments to guess at the sizes of the things, and their shapes, and other such matters long before they saw 'em. Some scientists thought—and still think—they are single molecules; big ones, of course—even bigger than the albumin ones—that's the white of egg, you know. I have read several darn good books on the subject; you might like to do the same."

"I would," replied Bob, still trying not to seem too eager. "Do you have any of them here?" The doctor got out of his chair and rummaged through another cabinet, eventually emerging with a thick volume, through which he leafed rapidly.

"There's a good deal here but I'm afraid it's a bit technical. You may take it if you want, of course. I had another that was much better in every way from your standpoint, but I guess I've already lent it out."

"Who has it?"

"One of your friends, as I recall—young Norman Hay. He's been getting interested in biology lately. Maybe you heard about his trying to get to the museum on Tahiti. I don't know whether he's after my job or Rance's over at the lab. He's had the book quite a while—several months, I think; if you can get it from him, take it."

"Thanks; I will." Bob meant the statement earnestly. "You couldn't tell me offhand more about the chemical separation you mentioned, could you? It sounds funny, identifying a living creature by chemistry."

"As I said, there's some doubt as to whether we should call the viruses living creatures. However, there's nothing unusual about the tests you mention. Haven't you ever heard of serums?"

"Yes, but I thought they were stuff that you used to make a person immune to some disease."

"That is frequently the case. However, a better way of looking at them is more or less as chemical fingerprints. The tissues of one type of creature try to fight off serums made from the tissues of another. You can get an animal used to human serum, for example, and then tell from the reaction between the serum of that animal and some unknown substance whether the substance contained human tissues or not. The details vary, of course, but that's one way of telling whether a bloodstain or other organic trace came from a man or some other animal."

"I see—I guess." Bob's eyes were narrowed in thought. "Does this book have anything about that?"

"No. I can give you something on it, but I warn you it's a little beyond high-school chemistry. Whose job are *you* after?"

"What? Oh, I see. Not yours, anyway. There was a problem I ran across, and I'd like to solve it myself if I can. If I can't, I'll be back for more help, I expect. Thanks, Doc."

Seever nodded and turned back to his desk as Bob went out; and for several minutes the doctor meditated.

The boy was certainly more serious than he had been. It would be nice to know just what his problem was. Very possibly—even probably— it accounted for the personality change that had worried the school authorities. That, at least, would be a comforting report to give the boy's father; and that, later in the afternoon, was just what the doctor did.

"I don't think you need worry at all, Art, if you were. The kid's gotten himself interested to the hilt in something that appears to have a scientific flavor—young Hay did the same a few months ago—and will simply soak it into his system. You probably acted the same, the last time you learned something big. He's presumably going to change the world, and you'll hear about it in due time."

Bob had no intention of changing the world to any great extent, not even the human portion of it. However, some problems which had arisen in the course of the afternoon's talk might make changes to individuals necessary, and once out of the doctor's office he wasted no time in putting them up to the Hunter.

"Can we use that serum trick of the doc's?"

"I doubt it. I am familiar with the technique, and know that since I have been with you so long your own blood serum might serve if it were not for one fact; but we would still have to decide where to use it. If we could do that, I could make the exploration faster by personal contact."

"I suppose that's true. Still, you wouldn't have to leave me—I might be able to make the check myself."

"You have a point there. We will bear the possibility in mind. Have you any idea about getting at young Teroa? When will he be leaving?"

"The tanker comes every eight days, which means it's due back a week from today. I suppose he'll be going then; certainly not any sooner. I don't think the *Beam* is around."

"The *Beam?*"

"She's a yacht owned by one of the company bigwigs, who sometimes comes to look things over. I left on her last fall—that's why we were so far from the island when you first looked around. Come to think of it, I know she's not near; she went into drydock in Seattle last fall, to get some sort of diving gear built into her bottom, and is there yet. I suppose you were going to ask who could have left on her while we were gone."

"Correct. Thanks for settling the question so quickly." The Hunter would have smiled had he been able.

Bob had no watch but was pretty sure it was nearly time for school to be dismissed, so he headed in that direction. He was early, and had to wait outside; but presently his friends came pouring out, giving vent to expressions of envy as they saw him.

"Never mind about how lucky I am not to be in school," Bob said. "Let's get to work on that boat. I've got to go back to school myself on Monday, and I'd like to have some fun first."

"You've brought us luck, anyhow," said Hay. "We'd been looking for a plank for weeks and didn't find one until you got here. What say, fellows? Hadn't we better get that thing into the boat while the luck holds?" There was a chorus of agreement and a general movement to collect bicycles. Bob rode on Malmstrom's handle bars—he had walked to the doctor's—as far as his own house, where he picked up his own machine and some tools. They waited at the culvert while Malmstrom and Colby went into their respective dwellings for equipment; when they returned, the bicycles were left, shoes removed, and trousers rolled up. There was a path from the road down to the place the boat was kept, but it ran through the shallower parts of the creek in spots to avoid the undergrowth, and the boys had never bothered to construct bridges.

Splashing and crashing through water and bushes, they finally dumped their collection of tools at the point where the little watercourse emptied into the lagoon. The boat was there drawn up on the sand, with the plank beside it. The boys were relieved to see the latter; there had been no risk of anyone's borrowing the boat, of course, even had it not been in its present condition, but the wood was another matter. The statement that Colby had stepped through the floor of the boat had been no exaggeration—a strip of planking four inches wide and more than two feet long was missing from the flat bottom.

The boys were not professional carpenters, but they had the boat turned over and the defective plank removed from its full length in record time. They found, however, that replacing the plank from the enormous board they had found was not such an easy matter. The first attempt came out too narrow in several places, because of their inability to saw straight near the line of the grain. The second try was started too wide, and after a good deal of labor with the plane was eventually reduced to a good fit. They had carefully salvaged the screws from the former piece and succeeded in attaching the replacement securely enough to satisfy them.

They immediately dragged the boat down to the water, brought the oars from the bushes, and the entire party piled in. The idea of letting the new plank soak for a while in order to swell, or at least to permit a guess at the seaworthiness of the new joints, occurred to them, but they were all excellent swimmers and much too impatient to hold up for any such consideration. There was some leakage at the seams, but it did not amount to more than the coconut-shell bailers could handle. The two youngest boys wielded these while Bob and Shorty rowed and Rice handled the tiller.

Bob suddenly realized that the figure which usually occupied the bow on these occasions was missing. Thinking back, he realized that this had been the case ever since his return. He spoke to Rice, who was facing him. "What's become of Tip? I haven't seen him since I got back."

"No one knows." The redhead's face clouded over. "He just disappeared quite a long time ago—well before Christmas. We've looked all over the place for him. I'm afraid he must have tried to swim over to the islet where Norm has his tank—we sometimes went there without him—and got picked off by a shark, though it doesn't seem very likely. The swim would be only a few yards, and I've never seen a live shark that close to shore. He just vanished."

"That's queer. Have you looked in the woods?"

"Some. You can't search there very well. Still, if he'd been there alive, he'd have heard us; and I can't think of anything that would hurt him there."

Bob nodded, and spoke half to himself. "That's right, come to think of it; there aren't even any snakes here." More loudly he asked, "What's this about Norm's tank? Is he going into competition with Pacific Fuels?"

"Course not," returned Hay, looking up from his job of bailing. "I cleaned out one of the pools on the reef a little way from the beach and fenced it off, and have been putting things in it to make an aquarium. I did it just for fun at first, but there are some magazines that want pictures of sea life, and I've sent for some color film. Trouble is, nothing seems to live very long in the pool; even the coral dies."

"I suppose you haven't seen it since the boat was out. Let's go over now and have a look."

"I've been swimming over every day or two with Hugh or Shorty. It's still not doing so well. I don't know whether we could get there and back now before supper; we must have been working a long time on the boat, and the sun's getting down a bit." The other boys looked up, noticing this fact for the first time; their parents had long since given up trying to keep them from exploring any part of the island inside the reef, but they had some sort of regulation about meeting mealtimes. Without further remark Rice headed the boat back toward the creek, and the rowers began to take longer strokes.

Bob rowed without thinking much. Everywhere he turned there was lots to see, but none of it seemed to bear on his problem; the Hunter seemed to feel that Teroa should be tested, of course, but even he had no definite suspicion—it was simply that the boy was going out of reach. The thought reminded him of the talk he had had with Charlie that morning; he wondered whether the Polynesian boy had found Rice during the lunch hour.

"Anyone seen Charlie Teroa today?" he asked.

"No." It was Malmstrom who answered. "He comes a couple of days a week for navigation, but this isn't one of them. Think he'll ever use it?"

"Not for anyone who knows him." Rice's voice was scornful. "I'd rather hire someone likely to stay awake on the job."

Bob concealed a smile. "He seems to get some work done in that garden of his," he remarked.

"Sure, with his mother watching and his sisters helping. Why, he went to sleep with a boatload of dynamite last fall, when they were clearing the east passage."

"You're crazy!"

"That's what you think. They sent him in alone for a case, and told him to stand by when he got back, and twenty minutes later my father found him moored to a bush on the reef, sound asleep, using the case for a footrest. He was lucky there weren't caps aboard and that he wasn't where a wave could have knocked the boat into the reef."

"Maybe that wasn't luck," Bob pointed out. "He knew he didn't have caps, and figured it was safe enough where he was."

"Maybe; but I haven't let him live it down yet." Rice grinned mischievously.

Bob looked at the redhead, who was rather short for his age. "Someday he'll throw you in the drink, if you don't stop riding him. Besides, wasn't that stowaway business *your* idea?"

Rice could have asked with some justice, what that had to do with matters, but he just chuckled and said nothing. A moment later the boat's flat bottom grated on the beach.

# XI. Slip!

Bob remembered after he got home that he had forgotten to ask Hay about the doctor's book, but reflected that there was plenty of time tomorrow. There probably would not be much of actual help in it anyway. He spent the evening in the house for a change, reading and talking to his parents; and the Hunter perforce did nothing but listen and think. The next forenoon was little better, from the detective's point of view; Bob worked around the house in the morning while his friends were in school, and neither of them thought of any means of getting Teroa long enough for a test. Bob, it is true, suggested leaving the Hunter near the other's home in the evening and coming back the next day, but the alien refused under any and all circumstances to place himself in a situation where Bob could see him either going or coming. He was sure what the emotional effect would be. Bob couldn't see it, but was convinced when the Hunter pointed out that there was no way for him to be sure that the mass of jelly which would return to him after the test was actually the detective. The boy bad no desire whatever to let their quarry get at his own body.

The afternoon was distinctly better. Bob met the others as usual, and they repaired immediately to the boat. There was no time problem on this occasion, and they set out northwest, paralleling the shore at a distance of a few rods, with Hay and Colby rowing. The new plank had swelled, and there was very little leakage this time.

They had well over a mile to go, and they had rowed most of it before the Hunter fully understood the geography which he had been picking up in snatches from the conversation. The islet on which Hay had made his aquarium was, as he had intimated, close to the beach; it was the first section of the reef which curved away to the north and east from the end of the sand strip where the boys usually swam. It was separated from the beach itself by a stretch of water not twenty yards wide, a narrow channel which was protected from the breakers by other ridges of coral a little farther out which barely appeared above water. This channel, the Hunter judged, must be the one in which the dog was supposed to have been taken by a shark; and remembering the monster he had ridden ashore and seeing the seething currents among the ridges on its seaward side, he shared Rice's doubt about that theory.

The islet itself was composed of coral, which had accumulated enough soil to support some bushes. It was not more than thirty or forty yards long and ten yards wide. The pool was at its widest part, almost circular, and about twenty feet across. It appeared to have no connection with the sea that raged a few yards away; Norman said he had blocked up two or three submarine passages with cement and that waves broke high enough and often enough at high tide to keep it full. As he had said, it was not doing well: a dead butterfly fish was floating near one side, and the coral that composed its walls showed no sign of living polyps.

"I thought it must be some sort of disease," he said, "but I never heard of one that attacks everything alike. Have you?"

Bob shook his head. "No. Was that why you borrowed that book of the doc's?"

Norman looked up sharply. "Why, yes. Who told you about that?"

"The doc. I wanted to find out something about viruses, and he said you had the best of his books on the subject, Are you still using it?"

"I guess not. What got you interested in viruses? I read what it had to say about 'em and couldn't get much out of it."

"Oh, I don't know. It was something about nobody being able to decide whether they were really alive or not, I guess. That sounded pretty queer. If they eat and grow, they must be alive."

"I remember something about that—" At this point the conversation was interrupted, sparing Bob the need for further invention.

"For gosh sakes, Norm, give him the book when you get home, but let's not get lost in the upper atmosphere now! Exercise your brains on this pool of yours if you like, or else let's go along the reef and see what we can find." It was Malmstrom who had cut in, and Rice supported him vocally. Colby, as usual, remained silent in the background.

"I suppose you're right." Hay turned back to the pool. "I don't know, though, what I'm likely to think of right now that I couldn't in the last three or four months. I was hoping Bob might have a new idea."

"I don't know much biology—just the school course," Robert replied. "Have you gone down in it to see if you could find anything? Have you brought up anything like a piece of coral, to see what's happened to the polyps?"

"No, I've never been swimming in it. At first I didn't want to disturb the fish I had collected, and later I thought that whatever disease affected so many different things might get me too."

"That's a thought. Still, you must have touched the water a lot before things got really bad, and nothing happened to you. I'll go in if you like." Once again the Hunter came close to losing his temper. "What would you like me to bring up?"

Norman stared at him for a moment. "You really think it's safe? All right, I'll go in if you will."

That gave Bob a jolt; he had, almost without thought, been assuming himself safe from any disease germ that might be around, but Hay, as far as anyone could tell, had no symbiote to protect him.

That thought gave rise to another—*did he?* Would that explain his courage? Bob thought not, since it seemed most unlikely that their quarry's host would have any idea of the alien's presence, but it was something to be considered when there was more time. For the moment the question was whether he should make good his offer of entering the questionable water if Hay were going to follow him.

He decided that he would; after all, the argument he had used against the trouble's being a disease seemed sound; and anyway there was a doctor on the island.

"All right," he said, starting to strip.

"Wait a minute! Are you fellows crazy?" Malmstrom and Rice yelled almost together. "If that water's been killing the fish, you're foolish to go in."

"It's safe enough," said Bob. "We're not fish." He was aware of the weakness of this argument but could not think of a better one on the spur of the moment. The two Kenneths were still expostulating as he slipped feet first into the pool, with Norman beside him—both knew better than to dive into a coral pool, however clear it might be. Colby, who had not contributed to the argument, walked over to the boat, got an oar, came back, and stood watching.

The trouble with the pool manifested itself with remarkable speed. Bob swam out to the middle and did a surface dive, a maneuver which should have taken him without effort to the bottom eight feet down. It did nothing of the sort; his momentum barely got his feet under water. He took a couple of strokes, reached the bottom, broke a sea fan loose, and bobbed back to the surface with remarkable speed. As was his custom, he started blowing out air just before his head broke water, and managed to get some of the liquid into his mouth in the process. That was enough.

"Norm! Taste this water!" he yelled. "No wonder your fish died." Hay obeyed hesitantly, and grimaced.

"Where did all the salt come from?" he asked. Bob swam to the edge of the pool, clambered out, and started to dress before answering.

"We should have guessed," he said. "Sea water comes in when the waves are high enough, but the only way it leaves is by evaporation. The salt stays behind. You shouldn't have blocked off all the passages to the sea. We'll have to chip out one of your plugs and find some wire netting, if you still want to take those pictures."

"My gosh," exclaimed Hay, "and I wrote a school report on Great Salt Lake only last year." He started to dress, indifferent as Bob to the fact that he was still wet. "What'll we do? Go back for a crowbar or something, or poke around the reef for a while now that we're here?"

A brief discussion resulted in the adoption of the second plan, and the group returned to the boat. On the way Norman pulled a large, battered bucket out of the bushes, laughing as he did so. "I used to fill up the pool with this sometimes, when I thought it was getting low," he said. "I guess we can find some other use for Mr. Bucket now." He tossed it into the bow of the boat after the others, entered, and shoved off.

For an hour they rowed along inside the reef, occasionally disembarking on one of the larger islets, more often coasting alongside the ridges and lumps of coral while using poles to keep them off the more dangerous sections. They had worked some distance along the reef away from the island itself and had reached another fairly large islet—this one actually supported half-a-dozen coconut palms—where they disembarked and pulled the boat well up on the gritty soil. Their loot up to this time had not been very impressive, consisting mainly of a few cowries and a weirdly colored fragment of coral for which Malmstrom had gone overboard in twelve feet of water. The Hunter's profit from the expedition had been even less, so far, which annoyed him, since the exploration of the reef for clues had been largely his idea.

He made the utmost use of Bob's eyes, however. They were nearing his arbitrary one-mile limit north of the beach, which meant that about half of the region in which he expected to find clues of his quarry's landing had been covered. There was still not very much to see, however. On one side of the irregular islet the breakers thundered; on the other was the relatively calm water of the lagoon, with the bulk of one of the great culture tanks a few hundred yards away. The scavenger barge was beside the tank at the moment, and the small figures of its crew were visible on the catwalks that crossed the paneled roof; beyond, and dwarfed by a distance of fully three miles, the houses of the island dwellers were barely visible.

These, however, could hardly be considered clues, it seemed to the Hunter, and he brought his attention back to the immediate surroundings. The present bit of land was similar to that on which Hay's pool was located, and, like it, had very irregular edges—clefts, walled with living coral, in which the water gurgled down almost out of sight and then spurted upward into the watchers' faces as another breaker came thundering against the barrier. Some of the openings were narrow at the outer edge and broadened farther in, so that the water in them was quieter, though there was always the endless up-and-down wash started by the waves.

It was in these larger openings that the boys did most of their searching—it would have been impossible to get anything out of the others, reckless as some of the youngsters tended to be.

Rice, the first one out of the boat, had run to one of the largest while the others were still pulling the little craft up and making it fast; and dropping into a prone position with his head over the edge, he shaded his eyes and looked down into the clear water. By the time the others came up he was already pulling off his shirt.

"My chance first," he said quickly as the others peered down to see what he had sighted. Before anyone was sure what he was looking at, Rice had slipped into the water, disturbing the surface so that nothing was clearly visible. He stayed down for some time, and finally reappeared asking for one of the poles that were carried in the boat. "I can't work it loose," he said. "It seems to be jammed in place."

"What is it?" several voices asked at once.

"I'm not sure; I've never seen anything like it. That's why I want to get it up." He received the pole which Colby handed down to him and slid under water once more. The object at which he was prying was about five feet below the surface—that is, it varied from about four to six feet as the water level rose and fell in response to the urge of the breakers.

Several times Kenneth came up for breath, without having dislodged the mysterious object; and finally Bob went down to help. He had one advantage over the other boy; thanks to the Hunter's prompt supplementing of the curvature of his eye lenses with some of his alien body material, Bob could see much better under water than usual. He could make out easily the shape of the object on which Kenneth was working but did not recognize it. It was a hollow hemisphere of dull metal eight or nine inches in diameter and half an inch thick, with the flat side protected over half its area by a plate of similar material. It was hung on a stubby branch of coral only a few inches from the bottom, rather like a cap on a peg; and another lump of the stuff had either fallen or grown so as to wedge it in place. Rice was prying at the upper lump with a pole.

After a few minutes of futile effort they stopped, got their breath, and planned a more co-operative method of attack. Bob, it was agreed, would go to the bottom and work the end of the pole behind the object; Kenneth, upon receiving his signal, would brace one foot against the steep side of the pool—they both wore their shoes, as any sane person would in a coral pool—and push outward, to get the thing out from under the heavy fragment that pinned it down. The first time the attempt failed; Bob did not have the pole well enough set and it slipped out. The second, however, succeeded—almost too well. The piece of metal popped free and rolled away from the wall into deeper water; Bob, who was approaching the end of his store of breath, came to the surface. He refilled his lungs and started to speak to Rice, and then realized that the redhead was not visible. For a moment he supposed the other boy had taken a quick breath and gone back down for his prize, but as the water sank abruptly Rice's head appeared.

"Help! My foot—" The words were cut off again as the water surged up, but the situation was crystal-clear. Bob immediately dived again, braced his feet on the bottom, and strove to lift the lump of coral, which had been freed by the removal of the piece of metal and had landed on Kenneth's foot. He was no more successful than before, and returned anxiously to the surface just as the water went down again.

"Don't talk! Get air!" Malmstrom yelled superfluously—Rice was too busy to do anything else when the opportunity to gulp air occurred. Bob was looking around for the pole, which had disappeared. He saw it floating a few yards away and went after it. Colby had disappeared toward the boat without saying anything; as Bob came back with the pole and prepared to dive once more, the young boy came back. He was carrying the bucket that Hay had brought from the pool.

Everything had happened so rapidly that Malmstrom and Hay had scarcely realized what was going on. They now looked at Hugh Colby and his bucket in astonishment. Colby wasted no time explaining. He threw himself face downward at the water's edge and reached out and downward to the trapped Rice. As the water receded he placed the inverted bucket over the other's head and spoke his only words during the entire incident.

"Hold it there!"

Rice, for a wonder, got the point, and followed orders; and as the water surged up again over his head he found his face enclosed in a bucket full of air. Bob had not seen this trick, as he was under water again prying at the lump of coral, but he came up a moment later, saw, blinked in bewilderment, and then understood.

"Shall we come in?" Hay asked anxiously.

"I think I can get it off this time," Bob replied. "I was worried at first because of his air supply, but he'll be all right now. Just a minute till I get my own breath." He rested a moment, while Hay yelled encouragement to his trapped comrade in the intervals that the latter's head was above water. Robert found time to mutter to the Hunter, "This is why I didn't want to come here alone!" Then he took a firmer grip on the pole, and submerged again.

This time he succeeded in finding a better point of leverage, and applied all his strength. The lump of coral started to shift, and he felt that the work was about done, when the pole broke, the splintered end raking down his own chest. For once the Hunter could raise no objection; the injury was clearly "line of duty," and he closed the scratches without resentment. Bob popped back to the surface.

"I guess you'd better come in at that. I got it started, and the pole broke. Get the other poles, or maybe an oar or two, and everyone who can get at it come in."

"Maybe we'd better go for a crowbar," suggested Malmstrom.

"Maybe we'd better do the work ourselves," retorted Bob. "The tide's coming in, and that bucket will be good just so long as the water gets below his head every few seconds. Come on."

Within a few seconds the four boys, armed with poles and oars, were in the water beside their comrade: Bob at the bottom placing the levers, the others supporting them and ready to lift when he gave the word. They knew nothing about his advantage in seeing under water, of course; they accepted his leadership simply because he had started telling them what to do and no one intended to argue at a time like that.

Heavy as the block was, it yielded to this concentration of effort, though the job nearly cost them an oar. For just a moment the fragment of coral lifted, and Kenneth was able to drag his numbed foot from beneath it. With the aid of his friends he scrambled out of the water and sat nursing the foot while the others gathered around.

Rice was remarkably pale, considering his normal tan, and it was some time before his breathing and heartbeat returned to normal and he felt like standing up. The other boys were almost as frightened, and for some time nobody suggested going back into the water for the piece of metal that had started the trouble. After ten minutes or so Rice suggested that it would be a pity if all that work were wasted, and Bob took the hint and went down again; but the thing was not visible among the sea fans and branching corals that covered the pool's bottom, and he stopped groping under things after encountering a sea urchin which believed in passive resistance. Rice had nothing to show for his afternoon's work but fright, which was not the sort of souvenir he had any intention of showing to his parents.

It was now almost half-past four, which left plenty of time before supper, but somehow the prospect of further search on the reef no longer attracted them. They decided, with very little argument, to row the two miles and a fraction that separated them from the big dock. "That ought to be fairly peaceful, with the ship not due for nearly a week," Hay innocently remarked. No one said anything in answer at the time, as all of them probably had some such idea in mind; but he heard a good deal about that remark later.

The Hunter hardly heard the statement, of course; for the past quarter hour his mind had been fully occupied with a generator casing he had just seen and felt and which had definitely not come from the flattened wreckage of his own ship.

# XII. And Fall!

There was little talk for the first half of the row, for they had been badly scared; but when Norman Hay passed a remark about his aquarium the conversation quickly blossomed full strength.

"Maybe we can find something here to get one of those cement plugs out of the pool," were his words.

"You'll need something pretty good," remarked Shorty. "That underwater cement you got is rugged stuff—at least they used it on the dock, and there's no mark yet where the tanker comes in."

"The tanker doesn't touch the dock, unless someone gets careless," pointed out Rice from the bow. "Still, Norm's right about needing some good tools. There's nothing around our house that'll do, I know."

"What'll we use, anyway—hammer and cold chisel?"

"You can't get much good out of a hammer under water. We need a long, heavy crowbar with a good point. Who knows where we can get one?" There was no answer to that, and Hay continued after a moment. "Well, we'll ask some of the dock crew, and if they don't know, the construction gang up on the hill is bound to."

"If we could snaffle a diving helmet we'd get the work done faster," Rice contributed.

"The only helmets on the island are the rescue rigs on the dock and at the tanks, and I don't think they'd appreciate our borrowing one of those," Bob said. "We could never get the suit, and anyway probably Shorty's the only one who could wear it."

"What's wrong with that?" Malmstrom wanted to know.

"You'd be kicking about doing all the work. Anyway, they wouldn't let us take it."

"Why don't we make one? There's not much to it."

"Maybe not; but we've talked about that for four or five years and wound up holding our breath every time we worked under water." It was one of Colby's rare contributions to the exchange; as usual, no one could think of an answer.

Rice broke the short silence with another question. "What are you going to use to keep your fish in? Bob said something about wire netting, but where are you going to get any?"

"I don't know that either. If there's any on the island, it ought to be in one of the storerooms on the dock. I'll try to scrounge a piece if there is, and we'll get some heavy wire and make it if there isn't. The hole won't be very big anyway."

They tied up at the foot of a ladder on the landward side of the structure, almost under the causeway leading from the shore; Rice and Bob made both bow and stern painters fast while the others went up to the main level without waiting. Ken had a little trouble with the ladder because of his foot, but managed to conceal it fairly well. Once on the dock, the group looked around, planning.

The dock was a large structure, even as such things go. The weekly production of oil was considerable, and expansion was still going on; storage space had been designed accordingly. Four enormous cylindrical tanks were the most striking features; their auxiliary pumping and control mechanisms looked tiny by comparison. There were no fire walls; the structure was built of steel and concrete, with numerous large drains opening on the water below, and the fire-fighting apparatus consisted principally of high-pressure hoses to wash burning oil into the lagoon.

Between and around the tanks were a number of corrugated-iron sheds similar in structure and function to the storage buildings on shore; and at the end opposite the causeway was a complicated and versatile apparatus which could be used to distill gasoline, heating, or lubricating oils from the crude products of the culture tanks—it was cheaper to make the small quantities of these which were used on the island on the spot rather than to ship the crudes for refining to Tahiti and then bring them back again and store them.

It was the storage buildings which interested the boys at the moment. None of them could think offhand of any normal use for wire netting on the island, but one never could be sure, and they intended to leave no stone unturned. They headed in single file down the narrow space between the tanks.

There was a slight interruption before they reached the storeroom they sought; as they passed the corner of one of the small sheds an arm reached out, attached itself to Rice's collar, and pulled him inside the building. The boys stopped in astonishment for a moment, then grinned understandingly at one another as the voice of Charlie Teroa reached their ears. He was saying something about "stowaways" and "jobs," and seemed quite emphatic; and for once a conversation lasting several minutes took place in Rice's neighborhood without his voice being audible. Bob had wondered whether he ought to give him a hint about Teroa's intentions but had been pretty sure no damage would be done—the older boy was too pleased with himself. Nevertheless, it was a very sheepish-looking redhead who rejoined the group. Teroa was behind him, with a faint grin on his face; he winked as he caught Bob's eye.

"You kids aren't supposed to be out here, are you?" he asked.

"As much as you," retorted Hay, who had no intention of leaving while there was a chance of getting what he wanted. "You don't work here, either."

"You can ask about that," returned Teroa severely. "At least I'm helping. I suppose you're after something." It was a statement, but there was a faint suggestion of question at the end.

"Nothing that anyone will miss," replied Hay defensively. He was going to enlarge upon this theme when a new voice cut in.

"Just how sure can we be of that?" The boys whirled to see the speaker, and discovered Bob's father standing behind them. "We're always glad to *lend* things," he went on, "as long as we know where they're going. What were you needing this trip?"

Hay explained without reluctance—his conscience was clear, as he had every intention of asking for the wire, though he had hoped to exercise a little selection of his own in deciding whom to ask.

Mr. Kinnaird nodded in understanding. "You'll probably have to go up to the new tank car for a crowbar or anything like it," he said. "I think we can do something about your grating, though. Let's look."

Everybody, including Teroa, trailed him across the somewhat slippery steel plates. As they went, Hay explained what had happened to his pool and the way in which they had discovered the cause of the trouble. Mr. Kinnaird was a good listener, but he shot a glance at his son, which that young man fortunately missed, when he heard about the question of entering the possibly disease-laden water. The conversation reminded Bob of the book he wanted, and he asked Hay about it when the latter stopped talking for a moment. Mr. Kinnaird could not restrain a comment.

"My word, are you going to be a doctor now? You don't seem to have been acting like one!"

"No—it's just something I wanted to find out," Bob said lamely (the Hunter's troubles were coming thick and fast; he wondered when he would get a chance to talk to his host—the present background was impossible).

Mr. Kinnaird smiled and turned to the door of one of the sheds they had reached. "There may be something in here, Norman," he said, and unlocked the door. It was dark inside, but a switch in the doorframe lighted a single bulb in the center of the ceiling. All eyes focused on the same thing immediately—a large roll of quarter-inch-mesh galvanized wire that might have been made to order for Norman's needs. Hay made a rush for it, while Bob's father stood back looking as though he had invented the stuff.

"How much will you need?"

"A piece eighteen inches square will be plenty," was the reply. Mr. Kinnaird took a pair of cutters from a bench at one side of the shed and went to work on the roll. It was awkward stuff to cut—the sharp ends of wire tended to discourage driving the cutters too far, but he handed Norman the desired piece after a few seconds' work and they went outside together.

"I didn't know that stuff was used anywhere on the island," Bob remarked as his father relocked the door behind them.

"Really?" asked the latter. "I thought you'd poked around here enough to rebuild the place if you had to." He led the way to the nearest of the storage tanks and indicated one of the safety drains beside it. "There," he said, pointing down the four-foot-square unguarded opening. The boys crowded around and looked down. A couple of feet below the opening, between them and the water a dozen feet farther down, was a protective net of the mesh that Norman was carrying.

"I shouldn't think that would be strong enough to hold a person who fell down there," remarked Bob.

"People aren't supposed to fall down there," retorted his father. "Or, if they do, they're expected to be able to swim. That's to catch tools, which do skitter around on these plates a good deal. People aren't allowed anywhere near these openings." He turned away from the drain as the boys drew back thoughtfully, and promptly demonstrated the truth of his own words.

He slipped; at least Malmstrom insisted that it was Mr. Kinnaird who slipped first, but no one was really sure. The group acted like a well-struck set of pins in a bowling alley; the only one to keep his feet was Teroa, and he was forced to move with remarkable speed to do so. Malmstrom was knocked against Hay, whose feet went out from under him and caught the ankles of Bob and Colby. Their shoes, in turn, failed to grip on the somewhat oily metal, and Bob gave a yell as he realized he was about to put the strength of the netting to practical test.

His reaction speed had earned him his position on the school hockey team, and that was what saved him now. He fell feet first; as his toes touched the mesh, he spread his arms wide and forward, reaching as far onto the solid part of the dock as he could. The edge of the plating caught him painfully across the ribs, but enough of his weight came on his arms so that the mesh was not overloaded, and it held.

His father, on hands and knees, made a lunge for Bob's hand, but he slipped again and missed his aim. It was Malmstrom and Colby, who had both fallen within reach, who seized his wrists without attempting to rise from their prone positions and gave him enough anchorage to let him work himself back onto solid footing.

Bob wiped sweat from his forehead, and his father appeared to brush something from his eyes as they looked at each other; then the man gave a rather forced smile. "You see what I mean," he said. Then, recovering himself a little, "I think one of us is going to be late for supper. I take it that that boat I saw tied up is yours and has to go back to the creek." The boys admitted that this was the case. "All right, you'd better charge along before something else happens. I'll be going home myself shortly, Bob. Had we better tell your mother? I thought not." There was no pause between question and answer, and they parted almost laughing.

The Hunter was not laughing, however, and could scarcely have felt less like it. He wanted to talk to Bob but had so much to say that he could hardly decide where to begin. He was intensely relieved when his young host took up his station in the bow of the boat rather than at an oar; and the instant Bob was looking away from his friends, the Hunter attracted his attention.

"Bob!" The projected letters were thick, slanted, and underlined. They would have been colored if there had been any way to do it; as it was, the boy got the desired impression of urgency and promptly directed his gaze toward the horizon.

"We will pass over," the Hunter began, "for the moment, at least, your tendency to expose yourself to minor injury because you know I will take care of it. The tendency itself is bad enough, but you have been practically broadcasting your confidence in your immunity. You offered publicly to go into that water this morning without the least hesitation; you have been announcing your new interest in biology in general and viruses in particular to all and sundry. Several times today I felt like forgetting my upbringing and paralyzing your tongue. At first I merely thought you might scare our quarry into a better hiding place; now I am not sure that the matter may not be even more serious."

"But what else could it do?" Bob muttered the question so that none of the others could hear.

"I am not certain, of course, but it seems odd that your near accident should follow so closely all that talk—particularly when the talk was in the hearing of some of our likeliest suspects." Bob absorbed that thought in silence for a minute or two. He had not previously considered that there might be personal danger in this mission. Before he could think of anything to say the Hunter added a point. "Even your examining that dead fish as closely as you did could easily attract the attention of a person as suspicious as our friend is likely to be."

"But Norm was examining the skate as much as I was," pointed out Bob.

"So I noticed." The Hunter did not enlarge upon that point, leaving his young host to derive any implications he might like from it.

"But anyway, what could he do? How could he have caused that fall—you said yourself that you couldn't make me do anything. Is he different from you?"

"No. It is quite true that he could not have forced any of those people to push you, or anything like it. However, he might have persuaded them; you have done much for me, remember."

"But you said he would not have made himself known."

"I didn't think he would—it would be risky for him. Still, he might have decided to chance it, and enlist his host's aid by some story or other—that would not be hard. How could the host prove he was lying?"

"I don't see, offhand; but what good would it have done him if I had gone into the drink back there? I can swim, and everyone there knows it; and if I couldn't, and got drowned, that wouldn't stop *you* for long."

"True; but he may have intended that you be slightly hurt, so that I would betray myself by repair activities. After all, no matter what story he told his host, he would be unlikely to persuade one of your friends to do you serious or permanent harm."

"You think, then, that maybe Charlie Teroa is trying to get that job off the island to suit our friend? I thought he was covering up that story about sleeping on the job because he really wanted to start working."

"The possibility exists, certainly. We definitely must find means of checking him before he goes—or keeping him from going." Bob did not pay too much attention to this statement. Not only had he heard it before, but another thought came swelling up into his mind—one that affected him quite enough to have been noticed by his friends had he been facing any of them.

The thought had been started by one of the Hunter's sentences a little earlier and had taken a little while to form; but now it sat there in his mind, glaringly clear. The Hunter had said his quarry would be able to deceive his host by a story and that there would be no way for the host to prove its falsehood. Bob suddenly realized that *he had no means of checking the Hunter's own tale.* For all he *knew,* the being now ensconced in his own body might be a fleeing criminal seeking to rid itself of legitimate pursuit.

He almost said something, but his natural common sense saved him at the last instant. This was something he must check himself; and until it was checked, he must appear to be as trustful and co-operative as ever.

He did not really doubt the Hunter seriously. In spite of communication limitations, the alien's very attitude and behavior had given the boy a remarkably good picture of his personality—as was evidenced by the fact that this was the first time Bob had thought to question his motives. Still, the doubt was there now and would have to be resolved in some way.

He was preoccupied when the boat reached the creek, and said little while they were pulling it up and stowing the oars. The fact did not cause remark; all the boys were fairly tired and not a little subdued by two accidents in one afternoon. They splashed up the creek to the culvert, retrieved their bicycles from the bushes, and went their various ways, after agreeing to meet at the same place after breakfast.

Alone at last, Bob could speak more freely to the little detective.

"Hunter," he asked, "if you think my talking and investigating are likely to make our friend suspicious of me, why do they worry you? If he tries anything, it will give us a clue to him! That might be the best way to find him—use me as bait. After all, the only smart way to hunt for a needle in a haystack is to use a magnet. How about it?"

"I thought of that. It is too dangerous."

"How can he hurt you?"

"I don't suppose he can. The danger that bothers me is yours. I don't know whether you are showing the bravery of maturity or the foolhardiness of youth, but understand, once and for all, that I will not expose you to any danger as long as I can see an alternative course of action."

Bob made no answer for a moment, and if the Hunter interpreted correctly the tightening of the muscles as the boy strove to suppress a smile of satisfaction, he did not mention the fact. There was one other thing Bob wanted settled, however, so he put the question as he turned up the drive to his home—he had walked the bicycle from Rice's drive, so there would be no danger in the Hunter's talking to him.

"In the boat you said something about paralyzing my tongue. Could you do it, or were you simply shooting off?"

The Hunter was not familiar with that bit of slang, but was able to guess correctly at its meaning. "I could paralyze any muscle in your body by pressing on the controlling nerve. How long the state would last after I stopped I cannot say, as I haven't tried it with you or any of your people."

"Show me." Bob stopped and kicked down the stand of the bike and stood expectantly.

"Go indoors and eat our supper and stop asking foolish questions!" Bob went, grinning openly now.

# XIII. Engineering Interlude

Saturday was not too profitable from the Hunter's point of view—at least as he judged it then—and even less so from that of Norman Hay. The boys met at the culvert as planned, Norman bearing his piece of netting, but nobody had brought anything that looked capable of doing much to the cement plugs Hay had installed.

It was decided, therefore, to go to the other end of the island, where a new culture tank was under construction, to see what might be available. They rode together down the road, across the larger creek, and past the school to Teroa's house. Here, instead of turning down toward the dock, they continued straight on, past some more corrugated-iron storage sheds, to the end of the paved surface. This left them on the shoulder of the island's highest hill though still on the lagoon side. Somewhat below and ahead of them was a row of three small tanks which had been there for some years; higher and still farther ahead was a new structure almost as large as the tanks in the lagoon. This had been completed only a month or two before; and another, the boys knew, was being built beyond it. This was their immediate goal.

While the hard-surfaced road stopped at the last of the sheds, the construction machinery had beaten a very plain trail which formed a continuation of it. It proved better, however, to traverse this section on foot, and the boys soon abandoned the bicycles rather than walk them. It was not far to go—three hundred yards to the big tank, seventy more along its lower wall, and as much farther to the scene of activity.

Like its neighbor, the new tank was on the hillside, partly cut into the ground and partly above it. The floor had been laid, reinforced, and the concrete cast; those portions of the walls that lay against the earth of the hillside were occupying the attention of the men at the moment. The boys noted with relief that digging seemed to have ended; it should, then, be possible to borrow the tools they needed. They had, as a matter of fact, surprisingly little trouble; they encountered Rice's father almost at once, and he readily located a couple of crowbars and gave permission to take them. He may have had ulterior motives; nearly all the children of the island between the ages of four and seventeen were underfoot at the time—the men were seriously considering having a local regulation passed ordering school to keep seven days a week—and anything that looked as though it might get rid of some of them would have been encouraged. The boys cared nothing about his reasons; they took the bars and returned the way they had come.

It was an encouraging start, but the rest of the morning was less so. They reached the pool without noteworthy delay, and went to work, diving by turns and pecking away at the concrete with the crowbars. They could not even work on the seaward side of the plug; anyone entering the water on that side of the islet would have been cut to pieces against the coral by the first breaker. They had chipped away enough to encourage them by dinnertime, but there was yet much to be done.

After the meal, however, meeting at the usual place, they found one of the jeeps parked by the culvert. Standing beside it were Rice and his father, and in the back seat was some equipment which the boys recognized.

"Dad's going to blast the gate for us!" called the younger Rice, quite superfluously, as the others arrived. "He got away from the tank for a couple of hours."

"Anything to get you out of my hair," remarked his father. "You'd better stick to your bikes—you, too, Ken. I'll ride the sticks."

"It's safe enough!" remonstrated Bob, who wanted to examine the plunger more closely.

The man looked at him. "No remarks from you," he said. "Your father would have the bunch of you stay here while he laid the charge and come back here with you to fire it! And I don't blame him a bit." He climbed under the wheel without further comment; and Bob, who knew that Mr. Rice had spoken the truth, mounted his bicycle and headed northwest, followed by the others.

At the Hay house the jeep was parked and its load removed. Mr. Rice insisted on carrying the dynamite and caps himself, though Bob thought he had a good argument when he claimed they should not be carried together. The wire and plunger were taken in charge by Bob and Malmstrom, and everybody headed for the beach on foot. They went a little to the left of the course the boys had followed Wednesday and emerged at the southern end of the strip of sand.

Here, as at the pool, the reef reappeared, curving away to the south and east, eventually to circle the island almost completely. On the southern side the lagoon was narrower, the reef never being more than half a mile from the shore, and no attempt had so far been made to build any installations on this side. Where the barrier started at the south end of the little beach was a passage from open sea to lagoon similar to that isolating the islet of the pool; but this was much narrower, offering at the base barely passage for a rowboat.

This was the "gate" to which Rice had referred. It looked, from a little distance, as though it were perfectly clear; but a closer inspection showed, as Rice had said, that there was an obstruction. The end of the passage toward the beach, which was exposed to the waves from the open sea to the west, had been neatly plugged by a brain coral about six feet in diameter, which had been dislodged from some point farther out in the reef and rolled about, probably by successive storms, until it had wedged securely where the waves could drive it no farther. Even the boys had not had to look twice to know they could never shift the huge thing by hand labor, though they had made some half-hearted attempts to break away enough coral to clear a passage around it.

It was possible, obviously, to reach the southern lagoon in a boat by rowing around the other end of the island, but it was generally agreed that clearing the gate would be worth the trouble.

Mr. Rice unbent sufficiently to allow Colby to place the charge—he did not want to go under water himself—after careful instruction; but he made everyone follow him back to the palm trees and take shelter behind the sturdy trunks before he fired it. The results were very satisfactory: a column of spray and coral chips fountained into the air, accompanied by a moderate amount of noise—dynamite is not particularly loud stuff. When the rain of fragments seemed to be over, the boys raced back to the gate and found that there would be no need of a second blast. About a quarter of the original piece was visible, rolled some distance from its original site; the rest had completely disappeared. There was ample room for the boat.

The boys controlled their exuberance sufficiently to help Mr. Rice pack the blasting equipment back into the jeep; but from that point their opinions were divided. Hay and Malmstrom wanted to go back to work on the pool; Bob and Rice wanted to take advantage of the newly opened gate to explore the southern reef. Colby, as usual, cast no vote. None of them thought of splitting up; and, oddly enough, Hay won the argument, his main point being that it was already well along in the afternoon, and it would be much better to start in the morning and spend the entire day on the reef.

Bob would have been considerably more insistent, in order to let the Hunter examine the rest of his "probable landing" area, but the detective had informed him the night before of the nature of the piece of metal that had indirectly caused Rice's accident.

"It was a generator casing from a ship similar to mine," he said. "And it certainly was not from my own. I am certain of my facts; if I had merely seen it, there might be a chance of error—I suppose your people might have apparatus that would look like it from a little distance—but I felt it while you were pulling at it barehanded. It had line-up marks etched into the metal, indicated by letters of my own alphabet."

"But how did it get there, when the rest of the ship isn't around?"

"I told you our friend was a coward. He must have detached it and carried it with him for protection, accepting the delay such a load would have caused. It was certainly good armor, I will admit; I cannot imagine any living creature breaking or piercing that metal, and he would have to stay so close to the bottom that there would be no chance of being swallowed whole. It was a rather smart move, except that it left us evidence not only of the fact that he has landed on the island, but also where."

"Can you judge what he would do then?"

"Exactly what I said before—pick up a host at the first opportunity, anyone he could catch. Your friends are still definitely under suspicion, including the young man who went to sleep near the reef with a boatload of explosive."

In consequence of this information, Bob was willing to forgo the examination of the southern reef, and to spend an afternoon at dull work. It would give him time to think; and thought seemed necessary. He was rewarded during the afternoon with one idea, but he was unable to speak clearly enough with the others around to get it across to Hunter. He finally gave up trying for the time being and concentrated on chipping concrete.

By the time they were ready to go home for supper they had actually penetrated the plug—at least a hole large enough to accommodate one of the crowbars was all the way through. The trip back to the creek was chiefly occupied with an argument whether or not this hole would be sufficient. The discussion was still unsettled when the boys separated.

Once alone Bob promptly put his suggestion up to the Hunter.

"You've been saying all along," he said, "that you would never leave or enter my body when I was awake—that you didn't want me to see you. I don't think I'd mind, but I won't argue the point any more.

"But suppose I put a container—a can, or box, or almost anything big enough—in my room at night. When I was asleep—I couldn't possibly fool you on that—you could come out and get in the box; if you like, I'll promise not to look inside. Then I could plant it next to the house of each of the fellows in turn and leave it there overnight. You could come out, do all the inspecting you wanted at that house, and get back to the can by morning. I could even put some sort of indicator on the can that you could move to tell me whether you wanted to come back to me or go on to the next house."

The Hunter thought for several minutes. "The idea is good, very good," he finally answered. "Its big disadvantages, at least as far as I can see, are only two: first, I could examine only one house each night, and would then be even more helpless than usual until the next night. Second, while I am making those examinations, you will be left unprotected. That might not ordinarily be too bad, but you must remember we now have reason to suspect that our quarry has identified you as my host. If he sprang a trap of some sort while I was away, it might be very bad."

"It might also convince him that I am not your host," pointed out Bob.

"And that, my young friend, might not do either of us the least good." As usual, the Hunter's implied meaning was plain.

At home, Bob found his father already eating, somewhat to his surprise.

"I'm not that late, am I?" he asked anxiously as he entered the dining room.

"No, it's all right, son; I came home to grab an early bite. I have to go back to the tank; we want to get the last of the forms for the back wall in place and pour tonight, so that the concrete can set over Sunday."

"May I come along?"

"We don't expect to be done till midnight anyway. Well, I guess it won't hurt. I expect if your mother were asked politely she would give her consent, and perhaps even double the sandwich order she's preparing at the moment."

Bob bounced toward the kitchen but was met halfway by his mother's voice.

"All right this time; but after you're back in school this sort of thing is out. Bargain?"

"Bargain." Bob seated himself opposite his father and began asking for further details. Mr. Kinnaird supplied them between mouthfuls. It had not occurred to Bob to wonder where the jeep was, but he understood anyway when its horn sounded outside. They went out together, but there was room for only one more in the vehicle. The fathers of Hay, Colby, Rice, and Malmstrom were already aboard. Mr. Kinnaird turned to Bob.

"I forgot to mention—you'll have to take your bike. You'll also have to walk it home, unless you have that light fixed, which I doubt. Still want to come?"

"Sure." Bob turned to the space under the porch where he stored the machine. The other men looked at Kinnaird with some surprise.

"You going to take a chance on having him around while we pour, Art?" asked the senior Malmstrom. "You'll be fishing him out of the cement."

"If he can't take care of himself by now, it's time we both found out," replied Bob's father, glancing in the direction his son had vanished.

"If there's anything in heredity, you won't find him in much danger," remarked the heavy-set Colby as he shifted to make room in the jeep. He spoke with a grin that was meant to remove the sting from the words. Mr. Kinnaird was apparently unaffected by the remark.

The red-haired driver turned the jeep and sent it down the drive, Bob pedaling furiously behind. Since the distance to the road was not great and the curve at that point sharp, he held his own down the drive; but once on the main road the men quickly drew ahead. Bob did not care. He rolled on through the village to the end of the road, parked the bicycle, and proceeded on foot along the path the boys had taken that morning. The sun had set during the ride, and darkness was closing in with typical tropic speed.

There was no lack of light at the scene of construction, however. Wherever there seemed the slightest need big portable fluorescents blazed. They were all powered from a single engine-driven generator mounted on a dolly parked at one side of the already smoothed floor; and for some time Bob occupied himself finding out all he could about this installation without actually taking it apart. Then he wandered over to the rear wall where the forms were going up, and, applying the principle the boys had long found best, helped for a while carrying the two-by-fours that were being used to prop the great, flat, prefabricated sections in place. He met his father several times, but no word either of approval or censure was passed.

Like the rest of the men, Mr. Kinnaird was far too busy to say much. He was a civil engineer by training, but, like everyone else on the island, he was expected to turn his hand to whatever job needed doing. For once the work came very near to his specialty, and he was making the most of it. The Hunter saw him occasionally, when Bob chanced to be looking somewhere near the right direction, and he was always busy—clinging precariously (it seemed to the alien) to the tops of ladders gauging the separation of the molds; stepping across the thirty-foot-deep chasm which the concrete was to fill, to climb the slope beyond and check the preparations of the men at the mixers; freezing over a spirit level or a theodolite as he gauged location or angle of stance of some newly positioned part; checking the fuel tank on the generator engine; even taking a turn at the power saw where the ends of the props were cut to the proper angles—jobs which would each have been done by a different man anywhere else, and jobs which sometimes scared even the watching Hunter. The alien decided that he had been overhasty in condemning the man for letting his son do dangerous work. Mr. Kinnaird just didn't think of that phase of the matter. Well, so much more work for the Hunter. Maybe someday he could educate the boy to take care of himself; but if he had had fifteen years of this example, the chances were smaller than the detective had hoped.

The man was not completely ignoring his son, however. Bob succeeded in concealing one yawn from everyone but his guest; but his father spotted the second and ordered him away from work. He knew what lack of sleep could do to a person's coordination, and had no desire to see the elder Malmstrom's prediction fulfilled.

"Do I have to go home?" asked Bob. "I wanted to see them pour."

"You won't be able to see if you don't get some sleep. No, you needn't go home; but stop working for a while and catch a nap. There's a good place up at the top of the hill there where you can see what's going on and lie down in comfort at the same time. I'll wake you before they pour, if you insist."

Bob made no objection. It was not yet ten o'clock, and he would never have ordinarily dreamed of sleeping so early; but the last few days had been a tremendous change in activity from the routine of the school, and even he was beginning to feel the results. Anyway, he knew that objecting would do him no good.

He climbed the hill accordingly, and on the very top found a spot which answered to his father's description. He stretched out on the soft grass, propped his head up on his elbows, and regarded the brilliant scene below him.

From here he could see almost everything at once. It was as though he looked down from a balcony onto a lighted stage. Only the area at the very foot of the wall to be was hidden by the molds; and there was plenty to watch elsewhere in the work area. Even outside this something could be seen; there was the faint glow from the water of the lagoon, with the nearer tanks silhouetted against it and the brighter band of luminosity that limned the outer reef. Bob could hear the breakers if he listened for them; but, like everyone else on the island, he was so accustomed to their endless sound that he seldom noticed it. To his left a few lights were visible, some on the dock and some in the half-dozen houses not hidden from his gaze by the shoulder of the hill. In the other direction, to the east, there was only darkness. The machines used to mow the lush vegetation grown there to feed the culture tanks were abandoned for the night, and the only sound was the rustling among the pithy stalks caused by small animals and vagrant breezes. There were a few mosquitoes and sand flies as well, but the Hunter also believed his host needed sleep, and frightened off with tiny pseudopods any that landed on the boy's exposed skin. It may have been listening to these faint noises which proved to be Bob's undoing, for in spite of the firmest determination merely to rest and watch, he was sound asleep when his father came up the hill to find him.

Mr. Kinnaird approached silently and looked down at the boy for some time with an expression that defied interpretation. At last, as the sound of the mixers below swelled abruptly, he nudged the prone figure with his toe. This proving ineffective, he bent over and shook his son gently; and eventually Bob emitted an audible yawn and opened his eyes. It took him a second or two to take in the situation, then he got to his feet at once.

"Thanks, Dad. I didn't think I'd go to sleep. Is it late? Are they pouring?"

"Just starting." Mr. Kinnaird made no comments about sleep. He had only one son but knew the minds of boys. "I'll have to go back to the floor; I suppose you'll want to watch from the top. Just to be sure someone's around to see you if you fall in." They started downhill together without further talk.

At the mixers Mr. Kinnaird bore off to the left, continuing down past the cut made for the tank, while Bob stayed by the machinery. It was already in action, and more of the lights had been moved up to the scene, so that every operation was clearly visible. The upper ends of the machines received apparently endless supplies of sand and cement from stock piles previously built up and of water pumped up from one of the big desalting units at the edge of the lagoon. A smooth, gray-white river of concrete poured from spouts at the lower end and into the chasm between the carefully placed mold boards. The scene of activity was gradually being obscured under a haze of cement dust. The men were protected from it by goggles, but Bob was not, and presently the penetrating stuff began to get into his eyes. The Hunter made a half-hearted attempt to do something about it, but it meant putting tissue on the outside of the boy's eyeballs which would interfere with sight from both their proper owner and himself, so he let the tear glands do the job. He had no particular ulterior motives, but was far from disappointed when his host moved a little way up the hill to get out of the dust cloud; for, as usual, Bob had been watching things with an annoying disregard for his own safety and had had to be ordered out of the way several times by some of the men.

Just before midnight, with the pouring almost done, Mr. Kinnaird reappeared and located Bob, who was asleep again. He did not fulfill his promise of making the boy ride home on his bicycle.

# XIV. Accidents

Sunday morning the boys met as planned, bringing lunches with them. The bicycles were cached as usual, and the group splashed down the creek to the boat, where all but Bob changed to bathing suits. He kept on shirt and slacks, as his sunburn was not quite at the stage where another layer would be advisable. He and Malmstrom took the oars, and they rowed along the shore toward the northwest. They stopped for a moment at Hay's tank and tasted the water, which seemed now to be ordinary sea water; then they headed the small craft between the islet and the north end of the beach. They were forced ashore at the seaward end of the passage, as the surf was too heavy for rowing; they splashed overside in water that one moment was knee deep and the next barely reached their ankles, and towed the boat for the half mile that lay between them and the gate. Here they re-embarked, and the exploration of the southern reef began.

This barrier ran much closer to the island than did that on the northern side, the stretch of water enclosed by it usually only a few hundred yards wide and never more than half a mile. The islets were fewer as well, the reef consisting for the most part of a forest of branching corals that appeared above water only at low tide, though it was wide enough to block even the heaviest breakers. It was a harder place to loot, from the boys' viewpoint, since the flotsam in which they were apt to be interested frequently lodged in the midst of a jagged, marble-hard labyrinth. The boat could not possibly be taken among those growths, and someone had to wade, wearing heavy shoes.

Bob, of course, was no longer seeking clues, but Hay had a box of wet seaweed and a number of jars which he hoped would accommodate specimens for his pool, and the others all had their plans. The section had not actually been deserted since the boat and gate had been out of commission, for other youngsters on the island had boats, and not all were too lazy to row around the long way; but these would have worked the east end of the reef first. It was very likely that the day might be profitable, and everyone was in high spirits.

They had worked their way a mile or so along the reef, and Hay in particular had had very good luck. His jars were all filled with sea water and specimens, and he was talking about going back early to establish them in the pool and get the screening in place—they had decided that the small hole would be enough. The others, naturally, wanted to continue with the original program. They thrashed the problem out while they ate their lunch on one of the few soil-covered islets available, and the result was a draw. The exploration was not continued, and they did not take the specimens to the pool.

The solution was taken out of their control quite unintentionally by Rice, who stood up in the bow of the boat after all were aboard, with the intention of shoving off from the coral ledge to which it was moored. It had not occurred to the boys that where one board had been rotten enough to yield to a fourteen-year-old's weight others might be in like state. They were reminded of the possibility when Rice's left foot, with a loud crack, went through the plank adjacent to the new one and he saved himself from falling overboard only by a quick snatch at the gunwales. He might as well have let himself go, for in a matter of seconds the craft had filled and left them sitting waist deep in the lagoon.

For a moment everyone was too startled for any reaction. Then Colby laughed, and the others, except Rice, joined in.

"That'll be the last I hear about stepping through the bottom of a boat, I hope," Hugh finally got out between chuckles. "At least I did it near enough to home so there was no trouble getting it there."

They waded to the shore only a yard or two away, taking the boat with them. There was no question of procedure. All could swim, all had had experience with swamped boats, and all knew that, even full of water, their craft was perfectly capable of supporting their weight if they kept their bodies low in the water. They simply made sure all their property was accounted for—most of Hay's specimens had escaped—re-entered the water, and pushed off across the narrow lagoon toward the main island. Once away from the reef and in water deep enough for swimming, they removed their shoes and placed them in the boat. Each clung to the gunwales with one hand, pushing it along as he swam. No particular difficulty was encountered, though somebody cheerfully pointed out, when they were about halfway across, that they had just finished eating.

Once ashore another disagreement arose, the question this time being whether they should leave the boat here and bring the wood and tools across the island, or take it around to the creek. The actual distance to their homes directly across the ridge was not great, but most of it was jungle; and carrying heavy loads through that would be no joke. The things could, of course, be brought around by the beach, but that involved extra distance. Since the next day was Monday, with school, they could not hope to do the job in one trip, and it was finally decided to take the boat back to the creek.

There was plenty of time before them, however, and before starting they pulled the craft up on the shore to examine the damage in more detail. Obviously the entire plank would need replacing. It had rotted away from the screws that held it to the sidepieces near the bow and cracked right in two midway between that point of attachment and the first cross-piece, opening downward like a double trapdoor. If Rice had tried to pull straight up without working his way loose carefully, the two pieces would probably have clamped firmly on his legs. It was fortunate, the boys agreed, that their craft was not a larger one carrying ballast.

It finally occurred to them to examine the rest of the woodwork; and the fact gradually forced itself upon them that satisfactory repair of the boat was going to amount almost to a rebuilding job. A good deal of scavenging was going to be necessary before the craft would once more be seaworthy, for the big plank they had been using would never be sufficient.

Bob came forth with a suggestion. "Why don't we leave it here for now and go over to the new tank? There's lots of scrap lumber there, and we can pick up what we need, take it to the creek, and bring the boat around either tonight or tomorrow."

"That would mean an extra trip over here," pointed out Malmstrom. "Why not do what we planned, and go up to the tank afterward?"

"Besides, there'll be no one there," added Colby. "We're going to need more than scraps, and we can't take the big stuff without permission."

Bob admitted the justice of this, and was willing to relinquish his suggestion, when Rice had another thought.

"I'll tell you what we might do," he said. "We're apt to be a long time finding just what we want. Why don't one or two of us go up like Bob says and pick out what we could use, and sort of put it to one side, while the others take the boat around—that won't need very many hands. Then after school tomorrow we can just ask for the stuff we've put aside all at once and be able to go to work without wasting time."

"That's O.K., if you think we can get it all at once. Sometimes it's better to ask for one thing at a time," Hay pointed out.

"Well, we can make more than one pile and ask different people. Who'll go up to the tank and who pushes the boat?"

It was eventually settled that Bob and Norman would set out at once for the construction site and the others would work the rowboat back to the creek. No one was in a hurry to start, but at last they dragged the wreck back into water deep enough to float it, and the two emissaries returned to shore, with Rice's voice behind them grunting the song of the Volga boatmen.

"I'm going home first and get my bike," said Norman as they headed away from the water. "It's easier, and'll save time."

"That's a thought," agreed Bob. "We'll lose a little cutting through the jungle, but the bikes should make up for it. I'll wait for you at my drive, shall I?"

"O.K., if you get there first. I know your place is closer to here, but the jungle is narrower up my way. I'll go up the shore till I'm opposite my house before I cut over."

"All right."

The boys separated, Norman walking rapidly along the beach in the direction taken by the others—whom he speedily overtook and passed—while Bob headed uphill into the heavy growth he had already shown to the Hunter. He knew the island as well as anyone, but no one could say he knew that jungle. Most of the plants were extremely fast-growing varieties and a path had to be in constant use to remain in existence. The larger trees were more permanent and would have made satisfactory landmarks had it been possible to proceed directly from one to the other; but the thorny undergrowth usually prevented it. The only really reliable guide was the slope of the ground, which enabled one to take a straight course with the assurance that he would come out somewhere. Bob, knowing where he was in relation to his house, was reasonably sure of reaching the road within a short distance of the dwelling—or even hitting it exactly if he bore enough to the right to cross the comparatively well-used trail he had employed a few days before. He plunged into the undergrowth without hesitation.

At the top of the ridge they paused, more to let Bob get his breath than his bearings. Ahead of them, down the slope where the houses should be, was a wall of brush. Even Bob hesitated at the sight and looked to each side; the Hunter cringed mentally and prepared himself for action. For the first time the boy went down on his hands and knees to thread his way through the barrier. It was a little better close to the ground, since the worst bushes tended to grow in clumps and spread as they rose, but it was still far from clear, and the scratches began mounting up. The Hunter had thought of something really biting to say on the subject of just how much time and effort were being saved by the short cut, when his attention was taken by something he saw from the corner of Bob's eye.

To the right of their line of travel was an area that, except for the thorns, looked more like a bamboo thicket than a lilac bush—the plants were separate stalks thrusting individually from the ground a few inches apart and shooting straight up. Like nearly everything produced in the first year or two of the island laboratory's existence, they possessed thorns—iron-hard, needle-sharp specimens an inch and a half long on the main stems and only a trifle shorter on the stubby, horizontal, thin-leafed branches that commenced within a foot of the ground. The object that had attracted the Hunter's attention lay at the edge of this patch of vegetation. He could not make it out exactly, since its image was well off the optical axis of Bob's eye lenses, but he saw enough to arouse his curiosity.

"Bob! What is that?" The boy turned his eyes in the direction indicated, and both recognized the pile of white objects instantly—Bob because he had seen such things before and the Hunter from his general knowledge of biology. Bob wormed his way over to it as quickly as he could, and then lay prone looking at the skeleton which lay partly in and partly out of the thicket of straight-growing shrubs.

"So that's what became of Tip," the boy said at last slowly. "Hunter, can you offer a guess at what killed him?"

The Hunter made no answer at first, but looked carefully over the bones. As nearly as he could tell from his memory of the dog's structure they were arranged naturally—even to the claws and the tiny bone that seemed to correspond to the hyoid in his host's tongue. The animal had apparently died in one piece and been undisturbed afterward.

"He doesn't seem to have been eaten, at least by any larger or medium-sized creature of his own general type," the Hunter advanced cautiously.

"That seems true enough. Ants, or something of the sort, could have cleaned the bones like that after he died, but we have none on this island that could have killed him first. Are you thinking what I am?"

"I'm no mind reader, though I've learned to know you well enough to predict your actions occasionally. I think I know what you mean, though. I admit that it is perfectly possible that the dog was killed and eaten by our friend after being ridden here from some part of the shore. I would point out, however, that I can see no reason for killing the dog *here* of all places; there could hardly be a less suitable place on the island for finding a new host. Also, the dog had flesh enough to last for weeks. Why should he stay here long enough to consume it all?"

"Panic. He might have thought you were right on his trail, and picked this for a hiding place." The Hunter had not expected such a prompt answer to what he had meant as a rhetorical question, but he had to admit that Bob's suggestion was distinctly possible. The boy had another idea before he could say any more.

"Hunter, couldn't you tell by examining these bones whether the flesh had been taken by one of your people or not? I'll hold one as long as you like, if you want to go over it thoroughly."

"Do that, please. Something might be learned."

Bob gingerly picked a femur out of the collection. The neighboring bones tended to adhere slightly; there were apparently traces of cartilage remaining in the joints. The boy held it firmly in his clenched hand, knowing how the Hunter would make his examination. It was the first time he had an opportunity actually to see part of his guest's body, but he nobly resisted the temptation to open his hand. As a matter of fact, it would have done him no good: the Hunter used exploratory filaments fine enough to reach through the pores in his host's skin and much too thin to be visible. The search took several minutes.

"All right; you may put it down."

"Did you find anything?"

"A little. Such evidence as there is suggests that our friend was not responsible. The marrow in the bone had decayed normally, as did blood and other organic material in the bone tubelets. It is hard to see why our friend should have remained long enough to consume the greater part of the available flesh but leave what I found. The evidence indicates, that your suggestion of ants is a very likely one."

"But not certain?"

"Of course not. It would be a most remarkable coincidence, but if you wish to believe that our arrival scared the fugitive away before he had time to finish his meal, I could not disprove it."

"Where would he have gone?"

"*I* am not defending this wild supposition. However, if we must dispose of it, then his most likely goal would be your body, and I can guarantee he has not tried that!"

"Maybe he guessed you were here." Bob could be irritating at times, the Hunter reflected, much as he liked the youngster.

"Maybe he did. Maybe he's flowing at top speed through this thicket to get away." The Hunter's voice would have been weary had it been audible. Bob smiled and headed downhill once more, but the detective noticed that he kept to the edge of the stand of plants he had mentioned. However improbable an idea might be, Bob was not going to leave it unchecked if checking were so easy!

"You have a friend waiting for you, you know."

"I know. This won't take long."

"Oh. I thought you might be planning to go entirely around this patch of spikes. I was going to point out that, if all the things we have been saying are true, you might also be walking into what I believe you call a booby trap. You don't have to be logical, but you might at least be consistent."

"Did I ever read those words?" countered Bob. "You'd better start teaching me English. If you'd listen, you'd realize we were coming to the creek, which should lead to the path we used the other day, which should lead to my house. I know it's not straight, but it's sure." He stopped talking and jumped as a small animal sprang out from almost underfoot and vanished into the thicket. "Darned rats. If there were a few million more of you, Hunter, you could do this island—not to mention a lot of other places—considerable good. They're too smart for any other animal small enough to catch 'em."

"In places like that I suppose you mean," the other supplemented. "We have similar pests where I come from. We work on them when they get too troublesome, or when there is nothing better to do. I'm afraid there is a rather more serious problem facing us just now. It begins to look as though we would have to employ your idea, at least to check young Teroa, in the next few nights."

Bob nodded thoughtfully and occupied his mind with details of this possibility as they traveled. The bush had opened out a little on their left, and it was possible to walk erect again as they approached the creek. The stream was already two or three feet wide, even this far up the hill; it had its origin in a spring surprisingly close to the top of the ridge, which occasionally dried up during prolonged rainless spells. These, as it happened, were rare. The creek itself had cut deep into the soil without spreading very wide; the roots of the thick vegetation held the steep and sometimes undercut banks. In many places saplings that had been unable to meet the fierce competition for soil had fallen over so that they made bridges across the stream or moss-draped inclines sloping from the banks into the water. Occasionally larger trees had fallen and damned the creek, making little dark pools with tiny waterfalls at their lower ends.

Such a pool was located a few yards above the spot where Bob and the Hunter reached the stream. The tree which formed it had fallen years before, and most of its few branches had fallen away or become buried in the soft soil as rain, insects, and worms did their bit. The water escaped from the pool on the side from which Bob and the Hunter had approached and had deeply undercut the bank at that point, and the buried branches— perhaps—aggravated the situation. There was no warning. Bob started to turn downstream at what should have been a perfectly safe distance from the bank even if he had had a thought of danger in his mind. As his weight came on his right foot the ground suddenly gave way and let him down, and something struck his ankle a heavy blow. He reacted rapidly enough to catch himself with his hands and the other leg as his right knee disappeared, then he paused to recover his wits.

As he did so he became aware of a severe pain in his leg; and as he started to stand up again the Hunter spoke urgently.

"Wait, Bob! Don't try to move your right leg!"

"What's happened? It hurts."

"I'm sure it does. Please give me opportunity to work. You have taken a bad cut from a buried branch and you cannot move without injuring yourself further." The Hunter had understated the matter, if anything. A comparatively thin piece of wood, buried almost vertically in the ground, had split diagonally under Bob's weight and the splintered end had been driven completely through his calf from a point about four inches above the ankle on the inside to one just below the knee, scraping along the rear side of the lower leg bones and severing the main artery at that point. Without the Hunter, as far as he was from help, the boy could easily have bled to death long before anyone would have missed him.

As it was, the only blood lost was carried out by the stick itself. The Hunter was on the job instantly, and there was plenty of work to be done. Much of it was routine—sealing leaks in the circulatory system, destroying the host of micro-organisms which had been carried into his host's flesh, and fighting off shock. There was also the fact that the stick extended apparently much farther into the ground below, and Bob was perforce pinned in one spot until it could be removed either from the ground or from his leg. The job was not going to be easy, and the alien sent an exploring tentacle down into the earth to find just how firmly the stick was lodged.

The results were not encouraging. He encountered water first. Then for six or eight inches the branch went nearly straight into hard earth; at that level it had been broken almost completely across and the tip section bent sharply upward again, still underground. It was as though the branch had been jabbed forcibly into the earth, bent and broken, and then pushed a little farther—which might, the Hunter realized, be exactly what had happened. In any case, there was no possibility of getting it out of the ground; he himself lacked the strength, and Bob was pinned in a position from which he could not work very well.

He believed in sparing his host as much physical damage as possible but knew that ignorance was seldom very helpful, so he now explained the situation completely to the boy.

"This is about the first time I've really been sorry I could do nothing about the pain without injuring your nervous system, or, rather, risking injury to it," he concluded. "This will hurt, I know. I will have to pull your muscle tissue away from the stick while you pull your leg out. I will try to tell you when and how much to pull."

Bob's face was pale, even though the alien was holding his blood pressure up. "Right now I think I'd take the chance of damage, if you were willing," he said.

The Hunter realized in a dim fashion just how much the youngster was standing, and decided some help was needed. "As a last resort, Bob, I will do it," he said. "Please try to hold on, though, for even if my work on your nerves does no permanent damage, it will interfere with your ability to control your leg at the moment; and I cannot possibly lift your leg out of this hole myself."

"All right; let's get it over with."

The Hunter set to work, forcing as much as possible of his body material around the splintery stick to prevent further tearing of his host's flesh as it was withdrawn. Bit by bit, tight-lipped with pain, Bob withdrew his leg, pulling when the Hunter indicated it was safe, waiting when he had to. It took many minutes, but at last the job was done.

Even Bob, knowing what he did, was a little startled at seeing his trouser leg stained only with dirt. He was going to roll up the cloth to see the injury, but the Hunter stopped him.

"A little later, if you must; but right now lie down and rest for a few minutes. I know you don't feel the need of it, but I assure you it is advisable."

Bob realized the alien probably knew what he was talking about and complied. By rights he should have fainted, for will power means nothing in the face of such an injury, but he did not, thanks to his guest; and as he relaxed obediently, he thought.

Things had been happening just a little too fast for Bob, but it was dawning on him that the events of the last half-hour had followed with remarkable fidelity the outline he and the Hunter had discussed, half-jokingly, just before they started—an outline based on one particular contingency. And even he was impressed by the coincidence.

# XV. Ally

To the Hunter, who had examined in detail both the bones of the unfortunate Tip and the splintered stick which had injured his own host so badly, the whole thing *was* coincidence. It was so obvious to him that his quarry had nothing to do with the matter that he never thought of saying so to Bob. The boy's line of thought, therefore, at this point began to diverge widely from the detective's—a fact that turned out to be extremely fortunate.

Bob had been lying motionless for some time when they were disturbed by a voice calling his name. The boy started to spring to his feet and almost collapsed as the injured leg sent a furious protest.

"I forgot we were meeting Norman!" he said. "He must have gotten tired waiting, and is coming uphill after us." More gingerly this time he put weight on the injured limb—a thing no doctor would have recommended and to which the Hunter also objected. "I can't help it," said Bob. "If you write me off as a cripple, they'll put me in bed and we can't do a thing. I'll favor it as much as I can—it can't get infected with you there and will just have more trouble growing together, won't it?"

"Isn't that enough? I admit that no permanent damage should result, but—"

"No buts! If anyone learns how bad this is they'll send me to the doctor; and he simply won't believe I made it home without bleeding to death. You've done too much to remain concealed from him now if he gets a chance to look me over!" The boy began limping downhill, and the Hunter pondered over the sad fact that the active member of a partnership was too apt to take control, regardless of qualifications.

Somewhat later it occurred to him that there might be worse things than the doctor's learning of his presence; it might even give them a most valuable ally. There was certainly enough evidence at the moment to prove to a stupider person than Dr. Seever that the Hunter was more than a figment of Bob's imagination. Unfortunately, by the time the thought occurred to him, it was too late to mention it—Bob and Hay had met.

"Where have you been?" was the greeting of Norman. "What happened to you? I got my bike and have been waiting in front of your house long enough to grow a beard. Did you get hung up on the thorns, or what?"

"I had a fall," Bob replied with perfect truth, "and hurt my leg a bit. It was a while before I could use it."

"Oh, I see. Is it all right now?"

"No, not quite. I can get around, I guess. I can ride a bike, anyway. Let's get back down to the house and pick mine up."

The meeting had taken place at no great distance from the Kinnaird house, since Hay had not dared go very far into the jungle for fear of missing Bob altogether. It took them only a minute or two to reach the dwelling, in spite of Bob's limp, and, once there, it proved fairly easy to ride the bicycle, provided Bob mounted from the left and pedaled with the instep of his right foot instead of the toe.

They made their way up to the construction site, amusing each other the while with speculation on the troubles the others would be having getting the swamped boat through the breakers at the beach, and began prowling for materials. These proved fairly plentiful, and well before suppertime they had placed the articles of their choice in a number of inconspicuous places, to insure their remaining unused until after school the next day. They were honest youngsters, in their way.

Two things happened to prevent Bob's getting back to the site immediately after school. One of them occurred Monday morning, when his father saw him limping as he descended to breakfast, and demanded the cause. Bob repeated the story he had given Hay; but the next demand was a little awkward.

"Let's see it." Bob, thinking fast, pulled his trouser leg halfway to the knee, exposing the entry wound. This, of course, did not look nearly so bad as it should have, since the Hunter had held the torn skin in place all night and was still on duty. To the boy's vast relief Mr. Kinnaird did not ask about the depth of the injury, taking for granted that nothing so obviously free from blood clots and infection could have been very deep. The relief was short-lived, however. The man turned away, saying, "All right. If you're still limping the next time I see you, you'd better be able to tell me you've seen Doc Seever." The Hunter's respect for Mr. Kinnaird was increasing daily.

Bob set out for school with that problem on his mind—nothing was more certain than the fact that his torn calf muscle would keep him limping for days to come, Hunter or no Hunter; and his father would certainly be at the construction site that afternoon. At the end of school another cause for delay materialized: the teacher who handled the older pupils requested that he remain for a time, so that his proper position in the group might be discovered. Bob requested a moment's excuse, hastily explained to the others, and saw them started for the new tank; then he returned to the schoolroom for the inquisition. It took some time. As frequently happens when a pupil changes from one school to another, the difference in programs had put him a year or so ahead in some subjects and as far behind in others. By the time a mutually satisfactory program had been worked out, Bob was pretty sure his friends would have obtained what they needed and taken it to the creek.

Even so, there remained the problem of the limp and his father's ultimatum. He had been trying all day to walk as though nothing were the matter, and had succeeded only in attracting more attention. He stood at the doorway of the school for some minutes, pondering this problem, and finally put it up to the Hunter. He was distinctly startled at the alien's answer.

"I suggest that you do exactly what your father said—go to Dr. Seever."

"But how can we get away with that? He's no dumbbell, and you won't make him believe in miracles. He won't be satisfied just to see one of those holes, either—he'll check the whole leg. How will I account for the shape it's in without telling about you?"

"I have been thinking about that. Just what, would you say, is wrong with the idea of telling him about me?"

"I don't want to be written off as cracked, that's what. I had trouble enough believing in you myself."

"You'll probably never have better evidence for your story than you have right now, if the doctor is as thorough as you say. I will back you up; and *I* can prove I am here to anyone's satisfaction, if necessary. I know we have been making strenuous efforts all along to keep my presence secret, and the reasons for that are still sound; I don't mean to broadcast the story. I think, however, that a doctor might be a remarkably good associate in our work. He has knowledge neither of us possesses and should be willing to use it—it is certainly no exaggeration to describe our quarry as a dangerous disease."

"And if he turns out to be the host of our quarry?"

"He is certainly one of the least likely candidates on the island. However, if that should be the case—I think I can find out very quickly and certainly. There is certainly a precaution we can take." He outlined this precaution at length to his host, and Bob nodded slowly in understanding.

The doctor's office was not far from the school. It would hardly have been worth using the bicycle had it not been for Bob's injury. There was a slight delay caused by the presence of another patient, then Bob and his invisible guest entered the pleasant room which Dr. Seever had turned into a consulting room and dispensary.

"Back again so soon, Bob?" greeted the doctor. "Is that sunburn still giving trouble?"

"No, sir, I'd forgotten about that."

"Not entirely, I hope." The two grinned in sympathy.

"This is something else. I had a fall in the woods yesterday, and Dad said I'd better either see you or stop limping."

"All right, let's see the damage." Bob seated himself in a chair facing the doctor and rolled up his trouser leg. At first Dr. Seever did not see the exit wound, but after a moment he did. He examined both openings carefully and at considerable length, then he sat back and eyed the boy.

"Let's have the story."

"I was up in the woods, near the head of the first creek. The bank had been undercut farther than I thought, and I broke through, and a sharp-pointed branch underneath went into my leg."

" 'Through' is the word you want. Go on."

"There's not much else. It hasn't bothered me too much, so I didn't come to you until Dad made me."

"I see." The doctor was silent for another minute or two. Then, "Did something like this happen at school back in the States?"

"We-e-ll——" It never occurred to Bob to pretend not to know what the doctor meant. "There was this." He extended the arm that had been cut the night the Hunter had made his first attempt at communication. The doctor silently examined the thin, barely visible scar.

"How long ago?"

"Three weeks about." Another period of silence, while Bob wondered what was going on in the other's mind. The Hunter thought he knew.

"You've discovered, then, that there's something unusual about you—something you couldn't understand; something that made injuries which should need stitches behave like scratches and punctures that should put you flat on your back 'not bother you much'; and you've been worried about it? Was that what got into you at school?"

"Not exactly, sir. You're almost right, but—I know what causes it." With the Rubicon crossed, Bob went ahead quickly and clearly with his story, and the doctor listened in rapt silence. At the end he had some questions.

"You have not seen this—Hunter yourself?"

"No. He won't show himself to me. Says it might disturb my emotions."

"I think I can see his point. Do you mind being blindfolded for a little while?" Bob made no objection, and the doctor found a bandage and tied it over his eyes. Then: "Please put your hand—either one—on the table here, palm up; let it relax. Now—Hunter, you understand what I want!"

The Hunter understood clearly enough and acted accordingly. Bob could see nothing, of course, but after a moment he felt a faint weight in the palm of the extended hand. His fingers started to close on it instinctively, and the doctor's hand promptly descended to pin them in place. "Hold on a moment, Bob." For a short time the weight could be detected, then the boy began to doubt whether or not it was actually there—it was rather like a pencil stowed behind the ear, which can be felt after it is gone. When the blindfold was removed, nothing was visible, but the doctor's face was even more sober than before.

"All right, Bob," he said. "Part of your story appears to be true anyway. Now, can you enlarge on this mission of your friend?"

"First, there is something I have to say," replied Bob. "This is really his speech, and I'll try to give it in his own words, as near as I can remember.

"You have been convinced, at least in one essential, of the truth of this story. You must be able to see why the secret has been kept so far and the risk we chose to face in telling you. There is certainly a chance, however small, that you are actually the person harboring our quarry.

"In that event, we see two possibilities. Either you know of his presence and are consciously co-operating with him because he has convinced you of the justice of his position, or you do not know. In the first case, you are now planning means to get rid of me. Your guest would be perfectly willing to do anything to my host in the process, but I know you would not; and that presents you with a problem that will take time to solve and will probably betray the truth to me in your attempts to solve it.

"In the second case, Doctor, your host now knows where I am. He also knows that you are a doctor, and will find some means to detect his presence in your body if anyone can. That, I fear, will mean that we have placed you in danger, for he will have no hesitation in doing whatever he thinks necessary to escape. I cannot suggest any precautions to you; you should be able to think of some yourself. Don't mention them aloud, though.

"I am sorry to have exposed you to this risk, but it seems to me to be one that falls within your normal duty as a doctor. If, however, you are not willing to take it, simply say so. We will leave at once. We will, of course, test you at the first opportunity; but with the fear of immediate discovery no longer pressing, he may at least leave your body without harming you, since he will be in no hurry. What is your decision?"

Dr. Seever did not hesitate an instant.

"I'll take any risks there may be. I think I can see how to test myself too. According to your story, you have been in Bob's body nearly six months; and your quarry, if he is in mine at all, is likely to have been there for several weeks at least. That is long enough for the formation of specific antibodies—you say you are, in effect, a virus. I can make a serum test with a sample of Bob's blood and my own that should give us an answer at once. Have you learned enough medical English to gather what I mean?"

Bob replied slowly, reading off the Hunter's answer as it came. "I know what you mean. Unfortunately, your plan won't work. If we had not long ago learned how to prevent the formation of antibodies for our particular cells, our way of life would never have been possible."

The doctor frowned at this. "I should have thought of that. I suppose there's no use expecting your friend to let any of his own tissue be caught in a section or a blood sample, either." He looked up sharply. "How did you plan to make identification? You must have some method."

Bob explained the Hunter's difficulty in that direction, then the alien finished: "I intended, when reasonably certain, to make a final check by personal inspection. He certainly could not hide for any length of time if I went into the same body in search of him."

"Then why not check me that way? I know you have no particular reason to suspect me, but it would be just as well to know one way or the other. You would know then that you could trust me; and, frankly, I should like to know myself. I've been rather afraid these last few minutes that I might find out the hard way as soon as you two leave the office."

"Your point is a good one," relayed Bob. "But the Hunter will not enter or leave any human body while its owner is awake. You seem to sympathize with him on that." The doctor nodded slowly, looking thoughtfully at his visible guest.

"Yes. Yes, I understand his reason. However, that situation can be arranged also." Dr. Seever left his chair and went to the front door, taking a small placard from a wall stand as he passed it. This he placed on a hook outside the door, closed and locked the latter, and returned to the office. He looked at Bob again, then went over to one of the numerous small cabinets.

"How much do you weigh, Bob?" he asked over his shoulder. The boy told him, and he made a brief calculation in his head, then he reached for a bottle of clear liquid. With this in his hand he turned back to the visitors.

"Hunter, I don't know whether this stuff will affect you as well. I would suggest that you get out of Bob's alimentary and circulatory systems before we take it. We will sleep for from one to two hours—I suppose that's longer than necessary, but I can't guarantee that any smaller dose would put us out at all. You can make your test while we're unconscious and get back to tell us the result—or maybe do something else, if necessary. All right? We won't be disturbed—I've seen to that."

"I'm afraid it is not quite all right," was the answer. "It means that my host would be helpless before I know for certain about you. However, I will concede that the test should be made, and I will relax my demand somewhat to get it over with. If you and Bob will sit side by side, holding hands tightly, and guarantee that you will not separate those hands for twenty minutes, I will shift enough of myself into your body to make the inspection and return."

The doctor agreed instantly—he had intended to use the drug only because of the Hunter's insistence that the hosts be insensible, and this alternative was both safer and pleasanter. He moved his chair out beside Robert's, therefore, took one of the boy's hands in his own, dropped the bandage that had served as a blindfold over the two hands as an added safeguard for the Hunter's peace of mind, and relaxed.

It took a little more than the promised twenty minutes, but to their relief the Hunter was able to give a negative report. Discussion for the first time flowed freely—at least between Bob and the doctor—and the general conditions of the problem were thrashed over so thoroughly that Dr. Seever almost forgot about Bob's injured leg. It was only at the end of the visit that he mentioned it.

"As I understand it, Bob, your friend can do nothing to speed up the processes of healing; he simply prevents bleeding and infection. My advice is to stay off that leg—you gave the muscle an awful beating."

"The only trouble is," said Bob, "I seem to be transportation division for this army and am vehicle for the commander in chief. I can't be immobilized."

"Well, it will certainly slow up the healing; I can't see that any other damage will result, under the circumstances. Use your own judgment; I know the situation is serious for someone. Just keep off it as much as possible." The doctor closed the door behind them and returned to his study, where he speedily immersed himself in a work on immunology. Maybe the Hunter's people knew what to do about antibodies, but there were other tricks to the medical trade.

It was not quite suppertime, and Bob and the Hunter made their way to the creek, where the boys should be. A sound of sawing gave evidence well before Bob was close enough to see that they were there; but work stopped as he came in sight.

"Where have you been? You've certainly ducked out of a lot of work this afternoon. Look at the boat!"

Bob looked. There was very little boat to see, as a matter of fact, for the removal of the bad timber had accounted for a remarkable percentage of the total, and very little replacement had as yet been accomplished. There was a reason for this, Bob noticed: there was very little replacement material on hand.

"Where's the stuff we picked out last night?" he asked Hay.

"A good question," said the other dryly. "Some of it was where we put it, and that's right here now. The rest had disappeared. I don't know whether the young kids cleaned it out or the men found it and used it. We didn't stay to get more; we thought we'd better get what was left down here and use it before it disappeared too. We'll have to go back for more— there isn't nearly enough here to finish."

"You're telling me," said Bob, looking at the rather forlorn framework lying on the beach before them. Its state reminded him of something else, and he turned to Rice.

"Red, I'm afraid I found Tip yesterday." The others laid down the tools with which they had been about to resume activity and listened with interest.

"Where?"

"Up in the woods, near the head of the creek. I had my fall just afterward and forgot everything else, or I'd have told you this morning. I don't really know it was Tip, since there wasn't much left, but it was a dog about his size. I'll show you the place after supper if you like—there isn't time now."

"Could you tell what killed him?" Rice had long since accepted the fact of the dog's death.

"No. Your guess is as good as mine when you've seen him. I think Sherlock Holmes himself would have trouble finding clues, but you can try."

The news put a final stop to work on the boat for that afternoon. As Bob had said, suppertime was approaching, anyway, and presently the group drifted back up the creek to the road, and its members went their ways. Rice, before vanishing, called after Bob a reminder that they were to visit the woods after the meal.

As it happened, everybody was there. Their curiosity had been aroused by Bob's extremely sketchy description of what he had found, and they all wanted to see. Bob led the way slowly along the path to the creek and up the watercourse to the point where he had had his accident, which he pointed out. Hay, groping curiously down the hole, encountered the branch which had caused so much trouble, and after considerable effort got the vertical part out.

"You just missed some bad trouble with this," he remarked, holding it up to view. Bob indicated his leg—the boys had all seen the lower puncture; as he had done with his father, he had avoided mentioning the other.

"I didn't quite miss it," he said. "I suppose that's what did this." Hay looked more closely at the stick. The sun was on the point of setting and the woods were already rather dark, but he saw the stains left from the accident.

"I guess you're right at that," he said. "You must have been a while pulling out: blood has gone down this thing a foot or more from the sharp end. I wonder why I didn't notice it on your pants leg when I met you yesterday."

"I don't know," Bob lied hastily, and began leading the way from the creek along the edge of the thicket. The other three followed, and Hay, after a moment, shrugged his shoulders, dropped the branch, and trailed along.

He found the others grouped around the skeleton of the dog exchanging theories. Bob, who had brought them here with a definite purpose m mind, was watching all the others sharply. He himself was quite sure, in spite of what the Hunter had said about the bones, that Tip had been killed by their quarry, who had then rigged the trap into which he had fallen. He even had an explanation for the fact that there had been no attempt to enter his body while he was helpless—the alien had found another host first: a host who used the creek as a highway through the jungle, as Bob and his friends used it. That implied, of course, that one of those friends had been in the neighborhood and motionless for some reason long enough for the creature's purpose. Bob had not heard of such an incident, but was hoping that here and now, if ever, someone might refer to it.

It was rapidly growing dark now, and the only conclusion reached by the boys was the obvious one that nothing much larger than insect life had disturbed the dog's body. No one had actually touched the bones as yet, but with seeing growing more difficult by the moment, Malmstrom decided to get a closer look. The skull was inside the thicket, but it was this he chose to examine, and he reached very gingerly among the thorns to pick it up.

Getting in gave little trouble, but it developed that the thorns on the short side branches pointed back in toward the main stems. This furnished about as efficient and unpleasant a trap as one could well hope not to encounter, and Malmstrom picked up several very nasty scratches as he withdrew hand and skull. He handed the latter to Colby and shook the injured member.

"There's something that would make a good fish spear," he remarked. "The darned thorns fold back against the branches easily enough, but they spring out again when you pull the other way. I bet that's what happened to Tip—he chased something in here and couldn't pull out."

The theory was a reasonable one, and even Bob was impressed by it. He suddenly remembered that he had not told his other idea to the doctor; what would Seever's opinion be? Perhaps by now he had worked out some medical test, and there would be no difficulty for him in finding an excuse to use it. Bob had hoped to give him some line on whom to test first; now he did not know what to think. He led the way back downhill in the darkness, his brain working furiously.

# XVI. Prospectus

Tuesday went as usual until the end of school, except for the fact that the Hunter was growing progressively more anxious about Charles Teroa. That one was due to leave the island on Thursday, and as far as the Hunter could see Bob had done nothing toward testing him or delaying his departure. There were only two more nights. . .

The boys, who had no such worries, departed on a search for more boatbuilding materials as soon as they were dismissed. Bob started with them, but stopped off at the doctor's office, ostensibly to have his leg checked. Here he told in full the story of the preceding evening and of his theory; and the detective realized for the first time that his host had been working along a line of thought radically different from his own. He hastily attracted the boy's attention and gave his own views, together with the evidence supporting them.

"I'm sorry I didn't realize the trend of your thoughts," he concluded. "I remember telling you that I didn't think the dog had been killed by our friend, but perhaps I did not mention the fact that your 'booby trap' also seemed to be entirely natural. I should say that the branch was driven into the ground that way when the tree fell. Is this why you have been ignoring the matter of Charles Teroa?"

"I guess so," Bob replied. He gave a brief summary of the Hunter's silent speech to the doctor.

"Young Teroa?" asked Seever. "He should be coming to me for shots tomorrow. Have you reason to suspect him?"

"At first it was simply the fact that he was to leave the island," replied the Hunter. "We wanted to be sure before he was out of reach. However, we learned later that he had slept at least once in a boat moored at the reef, which gives definite opportunity for our quarry to get at him. He

151

was also present when we nearly went through the drain on the dock, but that hardly involves him alone."

"That's right," mused the doctor. "We have quite a list of what you might call first-class possibles, with the whole island following right behind as slightly less probables. Bob, did nothing happen last night to give you ideas, one way or the other, about any of your friends?"

"Just one," replied the boy. "When Shorty Malmstrom pulled Tip's skull out of the thicket he got several gashes from the thorns; they bled like nobody's business. I kind of thought we needn't worry too much about him."

Seever frowned slightly, and addressed his next remark to the detective. "Hunter, just what sort of conscience has this friend of yours anyway? Could he or would he, for example, let an injury of that sort bleed just to make someone reach Bob's conclusion—that there was no one of your race there?"

"His conscience is non-existent," returned the alien. "However, the sealing of such minor injuries is so much a habit with us that he might have done it anyway if he were there. Certainly if he had any reason to believe his host were under suspicion, and if he thought of it, he would refrain from helping him regardless of the seriousness of the injury—he is looking out for just one creature's health. Bob's point is no positive proof either way, but we can list it as a minor point in Malmstrom's favor."

The doctor nodded. "That's about what I thought from your earlier story," he said. "Well, we seem to be left with the immediate problem of testing young Teroa. It would be nice to know what yellow-fever vaccine does to your people, Hunter. He's getting a dose of it tomorrow."

"I would gladly let you find out if the stuff will not harm Bob. However, I can guarantee that our friend will simply withdraw from the limb in which you inject the stuff and wait till it attenuates. Besides, the chances of its being harmful to us are very remote. I still think I had better examine him myself. Once we locate our quarry, we can find something that will damage him."

"Once you locate your quarry, you'd better be *ready* with something that will damage him," retorted the doctor. "All I can offer that may do it without harming his host are a few antibiotics and vaccines; and we can't test them all at once on Bob. We should have started this business days ago." He thought tensely for a moment. "I'll tell you. Suppose we start now, one substance at a time, with the things I know will not harm Bob. You can tell us the effect they have on you—we'll arrange things so you can leave his body in a hurry until he eliminates the particular substance you couldn't stand. We'll leave testing Teroa until we find one of them that works. If none of them do, we're no worse off anyway."

"But, as you say, that will take days, and Teroa leaves this island in less than forty-eight hours."

"Not necessarily. I don't like to do it, because I know how eager the fellow is to get going, but I can hold him on the island for observation until the next visit of the boat if necessary.

"That will give us ten days, with two drugs a day, and should give us a fair chance of finding something. We'll start with antibiotics, since vaccines are usually pretty specific in their likes and dislikes."

"Very good indeed, if you are willing, Bob," was the reply. "It is a pity we did not get you into the fight before, Doctor. Shall we make one test now?"

"Sure," replied Bob. He seated himself, and the doctor draped a cloth over his legs.

"I don't know whether it's worth the trouble to take your shoes off," he said as he was swabbing the boy's arm with antiseptic. "From what I gather about your friend, he can get out if he has to without their bothering him. All set?" Bob nodded, and Seever held the hypo syringe against his arm and pressed the plunger. The boy kept his eyes on the wall and waited for the Hunter's report.

"Just another kind of protein molecule to me," was the sentence that finally appeared. "You might ask the doctor if I should consume the stuff or if it's all right to leave loose in your system."

Bob relayed the message.

"It doesn't matter, as far as anyone knows," replied the doctor. "In fact, he would be doing me a favor if he let it go and reported any effect on your tissues to me. We believe it's harmless. Well, it's probably best not to try another today; you might as well get back to your friends. Keep your eyes open; Teroa isn't our only suspect, even if your own idea wasn't so good."

The boys were still at the construction site—Bob had kept an eye on the road to be sure of that. His leg gave a twinge as he mounted his bicycle. He realized with amusement that the doctor had forgotten the injury entirely. He wished he could himself. The ride did not take long, and he noted with satisfaction that there was already a fair-sized stack of loot at the point where the other machines had been left. He parked his own at the same point and sought his friends.

The four boys, it turned out, had called a temporary halt in the search for materials. They were on the hillside at the top of the wall which Bob had seen poured. The concrete had set and the forms were now being placed in preparation for the side walls; the boys were leaning over and looking down the smooth expanse of concrete. Bob, joining them, saw that the attraction was a crew of men busy with some peculiar apparatus at the bottom. They all wore breathing masks, but the man in charge was recognizable as Malmstrom's father. They seemed to have a pressure pump connected by flexible tubing to a drum of some liquid, which, in turn, was fed to a nozzle. One of the men was spraying the liquid on the concrete and the others were following with blowtorches. The boys had a rough idea of what was going on—many of the bacteria used in the tanks produced extremely corrosive substances, either as intermediate or final waste products. The glaze being applied to the wall was meant as protection from these. It consisted, actually, of one of the fluorine-bearing "plastics" developed a few years previously as a by-product of uranium isotope separation research; it was stored in the drum with one of the standard inhibitors and polymerized into a glassy varnish almost at once when this was boiled out. The fumes of the inhibitor were rather unhealthful, which was why the men were masked.

The boys, thirty feet above the scene of action, got an occasional whiff of the fumes. Not even the Hunter recognized the danger, but others did, and did something about it.

"First a sunburn that nearly toasts you alive and now this. You don't care much what happens to you any more, do you?" The group turned and looked up in surprise, to see the tall form of Bob's father looming over them. They had last noticed him well out on the floor of the tank, apparently busy, and none of them had seen him head their way. "Why do you suppose Mr. Malmstrom and his crew are wearing masks? You'd better come along with me. You may be safe enough at this distance, but there's no sense taking a chance on it." He turned and led the way along the wall, and the boys followed silently.

At the end of the finished section Mr. Kinnaird waved a hand at the far section of mold. "I'll meet you down there in a couple of minutes. I have to drive home to pick up something, and if you'd care to load up your loot in the jeep I'll drive it down to the creek with you." He watched the youngsters head downhill at top speed, and descended to the floor himself via one of the diagonal braces.

He picked up the T-shirt he had removed for comfort and stowed by one of the power saws, donned it, and walked down to the point he had indicated, where the jeep was parked. Only his son awaited him there; the others had gone on to the pile of material they had collected. Mr. Kinnaird sent the jeep along their trail, coasting most of the way.

The loading was quickly accomplished; the boys already had their hands full of the smaller scraps, and Mr. Kinnaird himself managed the longer stuff in a single armload. Then he headed on down the road, the five bicycles following. The boys, of course, made a race of it; the distance being short, they were not very far apart at the end, and even the jeep had not had to wait long for them.

Mr. Kinnaird, seeing the boys doff shoes and roll up their trouser legs, followed suit, and, with the same load of lumber under his arm, splashed behind them down the creek to the scene of operations. He looked over the skeleton of the boat, made a few constructive suggestions, and returned the way he had come, slapping as he went. "I think you kids keep trained bugs around, to discourage company," he said. The boys answered in the same vein, and finally got to work.

They paused to swim more than occasionally, and it was during one of these swims that the Hunter learned why human beings avoided jelly-fish. Bob failed to do so at one point, and his guest became intimately acquainted with the nettle cells of the Coelenterata. He blocked the spread of their poison, not because he felt that his host should be encouraged to ignore the creature, but in a half-sentimental recollection of the mistakes of his first day on earth. He felt that he was paying for knowledge.

In spite of sundry interruptions a good deal of work was accomplished in the first hour or so. Then another boat made its appearance, and Charles Teroa was with them, to the intense interest of the detective and his host.

"Hi, sleepy!" Rice greeted the newcomer boisterously, waving a saw in welcome. "Having a last look around?"

Teroa eyed him in none too friendly a fashion. "It's a pity that built-in danger signal of yours can't be seen by your tongue," he remarked. "You fellows having boat trouble again? Seems to me you got it fixed once." Four eager pairs of lungs vied in giving him the story, Rice suddenly fading into silence. The visitor simply looked at him when they had finished, and the expression on his brown face changed from annoyance to amusement. Nothing he could have said would have conveyed his thoughts more clearly, or made Rice feel sillier. Relations were a little strained between the two for the half-hour Teroa remained.

There was much talk and little work during that half-hour—Teroa enlarging on his future in great detail, with Hay and occasionally Colby contributing remarks in between times. Bob, whose knowledge of the doctor's intentions made him rather uncomfortable, said little; he spent most of the time reminding himself that it was for Teroa's own good. Rice had had his batteries silenced in the first exchange, and even Malmstrom was less talkative than usual. Bob put it down to the fact that he had always been on closer terms with Teroa than the others, and didn't like the idea of his friend's leaving. Sure enough, when Teroa returned to his boat, Malmstrom went with him, asking Colby to take home the bicycle he had left where the creek and road met.

"Charlie says we're going to meet the barge and get a tow around to the fields. He wants to see the fellows on the barge and then come back over the hill by the new tank and see the folks there. I'll go with him and walk home. I may be late, but what the heck."

Colby nodded, and the two departed, pulling strongly out into the lagoon to intercept the scavenger barge, which was making one of its periodic trips around the tanks. The others watched silently until contact was made.

"It's fun to ride him, but I'm sorry to see him go," remarked Rice at length. "Still, he'll be back every so often. Shall we get back to the boat?"

There was muttered agreement, but enthusiasm for the work seemed to have died out for the time being. They pottered around for a while, went swimming again, sawed a couple of boards to length, and eventually startled their parents by appearing at home well in advance of the evening meal.

Bob, instead of settling down to schoolwork after supper, went out again. To his mother's casual question he replied that he was going "down to the village." It was true enough, and he had no intention of worrying his parents by telling them he wanted to see Dr. Seever. The doctor had said that the next drug would not be tried until tomorrow, and Bob himself had nothing specific to tell or ask; but he was uneasy about something, and could not himself decide just what. The Hunter was a good and trustworthy friend, no doubt, but he was not even at the best of times an easy being to converse with; and Bob simply had to talk.

The doctor welcomed him with some surprise.

"Good evening, Bob. Are you getting impatient for another test, or do you have some news? Or are you just being sociable? Come in, whichever it is." He closed the door behind his young guest and motioned him to a seat.

"I don't exactly know what it is, sir. At least I do partly: it's this trick we're playing on Charlie. I know we have good reason, and it won't hurt him permanently, but I don't exactly feel right about it."

"I know. I don't pretend to like it myself—I'm going to have to lie, you know, in a way that goes very much against the grain. When I give a wrong diagnosis, I'd like it to be an honest mistake." He smiled wryly. "Still, I see no alternative, and deep down I know we are doing no wrong. You must realize that too. Are you sure there's nothing else on your mind?"

"No, I'm not," was the reply, "but I can't tell you what it is. I just can't seem to relax."

"That's natural enough; you are involved in a tense situation—more so than I, and I can certainly feel it. Still, it is possible that there is something of importance you have seen and can't bring back to mind—something you didn't notice at the time but which has some connection with our problem. Have you thought over carefully everything that has happened since you came home?"

"Not only that, but everything that's happened since last fall."

"Have you just *thought,* or have you talked it over with your friend?"

"Thought mostly."

"It might be a good idea to talk—it frequently gets one's thoughts in better order. We can at least discuss the cases against your friends, to see whether you've considered all the points. We have covered young Teroa pretty thoroughly, I should say—the facts that he slept near the reef and was present at your accident on the dock seem to be all we have against him. Besides, we already have a plan of action covering him.

"You mentioned a minor point in favor of Malmstrom, when he cut himself on those thorns. Have you anything else that could be given, either for or against him? He has not slept near the reef, for example?"

"All of us were sleeping on the beach the day the Hunter arrived, but come to think of it Shorty wasn't there that day. Anyway, that doesn't matter. I told you about finding that piece of the ship; it was a mile from the beach, and anyway the Hunter says it would have taken a long time for this creature to bring it ashore. He couldn't have landed until later." He paused. "The only other thing I remember noticing about Shorty was that he left us and went off with Charlie this afternoon; and they were always good friends, so there's nothing funny about his wanting to talk to him before he goes." The doctor was able to untangle this mess of pronouns, and nodded.

"Yes, I should say that everything you've dredged up on young Malmstrom is either immaterial or in his favor. How about the redhead—Ken Rice?"

"Pretty much the same as the rest, as far as haunting the reef and being there on the dock. I haven't seen him get injured, so—— Wait a minute; he did get his foot pretty badly bruised by that chunk of coral. He had his heavy shoes—the kind we always wear on the reef—on, though, so there's no reason to suppose he got any cuts. I suppose the bruise wouldn't mean any more than Shorty's scratches, though."

"When did all this take place? I don't recall your telling me about it."

"Out on the reef, the same time we found that generator shield— same place, in fact; I should have thought of that." He went on to tell the story in detail. "We've kept quiet about it, of course; after all, he did come pretty close to getting himself drowned."

"That is a very interesting little tale. Hunter, would you mind enlarging once more on your reasons for suspecting people who have *slept* on the outer reef?"

The alien could see what the doctor was driving at, but answered the question as it was asked.

"He must have come ashore somewhere on the reef; he could not possibly catch a human being who saw him first; and he would be too obsessed with the need for secrecy to waylay an intelligent host and enter his body regardless of objection—which would, of course, be physically possible. He would not mind terrifying his host, but he would not want to have anyone with the desire and ability to report his whereabouts to, say, a medical specialist. I think, Doctor, that if a lump of jelly had swarmed onto any one of these island people and soaked into his skin, you would have heard about it in very short order."

The doctor nodded. "That's what I thought. It occurs to me, however, that young Rice could very easily have been invaded without his own knowledge while his foot was trapped under water. Between the natural fear and excitement of the situation and the pain caused by the weight of the block on his foot, any sensations incident to such an attack would have passed unnoticed."

"That is perfectly possible," agreed the Hunter.

Bob transmitted this speech as he had the other, but continued with a remark of his own. "We can't have it both ways. If this creature entered Red's body only that afternoon, he couldn't have had anything to do with the trouble at the dock a few minutes later—first, because it would probably take him days, like the Hunter, before he would be well enough set up to look around; second, because he wouldn't have any reason for it—he could not possibly have begun to suspect that the Hunter was with me."

"That's true enough, Bob; but the dock affair might really have been an accident. After all, *all* these things that keep happening to you and your friends can't have been planned. I've known you all your lives, and if someone had asked me before you told me about this situation I would have had to admit that I was not the least surprised at the things that had been happening to you. The other kids on the island are pretty much the same. There are falls and cuts and bruises every day, and you know it."

Bob had to admit the justice of this point. "It was Ken who wrecked the boat this time too," he said, "though I can't see how that would connect with this business."

"Nor do I, at the moment, but we'll remember it. So far, then, young Rice has one of the best grounds for suspicion against him that we've dug up to date. How about the others? Norman Hay, for example? I've had a thought or two about him myself since you came up with this yarn."

"What's that?"

"Not being completely brainless, I now see why you were digging information about viruses from me the other day. It has occurred to me that Hay might have had a similar motive—you remember he had one of the books I wanted to lend you. I admit his sudden interest in biology might be natural, but it might be as much of a sham as yours. How about it?"

Bob nodded. "That's an idea. He had lots of opportunity too; he was often on the reef working on that pool of his, I understand. I don't know whether he ever took a nap on the job, but it's possible. He was willing to go in the water with me, too, that time we thought there might be some peculiar disease in his pool."

The doctor raised his eyebrows interrogatively, and Bob took time out to give the details of that occurrence.

"Bob," the doctor said when he had finished, "I may know more medicine, but I'd be willing to bet there's enough data right now in your memory to solve this problem if you could evaluate it properly. That's a darned interesting point. It would imply, of course, that Norman was in communication with his guest, as you are with the Hunter, but we've assumed that before without straining any of the known facts. The creature could easily have told a phony story to enlist Hay's sympathy."

It was at this point that Dr. Seever was first struck by the idea that the Hunter might have done just that; like Bob, he thought fast enough to keep the idea to himself; and, like Bob, he resolved to test the possibility at the first opportunity.

"I suppose Norman, like the others, was around on the dock that time, so he is even with them in opportunity there," the doctor went on without a perceptible pause. "Can you think of anything else about him—for or against? Not at the moment? All right, that leaves, I believe, Hugh Colby in your particular crowd, though we mustn't forget that there are plenty of others on the island who work or play around the reef."

"We can count out the workers," insisted Bob. "And none of the kids play around it—at least on that side of the island—anywhere near as much as we do."

"Well, granting that for the moment, what about Colby? I don't know him too well myself—I don't think I've exchanged more than about two words with him. He's never here professionally, and I don't think I've had to work on him since he was vaccinated."

"That sounds like Hugh all right," replied Bob. "We've heard more than two words, but not much more. He doesn't talk much and is always in the background. He thinks fast, though. He had gone after that bucket for Red's head before anyone else could figure out what was going on. He was at the dock, of course, but I can't think of anything else about him either way. I'm not too surprised, either; he's just not the sort of fellow you think much about, though he's a good enough guy."

"Well, we have Rice and Hay to think about anyway, and Charlie Teroa to work on. I don't know whether this has brought any of your worries into the open or not, but at least I have learned a lot, Bob. If you remember anything else, come around and we'll talk it over.

"I hadn't expected to see you again today, but it's several hours since we tested that last drug; it's probably out of your system by now. Do you want to try another?"

Bob was perfectly willing, and the preparations of the afternoon were repeated. The result were the same, except that the Hunter reported the new drug to be rather more "tasty" than the previous sample.

# XVII. Argument

Wednesday morning Bob left for school early and got another drug tested before appearing at that institution. He did not know just when Teroa was to appear for his shots and did not particularly want to meet him, so he wasted as little time as possible at the doctor's office. The school day went much as usual; afterward the boys decided to omit boat work for the afternoon and visit the new tank once more. Malmstrom was an exception to this; he vanished by himself without being very specific as to his plans, and Bob watched him go with considerable curiosity. He was tempted to follow, but he had no legitimate excuse for doing so, and anyway Rice and Hay rated higher on the suspect list.

Construction, it appeared, was not going quite so rapidly. The walls for which molds were now being set up were not only not backed on one side by the hill for the greater part of their length, but started from a floor which was itself some fifteen feet from the ground at its northern extremity. This involved the setting of diagonal braces considerably longer than had previously been necessary; and since none of the two-by-fours or two-by-sixes was long enough, piecing was required. The slope of the hill meant, further, that no two braces were of identical length; and Mr. Kinnaird was hustling from hillside to power saw with a slide rule in his hand and a steel tape popping in and out of his pocket.

Heavy boards were making rapid trips from lumber pile to saw to wall: and Bob, more or less indifferent to splinters, and Colby, who had borrowed a pair of work gloves, helped with these for some time. Hay and Rice equipped themselves with wrenches, and the persuasive redhead managed to get permission for them to tighten bolts on the conveyor troughs leading from the mixers up the hill down to the molds. These troughs ran on scaffolding, and much of their length was well off the ground, since some of the spouts delivered their contents at the end of the wall farthest from the mixers. Neither of the boys minded the height particularly, but some of the men did and were quite willing to have more active individuals take care of those sections. The scaffolding was solid enough to reduce risk of falling to a minimum.

The coating of the completed south wall was still under way and the boys were not allowed near this activity, but Bob was permitted once to drive down to the dock to refill the drum of fluor varnish. This material could not be kept for any length of time near the scene of the work, since it tended to polymerize at ordinary temperatures even with the inhibitor present. The reserve was stored in a refrigerated chamber near the diminutive cracking plant. The drive took only two or three minutes, but he had to wait nearly half an hour while the drum was cleaned and refilled; to leave any of the former contents in it was asking for trouble. There was literally no solvent known that could clean it out, once it hardened, without dissolving the metal of the drum first.

When he got back to the tank Bob found Rice no longer aloft; instead, he was about as low as he could get, driving stakes to butt the diagonal braces. Asked what had caused the change of occupation, he seemed more amused than otherwise.

"I dropped a bolt and nearly beaned Dad, and he told me to get down before I killed somebody. He's been lecturing me most of the time you were gone. He told me either to work down here or get away altogether; he said if I could drop anything on anyone from here he'd give up. I've been wondering what he'd say if the head came off this sledge on the upswing, which it seems to want to do."

"If he's in the way, he won't say a word. You'd better tighten it—that's a little too risky to be funny."

"I suppose you're right." Rice stopped swinging and busied himself with the wedges, while Bob looked around for something else to interest him. He held an end of the steel tape for his father for a while, was sternly forbidden to carry hundred-pound bags of cement to the stock pile near the mixers, and finally settled down at the top of a light ladder checking with a spirit level the trueness of each section of form before its braces were finally set. The work was important enough to make him satisfied with himself, easy enough so he could keep it up, and safe enough to keep his father from interfering.

He had been at this task for some time when he suddenly remembered that he should have seen the doctor immediately after school for another test. Now he was stuck here; as to most conspirators, however good their motives, it did not occur to him that there was no need for him to account for his movements. He stayed at the job therefore, trying to devise an excuse that would let him leave without arousing question in anyone's mind. The men might not notice, but there were his friends; and even if they didn't, there was a horde of smaller fry around who would be sure to want to know where he was going. Bob thought they would, anyway.

His reverie on these matters was interrupted by Colby, who was still working on the trough sections and happened to be nearly overhead.

"Say, there comes Charlie all by himself. I thought Shorty had probably gone to see him."

Bob looked down the hill toward the road extension and saw that Hugh was right. Teroa was coming slowly up toward the tank; his facial expression was hard to make out at that distance, but Bob was pretty sure from the aimless way he walked and his generally listless air that he had seen the doctor. Bob's own face tightened, and a pang of conscience went through him; for a moment he considered going up his ladder and out of sight over the forms. He managed to restrain the impulse and held his position, watching.

Teroa was now close enough to be seen clearly. His face was nearly expressionless, which in itself was something of a contrast to his usual good humor; he barely answered the greetings flung at him by the envious youngsters he passed. Two or three of the men, seeing that something must be wrong, tactfully said nothing; but tact was a word missing from the vocabulary of Kenneth Rice.

That young man was working perhaps thirty yards downhill from the foot of Bob's ladder. He was still driving stakes, using the sledge which he had repaired; it looked ridiculously large beside its wielder, for Rice was rather small for his age. He looked up from his work as Teroa approached, and hailed him.

"Hi, Charlie. All set for your trip?"

Charles did not change his expression, and answered in a voice almost devoid of inflection, "I'm not going."

"Weren't there beds enough on board?" It was a cruel remark, and Rice regretted it the instant it passed his lips, for he was a friendly and kind-hearted, if sometimes thoughtless, youngster; but he did not apologize. He was given no opportunity.

Teroa, as Bob had judged, had just seen Dr. Seever. For months the boy had been wanting the job; for nearly a week he had been planning his departure; and, what was worse, he had been announcing it to all and sundry. The doctor's statement that he must wait at least one more trip had been a major shock. He could not see the reason for the delay, which was not too surprising. He had been walking aimlessly for more than an hour since leaving the doctor's office before his feet had carried him to the construction site. Probably, if he had been giving any thought to his destination, he would have avoided the spot with its inevitable crowd of workers and children. Certainly he was in no fit mood to meet company; the more he thought, the less just the doctor's action seemed and the angrier the young man grew. Kenny Rice's raillery, quite apart from considerations of tact or courtesy, was extremely ill-advised.

Charles did not even pause to think. He was within a yard or two of Rice when the latter spoke, and he reacted instantly—he leaped and swung.

The smaller boy had quick reactions, and they were all that saved him from serious injury by that first blow. Teroa had put all his strength into it. Rice ducked backward, dropping his sledge and raising his arms in defense. Teroa, losing whatever shreds of temper that might have remained to him as his blow expended itself in empty air, recovered himself and sprang again with both fists flailing; and the other, with the molds forming an effective barrier to further retreat, fought back in self-defense.

The man whom Rice had been assisting was far too startled to interfere at first; Bob was too far away, as were all the other workers on that side of the tank; Colby had no ready means of descending from the scaffold. The fight, therefore, progressed for some moments with all the violence of which the combatants were capable. Rice stayed on the defensive at first, but he lost his own temper when the first of Teroa's blows got past his guard and thudded solidly against his ribs, and from then on he pulled no punches.

The fact that the other boy was three years older, a full head taller, and correspondingly heavier had considerable bearing on his success, of course. Neither belligerent was a scientific fighter, but some effective blows landed in spite of that. Most of them were Teroa's, who found his adversary's face on a very convenient level; but his own ribs sustained a heavy assault, and at least once the elder boy was staggered by a blow that landed fairly in the solar plexus.

Quite involuntarily he stepped back and dropped his guard over the afflicted region. For Rice, the fight reached a climax at that instant. He was not thinking and was not an experienced boxer, but he could not have reacted more rapidly or correctly if he had trained for years in the ring. As Teroa's arms went down momentarily, Rice's left fist jabbed forward, backed by the swimming-and-rowing muscles of his shoulders, waist, and legs, and connected squarely with his opponent's nose. It was a nice blow, and Rice, who had little to be pleased or proud about in connection with the fight, always remembered it with satisfaction. It was all the satisfaction he got. Teroa recovered his wind, his guard, and his poise, and responded with a blow so nearly identical in placement that it formed an excellent measure of the true effectiveness of Rice's guard. It was the last of the fight. The man with the other sledge had recovered his wits, and he flung his arms about Teroa from behind. Bob, who had had time to leap from his ladder and dash to the scene, did the same to Rice. Neither combatant made any serious effort to escape; the sharp action had winded them, the pause gave them a chance to evaluate the situation, and both presented rather shame-faced expressions—or what could be seen of their expressions—to the crowd which was still gathering.

The children, who formed the greater part of the group, were cheering both parties indiscriminately; but the men who appeared and shouldered their way through the smaller spectators showed no such enthusiasm. Mr. Rice, who was among them, bore a look on his face that would have removed any lingering trace of self-righteousness from his son's manner.

The son himself was not much to look at. Bruises were already starting to take on a rich purple color, which contrasted nicely with his red hair, and his nose was bleeding copiously. The bruises his adversary had collected were mostly concealed by his shirt, but he, too, had a nosebleed that said something for Rice's ability. The elder Rice, stationing himself in front of his offspring, looked him over for some time in silence, while the chatter of the crowd died down expectantly. He had no intention of saying what he had in mind where anyone but the intended recipient could hear it, however, and after a minute or so he simply said:

"Kenneth, you'd better get your face washed and the worst of the stains out of that shirt before your mother sees you. I'll talk to you later." He turned around. "Charles, if you'd go with him, and perhaps take the same advice, I'd appreciate it. I should like very much to hear exactly what caused this nonsense."

The boys made no answer, but started down toward the lagoon, now very much ashamed of themselves. Bob, Norman, and Hugh followed them. Bob and Hugh had heard the start of the trouble, but had no intention of telling anyone until the principals of the affair had decided what should be told.

Mr. Kinnaird knew his son and the latter's friends well enough to guess this, and it was only that knowledge which enabled him to keep quiet as he rounded the lower end of the tank and came face to face with the party. "I have some salt-water soap in the jeep," he remarked. "I'll get it, if one of you will take this blade up to Mr. Meredith at the saw." He moved as though to scale the disk-shaped object, which the boys had not noticed he was carrying, at Colby, who automatically slipped to one side. Recovering himself, Colby hooked a finger through the center hole of the blade and turned back uphill with it, while Mr. Kinnaird headed around the corner of his vehicle. The boys accepted the soap gratefully—Rice, in particular, had been worrying about his mother's reaction to the sight of his bloodstained shirt.

Half an hour later, the stains gone, he was worrying about her reaction to a pair of beautifully blacked eyes. He had kept his teeth by some miracle, but Bob and Norman, who were administering first aid, admitted that it would be some time before casual observers would quit asking him about his fight. Teroa was considerably better off in that respect; his face had been reached just once, and the swelling should go down in a day or two.

All animosity had vanished by this time; both combatants had spent much of the time apologizing to each other while their injuries were being worked on. Even Bob and Norman were amused to see them walking side by side back up the hill to face Mr. Rice.

"Well," Hay remarked at last, "we told Red he was asking for it. I hope he doesn't get into too much trouble, though; Charlie gave him enough. Those peepers are going to take a long time to forget, I'd say."

Bob nodded in agreement. "He certainly picked a bad time for his wisecracks—right after Charlie said he wasn't going. He must have been feeling pretty bad."

"I didn't hear that. Did he say why he wasn't going? It's news to me."

"No." Bob remembered in time that he was not supposed to know, either. "No, there wasn't time for explanations after that; things happened too fast. I don't suppose it would be smart to ask now, either, though he may have told Red by this time. Shall we go back up and see?"

"I don't think it would do much good. Besides, I still haven't put the grating in that pool of mine—we've been spending so much time fixing the boat and working up here. What say we go out and do that? We don't need the boat; the stuff is out there, and we can swim across from the beach."

Bob hesitated. This seemed a good opportunity of seeing the doctor and getting another drug written off the list—he was not very optimistic on this point, as may be seen—but he was still not quite sure how to get away from his friend; he still had an exaggerated fear of betraying his real motives.

"What about Hugh?" he asked. "He hasn't come down from delivering that saw blade yet. Maybe he'd like to go."

"He's probably found something else to do up there. I think I'll go back myself, if you don't want to work on the pool. You coming, or have you something else to do?"

"I did think of something," Bob replied. "I think I'll look after it now."

"O.K. I'll see you later." Hay went back up the hill after the still-visible fighters without a backward glance, while Bob, wondering how much the other suspected, turned along the shore toward the big dock.

He walked slowly, since he had much to think about; but he said nothing, and the Hunter forbore to disturb him. The alien had thoughts of his own, in any case.

At the shoreward end of the dock they turned up the road past the Teroa house, turned right there, and presently reached the home of the doctor. Here his plans, such as they were, were interrupted by the sight of a sign on the door which said the doctor was out on professional business, time of return uncertain.

The door was never locked, as Bob well knew. After a moment's consideration he opened it and went into the office. He could wait, and the doctor was bound to be back before too long. Besides, there were other books there, books which he had not read and which might prove interesting or useful. He investigated the shelves, helped himself to several promising titles, and sat down to deal with them.

He made heavy weather of the job: they were technical works, intended for professional readers, and they pulled no punches when it came to medical terms. Bob was far from stupid, but he simply did not have the knowledge needed to interpret very much of what they said. In consequence, his mind wandered frequently and far from the printed matter.

Naturally much of his thinking was about the afternoon's rather unusual events. More of it dealt with his problem. He had even asked the Hunter point-blank what he thought about the conclusions reached the night before—the strong suspicions Bob and Seever had developed toward Hay and Rice. He did so now.

"I have avoided criticizing your efforts," replied the Hunter, "since it seems to me that, however wrong your conclusions appear, you still have reason for them. I prefer not to tell you my opinions about Rice and Hay, or even about the other boys, for if I were to discourage your ideas on the grounds that they disagreed with mine, I might as well be working alone."

It was an indirect speech, but Bob suspected that the alien disagreed with their ideas. He could not see why—the logic used by the doctor and himself seemed sound—but he realized that the Hunter must have more knowledge about the creature they were seeking than he could impart in a lifetime.

Still, what could be wrong? Strictly speaking, they had reached no actual conclusions—they knew their limitations and had spoken only of probabilities. If the Hunter objected to that, then he should have a certainty!

"I have nothing certain," was the answer, however, when this line of reasoning was expounded to the detective, and Bob settled back to think some more. He got results, but this time he had no chance to discuss them with the Hunter, for just as the idea struck him, he heard the doctor's step on the front porch. Bob sprang to his feet, concentrating tensely; then, as the door opened, he turned to the entering figure.

"I've got some news," he said. "You can let Charlie go tomorrow, after all, and we can forget about Red too!"

# XVIII. Elimination

The doctor had stopped as he heard Bob's excited voice; now he finished closing the door behind him and moved to his usual chair.

"I'm glad to hear it," he said. "I have some news also. Suppose you give me the details first. Has the Hunter been making tests on his own?"

"No, I have. I mean, it's something I saw. I didn't realize what it meant until just now.

"Charlie and Red had a fight up by the new tank. It started when Red kidded him about not going away tomorrow—I suppose he must have seen you just before. Anyway, they both went right up in the air; they were swinging for all they were worth. They both picked up a lot of bruises—Ken has a beautiful pair of shiners—and they both had first-class nosebleeds when we got 'em apart!"

"And you feel that this display of injury means one of the Hunter's race can't be present? I thought we decided that our fugitive would refrain from stopping blood flow for fear of betraying himself. I don't see what your story proves."

"You don't get my point, Doc. I know that a cut or scratch bleeding wouldn't prove anything, but don't you see the difference between that and a nosebleed? There's no cut out in the open for the world to see; there'd be nothing surprising if a fellow got hit on the nose and it didn't bleed. Those two were regular fountains—he'd have been bound to stop 'em!"

There was a pause, while the doctor considered this point.

"There's one objection remaining," he said at last. "Would our friend *know* what you have just mentioned—that a blow on the nose does not necessarily cause bleeding? After all, he hasn't had a lifetime of human experience like you."

"I even thought of that." Bob was triumphant. "How could he be the sort of thing he is, and be where he is, without knowing? He just would have to know what causes a nosebleed and whether it's necessary or not. I haven't asked the Hunter yet, but how else could it be? How about it, Hunter?" He awaited the answer, at first with complete confidence, then with mounting doubt as the alien considered the wording of his response.

"I should say that you are quite right," the Hunter replied at last. "I had not considered that possibility before, and there was the chance that our friend had not, either; but even in that case he would certainly have seen that there was no danger in stopping the bleeding at any time. The boys who were fighting kept it up long after you were applying nose pressure and cold water and other odd remedies. You score first, Bob; I am willing to forget those two."

Bob repeated this to Dr. Seever, who received the information with a grim nod.

"I have an elimination candidate also," he answered. "Tell me, Bob, didn't you say your attention had been attracted to Ken Malmstrom yesterday?"

"Yes, a little. He didn't work so hard as usual on the boat and he seemed quieter, but I figured it was because Charlie was going away."

"And today?"

"I don't know. I haven't seen him since school."

"I'll bet you haven't," said Seever dryly. "You shouldn't have seen him in school, either. He had a temperature of a hundred and three right afterward, when he finally decided to tell his parents he wasn't feeling well."

"What—?"

"Your friend is down with malaria, and I'd like to know where in blazes he picked it up." The doctor glared as though Bob had been personally responsible.

"Well, there are mosquitoes on the island," pointed out that young man, uneasy under the glare.

"I know, though we keep 'em down pretty well. But where did *they* get it? I keep track of the people who leave this island or visit it; the crew of the tanker—some of 'em—come ashore for short periods. They're out, I'm sure; I know their medical histories. You've been away long enough to get anything and come back, but you can't be the one, unless the Hunter has been preserving the disease in your blood for fun."

"Is it a virus disease? The Hunter wants to know."

"No. It's caused by a flagellate—a protozoan. Here"—the doctor found a book with appropriate microphotographs—"look at these, Hunter, and see if anything like 'em were or are still in Robert's blood."

The answer was prompt.

"They are not now, and I really do not recall all the types of micro-organisms I destroyed months ago. You should recall whether or not he has ever shown symptoms of the disease. Your own blood contains many creatures that bear a superficial resemblance to that inert state illustrated, as I noticed yesterday, but with only those pictures to go by I could not say whether they were identical or not. I should be glad to help you more actively, if my problem were not so pressing."

"Bob," said the doctor when this had been transmitted, "if you don't hang onto that friend of yours after he finishes his job, and go to medical school yourself, you'll be a traitor to civilization. However, that's not germane to either of our problems. I don't like what you implied, Hunter, but I won't deny its possibility without further tests. That's my job. The point I started to make is that your friend cannot be inside Malmstrom's body; everything you've just said about nosebleed goes double for germ disease. You can't suspect anyone for *not* getting sick, and our fugitive must know it."

There was a silence of general agreement after this statement. This appeared ready to lengthen indefinitely; Bob broke it with the remark, "That leaves Norman and Hugh of our original top-priority list. I would have voted for Norm without question this afternoon; now I'm not so sure."

"Why not?"

The boy repeated the Hunter's words of a few minutes before, and the doctor shrugged them off.

"If you have your own ideas and won't tell us, Hunter, you can only expect us to act on ours," he said.

"That is just what I want," pointed out the detective. "You both have a tendency to regard me as all-knowing in this matter. That is not true. We are on *your* world, among your people. I will develop and test my ideas, with your help when necessary, but I want you to do the same with yours. You won't, if you let yourselves be influenced to any great extent by my opinions."

"A good point," agreed Seever. "All right, then, my present idea is the same as Bob's—that you make a personal examination, with the least practical delay, of Master Norman Hay. The only other candidate on our list always did seem the least likely. If this were a detective story, I suppose I'd be advising you to work on him. Robert, here, can take you up to a point near Hay's home as he planned before, and you can make the check tonight."

"You have forgotten your own argument—that I should be ready to do something about it if I find our friend there," responded the detective. "It seems to me that the testing of drugs had better go on, while you, Robert, and I keep our eyes open for evidence such as turned up today."

"I'm darned if I'll spread a malaria epidemic just for that," said the doctor. "Still, I suppose you're right. We'll try another drug—and don't tell me you like the taste; it's too expensive for candy." He set to work. "By the way"—he looked up from loading the gun—"wasn't Norman one of the stowaways a while back? How would that fit in?"

"He was," Bob replied, "but I couldn't tell you how it fits. The whole idea was Red's, and he backed out at the last minute from what I hear."

Seever applied the hypo thoughtfully. "Maybe that thing *was* with Teroa for a while and shifted to Hay. They must have slept at least once fairly close to each other while they were hiding on the ship."

"Why should he change?"

"He might have thought that Hay's chances of getting ashore were better. Remember Norman wanted to see the museum on Tahiti."

"That would mean that it had been with Charlie long enough to learn to understand English; and it would also mean that Norm's interest in biology had nothing funny about it, since it developed before he was invaded," pointed out Bob. The doctor was forced to concede this.

"All right," he said, "it was just an idea. I never claimed to have evidence for it. It's a pity we can't find the drug we're looking for. This malaria business would give me an excuse to administer it wholesale, if I had enough, which I probably wouldn't."

"You're no closer to finding it so far," reported the Hunter at that point. The doctor grimaced.

"We probably won't, either. Your structure is too different from that of any earthly creature, I suppose. I wish you would give us some of your own ideas; this seems too haphazard to me."

"I discussed my ideas with Bob a long time ago," the Hunter replied. "I have been following them. Unfortunately, they lead to such a wide field of possibilities that I am afraid to start testing them. I'd rather exhaust your field first."

"What, in Heaven's name, did you discuss with him that you haven't mentioned to me?" Seever asked the boy. "This is a fine time to learn that you have more clues."

"I don't think I have." Bob was frowning in perplexity. "All I remember discussing with the Hunter was the method of search; that was to guess the probable movements of our quarry and look for clues along those routes. We did that, and found the generator shield; it seems to me we're still doing it,"

"Me too. Well, if the Hunter wants us to run our ideas dry before he explains his any further, I suppose we'll have to do it. His reasons are good enough—except that one about the other field being too big. That's no excuse not to get started on it, it seems to me."

"I am started," pointed out the Hunter. "I just see no need of diverting your checking activities as yet. I am strongly in favor of observing Hay and Colby very closely indeed. I never did think very much of the case against Rice."

"Why not?"

"Your principal point against him was that he was helpless enough to be invaded for a time at the place our quarry came ashore. It seemed to me, however, that our friend would never enter the body of a person in the very considerable physical danger that was facing Rice at that moment."

"It would not be danger for him."

"No. But what use would a drowned host be to him at that point? I am not in the least surprised that your red-headed friend has been shown to be innocent—or uninfected, as I suppose Dr. Seever would put it."

"All right. We'll get the other two settled as quickly as possible, so we can really get to work," the doctor said, "but it still seems illogical to me."

Bob felt the same, but had come to develop a good deal of trust in the Hunter—except on one point. He made no further attempt to sway the alien's decision and went out from the doctor's office into the late-afternoon sunshine. Hay and Colby must be found and watched; that was all he could see to do.

He had left them at the tank. They might still be there; in any case, his own bicycle was. He would have to walk up there to get it, and could tell at the same time whether or not they had found something else to do.

Passing the Teroa house, he noticed Charles at his old occupation of gardening, and waved to him. The Polynesian boy seemed to have recovered his temper; Bob remembered that there had been no talk of letting him go, after all, and hoped the doctor would remember. Certainly there was no need for keeping him around now.

His bicycle was lying where he had left it. The other boys' bicycles had disappeared, which left him with the problem of just where they were likely to have gone. He remembered Hay's desire to work on his pool, and decided that that was as likely a probability as any, so he mounted his machine and headed back along the road he had come. At the doctor's he turned aside to make sure Seever had not forgotten about releasing Teroa; at the second creek he stopped to look for bicycles, though he was reasonably sure the others would not be working on the boat. Apparently he was right.

Norman had, of course, said that they would swim to the islet if they went at all. That would mean their machines would be, most probably, at

Hay's home, at the end of the road. Bob remounted and headed in that direction. The Hay residence was a two-storied, large-windowed building rather like that of the Kinnairds'. The principal difference was that it was not surrounded by jungle. It was situated at the end of the ridge, where the high ground sloped down to meet the beach, and the soil was already too sandy to accommodate so many of the heavy thorn growths of the higher ground. There was still vegetation enough to give ample shade, but walking around the house was not quite such a major undertaking. There was a spot in back where a rack had been constructed to accommodate a large number of bicycles—many of the adults on the island used them—and Bob automatically looked there first. He was pleased to see that his deductions had been at least partly right: the machines of Rice, Colby, and Hay were there. Bob racked his own beside the others and headed toward the beach. At the north end, where the reef recommenced, he was not surprised to see the trunk-clad figures of his three friends on the islet across the narrow strip of water.

They looked up at his hail, and waved him back as he started to strip. "Don't bother to come over! We're all done here!" Hay called. Bob nodded in understanding and stood waiting. The others looked around as though to make sure they had left nothing and made for the water. They had to pick their way gingerly among the coral growths that rimmed the islet and studded the passage before the water was deep enough to swim, and the few yards of swimming was rather awkward in shoes; but the beach side was clearer, and they presently waded out beside Bob.

"You got the wire in place?" Robert opened the conversation.

Hay nodded. "We made the hole a little bigger. It's about six or eight inches across now. I got some more cement and a piece of ordinary copper screening, and I cemented them both in together. The big mesh will serve as a support and the screening will keep practically anything in the pool."

"Do you have any specimens yet? And how about that color film?"

"Hugh got a couple of anemones in. I suppose I owe him a vote of thanks; I'm darned if I'd touch them."

"Neither would I, again," replied Colby. "I thought they always folded up when something big came near. One of 'em did, and I didn't have any trouble with it, but the other—wow!" He held up his right hand, and Bob whistled in sympathy. The inside of the thumb and the first two fingers were dotted with red points, where the stinging cells of the sea anemone had struck; and the whole hand up to the wrist was visibly swollen and evidently painful—the care with which Hugh moved the hand demonstrated that.

"I've been stung by the things, but never that bad," commented Bob. "What kind was it?"

"I don't know. Ask the professor. It was a big one. But big or little, he collects his own from now on!"

Bob nodded thoughtfully. It seemed peculiar, even to him, that everything should be happening on the same day; but it was hard to see around the apparent fact that four of the five chief suspects were now eliminated. Certainly if Hugh had transported one of the flowerlike creatures without injury or trouble, his hypothetical guest would have no reason for not acting on the stings of the second. Even if he were indifferent to his host's pain, he certainly would not want the hand disabled even temporarily.

It looked as though Norman Hay, by elimination, held star position. Bob resolved to put the point to the Hunter at the first opportunity.

In the meantime appearances had to be maintained.

"Did you fellows hear about Shorty?" he asked.

"No. What's happened to him?" returned Rice.

Bob promptly forgot his worries in the pleasure of bringing startling news. He told at great length, detailing their friend's illness and the doctor's mystification as to its source. The others were properly impressed; Hay even seemed a trifle uneasy. His biological interests had given him some knowledge of malarial mosquitoes. "Maybe we ought to look through the woods and drain or oil any still-water pools we find," he suggested. "If there is malaria on the island, and any mosquitoes get at Shorty now, we're in for trouble."

"We could ask the doc," replied Bob; "but it sounds good to me. It will be an awful job, though."

"Who cares? I've read what that stuff is like."

"I wonder if we can see Shorty," put in Rice. "I suppose we'd have to ask the doctor about that too."

"Let's go ask him now."

"Let's see what time it is first. It must be getting pretty late." This was a reasonable suggestion, and they waited at Hay's house, holding their bicycles, while he went inside to determine this important matter.

After a moment his face appeared at a window, "My folks are just starting supper. I'll see you afterward, in front of Bob's. O.K.?" And without waiting for an answer he disappeared again. Rice looked serious.

"If he's just on time, then I'm late," he remarked. "Let's go. If I'm not there after supper, fellows, you'll know why." He had approximately a mile to go, almost as far as Bob. Even Colby, who lived nearest to Hay, wasted no time, and the three machines rolled swiftly down the road. Bob had no means of telling how the others made out, but he had to get his own meal from the refrigerator and wash his dishes afterward.

Only Hay was waiting for him when he finally got out; and, though they remained for some time, neither of the others appeared. There had been ultimatums dangling over their heads for some time on the late-for-meals matter, and apparently the ax had fallen.

Eventually Norman and Robert decided there was no use waiting any longer and set out for the doctor's. He was in, as usual, though they had half-expected he might be at the Malmstroms'. It had not occurred to Hay to look up their drive to see whether his vehicle was present.

"Hello, gents; come in. Business is getting really brisk today. What can I do for you?"

"We were wondering if it was all right for Shorty to have visitors," replied Hay. "We just heard he was sick a little while ago and thought we'd better ask you before we went to his house."

"This was a good idea. I should think there would be no harm in your seeing him—you can't catch malaria just by breathing the same air. He's not very sick now—we have drugs that knock out our friend the plasmodium quite thoroughly these days. His temperature was down some time ago; I'm sure he'd be glad to see you."

"Thanks a lot, Doctor." It was Bob who spoke. "Norm, if you want to start along I'll be with you in a minute. There's something I want to check here."

"Oh, I don't mind waiting," replied Hay disconcertingly. Bob blinked, and for a moment found himself at a loss. The doctor filled the gap.

"I think Bob means that work has to be done on that leg of his, Norman," he said. "I'd prefer to work on that without witnesses, if you don't mind."

"But—well, I was sort of—that is, I wanted to see you about something too."

"I'll wait outside till you're done," said Bob, rising.

"No, that's all right. It may take a while. Maybe you'd better know anyway; I might have done the same thing to you. Stick around." Hay turned back to Dr. Seever. "Sir, could you tell me just what malaria feels like?"

"Well, I've never had it myself, thank goodness. It shows a period of chills. Then those die away, and usually alternate with fever and sweating, sometimes bad enough for the patient to be delirious; the whole thing has a fairly definite period, caused by the life cycle of the protozoan responsible for the disease. When a new batch of the organisms develop, the whole business starts over."

"Are the chills and fever always bad—that is, bad enough to make a person really sick?—or might he have it a long time without noticing it much?" The doctor frowned as he began to get an inkling of what the boy was driving at. Bob tightened up as though it were the last period of a tied hockey game—it was worse for him, since he had a piece of information not yet known to the doctor.

"Sometimes it seems to remain dormant for a long time, so that people who have had the disease once break out with the symptoms again years later. There's been some argument about how that happens, though, and I don't recall hearing of a person who was a carrier who had not had the symptoms at some time or other."

Hay frowned also, and seemed undecided how to phrase his next remark.

"Well," he said at last, "Bob said something about your not being sure where Shorty picked up the germ. I know it's carried by mosquitoes, and they have to get it from someone who already has malaria. I'm afraid that's me."

"Young man, I was around when you let out your first squall, and I've known you ever since. You've never had malaria."

"I've never been sick with it. I can remember having chills-and-fever sessions like you described, but they never lasted long and were never bad enough to bother me much—I just sort of felt queer. I never mentioned 'em to anyone, because I didn't think much of 'em, and didn't want to complain about something that seemed so small. Then, when Bob told us the story this afternoon, all the things I'd read and the things I remembered sort of ran together, and I thought I'd better see you. Can't you check some way to see if I really have it?"

"Personally, I think your idea is all wet, Norman, my boy; of course, with malaria so nearly wiped out, I don't pretend to be an expert on it, but I don't recall any case such as yours would be. However, if it will make you happy, I can take a blood specimen and have a look for our friend the plasmodium."

"I wish you would."

The two listeners did not know whether to be more worried or astonished at Norman's words and actions. Not only did they promise, if the boy were right, to remove him from the list of suspects, they also seemed out of character. The sight of a fourteen-year-old boy displaying what amounted to adult powers of analysis and social consciousness startled the doctor exceedingly and seemed odd even to Bob, who had always been fully aware of the fact that Norman was younger than he.

As a matter of fact, it was out of character; had the victim of the disease not been one of his best friends, Hay probably would not have devoted enough thought to the matter to recall his childhood chills; and if he had, it is more than doubtful whether he would have reported them to the doctor. At the present his conscience was bothering him; it is very probable that if he had not seen the doctor that night he would have changed his mind about doing so at all before morning. However that may be, he was now almost as eager as Seever drew the blood sample— whether or not he *was* responsible for Malmstrom's illness, he could feel that he was doing something to help.

"It will take quite a while to check," said the doctor. "If you have it at all, it must be very mild, and I might have to do a serum test as well. If you don't mind, I'd like to look over Bob's leg before I get to work on it. All right?"

Norman nodded, with a rather disappointed air, and, remembering the earlier conversation, got up and went reluctantly out the door. "Don't be too long, Bob," he called back. "I'll go slow."

The door closed behind him, and Bob turned instantly to the doctor. "Never mind my leg, if you ever meant to do anything to it. Let's find out about Norman! If he's right, it scratches him too!"

"That had occurred to me," replied Seever. "That's why I took so much blood—that serum-test story I told Norman was simply an excuse, though I suppose it wasn't necessary. I may want the Hunter to do some checking too."

"But he doesn't know the malaria parasite, at least act first-hand."

"If necessary, I'll get some from Malmstrom for him to compare. However, I'll do a microscopical right now. The trouble is, I wasn't kidding about the probable mildness of his case; I might look over a dozen slides or a hundred without seeing the parasite. That's why I wanted the Hunter—he can check the whole sample, if necessary, much faster than I can. I remember that trick of his you mentioned, of neutralizing the leucocytes in your body. If he can do that, he can look over every last one of these blood cells—or smell them, or whatever he does—in jig time." The doctor fell silent, brought out microscope and other apparatus, and set to work.

After two or three slides he looked up, stretched, and said, "Maybe one reason I'm not finding anything is because I don't expect to." He bent to his work again. Bob had time to think that Norman must long since have grown tired of waiting and gone on to pay his visit alone, when Seever finally straightened up once more.

"I find it hard to believe," he said. "But he may be right. There are one or two red cells which seem to be wrecked the way the plasmodium does the job. I haven't seen the brute himself, though there's everything else. I never cease to marvel"—he sat back in his chair and assumed a lecture-hall manner, oblivious of Bob's abrupt stiffening at his words— "at the variety of foreign organisms present in the blood stream of the healthiest individuals. If all the bacteria I have spotted in the last half-hour or so were permitted to reproduce unchecked, Norman would be down with typhoid, two or three kinds of gangrene, some form of encephalitis, and half-a-dozen types of strep infection. Yet there he walks, with mild chills at long enough intervals for him to need outside stimulation to recall them. I suppose you——" He stopped, as though the thought that had been striving to get from Bob's mind to the open air struck him.

"For Pete's sake! Malaria or no malaria, there's certainly *one* infection he doesn't have? And I've been straining my eyes for the last hour. With all that stuff in his blood—Bob, boy, tell me I'm an idiot if you like—I can see you've been on to the idea ever since I mentioned the critters." He was silent for a moment, shaking his head. "You know," he said at last, "this would be a beautiful test. I can't imagine our friend leaving a normal crop of germs in his host's blood just to meet this situation; that would be carrying caution just a mite too far. If I just had an excuse for making blood tests of everyone on the island—— Well, anyway, that leaves only one suspect on the list. I hope the principle of elimination is good."

"You don't know the half of it," said Bob, finding his voice at last. "It leaves no one on the list. I scratched off Hugh before supper." He gave his reasons, and the doctor had to admit their justice.

"Still, I hope he brings that hand to me. I'll get the blood smear if I have to lie like Ananias. Well, there's at least one good point: our ideas have run dry, and the Hunter will finally have to come across with some of his. How about it, Hunter?"

"You would seem to be right," the detective replied. "If you will give me the night to work out a course of action, I will tell you what I can tomorrow."

He was perfectly aware that the reason for delay was rather thin, but he had a strong motive just then for not telling his friends that he knew where their quarry was.

# XIX. Solution

Though Bob had no share in the turmoil of thoughts that were boiling through the Hunter's mind, he was a long time going to sleep. Hay had still been at Malmstrom's house, and they had chattered at the invalid's bedside until his mother had suggested that Kenneth could use some sleep; but very little of Robert's mind had been on the conversation.

The Hunter claimed to have carried their line of thought further and to be able to work out another line of action from it; Bob couldn't, and was wondering how stupid he must be compared to his guest. It bothered him, and he kept trying to imagine how the other alien's probable course could have been traced any further than the piece of metal on the reef—if Rice and Teroa were to be left out of consideration.

The Hunter felt stupid too. He himself had suggested that line of thought to Bob. True, he had not expected much to come of it, but it had contained possibilities for action on his host's part and should have left him free to work out ideas more in line with his training and practice. These last, however, had failed miserably, as he might have expected so far from the civilization which gave them technical backing; and he was now realizing that he had deliberately ignored the answer to his problem for some days, even with the diverse arguments of Bob and the doctor endlessly before him.

It was fortunate that Bob had been working on his own in the matter of the "trap" in the woods, of course; had he not been, the plan of having the Hunter check Teroa and the other boys individually would have been put to work before the doctor was in the secret. That would have meant that the Hunter was not with Bob for stretches of at least thirty-six hours at a time, and he would, he now realized, have missed clues that had been presented to him practically every day. Most of them meant little or nothing by themselves, but taken together. . .

He wished his host would go to sleep. There were things to be done, and done soon. Bob's eyes were closed, and the alien's only contact with his surroundings was auditory; but the boy's heartbeat and breathing proved clearly that he was still awake. For the thousandth time the detective wished he were a mind reader. He had the helpless feeling of a movie patron as the hero walks into a dark alley; all he could do was listen.

There was enough sound to give him a picture of his surroundings, of course: the endless dull boom of the breakers a mile away across the hill and even farther over the lagoon; the faint whine and hum of insect life in the forest outside; the less regular rustle of small animals in the undergrowth; and the much more distinct sounds made by Bob's parents as they came upstairs.

They had been talking, but they quieted down as they approached. Either Bob had been the subject of the conversation, or they just didn't want to disturb him. The boy heard them, however; the sudden ceasing of his restless motion and the deliberate relaxation that followed told the Hunter that. Mrs. Kinnaird glanced into her son's room and went on, leaving the door ajar; a moment later the Hunter heard another door open and close.

He was tense and anxious by the time Bob was definitely asleep, though not nearly enough to impair his judgment on that important matter. Once certain, however, he went instantly into action. His gelatinous flesh began to ooze out from the pores of Bob's skin—openings as large and convenient for the Hunter as the exits of a football stadium. Through sheet and mattress he poured with even greater ease, and in two or three minutes his whole mass was gathered into a single lump beneath the boy's bed.

He paused a moment to listen again, then flowed toward the door and extended an eye-bearing pseudopod through the crack. He was going to make a personal check of his suspect—or certainty, for he was morally certain he was right. He had not forgotten the argument of the doctor in favor of postponing such an examination until he was prepared to take immediate measures in disposing of what he found; but he felt that there was now one serious flaw in those arguments—if the Hunter's belief was correct, Bob must have betrayed himself time and again! There would be no more delay.

There was a light in the hall, but it was not nearly bright enough to bother him. Presently he was extended in the form of a pencil-thick rope of flesh along several yards of the baseboard. Here he waited again, while he analyzed the breathing sounds coming from the room where the elder Kinnairds slept; satisfied that both were actually asleep, he entered. The door of the room was closed, but that meant nothing to him—even had its edge been sealed airtight, there was always the keyhole.

He knew already the difference in rate and depth that served to distinguish the breathing of the two, and he made his way without hesitation to a point beneath the suspect's bed. A thread of jelly groped upward until it touched the mattress and went on through. The rest of the formless body followed and consolidated within the mattress itself; and then, cautiously, the Hunter located the sleeper's feet. His technique was polished by this time, and, if he had cared to do so, he could have entered this body far more rapidly than he had made himself at home in Bob's, for there would be no exploring to be done. However, bodily entry was not in his plans; and most of him remained in the mattress while the exploring tentacle started to penetrate. It did not get far.

The human skin is made of several distinct layers, but the cells which make up these are all of strictly ordinary size and pattern, whether they be dead and cornified like those in the outer layer or living and growing like those below. There is not, normally, a layer—or even a discontinuous network—of cells far more minute, sensitive, and mobile than the others. Bob had such a layer, of course—the Hunter had provided it for his own purpose; and the detective was not in the least surprised to encounter a similar net just beneath the epidermis of Mr. Arthur Kinnaird. He had expected it.

The cells he encountered felt and recognized his own tentacle. For an instant there was a disorganized motion, as though the web of alien flesh were trying to avoid the Hunter's touch; then, as though the creature of which it formed a part realized the futility of further concealment, it relaxed again.

The Hunter's flesh touched and closed over a portion of that net, bringing many of his own cells into contact with it; and along those cells, which could act equally well as nerves or muscles, sense organs or digestive glands, a message passed. It was not speech; neither sound nor vision nor any other normal human sense was employed. Neither was it telepathy; no word exists in the English language to describe accurately that form of communication. It was as though the nervous systems of the two beings had fused, for the time being, sufficiently to permit at least some of the sensation felt by one to be appreciated by the other—nerve currents bridging the gap between individuals as normally they bridged that between body cells.

The message was wordless, but it carried meaning as well and feeling much better than words could have done.

"I am glad to meet you, Killer. I apologize for wasting so much time in the search."

"I know you, Hunter. You need not apologize—particularly when you conceal a boast by it. That you have found me at all is of minor importance; that it took you half a year of this planet's time to do so amuses me exceedingly. I did not know just what had become of you; I can now picture you sneaking about this island for month after month, entering houses one after another—for no purpose, since you can do nothing to me now. I thank you for giving me information of such amusing character."

"I trust you will be equally amused to know that I have been on the island searching for seven days, and that this man is the first I have tested physically. I might have been faster if you had carried a sign, but not much." The Hunter was human enough to possess vanity and even to let it override normal caution. It did not occur to him until afterward that the other's speech had shown that it had not suspected Bob, and that his own answer had furnished far too much information for safety.

"I do not believe you. There are no tests you could have used on a human being from a distance; and this host has suffered no serious injuries or diseases since my coming. Had he done so, I should have found another rather than betray myself by helping."

"That I believe." The Hunter's nerves carried clearly the contempt and revulsion he felt at the other's attitude. "I did not say anything about *serious* injuries."

"The only ones I have worked on were those too minor to be noticed—if another human being was in a position to see the injury acquired, I left it alone. I even let parasitic insects take blood unobstructed while others were around."

"I know that. And you *boast* of it." The disgust was deeper, if possible.

"You know? You certainly don't like to admit you were beaten, do you, Hunter? But do you expect to fool me with your boasts?"

"You have been fooling yourself. I knew you had been letting mosquitoes bite your host when he had company, and not at other times; I knew you were in the habit of repairing unnoticeably small injuries which he received. I suppose you might be given credit for it, although you probably did it to save yourself from complete boredom. It was that, or attempt to control this host as you did with your last; and that would certainly betray you. No intelligent creature can spend its time doing nothing whatever without going mad.

"You were bright, in a way, to handle only inconspicuous injuries. However, there was one being who was bound to notice your activities, whether he attributed them to the true cause or not, and that was *your host himself!*

"I heard conversation—by the way, did you bother to learn English?— that described this man as a cautious individual who would take few chances himself and permit members of his family even fewer. Those words were spoken by men who have known him for years—two different men, my friend. Yet I have seen him rummage blindly in a container of sharp-edged tools for something he wanted; I have seen him climb down an inclined piece of wood full of splinters, and carry similar pieces in his hands and under his arm next to unprotected skin; I have seen him cut a piece of woven-wire mesh which could easily have taken the skin off his bare hand had it slipped at the pressure he was using; I have seen him carrying a sharp, toothed blade by the *edge* when even an adolescent, notoriously careless in matters pertaining to personal safety, held it at the center. You may have been concealing yourself from most of the human race, my friend, but your host knew you were there—whether he was aware that he knew it or not! He must have noticed subconsciously that nothing was apparently happening when he made minor slips in such matters and grew progressively more careless. I have evidence enough that human beings tend to act that way. I also heard your host mention on one occasion something to the effect that other people kept trained insects around to bother him; apparently he noticed that he was not bothered when he was alone.

"Really, you see, you never had a chance of staying hidden. You must either try to dominate and betray yourself, do a minimum of your duty and betray yourself, or do nothing at all except think for the rest of your life, and in that case you might as well surrender. Even on Earth, without skilled assistance, experience, or natives to help me, you were bound to be caught if only I came to the right neighborhood. You were foolish to run in the first place; at home you would simply have been restricted; here, I have no alternative but to destroy you."

The other might have been impressed by most of the Hunter's speech, but the last part aroused him to ridicule.

"Just how do you propose to do that? You have no selective drugs to drive me out of this body and no means of making—or at least of testing—any. Being what you are, you will not consider sacrificing this host to get rid of me; and I assure you I will have no such scruples about yours. It seems to me, Hunter, that finding me was a serious mistake on your part. Before, I was not even sure that you were on the planet; now I know you are here and cut off from home and help. I am safe enough, but watch out for yourself!"

"Since there is nothing I could or would say to disabuse you of that impression, I will leave you with it," replied the Hunter. Without further communication he withdrew, and in a few minutes was flowing back toward Bob's room. He expected momentarily to hear Mr. Kinnaird awaken, but the other apparently had decided there was too little chance of his host's doing the right thing even if he were aroused.

The Hunter was furious with himself. He had been sure, once he had decided that Mr. Kinnaird was the host of his quarry, that the accident on the dock had been deliberate—caused by the alien's interference with his host's eyesight and co-ordination. That would mean that Bob's secret was known, and there was no point in the doctor's plan of concealment until they were ready to strike. It had turned out that he was wrong—the fugitive had apparently not even suspected his pursuer's whereabouts; and the Hunter had certainly given enough data in the conversation to tell the other alien pretty accurately where he himself was. He could not even leave Bob now—the criminal would take no chances, and the Hunter must stay with the boy he had endangered, to protect him as far as possible.

The question now, he thought, as he re-established himself in Bob's still-sleeping body, was whether or not the boy should be told of the situation and of his danger. There was much to be said on both sides; knowledge that his father was involved might operate seriously against Bob's efficiency, but, on the other hand, ignorance was even more likely to do so. On the whole, the Hunter was inclined to tell the boy everything; and he relaxed into a state as close to sleep as he could come in that environment, with that intention in mind.

Bob took the information remarkably well, on the whole. He was shocked and worried, naturally, though his anxiety seemed greater for his father's plight than for his own danger. He was quick-minded enough, as the Hunter had long since realized, to perceive the situation in which he and his guest were caught, though he did not blame the Hunter for letting the cat out of the bag. He fully appreciated also the need for rapid action, and perceived one point which the Hunter had not considered—the extreme likelihood of their enemy's shifting his abode at any time, or at least at night. They would have, Bob pointed out, no assurance on any given day as to which of his parents would be harboring the creature.

"I don't think we need worry about that," the Hunter replied. "In the first place, he seems too sure of his safety to bother shifting; and, in the second, if he does, the fact will quickly become evident. Your father, suddenly deprived of the protection he has been enjoying for some months, is certainly going to provide plenty of notice of the fact, if he stays as careless as he has been."

"Speaking of that 'months' business, you still haven't told me how you settled on Dad as prime suspect."

"It was the line of reasoning I gave you. Our friend landed on the reef, as we know. The nearest sign of civilization was one of the culture tanks only a few hundred yards away. He would swim to that—at least I certainly would have, in his position. The only people who visit those tanks regularly are the operators of the fertilizer barge.

"He would have no opportunity to invade one of those men, but he would certainly go with the barge. That brings us to the field on the hill where the tank fodder is grown. I had to find someone who slept in that vicinity.

"There was a chance, of course, that he had made his way alone over the hill to the houses; in that case, we had the whole island to search. However, your father made a remark the other evening that showed he must have slept, or at least rested, at the hilltop above the new tanks. He was, therefore, the best suspect yet uncovered, to my way of thinking."

"It certainly seems obvious enough now," said Bob, "but I couldn't work it out. Well, we'll have to do some fast thinking today. With luck, he will stay with Dad until he's sure where you are—Dad is more suitable for research, since he moves around more. The trouble is we don't have any drugs yet. Isn't there anything else that would force one of your people out of a host, Hunter?"

"What would force you to leave home?" countered the detective. "There are probably lots of things, but they will have to be of earthly origin this time. You have at least as good a chance of hitting upon something as I. Certainly if I were our friend, I would stay right there—it's the safest possible place for him."

Bob nodded gloomily and went down to breakfast. He tried to act his normal self, even when his father appeared; he had no means of knowing how well he succeeded. It occurred to him that the other alien might not appreciate the fact that he was consciously aiding the Hunter; that might be one point in their favor, anyway.

He set out for school, still thinking. Actually, though he did not tell the Hunter so, he was trying to solve two problems at once, and that meant accepting quite a handicap.

# XX. PROBLEM TWO—AND SOLUTION

At the foot of the driveway a thought occurred to Bob, and he stopped to put a question to the Hunter.

"If we do make it impossible, or impossibly uncomfortable, for this thing to stay with Dad, how will it get out? I mean, is it likely to hurt him?"

"Definitely not. If he goes into such a situation, or we find a drug, it will simply leave. If he heads for something our friend thinks it won't like, it may thicken up the eye film to prevent him from seeing, or paralyze him in the manner I mentioned earlier."

"You say you are not sure of the aftereffects of this paralysis?"

"Not entirely, with your people," the Hunter admitted. "I told you why."

"I know you did. That's why I want you to try it on me right now, as soon as I get into the woods here so we can't be seen from the road." Bob's manner was utterly different from the half-humorous one in which he had made the same request a few days before, and the Hunter was not surprised at the futility of his objection.

"I told you long ago why I didn't want to do that."

"If you don't want to risk me, I don't want to risk Dad. I'm getting an idea, but I won't do a thing about it until I'm sure on that point. Let's go." He seated himself behind a bush out of sight from the road as he spoke.

The Hunter's reluctance to do anything that might harm the boy remained as great as ever, but there seemed to be nothing else to do. The threat not to continue with his own plan was minor; but he might also refuse to cooperate with the plans of the Hunter, and that would be serious. After all, the alien told himself, these people weren't too different from his former hosts, and he could be careful. He gave in.

Bob, sitting expectantly upright, quite suddenly experienced a total loss of sensation below the neck. He tried to catch himself as he went over backward, and found that his arms and legs might as well have belonged to someone else. The weird situation persisted for perhaps a minute, though it seemed longer to the victim; then, without the pins-and-needles feeling he had rather expected, sensation returned to his limbs.

"Well," he said as he arose, "do you think I'm any worse off?"

"Apparently not. You are less sensitive to the treatment than my former hosts and recover faster. I cannot tell whether that is a peculiarity of your own or a characteristic of your species. Are you satisfied?"

"I guess so. If that's all he does to Dad, I guess there's no objection. It still seems to me that he could kill him, but—"

"He could, of course, by blocking a major blood vessel or tightening up further on the nerves I just handled. Both methods are more work, though, and would take a little more time, at least from our friend's viewpoint. I don't think you need worry about them."

"All right." The boy emerged onto the road once more, remounted the bicycle he had left at the corner of the drive, and resumed his way to school. He was almost too deeply buried in thought to steer.

So the alien, if intelligent, would remain in his father's body because it was the safest possible refuge. Then what would it do if that refuge ceased to be safe? The answer seemed obvious. The difficulty was, of course, how to create a situation dangerous for the alien but not for Mr. Kinnaird; and that problem seemed, for the moment, at least, insuperable.

There was also the problem Bob had carefully refrained from mentioning to his guest. Strictly speaking, Bob did not actually *know* even now that the Hunter was what he claimed to be. The statement made earlier, to the effect that the criminal might have revealed himself to his host and enlisted his help with a false story, was too plausible to be considered with comfort. Something about whatever plan Bob finally devised must give him an answer to that question also—a better answer than the vague tests he had used a few days ago, when he had asked to be paralyzed. The whole attitude shown by the detective had been convincing, of course, but it just might be acting, whatever Bob wanted to believe. It must be seen whether he would carry that attitude into practice.

The Kinnaird record was not noticeably improved by that day's school session, and he very nearly alienated his friends during the lunch period. In the afternoon session he was as bad, until the threat of having to remain after dismissal time to complete some assignments focused his attention for the time being. He had reached a point in his cogitations where he very much wanted to be free as early as possible.

He certainly did not delay when school was dismissed. Leaving his bicycle where it was, he set out rapidly on foot toward the south across the gardens. He had a double reason for leaving the machine: not only would it be useless in his present project as he visualized it, but its presence would make his friends assume he would return shortly, so that they would be less likely to follow him.

Threading his way along the paths between garden patches until several houses hid him from the school, Bob began to work his way eastward. He was seen, of course—there were few people on the island who didn't know all the other inhabitants; but the ones to whom the boy nodded greeting as he passed were merely casual acquaintances, and there was no fear of their following him or becoming interested in his activities. Twenty minutes after leaving the school he was a mile from it and fairly close to the other shore, almost directly south of the dock. At this point he turned northeast, along the short leg of the island, and quickly put the rising ground of the ridge between himself and most of the houses. The unused ground on this side had not grown up into jungle quite so badly as the other leg; the brush was fairly heavy, but there were no trees. This section was narrow, and his original course would have carried him eventually into the fields of what the Hunter had aptly called "tank fodder."

However, as he came to a point directly south of the highest point of the ridge Bob turned straight uphill, and consequently he did not emerge from the undergrowth until almost at the top. Here he dropped face downward and wriggled his way to a point where he could look down the other side—almost the same point where he had slept for a time on the night the south wall of the tank had been poured.

Activity was much as usual, with men working and children getting underfoot. Bob looked carefully for his friends, and finally decided they must have gone either to work on the boat or to stock the pool. They did not appear to be on the scene below. His father was there, however, and on him the boy kept a careful eye while he waited for the opportunity that was sure to come. He was sure, from the amount of wall still unfinished the day before, that the glazing crew must still be at work; and sooner or later they were going to need a refill. It was not absolutely certain that Mr. Kinnaird would drive down for it, but the chances were pretty good.

The uncertainty about the matter affected Bob noticeably; the Hunter, who was in a uniquely good position to observe, realized that his host was more excited than he had been since they had met. The expression on his face was utterly serious; his eyes steadily roved over the scene as the few missing or weak details of his plan were filled in or repaired. He had not said a word to the Hunter since leaving school, and that individual was curious. He reminded himself that Bob was far from stupid, and his earthly experience might very possibly make him more fit for the present activity than the Hunter. The detective had been just a little smug about his ability to think out the probable course of the fugitive when Bob had been unable to do so; now he realized that the boy was off on a line of thought at least as far ahead of him. He hoped it was equally well founded.

Suddenly Bob started to move, though the Hunter could see no change in the scene below. Without obviously trying to hide, he went downhill inconspicuously. On the ground near the mixers were scattered a number of shirts which had been left there by the workmen; and Bob, indifferent to watchers, proceeded to go through the pockets of these. Eventually he came across a folder of matches, which appeared to be what he wanted. He cast his eyes around, met the gaze of the owner of the shirt, held up the folder, and raised his eyebrows interrogatively. The man nodded and turned back to his work.

The boy pocketed the matches and strolled a little way back up the hill, where he could see the greater part of the tank floor once more. There he seated himself, and once more concentrated his attention on the actions of his father.

At last the event he had been waiting for occurred. Mr. Kinnaird appeared with a metal drum on his shoulder, and as Bob stood up to see more clearly, he disappeared below the far edge of the flooring, at the point where the jeep was usually parked.

Bob began strolling toward the neighboring tank as casually as he could, keeping a careful eye downhill. He had been in motion only a few seconds when the little car appeared with his father at the wheel and the drum visible beside him. There was no question of his destination; and, as Bob remembered, he was sure to be gone at least half an hour. He disappeared almost at once below the neighboring tank, and, owing to Bob's nearness to this structure, did not reappear at all.

Bob himself used the same tank for concealment. He kept, with difficulty, to his casual pace until he had put the tank between himself and the scene of activity; then he turned slightly downhill and began running at the top of his speed.

A few moments brought him to the end of the paved road. Here the line of corrugated-iron storage sheds began; and, to the Hunter's bewilderment, Bob began inspecting them closely. The first few were normally used for construction machinery, such as mixers and graders; some of these were empty, their normal contents being in use. Several more, closer to the residential district, contained cans of gasoline and fuel and lubricating oils. The boy examined them all, stood looking around for a moment as though to get something straight in his mind, and then once more plunged into furious activity.

Choosing one of the empty sheds—he did not actually go in, but looked over about half the floor area from a point outside the door—he began carrying vast armfuls of five-gallon cans and stacking them beside the entrance. Even the Hunter wondered at the number he was able to carry, until the sound as he put them down disclosed the fact that they were empty. When the stack was built to his satisfaction, in a broad pyramid taller than the boy himself, he went to another shed and began reading very carefully the stenciled abbreviations on another set of cans. These, it turned out, were far from empty. They contained a fluid that would have passed anywhere for kerosene, although it had never been in an oil well. Two of these Bob placed at strategic points in his pyramid; another he opened, and began pouring the contents onto the stack of cans and over the adjacent ground. The Hunter suddenly connected this maneuver with the matches.

"Are you making a fire or not?' he asked. "Why the empties?"

"There'll be a fire, all right," was the reply. "I just don't want to flatten this part of the island."

"But what's the point? A fire can't hurt our friend without doing considerably worse to your father."

"I know it. But if he just thinks Dad is in a position where he can't escape the fire, I expect he might be tempted to leave. And I'm going to be standing by with another oil can and more matches."

"Fine." The sarcasm could not be described. "Just how do you expect to get your father into such a situation?'

"You'll see." Bob's voice went grim again as he spoke, and the Hunter began seriously to wonder just what was in his youthful ally's mind. As an afterthought, Bob dumped one more can of oil on the pyre, this time using a heavier fluid normally employed as a lubricant. Then he obtained a can of the kerosene, loosened its screw cap, and stationed himself across the road from his incipient bonfire at a point where he could see the dock between the sheds. He kept his eyes glued on this point, except for an occasional uneasy glance up toward the new tank. If anyone came down and found his handiwork just now, it would be embarrassing.

He had not bothered to check the time when his father went down on the errand, and had no idea how long the construction of his bonfire had taken, so he did not know how long he was likely to have to wait. Consequently, he dared not move from his station. The Hunter had asked no further questions, which was just as well; Bob had no intention of answering them until a time of his own choosing. He did not like to act in this way toward the alien, whom he liked, but the idea of killing an intelligent creature had begun to bother him now that the deed was imminent, and he wanted to be sure he attacked the right one. For a boy of his age Robert Kinnaird had a remarkably objective mind.

At last, to his immense relief, the jeep reappeared, far out on the dock. As it turned onto the causeway, the boy rose slowly to his feet and moved gradually across the road toward his fire, keeping the jeep in view; as it finally became hidden, close to shore, behind the nearer sheds, he took the last few steps to the pile of dripping cans and drew the folder of matches from his pocket. As he did so, he uttered his carefully prepared and carefully timed answer to the Hunter's question.

"It won't be difficult at all, Hunter, to make him come. You see, I'm going to be just inside the shed!" He twisted a match from the folder as he finished speaking. He rather expected to lose the control of his limbs about that time; certainly if the Hunter were not what he seemed but what the boy had feared he might be, Bob would never be allowed to strike that match. He had deliberately refrained from going where he could see the back windows of the shed, which he well knew existed; his guest should not know of them. The idea that a criminal of the sort which had been described to him would have the speed of mind to recognize his actual safety, or the courage to call the boy's bluff, did not occur to Robert. He had so timed his speech that the other should have no time to think; either he trusted the boy, which almost certainly no criminal could bring himself to do, or he would paralyze him instantly. The scheme had flaws, of course. Bob may even have recognized some of them; but, on the whole, it was a very promising one.

He struck the match without interference.

He bent over and touched the flaming tip to the edge of the pool of oil.

The match promptly went out.

Almost trembling with anxiety—the jeep would turn the corner at any moment—he lit another, and this time touched a place where the liquid had soaked into the ground, leaving a thin film instead of a deep pool. This time it caught, with a satisfactory "whoosh" of flame, and an instant later the pile was blazing merrily.

Bob leaped into the shed before the flames spread over the pool in front of the door and stood back from the already fierce heat, watching the road.

For the first time the Hunter spoke. "I trust you know what you're doing. If you suddenly can't breathe, it'll be me keeping smoke out of your lungs." Then he left his host's vision unobstructed. Bob was satisfied; things were moving too fast for him to find fault with the alien's reaction.

He heard the jeep before he saw it; Mr. Kinnaird had evidently seen the smoke, and stepped on the gas, as the little engine was whining merrily. He had no extinguisher in the vehicle capable of handling a blaze such as this appeared to be, and Bob realized, as the vehicle was almost level with the flame-blocked door, that his father was going up the hill for help. That, however, he was able to modify.

"Dad!" He said nothing else—if his father wanted to conclude that he was in danger, that was all right, but Bob was not going to lie about it. He was sure that the sound of his son's voice coming apparently from inside the inferno would induce Mr. Kinnaird to stop the car and come on foot to investigate or rescue; he underestimated both his father's reaction speed and resourcefulness. So, evidently, did someone else.

At the sound of Bob's voice from within the apparently blazing shed, the driver took his foot from the gas pedal and cut the steering wheel hard to the left. His intention was at once obvious to Bob and the Hunter: he meant to bring the vehicle's hood right up to the door, gaining momentary protection for both the boy and himself from the blazing pool beneath, and back out again the instant his son could leap aboard. It was a simple plan, and a very good one. It should have worked, and in that event Bob and his guardian angel would have to devise a new plan—and some rather detailed explanations.

Fortunately, from their point of view, another factor entered the situation. Mr. Kinnaird's hidden guest grasped the situation, or at least his host's plan, almost as rapidly as the two watchers; but that creature had no intention of risking itself any closer to a pile of flaming oil containers which, from all appearances, might be expected to blast a rain of fire all over the surrounding landscape at any moment. They were already within twenty yards of the blaze, and man and symbiote alike could feel the heat. There was literally no way on earth by which the latter could force his host to turn the jeep around and drive in the opposite direction. There was, likewise, no way by which he could be forced to stop the vehicle; but the creature did not realize this in the tension of the moment. At any rate, it did what seemed best.

Mr. Kinnaird took one hand from the wheel and brushed it across his eyes, which told the watchers in the shed more clearly than words what had happened; but he no longer needed eyes to hold a searingly clear mental picture of his son in the flames ahead, and the jeep neither swerved nor slowed. The symbiote must have realized almost instantly that blindness was insufficient, and a dozen yards from the shed Mr. Kinnaird collapsed over the wheel.

Unfortunately for his guest, the jeep was still in gear, as anyone who had paid normal attention to earthly matters would have foreseen unless utterly panic-stricken; and the little car continued its course, still turning slightly to the left, and thudded into the corrugated-iron wall of the shed several yards from the door. The fact that his foot had slipped off the gas pedal when he was paralyzed probably saved Mr. Kinnaird from a broken neck.

Things had been moving a little too fast for Bob; he had expected his father to be overcome while on foot and somewhat farther from the fire. He had intended using the oilcan in his hand to control the spread of the flames so that the fugitive would believe his helpless host in immediate danger of immolation. Now he could not fulfill this plan, since he could no longer get close enough to the pool of fire in the doorway to see the jeep, to say nothing of splashing oil in its neighborhood. To make the situation rather more awkward, one of the full cans that Bob had placed on the pile chose at this moment to let go. Since he had had the intelligence not to use gasoline, the container simply ruptured along a seam and let a further wave of liquid fire spread down the pile and over the ground; but that wave came closer to the stalled jeep than the boy could tell with certainty.

Almost frantic with his own anxiety, the boy suddenly remembered the windows whose existence he had so carefully concealed from the Hunter while the trap was being set. He whirled and dashed for the nearest, still clutching the oilcan and yelling at the same time in island French: "Don't worry! There's a window!" He managed to wriggle through the unglazed opening and drop to the ground outside. He landed on his feet and raced around the corner of the shed. What he saw as he made the turn brought him up short and restored the thought of his original purpose in his mind.

The fire had not yet reached the jeep, though it was spreading momentarily closer; but that was not the fact that drew the boy's eyes like a magnet.

His father was still slumped over the wheel, outlined clearly against the blaze beyond; and beside him, shielded by his body from the fierce, radiant heat, was something else. The Hunter had never allowed Bob to see him, but there was no doubt in the boy's mind what this was—a soft-looking mass of nearly opaque greenish jelly, swelling momentarily as more of its substance poured out of the man's clothing. Bob instantly drew back behind the corner, though he could see nothing resembling an eye, and peeked cautiously.

The alien creature seemed to be gathering itself for a plunge of some sort. A slender tentacle reached out from the central mass and groped downward over the side of the jeep. It seemed to cringe momentarily as it passed below the protection of the metal and felt the radiation; but apparently its owner felt that a little now was preferable to more later, and the pseudopod continued to the ground. There its tip seemed to swell coincidentally with the shrinking of the main mass on the seat, and Bob gathered himself for action. It took nearly a minute for the whole weird body to reach the ground.

The instant its last contact with the jeep was broken, Bob acted. He sprang from the concealment and sprinted toward the car, still bearing his oilcan. The Hunter expected him to pour its contents over the creature now flowing desperately away from the flames, but he passed it with scarcely a glance, pushed his father away from the steering wheel, got under it himself, started the jeep, and backed it a good thirty yards from the building. Then, and only then, did he give attention to the Hunter's main job.

The fugitive had covered a little distance during this maneuver. It had kept close to the wall of the shed and made the best possible time away from the heat, the disappearance of the shelter provided by the jeep spurring it to greater efforts. Apparently it saw Bob coming, however, for it stopped its flowing motion and gathered into a hemispherical mass from which a number of fine tendrils began to reach out toward the approaching human being. Its first idea must have been that this would be a satisfactory host, at least until it got away from this neighborhood. Then it must have realized the Hunter's presence in this purposeful and unswerving approach and tried for an instant to resume its flight. Realizing its limitations in speed, however, it humped together again; and even Bob could see, from his recollection of the Hunter's story of his own actions, that the creature must be trying to go underground.

There was a difference, however, between the well-packed, much-traveled ground by the shed and the loose sand of the beach. The spaces between grains were smaller, and most of them were full of water, which is soft only when there is somewhere to push it. Long before there was any appreciable diminution in the creature's size, it was being drenched by the stream of oil from the can Bob was carrying.

The boy poured until the container was almost empty, soaking the ground all about the thing for several feet; then he used the last of the oil to form a trail from the pool he had made toward the blaze. This accomplished. he stood back for a moment and watched the finger of fire reach slowly out toward its new playground.

It was too slow to satisfy Bob, and after a moment he took out the matches again, ignited the entire folder, and tossed it as accurately as he could onto the semifluid lump in the center of the oil pool. He had no reason for complaint this time; he barely got away from the sheet of flame himself.

# XXI. Problem Three

The Hunter wanted to stay until the fire had burned out, to make certain of results, but Bob, once he had done all he could, turned his attention at once to his father. A single glance at the inferno surrounding the fugitive's last known position was enough for him. He ran back to the jeep, glanced at his father's still motionless form, and sent the vehicle whirling toward the doctor's office. The Hunter dared make no remark; interference with his host's eyesight at this speed would have been a serious error.

Mr. Kinnaird had been able to see ever since the alien had left his body; he had been conscious the whole time. The paralysis, however, had endured considerably longer than the dose given to Bob by the Hunter, and he had not been in a position to see very well what went on by the shed. He knew Bob had stopped at what seemed to him dangerous proximity to the fire and had gone back for something, but he did not know what. He struggled all the way down the road to get the question past his vocal cords.

He recovered enough to sit up before they finished the short ride to the doctor's office, and the questions were beginning to pour forth as the jeep pulled up at the door. Bob, of course, was relieved to see the recovery, but he had developed another and rather serious worry in the meantime, and he merely said, "Never mind about what happened to the shed and me; I want to find out what happened to you. Can you walk in, or shall I help?"

The last sentence was a stroke of genius; it shut the elder Kinnaird up with a snap. He emerged with dignity from the car and stalked ahead of his son to the doctor's door. The boy followed; normally, he would have been wearing a grin of amused triumph, but an expression of worry still overcast his face.

Inside, the doctor finally got a more or less coherent idea of what had happened from their two stories, and from Bob's expression and a number of meaningful glances made a guess at the underlying phenomena; he ordered Mr. Kinnaird onto the examination table. The man objected, saying that he wanted to find out something from Bob first.

"I'll talk to him," Seever said. "You stay put." He went outside for a moment with the boy, raising his eyebrows interrogatively.

"Yes." Bob answered the unspoken question. "But you won't find anything now except maybe a lack of germs. I'll tell you all about it later; but the job's done."

He waited until the doctor had disappeared once more, and then spoke to the Hunter.

"'What are your plans, now that your job is finished here? Go back to your own world?"

"I can't. I told you that," was the silent answer. "My ship is totally wrecked, and even if the other were not, I could never find it. I have a rough idea of how a space ship works, but I am a policeman, not a physicist or construction engineer. I could no more make a space ship than you could build one of the airliners we traveled on together."

"Then——"

"I am on Earth for life, except for the ridiculously small chance of another ship's arriving from my old home. You can guess the likelihood of that if you will look at an astronomical picture of the Milky Way. Just what I do here and who my host is—and even if I have a host at all—depend on you. We do not thrust ourselves on those who do not want our company. What do you say?"

Bob did not answer at once. He looked back across the village to the pillar of smoke that was now thinning above the hill, and thought. The Hunter assumed that he was considering the pros and cons of the suggestion, and felt a little hurt that there should be any hesitation, even though he had begun to appreciate the human desire for privacy at certain times; but for once he had misunderstood his host.

Bob was intelligent for his age, as was evident enough, but he was still far from adult, and was apt to consider his immediate problems before indulging in long-term planning. When he spoke at last the Hunter did not know whether to be relieved, overjoyed, or amused; he never tried to find the words to describe his feelings.

"I'm glad you're staying around," Bob said slowly. "I was a little worried about it, particularly the last few minutes. I like you a lot, and was hoping you could help me out on another problem. You see, when I set up this booby trap we just sprung, there was one point I didn't consider; and it's one that has to be met awfully fast.

"In a few minutes Dad is going to come out that door with his mouth full of questions and his eyes full of fire. One of the questions is going to be, 'How did that fire get started?' I don't think my being fifteen will make any difference in what'll happen if I don't have an awfully convincing answer. I didn't stop to think of one before, and I can't seem to now, so please get your mind to work. If you can't do that, start toughening up that protective net of yours under my skin; I can tell you where it'll be needed most!"

# ICEWORLD

# I.

Sallman Ken had never been really sure of the wisdom he had shown in acceding to Rade's request. He was no policeman and knew it. He had no particular liking for physical danger. He had always believed, of course, that he could stand his share of discomfort, but the view he was now getting through the *Karella*'s port was making him doubt even that.

Rade had been fair enough, he had to admit. The narcotics chief had told him, apparently, everything he himself knew; enough so that Ken, had he used his imagination sufficiently, might even have foreseen something like *this*.

"There has never been much of it," Rade had said. "We don't even know what the peddlers call it—it's just a 'sniff' to them. It's been around for quite a few years now; we got interested when it first appeared, and then took most of our attention from it when it never seemed to amount to much."

"But what's so dangerous about it, then?" Ken had asked.

"Well, of course any habit-forming drug is dangerous—you could hardly be a teacher of science without knowing that. The special menace of this stuff seems to lie in the fact that it is a gas, and can therefore be administered easily without the victim's consent; and it seems to be so potent that a single dose will insure addiction. You can see what a public danger that could be." Ken had seen, clearly.

"I should say so. I'm surprised we haven't all been overcome already. A generator in a building's ventilation system—on board a ship—anything like that could make hundreds of customers for whoever has the stuff to sell. Why hasn't it spread?" Rade had smiled for the first time.

"There seem to be two reasons for that, also. There are production difficulties, if the very vague stories we hear have anything in them; and the stuff doesn't keep at normal temperature. It has to be held under extreme refrigeration; when exposed to normal conditions it breaks down in a few seconds. I believe that the active principle is actually one of the breakdown products, but no one had obtained a sample to prove it."

"But where do I come in? If you don't have any of it I can't analyze it for you. I probably couldn't anyway—I'm a school teacher, not a professional chemist. What else can I do?"

"It's because you're a teacher—a sort of jack-of-all-trades in scientific matters, without being an expert at any of them—that we think you can help us. I mentioned that there seemed to be production troubles with the drug.

"Certainly the producers would like to increase volume. They would like, of course, to get a first-rate production engineer. You know as well as I that they could never do it; no such person could be involved secretly in such a matter. Every competent engineer is well employed since Velio was discovered, and it would be too easy for us to trace one who was approached for such a purpose.

"You, however, are a comparatively inconspicuous person; you are on vacation, and will be for another year; no one will miss you—we expect these people to think. That's why we took such extreme precautions in arranging this interview."

"But you'll have to publicize me some way, or *they* would never know I existed, either," Ken pointed out.

"That can be done—in fact, has already started. I trust you'll forgive us for that; but the job is important. The whisper has already started in criminal circles that you are the manufacturer of the bomb that wrecked the Storrn plant. We can give you quite a reputation—"

"Which will prevent my ever getting an honest job again."

"Which will never be heard of by your present employers, or by any respectable person not associated with the police."

Ken was not yet sure why he had accepted. Maybe the occupation of policeman still carried a little subconscious glamour, though certainly it was now mostly laboratory work. This looked like an exception—or did it? He had as Rade expected been hired by an extremely short-spoken individual, who claimed to represent a trading concern. The understanding had been that his knowledge was to be placed at the disposal of his employers. Perhaps they would simply stick him in a lab with the outline of a production problem, and tell him to solve it. In that case, he would be out of a job very quickly, and if he were lucky might be able to offer his apologies to Rade.

For he certainly had learned nothing so far. Even the narcotics man had admitted that his people knew no one at all certainly connected with the ring, and it was very possible that he might be hired by comparatively respectable people—compared, of course, to drug-runners. For all Ken could tell at the moment, that might have happened. He had been shepherded aboard the *Karella* at the North Island spaceport, and for twenty-two days had seen nothing at all.

He knew, of course, that the drug came from off the planet. Rade had become sufficiently specific to admit that the original rush had been checked by examining incoming refrigeration apparatus. He did not know, however, that it came from outside the Sarrian planetary system. Twenty-two days was a long journey—if it had been made in a straight line.

Certainly the world that hung now beyond the port did not look as though it could produce anything. Only a thin crescent of it was visible, for it lay nearly between the ship and a remarkably feeble sun. The dark remainder of the sphere blotted out the Milky Way in a fashion that showed the planet to be airless. It was mountainous, inhospitable, and cold. Ken knew that last fact because of the appearance of the sun. It was dim enough to view directly without protection to the eyes; to Ken's color sense, reddish in shade and shrunken in aspect. No world this far from such a star could be anything but cold.

Of course, Rade's drug needed low temperature—well, if it were made here, Ken was going to resign, regardless. Merely looking at the planet made him shiver.

He wished someone would tell him what was going on. There was a speaker over the door of his room, but so far the only times it had been used was to tell him that there was food outside his room and the door was unlocked for the moment.

For he had not been allowed to leave his room. That suggested illegal proceedings of some sort; unfortunately it did not limit them to the sort he was seeking. With the trading regulations what they were, a mercantile explorer who found an inhabited system more often than not kept the find strictly for his own exploitation. The precaution of concealing its whereabouts from a new employee was natural.

At a venture, he spoke aloud. After all, the fact that they were hanging so long beside this world must mean something.

"Is this where I'm expected to work? You'll pardon my saying that it looks extremely unpleasant." A little to his surprise there was an answer, in a voice different from the one that had announced his meals.

"I agree. I have never landed there myself, but it certainly looks bad. As far as we know at present, your job will not require you to visit that world."

"Just what is my job? Or don't you want to tell me yet?"

"There is no harm in telling you more, anyway, since we have arrived at the proper planetary system." Ken cast an uneasy eye at the feeble sun as he heard these words, but continued to listen without comment.

"You will find the door unlocked. Turn to your right in the corridor outside, and proceed for about forty yards—as far as you can. That will take you to the control room, where I am. It will be more comfortable to talk face to face." The speaker's rumble ceased, and Ken did as he was told. The *Karella* seemed to be a fairly common type of interstellar flyer, somewhere between one hundred fifty and two hundred feet in length, and about one third that diameter. It would be shaped like a cylinder with slightly rounded ends. Plenty of bulk—usable for passengers, cargo, or anything else her owner cared.

The control room contained nothing worthy of comment, except its occupants. One of these was obviously the pilot; he was strapped to his rack in front of the main control panel. The other was floating free in the middle of the room, obviously awaiting Ken's arrival since he had both eyes on the door. He spoke at once, in a voice recognizable as the one which had invited the scientist forward.

"I was a little hesitant about letting you see any of us personally before having your final acceptance of our offer; but I don't see that it can do much harm, after all. I scarcely ever visit Sarr nowadays, and the chance of your encountering me if we fail to reach a final agreement is small."

"Then you are engaged in something illegal?" Ken felt that there could be little harm in mentioning a fact the other's speech had made so obvious. After all, they would not expect him to be stupid.

"Illegal, yes, if the law be interpreted—strictly. I feel, however, and many agree with me, that if someone finds an inhabited planet, investigates it at his own expense, and opens relations with the inhabitants, that he has a moral right to profit from the fact. That, bluntly, is our situation."

Ken's heart sank. It began to look as though he had stumbled on the very sort of petty violation he had feared, and was not going to be very useful to Rade.

"There is certainly some justice in that viewpoint," he said cautiously. "If that is the case, what can I do for you? I'm certainly no linguist, and know next to nothing of economic theory, if you're hitting trading difficulties."

"We are having difficulties, but not in that way. They stem from the fact that the planet in question is so different from Sarr that personal visits are impossible. We have had the greatest difficulty in establishing contact of a sort with even one group of natives—or perhaps a single individual; we can't tell."

"Can't tell? Can't you send a torpedo down with television apparatus, at least?"

"You'll see." The still nameless individual gave a rather unpleasant smile. "At any rate, we have managed to do a little trading with this native or natives, and found that they have something we can use. We get it, as you can well imagine, in trickles and driblets. Basically, your problem is—how do we get more of it? You can try to figure out some way of landing in person if you like, but I know you're not an engineer. What I thought you could do was get a good enough analysis of the planet's conditions—atmosphere, temperature, light, and so on—so that we could reproduce them in a more convenient location and grow our own product. That way, we wouldn't be forced to pay the price the native asks, too."

"That sounds simple enough. I notice you don't seem to want me to know what the product is—except that it seems to be of vegetable nature—but that doesn't bother me. I had a friend in the perfume business once, and the way he tried to keep secrets in elementary chemistry was a scandal. I'm certainly willing to try—but I warn you I'm not the Galaxy's best chemist by a long shot, and I've brought no apparatus with me, since I didn't know what you wanted me to do. Have you anything here in the ship?"

"Not in the ship. We discovered this place around twenty years ago, and have built a fairly comfortable base on the innermost planet of this system. It keeps the same hemisphere facing the sun all the time,* and we've been able to concentrate enough sunlight in a small valley to make the temperature quite bearable. There's a fairly respectable laboratory and shop there, with a very good mechanic named Feth Allmer; and if you find yourself in need of something we don't have, we can probably afford to get it for you. How does that sound?"

"Very good indeed. I'll take your job, and do what I can." Ken was a little happier at this point, partly because the job seemed interesting in itself and partly because of some of the other's statements. If this product was a plant, as seemed to be the case, there was at least a slight possibility that he was not on a blind run after all. The matter of the need for refrigeration, of course, had not come up specifically—for all that had been said so far, the planet was as likely to be too hot as too cold for comfort; but what he had seen of this system's sun made that seem doubtful. Then there was the reference to warming the *innermost* planet—no, the place was cold. Definitely. Chances improved again. He switched his attention from these thoughts, as he realized that his employer—if this were really the head of the concern—was speaking again.

---

*This is now known to be incorrect; it was the best knowledge at the time *Iceworld* was written.

"I was sure you would. You can give orders for anything you need, starting now. You may use this ship as you please, subject only to Ordon Lee's veto if he considers the vessel in danger." The pilot was indicated by the wave of a supple tentacle as the name was pronounced. "Incidentally, I am Laj Drai. You are working for me, and I am sure we will both be more comfortable if that fact is borne in mind. What do you think should be done first?"

Ken decided to ignore Drai's subtle implication of superiority, and answered the question with another.

"Do you have any samples of the atmosphere or soil of this planet?"

"Of the first, no. We have never been able to keep a sample; probably we did not collect it properly. One cylinder that was collected leaked and burned in our air, for what that may be worth. We do have bits of soil, but they were all exposed to our own air at one time or another, and may have been changed by that. You will have to decide that for yourself. All that I really know is that their atmosphere has a pressure around two thirds of Sarr-normal, and at its base the temperature is low enough to freeze most of the regular gases out of our own air—I believe it would even freeze potassium. Our mechanic claimed that was what happened to one device that failed to work."

"How about size?"

"Bigger than Sarr—the figures are all at the base on Planet One; it would be easier to look them over there. I don't pretend to remember any of them at all precisely—as a matter of fact, we don't *have* any of them too precisely. You're the scientist, as far as we are concerned; my people are just eyes and tentacles for you.

"We do have remote-controlled torpedoes, as you suggested. It might be well to tell me before you use them; we lost nineteen of the first twenty to reach the planet's surface. We planted a permanent transmitter at the point where the twentieth landed, and we always home down on it now. just what happened to the others we don't exactly know, though we have a pretty good guess. I'll tell you the whole story at the same time that you look over the other material. Is there anything you'd care to do before we leave the vicinity of the planet and go over to One?"

"Leave the vicinity? I thought you said that world was not the one in question." Ken waved a tentacle at the cratered crescent.

"That one isn't—that's a satellite of Three, the one we're interested in."

A chill came back to Ken's skin. The satellite had been frightening; the planet itself could be little if any warmer since it must be about the same distance from the sun. An atmosphere would help a little, of course; but still—cold enough to freeze potassium, and lead, and tin! He had not given real thought to that. His imagination was good—perhaps a little too good; and it began conjuring up out of nothing in particular an image of a world chilled to the core. It was rough, and an icy blizzard played over it, and nothing moved in the dim reddish light—a planet of death.

But that couldn't be right; there were natives. Ken tried to imagine the sort of life that could exist under such hideous conditions, and failed completely. Maybe Laj Drai was wrong about the temperature; after all, he hadn't been *sure*. It was just a mechanic's opinion.

"Let's see this place, since we're so close to it. I might as well learn the worst," he said at this point in his imagining. Laj Drai gestured to the pilot, and the hull of the *Karella* rotated slowly. The airless satellite slid out of sight, and stars followed it across the field of view. The ship must have spun a full hundred and eighty degrees before Planet Three itself hung in the apparent center of the port. They must be floating directly between planet and satellite, Ken thought. Not wise if the inhabitants had telescopes.

Since the sun was now behind them, the disc of the great world was fully illuminated. Unlike the bare moon, a fuzziness of outline showed that it possessed an extensive atmosphere, though Ken could not imagine what gases might be present. In spite of the definitely reddish sunlight, most of the surface had a decided blue tint. Details were impossible to make out; the atmosphere was extremely hazy. There were definite patches of white, and green, and brown, but there was no way of telling what any of them represented.

And yet, foggy as it was, there was something about the sight of the world which caused the shiver to caress the scientist's skin once more. Perhaps it was the things he had been told, and the things he had deduced from the appearance of the sun; perhaps it was nothing objective at all. Whatever it was, the very sight of the world made him shudder, and he turned away abruptly.

"Let's go to One, and look over that data," he said, striving to control his voice diaphragm. The pilot obeyed without comment.

Earth, really, is not as bad as all that. Some people are even quite fond of it. Ken, of course, was prejudiced, as anyone is likely to be against a world where water is a liquid—when he has grown up breathing gaseous sulfur and, at rare intervals, drinking molten copper chloride.

# II.

Roger Wing, for example, would probably have been slightly shocked at Ken's attitude. He was strongly in favor of Earth, at least the rather small portion which he knew. He had some justification, for the country around Lake Pend'Oreille is very much worth knowing, particularly in spring and summer. The first glimpse of the lake each June was something to look forward to; all the way up the highway from Hayden Lake the children maintained shrill rivalry over who would be the first to sight the Ear Drop. Even with only four of them this year, the noise was nearly as great as usual; for the absent Donald had never contributed too much to the racket. Roger, left the senior member by his older brother's absence, was determined to make the most of the opportunity; the more so since it was to last only another forty miles or so. Don was expected to fly to Sandpoint with a friend and meet the family there.

It was, all in all, a hilarious group; and the parents in the front seat had only moderate success in maintaining order. However, the northbound highway from Coeur d'Alene is a good one, and the disturbance in the rear was never really dangerous. The principal interruption occurred when the right rear tire of the station wagon went flat near Cocolalla. John Wing was a little slow in stopping the heavily loaded vehicle, and Roger got the first whiff of the sulfurous odor of burning rubber. He was to become much more familiar with sulfur during the course of the summer.

The children were a little quieter after that—the expression on their father's face suggested that his patience might not have much farther to go; but the journey was never really silent. The causeway across the tip of Pend' Oreille was greeted with ringing cheers, which ceased only momentarily while Mr. Wing purchased a new tire in Sandpoint. Then they proceeded to the small airport at the edge of the town, and the noise increased again as the youngsters caught sight of their oldest brother standing beside a Cub on the grass parking area.

He was tall, and rather slim, with dark hair and eyes and a narrow face like his father's. Roger, who had grown considerably since the last September, discovered to his chagrin that Donald still overtopped him by half a head; but he did not let the annoyance lessen the exuberance of his greeting. Don shook hands with his father and Roger, kissed his mother and sisters, and swung six-year-old Billy to his shoulder. No, the flight from Missoula had not been eventful. Yes, his final grades had been good, if not outstanding. No, he had no luggage except the little handbag beside him—a Cub has sharp load limitations. They might as well continue their journey, and he could answer questions on the way. He tossed the bag at Roger and moved toward the station wagon, Billy still on his shoulder; and with the crowd settled more or less comfortably, they rolled on.

North from Sandpoint; east fork to Kootenai; around the north end of the question-mark-shaped lake to Hope, and on to Clark Fork. There the car was left, in a building that partook of the characteristics of storehouse and garage.

Don and Roger disappeared, and returned with an imposing array of pack and saddle horses. These were accoutered with a speed which suggested the maneuver was not a new one to the family; and the Wings, waving farewell to their acquaintances who had gathered to see them off, headed northward into the woods.

Donald grinned at his father as the town vanished behind them.

"How many campers do you suppose we'll have this year?"

"It's hard to say. Most of the folks who know us have come to mind their own business pretty well, and I didn't notice any strangers in the town; but prospectors seem to turn up when least expected. I don't mind honest prospecting—it lends protective coloration. It's the ones who expect to benefit from our 'strike' that bother me. You boys will have to scout as usual—though I may want Don with me this time. If you've really gotten something out of freshman chemistry, Son, you may be able to help solve a problem or two. If he does go with me, Roger, you'll have a bigger responsibility than usual." The boy nodded, eyes shining.

He had only gradually come to realize the tremendous difference between the way his family and those of his schoolmates spent their summers. At first, the tales of trips to ranches, seashores, and mountains had aroused his envy; then he had begun to boast of his own mountain trips. When he finally realized the atmosphere of secrecy that surrounded certain aspects of those trips, his pride had exceeded his powers of restraint—until he had realized that his schoolmates simply didn't believe that his father had a "secret mine in the mountains." Pique had silenced his boasts for a while, and by the time he had developed a convincing argument he had realized that silence might be better for all concerned.

That had been the spring when he was ten years old. His father had somehow heard about the whole story, and seemed pleased for some reason; that summer he had extended to Roger the responsibility which Don had been carrying alone, of scouting the territory around their summer home before and during Mr. Wing's trips into the mountains. The find, their father had told him, was his own secret; and for reasons he would explain later it must be kept that way.

That summer and the two following he had continued to make his trips alone; now it looked as though there might be a change. Don, Roger knew, had been told a little just before leaving for college the preceding fall; his courses had been partly selected on the basis of that information—chemistry, astronomy and mathematics. The first seemed logical, but Roger failed to see the point of the others. Certainly astronomy seemed of doubtful value in anything connected with mining.

Still, he would find that out in due course; perhaps sooner than Don had, since their father seemed to be letting down the bars. His problem for the moment was to figure out a way by which one boy could keep himself informed about every person who came within a mile of the summer house in any direction—and farther than that in some directions. Roger, of course, knew the topography of the neighborhood quite well; but he began right then planning a series of exploration jaunts to make more certain of some points. He was a young man who took things seriously, if they were presented to him in that light.

Like anyone else of his own age, however, he tended even more strongly to fly off on the interests of the moment; and he was easily aroused from his reverie when Edie caught him in the face with a fir cone slyly tossed over her shoulder. She burst into laughter as he looked around fruitlessly for a means of retaliation—there seemed to be no more cones within reach, and the trail at this point was too narrow for the horses to travel side by side. The pack horse the girl was leading formed, for the time being, an impassable barrier.

"Why don't you wake up and join the party?" Edith finally gurgled out between spasms of laughter. "You looked as though you'd just remembered leaving your favorite fishpole in Spokane!" Roger assumed a mantle of superiority.

"Of course, you girls have nothing to do between now and September," he said. "There's a certain amount of men's work to be done, though, and I was deciding how to go about it."

"Men's work?" The girl raised her eyebrows in mock surprise. I know Dad will be busy, but what's that to you?" She knew perfectly well what

Roger's summer duties were, but had reasons of her own for speaking as she did. "Does it take a man to stroll around the house on sentry-go a couple of times a day?" Roger stiffened.

"It takes more than a girl to do a good job of it," he retorted. The words were hardly out when he regretted them; but he had no time to think of a way out of the corner into which he had talked himself.

"Evidence!" Edith responded quietly, and Roger mentally kicked himself. She had been playing for just that. Family rules required that any statement made by a member of the family be backed up with evidence if another member required it—a rule the elder Wing had instituted, with considerable foresight. He was seldom caught by it himself, being a thoughtful man by nature.

"You'll have to let me try, now," Edith remarked, "and you'll have to give me a fair amount of teaching. To be really fair, you'll have to let Margie try, too—" The last was an afterthought, uttered principally for its explosive effect. Roger almost left his saddle, but before he succeeded in expressing himself a thought struck him. After all, why couldn't the girls help? He could show them what he and Don had done in the past, and they might very well have ideas of their own. Roger's masculine pride did not blind him to the fact that girls in general, and his sisters in particular, did have brains. Edie and Marge could both ride, neither was afraid of the woods, and all things considered would probably make extremely useful assistants. Edith was so near to his own age that he could not dismiss her as too young for the work, and even the eight-year-old had at least sense enough to keep quiet when silence was needed and obey orders when argument would be injudicious.

"All right. You can both try it." Roger brought his cogitation to an end. "Dad won't mind, I guess, and Mother won't care if the work gets done. We'll have a conference tonight."

The conversation shifted to other matters, and the caravan wound on up the river. Two or three hours out of Clark Fork they crossed the stream and headed eastward toward the Montana border; and there were still several hours of daylight remaining when they reached the "summer cottage."

It was hardly a cottage. Built well up on a steep hillside, though still below the timber line, it boasted enough rooms to house the Wing family without any fear whatever of crowding. It possessed a gasoline-powered electric plant, a more or less limited supply of running water piped from a spring farther up the hill, and in general bore witness to Mr. Wing's luck or skill in the prospecting which was supposed to be the source of his income.

A short distance downhill from the dwelling was another building which combined the functions of storehouse and stable. Both structures were solidly built, and had never suffered serious damage from the Northwest winters. The foundation of the house was part of the bedrock core of the mountain, and its walls were well insulated. The family could easily have lived there the year round, and the parents had vague plans of doing so once the children had all finished school.

The first floor consisted of a big room which did duty as dining room and parlor, with a kitchen at one end and bedroom at the other. An open stair well by the kitchen door went down to a basement, containing work benches cluttered with woodworking and radio paraphernalia as well as the wherewithal for various games. The stair to the second floor was at the other end; this was divided into six much smaller rooms, one serving as bedroom for each of the children and the remaining one filled with the various odd articles of furniture and bric-a-brac which are apt to find their way into a spare room over a period of years.

The Wings dismounted by the porch which ran along the front of the dwelling, and promptly dispersed to their various duties. Mrs. Wing and the girls unlocked the front door and disappeared inside. Billy began unscrewing and removing the shutters on the more accessible windows— those along the porch, and the first-floor ones on the uphill side of the dwelling. Mr. Wing and Donald began unloading the pack animals, while Roger took the other horses down to the stable, unsaddled, and fed them.

By sunset, the house had assumed an inhabited air. Everyone had eaten, dishes had been washed, Billy and Marjorie were in bed, and the remaining members of the family had settled down for a few minutes of relaxation in the main room. There had been some debate as to whether the fireplace should be used, which had been won by the affirmatives— not so much because of the temperature, though even a June night can be chilly in the Cabinets, but simply because they liked to sit around a fire.

The parents were ensconced in their respective seats on each side of the stone fireplace. Donald, Roger and Edith sprawled on rugs between; Roger had just put forth the suggestion that the girls help in the scouting job. His father thought for a minute or two.

"Do you know your way around well enough, in directions other than toward town?" he finally asked Edith.

"Not as well as the boys, I suppose, but they had to learn sometime or other," she countered.

"True enough. I wouldn't want you to turn up missing, and your mother can't be expected to do all the housework herself. Well, Roger seems to have let himself in for proving a point, so let's put it this way. It will be a week or ten days before I go out for the first time. In that time the two of you, working together, will turn in a satisfactory map of the territory within three miles of this house, and a patrol schedule that will permit Edie's housework to be done at times satisfactory to your mother. Margie may go with you, but is not to go beyond the half-mile marks alone—the old rules hold for the younger people, still. That is subject to any additions or alterations your mother may see fit to make." He looked across at his wife, with a half smile on his face. She returned the smile, and nodded.

"That seems all right. Roger has a few duties of his own, I believe; hadn't they better be included in the last item?"

"Fair enough. Does that suit you, Rog? Edie? All right," as the two nodded, "time for bed. You seem to have the time for the next few days pretty well filled." The two youngsters grimaced but obeyed; Don and his parents remained. They talked seriously in low tones far into the night. The four younger children had been asleep for several hours when Donald finally climbed the stairs to his room, but the fact did not lessen his caution. He had no desire to spend the rest of the night ducking Roger's questions about what had gone on downstairs.

In spite of the rather strenuous day just finished, the entire family was up early the next morning. As a "special favor" to his younger brother, Donald volunteered to take the surplus horses back to town—they kept only a few at the summer house, as fodder was a little difficult to obtain. That left the younger boy free, once the shutters were removed from the upstairs windows, to get out on the mapping job, as far as his own work was concerned. Edith was delayed for a while dusting off china and washing cooking utensils—they had cleaned only enough for a sketchy meal the night before—but Roger conquered any slight distaste he might have had for women's work and helped out. The sun was not yet very high when they emerged onto the porch, consulted briefly, and started uphill around the house.

The boy carried a small Scout compass and a steel tape which had turned up in the basement workshop; his sister had a paper-covered notebook, a school relic still possessed of a few blank pages. Between his father's teaching and a year in a Scout troop, Roger was sure he could produce a readable map of the stipulated area with no further equipment. He had not considered at all carefully the problem of contours.

High as the Wing house was located, there was still a long climb above it; and both youngsters were quite willing to rest by the time they reached the top. They were willing, too, to sit and look at the view around them, though neither was a stranger to it.

The peaks of the Cabinets extended in all directions except the West. The elevation on which they were located was not high enough to permit them to see very far; but bits of Pend' Oreille were visible to the southwest and the easily recognized tip of Snowshoe Peak rose between east and south. Strictly speaking, there was no definite timber line; but most of the peaks managed to thrust bare rock through the soil for at least a few hundred feet. The lower slopes were covered with forest, principally the Douglas fir which is so prevalent in the Pacific Northwest. One or two relatively clear areas, relics of forest fires of the last few years, were visible from the children's point of vantage.

There were a number of points visible within the distance specified by Mr. Wing which looked as though they might serve as reference stations, and presently Roger took out the compass and began taking bearings on as many of these as he could. Edith was already making a free-hand sketch map of their surroundings, and the bearings were entered on this. Distances would come later; Roger knew neither his own altitude nor those of the points he was measuring, and could not have used the information had he possessed it. He knew no trigonometry and had no means of measuring angles of depression.

Details began to crowd the rough chart even before they left the hilltop; and presently the two were completely absorbed in their task. Mrs. Wing was not particularly surprised when they came in late for dinner.

# III.

The station on Planet One was a decidedly primitive installation though a good deal of engineering had obviously been needed to make it habitable at all. It was located in the bottom of a deep valley near the center of the planet's sunward hemisphere, where the temperature was normally around four hundred degrees Centigrade. This would still have been cold enough to liquefy the sulfur which formed the principal constituent of the atmosphere Ken's people needed; but the additional hundred degrees had been obtained by terracing the valley walls, cutting the faces of the terraces to the appropriate slope, and plating them with iron. The dark-colored metal dome of the station was, in effect, at the focus of a gigantic concave mirror; and between the angular size of the sun and the actual size of the dome, solar libration never moved the focus to a serious extent.

The interstellar flyer settled onto a smooth sheet of bare rock beside the dome. There were no cradling facilities, and Ken had to don vacuum armor to leave the vessel. Several other space-suited figures gathered in the airlock with him, and he suspected that most if not all of the ship's crew were "going ashore" at the same time though, of course, they might not be crew; one operator could handle a vessel of the *Karella's* class. He wondered whether or not this was considered safe practice on a foreign planet; but a careful look around as he walked the short distance from ship to dome revealed no defensive armament, and suggested that those manning the station had no anxiety about attack. If, as had been suggested, the post had been here for twenty years, they probably should know.

The interior of the dome was comfortable enough, though Ken's conductor made constant apology for the lack of facilities. They had a meal for which no apology was required, and Ken was shown private quarters at least as good as were provided by the average Sarrian hotel.

223

Laj Drai took him on a brief tour of the station, and made clear the facilities which the scientist could use in his assigned job.

With his "real" job usually in mind, Ken kept constant watch for any scrap of evidence that might suggest the presence of the narcotic he sought. He was reasonably certain, after the tour, that there was no complex chemical processing plant anywhere around; but if the drug were a natural product, there might not have to be. He could name more than one such substance that was horribly effective in the form in which it was found in nature—a vegetable product some primitive tribes on his own world still used to poison their arrows, for example.

The "trading" equipment, however, proved more promising, as might have been foreseen by anyone who had considered the planet with which the trading was done. There were many remote-control torpedoes, each divided into two main sections. One of these contained the driving and control machinery and was equipped with temperature control apparatus designed to keep it near normal; the other was mostly storage space and refrigeration machinery. Neither section was particularly well insulated, either from the other or the surrounding medium. Ken examined one of the machines minutely for some time, and then began asking questions.

"I don't see any vision transmitter; how do you see to control the thing on the planet's surface?"

"There is none," a technician who had been assisting Drai in the exposition replied. "They all originally had them, of course, but none has survived the trip to Three yet. We took them out, finally—it was too expensive. The optical apparatus has to be exposed to the planet's conditions at least partly, which means we must either run the whole machine at that temperature or have a terrific temperature difference between the optical and electrical elements. We have not been able to devise a system that would stand either situation—something goes completely haywire in the electrical part under those freezing conditions, or else the optical section shatters between the hot and cold sections."

"But how do you see to control?"

"We don't. There is a reflection altimeter installed, and a homing transmitter that was set up long ago on the planet. We simply send the torpedo down, land it, and let the natives come to it."

"And you have never brought any physical samples from the surface of the planet?"

"We can't see to pick up anything. The torpedo doesn't stay airtight at that temperature, so we never get a significant amount of the atmosphere back; and nothing seems to stick to the outer hull. Maybe it lands on a solid metal or rock surface—we wouldn't know."

"Surely you *could* make the thing hold air, even below the freezing point of sulfur?"

"Yes, I guess so. It's never seemed to be worth the trouble. If you want a sample, it would be easier to send a smaller container down, anyway—you can work with it better afterwards."

A thought suddenly struck Ken.

"How about the stuff you get from the natives? Doesn't that give any clue? Could I work with some of it?" Laj Drai cut in at this point.

"You said you were not a specialist. We have tried to get the stuff analyzed by people who were, without success. After all, if it were possible to synthesize the material, do you think we'd be going to all this trouble to trade for it? That's why we want you to get the planetary conditions for us—when you've done that, we'll figure out a means of getting seeds from the natives and growing our own."

"I see," Ken replied. The statement was certainly reasonable enough, and did not necessarily imply anything about the nature of the material they were discussing.

It did not refute anything, either.

Ken thought that one over for a time, letting his eyes wander over the exposed machinery as he did so. He had a few more questions in mind, but he wanted to dodge anything that might be interpreted as unhealthy curiosity, if these people actually were drug-runners.

"What do these natives get from you for this product?" he asked finally. "Is it a manufactured article they can't make, or a substance they don't have? In the latter case, I might be able to draw some conclusions about the planet." Drai sent a ripple down his tentacles, in a gesture equivalent to a human shrug.

"It's material—heavy metals that don't sulfide easily. We've been giving them platinum-group nuggets most of the time—they're easiest to come by; there's an outcropping of the stuff only a short distance from this station, and it's easy to send a man out to blast off a few pieces. I don't know what they use them for—For all I know they may worship the torpedo, and use the nuggets as priests' insignia. I can't say that I care, as long as they keep filling their end of the bargain." Ken made the gesture of agreement, and spoke of something which had caught his attention during the last speech.

"What in the Galaxy is a loudspeaker and microphone doing in that thing? Surely they don't work at the temperatures you mentioned—and you can't be speaking to these natives!"

The technician answered the first question.

"It works, all right. It's a crystal outfit without vacuum tubes, and should work in liquid hydrogen."

Drai supplemented the other answer. "We don't exactly talk to them, but they can apparently hear and produce sounds more or less similar to those of our speech."

"But how could you ever have worked out a common language, or even a code, without visual contact? Maybe, unless you think it's none of my business and will not be any help in what is, you'd better give me the whole story from the beginning."

"Maybe I had," Laj Drai said slowly, draping his pliant form over a convenient rack. "I have already mentioned that contact was made some twenty years ago—our years, that is; it would be nearer thirty for the natives of Planet Three.

"The *Karella* was simply cruising, without any particular object in view, when her previous owner happened to notice the rather peculiar color of Planet Three. You must have remarked that bluish tint yourself. He put the ship into an orbit at a safe distance beyond the atmosphere, and began sending down torpedoes. He knew better than to go down himself—there was never any doubt about the ghastly temperature conditions of the place.

"Well, he lost five projectiles in a row. Every one lost its vision connection in the upper atmosphere, since no one had bothered to think of the effect of the temperature on hot glass. Being a stubborn character, he sent them on down on long-wave instruments, and every one went out sooner or later; he was never sure even whether they had reached the surface. He had some fair engineers and plenty of torpedoes, though, and kept making changes and sending the results down. It finally became evident that most of them were reaching the surface—and going out of action the instant they did so. Something was either smashing them mechanically or playing the deuce with their electrical components.

"Up to then, the attempts had all been to make the landings on one of the relatively smooth, bluish areas; they seemed the least complicated. However, someone got the idea that this steady loss of machines could not be due to chance; somewhere there was intelligent intervention. To test the idea, a torpedo was sent down with every sort of detecting and protecting device that could be stuffed aboard—including a silver mesh over the entire surface, connected to the generators and capable of blocking any outside frequency which might be employed to interfere with control. A constantly changing control frequency was used from our end. It had automatic heat control—I tell you, it had *everything*. Nothing natural and darned little that was artificial should have been able to interfere with that machine; but it went out like the others, just as the reflection altimeter reported it as almost touching the surface.

"That was enough for the boss. He accepted as a working theory the idea that a race lived on the flatter parts of the planet; a race that did not want visitors. The next torpedo was sent to one of the darker, rougher areas that could be seen from space, the idea being that these beings might avoid such areas. He seems to have been right, for this time the landing was successful. At any rate, the instruments said the machine was down, it proved impossible to drive it lower, and it stayed put with power off.

"That was encouraging, but then no one could think of what to do. We still couldn't see, and were not certain for some time whether or not the microphone was working. It was decided not to use the loudspeaker for a while. There was a faint humming sound being picked up whose intensity varied without apparent system, which we finally decided might be wind rather than electrical trouble, and once or twice some brief, harsh, quite indescribable noises which have not yet been identified; the best guess is that they may have been the voices of living creatures.

"We kept listening for a full rotation of the planet—nearly two of our days—and heard nothing else except a very faint buzzing, equally faint scratching sounds, and an irregular tapping that might or might not have been the footsteps of a hoofed creature on a hard surface. You may listen to the records we made, if you like, but you'd better have company around when you do. There's something weird and unnerving about those noises out of nothing.

"I forgot to mention that the cargo port of the torpedo had been opened on landing, and microphones and weight detectors set to tell us if anything went in. Nothing did, however—a little surprising if there were small forms of wild life; the opening would have made a natural-looking shelter for them.

"Nothing even remotely suggestive of intelligence was heard during that rotation; and it was finally decided to use the loudspeaker. Someone worked out a schedule—starting at minimum power, repeating a tape for one rotation of the planet, then repeating with doubled output and so on until we reached the maximum which could be attained with that equipment. The program was followed, except that the boss was getting impatient and arranged to make the step-up each quarter rotation instead of the suggested time. Some humorist recorded a poem on the tape, and we started broadcasting.

"The first result was a complete cessation of the sounds we had tentatively associated with life forms. Presumably they *were* small animals, and were scared away by the noise. The wind, if that's what it was, continued as expected. The first time we increased the noise, after a quarter rotation of the planet, we began to get a faint echo. That suggested that the sound was at least not being muffled very close to the speaker, and if any intelligent beings came within a considerable radius they would hear it.

"To make a long story short, we got a response after the fourth increase of power. We thought it was a distorted echo at first, but it got louder while our power remained constant, and finally we could tell that the sounds were different. They formed a tremendously complex noise pattern, and every one of us who heard them was sure from the beginning that they represented intelligent speech.

"Eventually we began to hear more footstep-sounds between the bursts of alien language, and we cut off our own broadcast. It became evident that the creature was close enough to detect the torpedo by other means than hearing, for the footsteps continued to approach. At first they were interrupted every few seconds by a loud call; but presently the thing must have actually reached the machine, for the sounds suggested that it was walking around at a nearly constant distance, and the calls were replaced by much less powerful but longer and more complex speech-noises. Probably the creatures can see much as we do, though the light is so much weaker on that planet.

"Presently the photocell inside the cargo compartment indicated that something had cut off much of the fight. One of the operators moved to close the door, and the boss knocked him clean out of the control room. He took the torpedo controls himself, and began attempting to imitate the voice sounds of the creature we couldn't see. That produced results, all right! If noise means anything, the native got wildly excited for a minute or two; then he buckled down to producing apparently as wide a variety of sounds as his vocal apparatus would permit. Certainly we couldn't imitate them all.

"That lasted for some time, with nobody making any real progress. Nobody had any way of telling what any of the other fellow's noises meant, of course. It began to look as though we'd gone as far as we could, in learning about the planet, and that the knowledge was not going to do anyone any good.

"Then someone remembered the old swap-boxes. I don't know whether you've heard of them; they were used, I guess, before our race ever left the home planet, when people who didn't speak each other's language wanted to trade. They are simply two trays, hinged together, each divided into a number of small compartments. One side is empty, while the compartments of the other are filled with various articles that are for sale. A glass lid covers each of the full compartments, and cannot be removed until something has been placed in the corresponding compartment of the other tray. It takes a pretty stupid savage not to get the idea in fairly short order.

"We didn't have any such gadget, of course, but it was not difficult to rig one up. The trouble was that we could not tell what had been put in the empty tray until the box came back to us. Since we were more interested in talking than trading, that didn't matter too much at the time. We sent the box down in another torpedo, homing it on the location signal of the first and hoping the flatland people wouldn't detect it, opened the thing up, and waited.

"The native promptly investigated; he was apparently intelligent enough to put curiosity ahead of fear, even though he must have seen the second torpedo in flight. He behaved exactly as expected with the box, though of course we couldn't watch him—he put something in every compartment of the empty section, and presumably cleaned out the other; but he put most of the stuff back. One of the things he gave us proved useful—the stuff we still trade for—so we sent the box back with only the compartment corresponding to the one he had put that stuff in full. He got the idea, and we've been on fine terms ever since."

"But about the language?"

"Well, we know his words for 'yes' and 'no,' his names for a few metals, and his name for the stuff he sells us. I can give you either a tape of his pronunciation or a written record, if you want to talk to him."

"Thanks a lot. That makes the whole situation a good deal clearer. I take it you have had no more trouble from these flatlanders?"

"None. We have carefully avoided contacting any other part of the planet. As I said, our interests are now commercial rather than scientific. Still, if you want to send down machines on your own, I suppose we shouldn't interfere with you. Please be careful, though; we'd hate to have contact cut off before we were in a position to do our own producing."

Ken gave the equivalent of a grin. "I notice you are still carefully refraining from telling me what the stuff is. Well, I won't butt in. That's none of my business, and I don't see how knowing it could help me out. Right now, I guess, it would be best for you to give me all the physical data you have on the planet. Then I can make a guess at its atmosphere, and send a torpedo down with equipment to confirm or deny the guess. That will be easier than trying to bring back samples for analysis, I imagine."

Drai pulled himself together from the rack on which he was sprawled, and gave the equivalent of an affirmative nod. "I'm not saying you shouldn't know what we get from the planet," he said. "But I shall most certainly make a hammock from the skin of the first member of this organization who lets you find out!" The technician, who had been listening in the background, turned back to the mechanism of another torpedo, and spoke for the first time without looking up.

"That won't be difficult; there's little to tell. The planet is about three-tenths larger than ours in diameter, making its volume rather over twice as great as that of Sarr. Its mass is also over twice ours, though its average density is a shade less. Surface gravity is one and a quarter Sarr normal. Mean temperature is a little below the freezing point of potassium. Atmospheric pressure uncertain, composition unknown. Period of rotation, one point eight four Sarr days."

"I see. You could duplicate temperature readily enough on this planet, by choosing a point far enough around toward the dark side; and if necessary, there wouldn't be too much trouble in reproducing the periodicity of night and day. Your problem is atmosphere. I'll spend some time thinking out ways and means of getting that, then." Sallman Ken moved slowly away in the direction of his assigned quarters. His thoughts were not exclusively occupied with the problem of atmosphere analysis; he was thinking more of a mysterious race inhabiting the flat, bleak plains of Planet Three and the possibility of cutting off trade with the planet—always, of course, assuming that its mysterious product was what he feared.

He was also wondering if he had overdone his disclaimer of interest in the planet's chief export.

# IV.

A circle of three-mile radius has an area of slightly over twenty-eight square miles, or roughly eighteen thousand acres. It follows that the map prepared by Roger and Edith Wing was not as detailed as it might have been. On the other hand, as their father was forced to admit, a tree-covered mountain side does not offer too many details to put on a map; and the effort the children turned in did show every creek and trail of which Mr. Wing had knowledge. Still more to the point, it showed clearly that they had actually travelled over the area in question. This was the defect in the girl's experience which he had wanted corrected before she was released from the "stick-to-the-trail" rule.

He looked up presently from the tattered notebook. The family was gathered around the fireplace again, and the two cartographers were ensconced on either arm of his chair. Don was on the floor between the seats with Billy draped across his neck; Marjorie was in her mother's lap. All were listening for the verdict.

"You seem to have done a pretty good job here," Mr. Wing said at last. "Certainly anyone could find his way around the area with the aid of this map. Edie, how do you think you could do *without* it?"

"All right, Dad, I'm sure," the girl replied in a slightly surprised tone. "Do I have to?" Her father shrugged.

"You know best whether you want to carry this with you all the time. No, you don't have to, as far as I'm concerned. How have the two of you made out on the patrol schedule?" Roger took over the conversation, curling a little closer to his father's shoulder and using the map to illustrate his points.

"There are eight trails leading into the three-mile circle at different points. Don and I used to go around the circle each day, going along each one far enough to be sure no one had been using it. There are spots on each which it's practically impossible to go through without leaving some sort of trail. Going from one trail to another we'd try to cut across places of the same sort—where we could tell if people had been through.

"This time we're working it a little differently. I'm still checking the ends of those trails, but we've been listing places from which people could watch anyone bound away from here—there aren't nearly so many of those. Edie can cover nearly all of them in two hour-and-a-half walks morning and afternoon—we've tried it; and I can do the rest when I take the outer trails. That's a lot like the way you've always worked it when you were going out, anyway; you took a zigzag path, and had us checking for watchers, so that one of us could cut across and warn you if we saw anyone— we never have, that I can remember, but I don't suppose that proves anything." Mr. Wing smiled briefly.

"I may be stretching the precautions a little too far," he said. "Still, I have certain reasons for not wanting the place I get the metal to become known. Half a dozen of the reasons are in this room with me. Besides, I think you get fun out of it, and I know it keeps you outdoors where you ought to be this time of year. If two or three more of you grow up to be scientists, we may be able to do some work together that will let us forget about secrecy."

The younger girl, who had been displaying increasing signs of indignation during her brother's talk, cut in the instant she thought her father had finished.

"Daddy, I thought I was supposed to be helping with this. I heard Roger say so yesterday, and you said it the first night."

"Oh? And how did you hear what I said that night? As I recall, the matter was not discussed until after you were in bed. What I said then goes—you can go with either Roger or Edie on their walks, but you still observe the limits when you're by yourself. Billy, you too! There'll be plenty of long trips for all of you, without your having to go off on your own, and there's always been plenty to keep you occupied around here. I've been promising for five or six years to get a load of cement up here if you folks would get enough loose rock together to make a dam out here—I'd like a swimming pool myself. Don doesn't think we need cement for it, but that's something he'll have to prove. I'll be glad if he can do without it, of course." He leaned back and stretched his legs. Billy promptly transferred his perch from Don's shoulders to his father's shins, and put his own oar into the conversation. He wanted one of the trips before his father went prospecting, and expressed himself at considerable length on the subject. Mr. Wing remained noncommittal until the striking of the clock brought relief. He pulled in his legs abruptly, depositing the youngster on the floor.

"Small fry to bed!" he pronounced solemnly.

"Story!" yelled Margie. "You haven't read since we got here!" Her father pursed his lips.

"How long do you suppose it would take them to be ready for bed?" he asked, as though to himself. There was a flurry of departing legs. Mr. Wing turned to the bookcase beside the fireplace, and encountered the grinning face of his second son. "All right, young man, we need some fun—but some of us need discipline, too. Suppose you and Edie save time by popping upstairs and imitating the excellent example of your juniors!" Still chuckling, the two did so.

For some reason, the story lasted until quite late. The beginning was vastly exciting, but the pace calmed down later, and Billy and Margie were both carried up to bed at the end—though they refused to believe the fact in the morning.

Roger tried at breakfast to make the small boy tell the end of the story, and was surprised when Billy refused to accept his inability to do so as evidence that he had been asleep. The older boy gave up at last and went to saddle the horses; he was constitutionally unfitted to hold his own in an argument where the opponent's only words were "I was not either!"

It was shopping day, and Roger's turn to go down to Clark Fork with his mother to obtain the necessities for the next week. They left as soon after breakfast as the animals could be readied. Edie and the younger children went off on their own; as soon as everyone was away from the house, Mr. Wing and Don dressed themselves in hiking clothes and headed east. Roger would have given much to see them go.

The trails were good, and for a couple of hours the two made very satisfactory progress. For the most part they followed the creeks, but once or twice the older man led the way over open spurs of rock which involved considerable climbing.

"This is about the quickest way to the transmitter, Don," he said at one point. "It's a lot closer to the house than even your mother realizes—though goodness knows I wouldn't hide it from her if she cared to come on one of these hikes. On the regular trips, I follow a very roundabout path I worked out years ago when I was really afraid of being followed. That was just after the first World War, long before I'd even met your mother. There were a number of people around this part of the country then who would cheerfully have tossed me off a hilltop for a fraction of the value I brought back from the first trip. I tell you, I did some pretty serious thinking on the way in from that trip. You'll see why very shortly."

Don made no immediate answer to this. His attention seemed to be fully taken up with negotiating the slope of loose rock they were traversing at the moment. It was a section practically impossible to cross without leaving prominent traces, and he had been a little puzzled at his father's going this way until he realized that the idea was probably to permit a check on any trailers as they returned. Once across the treacherous stuff and angling back down the slope, he finally spoke.

"You said a while back, Dad, that we were the reasons you didn't make public this source of metal. It seems to me that even that shouldn't have carried weight while the war was on—it might have been better to let the government develop the find and use it. I don't mean that I don't appreciate getting a college education, but—well—" he paused a little uncomfortably.

"You have a point, son, and that was another matter for thought when the war started, with you in high school and Billy just learning to walk. I think I might have done as you suggest, except for the fact that the most probable result of publicity would be to remove the source of metal. Just be patient a little longer—we'll be there in a few minutes, and you will see for yourself."

Donald nodded acceptance of this, and they proceeded in silence for a short time. The course Mr. Wing was following had led them into a narrow gully after crossing the scree; now he turned up this, making his way easily along the bank of the tiny brook which flowed down its center. After some ten minutes' climb the trees began to thin out, and a few more rods found them on practically bare rock. This extended for some distance above them, but the older man seemed to have no desire to get to the top of the hill.

Instead, he turned again, moving quickly across the bare rock as though a path were plainly marked before him; and in a few steps reached the edge of a shallow declivity which appeared to have acted as a catch basin for rocks which had rolled from farther up the hill. Winding his way among these, with Donald close at his heels, he finally stopped and moved to one side, permitting his son to see what lay before them.

It was an almost featureless structure of metal, roughly cubical in shape and a little less than a yard on each edge. There was a small opening on one side, containing a single projection which had the appearance of a toggle switch. Several bolt heads of quite conventional appearance were also visible on different parts of the surface.

After allowing his son to look the object over for a few moments, Mr. Wing took a small screwdriver from his pocket and set to work on the bolts, which seemed very loose. Don, lacking tools, tried a few of the projecting heads with his fingers and had little difficulty with them; in two or three minutes, the older man was able to remove several metal plates and expose the interior of the block to view. Don looked, and whistled.

"What is it, Dad? Not an ordinary radio, certainly!"

"No. It seems to be a radio of some sort, however. I don't know what sort of wave it uses, or its range, or its power source—though I have some ideas about the last two. There's nothing to using it; I imagine the makers wanted that to be easy, and there is only the single control switch. I'm not so sure that the interior was meant to be so accessible."

"But where did it come from? Who made it? How did you get hold of it?"

"That's a rather long story, and happened, as I said, before you were born.

"I was just out of college, and had gotten interested in this part of the country; so I decided to see some of it first hand, and eventually found myself here in the hills. I started at Helena, and went on foot up to Flathead, through Glacier Park, west along the border to the Kootenai, and back along the river past Bonner's Ferry into the Cabinets. It wasn't a very exciting jaunt, but I saw a lot and had a pretty good time.

"I was crossing the brook we just followed up here, just after I had gotten under way one morning, when I heard the weirdest racket from up the hill. I really didn't know too much about the neighborhood, and was a bit on the uneasy side; but I had a rifle, and managed to convince myself that I was out to satisfy my curiosity, so I headed up toward the noise.

"When I got out from among the trees, the noise began to sound more and more like spoken language; so I yelled a few words myself, though I couldn't understand a word of it. There was no answer at first— just this tremendous, roaring voice blatting out the strangely regular sounds. Finally, a little way up the hill from here, on a rather open spot, I saw the source; and at almost the same instant the noise stopped.

"Lying out in the open, where it could be seen from any direction, was a thing that looked like a perfectly good submarine torpedo—everyone was familiar with those at the time, as they played a very prominent part in the first World War. Science-fiction had not come into style then, and Heaven knows I wasn't much of a physical scientist, but even so I found it hard to believe that the thing had been carried there. I examined it as thoroughly as I could, and found a few discrepancies in the torpedo theory.

"In the first place, it had neither propellers nor any type of steering fin. It was about twenty feet long and three in diameter, which was reasonable for a torpedo as far as I knew, but the only break in the surface was a section of the side, near what I supposed to be the front, which was open rather like a bomb bay. I looked in, though I didn't take a chance on sticking an arm or my head inside, and saw a chamber that occupied most of the interior of the nose section. It was empty, except for a noticeable smell of burning sulfur.

"I nearly had a heart attack when the thing began talking again, this time in a much lower tone—at any rate I jumped two feet. Then I cussed it out in every language I knew for startling me so. It took me a minute or two to get command of myself, and then I realized that the sounds it was making were rather clumsy imitations of my own words. To make sure, I tried some others, one word at a time; and most of them were repeated with fair accuracy. Whoever was speaking couldn't pronounce 'P' or 'B,' but got on fairly well with the rest.

"Obviously there was either someone trapped in the rear of the torpedo, or it contained a radio and someone was calling from a distance. I doubted the first, because of the tremendous volume behind the original sounds; and presently there was further evidence.

"I had determined to set up camp right there, early as it was. I was going about the business, saying an occasional word to the torpedo and being boomed at in return, when another of the things appeared overhead. It spoke, rather softly, when it was still some distance up—apparently the controllers didn't want to scare me away! It settled beside the first, trailing a thin cloud of blue smoke which I thought at first must have to do with driving rockets. However, it proved to be leaking around the edges of a door similar to that in the first torpedo, and then a big cloud of it puffed out as the door opened. That made me a little cautious, which was just as well—the metal turned out to be hot enough to feel the radiation five feet away. How much hotter it had been before I can't guess. The sulfur smell was strong for a while after the second torpedo landed, but gradually faded out again.

"I had to wait a while before the thing was cool enough to approach with comfort. When I did, I found that the nose compartment this time was not empty. There was an affair rather like a fishing-box inside, with the compartments of one side full of junk and those on the other empty. I finally took a chance on reaching in for it, once it was cool enough to touch.

"When I got it out in the sunlight, I found that the full compartments were covered with little glassy lids, which were latched shut; and there was a tricky connection between the two sides which made it necessary to put something in an empty compartment and close its lid before you could open the corresponding one on the other side. There were only half a dozen spaces, so I fished out some junk of my own—a wad of paper from my notebook, a chunk of granite, a cigarette, some lichen from the rocks around, and so on—and cleaned out the full compartments. One of the things was a lump of platinum and related metals that must have weighed two pounds.

"Right then I settled down to some serious thinking. In the first place, the torpedo came from off this planet. The only space ship I'd ever heard of was the projectile in Jules Verne's story, but people of this planet don't send flying torpedoes with no visible means of propulsion carrying nuggets of what I knew even then was a valuable metal; and if they do, they don't call attention to the practice by broadcasting weird languages loudly enough to be heard a mile away.

"Granting that the torpedo came from outer space, its behavior seemed to indicate only one thing—its senders wanted to trade. At any rate, that was the theory I decided to act on. I put all the junk except the platinum nugget back where it came from, and put the box back in the nose of the torpedo. I don't yet know if they could see me or not—I rather doubt it, for a number of reasons—but the door closed almost at once and the thing took off—straight up, out of sight. I was sorry I hadn't had much of value to stuff in my side of the box. I had thought of sending them a rifle cartridge to indicate we had a mechanical industry, but remembered the temperature at which the thing had arrived and decided against it.

"It took two or three hours for the torpedo to make its round trip. I had set up my tent and rounded up some firewood and water by the time it came back, and I found out my guess was right. This time they had put another platinum nugget in one compartment, leaving the others empty; and I was able to remember what I had put in the corresponding space on the previous visit.

"That about tells the story." Mr. Wing grinned at his son. "I've been swapping cigarettes for platinum and iridium nuggets for about thirty years now—and you can see why I wanted you to study some astronomy!" Don whistled gently.

"I guess I do, at that. But you haven't explained this." He indicated the metal cube on which his father was sitting.

"That came down a little later, grappled to a torpedo, and the original one took off immediately afterwards. I have always supposed they use it to find this spot again. We've sort of fallen into a schedule over the years. I'm never here in the winter any more, and they seem to realize that; but from two to three days after I snap this switch off and on a few times, like this," he demonstrated, "the exchequer gets a shot in the arm."

Don frowned thoughtfully, and was silent for a time.

"I still don't see why you keep it a secret," he said at last. "If the affair is really interplanetary, it's tremendously important."

"That's true, of course. However, if these people wanted contact with mankind in general, they could certainly establish it without any difficulty. It has always seemed to me that their maintaining contact in this fashion was evidence that they did not want their presence generally known; so that if experts began taking their transmitter apart, for example, or sending literature and machinery out to them in an effort to show our state of civilization, they would simply leave."

"That seems a little far-fetched."

"Perhaps; but can you offer a better suggestion why they don't land one of these things in a city? They're paying tremendous prices for darned small quantities of tobacco—and a corner drug store could stock them for years at their rate of consumption.

"Don't get me wrong, son; I certainly appreciate the importance of all this, and want very much to find out all I can about these things and their machines; but I want the investigating done by people whom I can trust to be careful not to upset the apple cart. I wish the whole family were seven or eight years older; we'd have a good research team right here. For the moment, though, you and I—principally you—are going to have to do the investigating, while Rog and Edie do the scouting. I expect they'll sneak over to watch us, of course; Roger's curiosity is starting to keep him awake nights, and he has the makings of a man of action. I'm wondering whether we don't find his tracks or Edie's on the way back—he might have persuaded her to go to town for him. There's nothing more to be done here, unless you want to look this communicator over more closely; we might as well head back, and find out how enterprising the younger generation is."

"There's no hurry, Dad. I'd like to look this thing over for a while. It has some of the earmarks of a short wave transmitter, but there are a lot of things I'd like to get straight."

"Me, too. I've learned a good deal about radios in the last twenty years, but it's a bit beyond me. Of course, I've never dared take off more than the outer casing; there are parts too deeply stowed to be visible, which might be highly informative if we could see them."

"Exactly what I was thinking. There should be some way to look into it—we ought to dig up one of those dentist's mirrors."

"You don't catch me sticking anything made of metal into a gadget that almost certainly uses astronomical voltages."

"Well—I suppose not. We could turn it off first, if we were sure which position of that switch were off. We don't really know whether you're calling them with a short transmission when you move it, or whether you're breaking a continuous one. If they use it for homing, it would be the latter; but we can't be sure."

"Even if we were, turning it off wouldn't be enough. Condensers can hold a nasty bite for a long time."

Don admitted the justice of this point, and spent only a few minutes peering through the openings left by the removal of the plates.

"Most of the inside seems to be blocks of bakelite anyway," he said at last. "I suppose they have everything sealed in for permanence. I wonder how they expect to service it? I guess you're right—we may as well go home until the torpedo comes." He slung the pack that had contained their lunch—or rather, the sandwiches they had eaten en route—over his shoulder, and straightened up. His father nodded in agreement, and they began to retrace their steps down the hillside.

Don was wrapped in thought, and his father forbore to interrupt. He knew how he had reacted to the events he had just described, when he had been very little older than his son was now; also, he had a high opinion of his children's intelligence, and believed firmly in letting them solve problems for themselves as much as was safe. He reflected somewhat ruefully that nothing he could say would be too much help, in any case.

There was no trace of anyone's having followed them at any point on the trail home, though they split up to take opposite sides of the scree they had deliberately crossed on the way out. Neither found this very surprising, for it turned out that Edith had made her scheduled patrols and spent the rest of the day with the younger children, while Roger had gone to town as expected. If he had thought of finding a substitute and following his father, nothing had come of it. Mr. Wing was not sure whether he ought to be pleased or disappointed.

# V.

Laj Drai found his hired schoolteacher beside one of the torpedoes, checking off its contents with loops of one tentacle. The mechanic was listening as he named off the items.

"Magnesium cell; titanium cell; sodium—oh, hello, Drai. Anything going on?"

"Hard to say. You are setting up a research project, I take it?"

"Just checking some hypotheses. I've listed all the elements that would be gaseous under the conditions of Planet Three, and as many compounds as I could find in the Tables. Some are a little doubtful, since I have no pressure data; they might be liquid. Still, if they are there in any quantity, their vapors should be present.

"Then I eliminated as many as possible on theoretical grounds, since I can't test for everything at once."

"Theoretical grounds?"

"Yes. For example, while fluorine is still gaseous under those conditions, it's much too active to be expected in the free state. The same is true of chlorine—which may be liquid—and oxygen. On the other hand, hydrogen seems very likely, along with hydrogen sulfide and other volatile compounds of both those elements. Nitrogen should be present, and the inert gases—though I don't know how I can test for those.

"I've built little cells containing various materials, along with built-in heaters; and I'm going to warm them up one at a time after landing this torpedo and opening it to the atmosphere. Then I'll bring it back and see what the air did to my samples. I have magnesium and titanium, which should detect the nitrogen, and sodium, and a couple of sulfides which should be reduced if there's much hydrogen, and so on. The report may not be complete, but we should learn something."

241

"So I should say, from what little I know about it. Were you planning to send the torpedo out right away?"

"Yes; everything seems to be ready, unless there are complications from your department."

"Nothing much. We were just going to send one out ourselves; our native signalled a short time ago."

"Can you control two torpedoes at once?"

"Yes, easily. It occurs to me, however, that it might be best for you to keep a mile or two away from our homing station, and make your descent when that part of the planet is in darkness. The natives are diurnal, we are sure; and it would be a pity to scare them off if any of your chemical reactions are bright or noisy or smelly."

"Or affect some sense we don't know about. All right, you have a good point. Do you want me to wait until you have finished your trading, or go ahead of you if the chance occurs?"

"I don't see that it matters much. I don't remember whether it will be night or day there when the torpedoes arrive overhead; there's a table for figuring it up in the office, and we'll check before arrival time. I'd say if it was day, we'd go right down while you waited, and if it's night you get first shot."

"All right with me."

"You'll have to control from down here—there's only one unit up in the observatory. It won't matter, since you'll be working blind anyway. I'll go up and tell them that you're operating too—we have a relay unit with detection apparatus circling the planet now, and there's no point in having the observers think the flatlanders are out in space."

"Have you been getting activity from them?"

"Not much. Within the last three or four years we have picked up some radiation suspiciously like radar, but it's all been constant frequency so far. We put quarter-wave coatings of plastic with a half-reflecting film of metal on all the torpedoes, and we haven't had any trouble. They only use a dozen different frequencies, and we're set up for all of them—when they change, we simply use another drone. I suppose they'll start using two or more wave lengths in one area or maybe frequency modulation eventually, and we'll have to get a non-reflective coating. That would be simpler anyway—only it's more expensive. I learned that when I had the *Karella* coated. I wonder how we'll get around it if they learn to pick up infra-red? The torps are enough hotter than the planet to show up like novae, when we happen to start them from the ship just outside the atmosphere."

"Let 'em hang in space until they cool off," Ken and the mechanic replied in chorus. "Or send them all from here, as we've been doing," added the latter. Laj Drai left without further remark.

"That fellow needs a whole scientific college," the mechanic remarked as the door closed. "He's so darned suspicious he'll hire only one man at a time, and usually fires them before long."

"Then I'm not the first?"

"You're the first to get this far. There were a couple of others, and he got the idea they were poking into his business, so I never even found out what ideas they had. I'm no scientist, but I'm curious—let's get this iron cigar into space before he changes his mind about letting it go."

Ken gestured agreement, but hung back as the mechanic cut the test controller into the main outside beam circuit—two multiphase signals could be handled as easily as one on the beam, and both torpedoes would be close enough together so that one beam would suffice. The mechanic's information was interesting; it had never occurred to him that others might have preceded him on this job. In a way, that was good—the others had presumably not been narcotics agents, or Rade would have told him. Therefore he had better protective coloration than he had supposed. Drai might even be getting used to having outsiders connected with his project.

But just what did this mechanic know? After all, he had apparently been around for some time, and Drai was certainly not afraid to talk in his presence. Perhaps he might be worked up into a really effective source of information; on the other hand, it might be dangerous to try—quite conceivably one of his minor duties was keeping a watchful eye on Sallman Ken's behavior. He was a rather taciturn individual, and Ken had not given him much attention so far.

At the moment he was all technician. He was draped over the rack in front of the control board, his tentacles resting on the various toggles and verniers, and a rising hum indicated that the tubes were warming. After a moment, he twisted a vernier knob slightly, and the torpedo on which Ken had been working lifted gently from the cradle. He spoke without turning his eyes backward:

"If you'll go to the far end of the room, I'll run it down there and we can test the microphone and speaker. I know you don't plan to use them, but we might as well have them serviceable."

Ken followed the suggestion, testing first the sound apparatus and then the various recorders and other instruments in the cargo chamber which were intended to tell whether or not any violent chemical reactions took place—photocells and pyrometers, and gas pumps connected to sample flasks and precipitators. Everything appeared in working order and was firmly clamped in place.

Assured of this, the operator guided the little vessel to a tunnel-like air lock in one wall of the room, maneuvered it in, pumped back the air, and drove the torpedo out into the vacuum of Mercury's surface. Without further ado he sent it hurtling away from the planet, its control keyed in with a master achronic beam running from the station to the relay unit near Earth. No further attention would be needed until it approached the planet.

The mechanic rose from in front of the panel, and turned to Ken.

"I'm going to sleep for a while," he said. "I'll be back before arrival time. In case you care, you'll be making the first landing. It takes one and a half revolutions of Planet Three, more or less, to get the torpedo there when the planets are in their present relative positions—we can't use overdrive on the drones—and the signal must have come during the local daytime. I'll see you. Have me paged if you want me for anything."

Ken gave the equivalent of an affirmative nod.

"All right—and thanks. Your name is Allmer, isn't it?"

"Right—Feth Allmer." Without further speech the mechanic disappeared through the door, moving with the fluid ease of a person well accustomed to Mercury's feeble gravity, and leaving Sallman Ken in a very thoughtful mood behind him.

Almost unconsciously the investigator settled onto the rack deserted by Allmer, and stared blankly at the indicators in front of him. One of his troubles, he reflected ruefully, was his tendency to get interested in two problems at once. In one way, that might be good, of course; the genuine absorption in the problem of Planet Three was the best possible guard against suspicion of his other job; but it didn't help him to concentrate on that other. For hours now he had thought of practically nothing but his test project, until Allmer's parting remarks had jarred him back to duty.

He had assumed Allmer was a competent technician, but somehow he had not expected the acuity the elderly fellow had just displayed. Ken himself had missed the implication of Drai's statement concerning the habits of the natives of the third planet; apparently Drai had not even thought of doing his own reasoning.

But could he be that stupid? He, unlike Ken, knew the distances involved in a flight to that world, and the speed of the torpedoes; he had, on his own word, been trading here for years. What purpose could he have in trying to appear more stupid than he really was?

One possibility certainly existed. Ken might already be under suspicion, and facing a conspiracy to make him betray himself by overconfidence. Still, why in that case had the mechanic betrayed his own intelligence? Perhaps he was building himself up as a possible confidant, in case Ken were to grow communicative. If that were so, Feth was his greatest danger, since he was most in Ken's company and in best position to serve as a spy. On the other hand, the fellow might be completely innocent even if the group as a whole were engaged in smuggling, and his recent words might have been motivated by a sincere desire to be helpful. There seemed no way of telling at the moment which of these possibilities was the more likely; Ken gave the problem up for the moment as insoluble with the data on hand.

The other problem was demanding his attention, anyway. Some of the indicators on the board in front of him were fluctuating. He had learned the panel fairly well in the last day or two, and was able to interpret the readings himself. It seemed, he noted, that pressure and temperature were both going down in the cargo chamber of the projectile. Well, that was reasonable. There were no heaters working, and the pressure would naturally drop as the gas cooled. Then it occurred to him that the temperature of Planet Three was low enough to freeze sulfur, and his test units would be covered with a crust of the stuff. Something should be done about that.

As a matter of fact, most of the pressure drop was due to leakage; the cargo door had cooled and contracted sufficiently to let air escape slowly around its edges. Ken, however, did not think of that; he found the appropriate switch and tripped it, watching the pressure drop instantly to zero as the door opened. The temperature was almost unaffected—if anything, it dropped more slowly, for the recording pyrometers were now insulated by a vacuum and the expansion of the gaseous sulfur into empty space had had no cooling effect to speak of. A touch on some of the switches which were designed to heat the test substances showed that the little furnaces were still in working order, and after a moment's thought Ken allowed the magnesium and titanium specimens to come up to melting temperature. Then, sure that they were as free of contaminating gases as could be managed, he watched the recorders as the samples cooled again. Through all this, the torpedo hurtled on, unaffected by the extra drain on its power.

For some minutes Ken continued to wait, one eye roving over the dials and the other glancing casually about the great room; but finally he decided that Allmer had picked a good time to go off duty. He did not feel tired himself, but gradually he became convinced that there must be something a little more constructive to do. He suspected that, even if there were to be any drugs around the station, they would not have arrived yet, so there was no use making a search for them; but preparations might be made to see just what came back in the other torpedo.

As a first step, it might be well to go up to the observatory to find out just who was guiding that missile. If it were Drai himself, it would be a point in favor of Rade; if not, it would be another person from whom information might be obtained. There seemed little doubt that no one would be allowed to run the trading torpedo who did not know exactly what was being obtained on the third planet—the Planet of Ice, as Ken was coming to think of it (not that he thought of ice as a substance; he bad never seen the material and would have thought of it as hydrogen oxide in any case. Planet of Solid Sulfur comes closer to the way he would have expressed the thought).

Ken was basing his supposition on his memory of how Drai had refrained from naming the substance obtained from the planet; and, determined to find at least one small brick of data to add to his edifice of information, the investigator headed up the spiral ramp toward the observatory at the station's highest level. No one attempted to stop him on the way, though he met a couple of workers who flipped tentacles in casual recognition. The door of the observatory was not locked, as a trial push showed, and he entered, still without opposition. He was braced for a prompt request to depart, and was a little surprised when nothing at all was said. A moment later, when his eyes had become accustomed to the dimness of the big room, he realized to his chagrin that no one was there.

"No business secrets loose so far," he muttered.

He was about to return the way he had come, when it occurred to him that he might as well make sure of that fact. There were not many places where paper work of any sort could be kept, at least at first glance; and these he rapidly covered. They were mostly cabinets built under instrument panels, and seemed to contain nothing but tables of the motions of the planets of this system. These seemed rather valueless; their most probable use would be in navigation, and Ken could not imagine anyone's wanting to navigate anywhere in this system except to the world of Ice. They could also be used to direct the instruments, if anyone wanted to look at the planets in question; but that seemed even less helpful.

Under the beam setting controls was a small drawer which also contained two sets of numbers—again, spatial coordinates; but this time Ken froze to attention as he realized that one set at least did not refer to planets—they contained no cyclic term. The set was short, consisting of six groups of numbers containing from six to ten digits each; but he *recognized* them. The first identified by spectrum a beacon star; the next three were direction cosines, giving the three-dimensional bearing to another sun; the fifth gave a distance. Normally he might not have recognized or remembered the lengthy figures; but those were the coordinates of the blazing A-class sun which warmed Sarr, his home planet. The final number was another range; and beyond question it represented the distance from the present point of observation to the listed star. Ken knew enough of the standard navigational notations to be sure of that.

The other set of numbers, then, must give the direction of the same sun relative to some local set of coordinates; and not only was he ignorant of the coordinates, but the numbers were too long to remember. To copy them would be suicide, if anything more than commercial secrecy were involved. For long minutes Sallman Ken stood frozen in thought; then, abruptly, he slipped the sheet back into the drawer, closed the latter, and as quickly as was compatible with caution left the observatory. Since the information was there, it would not do for anyone to get the idea he had been there for any great length of time. It would be better if no one knew he had been there at all, but he had been seen on the way up the ramp. He proceeded to get back to his own quarters and assume an attitude of repose, though his mind still raced furiously.

He knew his distance from home. Evidently the twenty-two days of the journey to this system had not been spent in straight-line flight; the distance was only two hundred twelve parsecs. Score one for Rade; that would be an expensive business precaution, but a normal criminal one.

The direction home *from* this system he did not know. It did not matter too much anyway; what the Narcotics Bureau would want would be the opposite direction, on Galactic coordinates, and there would be no mathematical connection between the two except a purely arbitrary formula which would be harder to memorize than the direction itself.

Of course, the beacon listed in the stellar coordinates was probably visible from here; but could he recognize it with any certainty without instruments? The instruments were available, of course, but it might not be wise to be caught using them. No, orientation was definitely the last job to be accomplished in his present location.

At any rate, one fact had been learned and one point of probability had been added to the Rade theory. Sallman Ken decided that made a good day's work, and allowed himself to relax on the strength of it.

# VI.

Nearly three of Sarr's thirteen-hour days passed uneventfully before the relay station circling Earth picked up the approaching torpedoes. As Feth Allmer had predicted—and Laj Drai had confirmed, after checking with his tables—the signals from the planted homing unit were coming from the dark side of the planet. Drai phoned down from the observatory to the shop, where Ken and Allmer were engaged in decelerating their missile.

"You may as well drop straight down as soon as you swing around to the dark side," he said. "You will pick up the beacon if you spiral in, keeping between forty and fifty-five degrees above the plane of the planet's orbit, measured from the planet's center. The beam can be picked up by your torpedo more than forty diameters out, so you can't possibly miss it. You'd better ride the beam down automatically until you're into atmosphere, then go manual and move off a couple of miles if you plan to go all the way to the ground. If the natives are camping near the beam transmitter, it would be a pity to touch off your chemicals right in their midst."

"True enough," Ken replied. "Feth is swinging around into the shadow now, still about five diameters out. I wish there were a vision transmitter in that machine. Some time I'm going down close enough to use a telescope, unless someone builds a TV that will stand winter weather."

"You'll get worse than frostbite," Drai responded sincerely. "The time you were really looking at that world, you didn't seem quite so anxious to get close to it."

"I hadn't gotten curious then," responded Ken.

The conversation lapsed for a while, as Feth Allmer slowly spun the verniers controlling the direction of thrust from the torpedo's drivers. The machine was, as Ken had said, cutting around into the shadow of the big planet, still with a relative speed of several miles per second to overcome.

Allmer was navigating with the aid of a response-timer and directional loop in the relay station, whose readings were being reproduced on his own board; the torpedo was still too far from Earth for its reflection altimeter to be effective. For some minutes Ken watched silently, interpreting as best he could the motions of the flickering needles and deft tentacles. A grunt of satisfaction from the operator finally told him more clearly than the instruments that the beam had been reached; a snaky arm promptly twisted one of the verniers as far as it would go.

"I don't see why they couldn't power these things for decent acceleration," Feth's voice came in an undertone. "How much do you want to bet that we don't run all the way through the beam before I can match the planet's rotation? With nine-tenths of their space free for drivers and accumulators, you'd think they could pile up speed even without overdrive. These cheap—" his voice trailed off again. Ken made no reply, not being sure whether one was expected. Anyway, Allmer was too bright for his utterances to be spontaneous, and any answer should be carefully considered purely from motives of caution.

Apparently the mechanic had been unduly pessimistic; for in a matter of minutes he had succeeded in fighting the torpedo into a vertical descent. Even Ken was able to read this from the indicators; and before long the reflection altimeter began to register. This device was effective at a distance equal to Sarr's diameter—a trifle over six thousand miles—and Ken settled himself beside the operator as soon as he noted its reaction. There was not far to go.

His own particular bank of instruments, installed on a makeshift panel of their own by Allmer, were still idle. The pressures indicated zero, and the temperatures were low—even the sodium had frozen, apparently. There had been little change for many hours—apparently the whole projectile was nearly in radiative equilibrium with the distant sun. Ken watched tensely as the altimeter reading dropped, wondering slightly whether atmosphere would first make itself apparent through temperature or pressure readings.

As a matter of fact, he did not find out. Feth reported pressure first, before any of Ken's indicators had responded; and the investigator remembered that the door was shut. It had leaked before, of course, but that had been under a considerably greater pressure differential; apparently the space around the door was fairly tight, even at the temperature now indicated.

"Open the cargo door, please," Ken responded to the report. "We might as well find out if anything is going to react spontaneously."

"Just a minute; I'm still descending pretty fast. If the air is very dense, I could tear the doors off at this speed."

"Can't you decelerate faster?"

"Yes, now. Just a moment. I didn't want to take all night on the drop, but there's only about twenty miles to go now. You're the boss from here in." The needle of the altimeter obediently slowed in its march around the dial. Ken began warming up the titanium sample—it had the highest melting point of all. In addition, he was reasonably sure that there would be free nitrogen in the atmosphere; and at least one of the tests ought to work.

At five miles above the ground, the little furnace was glowing white hot, judging from the amount of light striking the photocell inside the nose compartment. Atmospheric pressure was quite measurable, though far from sufficient from the Sarrian point of view, if the Bourdon gauge could be trusted; and Feth claimed to have worked out a correction table by calibrating several of them on the dark side of Planet One.

"Can you hold it at this height for a while?" Ken asked. "I'm going to let this titanium act up here, if I possibly can. There's atmosphere, and we're high enough not to be visible, I should think." Allmer gestured to the reading of the photocell.

"The door is open, and that furnace is shining pretty brightly. You'd do better to shut the door, only that would keep air pretty well out. A light like that so far from the ground must show for scores of miles."

"I never thought of that." Ken was a trifle startled. He thought for a moment, then, "Well, let's close the door anyway. We have a pressure reading. If that drops, we'll know that some sort of action is taking place."

"True enough." Allmer snapped the toggle closing the door and waited silently while Ken manipulated his controls. Deprived of the opening through which a good deal of heat had been radiating, the compartment temperature began to climb. By rights, the pressure should have done the same; but to Ken's intense satisfaction, it did not—it fell, instead. At his request, the door was opened for an instant and promptly closed again; results were consistent. The pressure popped back to its former value, then fell off once more. Apparently the titanium was combining with some gaseous component of the surrounding atmosphere, though not violently enough for the reaction to be called combustion.

"If you're far enough to one side of the beam, let's go down to the surface," the investigator finally said. "I'd like to find out what percentage of the air will react this way, and for any sort of accuracy I'll need all the atmospheric pressure I can get to start with."

Feth Allmer gave the equivalent of a nod.

"We're a couple of miles to one side," he said. "I can drop straight down whenever you want. Do you want the door open or closed?"

"Closed. I'll let the sample cool a little, so we can get normal pressure after landing without using it all up. Then I'll warm it up again, and see how much of the air in the compartment is used up." Feth gestured agreement, and a faint whistling became audible as the torpedo began to fall without power—like the others, it had speaker and sound pickups, which Allmer had not bothered to remove. Four miles—three—two—one—with deceptive casualness, the mechanic checked the plunge with a reading of one hundred fifty feet on the altimeter, and eased it very cautiously downward. As he did so, he gestured with one tentacle at another dial; and Ken, after a moment, understood. The projectile was already below the level of the homing station.

"I suppose the transmitter is on a mountain, and we're letting down into a valley," Feth elaborated, without taking his eyes from his work.

"Reasonable enough—this was always supposed to be a rough section of the planet," agreed Ken. "It's good—there's that much less chance of being visible from a distance. What's the matter—aren't you down, after all?"

The altimeter had reached zero, but nothing had checked the descent. Faint rustlings had become audible in the last few seconds, and now these were supplemented by louder snappings and cracklings. Descent ceased for a moment. Apparently an obstacle sufficient to reflect radar waves and take the machine's weight had been encountered; but when a little downward drive was applied, the crackling progress continued for some distance. Finally, however, it ceased—noise and motion alike—even when Allmer doubled and quadrupled the power for several seconds. He opened his drive switches and turned to Ken with a gesture equivalent to a shrug.

"We seem to be down, though I can't guarantee it's ground as we know it. It seems to be as low as we can get, though. There's the door switch, in case you didn't know. You're on your own, unless you don't mind my hanging around to watch. I suppose the boss will be here soon, too; he should have his machine in an orbit by this time."

"Sure—stick around. I'll be glad to have you. Maybe we'll have to move the thing around, for all I can tell at the moment." He had opened the door as he spoke, and watched with interest as the pressure gauge snapped up to a value about two thirds of Sarr normal. At the same instant, the temperature dial of the still hot titanium furnace began to rise spontaneously—apparently the greater atmospheric density was more than able to offset the slight amount of cooling that had taken place; the metal was actually burning. Ken hastily shut the door.

The temperature continued to rise a short distance, while the light intensity in the cargo compartment of the torpedo held at a value that would have been intense even to eyes accustomed to Sarr's fervent sun. The most interesting information, however, came from the pressure gauge; and it was on this that Ken kept his attention glued.

For perhaps twenty seconds the reaction continued unabated; then it began to die out, and in ten more the temperature began once more to drop. The reason was evident; pressure had dropped to less than two percent of its former value. There was literally nothing left to carry on the reaction.

Ken emitted the booming drone from his sound-diaphragm that was the Sarrian equivalent of a whistle of surprise.

"I knew molten titanium would react to completion in our atmosphere, but I didn't think it would possibly do it here. I guess I was wrong—I was rather expecting a mixture of compounds, whose heats of formation would prevent any such reaction. Still, I suppose at this planet's temperature, they wouldn't have to be very stable from our point of view. . ." his voice trailed off.

"Means nothing to me, but it certainly burned," Feth Allmer remarked. "How about your other samples? Are you going to run them off right away, or wait for things to cool down again to planet-normal?" Another dial caught Ken's eye before he could answer.

"Hey—who lit the sodium?" he asked, heedless of Allmer's query. "It's cooling now, but it must have been burning, too, for a while when there was air."

"Let more in and see." The toggle snapped over, and there was a distinct popping sound as air rushed into the near-vacuum. The sodium continued to cool.

"Maybe a spark from the titanium pot lighted it up." Without answering, Ken closed the door once more and began to warm up the sodium container. Apparently Feth's suggestion was not too far from the mark; very little additional heat was needed to ignite the metal. This time the reaction stopped after pressure had dropped about a sixth. Then the door was opened again, and another touch of artificial heat caused the reaction to resume. This time it continued, presumably, until the sodium was consumed.

"I want enough material to work on when we get it back," Ken explained. "I'm not the Galaxy's best analytical chemist."

The crucible of carbon dust gave decidedly peculiar results. *Something* certainly happened, for the material not only maintained but even increased its temperature for some time after the heating current was cut off; but there was no evidence either of consumption or production of gas in the closed chamber. Both Ken and Feth were slightly startled. The former, in response to the mechanic's quizzical expression, admitted the fact was probably significant but could offer no explanation.

Samples of iron, tin, lead, and gold followed in due course. None of these seemed greatly affected by the peculiar atmosphere at any temperature, with the possible exception of the iron; there the pressure drop was too small to be certain, since in each of these cases the heating had caused an increase in pressure which had to be allowed for. Magnesium behaved remarkably like sodium, except that it burned even more brightly than the titanium.

Here again Ken decided to finish off the metal by re-lighting it with the door open; and here the testing program received a sudden interruption.

Both Sarrians were perfectly aware that with the door open a beam of light must be stabbing out into the darkness. Both had ceased to worry about the fact; it had been equally true, though perhaps the radiance was fainter, with the blazing sodium and almost as much so when the sheer heat of the samples of iron and gold had been exposed. They had completely ceased to worry about being seen; a full hour had already passed since they had landed the torpedo, owing to the cooling periods necessary between tests, and there had been no sign that any attention had been attracted. Ken should have remembered the difficulty that had been encountered in reaching the ground.

The possibility was brought back to their attention with the re-lighting of the magnesium sample. As the photocell reported the reestablishment of combustion, a shrill sound erupted from the speaker above the control board and echoed through the ship. Neither had to be told what it was; both had heard the recordings of the voice of the Third Planet native who had found the original torpedo.

For an instant both remained frozen on their racks, exploring mentally the possibilities of the situation. Feth made a tentative gesture toward the power switches, only to be checked by an imperious snap of Ken's tentacles.

"Wait! Is our speaker on?" The words were whispered.

"Yes." Feth pulled a microphone down to chest level and retreated a step. He wanted no part in what Ken seemed about to do. Sallman himself, however, had once more become completely absorbed in the mystery of the World of Ice, to the exclusion of all other matters; he saw no reason for leaving the site where his activities had been discovered. it did not even occur to him not to answer the native who appeared to have made the discovery. With his speaking diaphragm close to the microphone, he emulated the "boss" of so many years before, and tried to imitate the sounds coming from the speaker.

The result was utter silence.

At first neither listener worried; the native would naturally be surprised. Gradually, however, an expression of mild anxiety began to appear on Ken's features, while an "I-told-you-so" air became manifest about Feth.

"You've scared him away," the latter finally said. "If his tribe stampedes with him, Drai won't be very happy about it."

A faint crackling which had preceded the alien's call, and which his concentration of chemical problems had prevented reaching Ken's conscious mind, suddenly ballooned into recollection, and he snatched at the straw.

"But we heard him coming—the same sort of noise the torpedo made landing—and we haven't heard him leave. He must still be waiting."

"Heard him coming? Oh—that? How do you know that's what it was? Neither of us was paying any attention."

"What else could it have been?" This was a decidedly unfair question, to which Feth attempted no direct answer. He simply countered with another.

"What's he waiting for, then?" Fate was unkind to him; Ken was spared the necessity of answering. The human voice came again, less shrill this time; history seemed to be repeating itself. Ken listened intently; Feth seemed to have forgotten his intention of dissociating himself from the proceedings and was crowded as close as the detective to the speaker. The voice went on, in short bursts which required little imagination to interpret as questions. Not a word was understandable, though both thought they recognized the human "no" on several occasions. Certainly the creature did not utter any of the names that the Sarrians had come to associate with trade items—Feth, who knew them all, was writing them on a scrap of paper. Ken finally grew impatient, took the list from the mechanic, and began to pronounce them as well as he could, pausing after each. "Iridium—Flatinum—Gold—Osmium—"

"Gold!" the unseen speaker cut in.

"Gold!" responded Ken intelligently, into the microphone, and "which one is that?" in a hasty aside to Feth.

The mechanic told him, also in a whisper. "There's a sample in the torpedo. We can't trade it off—I want to analyze it for traces of corrosion. Anyway it was melted a little while ago, and he'll never get it out of the crucible. What's the name for the stuff you get from them?"

"Tofacco," Feth answered without thinking—but he started thinking immediately afterward. He remembered Drai's promise of the fate of anyone who gave Ken information about "the stuff" obtained from Earth, and knew rather better than Sallman just how jocular Laj was likely to be. The memory made him itch, as though his hide were already coming loose. He wondered how he could keep news of his slip from reaching the higher levels, but had no time to get a really constructive idea. The speaker interrupted him again.

If the previous calls had been loud, this was explosive. The creature must have had his vocal apparatus within inches of the torpedo's microphone, and been using full voice power to boot. The roar echoed for seconds through the shop and almost drowned out the clanking which followed—a sound which suggested something hard striking the hull of the torpedo. The native, for some reason, seemed to have become wildly excited.

At almost the same instant, Ken also gave an exclamation. The thermometer dial for the gold sample had ceased to register.

"The blasted savage is stealing my sample!" he howled, and snapped over the switch closing the cargo door. The switch moved, but the door apparently didn't—at least, it failed to indicate "locked." There was no way of telling whether or not it had stopped at some partly-closed position.

The native was still jabbering—more than ever, if that were possible. Ken switched back to "open" position, waited a moment, and tried to close again. This time it worked. The Sarrians wondered whether the relatively feeble motor which closed the portal had been able to cause any injury. There seemed little doubt about the cause of the first failure; if there had been any, the noise would have removed it.

"I don't think he was trying to steal," Feth said mildly. "After all, you repeated the name of the stuff more than once. He probably thought you were offering it to him."

"I suppose you may be right." Ken turned back to the microphone. "I'll try to make clear that it's market day, not a wedding feast." He gave a chirruping whistle, then "Tofacco! tofacco! Gold—tofacco!" Feth shriveled internally. If he could only learn to keep his big diaphragm frozen—.

"Tofacco! Gold—tofacco! I wonder whether that will mean anything to him?" Ken turned a little away from the microphone. "This may not be one of the creatures you've been trading with—after all, we're not in the usual place."

"That's not the principal question!" Feth's tentacles coiled tightly around his torso, as though he were expecting a thunderbolt to strike somewhere in the neighborhood. The voice which had made the last statement was that of Laj Drai.

# VII.

Roger Wing, at thirteen years of age, was far from stupid. He had very little doubt where his father and brother had been, and he found the fact of considerable interest. A few minutes' talk with Edie gave him a fairly accurate idea of how long they had been gone; and within ten minutes of the time he and his mother returned from Clark Fork, he had sharply modified his older ideas about the location of the "secret mine." Hitherto, his father had always been away several days on his visits to it.

"You know, Edie, that mine can't be more than eight or ten miles from here, at the outside." The two were feeding the horses, and Roger had made sure the younger children were occupied elsewhere. "I talked to Don for about two minutes, and I know darned well Dad was showing him the mine. I'm going to see it, too, before the summer's out. I'll take bets on it."

"Do you think you ought to? After all, if Dad wanted us to know, he'd tell us."

"I don't care. I have a right to know anything I can find out. Besides, we can do a better job of scouting if we know the place we're supposed to be protecting."

"Well—maybe."

"Besides, you know Dad sometimes sets things up just so we'll find things out for ourselves. After it's all over he just says that's what we have brains for. Remember he never actually *said* we weren't to go looking for the mine—he just said he'd tell us when the time came. How about that?"

"Well—maybe. What are you going to do about it? If you try to follow Dad you'll be picked up like a dime in a schoolroom."

"That's what you think. Anyway, I'm not going to follow him. I'll lead him. I'll go out the first thing tomorrow morning and look for any traces they may have left. Then the next time they go, I'll be waiting for them at the farthest trace I could find, and go on from there. That'll work, for sure!"

"Who does the patrolling?"

"Oh, we both do, same as before. This won't take long. Anyway, like I said, since I'll be watching the trail they take, it'll be even better than the regular patrol. Don't you think?" Edie looked a little dubious as she latched the door of the feed bin.

"You'll probably get away with it, but I bet you'll have to talk fast," was her verdict as they headed for the house.

Twenty-four hours later Roger was wondering whether any excuses would be needed at all. Things had not gone according to his sweepingly simple forecast.

In the first place, he had not had time to check any trail his father and Don might have left; for the two started out at daybreak the next morning. They did not follow the previous day's route, but the one Mr. Wing had always taken in years past—the admittedly zigzag path specifically designed to permit his scouts to take short cuts to warn him, in the event that anyone followed. Roger and Edith were given stations which were to be watched for one hour after the two men had passed; each was then to intercept the trail and make a report, whether or not anyone had been seen. Roger looked suspiciously at his sister for an instant when those orders were received, but decided she would never have told his plans. His father was simply one jump ahead, as usual.

A good fraction of the morning had passed by the time he had made his report, and watched his father and brother disappear to the north. This was not the direction they had gone the day before, according to Edith; now the question was whether or not they had bothered to lay a false trail on that occasion, too. The only way to settle that appeared to be a straightforward search for traces. That was not too hopeless; as Roger had said while telling his father about the new patrol arrangements, there were places practically impossible to cross without leaving some sort of track, and the mere act of avoiding all those places would narrow down considerably the routes a person could take.

In spite of this, the boy had decided by dinner time that either he knew less about tracking than he had supposed or else the two he sought had spent the day in the attic. Certainly he had found nothing to which he could point with confidence as being evidence of their passage.

After the meal he had abandoned that line of research, and simply headed eastward. His sister had said they had taken this direction, and there was the remote chance that they might have abandoned precautions just that once. He traveled without pause for nearly half the afternoon, following what seemed to be natural trails, and finally stopped some eight miles from home.

He found himself in a valley, its center marked as usual by a noisy brook. The hills on either side were high, though by no means as high as some of their neighbors—six to seven thousand feet was a common height in this part of the range. He had not been here before, either alone or with his father, but still felt he had a good idea of his location. His principal worry was the fact that he had as yet seen no sign of his father or brother.

His intention was to work back toward the house from this point, zigzagging to cover as much territory as possible before dark. The first zig, he decided, should take him straight up the side of the hill to the south, thus crossing any possible trails cutting around this side of the mountain. After reaching the top, he could decide whether to go down the other side at once, or head west a short distance before sweeping back to the north. As it turned out, he never had to make that decision.

Roger Wing was not, of course, as competent a tracker as he liked to believe. As a matter of fact, he had crossed the trail he was so diligently seeking four times since leaving the house. His present location was at the foot of the hill bearing the open slope which the "miners" had crossed the day before, and within a mile of the Sarrian homing station. The course he now took uphill would have led him within a few rods of the transmitter.

However, he didn't get that far. Donald had been perfectly correct in concluding that no one could cross that slope of loose rock without leaving traces. Roger failed to recognize the marks left by the two on the way out, but he did find where his brother had forced his way through an unusually thick patch of brush at the top of the scree on the way back. It was carelessness on the older boy's part, of course; his attention at the time had been mainly taken up with the search for tracks left by the possible followers, and he had paid no attention to those he himself was leaving. While the broken bushes gave Roger no clue to the traveller's identity, they indicated his direction very clearly; and the boy promptly turned westward. Had he stopped to think, it would have occurred to him that a trail in this direction hardly jibed with the assumption that his father and brother were going straight to the "mine"; but he was not thinking at the moment. He was tracking, as he would have told anyone who might have asked.

Once out of the patch of brush, the trail was neither more nor less obvious than it had been all along; but Roger was able to follow it. Probably the assurance that there was a trail to follow had something to do with that. He still did not know whether the traces had been left by his father, his brother, or both. He also failed to recognize the point where the two had come together after covering both sides of the scree. He simply went on, picking out the occasional scuff in the carpet of fir needles or snapped twigs where the bushes were thicker. He descended the west side of the hill, after following it around from the point where the first traces had appeared. He crossed the narrow valley on this side, leaping the inevitable brook with little difficulty. Here he found the only assurance that he was actually following two people, in the indentations where they had landed on the bank after a similar leap. The marks were just dents, for the needles did not retain any definite shoe patterns, but there were four of them. They were in two pairs, one of each deeper than its fellow, as though the jumper had taken the shock of landing principally on one foot.

Up the side of the next hill the boy went. It was darker now under the trees, for the sun was already concealed by the peak ahead of him; and presently he began to wonder whether he were really on the right trail. He stopped, looking about, and saw first to one side and then the other marks of the sort he had been following. He could not, he found, convince himself that those ahead of him were the right ones.

He tried to go on, then hesitated again. Then he began to backtrack— and reached the brook many yards from the spot at which he had jumped it. He spent some minutes searching for the marks, and when he had found them realized that he had not even followed his own back trail with any accuracy.

He should, of course, have headed for home right then. Equally, of course, he did nothing of the sort. While the gloom on the mountain's eastward face grew ever deeper, he cast about for tracks. Every few minutes he found something, and spent long seconds over it before deciding to make sure—and then he always found something else. Gradually he worked his way up the mountain side, finally reaching open rock; and after deep thought, he moved around to the other side where it was lighter, and resumed his search. After all, the men had been heading westward.

He had crossed another valley—this time its central watercourse was dry, and there was no sign of anyone's jumping over—and was near the top of the unusually low hill on its farther side when he finally realized the time. He had been searching with a single-mindedness which had prevented even hunger from forcing itself on his attention. The sheer impossibility of seeing details on the shadowed ground was all that finally compelled him to consider other matters. He had no flashlight, as he had not contemplated remaining out this late. Worse, he had neither food, water, nor a blanket. The first two were serious omissions, or would be if his father heard of his venturing any distance into the woods without them.

It was quite suddenly borne in upon Roger Wing, as he saw the first stars glimmering in the deepening blue between the tree tops, that he was not another Daniel Boone or Kit Carson. He was a thirteen-year-old boy whose carelessness had gotten him into a situation that was certainly going to be uncomfortable and might even be serious.

Though rash, Roger was not stupid. His first action upon realizing the situation was not a wild break for home. Instead he sensibly stood where he was and proceeded to plan a course of action.

He was certainly going to be cold that night. There was no help for that, though a shelter of fir branches would make some difference. Also, there was no food, or at least none that he would be able to find in the dark. Water, however, should be findable; and, after all, it was the greatest necessity. Remembering that the valley he had just crossed lacked a stream, the boy started on again over the low top in front of him and began to pick his way down the other side. He was forced to rely almost entirely on touch before he reached the bottom, for the lingering twilight made little impression on the gloom beneath the firs. He found a brook, as he had hoped, partly by sound and partly by almost falling over the bank.

He did have a knife, and with this he cut enough fir branches to make a bed near the stream, and to lean against a fallen log beside it as a crude roof—he knew that anything at all to break air circulation immediately over his body would be a help. He then drank, loosened his belt, and crawled under the rude shelter. All things considered, he was not too long in going to sleep.

He was a healthy youngster, and the night was not particularly cold. He slept soundly enough so that the crackling and crashing of branches in the forest roof failed to awaken him, and even the louder crunching as Ken's torpedo settled through the underbrush forty yards away only caused him to mutter sleepily and turn over.

But he was awakened at last, by the stimulus which sends any forest resident into furious activity. The cargo door of the torpedo faced the boy's shelter. The light from burning sodium and glowing gold and iron did not disturb him—perhaps they only gave him bad dreams, or perhaps he was facing the other way at the time. The blazing radiance of the burning magnesium, however, blasted directly onto his closed eyelids, and enough of it got through to ring an alarm. He was on his feet yelling "Fire," before he was fully awake.

He had seen the aftermath of more than one forest fire—there had been a seventy-five-hundred-acre blaze the summer before north of

Bonner's Ferry, and a smaller but much closer one near Troy. He knew what such a catastrophe meant for life in its path, and for several seconds was completely panic-stricken. He even made a leap away from the direction of the radiance, and was brought to his senses by the shock of falling over the tree trunk beside which he had been sleeping.

Coming to his feet more slowly, he realized that the light was not the flickering, ruddy glow of wood flames, that there was none of the crackling roar he had heard described more than once, and that there was no smell of smoke. He had never seen magnesium burn, but the mere fact that this was not an ordinary forest fire allowed his curiosity to come once more into the foreground.

The light was sufficient to permit him to clear the little stream without difficulty, and in a matter of seconds he had crashed through the underbrush to its source, calling as he went, "Hello! Who's that? What's that light?"

The booming grumble of Sallman Ken's answer startled him out of his wits. The drumlike speaking diaphragm on the Sarrian torso can be made to imitate most human speech sounds, but there is a distortion that is readily apparent to any human ear; and the attempt to imitate his words in those weird tones sent prickling chills down the boy's spine. The fact that he *could* recognize his own words in the booming utterance made it, if anything, rather worse.

He stopped two yards from the torpedo, wondering. The blue-white glare from the rectangular opening had died away abruptly as he approached, and had been replaced by a fading yellow-white glow as the crucible which had contained the magnesium slowly cooled. He could just see into the door. The chamber beyond seemed to occupy most of the interior of that end of the structure, as nearly as he could tell from his inadequate view of the outside, and its floor was covered with roughly cylindrical objects a trifle larger than his fist. One of these was the source of the white-hot glow, and at least two others still radiated a dull red. He had noticed only this much when Ken began to go through his precious-metals list.

Roger knew, of course, what platinum and iridium were, even when the former suffered from the peculiarities of the Sarrian vocal apparatus; but like many other human beings, it was the mention of gold that really excited him. He repeated the word instantly.

"Gold!"

"Gold." The booming voice from the torpedo responded, and Roger found the courage to approach the still radiant doorway, and look in. As he had guessed, the little cylindrical crucibles were everywhere. The chamber was covered with white dust, the oxides of titanium and magnesium which had sprayed from the containers during the energetic reactions which had produced them. Tiny yellowish globules of sodium peroxide were spread almost as widely. A noticeable wave of heat could still be felt coming from the chamber along with a faint sulfurous smell, but when Roger laid a cautious hand in the dust of its floor the temperature proved to be bearable. He saw almost instantly what he supposed the hidden speaker had been talking about—the gold which had already solidified in its small container. The light was bright enough for him to recognize it, particularly since there was nothing else of even approximately the same color in the chamber.

The boy acted instantly, but with more forethought than might have been expected. A dead branch which he picked up as he approached was put to use—the door of the compartment reminded him too much of a trap, and he propped it open. Then he made a grab for the pot of gold.

He did not see the wires which connected its heater to the power source of the torpedo. After touching the crucible, he did not even look for them, though they were the only reason he did not succeed in getting the container out. He had time for one good tug before the fact that the metal had only recently been melted made itself felt.

Roger, his face almost inside the compartment, yelled even more whole-heartedly than he had before, released the crucible, delivered a furious kick on the hull of the torpedo, and danced about, holding his scorched hand and hurling abuse at the unseen beings who had been responsible for the injury. He did not notice the stick which he had used as a prop suddenly snap as the door started to close, or the thud as the portal jammed against the fragments of wood. The sudden cutting off of nearly all the light, however, did catch his attention, and he saw what had happened when the door opened again. Without quite knowing why he did so, he swept the pieces out of the way with his uninjured hand, and a moment later he was left in darkness as the door closed completely. He had an uneasy idea that he was being watched.

Again the voice boomed out. He recognized the word "gold" again, but the syllables which alternated with it were too much distorted for him to understand. He had, after all, no tobacco on his person, and there certainly was none in the torpedo, so that there was nothing to bring the substance to mind. He made no attempt to imitate the alien-sounding word, and after a moment the utterance ceased.

It was replaced by fainter sounds, which somehow did not seem to be directed at him, although they had the complexity of speech. Roger would not, of course, have analyzed them in just that way, but he got the distinct impression that they represented a conversation he could not understand.

This lasted for what seemed to the boy a long time; then the earlier refrain broke out again. "Gold—tofacco—gold—tofacco!" Eventually it got on even Roger's nerves, and he yelled at the dark hulk.

"I don't know what you're saying, darn you! I'm darned if I'll touch your gold again, and I don't know what the other words are. Shut up!" He kicked the hull again, to emphasize his feelings, and was rather startled when the voice fell silent. He backed away a little farther, wondering what this presaged. It was well he did.

An instant later, without preliminary sound, the dark shape of the torpedo lunged upward, crashed through the overhanging branches, and vanished into the black sky with a whistle of protesting air. For minutes the boy stood where he was, gazing up through the gap smashed in the limbs; but nothing rewarded his efforts except the stars.

Roger Wing got very little sleep that night, and the fact that he got his feet wet finding his shelter was only partly responsible.

# VIII.

"No, that's not the principal question." Laj Drai repeated the statement rather thoughtfully, as he glided into the shop and absently closed the door behind him.

"Sir, I—" Feth got no farther with his expostulation.

"Oh, don't let me interrupt. Go right ahead, Ken—you have a problem on your hands, I see. Get it out of the way, and we'll tackle the other afterwards. There'll be no interruptions then."

Rather puzzled, for he had completely forgotten Drai's threat, Ken turned back to his microphone and resumed the apparently endless chant. While he did not understand the words with which Roger finally interrupted, the thing had gone on long enough so that he shared the boy's impatience to some extent. Also, the clank as Roger kicked the torpedo was at least suggestive.

It was Drai who drove the projectile into the air, an instant later. He had never heard those words, either; but they were different enough from the usual human conversation to start him shivering. The thought of strained or severed relations with Planet Three was one he could not face— and this being was definitely excited and more than probably angry. That blow on the hull of the torpedo—

Drai's tentacle whipped past Sallman Ken at the thought, and the main power and drive director switches closed as one. The investigator swivelled around on the control rack, and eyed his employer curiously.

"You seem almost as excited as the native. What's the matter?" Laj drew a deep breath, and finally got his voice under control. He was just beginning to realize that his dramatic entry had not been the wisest of moves. It was perfectly possible that his hired expert had learned the name of Earth's product quite innocently; and if that were the case he would be ill-advised to attach too much weight to the incident—publicly, at least. He shifted ground, therefore, as smoothly as he could.

"Your chemical analysis seems to have encountered complications."

"It would seem so. Apparently your natives are not quite so completely diurnal as you gave me to understand." Ken was not intentionally defending his actions, but he could have found no better answer. Laj Drai paused momentarily.

"Yes, that is a point that surprises me a little. For twenty years they have never signalled except during their daytime. I wonder if the flatlanders had anything to do with it? I can't imagine what or how, though. Did you finish your tests?"

"Enough, I guess. We'll have to bring the torpedo back here, so I can find out just what that atmosphere did to my samples. Some of them burned, we already know, but I'd like to know what was produced."

"Of course it couldn't be sulfides. That's what one thinks of as the natural product of combustion."

"Not unless frozen sulfur dust is suspended in the atmosphere in tremendous quantities. I hadn't thought of that, though—I'll check for it when the samples come back. Actually, I'm a little bothered by the results so far. I couldn't think of anything gaseous at that temperature which would support combustion, and something definitely does."

"How about fluorine?" Laj was digging in the dim memories of an elementary science course.

"Maybe—but how come it exists free in the atmosphere? I should think it would be *too* active, even at that temperature. Of course, I suppose the same would be true of anything which would support combustion, so we'll simply have to wait until the samples are back. You know, I'm almost at the point where I'd be willing to risk a landing there, to *see* what the place is like." Drai shrugged expressively.

"If you and Feth can figure out a way of doing it, I won't stop you. We might even see our way to offering a bonus. Well, it'll be nearly three days before your stuff is back here, and there won't be much to do in the meantime. Feth will cut it in on the beam when it's far enough from Three."

Ken took this as a hint to leave, and drifted aimlessly out into the corridors. He had some thinking of his own to do. As Drai had said, nothing could be done about Planet Three until the return of the torpedo, and he had no excuse for not considering Rade's problem for a while.

The product was called "tofacco." That, at least, was information. Rade had had no name for the narcotic he sought, so the information was of questionable value so far.

This planetary system was relatively close to Sarr. Another fact. The precautions taken by Drai and his people to conceal that fact might or

might not be considered reasonable for a near-legal commercial enter-
prise, but were certainly natural for anything as blatantly criminal as drug-
running.

Planet Three was cold—to put it feebly—and the drug in question
could not stand normal temperatures. That was a link of rather uncertain
strength, reinforced slightly by Drai's tacit admission that "tofacco" was a
vegetable product.

Think as he would, he could recall no other information which could
be of the slightest use to Rade. Ken was mildly annoyed at the narcotics
chief anyway for involving him in such a matter, and was certainly more
willing than a professional policeman would have been to go back to the
purely astronomical and ecological problem that was facing him.

How about his pesky Planet Three? Certainly it was inhabited—a
fantastic enough fact in itself. Certainly it was not well known; no vision
transmitter and no manned ship had ever gotten through its atmosphere.
That seemed a little queer, now that Ken considered the matter again.
Granted the fearful cold, and the fact that an atmosphere would conduct
heat away as space could not, he still found it hard to believe that a competent engineer could not design apparatus capable of the descent. Feth
was supposed to be a mechanic rather than an engineer, of course; but
still it seemed very much as though the organization were singularly lacking in scientific resource. The very fact that Ken himself had been hired
made that fact even more evident.

Perhaps he was not so far from Rade's problem after all. Certainly
any regular interstellar trading organization could and always did have
its own ecological staff—no such concern could last without one, considering the rather weird situations apt to arise when, for example, metal-
rich Sarr traded with the amphibious chemistry wizards of Rehagh. Yet
he, Sallman Ken, a general science dabbler, was all that Laj Drai could
get! It was not strange; it was unbelievable. He wondered how Drai had
made the fact seem reasonable even for a moment.

Well, if he found out nothing they would probably not bother him.
He could and would investigate Planet Three as completely as he could,
go home, and turn his information over to Rade—let the narcotics man
do what he wanted with it. Planet Three was more interesting.

How to land on the blasted planet? He could see keeping large ships
out of its atmosphere, after the trouble with the natives of the flat, bluish
areas. Still, torpedoes had been running the gauntlet without loss for
twenty years, and the only detectable flatlander activity had been radar
beams in the last two or three. Those were easily fooled by quarter-wave
coatings, as Drai had said. No, the only real objections were the frightful
natural conditions of the world.

Well, a standard suit of engineer's armor would let a Sarrian work in a lake of molten aluminum for quite a while. There, of course, the temperature difference was less than it would be on the Planet of Ice; but the conductivity of the metal must be greater than that of the planet's atmosphere, and might make up the difference. Even if it did not, the armor could be given extra heating coils or insulation or both. Why had this never been tried? He would have to ask Feth or Laj Drai.

Then, granting for the moment that a landing could not be made even this way, why was television impossible? Ken refused to believe that the thin glass of a television tube could not be cooled down sufficiently to match the world's conditions without shattering, even if the electrical parts had to be kept hot. Surely the difference could be no greater than in the ancient incandescent bulbs!

He would have to put both these points up to Feth. He was heading purposefully back toward the shop with this plan in mind, when he encountered Drai, who greeted him as though there had been no suspicious thoughts in his own brain that day.

"Feth has cut you in to the main beam, and no piloting will be needed for nearly three days," he said. "You looked as though you were going back to your controls."

"I wanted to talk to Feth again. I've been thinking over the matter of armor and apparatus withstanding Planet Three's conditions, and it seems to me something could be done." He went on to give a censored version of his recent thoughts to his employer.

"I don't know," the latter said when he had finished. "You'll have to talk to Feth, as you planned. We've tried it, since he joined us, and the failures occurred just as he said in the matter of television. He was not with us on the original expedition, which did no investigating except as I originally told you—it was strictly a pleasure cruise, and the only reason there were so many torpedoes available was that the owner of the ship preferred to do his sightseeing in comfort—he'd send out a dozen at once, when we entered a planetary system, and keep the *Karella* in space until he found something he wanted to see or do personally."

"I've never met him, have I?"

"No—he died long ago. He was pretty old when we hit this place. I inherited the ship and got into this trading business."

"When did Feth join you?"

"A year or two after I got started—he's the oldest in the crew in point of service. He can tell you all about the engineering troubles, you see, and I certainly can't. You'd better see him, if he feels like talking." Without explaining this last remark, Drai disappeared down the corridor. Ken did not wonder at the words—he had already come to regard Feth as a taciturn personality.

The mechanic did not appear to be busy. He was still draped in the rack in front of the torpedo controls, and seemed to be thinking. He rose as Ken entered the room, but said nothing, merely giving the equivalent of a nod of greeting. Not noticing anything unusual in his manner, Ken began immediately to spill forth his ideas. He was allowed to finish without interruption.

"Your points all sound good," the mechanic admitted when he had heard them, "and I certainly can't bring any theory against them. I can merely point out that the tubes do break. If you want to send down a suit of armor full of thermometers and pressure gauges, that's all right with me, but I trust you'll pardon a pessimistic attitude. I used up a lot of good TV equipment in that atmosphere."

"Well, I admit your superior practical knowledge," replied Ken, "but I do think it's worth trying."

"If the instruments read all right, who goes down in the armor the next time? The thought makes my knee-joints stiff. I'm scared of the idea, and don't mind admitting it."

"So am I." Ken remembered the uncontrollable emotion that had swept his being the first time he had seen Planet Three. "It's a ghastly place, beyond doubt; but I still like to find things out, and I'm willing to take a chance on my health to do it."

"Health—huh! You'd be a ready-made memorial statue five seconds after the first pinhole appeared in your suit," retorted the mechanic. "I almost feel it's a dirty trick to send good instruments down into that, even when I know they can take it. Well, I'll break out a suit of armor, if you really want to try it. There are are plenty of torpedoes."

"How can you carry it by torpedo? You can't possibly get it inside, surely."

"No; there are rings on the outer hull, and we can clamp the suit to those. We'll just have to be careful and go through the atmosphere more slowly, this time." He glided down the length of the shop to a set of lockers at the far end, and from one of these wrestled a suit of the much-discussed armor into view.

Even under Mercurian gravity it was difficult to handle. Owing to the peculiarities of the Sarrian physique, a greatly superior leverage could be obtained from inside the garment; but even knowing this, Ken began to wonder just what he was going to do if he succeeded in reaching the surface of the massive Planet Three in that metal monstrosity, under nearly four times his present gravity. That thought led to a question.

"Feth, what sort of body chemistry do you suppose these natives have? They move around—presumably—under a whopping gravity in a temperature that should freeze any organic material. Ever thought about it?" The mechanic was silent for some time, as though considering his reply.

"Yes," he said at last, "I'll admit I've thought about it. I'm not sure I want to talk about it, though."

"Why not? The place can't be that repulsive."

"It's not that. You remember what Drai said he'd do if anyone gave you information about the stuff we got from the planet?"

"Yes, vaguely; but what does that have to do with it?"

"Maybe nothing, maybe not. He was pretty sore about my telling you the name of the stuff. I wouldn't have done it if I'd stopped to think. The situation just seemed to call for a quick answer, so I gave it."

"But your ideas on the native chemistry could hardly tell—or I suppose perhaps they could. Still, Drai knows perfectly well I've never worked for another trading company and I'm not a trader myself—why should I be treated like a commercial spy? I don't care particularly what your stuff is—I'm interested in the planet."

"I don't doubt it. Just the same, if I ever make any more slips like that, please keep whatever you learn to yourself. I thought there'd be a nuclear explosion when Drai walked in with you yelling 'Tofacco!' into the mike."

"He couldn't really do much, though." This was a ranging question; Ken had started to think again.

"Well—" Feth was cautious about his answer—"he's the boss, and this isn't such a bad job. Just do the favor, if you don't mind." He turned back to the armor, with an expression on his face which indicated he was through talking for the time being. Ken found himself unable to get anything definite from the mechanic's answer.

He didn't think about it very hard anyway, for the other problem proved too interesting. Feth was certainly a good mechanic; as good as some rated engineers Ken had known. He had opened the armor completely and removed all the service plates, and started the job by giving it a full overhaul inspection. That completed, he refilled the zinc circulating system and replaced and safetied the plates he had removed, but left the armor itself open. One eye rolled questioningly at the watcher, and he spoke for the first time in two hours.

"Have you any ideas about instrument arrangement? You know best what you want to find out."

"Well, all we really need to know is whether the suit can maintain temperature and pressure. I suppose a single pressure gauge anywhere inside, and thermometers at the extremities, would tell enough. Can you use telemetering instruments, or will we have to wait until this torpedo gets back, too?"

"I'm afraid we'll have to wait. The instruments themselves would be easy enough to install, but the voice transmitter in the armor couldn't handle their messages. I can put a multiple recorder in the body, connect the instruments to that, and arrange so you can turn it on and off by remote control—I'll simply tie it in to one of the suit controls. I suppose you'll want to be able to manipulate the suit heaters, as well?"

"Yes. If it takes anywhere near full power to maintain livable temperature, we ought to know it. I suppose extra heaters could be installed, if necessary?"

"I expect so." For the first time, Feth wore an expression approximating a grin. "I could probably mount blast furnaces on the feet. I'm not so sure you could walk around with them."

"Even if I can't I can at least see."

"If you don't have the same trouble with your visor that I did with TV tubes. Even quartz has its limitations."

"I still think it can take it. Anyway, it won't cost us anything to find out. Let's go ahead and mount those instruments—I'm rather curious to see which of us is right. Is this recorder all right?" He took from a cabinet a minute machine whose most prominent feature was the double reel of sensitized tape, and held it up as he spoke. Feth glanced at it.

"Only one record. Get an L-7. You can recognize it by the reel—its tape is about five times as wide. I'm using the single barometer you suggested, and thermometers in head, trunk, one foot, and one sleeve as far out as I can mount it. That leaves a free band on the tape that you can use for anything you want." The mechanic was working as he spoke, clamping tiny instruments from a well-stocked supply cabinet into the places he had mentioned. For a moment Ken wondered whether the existence of this more than adequate instrument stock did not invalidate his argument about the lack of scientific facilities; then he recognized that all the devices were perfectly standard engineering instruments, and represented nothing but a respectable financial outlay. Anyone could buy and almost anyone could use them.

In spite of Feth's evident skill, the job was a long one. They did not sleep, being Sarrians, but even they had to rest occasionally. It was during one of these rests that Ken happened to notice the time.

"Say," he remarked to his companion, "it must be daylight on that part of the planet by now. I wonder if Drai has made his landing yet?"

"Very probably," Feth replied, one eye following Ken's gaze toward the clock. "He is more than likely to be back in space again—he doesn't waste much time as a rule."

"In that case, would I be likely to be skinned for dropping in to the observatory?" Feth gazed at him narrowly for long enough to let Ken regret the question.

"I probably would be if Drai found out I'd encouraged you," was the answer. "I think it would be better if you stayed here. There's plenty for us to do." He rose and returned to his labors, although the rest period had scarcely started. Ken, realizing he did not intend to say any more, joined him.

The work turned out to be timed rather nicely. By the time the armor had survived a one-hour leakage and radiation-loss test in the vacuum of the shadowed airlock, had been clamped to the load rings of another torpedo, and launched into the void on automatic control, the other projectile was on the point of landing. The automatic control, in fact, was necessary—the second missile could not be handled by radio until the first had been docked, since the other controlling station was still being used by Drai to bring his own load back to Mercury.

A single rest period fitted nicely between the launching of the suit and the landing of the mobile laboratory; and Ken was awaiting the latter with eagerness when it finally drifted through the air lock under Feth's expert control. He would have pounced on it at once, but was restrained by a warning cry from the mechanic.

"Hold on! It's not as cold as it was out on Planet Three, but you'll still freeze to it. Look!" A tentacle waved toward the gleaming hull, on which drops of liquid sulfur were condensing, running together and trickling to the floor, where they promptly boiled away again. "Let that stop, first."

Ken stopped obediently, feeling the icy draft pour about his feet, and backed slowly away. The air that reached him was bearable, but the hull of the torpedo must be cold enough to freeze zinc, if it had reached radiative equilibrium for this distance from the sun.

Long minutes passed before the metal was warmed through and the drip of liquid sulfur ceased. Only then did Feth open the cargo door, whereupon the process was repeated. This time the straw-colored liquid made a pool on the floor of the cargo compartment, flooding around the crucibles and making Ken wonder seriously about the purity of his samples. He turned on all the heaters at low strength to get rid of the stuff as fast as possible. Since there was a serious chance of further reaction with the air if a high temperature were attained, he opened the switches again the moment the hissing and bubbling of boiling air ceased; and at last he was free to examine his results. As Roger Wing could have told him, they were quite a sight!

# IX.

Some of the little pots were full; most of these appeared to be unchanged. Others, however, were not. The contents of most of these were easy to find, but Ken could see that they were going to be hard to identify.

A white powder was literally over everything, as Roger had already seen. The yellow flecks of sodium peroxide were turning grayish as they decomposed in the heat. The gold crucible had been pulled from its base, but was otherwise unchanged; the iron had turned black; sodium, magnesium and titanium had disappeared, though the residue in each crucible gave promise that some of the scattered dust could be identified. There was still carbon in the container devoted to that substance, but much less of it than there had been.

All these things, however, interesting and important as they might be, only held the attention of Feth and Ken for a moment; for just inside the cargo door, imprinted clearly in the layer of dust, was a mark utterly unlike anything either had ever seen.

"Feth, dig up a camera somewhere. I'm going to get Drai." Ken was gone almost before the words had left his diaphragm, and for once Feth had nothing to say. His eyes were still fixed on the mark.

There was nothing exactly weird or terrifying about it; but he was utterly unable to keep his mind from the fascinating problem of what had made it. To a creature which had never seen anything even remotely like a human being, a hand print is apt to present difficulties in interpretation. For all he could tell, the creature might have been standing, sitting, or leaning on the spot, or sprawled out in the manner the Sarrians substituted for the second of those choices. There was simply no telling; the native might be the size of a Sarrian foot, making the mark with his body—or he might have been too big to get more than a single appendage into the compartment. Feth shook his head to clear it—even he be-

273

gan to realize that his thoughts were beginning to go in circles. He went to look for a camera.

Sallman Ken burst into the observatory without warning, but gave Drai no chance to explode. He was bursting himself with the news of the discovery—a little too much, in fact, since he kept up the talk all the way back to the shop. By the time they got there, the actual sight of the print was something of an anticlimax to Drai. He expressed polite interest, but little more. To him, of course, the physical appearance of Earth's natives meant nothing whatever. His attention went to another aspect of the compartment.

"What's all that white stuff?"

"I don't know yet," Ken admitted. "The torpedo just got back. It's whatever Planet Three's atmosphere does to the samples I sent down."

"Then you'll know what the atmosphere is before long? That will be a help. There are some caverns near the dark hemisphere that we've known about for years, which we could easily seal off and fill with whatever you say. Let us know when you find out anything." He drifted casually out of the shop, leaving Ken rather disappointed. It had been such a fascinating discovery.

He shrugged the feeling off, collected what he could of his samples without disturbing the print, and bore them across the room to the bench on which a makeshift chemical laboratory had been set up. As he himself had admitted, he was not an expert analyst; but compounds formed by combustion are seldom extremely complex, and he felt that he could get a pretty good idea of the nature of these. After all, he knew the metals involved—there could be no metallic gases except hydrogen in Planet Three's atmosphere. Even mercury would be a liquid, and no other metal had a really high vapor pressure even at Sarrian temperature. With this idea firmly in mind like a guiding star, Ken set blithely to work.

To a chemist the work or a description of it would be interesting. To anyone else, it would be a boringly repetitious routine of heating and cooling, checking for boiling points and melting points, fractionating and filtering. Ken would have been quicker had he started with no preconceived notions; but finally even he was convinced. Once convinced, he wondered why he had not seen it before.

Feth Allmer had returned long since, and photographed the hand print from half a dozen angles. Now, seeing that Ken had stopped working, he roused himself from the rack on which he had found repose and approached the work bench.

"Have you got it, or are you stumped?" he queried.

"I have it, I guess. I should have guessed long ago. It's oxygen."

"What's so obvious about that? Or, for that matter, why shouldn't it be?"

"To the latter question, no reason. I simply rejected it as a possibility at first because it's so active. I never stopped to think that it's little if any more active at that temperature than sulfur is at ours. It's perfectly possible to have it free in an atmosphere—provided there's a process constantly replacing what goes into combination. You need the same for sulfur. Blast it, the two elements are so much alike! I should have thought of that right away!"

"What do you mean—a replacement process?"

"You know we breathe sulfur and form sulfides with our metabolic processes. Mineral-eating life such as most plants, on the other hand, breaks down the sulfides and releases free sulfur, using solar energy for the purpose. Probably there is a similar division of life forms on this planet—one forming oxides and the other breaking them down. Now that I think of it, I believe there are some microorganisms on Sarr that use oxygen instead of sulfur."

"Is it pure oxygen?"

"No—only about a fifth or less. You remember how quickly the sodium and magnesium went out, and what the pressure drop was with them."

"No, I don't, and I can't say that it means much to me anyway, but I'll take your word for it. What else is there in the atmosphere? The titanium took about all of it, I do remember."

"Right. It's either nitrogen or some of its oxides—I can't tell which without better controlled samples for quantity measurement. The only titanium compounds I could find in that mess were oxides and nitrides, though. The carbon oxidized, I guess—the reason there was no pressure change except that due to heat was that the principal oxide of carbon has two atoms of oxygen, and there is therefore no volume change. I should have thought of that, too."

"I'll have to take your word for that, too, I guess. All we have to do, then, is cook up a four-to-one mixture of nitrogen and oxygen and fill the caves the boss mentioned to about two-thirds normal pressure with it?"

"That may be a little oversimplified, but it should be close enough to the real thing to let this tofacco stuff grow—if you can get specimens here alive, to start things off. It would be a good idea to get some soil, too—I don't suppose that powdering the local rock would help much. I may add in passing that I refuse even to attempt analyzing that soil. You'll have to get enough to use." Feth stared.

"But that's ridiculous! We'd need tons, for a decent-sized plantation!" Sallman Ken shrugged.

"I know it. I tell you clearly that it will be easier to get those tons than to get an accurate soil analysis out of me. I simply don't know enough about it, and I doubt if Sarr's best chemist could hazard a prediction about the chemicals likely to be present in the solid state on that planet. At that temperature, I'll bet organic compounds could exist without either fluorine or silicon."

"I think we'd better get Drai back here to listen to that. I'm sure he was planning to have you synthesize both atmosphere and soil, so that we could set up the plantation entirely on our own."

"Perhaps you'd better. I told him my limitations at the beginning; if he still expects that, he has no idea whatever of the nature of the problem." Feth left, looking worried, though Ken was unable to understand what particular difference it made to the mechanic. Later he was to find out.

The worried expression was still more evident when Feth returned.

"He's busy now. He says he'll talk it over with you after that suit comes back, so that any alternatives can be considered, too. He wants me to take you out to the caves so you can see for yourself what he has in mind for making them usable."

"How do we get there? They must be some distance from here."

"Ordon Lee will take us around in the ship. It's about two thousand miles. Let's get into our suits."

Ken heroically swallowed the impulse to ask why the whole subject should have come up so suddenly in the midst of what seemed a totally different matter, and went to the locker where the space suits were stowed. He more than suspected the reason, anyway, and looked confidently forward to having the trip prolonged until after the return of the trading torpedo.

His attention was shifted from these matters as stepped onto the surface of Mercury, for the first time since his arrival at the station. The blistered, baked, utterly dry expanse of the valley was not particularly strange to him, since Sarr was almost equally dry and even hotter; but the blackness of the sky about the sun and the bareness of the ground contributed to a *dead* effect that he found unpleasant. On Sarr, plant life is everywhere in spite of the dryness; the plants with which Ken was familiar were more crystalline than organic and needed only the most minute amounts of liquid for their existence.

Also, Sarr has weather, and Mercury does not. As the ship lifted from the valley, Ken was able to appreciate the difference. Mercury's terrain is rugged, towering and harsh. The peaks, faults and meteor scars are unsoftened by the blurring hand of erosion. Shadows are dark where they exist at all, relieved only by light reflected from nearby solid objects. Lakes and streams would have to be of metals like lead and tin, or simple compounds like the "water" of Sarr—copper chloride, lead bromide, and sulfides of phosphorus and potassium. The first sort are too heavy, and have filtered down through the rocks of Mercury, if they ever existed at all; the second are absent for lack of the living organisms that might have produced them. Sallman Ken, watching the surface over which they sped, began to think a little more highly even of Earth.

A vessel capable of exceeding the speed of light by a factor of several thousand makes short work of a trip of two thousand miles, even when the speed is kept down to a value that will permit manual control. The surface was a little darker where they landed, with the sun near the horizon instead of directly overhead and the shadows correspondingly longer. It looked and was colder. However, the vacuum and the poor conducting qualities of the rock made it possible even here to venture out in ordinary space suits, and within a few moments Ken, Feth and the pilot were afoot gliding swiftly toward a cliff some forty feet in height.

The rock surface was seamed and cracked, like nearly all Mercurian topography. Into one of the wider cracks Lee unhesitatingly led the way. It did not lead directly away from the sun, and the party found itself almost at once in utter darkness. With one accord they switched on their portable lamps and proceeded. The passage was rather narrow at first, and rough enough on both floor and walls to be dangerous to space suits. This continued for perhaps a quarter of a mile, and quite suddenly opened into a vast, nearly spherical chamber. Apparently Mercury had not always been without gases—the cave had every appearance of a bubble blown in the igneous rock. The crack through which the explorers had entered extended upward nearly to its top, and downward nearly as far. It had been partly filled with rubble from above, which was the principal reason the going had been so difficult. The lower part of the bubble also contained a certain amount of loose rock. This looked as though it might make a climb down to the center possible, but Ken did not find himself particularly entranced by the idea.

"Is there just this one big bubble?" he asked. Ordon Lee answered.

"No; we have found several, very similar in structure, along this cliff, and there are probably others with no openings into them. I suppose they could be located by echo-sounders if we really wanted to find them."

"It might be a good idea to try that," Ken pointed out. "A cave whose only entrance was one we had drilled would be a lot easier to keep airtight than this thing." Feth and Lee grunted assent to that. The latter added a thought of his own. "It might be good if we could find one well down; we could be a lot freer in drilling—there's be no risk of a crack running to the surface."

"Just one trouble," put in Feth. "Do we have an echo-sounder? Like Ken on his soil analysis, I have my doubts about being able to make one."

Nobody answered that for some moments.

"I guess I'd better show you some of the other caves we've found already," Lee said at last. No one objected to this, and they retraced their steps to daylight. In the next four hours they looked at seven more caves, ranging from a mere hemispherical hollow in the very face of the cliff to a gloomy, frighteningly deep bubble reached by a passageway just barely negotiable for a space-suited Sarrian. This last, in spite of the terrors of its approach and relative smallness, was evidently the best for their purpose out of those examined; and Lee made a remark to that effect as they doffed space suits back in the *Karella*.

"I suppose you're right," Ken admitted, "but I'd still like to poke deeper. Blast it, Feth, are you sure you couldn't put a sounder together? You never had any trouble with the gadgets we used in the torpedoes."

"Now you're the one who doesn't realize the problem," the mechanic replied. "We were using heating coils, thermometers, pressure gauges, and photocells for the other stuff. Those come ready made. All I did was hook them up to a regular achronic transmitter—we couldn't use ordinary radio because the waves would have taken ten or twelve minutes for the round trip. I didn't make anything—just strung wires."

"I suppose you're right," Ken admitted. "In that case, we may as well go back to the station and lay plans for sealing off that last cavern." He kept a sharp look on his two companions as he said this, and succeeded in catching the glance Feth sent at the clock before his reply. It almost pleased him.

"Hadn't we better get some photographs and measurements of the cave first?" Ordon Lee cut in. "We'll need them for estimates on how much gas and soil will be needed, regardless of how it's to be obtained." Ken made no objection to this; there was no point in raising active suspicion, and he had substantiated his own idea. He was being kept away from the station intentionally. He helped with the photography, and subsequently with the direct measurement of the cave. He had some trouble refraining from laughter; affairs were so managed that the party had returned to the ship and doffed space suits each time before the next activity was proposed. It was very efficient, from one point of view. Just to keep his end up, he proposed a rest before returning to the base, and was enthusiastically seconded by the others. Then he decided to compute the volume of the cave from their measurements, and contrived to spend a good deal of time at that—legitimately, as the cave was far from being a perfect sphere. Then he suggested getting some samples of local rock to permit an estimate of digging difficulties, and bit back a grin when Feth suggested rather impatiently that that could wait. Apparently he had outdone the precious pair at their own game—though why Feth should care whether or not they stayed longer than necessary was hard to see.

"It's going to take quite a lot of gas," he said as the *Karella* lunged into the black sky. "There's about two million cubic feet of volume there, and even the lower pressure we need won't help much. I'd like to find out if we can get oxygen from those rocks; we should have picked up a few samples, as I suggested. We're going to have to look over the upper area for small cracks, too—we have no idea how airtight the darn thing is. I wish we could—say, Feth, aren't there a lot of radar units of one sort or another around here?"

"Yes, of course. What do you want them for? Their beams won't penetrate rock."

"I know. But can't the pulse-interval on at least some of them be altered?"

"Of course. You'd have to use a different set every time your range scale changed, otherwise. So what?"

"Why couldn't we—or you, anyway—set one up with the impulse actuating a sounder of some sort which could be put in contact with the rock, and time *that* return-echo picked up by a contact-mike? I know the impulse rate would be slower, but we could calibrate it easily enough."

"One trouble might be that radar units are usually not very portable. Certainly none of the warning devices in this ship are."

"Well, dismantle a torpedo, then. They have radar altimeters, and there are certainly enough of them so one can be spared. We could have called base and had them send one out to us—I bet it would have taken you only a few hours. Let's do that anyway—we're still a lot closer to the caves than to the base."

"It's easier to work in the shop; and anyway, if we go as far underground as this idea should let us—supposing it works—we might as well scout areas closer to the base, for everyone's convenience." Ordon Lee contributed the thought without looking from his controls.

"Do you think you can do it?" Ken asked the mechanic.

"It doesn't seem too hard," the latter answered. "Still, I don't want to make any promises just yet."

"There's a while yet before that suit comes back. We can probably find out before then, and really have some material for Drai to digest. Let's call him now—maybe he'll have some ideas about soil."

The eyes of the other two met for a brief moment; then Lee gestured to the radio controls.

"Go ahead; only we'll be there before you can say much."

"He told me you were going to manufacture soil," reminded Feth.

"I know. That's why I want to talk to him—we left in too much of a hurry before." Ken switched on the radio while the others tried to decide whether or not he was suspicious about that hasty departure. Neither dared speak, with Ken in the same room, but once again their eyes met, and the glances were heavy with meaning.

Drai eventually came to the microphone at the other end, and Ken began talking with little preliminary.

"We've made measurements of the smallest cave we can find, so far at least, and figured out roughly how much air you're going to need to fill it. I can tell you how much soil you'll need to cover the bottom, too, if you plan to use all of it. The trouble is, even if I can analyze the soil—even as roughly as I did the air—you're facing a supply problem that runs into tons. I can't make that much in the laboratory in any reasonable time. You're going to have to get it ready-made."

"How? We can't land a person on Planet Three, let alone a freighter."

"That we'll see presently. But that's not the suggestion I wanted to make—I see we're nearly there, so we can finish this chat in person. Think this over while we're going in: whatever sort of atmosphere a planet may have, I don't see how the soils can be *too* different—at least in their principal constituents. Why don't you get a shipload of Sarrian soil?" Drai gaped for a moment.

"But—bacteria—"

"Don't be silly; nothing Sarrian could live at that temperature. I admit it would be safer to use soil from Planet Three, and we may be able to. But if we can't, then you have my advice, if you're interested in speed—even if I knew the composition, it would take me a lot longer than a week to make a hundred tons of dirt!" He broke the connection as the *Karella* settled to the ground.

# X.

Ken wasted no time donning his space suit and leaving the ship with the others. Once inside the station and out of the heavy garment, he hastened to the shop to see how far out the returning test suit was; then, satisfied with its progress as recorded there, he headed for the observatory to continue his conversation with Laj Drai. He met no one on the way. Lee had stayed on the ship, Feth had disappeared on some errand of his own the moment the lock had closed behind them, and the rest of the personnel kept pretty much to themselves anyway. Ken did not care this time whether or not he were seen, since he planned a perfectly aboveboard conversation.

He was interrupted, however, in planning just how to present his arguments, by the fact that the observatory door was locked.

It was the first time he had encountered a locked door in the station since his arrival, and it gave him to think furiously. He was morally certain that the trading torpedo had returned during the absence of the *Karella*, and that there was a load of tofacco somewhere around the building. If this were the only locked door—and it was, after all, the room Drai used as an office—

Ken pressed his body close to the door, trying to tell by sound whether anyone were in the room. He was not sure; and even if there were not, what could he do? A professional detective could probably have opened the door in a matter of seconds. Ken, however, was no professional; the door was definitely locked, as far as he was concerned. Apparently the only thing to do was seek Drai elsewhere.

He was ten yards down the ramp, out of sight of the observatory door, when he heard it open. Instantly he whirled on his toes and was walking back up the incline as though just arriving. Just as he reached the bend that hid the door from him he heard it close again; and an instant later he came face to face with Feth. The mechanic, for the first time since Ken had known him, looked restless and uneasy. He avoided Ken's direct gaze, and wound the tip of one tentacle more tightly about a small object he was carrying, concealing it from view. He brushed past with a muttered greeting and vanished with remarkable speed around the turn of the ramp, making no answer to Ken's query as to whether Drai were in the observatory.

Ken stared after him for seconds after he had disappeared. Feth had always been taciturn, but he had seemed friendly enough. Now it almost seemed as though he were angry at Ken's presence.

With a sigh, the pro tem detective turned back up the ramp. It wouldn't hurt to knock at the door, anyway. The only reason he hadn't the first time was probably a subconscious hope that he would find Drai somewhere else, and feel free to investigate. Since his common sense told him he couldn't investigate anyway, he knocked.

It was just as well he hadn't made any amateur efforts at lock-picking, he decided as the door opened. Drai was there, apparently waiting for him. His face bore no recognizable expression; either whatever bothered Feth had not affected him, or he was a much better actor than the mechanic. Ken, feeling he knew Feth, inclined to the former view.

"I'm afraid I'm not convinced of the usability of any Sarrian soil," Drai opened the conversation. "I agree that most of the substances present in it, as far as I know, could also be present at Planet Three's temperature; but I'm not so sure the reverse is true. Mightn't there be substances that would be solid or liquid at that temperature and gaseous at ours, so that they would be missing from any we brought from home?"

"I hadn't thought of that," Ken admitted. "The fact that I can't think of any such substances doesn't mean they don't exist, either. I can skim through the handbook and see if there are any inorganic compounds that would behave that way, but even that might miss some—and if their life is at all analogous to ours, there are probably a couple of million organic compounds—for which we *don't* have any catalogue. No, blast it, I guess you're right; we'll have to take the stuff from the planet itself." He lapsed into silent thought, from which Drai finally aroused him.

"Do you really think you're going to be able to get to the surface of that world?"

"I still can't see why we shouldn't," replied Ken. "It seems to me that people have visited worse ones before, bad as that is. Feth is pessimistic about it, though, and I suppose he has more practical knowledge of the problem than I. We can make more definite plans in that direction when the suit comes back, which shouldn't be long now. According to the instruments it started back a couple of hours ago."

"That means nearly three days before you're sure. There must be something else—say! You claim it's the presence of a conducting atmosphere that makes the heat loss on Planet Three so great, don't you?"

"Sure. You know as well as I that you can go out in an ordinary space suit light years from the nearest sun; radiation loss is easy to replace. Why?"

"I just thought—there are other planets in this system. If we could find an airless one roughly the same temperature as Three, we might get soil from that."

"That's an idea." Ken was promptly lost in enthusiasm again. "As long as it's cold enough, which is easy in this system—and Three has a satellite—you showed it to me. We can go there in no time in the *Karella*—and we could pick up that suit in space while we're at it. Collect Feth, and let's go!"

"I fear Feth will not be available for a while," replied Drai. "Also," he grimaced, "I have been on that satellite, and its soil is mostly pumice dust; it might have come straight from the Polar Desert on Sarr. We'd better consider the other possibilities before we take off. The trouble is, all we've ever noted about the other planets of the system is their motions. We wanted to avoid them, not visit them. I do remember, I think, that Five and Six do have atmospheres, which I suppose writes them off the list. You might see where Four is just now, will you? I assume you can interpret an ephemeris."

Ken decided later that courtesy was really a superfluous facet of character. Had it not been for the requirements of courtesy he would not have bothered to make an answer to this suggestion, and had not most of his attention been concentrated on the answer he would never have made the serious error of walking over to the cabinet where the table in question was located, and reaching for it. He realized just as he touched the paper what he was doing, but with a stupendous effort of will he finished his assurance that he could read an ephemeris and completed the motion of obtaining the document. He felt, however, as though a laboratory vacuum pump had gone to work on his stomach as he turned back to his employer.

That individual was standing exactly where he had been, the expression on his face still inscrutable.

"I fear I must have done our friend Feth an injustice," he remarked casually. "I was wondering how you had come to imply that a round trip to Sarr would take only a week. I realize of course that your discoveries were made quite accidentally, and that nothing was farther from your plans than vulgar spying; but the problem of what to do about your unfortunate knowledge remains. That will require a certain amount of thought. In the meantime, let us continue with the matter of Planet Four. Is it in a convenient position to visit, and could we as you suggested pick up the torpedo carrying your suit without going too far from course?"

Ken found himself completely at a loss. Drai's apparently unperturbed blandness was the last attitude he expected under the circumstances. He could not believe that the other was really that indifferent; something unpleasant must be brewing between those steady eyes, but the face gave him no clue. As best he could he tried to match his employer's attitude. With an effort he turned his attention to the ephemeris he was holding, found the proper terms, and indulged in some mental arithmetic.

"The planets are just about at right angles as seen from here," he announced at length. "We're just about between the sun and Three, as you know; Four is in the retrograde direction, roughly twice as far from us. Still, that shouldn't mean anything to the *Karella*."

"True enough. Very well, we will take off in an hour. Get any equipment you think you will need on board before then—better use engineering armor for Planet Four, even if it doesn't have air. You'll have to point out where they are to whomever I get to help you."

"How about Feth?" Ken had gotten the idea that the mechanic was in disgrace for betraying the secret of their location.

"He won't be available for some time—he's occupied. I'll give you a man—you can be picking out what you want in the shop; I'll send him there. One hour." Laj Drai turned away, intimating that the interview was at an end.

The man he sent proved to be a fellow Ken had seen around, but had never spoken to. The present occasion did little to change that; he was almost as taciturn as Feth, and Ken never did learn his name. He did all he was asked in the way of moving material to the *Karella,* and then disappeared. The takeoff was on schedule.

Ordon Lee, who evidently had his orders, sent the vessel around the planet so rapidly that the acceleration needed to hug the curving surfaces exceeded that produced by the planet's gravity; the world seemed to be above them, to the inhabitants of the ship. With the sun near the horizon behind and the glowing double spark of Earth rising ahead, however, he discontinued the radial acceleration and plunged straight away from the star. Under the terrific urge of the interstellar engines, the Earth-Luna system swelled into a pair of clearly marked discs in minutes. Lee applied his forces skillfully, bringing the vessel to a halt relative to the planet and half a million miles sunward of it. Drai gestured to Ken, indicating a control board similar to that in the shop.

"That's tuned in to your torpedo; the screen at the right is a radar unit you can use to help find it. There's a compass at the top of the panel, and this switch will cause the torpedo to emit a homing signal." Ken silently placed himself at the controls, and got the feel of them in a few minutes. The compass gave rather indefinite readings at first because of the distance involved; but Lee was quickly able to reduce that, and in a quarter of an hour the still invisible projectile was only a dozen miles way. Ken had no difficulty in handling it from that point, and presently he and Drai left the control room and repaired to a cargo chamber in the *Karella*'s belly, where the torpedo was warming up.

This time it was the suit still clamped to the outside that took all their interest. The whole thing had been left at the bottom of the atmosphere for a full hour, and Ken felt that any serious faults should be apparent in that time. It was a little discouraging to note that air was condensing on the suit as well as the hull; if the heaters had been working properly, some sort of equilibrium should have been reached between the inner and outer layers of the armor during the few hours in space. More accurately, since an equilibrium had undoubtedly been reached, it should have been at a much higher temperature.

The trickling of liquid air did cease much sooner on the armor, however, and Ken still had some hope when he was finally able to unclamp the garment and take it in for closer examination.

The outer surface of the metal had changed color. That was the first and most obvious fact. Instead of the silvery sheen of polished steel, there was a definitely bluish tint on certain areas, mostly near the tips of the armlike handling extensions and the inner surfaces of the legs. Ken was willing to write off the color as a corrosion film caused by the oxygen, but could not account for its unequal distribution. With some trepidation he opened the body section of the massive suit, and reached inside.

It was cold. Too cold for comfort. The heating coils might have been able to overcome that, but they were not working. The recorder showed a few inches of tape—it had been started automatically by a circuit which ran from a pressure gauge in the torpedo through one of the suit radio jacks as soon as atmospheric pressure had been detectable—and that tape showed a clear story. Temperature and pressure had held steady for a few minutes; then, somewhere about the time the torpedo must have reached the planet's surface, or shortly thereafter, they had both started erratically downward—very erratically, indeed; there was even a brief rise above normal temperature. The recorder had been stopped when the temperature reached the freezing point of sulfur, probably by air solidifying around its moving parts. It had not resumed operation. The planet was apparently a heat trap, pure and simple.

There was no direct evidence that the suit had leaked gas either way, but Ken rather suspected it had. The bluish tint on portions of the metal might conceivably be the result of flame—flaming oxygen, ignited by jets of high-pressure sulfur coming from minute leaks in the armor. Both sulfur and oxygen support combustion, as Ken well knew, and they do combine with each other—he made a mental note to look up the heats of formation of any sulfides of oxygen that might exist.

He turned away from the debacle at last.

"We'll let Feth look this over when we get back," he said. "He may have better ideas about just how and why the insulation failed. We may as well go on to Planet Four and see if it has anything that might pass for soil."

"We've been orbiting around it for some time, I imagine," Drai responded. "Lee was supposed to head that way as soon as we got your suit on board, but he was not to land until I returned to the control room." The two promptly glided forward, pulling their weightless bodies along by means of the grips set into the walls, and shot within seconds through the control room door—even Ken was getting used to non-standard gravity and even to none at all.

Drai's assumption proved to be correct; drive power was off, and Mars hung beyond the ports. To Sarrian eyes it was even more dimly lighted than Earth, and like it obviously possessed of an atmosphere. Here, however, the atmospheric envelope was apparently less dense. They were too close to make out the so-called canals, which become river valleys when observation facilities are adequate, but even rivers were something new to the Sarrians. They were also too close to see the polar caps from their current latitude, but as the *Karella* drifted southward a broad expanse of white came into view. The cap was nowhere near the size it had been two months before, but again it was a completely strange phenomenon to the gazing aliens.

Or, more accurately, almost completely strange. Ken tightened a tentacle about one of Drai's.

"There was a white patch like that on Planet Three! I remember it distinctly! There's *some* resemblance between them, anyway."

"There are two, as a matter of fact," replied Drai. "Do you want to get your soil from there? We have no assurance that it is there that the tofacco grows on Planet Three."

"I suppose not; but I'd like to know what the stuff is anyway. We can land at the edge of it, and get samples of everything we find. Lee?"

The pilot looked a little doubtful, but finally agreed to edge down carefully into atmosphere. He refused to commit himself to an actual landing until he had found how rapidly the air could pull heat from his hull. Neither Drai nor Ken objected to this stipulation, and presently the white, brown and greenish expanse below them began to assume the appearance of a landscape instead of a painted disc hanging in darkness.

The atmosphere turned out to be something of a delusion. With the ship hanging a hundred feet above the surface, the outside pressure gauges seemed very reluctant to move far from zero. Pressure was about one fiftieth of Sarr normal. Ken pointed this out to the pilot, but Ordon Lee refused to permit his hull to touch ground until he had watched his outside pyrometers for fully fifteen minutes. Finally satisfied that heat was not being lost any faster than it could be replaced, he settled down on a patch of dark-colored sand, and listened for long seconds to the creak of his hull as it adapted itself to the changed load and localized heat loss. At last, apparently satisfied, he left his controls and turned to Ken.

"If you're going out to look this place over, go ahead. I don't think your armor will suffer any worse than our hull. If you have trouble anywhere, it will be with your feet—loss through the air is nothing to speak of. If your feet get cold, though, don't waste time—get back inside!"

Ken cast a mischievous glance at Drai. "Too bad we didn't bring two suits," he said. "I'm sure you'd have liked to come with me."

"Not in a hundred lifetimes!" Drai said emphatically. Ken laughed outright. Curiously enough, his own original horror of the fearful chill of these Solar planets seemed to have evaporated; he actually felt eager to make the test. With the help of Drai and Lee he climbed into the armor they had brought from Mercury, sealed it, and tested its various working parts. Then he entered the air lock of the *Karella,* and observed his instruments carefully while it was pumped out. Still nothing appeared to be wrong, and he closed the switch actuating the motor of the outer door.

For some reason, as the Martian landscape was unveiled before him, his mind was dwelling on the curious discoloration of the suit that had been exposed to Planet Three's atmosphere, and wondering if anything of the sort was likely to happen here.

Curiously enough, one hundred sixty million miles away, a thirteen-year-old boy was trying to account for a fire which seemed to have burned over a small patch of brush, isolated by bare rock, on a hillside five miles west of his home.

# XI.

Even to an Earth man, Mars is not a world to promote enthusiasm. It is rather cold at the best of times, much too dry, and woefully lacking in air—breathable or otherwise. The first and last of these points struck Ken most forcibly.

The landscape in front of him was very flat. It was also very patchy. In some spots bare rock showed, but those were few and far between. Much of the area seemed to be dark, naked soil, with bits of green, brown, red and yellow mingling in the general background. Nearly half of the landscape seemed to be composed of the patches of white, which had seemed to be a solid mass from space. Probably, Ken realized, they formed a solid covering closer to the center of the white region; they had landed on its edge, as planned.

He took a careful step away from the ship's side. The gravity was less than that of Sarr, but distinctly greater than on Mercury, and the armor was a severe burden. The two tentacles inside his right "sleeve" forced the clumsy pipe of steel downward almost to the ground, and manipulated the handlers at the end. With some difficulty, he scraped loose a piece of dark brown soil and raised it to eye level. He locked the "knees" of the armor and settled back on the tail-like prop that extended from the rear of the metal trunk, so that he could give all his attention to examining the specimen.

The glass of his face plate showed no signs of differential contraction so far, but he carefully avoided letting the soil touch it during the examination. He almost forgot this precaution, however, when he saw the tiny varicolored objects on the surface of the sample. Weird as they were in shape, they were unquestionably plants—tiny, oddly soft-looking compared to the crystalline growths of Sarr, but still plants. And they lived in this frightful cold! Already those nearest the metal of his handler were shriveling and curling, cold as the outside of his armor already must be. Eagerly Ken reported this to the listeners inside.

"This life must have something in common with that of Three," he added. "Both must run on chemical energy of the same general sort, since there's no important difference in their temperatures. This soil must have all the elements necessary, even if the compounds aren't quite right for what we want—who ever heard of a life form that didn't have a good deal of latitude that way?" He looked back at the sample he was holding. "It looks a little different around the edges, as though the heat of my armor were making some change in it. You may be right, Drai—there may be some volatile substance in this soil that's evaporating now. I wonder if I can trap it?" He lapsed into thought, dropping his specimen.

"You can try afterward. Why not investigate the white patches?" called Drai. "And the rocks, too; they might be something familiar—and soils are made from rock, after all." Ken admitted the justice of this, hitched himself off the rear prop, unlocked his leg joints, and resumed his walk away from the ship.

So far, he had felt no sign of cold, even in his feet. Evidently the soil was not a very good conductor of heat. That was not too surprising, but Ken made a mental note to be careful of any patches of solid rock he might encounter.

The nearest of the white areas was perhaps thirty yards from the air lock door. Reaching it quickly enough in spite of the weight of his armor, Ken looked it over carefully. He could not bend over to examine its texture, and was a little uneasy about picking it up; but remembering that the handlers of his armor extended some distance beyond the actual tips of his tentacles, as well as the fact that the first sample had been harmless, he reached down and attempted to scrape up a piece.

This seemed easy enough. The handler grated across the surface, leaving a brown streak behind—evidently the white material formed a very thin layer on the ground. Raising the sample to eye level, however, Ken discovered that he had nothing but dark-colored sand.

Excusably puzzled, he repeated the process, and this time was quick enough to see the last of the white material vanish from the sand grains. "You were right, Laj," he said into his transmitter. "There's something here that's really volatile. I haven't got enough for a good look, yet—I'll try to find a deeper deposit." He started forward again, toward the center of the white patch.

The expanse was perhaps fifty yards across, and Ken judged that the volatile coating might be thicker in the, center. This proved to be the case, but it never became heavy enough to impede even his progress. His trail was clearly marked by bare soil, as the stuff faded eerily out of sight around each footprint. Ken, though he could have looked behind in his armor without turning his whole body, did not notice this, but the watchers from the ship did. Drai remarked on it over the radio, and Ken responded:

"Tell me if it stops—maybe that will be a place where it's thick enough to pick some of the stuff up. I'd like to get a close look at it before it evaporates. Right now, I can't imagine what it might be, and I need information badly in order to make even an educated guess."

"The trail is getting narrower now—there are separate spots which outline the shape of the feet of your armor, instead of broad circular areas that blend into each other. A little farther ought to do it."

A little farther did. Ken was not quite to the center of the white patch when Drai reported that he had ceased to leave a trail. He promptly stopped, propped himself as he had before, and scooped up a fresh handful of the evanescent substance. This time there was practically no sand included; the material was fully an inch deep. The mass on his handler began to shrink at once, but not so rapidly as to prevent his getting a fairly long look. It was crystalline, millions of minute facets catching and scattering the feeble sunlight; but the individual crystals were too tiny to permit him to determine their shape. It was gone before he was really satisfied, but there seemed little likelihood of his getting a better look. Somehow a sample would have to be obtained—and analyzed. He thought he saw how that might be done, but some careful preparation would be necessary. Announcing this fact over his suit radio, he prepared to return to the ship.

Perhaps, in the half-seated attitude he had been holding, his feet had been partly out of contact with the armor; perhaps in his single-minded interest in things outside he simply had not noticed what was happening. Whatever the cause, it was not until he stood up that the abrupt, stabbing blade of cold seared straight from his feet to his brain. For an instant he settled back on his prop, trying to draw his feet from the biting touch of what was supposed to be insulation; then, realizing that matters would only grow worse if he delayed, he forced himself into action. Barely able to bite back a scream of anguish, he strained every muscle forcing the unwieldy mass of metal toward the air lock; and even through his pain, the thought came driving—no wonder the trail had become narrower; the feet of his armor must be nearly at the temperature of their surroundings. From five hundred degrees above zero Centigrade to fifty below is quite a temperature gradient for a scant three inches of steel, vacuum space, fluid coils, and insulating fiber to maintain, even with a powerful heating coil backing up the high-temperature side of the barrier.

The pain grew less as he struggled toward the lock, but the fact did not make him any happier; it terrified him. If he should lose control of his feet, he would die within sight of the *Karella's* crew, for there was not another suit of special armor aboard that could be worn to rescue him.

Now his face was cold, too—he must be losing radiation even through the special glass of the face plate. His tentacle tips were feeling the chill, but not so badly; the fact that the deadly whiteness had touched only the handlers, inches beyond the "inhabited" parts of the sleeve, was helping there. He had reached the edge of the area of death, and only thirty yards of bare ground lay between him and the lock. That ground was cold, too. It must be as cold as the other area; but at least it did not seem to drink heat. The lock door was open as he had left it, a metal-lined cavern that seemed to draw away as he struggled forward. He was numb below the lower knees, now; for the first time he blessed the clumsy stiffness of the armor legs, which made them feel and act like stilts, for that was all that enabled him to control the feet. Once he stumbled, and had time to wonder if he would ever be able to get the clumsy bulk erect again; then he had caught himself in some way—he never learned how, and no one on the ship could tell him—and was reeling forward again. Ten yards to go—five—two—and he brought up against the hull of the *Karella* with a clang. One more step and he was inside the lock. Two, and he was out of the swing of the massive door. With frantic haste he swung the sleeve of his armor at the closing switch. He hit it—hit it hard enough to bend the toggle, but the circuit was closed and the door thudded shut behind him, the sound of its closing coming through the metal of floor and suit. Then came the air, automatically, pouring into the lock chamber, condensing on the body of his armor, freezing into a yellow crust on the extremities. With the pressure up, the inner door swung wide, revealing Drai and Ordon Lee in the corridor beyond. The former shrank from the fierce chill that poured from the chamber; the pilot, thinking faster, leaped to a locker nearby and seized a welding torch. Playing the flame of this ahead of him, he approached Ken carefully.

The crust of sulfur boiled away instantly in the flame, to be replaced almost as fast when the tongue of light swung elsewhere. Long seconds passed before the metal was warm enough to stay clear, and more before it could be touched, and the almost unconscious Ken extracted. Minutes more passed before the throbbing agony receded from his limbs, and he was able to talk coherently, but at last he was satisfied that no permanent damage had been done. He had not actually been frost-bitten, though judging by the color of his skin he had come dangerously near to it.

Drai and Lee, amazed and horrified at the results of the brief sortie, felt both emotions redoubled as they heard of his plans for another. Even Drai, interested as he was in obtaining useful information, made a half-hearted attempt to dissuade him from the project. Ken refused to be dissuaded, and his employer did not have too much difficulty in consoling himself—after all, it was Ken's health.

The instructions to bring "whatever he thought he would need" had been obeyed, and Ken spent some time searching through the pile of apparatus from the Mercurian laboratory. What he found seemed to satisfy him, and he made a number of careful preparations which involved some very precise weighing. He then carried several items of equipment to the air lock, and finally donned the armor again, to Ordon Lee's undisguised admiration.

From the control room port, Drai and the pilot watched Ken's hasty trip back to the scene of his earlier trouble. He followed his earlier trail, which was still clearly visible, and carefully avoided touching the whiteness with any part of his armor. Arrived at the point where his cooling boots had been unable to boil their way down to solid ground, he stopped. The watchers were unable to make out his actions in detail, but apparently he set some object on the ground, and began rolling it about as the white substance evaporated from around it. Presently this ceased to happen, as its temperature fell to that of its surroundings; then Ken appeared to pick it up and separate it into two parts. Into one of these he scooped a quantity of the mysterious stuff, using an ordinary spoon. Then the two halves of the thing were fastened together again, and the scientist beat a hasty retreat toward the air lock.

Drai was promptly headed for the inner door of the chamber, expecting to see what was going on; but the portal remained closed. He heard the hissing of air as pressure was brought up, and then nothing. He waited for some minutes, wondering more and more, and finally went slowly back to the control room. He kept looking back as he went, but the valve remained sealed.

As he entered the control room, however, Lee had something to report.

"He's pumping the lock down again," the pilot said, gesturing to a flaring violet light on the board. Both Sarrians turned to the port of the side toward the air lock, Lee keeping one eye on the indicator that would tell them when the outer door opened. It flashed in a matter of seconds, and the watchers crowded eagerly against the transparent panel, expecting Ken's armored figure to appear. Again, however, nothing seemed to happen.

"What in the Galaxy is the fellow up to?" Drai asked the world at large, after a minute or so. Lee treated the question as rhetorical, but did shift part of his attention back to the control board. Even here, however, fully five minutes passed without anything occurring; then the outer door closed again. Calling Drai's attention to this, he looked expectantly at the pressure indicator, which obediently flashed a report of rising pressure. They waited no longer, but headed down the corridor side by side.

This time Ken appeared to have finished his work; the inner door was open when they reached it. He had not permitted his suit to get so cold this time, it seemed; only a light dew dimmed its polish. Within a minute or so Lee was able to help him emerge. He was wearing a satisfied expression, which did not escape the watchers.

"You found out what it was!" Drai stated, rather than asked.

"I found out something which will let me figure out what it is, very shortly," replied Ken.

"But what did you do? Why did you go out twice?"

"You must have seen me putting a sample into the pressure bomb. I sealed it in, and brought it inside so it would all evaporate and so that the pressure gauge on the bomb would be at a temperature where I could trust it. I read the pressure at several temperatures, and weighed the bomb with the sample. I had already weighed it empty—or rather, with the near-vacuum this planet uses for air inside it. The second time I opened the door was to let off the sample, and to make a check at the same temperature with a sample of the planet's air—after all, it must have contributed a little to the pressure the first time."

"But what good would all that do?"

"Without going into a lot of detail, it enabled me to find out the molecular weight of the substance. I did not expect that to be very conclusive, but as it happened I think it will be; it's so small that there aren't many possible elements in it—certainly nothing above fluorine, and I think nothing above oxygen. I'll concede that I may be off a unit or so in my determination, since the apparatus and observing conditions were not exactly ideal, but I don't think it can be much worse than that."

"But what is it?"

"The molecular weight? Between eighteen and nineteen, I got."

"What has that weight, though?"

"Nothing at all common. I'll have to look through the handbook, as I said. Only the very rarest elements are that light."

"If they're so rare, maybe the stuff is not so important for life after all." Ken looked at Drai to see if he were serious.

"In the first place," he pointed out, seeing that the other had not been joking, "mere rarity doesn't prove that life doesn't need it. We use quite respectable quantities of fluorine in our bodies, not to mention zinc, arsenic and copper. This other form of life may well do the same. In the second place, just because an element is rare on Sarr doesn't prove it would be so on Planet Three—it's a much bigger world, and could easily have held considerable quantities of the lighter elements during its original formation, even if they had been there as uncombined gases." The group had been walking toward Ken's room, where he had stored most of his apparatus, as they talked. Reaching it at this point, they entered. Ken draped himself without apology on the only rack, and began to flip through the pages of the chemical handbook, in the section devoted to inorganic compounds. He realized that his mysterious substance could contain carbon, but it certainly could not contain more than one atom per molecule, so there was no danger of its being a really complex organic material.

There were, in fact, just eight elements likely to be present; and the laws of chemistry would put considerable restriction on the possible combinations of those eight. The lightest of these was hydrogen, of course; and to the hydrogen compounds Ken turned, since they came first in that section of the handbook.

Drai had moved to a position from which he could oversee the pages that Ken was reading; the less interested or less excitable Lee stayed near the door and waited silently. He was more prepared than his employer for a long wait while the scientist made his search; and he was correspondingly more surprised when Ken, almost as soon as he began reading, suddenly stiffened in a fashion which indicated he had found something of interest. Drai saw the action as well.

"What is it?" he asked at once. Both Ken and Lee realized that the "it" referred to the substance, not the cause of Ken's interest; Drai assumed without thought that his scientist had found what he was seeking.

"Just a moment. There's something that doesn't quite agree—but the rest is too perfect—wait a minute—" Ken's voice trailed off for a moment; then, "Of course. This is under normal pressure." He looked up from the book.

"This appears to be the stuff—it's almost completely unknown on Sarr, because of its low molecular weight—most of it must have escaped from the atmosphere eons ago, if it ever was present. According to this handbook, it should be liquid through quite a temperature range, but that's under our atmospheric pressure. It's quite reasonable that it should sublime the way it did in this vacuum."

"But what is it?"

"One of the oxides of hydrogen—$H_2O$, apparently. If it proves to be essential for the form of growth you're interested in, we're going to have a very interesting time handling it."

"We have cargo shells that can be kept at outside conditions, and towed outside the ship," Drai pointed out.

"I assumed you did," replied Ken. "However, normal 'outside' conditions in the space near Planet One would almost certainly cause this stuff to volatilize just as it did from the comparatively faint heat radiating from my armor. Your shells will have to be sealed airtight, and you will, as I said, have an interesting time transferring their contents to any cave we may pick."

Laj Drai looked startled for several seconds. Then he appeared to remember something, and his expression changed to one of satisfaction.

"Well," he said, "I'm sure you'll be able to figure that one out. That's what scientists are for, aren't they?" It was Ken's turn to look startled, though he had known Drai long enough by this time to have expected something of the sort.

"Don't you ever solve your own problems?" he asked, a trifle sourly. Drai nodded slowly.

"Yes, sometimes. I like to think them over for quite a while, though, and if they're scientific ones I don't have the knowledge to think with. That's why I hire people like you and Feth. Thanks for reminding me— I do have a problem at the moment, on which I have spent a good deal of thought. If you'll excuse me, I'll attend to the finishing touches. You can stay here and work on this one."

"There's nothing more we can do on this planet for the present."

"That I can believe. We'll head back for Planet One and the rest of your laboratory facilities. Come on, Lee—we'll leave the scientist to his science."

Ken, unsuspicious by nature, did not even look up as the two left his room. He had just found ammonia on the list, and was wondering whether his measurement could have been far enough off to permit the true molecular weight to be only seventeen. Melting-point data finally reassured him. For safety's sake, however, he went through all the hydrogen, lithium, beryllium, boron, nitrogen, and oxygen compounds that were listed in the handbook. The faint disturbance incident to the vessel's takeoff did not bother him at all. The silent opening of his door made no impression on him, either.

In fact, the door had closed again with a crisp snap before anything outside the printed pages registered on his consciousness. Then a voice, coincident with the closing door, suddenly shattered the silence.

"Sallman Ken!" The mechanical speaker over the entrance boomed the words; the voice was that of Laj Drai. "I said when we parted a moment ago that I occasionally solve my own problems. Unfortunately, you have come to represent a problem. There seems to be only one solution which will not destroy your usefulness. In a way I regret to employ it, but you have really only your own unwarranted curiosity to thank. When you wake up, we will talk again—you can tell me what you think of our commercial product!" The voice ceased, with a click which indicated that the microphone had been switched off.

Ken, fully aroused, had dropped the book and risen to his feet—or rather, left his rack and floated away from the floor, since they were in weightless flight. His eyes roved rapidly to all quarters of the room in search of something that might furnish meaning to Drai's rather ominous words. Several seconds passed before he saw it—a rectangular yellow brick, floating in the air near the door. For a moment he did not recognize it, and pushed against a wall to bring himself nearer to it; then, as he felt the chill emanating from the thing, he tried futilely to check his drift.

Already the brick was losing shape, its corners rounding with the heat and puffing off into vapor. It was frozen sulfur—harmless enough in itself if contact were avoided, but terrifying when considered with his background of knowledge and suspicion. With a frantic flailing of his tentacles, he managed to set up enough of an air current to cause the thing to drift out of his path; but an equally anxious look about the room for something which might serve as a gas mask disclosed nothing.

He found himself unable to take his eyes from the dwindling object, now a rather elongated ellipsoid. It continued to shrink remorselessly, and suddenly there was something else visible in the yellow—the end of a small white cylinder. As the last of the protective box vanished, this began to turn brown and then black over its entire surface, and a spherical cloud of smoke enveloped it. For an instant a wild hope flashed in Ken's mind; the thing had to burn, and a fire will not maintain itself in weightless flight. It requires a forced draft. Perhaps this one would smother itself out—but the cloud of smoke continued to swell. Apparently the thing had been impregnated with chips of frozen air in anticipation of this situation.

Now the edges of the smoke cloud were becoming fuzzy and ill-defined as diffusion carried its particles through the room. Ken caught the first traces of a sweetish odor, and tried to hold his breath; but he was too late. The determination to make the effort was his last coherent thought.

# XII.

"So they decided to keep you." There might or might not have been a faint trace of sympathy in Feth Allmer's tone. "I'm not very surprised. When Drai raised a dust storm with me for telling you how far away Sarr was, I knew you must have been doing some probing on your own. What are you, Commerce or Narcotics?" Ken made no answer.

He was not feeling much like talking, as a matter of fact. He could remember just enough of his drug-induced slumber to realize things about himself which no conscientious being should be forced to consider. He had dreamed he was enjoying sights and pleasures whose recollection now gave him only disgust—and yet under the disgust was the hideous feeling that there had been pleasure, and there might be pleasure again. There is no real possibility of describing the sensations of a drug addict, either while he is under the influence of his narcotic or during the deadly craving just before the substance becomes a physical necessity; but at this moment, less than an hour after he had emerged from its influence, there may be some chance of his frame of mind being understandable. Feth certainly understood, but apparently chose not to dwell on that point.

"It doesn't matter now which you were, or whether the whole gang knows it," he went on after waiting in vain for Ken's answer. "It won't worry anyone. They know you're ours for good, regardless of what you may think at the moment. Wait until the craving comes on—you'll see."

"How long will that be?" The point was of sufficient interest to Ken to overcome his lethargy.

"Five to six days; it varies a little with the subject. Let me warn you now—don't cross Laj Drai, ever. He really has the ship. If he keeps the tofacco from you for even half an hour after the craving comes on, you'll never forget it. I still haven't gotten over his believing that I told you where we were." Again surprise caused Ken to speak.

299

"You? Are you—?"

"A sniffer? Yes. They got me years ago, just like you, when I began to get an idea of what this was all about. I didn't know where this system was, but my job required me to get engineering supplies occasionally, and they didn't want me talking."

"That was why you didn't speak to me outside the observatory, just after we got back from the caves?"

"You saw me come out of the office? I never knew you were there. Yes, that was the reason, all right." Feth's normally dour features grew even grimmer at the memory. Ken went back to his own gloomy thought, which gradually crystallized into a resolve. He hesitated for a time before deciding to mention it aloud, but was unable to see what harm could result.

"Maybe you can't get out from under this stuff—I don't know; but I'll certainly try."

"Of course you will. So did I."

"Well, even if I can't Drai needn't think I'm going to help him mass produce this hellish stuff. He can keep me under his power, but he can't compel me to think."

"He could, if he knew you weren't. Remember what I told you—not a single open act of rebellion is worth the effort. I don't know that he actually enjoys holding out on a sniffer, but he certainly never hesitates if he thinks there's need—and you're guilty until proved innocent. If I were you, I'd go right on developing those caves."

"Maybe you would. At least, I'll see to it that the caves never do him any good."

Feth was silent for a moment. If he felt any anger at the implication in Ken's statement, his voice did not betray it, however.

"That, of course, is the way to do it. I am rather surprised that you have attached no importance to the fact that Drai has made no progress exploring Planet Three for the seventeen years I have been with him."

For nearly a minute Ken stared at the mechanic, while his mental picture of the older being underwent a gradual but complete readjustment.

"No," he said at last, "I never thought of that at all. I should have, too—I did think that some of the obstacles to investigation of the planet seemed rather odd. You mean you engineered the television tube failures, and all such things?"

"The tubes, yes. That was easy enough—just make sure there were strains in the glass before the torpedo took off."

"But you weren't here when the original torpedoes were lost, were you?"

"No, that was natural enough. The radar impulses we pick up are real, too; I don't know whether this idea of a hostile race living on the blue plains of Planet Three is true or not, but there seems to be some justification for the theory. I've been tempted once or twice to put the wrong thickness of anti-radar coating on a torpedo so that they'd know we were getting in—but then I remember that that might stop the supply of tofacco entirely. Wait a few days before you think too hardly of me for that." Ken nodded slowly in understanding, then looked up suddenly as another idea struck him.

"Say, then the failure of that suit we sent to Three was not natural?"

"I'm afraid not." Feth smiled a trifle. "I overtightened the packing seals at knees, hips and handler joints while you were looking on. They contracted enough to let air out, I imagine—I haven't seen the suit, re-member. I didn't want you walking around on that planet—you could do too much for this gang in an awfully short time, I imagine."

"But surely that doesn't matter now? Can't we find an excuse for re-peating the test?"

"Why? I thought you weren't going to help."

"I'm not, but there's an awfully big step between getting a first-hand look at the planet and taking living specimens of tofacco away from it. If you sent a person to make one landing on Sarr, what would be the chance of his landing within sight of a *Gree* bush? or, if he did, of your finding it out against his wish?"

"The first point isn't so good; this tofacco might be all over the place like *Mekko*—the difficulty would be to miss a patch of it. Your second consideration, however, now has weight." He really smiled, for the first time since Ken had known him. "I see you are a scientist after all. No narcotics agent would care in the least about the planet, under the cir-cumstances. Well, I expect the experiment can be repeated more success-fully, though I wouldn't make the dive myself for anything I can think of."

"I'll bet you would—for one thing," Ken replied. Feth's smile disap-peared.

"Yes—just one," he agreed soberly. "But I see no chance of that. It would take a competent medical researcher years, even on Sarr with all his facilities. What hope would we have here?"

"I don't know, but neither of us is senile," retorted Ken. "It'll be a few years yet before I give up hope. Let's look at that suit you fixed, and the one I wore on Four. They may tell us something of what we'll have to guard against." This was the first Feth had heard of the sortie on Mars, and he said so. Ken told of his experience in detail, while the mechanic listened carefully.

"In other words," he said at the end of the tale, "there was no trouble until you actually touched this stuff you have decided was hydrogen oxide. That means it's either a terrifically good conductor, has an enormous specific heat, a large heat of vaporization, or two or three of those in combination. Right?" Ken admitted, with some surprise, that that was right. He had not summed up the matter so concisely in his own mind. Feth went on: "There is at the moment no way of telling whether there is much of that stuff on Three, but the chances are there is at least some. It follows that the principal danger on that planet seems to be encountering deposits of this chemical. I am quite certain that I can insulate a suit so that you will not suffer excessive heat loss by conduction or convection in atmospheric gases, whatever they are."

Ken did not voice his growing suspicion that Feth had been more than a mechanic in his time. He kept to the vein of the conversation.

"That seems right. I've seen the stuff, and it's certainly easy to recognize, so there should be no difficulty in avoiding it."

"You've seen the solid form, which sublimed in a near vacuum. Three has a respectable atmospheric pressure, and there may be a liquid phase of the compound. If you see any pools of any sort of liquid whatever, I would advise keeping clear of them."

"Sound enough—only, if the planet is anything like Sarr, there isn't a chance in a thousand of landing near open liquid."

"Our troubles seem to spring mostly from the fact that this planet *isn't* anything like Sarr," Feth pointed out drily. Ken was forced to admit the justice of this statement, and stored away the rapidly growing stock of information about his companion. Enough of Feth's former reserve had disappeared to make him seem a completely changed person.

The suits were brought into the shop and gone over with extreme care. The one used on Planet Four appeared to have suffered no damage, and they spent most of the time on the other. The examination this time was much more minute than the one Ken had given it on board the *Karella*, and one or two new discoveries resulted. Besides the bluish deposit Ken had noted on the metal, which he was now able to show contained oxides, there was a looser encrustation in several more protected spots which gave a definite potassium spectrum—one of the few that Ken could readily recognize—and also a distinct odor of carbon bisulfide when heated. That, to the chemist, was completely inexplicable. He was familiar with gaseous compounds of both elements, but was utterly unable to imagine how there could have been precipitated from them anything capable of remaining solid at "normal" temperature.

Naturally, he was unfamiliar with the makeup of earthly planets, and had not seen the fire whose remains had so puzzled Roger Wing. Even the best imaginations have their limits when data are lacking.

The joints had, as Feth expected, shrunk at the seals, and traces of oxides could be found in the insulation. Apparently some native atmosphere had gotten into the suit, either by diffusion or by outside pressure after the sulfur had frozen.

"Do you think that is likely to happen with the packing properly tightened?" Ken asked, when this point had been checked.

"Not unless the internal heaters fail from some other cause, and in that case you won't care anyway. The overtightening cut down the fluid circulation in the temperature equalizing shell, so that at first severe local cooling could take place without causing a sufficiently rapid reaction in the main heaters. The local coils weren't up to the job, and once the fluid had frozen at the joints of course the rest was only a matter of seconds. I suppose we might use something with a lower freezing point than zinc as an equalizing fluid—potassium or sodium would be best from that point of view, but they're nasty liquids to handle from chemical considerations. Tin or bismuth are all right that way, but their specific heats are much lower than that of zinc. I suspect the best compromise would be selenium."

"I see you've spent a good deal of time thinking this out. What would be wrong with a low-specific-heat liquid?"

"It would have to be circulated much faster, and I don't know whether the pumps would handle it—both those metals are a good deal denser than zinc, too. Selenium is still pretty bad in specific heat, but its lower density will help the pumps. The only trouble is getting it. Well, it was just a thought—the zinc should stay liquid if nothing special goes wrong. We can try it on the next test, anyway."

"Have you thought about how you are going to justify this next trial, when Drai asks how come?"

"Not in detail. He won't ask. He likes to boast that he doesn't know any science—then he gloats about hiring brains when he needs them. We'll simply say that we have found a way around the cause of the first failure—which is certainly true enough."

"Could we sneak a televisor down on the next test, so we could see what goes on?"

"I don't see how we could conceal it—any signal we can receive down here can be picked up as well or better in the observatory. I suppose we might say that you had an idea in that line too, and we were testing it out."

"We could—only perhaps it would be better to separate ideas a little. It wouldn't help if Drai began to think you were a fool. People too often connect fools and knaves in figures of speech, and it would be a pity to have him thinking along those lines."

"Thanks—I was hoping you'd keep that point in mind. It doesn't matter much anyway—I don't see why we can't take the *Karella* out near Three and make the tests from there. That would take only a matter of minutes, and you could make the dive right away if things went well. I know it will be several days before the ship will be wanted—more likely several weeks. They get eight or ten loads of tofacco from the planet during the 'season,' and several days elapse between each load. Since all the trading is done by torpedo, Lee has a nice idle time of it."

"That will be better. I still don't much like free fall, but a few hours of that will certainly be better than days of waiting. Go ahead and put it up to Drai. One other thing—let's bring more than one suit this time. I was a little worried for a while, there, out on Four."

"A good point. I'll check three suits, and then call Drai." Conversation lapsed, and for the next few hours a remarkable amount of constructive work was accomplished. The three units of armor received an honest preservice check this time, and Feth was no slacker. Pumps, valves, tanks, joints, heating coils—everything was tested, separately and in all combinations.

"A real outfit would spray them with liquid mercury as a final trick," Feth said as be stepped back from the last suit, "but we don't have it, and we don't have any place to try it, and it wouldn't check as cold as these are going to have to take anyway. I'll see what Drai has to say about using the ship—we certainly can't run three torpedoes at once, and I'd like to be sure all these suits are serviceable before any one of them is worn on Three." He was putting away his tools as he spoke. That accomplished, he half turned toward the communicator, then appeared to think better of it.

"I'll talk to him in person. Drai's a funny chap," he said, and left the shop.

He was back in a very few minutes, grinning.

"*We* can go," he said. "He was very particular about the plural. You haven't been through a period of tofacco-need yet, and he is afraid you'd get funny ideas alone. He is sure that I'll have you back here in time for my next dose. He didn't *say* all this, you understand, but it wasn't hard to tell what he had in mind."

"Couldn't we smuggle enough tofacco aboard to get us back to Sarr?"

"Speaking for myself, I couldn't get there. I understand you don't know the direction yourself. Furthermore, if Drai himself can't smuggle the stuff onto Sarr, how do you expect me to get it past his eyes? I can't carry a refrigerator on my back, and you know what happens if the stuff warms up."

"All right—we'll play the game as it's dealt for a while. Let's go."

Half an hour later, the *Karella* headed out into the icy dark. At about the same time, Roger Wing began to feel cold himself, and decided to give up the watch for that night. He was beginning to feel a little discouraged, and as he crawled through his bedroom window a short time later—with elaborate precautions of silence—and stowed the rope under his bed, he was wondering seriously if he should continue the vigil. Perhaps the strange visitor would never return, and the longer he waited to get his father's opinion, the harder it would be to show any concrete evidence of what had happened.

He fell asleep over the problem—somewhere about the time the test torpedo entered atmosphere a few miles above him.

# XIII.

The *Karella* hung poised deep in Earth's shadow, well beyond measurable air pressure. The spherical compass tuned to the transmitter on the planet far below pointed in a direction that would have been straight down had there been any weight. Ordon Lee was reading, with an occasional glance at his beloved indicator board whenever a light blinked. This was fairly often, for Ken and Feth had put the testing of cold-armor on a mass-production basis. One of the suits had already returned and been checked; Feth was now in the open air lock, clad in an ordinary space suit, detaching the second from the cargo rings and putting the third in its place. He was in touch with Ken, at the torpedo controls, by radio. The scientist was holding the torpedo as well as he could partly inside the lock, which had not been designed for such maneuvers and was not large enough for the full length of the projectile. Feth was having his troubles from the same fact, and the lock-obstruction light on Lee's board was flashing hysterically.

With the torpedo once more plunging toward the dark surface below, things quieted down a little—but only a little. Feth brought the second suit inside, necessarily closing the outer door in the process and occasioning another pattern of colored light to disturb the pilot's reading. Then there was nothing but the fading proximity light as the torpedo receded, and the burden of divided attention was shifted to Ken. He had to stay at his controls, but he wanted desperately to see what Feth was doing. He already knew that the first of the suits was wearable—its interior temperature had dropped about forty degrees, which represented an actual heat loss his own metabolism could easily make up; and there was a governor on the heater unit which Feth had deliberately set down so that the heat loss should be measurable. With that limitation removed, he should be as comfortable on the Planet of Ice as anyone could expect to be while encased in nearly three hundred pounds of metal.

307

Knowing this, he was less worried about the second suit; but he found that he was still unable to concentrate completely on the job in hand. He was quite startled when a buzzer sounded on his own board, which proved to be announcing the fact that his torpedo had encountered outside pressure. As Ken had not reduced its speed to anything like a safe value, he was quite busy for a while; and when he had finally landed the messenger—safely, he hoped—Feth had finished his work. There were now two usable suits.

That removed the greatest load from the minds of both scientist and mechanic, and they were not too disappointed when the third unit failed its test. Ken had a suspicion of the reason—Feth found that leakage had occurred at leg and "sleeve" joints, which would have been put under considerable stress by high acceleration. He did not volunteer this idea, and Feth asked no questions. Ken had an uneasy idea that the mechanic with the rather surprising chemical and physical background might have figured the matter out for himself, however.

This worry, if it could be dignified by such a name, was quickly submerged in the flurry of final preparations for the descent. Ordon Lee still refused flatly to lower his ship into the heat-trap of Earth's atmosphere, even after the success of two of the suits; it would therefore be necessary for Ken to ride down as the empty armor had done—clamped to the outside of a torpedo. The attachments would have to be modified so that he could manipulate them himself, and that took a little time. Ken ate a good meal, and took the unusual precaution of drinking—the Sarrians manufactured nearly all the liquid they needed in their own tissues.

If the scientist felt any slight doubts as he stepped into the metallic bulk which was to be his only shield for the next few hours from the ghastliest environment he could imagine, his pride prevented them from showing. He was silent as Feth carefully dogged the upper section in place—entry was effected through the top—and listened with a tiny stethoscope to each of the equalizer pumps as they were turned on. Satisfied, he nodded approval at the armored scientist, and Ken reached out, seized a stanchion with one of his handlers, and pulled his personal tank into motion toward the air lock. He had to wait in the corridor while Feth redonned his own suit, and then patiently inside the lock while the mechanic carefully attached the armor to the hull of the torpedo. Lee had finally become helpful, and was holding the projectile inside the lock against the pull of the meteor repellers, which he still refused to turn off for an instant.

Even when the outer door closed between Ken and the rest of the livable space within several million miles, he managed to keep his self-control. He was now used to weightlessness, fortunately; the endless-fall sensation has serious mental effects on some people. Even the relative emptiness of the surrounding space he could stand, since he could see enough objects to keep himself oriented. There were about as many stars visible here as near his home planet, since two hundred parsecs mean little in the size of the Galaxy. In fact, he retained his calm until his eyes as well as his sense of balance agreed to tell him he was falling. The *Karella* had long since vanished behind—or above—him. The sun was in almost the same direction, since there had been no discussion needed to settle that the landing should be made on the day side of the planet. Rather more had been needed before the same old landing place had been selected—Ken, of course, wanted to see the natives, but even his scientific curiosity had been tempered with caution. Feth, regarding the trip chiefly as another test of the armor, had been rather against natives as an added complication; but curiosity had won out. Ken was falling toward the homing transmitter at which the trading was done, with the understanding that he would be carried a little to the west, as before—he was willing to meet "his" native, but did not want to interfere more than necessary with trade. He realized, of course, that the creatures probably moved around, but he resolutely declined to think about the probable results if the one he had frightened had met the traders; he regarded it as profitless guesswork, which it certainly would have been.

The result of all the discussion, however, meant that he could see clearly the expanding world below—it felt like below, since Feth was now slowing the torpedo's descent. He could not see the torpedo at all easily, as his armor was facing away from it and the back view ports in the helmet were too close to the hull for real vision. He was beginning to feel, therefore, like a man hanging from the ledge of a high roof on a rope of questionable strength. If his vocal apparatus had been as closely connected with his breathing mechanism as is that of a human being, his state of mind would certainly have been betrayed by the radio to the listeners above. As it was they could not hear his tense breathing, and be endured his terror in silence and alone. It was probably just as well; Ordon Lee's reaction would hardly have been a sympathetic one, and whatever helpful feeling Feth might have had he would not have been likely to express aloud.

There was air around him now—at least the gaseous mixture this world used for air. It was whistling upward, audible even through the armor. He could not be much more than five miles from the ground, and the descent was still rapid—too rapid, he was beginning to feel. As if in answer to the thought, his weight increased abruptly, and he knew that Feth far above had added power. With an effort greater than he had thought himself capable of making, Ken wrenched his attention from the rapid expansion of the landscape below and the creaking of the taut chains above, and concentrated on details. Once started, this proved easy, for there was more that was fantastic around him than mere temperature.

He could not see too far, of course. Eyes whose greatest sensitivity lies in the blue and near ultra-violet are at a considerable disadvantage in Earth's hazy atmosphere. Still, the ground below was taking on detail.

It was rough, as they had deduced. Even though mountains do not show to best advantage from overhead, Ken was experienced enough to judge that these were quite respectable heights by Sarrian standards. The surface was buried in a riot of color, largely varying shades of green, brown, and gray. Here and there a patch of metallic sheen reminded him disquietingly of the vast, smooth areas where the mysteriously hostile intelligences of the planet dwelt. If these were outposts—but they had never interfered with the trading torpedoes which had been descending for years in this same area, Ken told himself.

As be dropped lower, he saw that some of the gray elevations were of remarkable shape and form—many of them were actually broader above than lower down. He was quite low before he could see that these objects were not part of the landscape, but were actually suspended in the air. The only clouds he had ever seen were the vast dust storms raised by Sarr's furious winds, but he judged that these must be of somewhat similar nature. Probably the particles were smaller, to permit them to remain in suspension—a planet this cold could hardly have very strong winds. He described the phenomena as minutely as he could to the listeners above. Feth reported that he was putting Ken's broadcasts on record, and added some more pertinent information.

"Your descent has been almost stopped, now. You are about one mile above the transmitter, and a few hundred feet higher above the place where the atmosphere tests were made. Do you want to go straight down now, or stay there and observe for a while?"

"Down with moderate speed, please. It is not possible to see too far, and I'd like to get down to where real details are visible. It seems to be mountainous country—I'll try to guide you in landing me near some peak, so that I can observe for a reasonable distance from a stable spot."

"All right. You're going down." Two or three minutes passed silently; then Ken spoke again.

"Are you moving me horizontally?"

"No. You are already away from over the transmitter—three or four miles."

"Then this atmosphere has stronger currents than I expected. I am drifting visibly, though not rapidly. It's rather hard to specify the direction—the sun is not very far from straight up, and the torpedo hides it."

"When you're nearly down, give me the direction with respect to the torpedo's orientation. I'll stop you before you touch."

Gradually details grew clearer. The greenness seemed to be a tangled mass of material somewhat resembling chemical growths Ken had prepared in various solutions; he tentatively identified it as plant life, and began to suspect what had caused the crackling sound when the test torpedo had been landed.

Standing out from the green were areas quite obviously of bare rock. These seemed to be located for the most part at and near the tops of the mountains; and with infinite care Ken directed his distant pilot in an approach to one of these. Finally, hanging motionless twenty feet above a surface which even in this relatively dim light was recognizable as rock, he gave the order to lower away.

Six feet from the ground, he had the machine stopped again, and carefully released the leg chains. The lower part of his armor dropped, almost touching; a word into the microphone brought the metal feet into contact with the ground. Releasing one of the upper chains caused him to swing around, still leaning at a sharp angle, with one side up toward the supporting hull. By a species of contortionism he contrived to make a workable tripod of his legs and the rear prop of the armor, and at last released the final chain. He was standing on the Planet of Ice, on his own two feet.

He felt heavy, but not unbearably so. His extreme caution not to land in a recumbent position was probably well founded—it was very unlikely that he could have raised himself and the armor to a standing posture with his own muscles in this gravity. Walking was going to be difficult, too—possibly even dangerous; the rock was far from level.

This, of course, was not the principal matter. For several minutes after he had severed connections with the torpedo, Ken made no attempt to move; he simply stood where he was, listening to the almost inaudible hum of his circulation motors and wondering when his feet would start to freeze. Nothing seemed to happen, however, and presently he began to take a few cautious steps. The joints of his armor were still movable; evidently the zinc had not yet frozen.

The torpedo had drifted away from overhead; apparently a slight wind was blowing. At Ken's advice, Feth brought the machine to the ground. Even with his fear lost in curiosity, Ken had no intention of becoming separated by any great distance from his transportation. Once assured that it was remaining in place, he set to work.

A few minutes' search located several loose rock fragments. These he picked up and placed in the torpedo, since anything might be of some interest; but he principally wanted soil—soil in which things were visibly growing. Several times he examined rock specimens as closely as he could, hoping to find something that might resemble the minute plants of Planet Four; but he failed utterly to recognize as life the gray and black crustose lichens which were actually growing on some of the fragments.

The landscape was not barren, however. Starting a few hundred yards from his point of landing, and appearing with ever-increasing frequency as one proceeded down the mountainside, there were bushes and patches of moss which gradually gave way to dwarfed trees and finally, where the rock disappeared for good beneath the soil, to full-grown firs. Ken saw this, and promptly headed for the nearest clump of bushes. As an afterthought, he told Feth what he was doing, so that the torpedo could be sent along. There was no point, he told himself, in carrying all the specimens back up the hillside.

Progress was quite difficult, since a gap a foot wide between rocks presented a major obstacle to the armor. After a few minutes of shuffling punctuated with frequent pauses for rest, he remarked:

"The next time, we'd better have longer shoulder chains. Then I can hang right side up from the torpedo, and be spared all this waddling."

"That's a thought," replied Feth. "It certainly will be easy enough. Do you want to come back up now and make the change, or collect a few things first?"

"Oh, I'll stay a while, now that I'm here. I haven't much farther to travel to get to these plants, if they are plants. The darned things are green, at least partly. I suppose, though, that objectively speaking there should be nothing surprising about that. Well, here we go again."

He lifted his prop from the ground and shuffled forward once more. Another minute or two sufficed to bring him within reach of the strange growth. It was only about a foot high, and he was even less able to bend down to it than he had been on Planet Four; so he extended a handler to seize a branch. The results were a trifle startling.

The branch came away easily enough. There was no trouble about that. However, before he had time to raise it to his eyes a puff of smoke spurted from the point where the handler was touching it, and the tissue in the immediate neighborhood of the metal began to turn black. The memories aroused by this phenomenon caused Ken to drop the branch, and he would undoubtedly have taken a step backward had the armor been less cumbersome. As it was, he remembered almost instantly that no gas could penetrate his metal defenses, and once more picked up the bit of vegetation.

The smoke reappeared and grew thicker as he lifted it toward his face port, but he had several seconds to examine its structure before the smoldering wood burst into flame. Although this startled him almost as much as the earlier phenomenon had, he retained his hold on the fragment. He watched with interest as the main branch curled, blackened, glowed, and flamed away, the drier leaves following suit while the green ones merely browned slightly. He made an effort to capture some of the traces of ash that remained when the process was completed, but all he was able to save were some bits of charcoal from the less completely burned portions. This he also stowed in the torpedo, Feth guiding the little vessel over to him in response to spoken directions.

A bit of soil, scraped up from beneath the plant, smoked but did not burn. Ken obtained a number of airtight cans from the cargo compartment of the torpedo and spent some time scooping bits of soil up in these. He also compressed some of the air into a cylinder, using a small piston-type pump from which Feth had carefully removed all traces of lubricant. It leaked a trifle, but its moving parts moved, which was a pleasant surprise.

"There," said Ken, when the task was completed. "If there are any seeds in that earth, we should be able to build a little vivarium and find out at least something about this life and its needs."

"Do you have a balance between makers and eaters?" asked Feth. "Suppose these plants are all—what would you call them? oxidizers?—and you don't have the corresponding reducers. I should think you'd need a balance of some sort, with any sort of life—otherwise you'd have perpetual motion."

"I can't tell that, of course, until we try. Still, I might go down this mountain a little farther and try to pick up a wider variety. There are still some empty cans."

"Another point—I don't recall your making any arrangement to keep them at the proper temperature. I know they're almost as cold as outer space, but there's a difference between almost and all the way."

"We'll leave the cans in the torpedo until we get back to One. With no air, they'll change temperature very slowly, and we can leave the torpedo somewhere on the twilight zone of One where it'll stay about the right temperature until we can build a chamber with thermostats and a refrigerator—it won't be very large; I have only a couple of cubic yards of air."

"All right, I guess you win. If it doesn't work, it will be small loss anyway. Are your feet getting cold yet?"

"Not so far—and believe me, I'm looking for it!"

"I'm not sure I believe you. I have a pretty good idea of where most of your attention is. Have you seen any animal life? I've heard the old buzzing once or twice."

"Have you? I hadn't noticed it. All I can hear comes from the mike in the torpedo, so I should get anything you do."

"I told you where your attention was. Well, I'll call you if I hear it again." He fell silent, and Ken resumed his laborious journey downhill. With frequent rests, he finally succeeded in filling and sealing all his containers and depositing them in the cargo space of the torpedo. He was interrupted once by Feth, who reported that the buzzing was again audible; but even though Ken himself could hear it when he listened, he was unable to find the source. Flies are not very large creatures, and the light was very dim anyway by Sarrian standards. Since there was nothing very appetizing even for a fly in the cargo compartment above which the microphone was located, the buzzing presently ceased.

Ken took a final look at the landscape, describing everything as completely as he could so that the record being made far above would be useful. The peaks stood out far more prominently now, since some of them were higher than he was. By ignoring the vegetation with which their slopes were clothed and imagining that it was sunset just after a particularly good dust storm, he was even able to find something almost homelike in the scene—there were times when even Sarr's blue-white sun could look as dull as the luminary of this icy world. At such times, of course, there was always a wind which would put Earth's wildest hurricane to shame, and the silence around him was out of place on that score; but for just a moment his imagination was able to carry him across two hundred parsecs of emptiness to a world of warmth and life.

He came to himself with a little start. This place was nothing like home—it wasn't exactly dead, but it should be; dead as the vacuum of space it so greatly resembled. Its cold was beginning to creep into him, mentally in the form of a return of the horror he had felt the first time he had seen the planet and physically by a slight ache in his feet. Even the engineering miracle he was wearing could not keep out the fingers of the cold indefinitely. He started to call Feth, to have the torpedo lifted so that he could get at the chains and clamps; but the request was not uttered.

As suddenly as it had done a few days before, a human voice cut sharply through the stillness of the Planet of Ice.

# XIV.

It was not, in the end, his own discouragement which caused the cessation of Roger's nocturnal watchings. The night on which the Sarrians tested the armor was, indeed, the last of these journeys; but this was owing to reasons beyond the boy's control. When he descended in the morning, his father met him and accompanied him outside. There he pointed out certain footprints. Then they went up to Roger's room together, and the rope came to light. Mr. Wing concluded the proceedings with a request for an explanation.

"Don't get the idea that anyone tattled," he added. "I don't know whether you have anyone in your confidence, even. Both your mother and I saw that you were getting most of your sleep done daytimes. Well, what's the story?"

Roger never even thought of lying. The family custom of proving questionable statements on challenge had taught him, as it had the other children, to recognize evidence and forgo useless denial. The only question in his mind was whether to tell or not. He knew there would be no punishment if he refused; but also, there would be no help from his father on a problem that was decidedly beyond his own abilities, and there would most certainly be no more night journeys in search of landing torpedoes. He told what had happened, with all the detail the near-eidetic memory of childhood could evoke. His father was silent for a minute or two when he had finished.

"We'll say nothing about your following Don and me," he said at last. "You were never told in so many words not to, and curiosity is a healthy trait. Of course you let yourself get caught in the woods at night without food, water or light, and that is a more serious matter in view of the fact that you're supposed to know better. However, the story being as

315

interesting as it is, I guess we'll suspend sentence on that offense." Roger grinned.

"What would the sentence have been?"

"The logical one would be restriction to the half-mile circle for a week or two. You certainly behaved like a six-year-old. Let's consider that that's hanging over your head, and go on to more immediate matters. I suppose Edie knows all about this?"

"She knows about what happened that night. Not about the times I've gone out since."

"All right. After breakfast, get her and come with me. We have a number of things to talk over."

It turned out that Don was also at the meeting. This was held in a little natural amphitheater a few yards uphill from the house, which had been fitted with split-log benches. Mr. Wing wasted no time, but told the younger children the same story he had told Donald a few days before. Then Roger repeated his tale, mostly for his older brother's benefit. Don had, of course, seen a Sarrian torpedo by this time, as he had been present when the first load of tobacco had been delivered a few days before; and there seemed to be little doubt that the structure Roger had encountered was of the same origin.

"I don't understand why they're shifting their base of operations after all these years." Mr. Wing looked puzzled. "They've been coming back to that same gadget which we think is a directional transmitter every summer since before Don was born."

"You don't really know that they haven't landed anywhere else, though," pointed out Donald. "It just happened that Roger met one of their torpedoes. There might have been any number of others, anywhere on the Earth."

"That's true, of course. Rog, you didn't find any traces of other landings on these night walks of yours, did you?"

"I'm not sure, Dad. There's a little patch of bushes all by itself on a hilltop out that way, that's been burnt over. I couldn't find any sign of a campfire, and there haven't been any thunderstorms. I thought maybe one of the things had dropped something like the thing that burned my hand, and started the fire; but I couldn't find anything of the sort. I don't really know what started it."

"I see. Then to sum up, we've been trading with creatures not native to this world for a long time; we may or may not be the only ones doing so; on at least one occasion they sent down a craft whose primary mission does not seem to have been trade."

"Unless the light that Rog saw was intended to attract attention, as it did," cut in Donald.

"In that case they would hardly have had their gold too hot to be touched. Furthermore, I've always refused gold—regular prospectors are competition enough without starting a rush of amateurs."

"We don't know that other people, if there have been any, felt the same way. But I guess you're right about the temperature. They must have been conducting an experiment of their own, and the offer to trade was an afterthought when they heard Rog's voice."

"It was a dirty trick," commented Roger."

"It may have been unintentional. Their knowledge of our language is extremely limited, and apparently they can't see down here. Either they don't know about television or can't mount a transmitter in those torpedoes. Besides, if you came on them unexpectedly, they may have forgotten in the excitement of the moment that the gold would be hot. You said it was another container which was providing the light. However, that's a point there's not much use discussing.

"I had not planned to take this step until both Roger and Edie were older, and had had training enough to be of more help; but the matter seems to have been taken out of my control in that respect. What I want to do, and will need the help of all of you in doing, is to find out where these things are from, what sort of people are running them—and, if possible, how they work. I don't have to tell you how important that knowledge would be. I have never tried to get outside experts on the job, because, as I told Don, I was afraid they'd let curiosity overcome prudence. I don't want the torpedoes scared away by any hasty action. I'm too old to learn a new trade, for one thing."

"Nuts!" It was Edie's first contribution to the discussion, though she had listened intently to all that had gone before.

"What are we going to do?" Roger asked, rather more practically.

"First of all, you two will come with us the next time we trade. I may take the younger kids along too, only it's quite a walk for them. You can listen in, watch, and generally see the whole thing for yourselves. After that, ideas will be in order. I was hoping, Rog, that you'd be an electronics expert by the time this happened. However, we'll use what we have."

"Maybe my trouble the other night could be put to use," Roger suggested. "If they want tobacco badly enough to pay for it in platinum and iridium, they might be in a mood to apologize."

"Supposing they realize they hurt you, and could think of a way to transmit the apology. I won't refuse an extra nugget or two if they choose to send them, but that won't be very informative."

"I suppose that's so. Well, anyway, I'm going to go over the whole neighborhood of where I saw it and where you do your trading, by daylight. If they've made any other landings in the woods, I'll find 'em—

that one broke a lot of branches, and left a dent in the ground the shape of the torpedo."

"If you think it's worth doing," remarked Don. "Why should they have landed in this neighborhood? Earth's a pretty big place."

"They did once, and I bet I know why!" retorted Roger. 'That transmitter is right here! If you were exploring a new world or a new country even, would you make one landing here and another five hundred miles away? You would not. You'd get to know one neighborhood first, and plant an outpost, and then spread out from there."

There was silence for two or three minutes while the others absorbed this.

"You're assuming, then," said Mr. Wing at last, "that after twenty years of mere trading, they suddenly are starting to explore? Why didn't they do it sooner?"

"Unfair question."

"True enough. All right, it's certainly a usable working hypothesis. You may go ahead with your exploring—so may Edie if she wants. I'm not sold enough on your idea to spend the effort myself, but in a day or two I'll signal for another torpedo. That will give you time to do any looking you want, I suppose?"

"Well—" Roger's recent mapping activities had given him a much clearer idea than he had formerly held just what the examining of one square mile meant. "We can look around a bit, anyway. I'm going right now, if no one has any real ideas. Coming, Edie?" The girl stood up silently, and followed him back to the house. Their father watched them go with some amusement.

"I wish I didn't have a nagging worry about Rog's theory," he said suddenly to Donald. "He might just be right—these creatures might be tired of paying for tobacco, and they certainly know more of physical science than we do."

"They'll have a fine time looking for the living weed in this neighborhood," replied his son. "They'll do better to stay on peaceful terms."

"Just tell 'em that, will you?" murmured Mr. Wing.

Roger and his sister wasted no time. This time there was no mistake in the matter of food; they hastily prepared some sandwiches—their mother had long since resigned herself to the fact that raids on the pantry were inseparable from common-sense rules of forest life—and with a canteen of water apiece they set out eastward. Billy and Marge were playing somewhere out of sight, so there was no trouble about leaving them home. Their father's description had been clear enough so that they had no trouble in finding the Sarrian transmitter, and from there the two began their search. At Edie's suggestion they split up, she taking the southern slopes on the line back to their home and Roger taking the northern. They agreed to keep to high ground as much as possible, and thus remain in earshot of each other most of the time. There was little point, in the time available, to look for traces in the woods; but it might be possible to sight either burned spots such as Roger had already seen or traces of disturbance in the upper branches of trees while looking from above. At any rate, more territory could be examined. Neither youngster had spent any time debating the question of whether it was better to know about a small area or guess about a large one.

Neither Roger nor Edith was on the hill where Ken landed at the time of his descent. Nature had arranged that they should be in the neighborhood, but coincidence refused to carry matters farther. However, Nature still had a trick in reserve.

Roger, until that morning, had taken more or less for granted that any future visits of the torpedo would be at night, as the first had been. His father's story had changed that idea; and since he had heard it only three or four hours before, he had not given up taking rather frequent looks at the sky. It was not too surprising, therefore, that he saw the descending torpedo.

It was nearly a mile and a half away, and he could make out no details; but he was certain it was no bird. The irregularity caused by Ken's dangling form gave just a suggestion of oddness at that distance. Detailed or not, however, Roger never thought of doubting what it was; and with a whoop that might or might not reach his sister's ears for all he cared at the moment, he headed downhill at a breakneck pace.

For a short time he made excellent speed, the irregularity of the rocks offering no obstacle that his alert eyes and active muscles could not overcome without trouble. Then he reached the forest, and was slowed considerably, For a short distance he kept up the furious effort with which he had started; then, realizing that he had at least one hill to cross and another to climb, he eased off a little.

He had wet feet, thoroughly scratched legs, and a decided shortness of wind when he reached the hilltop toward which the torpedo had seemed to be descending, some three quarters of an hour later. He had seen no sign of Edith—he had, in fact, completely forgotten her. She might have come back to mind as he paused at the top of the small mountain to gain his breath and look around for the object of his search; but as it happened, the torpedo was in sight, only a short distance down the other side. So was Sallman Ken.

Roger had seen pictures of the tremendous pressure suits which have from time to time been constructed for deep-sea exploration. The sight of Ken, therefore, did not astonish him too much—certainly less than the sight of a Sarrian without armor would have done. The suit the scientist was wearing humanized his appearance considerably, since a human being would not have had to be too greatly distorted to get into it.

The legs, for engineering reasons, bad only a single "knee," corresponding to the upper joint of the Sarrian limb; the body was about human size, and cylindrical in shape; there were only two upper limbs. These were more flexible than a human being would have needed in a similar suit, but they at least gave no indication that the creature wearing them was controlling them with two tentacles each. The handlers at their extremities were natural enough, though more complicated than the claw-like devices the boy had seen in the diving suit pictures.

At his distance, he could not see clearly through the transparent ports in the helmet; and so for some moments he failed to realize just how unhuman the wearer of the clumsy garment was.

For perhaps half a minute, Roger simply stared; then he unloosed the yell which interrupted Ken's "embarkation." The scientist's attention had been completely taken up with this task, and he had not seen Roger at all before the cry; after it, he saw nothing else. He himself was not facing the direction from which the sound had come, but one of the transparent ports in his helmet was; and he was much too interested to devote attention to anything like turning the armor, after his first look at the being charging downhill toward him. He simply stood, watching with the one eye he could bring to bear. It never occurred to him for an instant that the creature might be hostile.

Roger never thought of the possibility either. His mind resembled that of Ken much too closely, in spite of the overwhelming physical differences. They simply stood facing each other—Ken finally did swing his armor around, so he could use both eyes—and silently absorbed all the details their respective optics could pick out. Each had an advantage— Roger in the fact that the light was normal for him, Ken in that the boy was not concealed in a couple of hundred pounds of metal. Roger could see the Sarrian's face now, and his attention was taken up completely with the great, wide-spread, independently movable eyes, the blank where a nose should have been, and the broad, thin-lipped, surprisingly human mouth. The silence stretched out.

It was interrupted by Feth, whose anxiety had been increasing with each second that passed after Roger's call.

"What's happened? Is anything wrong? Are you all right, Ken?" The scientist found his voice.

"Perfectly all right. We have company, as I suppose you guessed." He began to describe Roger as completely as possible, and was interrupted within a minute by the mechanic.

"It can't be done. We'll get a television set or a camera down there if I have to invent a whole new system. Never mind describing the thing—see if you can talk to it!"

Roger had heard none of this, since Feth had not energized the speaker in the torpedo. This oversight he now rectified, and Ken's next words reached the boy clearly.

"What in the Galaxy can I say? Suppose this one has heard about our mistake the other night—suppose it's even the same one? If I use the word 'Gold' it'll either run or start fighting. I'm not afraid of it, but that certainly wouldn't help the process of getting acquainted."

"Well, you've just used the word. How did he take it? I have the main speaker on." Ken, who had had no means of knowing that fact, cast a startled glance at Roger.

The boy, of course, had understood just the one word "Gold." He probably would have missed that, except for the fact that Ken had accentuated it as one does a foreign word; but as it was, he thought that the previous conversation had been addressed to him. He had not distinguished the two voices, and all the sounds had come from the torpedo still poised just above Ken's head.

"I don't want any of your gold—not if it's like the last batch!" Again only one word was understood by the listener. Ken grew hopeful. Maybe this creature hadn't heard, or maybe they had completely misinterpreted the sounds he and Feth had heard during the atmosphere test.

"Gold?" he asked.

"NO!" Roger shook his head negatively and backed away as he gave the emphatic answer. The first gesture meant nothing to the watching Sarrian, but the second seemed clear enough.

"Did you get that last sound of his on record, Feth? judging by his actions, that's the negative in their language. No gold!" He addressed the last two words after a brief pause. Roger relaxed visibly, but still spoke emphatically.

"No gold, no platinum—I have no tobacco." He spread empty hands and turned out his pockets, giving the Sarrian scientist a clue he had been waiting for on just how much of his covering was artificial.

"Point to things and name them!" Feth cut in from above. "How else can you learn a language? This chatter sounds as silly as anything I've ever heard!"

"All right—only remember, I can see as well as hear. That makes a bit of difference. If you expect any results, keep quiet; how's this thing going to tell who's talking? It all comes from the same loudspeaker. I'll call you when I want to hear from you." Feth gave no answer to this very sound point, and after waiting a minute Ken began to follow the mechanic's suggestion.

Since Roger had been thinking of exactly the same thing, he caught on at once, and thereby gave the Sarrian a higher opinion of human intelligence than his conversations with Laj Drai had caused him to hold previously. The English words for rock, tree, bush, mountain, cloud, and the numbers up to ten were learned in short order. A few verbs were managed easily enough. At this point operations seemed likely to be suspended, and Roger was rather relieved to have the subject changed by a distant hail.

"My gosh! I forgot all about Edie! She must think I fell off a cliff or something!" He turned in the direction from which the faint voice seemed to be coming, and put all the strength of his lungs into an answering hail. His sister heard it and responded; and ten or fifteen minutes of lung strain brought her to the scene. She seemed a little dubious about approaching Ken at all closely, to Roger's surprise.

"What's the matter with you? He just wants to talk, as far as I can see."

"Haven't you got burned again?"

"No; why should I?"

"Can't you feel the heat?"

Oddly enough, Roger hadn't. He had never come closer than about fifteen feet to the scientist. The radiation from the armor was easily detectable at that distance without being uncomfortable, but he simply had not noticed it in the press of other interests. For Edith, whose strongest impression of the aliens had been derived from her brother's experience of a few nights before, it was the most prominent characteristic of the thing standing before them.

With the matter brought to his notice, Roger approached the alien more closely, and extended a cautious hand toward the metal. He stopped it more than a foot away.

"My gosh, he certainly *is* hot. Maybe that's what caused the trouble—they never thought the gold would burn me. Do you suppose that's it?"

"Maybe. I'd like to know how it can live when it's that hot, though. So would Dad. He ought to be here anyway. Had I better go tell him, while you keep the thing here?"

"I don't know how I'd keep it. Besides, it would be awful late by the time he got here. Let's try to make a date for tomorrow." He turned back to Ken without waiting for Edie's rather sensible question, "How?"

Actually the "how" proved not too difficult. Time is an abstract quantity, but when it is measured by phenomena like the apparent movement of the sun it can be discussed in signs quite clearly enough for practical purposes. Ken understood without difficulty by the time Roger had finished waving his arms that the two natives would return to the present location shortly after sunrise the following day. The scientist was just as glad to break off the interview, since his feet were now quite numb with cold. He resumed the task of fastening himself to the hovering torpedo, and the children, turning back for a last look as they reached the trees, saw the odd-looking assemblage of suit and carrier drifting upward with ever-increasing velocity. They watched until it had dwindled to a speck and vanished; then with one accord they headed for home.

# XV.

Mr. Wing was not merely interested; he was enthralled by the young-sters' report. He was sensible enough to realize that nothing any of his family had done could possibly be responsible for the aliens' starting to make personal exploration of the Earth, but the fact that they were doing so seemed likely to be very helpful to his plans. The evening meal con-sisted very largely of conversation, for all attempts to keep the details from any of the family were abandoned. Mrs. Wing, of course, had known everything from the beginning; Roger and Edie had been pretty well briefed that morning; but Billy and Marge lacked both specific informa-tion and basic knowledge to appreciate the situation. Their questions tended to break up the general train of thought, but only Roger showed any impatience. Since even he did not dare become openly contemptu-ous of their ignorance, the general tone of the conversation remained peaceful, and several important decisions were made.

"It seems to me," Mr. Wing said, "that these things—maybe we can think of them as people, now that we have some idea what they look like—must at last have some scientists on the job. I can't even guess at the rea-son for the delay—"

"Look at an astronomical photo of the Milky Way some time, and you might guess," cut in Don.

"Reason or no reason, the fact itself may be useful. There will be both explorers and apparatus coming down, beyond reasonable doubt; and they must expect to lose a certain amount of the latter. I don't mean to en-courage dishonesty in my offspring, but if we could acquire some of that apparatus long enough to perform dissection I would be very pleased."

"I take it you are no longer afraid of scaring them off," Mrs. Wing stated rather than asked.

"No. Whether they continue trading or not is out of my hands—it will probably depend on the results that their scientists get. I am not worried; they obviously want tobacco badly, and I doubt very much if it grows on any other planet. I could be surer of my ground, of course, if I knew what they wanted it for. I used to think they smoked it as we do, but this knowledge of their normal temperature makes that sound a trifle unlikely.

"But back to the original point. Anyone who talks to them from now on might well suggest that another transmitter be brought down, so they can home on this house. I see no point in walking five or six miles out and the same distance back just for a daily conversation. Incidentally, Rog, I'm wondering whether we mightn't have made a better impression if we'd tried learning their words for things instead of teaching them ours."

"Maybe. I didn't think of that."

"How about the trading, Dad?" asked Don. "Are you going to keep it up as usual, or try to get these investigators to take our stuff?" His father considered for a moment.

"I think we'd better stick to the old routine," he said finally. "We have no assurance that the traders and scientists are in with each other, and it would be a pity to disappoint our customers. Perhaps, when we go to keep this date tomorrow, you'd better go on to the transmitter and give the signal. You'd better carry a pack of cigarettes with you; normally, of course, they're two or three days answering, but if they should be in with the science crowd they may be a lot closer at the moment. You'd better be prepared, in case they answer at once."

"You mean I'd better stay by the transmitter all day, if necessary?"

"Well—no, not that. Hang around for a while, and then come back to where we'll be. We can keep an eye in the right direction in case another torpedo comes down—it can't be more than a couple of miles in a straight line, so we stand a fair chance of seeing it."

"All right. I signal, and everybody talks, with emphasis on suggesting that another communicator be brought down—always supposing either party learns enough of the other's language to get any such idea across." Don shifted the subject suddenly. "Say, Dad, I just had an idea. You say it doesn't always take the same length of time between the signal and the arrival of the torpedo?"

"That's right. Never less than two days, never much more than three."

"Could you give me any specific signaling dates, with the time of arrival? The more the better. I think I can do something with them." Mr. Wing thought for a moment.

"Some, anyway. I can remember those of the last couple of years pretty well, and probably some odd ones from earlier years if I try. What's your idea?"

"I'd rather not tell until I'm a little more certain of it. Let's have what you can recall."

With the aid of the family, who were able to supply clues on his dates of absence—a diary kept by Edie was very helpful—about two dozen of the dates were fixed with sufficient accuracy to satisfy Don. He immediately went up to his room, carrying the notes he had taken.

From that point the conversation drifted by imperceptible degrees into pure fantasy, and by bed-time a number of wonderful pictures had been drawn about the home life of the fiery visitors. Little Margie's was the most interesting, if the least accurate.

Sallman Ken, however, was wasting no time on fantasy. He had not yet worked out a really detailed course of action, but certain ideas were gradually taking shape in his mind as he worked.

The moment he entered the *Karella* and had emerged from his bulky armor, he went into a close conference with Feth. Lee was present at first, even following them to Ken's quarters where the scientist began; but a glance of understanding passed between Ken and Feth, and the conversation took a remarkably abstruse turn. It had just enough meaning to give the impression that matters of highly advanced physics and chemistry were being covered, in connection with the problem of keeping the seeds— if any—in the soil samples alive and healthy. For a few minutes it looked as though Lee were going to stay and take it, but Feth suddenly had the inspiration to ask the pilot's opinion of occasional matters. After a little of this, Ordon Lee drifted back to his control room. "He's not stupid," Feth said, looking after his retreating form, "but he certainly lacks confidence in his education! Now; what did you want to keep from Drai?"

"It has occurred to me," Ken said, "that our employer is going to want to hear everything that goes on on Planet Three, as soon as we are in halfway decent communication with the natives. I have some vague ideas about the uses to which those creatures can be put, and I'd rather not have Drai listening in to all our conversations. Since at the moment there's no way of preventing that, I'd like to know whether it might not be possible to connect me up with that speaker on the torpedo *without* having everything audible up here as well. It would be best, I suppose, if I could turn your contact on and off at will, so that he'll hear enough to keep him from getting suspicious."

"I suppose it could be done, all right," the mechanic said slowly. "I'm afraid it would take more work than it's worth, though. Wouldn't it be a great deal simpler to take another set down with you in the torpedo? You already have means for tuning both transmitter and receiver in the armor, so you could switch from one set to the other whenever you pleased."

"Wouldn't they miss the extra set?"

"Not unless Drai starts paying a great deal more attention to the technical supplies than he has in the past."

"All right, let's do it that way. Now, let's see. I already suggested suspending the armor vertically instead of horizontally from the torpedo, so I can be carried around instead of having to lug that hardware against extra gravity, didn't I?"

"Yes. That will be easy enough."

"It will have another good point, as well. The only discomfort I've felt so far on that planet has been in my feet, in spite of what we feared. This way we can keep them off the ground, so they don't lose so much by conduction.

"The only other thing I had in mind had to do with torpedo control. Could a unit be made small enough for me to carry, so I could move myself around down there instead of having to tell you where I want to go?"

Feth frowned at this suggestion. "I thought of that, too, while I was trying to keep the torpedo near you this time," he said. "Frankly, I doubt it—not that the set could be made small enough, but that I could do it with the materials I have at hand. Still, I'll look into the possibility when we get back to One. I take it you have no objection to Drai's hearing about these last two suggestions?"

"Of course not. They ought to keep him happy. I suppose it would be too much to hope that he'd take a trip down there himself, once we showed it was safe enough?" Feth smiled broadly at the scientist's suggestion.

"It would take a better psychologist than either of us to endue him with that much trust in his fellows, I fear. Besides, what good would it do? We wouldn't gain anything by leaving him there, pleasant as the idea sounds, and there'd be no use trying to threaten him, since he'd never dream of keeping any inconvenient promises you might wring out of him."

"I didn't really expect much from the idea. Well, with the other matter understood, I suppose we'd better take those samples back to One before they freeze, and get a vivarium knocked together. If we can grow anything at all, it ought to keep Drai quiet for a little while."

The torpedo which had transported Ken and his specimens had been allowed to drift to the edge of the repeller field as soon as he had detached himself from it. Feth now returned to the control room and began to monitor the little vessel, holding it close against the hull of the large ship so that it would be dragged along in the *Karella's* drive fields; and Lee, at Ken's request, headed sunward once more. A thousand miles from the surface of Mercury the torpedo was cast loose again, and Feth eased it down to a landing near the caves—a televisor had been set up there some time since, and he was able to guide the landing with the aid of this. He arranged matters so that about three feet of the torpedo's nose was in sunlight, while the rest was in the shadow of a large mass of rock. That, he judged, should maintain somewhere near the right temperature for a few hours at least. As soon as the *Karella* was grounded, he and Ken adjourned at once to the shop. There, a metal case about a yard square and two feet high was quickly assembled. Feth very carefully welded all seams and tested them against full atmospheric pressure. A glass top was provided, sealed in place with a silicone vacuum wax that was standard equipment on any space ship; this also checked out against a pressure equivalent to an earthly barometric reading of twelve hundred fifty millimeters of mercury. A second, similar case large enough to enclose the first was under construction when Drai appeared. He had evidently noticed at last that the ship was back.

"Well, I understand from Lee that you actually talked to a native. Good work, good work. Did you find out anything about how they make their tofacco?"

"We haven't learned their language too well, yet," Feth replied with as little sarcasm as he could manage. "We were operating on a slightly different line of investigation." He indicated the partly constructed vivarium. Drai frowned at it, as though trying to gather its purpose. "It's a small chamber where we can reproduce Planet Three's conditions, we hope; more or less of an experiment. The larger one goes outside, and we'll maintain a vacuum between the two. Feth says one of the sulfur hexafluoride refrigerators he knocked together years ago will get the temperature low enough, and we got enough of the planet's air to fill it a couple of times at their pressure." Drai looked puzzled still.

"But isn't it a little small for one of the natives? Lee said you'd described them as nearly five feet tall. Besides, I didn't hear about these plans at all."

"Natives? I thought you wanted us to grow vegetation. What good would a native do us here?" The master's face cleared.

"Oh, I see. I didn't know you'd picked up vegetation already. Still, now that I think of it, it mightn't be a bad idea to have a native or two. If the race is at all civilized, they could be used for a really stupendous ransom in tofacco—and we could use them in the cave, once it was conditioned, to take care of the tofacco and harvest it. Thanks for the idea."

"I don't know just how intelligent the natives are, as yet," replied Ken, "but I don't think they're stupid enough to walk into any sort of cage we might leave open for them. If you don't mind, I'll leave that as a last resort—we're going to have trouble enough getting our soil and seeds from their present containers into this thing without exposing them either to our atmosphere or to empty space. It would be a hundred times worse getting a native into one of those caves."

"Well, you may be right. I still think it would get us more tofacco, though."

"I'm sure it would, if they are at all civilized. I don't see why you're complaining about that, though—you're getting it cheap enough now, goodness knows."

"I don't mind the price—it's the quantity. We only get a couple of hundred cylinders a year—one of Three's years, that is. That doesn't let us operate on a very large scale. Well, do what you think best—provided you can convince me it's best, too." He left on that note, smiling; but the smile seemed to both Feth and Ken to have a rather unpleasant undertone. Feth looked after him a little uneasily, started to return to the job in hand, stopped once more, looked rather apologetically at Ken, and then went after Drai. The scientist remembered that Feth's last dose of the drug had come some time before his own.

That set him to wondering about when he himself could expect to feel the craving. Feth had said the interval was five or six Sarrian days—which were about thirteen Earthly hours in length. About half a day had been consumed after his first recovery in general talk, checking of the big suits, and travelling out to Three; rather more than a day in the actual tests and the meeting with which they had culminated; another half day since. Looking into the future, at least a full day must pass before the planned meeting with the natives of Three. No one could tell how long that would last, but apparently he had a couple of days' leeway in any case. He stopped worrying and turned his attention back to the partly completed vivarium.

He was not an expert welder, but the specimens waiting patiently two thousand miles away would only last so long, and he did not know how long Feth would be incapacitated. He took the torch and resumed work on the outer case. He had learned from watching Feth how the testing equipment was used, and was pleasantly surprised when his seams proved airtight. That, however, was as far as he could go; the mechanic had made no written plans, and Ken had no idea of his ideas on the attachment of the various refrigerating and pumping mechanisms. He stopped work, therefore, and devoted his mind to the problem he had mentioned to Drai—how to transfer the samples to the beautiful little tank after it was completed.

He spent some time trying to invent a remote-controlled can opener before the solution struck him. Then he kicked himself soundly for not having thought of it before—his double-kneed legs gave him a noticeable advantage in that operation. After that he relaxed until Feth returned, coming as close to sleep as his race ever did.

The mechanic was back in less than four hours, as a matter of fact. He seemed to be in fairly good shape; the tofacco apparently had few visible after-effects, even after years of use, which was a comforting thing to think about.

Ken showed him what had been done on the vivarium during his absence, and Feth expressed approval. He looked a little disappointed, however, at hearing the scientist's plan for stocking the device; as it turned out, he had had one of his own.

"I don't know why we were fools enough to get the specimens before we had a place to put them," Ken said. "We run the risk of ruining them in the cans, and have the transfer problem. We'd have been a lot smarter to make this thing first, and take it down to Three's surface for stocking on the spot. Why didn't we?"

"If you want an answer to that, we were probably too eager to make the trip," was the plausible answer. "Are you going to forget about the specimens we have, then?"

"We might check their temperatures. If those are still reasonable, we might as well take them back to Three and make the transfer there. It will be interesting to see how the seeds, if any, stood their trip—not that anything will be proved if they don't come up."

"You could make a microscopic check for anything resembling seed," Feth suggested, forgetting the situation for a moment.

"Do I cook the specimen or freeze the observer?" queried the scientist in an interested tone. Feth did not pursue the matter. Instead, he turned back to his work, and gradually the vivarium took shape under his skilled tentacles. Both the refrigerator and the pump were remarkably tiny devices, each solidly attached to a side of the box-like affair. Their controls were simple; an off-on toggle for the pump, and a thermostat dial for the refrigerator.

"I haven't calibrated that," Feth said, referring to the latter. "I'm mounting a thermometer inside where it can be seen through the lid, and you'll just have to fiddle with the knob until it's right."

"That's all right—for supposedly haywire apparatus, you certainly turn out a factory job. There's nothing to apologize for that I can see."

There were several hours yet to go before they were actually due at the meeting place on Planet Three. They loafed and talked for a while, Ken's plan coming gradually into more definite shape as they did so. They discussed the peculiarities of the Planet of Ice. Feth looked through his stock cabinets and reported that there was nothing he could turn into a portable control set so that Ken could handle his own torpedo. It was his turn to kick himself when the scientist suggested that he *wire* contacts to the controls—he (Ken) did not *insist* on sending the impulses by radio.

Thirty minutes later a torpedo was sitting in the shop with a long cable extending from a tiny opening in its hull, and ending in a small box with half a dozen knobs studding its surface. Ken, manipulating the knobs, found no difficulty in making the projectile do whatever he wanted.

"I guess we're even in the matter of overlooking the obvious," he said at last. "Had we better be getting ready to go?"

"I suppose so. By the way, since you can't read the torpedo's instruments, maybe you'd better let me navigate you to the ground. Then you can do what you please."

"That would be best. I certainly could not judge either distance or speed at three thousand miles from the surface."

They donned space suits, and carried their apparatus out to the *Karella*. The vivarium they left in the air lock, since it was going to have to be fastened to the torpedo anyway; but Lee found it there a little later and delivered a vitriolic comment on people who obstructed the exits from a space ship. Ken humbly carted the box inside by himself, Feth having gone up to the control room to direct the newly modified torpedo to its cradle.

They were ready to go, except for one thing, and neither of them realized the omission. It was brought home to them only a minute before the planned take-off time, when another space-suited figure glided from the air lock of the station to that of the ship. Lee waited, apparently unsurprised; and a moment later Laj Drai entered the control room.

"We may as well go, if all your apparatus is on board," he said.

Without comment, Ken nodded to the pilot.

# XVI.

Ken paused halfway into his armor to wave all four tentacles in expostulation.

"If you don't think I know what I'm talking about, why did you hire me?" he asked. "I'll get and grow plants for you as fast as I can. Our tank is only so big—there are growths down there that wouldn't fit in this ship, whether you believe it or not. I don't know any better than you what tofacco looks like when it's growing—I'm not even as sure as you seem to be that it's a plant. Just get out of your head the idea that I'm going to pack plants into this case until they have no room to breathe, and try to develop a little patience. It took two thousand years to explore Sarr, and the exploring was a darn sight easier than this!" He resumed the task of sliding into his metal shell.

"You'll do what you're told, Mr. Ken. I don't care how you do it, as I said before; but if we're not growing tofacco in a reasonable time, someone's going to be awfully sorry."

Ken's response was slightly muffled, as only his head was now protruding from the suit. "That, of course, you can do; I can't stop you. However, if you'll let me do this my own way, I honestly think things will go faster. Use your head, after all—who does know this planet?" He paused too briefly for the question to have any but rhetorical significance, and went on: "The natives, of course. They not only know the planet, they presumably know where the tofacco can be obtained, since they sell it to you. You'll have to work hard to convince me that there's any better way of learning what we want to know than getting the information from the natives."

"But it takes so long to learn a language!"

"True. It also takes quite a while to explore two hundred million square miles of territory, even if you count out the three quarters of it that seems to be flatland—and you can't really do that; these natives may be on good enough terms with the flatlanders to get the tofacco from them by trade. How about that? I understand you had your fill of exploring the flatlands quite a while ago—what was it, nineteen out of nineteen torpedoes lost, or twenty out of twenty? The percentage was embarrassing in either case."

"But suppose they don't want us to learn where it can be obtained? They might be afraid we'd get it ourselves, instead of paying them for it."

"That would not be too stupid of them. Sure, they may suspect just that. I never denied that a certain amount of tact would be needed. If you don't think I can exercise it, I repeat—do it yourself. We have more suits. I want to go down anyway, to study the place, but come right along—the torpedo will carry you and me and the tank easily enough!"

"I may not be a genius, but I'm not completely insane. I'll be there by proxy. If I don't like your tact, you needn't bother to come back."

"Don't you want the suit? I thought they were expensive," Ken said sweetly, and pulled the massive helmet into place with a clang.

Feth, who had been listening in, dogged the piece in place. He was just a trifle worried; he himself had not talked to Drai like that for years, and still retained unpleasant memories of the last time he had done so. He knew, of course, the purpose behind Ken's attitude; the scientist wanted to annoy Drai sufficiently so that he would not suspect more than one thing at a time. That one thing was to be exactly what Ken wanted. Feth admitted to himself that that part of the conversation had been well handled. Nevertheless, he was not too sure he liked the expression of Laj Drai's face as that individual draped himself within easy earshot of the radio.

His attention was shifted from the matter as Ken called in from the air lock, reporting that he was attached.

"Let me get out of here with my own controls, and move around a bit while I'm close enough to judge results," he finished. "I'd better get the feel of this thing while I have just inertia for trouble, and before there's weight as well."

"Sound enough," Feth approved, and took his tentacles from his own controls. One eye remained on the indicators, while the other sought the nearest port. In a few seconds the cigar-shaped bit of metal came into view, darting this way and that, swinging the clumsy figure of the armored scientist from a point near its bow and the rectangular box of the vivarium a few feet farther aft—it, too, was too large to go into the cargo compartment. Ken seemed to be having no trouble in controlling the sloppy-looking assembly, and presently signified that he was ready for the dive.

"All right," Feth replied, "I have it. Be sure all your own controls are neutral—they're not cross-connected, and impulses will add algebraically. By the way, *all* the stuff is in the cargo compartment."

The other torpedo with the first batch of samples had been salvaged from its lonely perch on Mercury, and Laj Drai knew that; so Feth hoped he would not notice the slight accent on the "all." The mechanic had placed the extra radio in with the other objects, but had done so at the last moment and had had no time to tell Ken about it. He hoped the fellow knew how to operate the set.

Ken, as a matter of fact, had not realized what Feth was implying. He was much too occupied in bracing his nerves for the descent that had been so hard on them the previous time. He succeeded better on this occasion, largely because he was able to keep most of his mind on the problems that would be facing him after he was down. They were numerous enough.

He had little trouble finding the scene of the previous meeting, though Feth did not succeed in lowering him exactly over it. He was, he realized, early; the sun was barely up. All to the good. He reported his arrival to Feth to make sure, announced that he was resuming control, and went to work.

His first step was to guide the torpedo downhill to the edge of a fairly extensive patch of plant growth. Before doing anything else, he made sure that the patch was isolated; the reaction of the vegetable matter of this world to hot metal had impressed him strongly, and he had a good imagination. Then he lowered the carrier until the vivarium was touching the ground, and detached the clumsy box. The double lids opened without difficulty—Feth had allowed for the probable effect of low temperature on the metal hinges—and set to work.

The samples of earth came speedily from the cargo compartment, and were dumped into the box—all at one side. Using a strip of metal he had brought along for the purpose, Ken leveled out the dark pile into a layer some three inches deep and a foot wide along one side of the container; then he began to use the strip as a crude shovel. Tiny bushes, patches of moss, and other growths were pried out of the ground, the scientist carefully refraining from allowing his armor to contact them and laying the strip down to cool at frequent intervals. He investigated the widely varying root systems, and carefully dug an extra allowance of soil from the spot where each plant had been removed, so that there would be a sufficient depth in the box beneath it. One by one he transferred his specimens to the vivarium, placing them much too close together to have pleased a human gardener, but setting them firmly into the soil so that they stood up as they had before. Once or twice he looked longingly at larger bushes, but gave up. They were too tall, and a brief investigation showed that their roots were too long.

He had covered perhaps two of the six square feet he had to fill when the Wings arrived. Roger and Edie were noticeably in advance of the rest;

the two youngest would probably have been close behind them if the scene had not been so far from home. As it was, they had begun to get a little tired, and arrived at the same time as their parents.

Ken did not hear them coming; the microphone in the torpedo was not as sensitive as it might have been, and this time Roger did not call as soon as he saw the scientist. Instead, the children came as close as they dared, trying to see what he was up to. That proved obvious enough, but it was only after his curiosity was satisfied on that point that Roger gave an audible greeting.

"I see you're here early."

"Why didn't you tell me they were coming?" snapped the voice of Laj Drai from the speaker.

"I didn't see them; I've been working," replied Ken quietly. "Now, if you expect us to get anywhere with communication, kindly keep quiet. They have no means of telling when I'm the one who's talking, and extra sounds will just confuse them." He fell silent, and watched solemnly as the rest of the human beings arrived. The size of Mr. and Mrs. Wing surprised him a little; it took him some seconds to decide that the individuals he had seen first were probably children. The adults were more impressive, if one was impressed by mere size; Ken decided that either one would outweigh the average Sarrian by fully a quarter, assuming that they really filled their queer clothing and had flesh of comparable density. There was something a little more commanding about the manner of the older natives, also; a dignity and seriousness of purpose which he now realized had been decidedly lacking in the immature specimens. For the first time, Ken really thought of the natives of Earth as possibly civilized beings.

Certainly the actions of the largest one suggested a well-disciplined mind. Mr. Wing wasted little time. He seated himself in front of Ken, pulled out a notebook in which he had already noted the words Roger claimed to have taught the alien, and checked through them. He looked up at Ken as he pronounced each; the scientist responded by pointing to the appropriate object. Satisfied that these words were understood, the man promptly embarked on a language lesson with a singleness of purpose and efficiency of execution that had Ken regarding him as a fellow being long before they were in real communication. This was not accomplished at once, but it took far less time than many people would believe possible. As any proponent of Basic English will agree, most everyday matters can be discussed quite easily with a vocabulary of less than a thousand words. The present situation was not quite everyday in any sense of the term, but between Mrs. Wing's sketching ability and the willingness of the children to illustrate practically any actions required, progress was quite satisfactory to both parties.

Since Ken had stood in the same place throughout the lesson, he had warmed up the rock around his feet; consequently it was fully three hours before he felt the first warning ache of cold. When he did, however, he suddenly realized that he had done nothing toward the filling of his specimen box since the natives had arrived; and waiting courteously until Mr. Wing had finished an explanation, he indicated the dearth. The man nodded, and pointed to the ground beyond.

Ken had paid no attention to the actions of the smallest children since shortly after the lesson had started; he had judged that they were playing, as the children of his own race did. Now he was startled to see, spread out on the rock at a little distance from the case, several score plants of assorted shapes and sizes. Apparently the youngsters had seen what he was doing, and decided to help. With growing surprise, he discovered that there were no duplicates among the specimens. The race must really have brains; he had not seen either of the adults give instructions. With an oral expression of gratitude which he was sure must be lost on them, he began clumsily placing them in the box with the aid of his metal strip. As he picked up the first, he pointed to it with his free handler and said, "Word!" All understood his meaning, and Roger replied, "Fern."

After watching his clumsy actions for a moment, Mr. Wing waved him away from the box, and put the children to work. Ken watched them with tremendous interest, for the first time realizing what an efficient prehensile organ the human hand could be. The deft fingers of the girls in particular were setting the plants firmly in the earth at a rate and with an ease he himself could not have managed even without the handicap of armor and temperature difference. As each was picked up, a name was given it. It did turn out afterward that the same name had been used over several times in many cases for plants that bore either a merely superficial resemblance or none at all. It took him some time to solve that one, though he already knew that the native language had both particular and generic terms.

A very few minutes were required to cover the base of the box with neatly set plants; and not once had Ken heard the word that would have meant so much to the listening Drai. He himself was just as satisfied; the mention of "tofacco" by a native in a place where Drai could have heard it would have put a serious crimp in Ken's now rapidly maturing plans.

In spite of his having taken the cans containing the earlier specimens from the cargo section of the torpedo, it was not until he was putting the empty containers back that Ken saw the other radio Feth had placed there. For a moment he was irritated with both himself and the mechanic, since by then he had forgotten the latter's words at the time of Ken's departure; then he decided that it might be for the best. If Drai had been listening ever since the start of the language lesson, he should by now be pretty well convinced that Ken was not up to any funny business. There had been no breaks to make him suspicious.

While these thoughts were passing through his mind, Mr. Wing was also doing some thinking. It seemed fairly evident that the alien—they had not yet learned each other's names—was on the point of departure. This trip had been a pleasant enough outing for the family, it was true; but a daily repetition would be too much of a good thing, and there were more objects at their home which could be used in language instruction as well. It seemed, therefore, that it might be worth while to make the attempt he had suggested earlier to the family—persuading the aliens to land closer to the house. In consequence, when Ken turned from his task of replacing the empty cans and fastening the sealed vivarium back in place, he found the largest native facing him with a neatly drawn but quite unintelligible diagram in his hand and an evident desire to transmit intelligence of some sort.

It took four or five minutes to make clear exactly what the map represented, though Ken got the general idea after a few seconds. Scale was the principal difficulty. At last, however, the alien understood—he spent two or three minutes describing the map in detail to Feth, first, so that it could be studied and reproduced later—and then said, "Yes," to Mr. Wing.

"Tomorrow—one day after now—*here,*" the man reiterated, and Ken nodded his head (he had not been too surprised to find that visual signs supplemented the spoken language of these creatures).

"Here." He indicated the same spot as well as he could with a handler, and the paper turned brown before he hastily snatched it away. Then he remembered something else. "Not tomorrow. Not one day after now. Two days." Mr. Wing frowned.

"Not tomorrow?"

"No. Two days. Go now; cold." And Sallman Ken turned, took the extra radio from the cargo compartment, placed it on the ground, said, "Carry!" and addressed himself to the task of attaching himself to the torpedo once more. He had detached himself, in spite of his original plan, when he found that he could not reach the cargo compartment while chained to the hull of the carrier.

The native mercifully said nothing as he completed this task. As a matter of fact, Mr. Wing was too dumbfounded at this turn of events to say anything; and even the children wondered how he had done it. Ken rose into the air amid a dead silence, until the two youngest children remembered their training and shrilled, "Good-bye!" after the vanishing form. He barely heard the words, but was able to guess at the meaning.

Back at the *Karella,* his first care was to get the vivarium inside. He had already evacuated the space between the walls by opening a small valve for a time during the journey through space; now he started the refrigerator, and refused to take his eyes from the inside thermometer until he had satisfied himself that all fluctuation had ceased. Then, and then only, did he start going over the tape record with Feth to make sure be remembered the hundred or so words be had been taught during his brief dive. Laj Drai, rather to Ken's surprise, forbore to interrupt, though Feth said he had listened carefully during the entire stay on the planet. During this session, Ken managed to tell the mechanic what he had done with the radio, and the latter agreed that it had been a wise move. There was now no need to fear a casual check on the contents of the torpedo by Drai or Lee.

It seemed that Ken had been more convincing than he had expected, in his speech to Drai just before leaving. He had been a little surprised when the boss had failed to interrupt him after his return; now he found that Drai had been itching to do just that, but had been afraid of putting himself in the wrong again. The moment the conference between Ken and Feth came to an end, he was at the scientist's side, asking for an eye-witness account to supplement what he had heard on the radio.

"I really need a camera to give a good idea of appearances," Ken replied. "I seem to have been wrong about their size; the ones I saw before appear to have been children. The adults are a trifle bulkier than we are.

"I don't think the language is going to be difficult, and it looks as though this group, at least, is very cooperative." He told about the help he had received in making the plant collection.

"I was looking at that," said Drai. "I don't suppose any of those things is what we're after?"

"No, unless they use different names for the living plant and the product. They named each of these to me as they set them in, and you'd have heard as well as I if they'd said 'tofacco' once." Drai seemed thoughtful for a moment before he spoke again.

"Children, eh? Maybe if you can work with them and get rid of the adults you could find things out more easily. They should be easier to fool."

"Something like that crossed my mind, too," Ken said. "Perhaps we ought to make a few more collection boxes to take down; I could give them to the kids to fill while I was having another language lesson, and then when they came back I'd have a good excuse to talk it over with each in turn. Something might very well crop up if the parents don't interfere."

"Parents? How do you know?"

"I don't, of course; but it seems likely. But what do you think of the idea?"

"Very good, I should say. Can you get enough boxes for all the children ready by their next morning?"

"I'm not going down that soon. I was making allowances for what Feth told me was the effect of tofacco on the system, and thought I might not be able to make it." Drai paused long enough to do some mental arithmetic.

"You're probably right. We'll have to go back to One to get your dose, too; I somehow can't bring myself to keep the stuff around where it might fall into the wrong hands." He smiled, with the same ugly undertone that was making Ken hate the drug-runner a little more each time he saw it.

# XVII.

"Dad, will you kindly tell me just how on Earth you worked that?" Don stared at the Sarrian radio, which was all that was visible of the aliens by the time he got back from giving the trade signal. Roger chuckled. "He didn't work it. He spends all afternoon teaching the thing to talk English, and just as it's going it turns around and puts this on the ground. 'Carry,' it booms, and takes off. What do you suppose it is, Dad?"

"I can't possibly be sure, Son, until he comes back. It may be a piece of apparatus he intends to use on his next visit; it may be a gift in return for our aid with the plant collection. I think we'd best get it home, as he seemed to want, and do nothing at all to it until he comes back."

"But if he's not coming back until the day after tomorrow—

"I know curiosity is a painful disease, Rog; I suffer from it myself. But I still think that the one who'll come out ahead in this new sort of trading is the one who steps most cautiously and keeps his real aims up his sleeve the longest. We're still not certain that this scientific investigation isn't aimed at just one end—to relieve them of the need for paying us for tobacco. After all, why did this fellow start with plants? There are lots of other things he might have shown interest in."

"If he's as different from our sort of life as he seems to be, how would he know that tobacco is a plant?" countered Roger. "It certainly doesn't stay unburned long enough at his temperature to let him look at the crumbs with a microscope or anything, and a cigarette doesn't much look like a plant."

"That's true," his father admitted. "Well, I only said we don't *know* he hasn't that up his sleeve. I admit it doesn't seem likely."

Curiously enough, Ken thought of one of those points himself before the next visit; and when he descended in the clearing by the Wing home with four collecting boxes attached to his torpedo, the first thing he did was to make clear he wanted minerals in one that was not equipped with refrigeration apparatus. Pointing to another similarly plain he said, "Thing—good—hot—cold." The Wings looked at each other for a moment; then Edith spoke.

"You mean anything that stays good whether it's hot or cold? Stuff that you don't have to keep in a refrigerator?" There were too many new words in that sentence for Ken, but he took a chance. "Yes. Hot, good." He was still drifting a foot or two from the ground, having so arranged the load this time that he could detach it without first freeing himself. Now he settled lightly to the ground, and things began to happen.

The ground, like most of that in evergreen forests, was largely composed of shed needles. These had been cleared away to some extent around the house, but the soil itself was decidedly inflammable. Naturally, the moment Ken's armored feet touched it a cloud of smoke appeared, and only lightning-like action in lifting himself again prevented its bursting into flame. As it was, no one felt really safe until Roger had soaked the spot with a bucket of water.

That led to further complications. Ken had never seen water to his knowledge, and certainly had never seen apparatus for dispensing apparently limitless amounts of any liquid. The outside faucet from which the bucket had been filled interested him greatly; and at his request, made in a mixture of signs and English words, Roger drew another bucketful, placed it on the flat top of one of the cement posts at the foot of the porch steps, and retreated. Ken, thus enabled to examine the object without coming in contact with anything else, did so at great length; and finished by dipping a handler cautiously into the peculiarly transparent fluid. The resulting cloud of steam startled him almost as much as the temporary but intense chill that bit through the metal, and he drew back hastily. He began to suspect what the liquid was, and mentally took off his hat to Feth. The mechanic, if that was all he really was, really could think.

Eventually Ken was installed on top of an outdoor oven near the house, the specimen boxes were on the ground, and the children had disappeared in various directions to fill them. The language lesson was resumed, and excellent progress made for an hour or so. At the end of that time, both parties were slightly surprised to find themselves exchanging intelligible sentences—crude and clumsy ones, full of circumlocutions, but understandable. A faint smile appeared on Mr. Wing's face as he realized this; the time had come to administer a slight jolt to his guest, and perhaps startle a little useful information out of him. He remembered the conversation he had had with Don the night before, and felt quiet satisfaction in the boy—the sort of satisfaction that sometimes goes to make a father a major bore.

"You didn't have too many times, Dad," his son had said, "but there were enough. It ties in with other things, anyway. The intervals between signalling and the arrival of the trading torpedo have been varying in a period of just about a hundred and twenty days, taking several years into account. Of course, a lot of those 'periods' didn't have any trading occur, but the period is there; first two days, then three. That hundred and twenty days is the synodic period of Mercury—the length of time it takes that planet to catch the Earth up on successive trips around the sun. I remembered Mercury's position when we studied it this spring, and did some figuring; your short times came when it was closest to us, the long ones when it was on the other side of the sun, about twice as far away. Those torpedoes seem to be coming from there at about one and a quarter G's of acceleration." Mr. Wing, though no physicist, understood this clearly enough. The concept had been publicized sufficiently in connection with airplanes.

He had looked over Don's figures, which were easy enough to follow, and agreed with his results; and the boy had, at his request, drawn a diagram of the orbits of inner planets of the Solar System showing the current positions of the planets themselves. This he now had in his pocket.

The word "home" had just been under discussion, more or less as a result of chance. Mr. Wing had made the concept reasonably clear, he believed; and it seemed to him that the time had come to put one of his cards on the table.

He began by waving an arm to encompass the whole horizon. "Earth," he said. The Sarrian repeated the word, but without any gesture of his own suggesting that he understood. The man repeated the word, stamping on the ground as he did so; then he took a new page in the notebook and made a sketch of the planet as he thought it would appear from space. As a final illustration, he molded a sphere from a lump of modeling clay which had been found in the playroom and had already been put to good use. Then be pointed to the sphere, drawing, and the ground, repeating the word after each in turn.

Ken understood. He proved it by scratching a picture of his own on the ground, reaching as far as he could over the side of the oven and using his strip of metal. It was a perfectly recognizable drawing of the sun and orbits of the first three planets. He knew be might be exceeding the local knowledge of astronomy, but the fact that the native seemed to know the shape of his world was encouraging.

Mr. Wing promptly pulled out Don's diagram, which was substantially the same as Ken's except that Mars' orbit and position were shown. He spent some minutes naming each of the planets, and making the generic name clear as well. Then they spent some more time in a sort of game; Ken added

Jupiter and Saturn to the diagram, in an effort to find out how much astronomy the human being knew. Mr. Wing named those, and added Uranus, Neptune and Pluto; Don, who had made no contribution up to this point, made a correction in the orbit of Pluto so that it crossed that of Neptune at one point, and began adding satellites at a furious rate. They took the burst of Sarrian speech that erupted from the speaker as an indication of the alien's surprise, and were gratified accordingly.

Ken was surprised for more reasons than one.

"Drai, if you're listening, these folks are not any sort of savage. They must have a well-developed science. They seem to know of nine planets in this system, and we only knew about six; and there are an awful lot of moons one of them is busy telling me about right now—he's even put two with Planet Four, and we didn't notice any. They either have space travel or darned good telescopes."

"We haven't seen a space ship here in twenty years," Feth's voice reminded him. Ken made no answer; Mr. Wing had started to talk again. He was pointing to Planet Three on his own diagram, and repeating the name he had given it.

"Earth—my home." He indicated himself with one hand to emphasize the personal pronoun. Then he moved the finger to the innermost world. "Mercury—your home." And he pointed to Sallman Ken.

He was a little disappointed in the reaction, but would not have been had he known how to interpret Sarrian facial expressions. The scientist was dumbfounded for fully ten seconds; when he did regain control of his voice, he addressed the distant listeners rather than the Earth man.

"I'm sure that you will also be interested in knowing that he is aware we come from Planet One. I believe he thinks we live there, but the error is minor under the circumstances." This time Drai's voice responded.

"You're crazy! You must have told him yourself, you fool! How could he possibly have learned that without help?"

"I did not tell him. You've been listening and ought to know. And I don't see why I should be expected to explain how he found out; I'm just telling you what's going on here at the moment."

"Well, don't let him go on thinking that! Deny it! He knows too much!"

"What's wrong with that?" Ken asked, reasonably enough.

"Suppose they do have space travel! We don't want them dropping in on us! Why—I've been keeping this place a secret for twenty years."

Ken forbore to point out the flaws in that line of reasoning. He simply said:

"Not knowing how certain they are of their facts, I think a denial would be foolish. If they are really sure, then they'd know I was lying; and the results might not be good." Drai made no answer to that, and Ken turned back to the Earthman, who had been listening uncomprehendingly to the conversation.

"Mercury. Yes," the Sarrian said.

"I see. Hot," replied Mr. Wing.

"No. Cold." Ken paused, seeking words. "Little hot. Hot to you. Hot to—" he waved a sleeve of his armor in a wide circle—"plants, these things. Cold to me."

Don muttered to his father, "If he regards Mercury as too cold for comfort, he must come from the inside of a volcano somewhere. Most astronomers are satisfied that there's no planet closer to the sun, and he didn't show one on his diagram, you'll notice."

"It would be nice if we knew just how hot he liked it," agreed the older man. He was about to address Ken again in the hope of finding out something on this point when a burst of alien speech suddenly boomed from the torpedo's speaker. Even to Ken, it carried only partial meaning.

"Ken! This—" Just those two words, in Feth's voice; then the transmission ceased with the click that accompanies a broken circuit. Ken called Feth's name several times into his own microphone, but there was no response. He fell silent, and thought furiously.

He suspected from the fact that the natives were simply looking at him that they realized something had gone wrong; but he did not want to worry about their feelings just then. He felt like a diver who had heard a fight start among the crew of his air-pump, and had little attention for anything else. What in the Galaxy were they about, up there? Had Drai decided to abandon him? No, even if the drug-runner had suddenly decided Ken was useless, he would not abandon a lot of expensive equipment just to get rid of him. For one thing, Ken suspected that Drai would prefer to see him die of drug hunger, though this may have been an injustice. What then? Had Drai become subtle, and cut off the transmitter above in the hope that Ken would betray himself in some way? Unlikely. If nothing else, Feth would almost certainly have warned him in some fashion, or at least not sounded so anxious in the words he had managed to transmit.

Perhaps Drai's distrust—natural enough under the circumstances— had reached a point where he had decided to check personally on the actions of his tame scientist. However, Ken could not imagine him trusting himself in armor on the surface of the Planet of Ice no matter what he wanted to find out.

Still, there was another way of coming down personally. Lee would not like it, of course. He might even persuade his employer that it was far too dangerous. He would certainly try. Still, if Drai really had the idea in his mind, it was more than possible that he might simply refuse to listen to persuasion.

In that case, the *Karella*'s shadow might fall across them at any moment. That would fit in with Feth's attempt to warn him, and its abrupt interruption. If that were actually the case, he need not worry; his conscience was clear, and for all that was going on at the moment Drai was perfectly welcome to look on until his eyes froze to the ports. There had been no sign of tofacco anywhere, although the native children had been coming back at frequent intervals with new specimens for the boxes and had named them each time. He himself had not done a single thing in furtherance of his plan.

He had just relaxed with this realization firmly in mind when the native who had been doing most of the talking produced and lighted a cigarette.

Mr. Wing had had no intention of doing anything of the sort. He had a pretty good idea of the value placed by these creatures on tobacco, and he did not want to distract the scientist from what might prove a valuable line of talk. As a matter of fact, he would have been perfectly satisfied to have the creature assume that it was someone else entirely who did the trading. Habit, however, defeated his good intentions; and he was only recalled from his speculations on the nature of this new interruption by the realization that he had taken the first puff.

The Sarrian had both eyes fixed on the little cylinder—an unusual event in itself; usually one was roving in a way calculated to get on the nerves even of someone like young Roger. The reason seemed obvious; Mr. Wing could imagine the alien running mentally over the list of things he had brought with him, wondering what he could trade for the rest of the pack. He was closer to being right than he should have been.

That line of thought, however, was profitless, and no one knew it better than Ken. The real problem of the moment was to get the infernal stuff out of sight before Drai arrived—if he were coming. For a moment Ken wondered if the other radio, which he had seen lying on the porch when he arrived, could be put to use in time. Common sense assured him that it could not; even if he could persuade one of the natives to bring it and tow the torpedo out of earshot, he certainly could not make his wish clear in time. He would have to hope—the cylinder was vanishing slowly, and there was a chance that it might be gone before the ship arrived. If only he could be sure that the receiver as well as the transmitter aboard the space ship had been cut off!

If Drai were still listening, the silence of the last few seconds would probably make him doubly suspicious. Well, there was nothing to be done about that.

As it happened, there was plenty of time for the cigarette to burn out, thanks to Ordon Lee. Feth had tried to give his warning the instant be realized what Drai was thinking; and the other's lashing tentacles had hurled him away from the board and across the control room before he could finish. When he had recovered and started to return, he had found himself staring into the muzzle of a pistol, its disc-shaped butt steadied against the drug-runner's torso.

"So the two of you *are* up to something," Drai had said. "I'm not surprised. Lee, find the carrier of that torpedo and home down on it!"

"But sir—into Three's atmosphere? We can't—"

"We can, you soft-headed field-twister. That tame brain of mine stood it for three hours and more in a suit of engineering armor, and you want me to believe the hull of this ship can't take it!"

"But the ports—and the outer drive plates—and—"

"I said *get us down there!* There are ports in a suit of armor, and the bottom plates stood everything that the soil of Planet Four could give them. And don't talk about risk from the flatlanders! I know as well as you do that the hull of this barrel is coated even against frequency-modulated radar, to say nothing of the stuff these things have been beaming out—I paid for it, and it's been getting us through the System patrol at Sarr for a long time. Now punch those keys!" Ordon Lee subsided, but he was quite evidently unhappy. He tuned in the compass with a slightly hopeful expression, which faded when he found that Ken's torpedo was still emitting its carrier wave. Gloomily he applied a driving force along the indicated line, and the gibbous patch of light that was Planet Three began to swell beyond the ports.

As the board flashed a warning of outside pressure, he brought the vessel to a halt and looked hopefully at his employer. Drai made a downward gesture with the gun muzzle. Lee shrugged in resigned fashion, switched on the heaters in the outer hull, and began feeling his way into the ocean of frigid gas, muttering in an undertone and putting on an I-told-you-so expression every time a *clink* told of contracting outer plates.

Feth, knowing he would get no further chance at the radio, glued his attention to one of the ports. One of Drai's eyes did likewise, but no change appeared in his expression as the evidence began to pile up that Ken had been telling the truth. Great mountains, hazy air, green vegetation, even the shiny patches so suggestive of the vast blue plains where the flatlanders had downed the exploring torpedoes; all were there, as the scientist had said, dimly illuminated by the feeble sun of this system but clearly visible for all that. Feth, heedless of the gun in Drai's hand, suddenly leaped for the door, shouting, "Camera!" and disappeared down the corridor. Drai put the gun away.

"Why can't you be like those two?" he asked the pilot. "Just get them interested in something, and they forget that there's anything in the universe to be afraid of." The pilot made no immediate answer; apparently Drai expected none, for he strolled to the port without waiting. Then without looking up from his controls the pilot asked sourly:

"If you think Ken is interested in his job and nothing else, why are you so anxious to check up on him all of a sudden?"

"Mostly because I'm not quite sure whose job he's doing. Tell me, Lee, just who would you say was to blame for the fact that this is the first time we're landing on this world which we've known about for twenty years?"

The pilot made no verbal answer, but one eye rolled back and met one of his employer's for a moment. The question had evidently made him think of something other than frostbite and cracked plates: Laj Drai may not have been a genius, as he had been known to admit, but his rule-of-thumb psychology was of a high order.

The *Karella* sank lower. Mountain tops were level with the port now; an apparently unbroken expanse of green lay below, but the compass pointed unhesitatingly into its midst. At five hundred feet separate trees were discernible, and the roof of the Wing home showed dimly through them. There was no sign of Ken or his torpedo, but neither being in the control room doubted for an instant that this was the house he had mentioned. Both had completely forgotten Feth.

"Take us a few yards to one side, Lee. I want to be able to see from the side ports. I think I see Ken's armor—yes. The ground slopes; land us uphill a little way. We can see for a fair distance between these plants." The pilot obeyed silently. If he heard the shriek of Feth, echoing down the corridor from the room where the mechanic was still taking pictures, he gave no sign; the words were rendered indistinguishable by reverberation in any case. The meaning, however, became clear a moment later. The sound of the hull's crushing its way through the treetops was inaudible inside; but the other token of arrival was quite perceptible. An abrupt cloud of smoke blotted out the view from port, and as Laj Drai started back in astonishment a tongue of flame licked upward around the curve of the great hull.

# XVIII.

Feth was not the only one who called to the pilot to hold off. Ken, realizing only too clearly that the hull of the vessel would be nearly as hot as his own suit in spite of its superior insulation, expressed himself on the radio as he would never have done before his pupils; but of course no one on board was listening. Mr. Wing and Don, guessing the cause of his excitement, added their voices; Mrs. Wing, hearing the racket, appeared at a window in time to see the glossy black cylinder settle into the trees fifty yards above the house. No one was surprised at the results—no one outside the ship, at least.

Don and his father raced at top speed for the stable, where the portable fire pumps were kept. Mrs. Wing appeared on the porch, calling in a fairly well controlled voice, "Don, where are the children?" This question was partially answered before either man could make a response, as Margie and Billy broke from the woods on opposite sides of the clearing, still carrying plants which they had forgotten to drop in their excitement.

"Daddy! See the fire!" The boy shrilled as soon as he saw his father.

"I know, Billy. Both of you go with your mother, start the pump, and help her spray everything near the house. I don't think the fire will come downhill with the wind the way it is, but we mustn't take chances."

"Where are Roger and Edith?" Mrs. Wing asked the younger children.

"They were going to get rocks for the fire-man," Margie replied. I don't know where they were going to get them. They'll come back when they see the fire."

"I suppose so." Their mother was obviously unhappy about the matter, but she took the youngsters in tow and went after the hoses. Don and his father continued on their way, slung the always filled fire pumps across their shoulders, and headed back uphill toward the ever-thickening cloud of smoke and flame.

Ken had not waited for the human beings to go into action. Pausing only to make certain his armor was still firmly attached to the torpedo, he had seized the control spindle and shot straight upward. He was taking a chance, he realized; but with the relatively cold torpedo hull to smash the initial path through the thin overhanging branches he felt that he could avoid contact with any one of them except for periods too brief to set them ablaze. He succeeded, though a suspicion of smoke floated upward in his wake as he soared clear. The *Karella,* he noted, had done likewise; it now floated a quarter of a mile above the blaze it had started. He wasted no further time on recriminations, even though the chances seemed good that those on board would be listening again.

The fire was not spreading as rapidly as he had feared it might in most directions. On the side toward the house it seemed to have made no progress at all, while along the contours of the mountain its advance was very slow. Upward, however, under the combined influence of its own convection currents and the breeze which had already been blowing in that direction, it was leaping from growth to growth in fine style. Ken saw flaming bits of vegetable tissue borne far aloft on the hot air pillar; some burned out in flight, others settled into the trees farther up the mountain and gave rise to other centers of combustion. A dark-colored growth, apparently dead, a few yards in advance of the main blaze, smoked briefly in the fierce radiation and suddenly exploded with an audible roar, burning out in less than fifteen seconds and crumbling into a rain of glowing coals. Ken, unmoved by the prospect of being involved in the uprushing hot gases, maneuvered closer to the blaze. At least part of the reason for the slow advance downhill became evident; the two natives with whom he had been talking were visible through the trees, spraying everything in sight with apparently tiny streams of a liquid at whose nature Ken could only make an educated guess. He watched them for some time, noting that they refilled their containers of liquid every few minutes at a stream of the stuff flowing down near the house, which Ken had not noticed earlier. He wondered where the liquid could have its source, and decided to follow the stream uphill to find out.

As he rose, the extent of the forest country once more was impressed on him, and he began to wonder at the magnitude of the catastrophe the *Karella* had caused. If this combustion reaction were to spread over the whole countryside, the effect on the natives would undoubtedly be quite serious, he decided. He noted that it had spread across the little stream a short distance farther up; apparently the liquid had to be in actual contact with vegetation in order to stop combustion. The flame and smoke made it impossible to follow the watercourse; Ken dropped lower, reasoning with some justice that the temperature of his armor would do no damage to vegetation already burning, and drifted along only a few feet above the stream bed, barely able to see even then. For the first time he saw animal life other than the intelligent natives; tiny creatures, usually four-legged when they were moving slowly enough for him to see the legs, all fleeing madly uphill. Ken wondered that they could breathe—the smoke suggested that the air should be full of combustion products, and probably was too hot for them; he knew nothing about the fairly common phenomenon of relatively pure air near the ground ahead of a fire. Large-scale conflagrations occurred on Sarr, but he was no fireman.

He was ahead of the flames but still in smoke-filled air, when he found the source of the stream. He had trouble realizing that it *was* the source; he was no geologist, and a real geologist of his race would have had difficulty in figuring out the mechanism of a spring. Ken rather suspected artificial backing for the phenomenon, but he did not dare touch the liquid to investigate very closely. He would have had grounds for serious worry had he known that a forest fire can sometimes cause a local rainstorm; but that, too, was too far outside his experience. The closest approach to such a thing on Sarr occurred near the poles, where on very rare occasions meteorological forces so combined as to raise the pressure and drop the temperature enough to cause a slight precipitation of liquid sulfur.

Realizing that nothing more could be learned here at the moment, Ken rose once more into clearer air. Downhill, the natives seemed to be winning; there was a narrow band of blackened vegetation at the edge of the region of flame which suggested that the fire had burned out in that direction. At the sides, progress was less obvious; but the fire in general had taken on the outline of a great fan, with its handle pointing toward the house and the ribs spreading to a breadth of three or four hundred yards at a roughly equal distance up the mountainside Through the billowing smoke, Ken could see that the large trees were thinning out at this point, giving way to smaller growths which in turn seemed to follow the usual pattern of yielding to bare rock near the top of the hill. Ken, looking the situation over from his vantage point, decided that the blaze stood a very good chance of eating itself into starvation territory in a very few hours; the natives might very well dispose of the fringes without assistance.

The thought of possible assistance gave rise to another; the smoke was rising in a pillar that must be visible for many miles. Was this likely to bring other natives to help, or would it be mistaken for an ordinary cloud? Ken's eyes, with their color balance differing as it did from the human, could not be sure of the distinction in hue; but the shape of the smoke pillar seemed distinctive enough to attract attention. With this thought in mind, he decided to call the ship; but when he looked up, the vessel was nowhere in sight. He moved the torpedo back and forth rapidly enough to cause his armor to swing pendulum fashion and give him a glimpse of the sky directly overhead, but there was still no sign of the black cylinder. Apparently Laj Drai's brief taste of Planet Three had been enough. To make sure, Ken broadcast his thought on the matter of further natives arriving, and then returned to his examination of the fire. Within seconds, he had once more forgotten the vessel's existence.

He had found that little could be seen inside the fire itself. This time, therefore, he descended just ahead of the actual blaze, watching through the eddying smoke clouds as the leaves of bushes and small trees in its path shriveled, smoked, and burst into flame sometimes many feet from the nearest actual tongue of fire. Usually, he noticed, the thicker stems did not ignite until they were actually in contact with flame from some other source, but there were exceptions to this. He remembered the exploding tree. He regretted that he had no thermometer, with which he could get some idea of the kindling point of the growths. He wondered if the oxygen alone could be responsible for such a furious reaction, or whether the nitrogen which made up such a large part of the atmosphere might be playing a part. It had combined with his titanium specimen, after all. There seemed no way of collecting samples of the combustion gases, but perhaps some of the solid residue would tell. Ken landed in the midst of the fire, brought the torpedo down beside him, opened the cargo door, and threw in several pieces of charred wood. Then he went downhill a short distance, located some grayish ash, and added that to the collection. Satisfied for the moment, he rose clear of the ground again, wondering vaguely how much time, if any, his brief sojourn in the flames would add to the few hours he could remain down. He had heard the thermostats in his armor cutting off several of the heaters during those few minutes; the outer layers must have been warmed up considerably.

In an attempt to guess how long the fire would take to burn out, Ken moved fifty or sixty yards ahead of the flame front and began timing its rate of progress at several points. This proved deceptive, since the rate of travel varied greatly—as any forester could have told him. It depended principally on the sort of fuel available in a given spot and on the configuration of the ground, which influenced the air currents feeding the fire; and those points were both too difficult to observe for Ken to learn very much about them. He gave up that attempt, moved a little farther ahead, and tried to see what he could of the animals still scurrying away from the most frightful menace that ever threatened their small lives.

It was here that the torpedo microphone picked up a cracking that differed from that of the fire, and a heavy panting that reminded Ken of the sounds he had heard just after his first meeting with Roger. Remembering that he had not seen two of the natives just after the blaze had started, the scientist became a trifle anxious; and two or three minutes' search showed that his worry was only too well founded. Roger and Edith Wing, gasping and coughing from smoke and exhaustion, were struggling almost blindly through the bushes. The boy's original intention had been to travel across the path of the blaze, to get out of its way—the most sensible course under the circumstances. Several things, however, had combined to make this a trifle difficult. For one thing, after the smoke had become thick enough to prevent their seeing more than a few yards, they had blundered into a little hollow. Using the slope of the ground for guidance, they had made several complete circles of this spot before realizing what had happened. By that time the flames were actually in sight, and they had no choice but to run straight before them. They simply did not know by then how wide the flame front was; to parallel it at a distance of only a few yards would have been the height of insanity. They had been trying to work their way to one side while keeping ahead of the flames, but they were rapidly approaching a state of exhaustion where merely keeping ahead demanded all that their young bodies could give. They were nearly blind, with tears streaming down their soot-stained faces. In Edith's case the tears were not entirely due to smoke; she was crying openly from fatigue and terror, while the boy was having a good deal of trouble keeping his self-control.

None of these facts were very clear to the scientist, since even the undistorted human face was still quite strange to him; but his sympathy was aroused just the same. It is possible that, had the same situation occurred just after his first meeting with the natives, he might have remained an impassive observer in order to find out just what the creatures would and could do in an extremity. Now, however, his talk with Mr. Wing and the evidence of culture and scientific knowledge the native had shown gave the Sarrian a feeling of actual intellectual kinship with the creatures below him; they were people, not animals. Also, they had fallen into their present plight while working for him; he remembered that these two had departed in search of specimens for him. He did not hesitate an instant after seeing them.

He dropped toward the stumbling children, using one of his few English verbs for all it was worth. "Carry!" the torpedo speaker boomed, again and again. He stopped just ahead of the startled youngsters, poised just out of contact with the vegetation. Edith started to reach toward him, but Roger still retained some presence of mind.

"No, Edie! You'll be burned that way, too. We'll have to ride the thing that carries him, if we can get up to it." Ken had already realized this, and was manipulating his control spindle in an effort to bring the torpedo's tail section within their reach, while he himself was still supported safely above the bushes. He had no intrinsic objection to igniting them, since they were doomed in a few minutes anyway, but it looked as though the young natives were going to have trouble enough without an extra fire right beside them. The problem was a little awkward, as his armored feet hung two yards below the hull of the torpedo, and the carrier itself contained automatic circuits designed to keep it horizontal while hovering in a gravitational field. It could be rotated on any axis, however; the main trouble was that Ken had had no occasion to do so as yet, and it took a little time to solve the necessary control combination. It seemed like an hour, even to him, before he succeeded in the maneuver, for he had thrown his full heart into the rescue and was almost as anxious as the children themselves; but at last the rear end of the yard-thick cylinder hung within its own diameter of the ground.

The children at once made frantic efforts to climb aboard. They had no luck; the composition was too slippery, the curve not sharp enough to afford a real grip, and they themselves too exhausted. Roger made a hand-stirrup for his sister, and actually succeeded in getting her partly across the smooth hull; but after a moment of frantic, futile clutching she slipped back and collapsed on the ground, sobbing. Roger paused, indecisive. A blast of hot, smoky air made him gasp for breath; there remained bare moments, it seemed to him, before the flames would be on them. For a second he stared enviously at the helpless being hanging from the other end of the torpedo, to whom the fire's breath was probably a cooling breeze; then he saw the clamps from which the specimen boxes had hung.

For a moment even these seemed useless. He doubted whether he could hang by hand grip alone from those small metal projections for any length of time, and was sure his sister in her present condition could not do so for a moment. Then he had an idea. The clamps were really hook-like, lockable devices rather like the clasp of a brooch; fastened, they made complete rings. Roger fastened the nearest, pulled his belt off with a savage jerk, threaded it through the ring, and buckled it again. Hastily urging Edie to her feet—she gained a little self-possession as she saw what he was doing—he did the same with her belt in another ring, not stopping to give thanks that she was wearing dungarees. All the children did in the woods. Then he helped support her while she held to one of the loops of leather and thrust both legs through the other. Some work would still be needed to hold on, but the leg-strap was carrying most of her weight. Satisfied, he waved the Sarrian off.

Ken understood, and his admiration for the human race went up another notch or two. He did not hesitate or argue, however; he knew perfectly well that the boy had found the only likely method of transporting either of them, and even if Ken could speak his language well enough, argument would be a waste of time. He took off at once, the dazed girl hanging behind him.

He rose first out of the smoke, to give his passenger a chance to breathe; then he took a good look at his surroundings, to be sure of finding the spot again. A momentary break in the smoke below showed Roger struggling uphill once more; and without waiting for further observation Ken sent the torpedo plunging downhill toward the house. Mrs. Wing saw them coming, and he was on his way back for a second load in three quarters of a minute.

In spite of the brief interval and his careful observations, he realized as he arrived overhead that finding the other native was not to be an easy job. His original point of observation was reached easily enough; but he discovered when be arrived there that with the total lack of instruments at his disposal and the moderately strong and erratic air current obviously present there was no way for him to tell whether he had risen vertically to that point, or whether he would be descending vertically from it. He had, of course, seen Roger after getting there, but the boy had already been in motion. He could also cut his lift entirely and fall vertically; but that line of action did not recommend itself. The torpedo was a heavy machine, and he had no desire to have it drop on his armor, especially in the gravity of this planet. He did the best he could, letting down to ground level as rapidly as seemed safe and starting a regular search pattern over the area.

Where he landed, the fire had not quite reached, though the bushes were beginning to smoke. There was no trail such as the boy might have left, or at least none that Ken could recognize. Playing safe, he moved downhill to the very edge of the fire and searched back and forth across it for fifty yards each way—a considerable distance, when the visibility was less than a tenth of that. Then he began moving his sweep gradually up the hill.

Roger had made more progress than might have seemed likely, considering the condition in which Ken had left him; it was fully ten minutes before the scientist found him, still struggling on but making practically no headway. He must have actually gained on the fire during at least part of that time, however, the Sarrian realized.

He sent his booming call downward, and once more lowered the tail of the torpedo. Roger, with a final effort, got his legs through one of the straps, and folded his arms through the other. His face was within an inch or two of the torpedo hull, which had been heated considerably by its recent passage along the flame front; but anything was better than staying where he was, and Roger was scarcely conscious of the blistering on his hands and face. Ken, once sure that the boy had a good grip, plunged up into clear air and bore his second burden down to the house. Roger was still holding on when they arrived, but it was hardly a conscious effort—his mother had to unlock his frantic grip by force.

Ken, knowing he could do no good around the house, went back uphill above the treetops to see how the others were making out in their fire fighting, leaving the presumably competent adult to care for the rescued children. The need for effort seemed to be decreasing; the lower portion was definitely burned out, it seemed to him, and the only activity was along the upper edge. The men were still at work soaking down the edges as they worked upward, but the really lively area had long since outrun them. It was, as Ken had rather expected, heading for bare rock and fuel starvation; but it would be many hours yet before it died completely. As the Wings were perfectly aware, it would be a source of danger for days if the wind should shift, and they did not let up for an instant in their effort until forced to do so by sheer exhaustion. Twice during that period Ken landed on bare patches near Mr. Wing and sketched a rough map of the situation on the ground. Once he hugged ground between trees himself for many minutes while a stiff-winged, three-engined metal machine droned overhead; again he concealed himself as a group of men bearing water pumps and other fire-fighting tools, appeared on the trail from Clark Fork and passed on uphill to help. Ken remained in the vicinity of the house after that; he did not particularly want to be seen by these new natives, reasoning that much delay to his language progress would ensue. He may have been right.

It was shortly after the arrival of the new group that Mr. Wing and Don appeared at the house, almost ready to drop. They were scratched, soot-stained, and scorched; even Ken could appreciate the difference from their former appearance, for they appeared in even worse shape than Roger and Edie had been. It was then, for the first time, that Mr. Wing learned of the danger and rescue of the two, for Ken had made no attempt to apprise him of the matter—it was too difficult, with his limited grasp of English, to manufacture adequate phrases.

Mr. Wing had the same trouble, after he heard the story. Ken had already judged that the race must have strongly developed ties of affection; now he was sure of it. Mr. Wing could not find the words to express himself, but he made the fact of his gratitude amply clear.

# XIX.

The *Karella* had indeed left the earth's atmosphere, but had not returned to her previous height. Two-way communication had been reestablished—Ken wished he knew just when—and Feth was once more controlling the torpedo which carried the scientist. The process of getting aboard was no more complicated than usual. Ken left the two "live" boxes in the air lock for the time being, having set their refrigerators to the same power as the first had seemed to require; the other two, partly filled with mineral specimens, he brought inside. Drai greeted him rather sourly as he emerged from his metal chrysalis.

"So you're finally back. What did you get, if anything?" Ken eyed him with the closest approach to a defiant expression he had yet worn.

"Very little. Thanks to the slight distraction you seem to have engineered, the natives had other things to do than talk to me."

"How was I to know that the ship's hull would set off a chain reaction in the local vegetation? I should think if anything could do it, it would have happened long ago from some other cause."

"I seem to recall telling you of the danger myself. And it may have happened before; the natives seemed to have fairly well organized means of dealing with it."

"Then the fire is out?"

"Not quite. It will probably react for some hours yet. What I dislike is your habit of assuming that I am either a liar or a fool. I told you what happened to the piece of vegetation I picked up; I told you what I was doing with the native in the matter of learning his language. You were listening to me most if not all of the time. What possessed you to come down the way you did?"

"Because I doubted what you told me." Drai made the statement without circumlocution; he apparently felt he was on secure ground. "You said that there had been no talk between you and the native on the subject of tofacco; you even said that you doubted that this was the same native we've been trading he with."

"I said I wasn't sure he *was* the same. That's minor, though—go ahead."

"The first day, while you were down talking to him, the signal came from the fixed transmitter, indicating that they were ready to trade."

"I should think that would support my veracity. I was not near the transmitter. Ask Feth—he landed me."

"That's what I thought, for a while. But today, which was the usual interval after a signal, I sent down another torpedo while you were having your 'language lesson' and nothing happened! There was no one there."

"You mean no one gave you any tofacco."

"No one took the metal, either. I'd be willing to believe they were trying to cheat me, if it had gone without anything in return; but that doesn't fit. I decided you had let something slip while I wasn't listening, and came down to see what you were up to."

"Skipping for the moment the question of how I could possibly tell whether or not you were listening, I'm not sure whether to be glad you think me stupid rather than dishonest. I agree that my native may be your trader, in that case; he might have decided to go to the transmitter later in the day, after he had talked to me. He knew I couldn't stay long. In that case, you have only yourself to thank that he didn't go later—he was too busy. Also, a couple of the young ones were nearly killed by the chain reaction; he may not be too pleased with you now, if he's connected the ship and the trading business. After all, remember he knows we come from Planet One on these trips."

"That I don't believe. He couldn't possibly know it, That's another reason I decided you were trying to cover up your own indiscretion. How do you know that two of the natives were endangered by the fire?"

"I saw them. As a matter of fact, I rescued them—rode them out of the way on the torpedo. I spent quite a while investigating the whole thing, since once you'd started it there was nothing else for me to do. I can prove that—I got some specimens of vegetation residue that may give some more information about the planet." Drai eyed him silently for some moments.

"I'm not convinced yet, and you'd better convince me before your next drug-hunger comes due. If they're going to stop trading, I'm going to stop distributing free samples." Feth, in the background, emitted an uncontrolled sound that was the equivalent of a gasp of dismay; Ken permitted an anxious expression to reach his face for a moment. He had had one brief experience of tofacco-hunger now, and did not want a prolonged one. Drai nodded as he saw the expression. "Yes. The stock is not very high, and if it's to be the last, I'm going to get value for it. I have been given an idea from what you just told me. If this tale of having rescued two natives from death by overheating is true, you can just go back down and play on their gratitude. You can make out that *you* want to trade for tofacco. Surely they will gratify the hero who pulled them from terrible death. Particularly if he makes it clear that he's in for a very uncomfortable time if they don't. You go right back down—your armor's warmed up by this time. We haven't pulled in the other torpedo yet; as soon as you go on local control down there, we'll send it over to you with the metal, and you can haggle to your heart's content." He ceased, still wearing a definite sneer.

"That fact that my knowledge of the language is still fragmentary does not bother you?"

"No. I think you know more than you say."

"How about the fact that there are, at the moment, many other natives at the scene of the fire? I kept among the trees when they arrived so as not to be seen, but I can't do that and trade at the same time. Do you want me to work out in the open? They'll all be fire-fighting for a while, but I suppose they'll want metal afterward." He paused. "I don't see how they can *all* be the one you've been trading with. But I suppose you don't mind opening new bargains with the others—" Laj Drai interrupted.

"You can wait."

"Oh, it wouldn't take very many torpedo loads of metal to satisfy them all, I'm sure."

"I said you could wait." Drai must have seen the satisfied expression that flickered for an instant on the scientist's face, for he added, "I have another idea. The *Karella* will go down with you, and both watch and listen. Possibly if the native becomes recalcitrant, we can suggest lighting another fire."

"Now you want the natives to get a good look at a full-sized space ship. You don't care much about the law, do you?"

"You ought to know. Besides, they've seen it already. However, we'll wait—for a while. I rather think we'll land at a little distance from the scene of the fire, and drop in when it's out. That way," both eyes fixed themselves on Ken, "we'll be sure who talks, and for how long." He turned, pushed off from a convenient wall, and glided out of sight along the corridor. Feth followed him with one troubled eye.

"Ken, you shouldn't use that tone of voice to him. I know you don't like him—no one could—but remember what he can do. I thought, after you'd had a taste of that, you'd calm down a bit. Now he's likely to hold out on you just for the fun of it."

"I know—I'm sorry if I've gotten you in trouble too," replied the scientist. "I just think he's safer when angry. While he's gone, now, we'll have to talk fast. There's work to be done. First of all, was he telling the truth about the short supply of tofacco? Does he keep it all in that refrigerated safe that he hands out our doses from?"

"Yes, And he's probably telling the truth; most of the stuff goes back to the Sarrian system at the end of the season, and he doesn't keep much on hand."

"How much constitutes a dose? I didn't get a really good look at what was inside the brick of frozen air, either time."

"A little cylinder about so big." Feth illustrated. "It comes that way, only in longer sticks—he cuts them into ten sections, and freezes each one up for a separate dose."

"All right—that's what I wanted to make sure of. Now, how good are the little refrigerators on those vivaria of mine? Will they freeze air?"

"Sure. Why?"

"You'll see. Right now, I imagine I have another acting job to do; I don't suppose anything would stop Drai from going down to the surface of Three, as he said." Without explaining anything more, Ken headed toward the control room of the interstellar flyer.

He was quite right; the impatient drug-runner had already ordered the pilot down once more. Lee was making no objection this time, though his expression was not actually one of delight. The descent was uneventful, practically a repetition of the earlier one, except that they were homing on the fixed transmitter and consequently were some eight miles east of their former point of landing. They stopped at a height of two miles above the nearest peaks, and looked around for the smoke cloud. Rather to Drai's disappointment, they saw it; even their eyes could distinguish it from the regular clouds without much difficulty.

"It still seems to be burning," Ken remarked innocently. "Are we going to drift here in full sight until they put it out?"

"No. We'll go down and hide."

"Among the plants? That doesn't seem to work so well, as a method of concealing this ship." Drai eyed the scientist for some time, obviously near the limit of exasperation.

"I'm looking after the matter, thank you. The vegetation does not grow everywhere, as even you should be able to see. There, for example." He pointed to the south. A triangular patch which gave a metallic reflection of the sky light lay in that direction. It was one of those Ken had noticed on his first descent. "We'll look that over. It seems to be lower than the surrounding territory, and would make a very good hiding place.

If it's really like the sort of ground the flatlanders live on, these other natives may very well avoid it. How about that, scientist?"

"You seem to have some logic on your side," Ken replied equably. Drai made no answer to this; he simply gestured to Lee, and the pilot obediently slanted their line of descent toward the shiny patch.

With the radio altimeter registering five hundred feet, Ken began a careful examination of the area. It was larger than he had guessed from a distance, and he found himself unable to decide on its nature. The planet had some queer minerals, of course; the brief look he had had of the specimens he had just brought in showed that. Directly below he could make out no details at all; but over near the edge of the area, the trees that rimmed it were reflected—

"*Lee! Hold up!*" The pilot obeyed without thought, stung by the urgency of his tone.

"What is it?" The eternal suspicion was lacking even from Drai's voice, this time.

"It's a liquid—see how the reflection at the edge trembles in the air currents!"

"So what?"

"The only liquid I've encountered on this planet behaved an awful lot like that queer oxide we found on Four—the one that nearly froze my feet. I saw some before here, and dipped a handler in it; the stuff vaporized instantly, and it was minutes before I could put a tentacle in the sleeve again. I think it's that heat-drinking stuff—hydrogen oxide."

"Why didn't you mention this before?" The suspicion was back in Drai's tone.

"What chance have I had? Besides, I don't care if you leave yourself a frozen memorial on this planet—it's just that I'm with you at the moment. If you don't want to believe me, at least put a torpedo down on it first. You must have plenty of those."

Even Drai could find no fault with this suggestion, and he gestured to Feth. The mechanic, with a censorious glance at Ken, went to his control board and without comment launched another of the projectiles. The one Ken had used was available, but it was the only one fitted with manual control, and he did not want to waste it. He was already convinced of the correctness of Ken's hypothesis.

The slim projectile appeared outside the control room port, and drifted gently down to the surface of the lake. It was still hot, having been stowed inside the ship; and contact with the liquid surface was heralded by a burst of steam. Feth hastily lifted it a short distance, and waited for it to cool somewhat.

"Hardly a fair test to cool it off that fast," he said. "Something's bound to give."

Presently he lowered the machine again. This time only ripples marked the contact. Very cautiously Feth forced it still lower, while the others watched silently. Apparently the cold did not matter.

But something else did. Quite suddenly another cloud of steam arose, and a wave of considerable size spread from the place where the torpedo had been. *Had been* was the right expression; there was no response when the mechanic manipulated the controls to bring it up again. He glanced up, presently.

"It's a pity, that only the cargo compartments of those things are airtight. Apparently the liquid bothers electrical machinery. Maybe it dissolves insulation." Laj Drai was looking as though he had seen a ghost. He made no direct answer to the mechanic's remark.

"Ken!" he spoke suddenly, still looking preoccupied. "When you first described this patch of stuff, you said its appearance reminded you of the flat country. Right?"

"Right." Ken saw what the drug-runner had in mind.

"Would it—would it be possible for a planet to have so much liquid that three quarters of its surface would be covered?"

"I certainly can't say it's impossible. I admit it's hard to imagine. Any liquid at all—and particularly something as rare as that stuff is with us. Still, this is a larger planet than Sarr, and would have a greater velocity of escape, and is colder, so the average speed of the gas molecules would be slower—let's see—" His voice trailed off as he became involved in mental arithmetic. "Yes, this planet would hold the stuff easily enough; and hydrogen and oxygen are common elements in the universe. I'm afraid it's very possible, Drai." The other did not answer; everyone else knew what he was thinking. When he did speak, Ken felt smug—he had predicted the subject correctly.

"But the flatlanders—could they live in the stuff?—but maybe there aren't any; the liquid must have destroyed the torpedoes—but their radar beams! We've detected those!" He looked at Ken suddenly, as though he had made a telling point in an argument. Ken had been following his thoughts well enough to answer.

"You have no evidence whatever that those beams were not generated by the same race with which you have been trading. I have already pointed out that they are competent astronomers. I think you have been developing a very interesting mythology for the last twenty years, though I admit the idea could do with a little more proof."

Keeping one eye on the enigmatic liquid beyond the port, Drai rolled the other toward the pilot.

"Lee, go up about ten miles, and start travelling. It doesn't matter which way, I guess." He was obeyed in silence. Even though Lee did not take the shortest route to the ocean, the speed of the ship even within the atmosphere was such that only minutes passed before the fabulous "flatland" lay beneath them—the closest any of them had dared to approach it in twenty Sarrian years. Dumbly the commander gestured downward, and presently they hung a few hundred feet above the waves. Drai looked for a long time, then spoke three words to Ken: "Get a sample."

The scientist thought for a moment; then he found the small bomb in which he had taken the frost sample on Mars, pumped out the air, and closed the valve. Redonning his armor, he clumped into the air lock after voicing dire warning to Lee about keeping the vessel level. He fastened a wire to the bomb itself and another to the valve handle; then, opening the outer door, he lowered away until the loss of weight told him the bomb was submerged. He pulled the other wire, waited a moment, pulled up the filled bomb, closed the valve again, and sealed the outer door of the air lock.

Naturally, the bomb exploded violently within a few seconds of the time that sulfur ceased condensing on its surface. Ken felt thankful that he had not yet removed the armor—parts of the bomb had actually scored the metal—and after some thought tried again. This time he let down a tiny glass wool sponge, hoping the liquid had a significant amount of natural capillary action. He placed the sponge in another bomb, and by the same method he had used with the Martian sample eventually determined the molecular weight of the substance. It came out higher than before, but eventually he found the deposit of salts on the sponge and allowed for their weight. The result this time left little doubt that the substance was indeed hydrogen oxide.

He looked down for a minute at the tossing blue expanse, wondering how deep it might be and whether it would have any real effect on the conditions of the Planet of Ice; then he turned, climbed out of the armor—he had stayed in it for the rest of his experiment, after the first blast—and went to report to Drai.

The drug-runner heard him in silence. He still seemed a little dazed by the overthrow of his former belief. It was many minutes before he spoke, and then he simply said, "Take us back to One, Lee. I have to think." Ken and Feth eyed each other, but kept all expression of glee from their faces.

# XX.

"Well, you seem to have done it now." Feth was still unhappy.

"In what way?" queried Ken. The two were ostensibly engaged in checking the mechanical adequacy of the refrigerated vivaria.

"I've been working for years to support this flatland myth—I realized it was never more than a theory, but Drai had to be shown the difference between that and fact—and I've been doing my level best to keep the production of tofacco down to a minimum."

"Provided it was not cut off entirely," Ken interjected rather unkindly.

"True. Now you blow up the story that kept him scared of really exploring the planet, and at the same time give him a tool for getting what he wants from the inhabitants by threats and force. If you had any ideas in mind at all, they seem to have flopped badly."

"Oh, I wouldn't say that. You saw the way Drai was feeling when he left the ship."

"Oh, yes, he was regretting the wasted years and the money that went with them, I suppose. That won't last much longer; he's been mooning for days now. Then he'll—" Ken had been thinking furiously as the mechanic delivered his gloomy discourse; now he interrupted abruptly.

"Then he'll be too late to do anything. Feth, I want you to take me on trust for a while. I promise you won't miss your sniff. I'm going to be very busy in the air lock for at least a couple of hours, I imagine. Lee is still aboard. I want you to find him, and keep him occupied in any way you see fit for at least that length of time. I don't want him to see what I'm doing. You have known him longer than I, and can figure out something to interest him. Just don't kill him; we're going to need him later."

Feth looked at the scientist for several seconds, obviously doubtful. Ken wisely said nothing more, letting him fight his own battle with a perfectly natural fear. He was pleased but not too surprised when the mechanic finally said, "All right," and disappeared toward the control room. Ken waited a moment; then, reasonably sure of not being interrupted, he closed the inner door of the air lock, donned a regular space suit, and set briskly to work. He was rather regretful of the need for sacrificing some of his living specimens, but he consoled himself with the thought they could easily be replaced later. Then, too, the vivarium he had to use was the one containing only a few plants—the fire had interrupted before the human children had made much progress with it. That was foresight, not good fortune; he had had to decide which of them he was going to use, before be had left the planet.

In the control room, Feth did not find his task too difficult. He was not on the best of terms with the pilot, but had never held toward him the blazing hatred he had felt toward his chief. Lee was not particularly scrupulous, as he had shown in the past, but Feth knew of nothing in his record to call forth whole-souled detestation. In consequence, there was nothing strange in the mechanic's entering the control room and settling down for a talk. The pilot was reading, as usual when off duty; to his question concerning Ken's whereabouts, the mechanic responded that he was "fooling with his vegetables in the air lock."

"Why does he have to use the lock for a laboratory?" the pilot asked plaintively. "I've already told him it's bad practice. He's got a lab in the station—why doesn't he take them there?"

"I guess he figures if a refrigerator breaks down he can pump the air out of the lock and have a chance of the specimen's lasting until he can make repairs," Feth replied. "I imagine you'd have to ask him, to be really sure. I wouldn't worry—there are just the three of us aboard, and those cases aren't too big to get around if your engines start to get out of hand." The pilot grunted, and returned to his reading; but one eye flickered occasionally to the board of telltale lights. He knew when Ken evacuated the lock and opened the outer door, but apparently did not consider it worth while to ask why. Feth, as a matter of fact, did not know either; he was wondering a good deal harder than Lee. Fortunately the pilot was used to his taciturnity and habitual glumness of expression, or his attitude might have aroused suspicion. It was, as a matter of fact, his awareness of this fact that had caused Ken to refrain from telling his whole plan to Feth. He was afraid the mechanic might look too happy to be natural.

The next interruption caused the pilot to put down his book and rise to his feet. "What's that fool doing now?" he asked aloud. "Drilling holes in the hull?" Feth could understand the source of his worry; the outer door of the air lock had been closed again, and pressure had returned to normal some time before—but now the pressure was dropping rapidly, as though through a serious leak, and air was being pumped *into* the chamber. The outer door was still closed.

"Maybe he's filling some portable tanks," suggested Feth hopefully.

"With what? There isn't a pump on board that could take air faster than the lock bleeders can deliver it, except the main circulators. He's not using those, where he is."

"Why don't you call him and ask, then? I notice the inner door is sealed, too; he'll probably have a fit if you opened it in the middle of his work."

"I'll have one myself if this goes on," growled Lee. He watched the indicators for another moment, noting that the pressure now seemed to be holding steady at about half normal. "Well, if it's a leak, he had sense enough to plug it." He turned to the microphone, switched to the local wavelength used in the suit receivers, and made the suggested call. Ken answered promptly, denying that he had bored any holes in the hull and stating that he would be through shortly. Lee was able to get nothing else from him.

"One would almost think you didn't trust him," gibed Feth as the pilot turned away from the microphone. "You have as much reason to believe him as you have to believe me, and I notice you don't worry much about me."

"Maybe after he's had a few more sniffs I'll feel the same about him," Lee replied. "Right now, just listening to him makes me think he's not convinced yet about being under the influence. I never heard anyone talk like that to Drai before."

"I did—once."

"Yeah. But he's done it more than once. Drai feels the same way—he told me to camp in this control room as long as you two were on board. I don't think it matters, myself—I've got the key, and if anyone can short the whole control system out from under a Bern lock he's darned good. However, orders are orders." He relaxed once more with his book. Feth resumed his gloomy train of thought.

"So they're trusting on just that one hold on us. As if I didn't know it. If Ken could figure out some means of getting at Drai's cold-safe—I certainly have never been able to—but then, we couldn't find Sarr anyway—if only we were looking for a sun like Rigel or Deneb, that a fellow could recognize at thousands of parsecs instead of having to get close enough to spot planets—" his thoughts rolled on, consisting largely of "If only's" as they had now for years. The drug had done little if anything to Feth's mind, but the fact of his subjection to it had long since given him an apathetic attitude toward all suggestions for escape. He wondered why he had consented to do as Ken asked—how could the scientist possibly keep the assurance he had given?

Ken's own voice eventually interrupted this line of cogitation. "Feth, could you come down here to help me for a moment? I'm nearly through; there's some stuff I want to take out of the lock." Both Sarrians in the control room glanced at the indicators. The lock pressure was rising again.

"All right, I'm coming," replied Feth. "Get the inner door open as soon as pressure's up." He started down the corridor, leaving the pilot behind. Ken's message had been well worded.

He was not gone long enough to make the pilot suspicious; within two or three minutes Lee heard both mechanic and scientist returning. They were not talking, and as they approached the pilot grew curious. He started to rise to meet them, but had time just to reach his feet before the two entered the door. The gloomy expression had left Feth's face, to be replaced by one much harder to decipher. Lee, however, spent no time trying to solve its meaning; his eyes were both drawn instantly to the object the two were carrying in a cloth sling between them.

It was roughly cubical, perhaps a foot on a side. It was yellow in color. It trailed a visible stream of mist, and yellow droplets appeared and grew on its surface—droplets of a deeper, honey-colored hue; droplets that gathered together, ran down the sides of the block, soaked into the sling, and vanished in thin air. For an instant Lee, watching it, showed an expression of bewilderment; this changed almost at once to one of horror; then he regained control of himself.

"So that's where the air was going," he remarked. "What's the idea?"

Ken, who was clad in a space suit except for the helmet, did not answer the question directly. Instead, he asked one of his own.

"You know the coordinates of Sarr, and could get there from here, don't you?"

"Of course. I've made the trip often enough. So what?—I hope you don't think I'm going to tell you in order to get out of a frostbite."

"I don't care whether you want to tell us or not. I plan for you to do the piloting. And I don't plan to freeze you on this block—in fact, we'll put it down right here. You have until it evaporates to make up your mind. After that, we'll be in a position to make it up for you."

The pilot laughed. "I was expecting that one. Am I supposed to believe you have some tofacco in the middle of that? You just made the block a couple of minutes ago."

"Quite true. Since you bring up the matter, there *is* a cylinder of tofacco inside the block. I put it there myself—a few minutes ago, as you say."

"I suppose you broke into Laj Drai's safe and borrowed it." The pilot was obviously incredulous.

"No. However, Drai's suggestion of playing on the sympathies of the natives of Planet Three was a very good idea."

"I suppose they gave you a hundred units for rescuing their kids."

"As a matter of fact, it seems to be more like two thousand. I didn't exactly count them, but they're very neatly arranged; and if the unit you mean is one tenth of one of the cylinders they come in, that figure is about right."

The pilot might have been just a trifle uneasy. "But there weren't any landings after Drai had the idea—you couldn't have asked for it."

"Are you trying to insult me by saying I had to wait for Drai to have such an idea? I thought of it myself, but having been brought up with a conscience I decided against trying it. Besides, as I keep saying, I don't know their language well enough yet. As it happened, the native I'd been talking to gave me a container of the stuff without my mentioning it at all. He seems to be a nice fellow, and apparently knows the value we place on tofacco. I fear I forgot to report that to Drai."

Lee looked positively haggard as the likelihood of the story began to impress him; Feth, on the other hand, had brightened up amazingly. Only a slight expression of doubt still clouded his features—could the scientist be running a bluff? It seemed impossible; it was hard to see how getting started for Sarr would do any good unless he had a supply of the drug, and he had made no mention of forcing Lee to help them get it from Drai's safe.

These points must have crossed the pilot's mind, too; he was looking at the dwindling lump of sulfur with a growing expression of terror. He made one last objection, knowing its weakness even before he spoke.

"You won't dare let it out—Feth has no suit, and you don't have a helmet."

"What difference does it make to us?"

With that, Lee made a sudden, frantic break for the door. He dived headlong into Feth, and for a few seconds there was a nightmarish swirling of legs and tentacles. Ken stood by, but his assistance was not needed. The pilot suddenly rolled back almost to his control board, tentacles lashing madly; but when he regained his feet, he did not seem eager to renew the struggle.

"If I'd only had—"

"Yes—it would have been very nice if Drai had let anyone but himself carry a gun. The fact is, he doesn't and you haven't too much time. How about it?" Feth emphasized his words by turning up the control room thermostat, which was within his reach.

The pilot gave in. If any shred of doubt about Ken's truthfulness remained in his mind, he did not dare gamble on it—he had seen drug addicts other than Feth, and remembered some harrowing details.

"All right—take it away!" he gasped. "I'll do whatever you want!"

Without comment Ken picked up both ends of the sling and carried the now much lighter bundle back toward the air lock. He was back in two or three minutes.

"Made it!" he said. "I was wondering if it might not boil through before I got there—you held out longer than I thought you would, Lee. However, the air is clear after all. I may mention that that particular block is the top one in my little refrigerator, and it will take remarkably little time to bring it into action.

"Well, let's make plans. I'd rather like to arrest our friend Drai, but I don't quite see how we're to go about it. Any ideas?"

"*Arrest* him?" A faint smile suddenly appeared on Feth's face.

"Yes. I'm afraid I'm some sort of deputy narcotics investigator—not that I asked for the job, and certainly I'm not a very efficient one. Maybe I ought to swear you in, too, Feth—I guess I can do it legally."

"You needn't bother. It was done more than eighteen years ago. Apparently they didn't bother to tell you that the stunt of taking an innocent general science dabbler and trying to make a policeman out of him had been tried before, with no visible results?"

"No, they didn't. I'll have something to say to Rade when we get back. If he knew that—"

"Take it easy on him. Under the circumstances, I'm very glad he tried again. You haven't done such a bad job, you know."

"Maybe not, but the job's not done. I see the reason now for a lot of things that puzzled me about you. As far as I'm concerned, this is your show as much as mine, from now on. How do we go about collecting Drai? I suppose the others aren't worth bothering with."

"Why not leave him where he is? There's no other ship; he's stuck as long as we have this one, unless he wants to take a ride in a torpedo. Since there's nowhere else in this system where he could live for any length of time, I don't think he'll do that. My advice would be to take off right away, and let him worry about what's happened until we get back with official support."

"The motion is carried—except for one thing. I have to run a little errand first. Feth, you keep an eye on our friend and pilot while I'm gone." He disappeared toward the air lock before any questions could be asked.

As a matter of fact, his absence was quite long, and eventually the ship had to go after him. He was in a valley adjacent to that of the station, with a problem he could not handle alone. Sallman Ken liked to pay his debts.

None of the Wings, of course, felt that the strange "fire-man" owed them anything. On the contrary. They did not blame him for the fire— he had been on the ground, talking to them, when the ship started it.

The blaze was out by night, anyway, with the aid of the crew from Clark Fork. The only real concern the family felt was whether or not the alien would return.

It was not until evening that anyone remembered that a torpedo load of metal should have arrived that day. Don and Roger went out in the morning to the site of the transmitter, and found a torpedo, but its cargo door was closed and there was no answer to their shouts. This, of course, was the one Drai had sent down, and which he had completely forgotten in the rush of events. It had been operating on radio rather than achronic transmitter control, since the *Karella* had been so near at the time, and there was no way to switch it back from a distance even if the drug-runner's memory should improve. Ken himself, with his "payment" safely on board the *Karella,* never thought of it; his attention had promptly switched to the obvious need for a survey of the Solar System before he left it. A full Earth day had been spent looking briefly over Sol's frozen family, before he could be persuaded to start for home—Feth did not try very hard to persuade him, as a matter of fact, since he had his own share of scientific curiosity. At last, however, they plunged back to make the final call at Planet Three. The transmitter was just emerging into sunlight; this time even Lee appeared willing to home down on it. A mile above the peaks, Ken guided him on a long downward slant to a point above the Wing home.

The natives had seen them coming; all seven of them were standing outside, watching the descent with emotions that Ken could easily guess. He waved Lee into a position that brought the air lock directly over the clearing in front of the house, and the lowest part of the ship's hull thirty feet above the treetops. Then he climbed into his armor, entered the air lock with his "payment," and opened the outer door without bothering to pump back the air. For a moment he was enveloped in a sheet of blue fire, which burst from the port and caused the natives to exclaim in alarm. Fortunately the flame of burning sulfur licked upward, and was gone in a moment. Then Ken, waving the natives away from directly below, rolled his payment over the sill of the lock. It made quite a hole in the ground. A carefully made diagram, drawn on the fluo-silicone material the Sarrians used for paper, followed; and when the Wings looked up after crowding around this, the *Karella* was a dwindling dot in the sky, and Ken was already preparing a report for the planetary ecologists and medical researchers who would return with them. Perhaps a cure for the drug could be found, and even if it weren't he was on good enough terms with the natives so that he needn't worry too much. Not, of course, that that was his only interest in the weird beings; they seemed rather likable, in their own way—

He even remembered to write a brief report for Rade.

On the ground, no one spoke for some time.

"I can't budge it, Dad," were the first words finally uttered. They came from Roger, who had been vainly trying to move the grayish lump that had landed at their feet.

"It must weigh two hundred pounds or so," supplemented Don. "If it's all platinum—"

"Then we'll have a fine time breaking it up into pieces small enough to avoid comment," finished his father. "What interests me right now is this picture." The others crowded around once more.

It was a tiny diagram of the Solar System, such as they had drawn before the fire two days ago. Beside it was the unmistakable picture of a space ship like the *Karella*—heading away from it. Then another diagram, apparently an enlarged view of the orbits of the inner planets, showed the arcs through which each would move in approximately a month; and finally a third picture reproduced the first—except that the space ship was pointing *toward* the system. The meaning was clear enough, and a smile broke out on Mr. Wing's face as he interpreted it.

"I guess we continue to eat," he remarked, "and I guess our friend wants to learn more English. He'll be back, all right. I was afraid for a little while he'd take that carton of cigarettes in the wrong spirit. Well—" he turned to the family suddenly.

"Don—Roger—let's go. If he's going to be away a month, and that torpedo is still lying where you found it, we have a job of tinkering to do. Roger, by the time you're Don's age you may be able to pilot us on a return visit to your hot-blooded friend—we're going to find out how that gadget works!"

# CLOSE TO CRITICAL

# PROLOGUE: INVESTIGATION; ANNEXATION

Sol, seen at a distance of sixteen light-years, is a little fainter than the star at the tip of Orion's sword, and it could not have been contributing much to the sparkle in the diamond lenses of the strange machine. More than one of the watching men, however, got a distinct impression that the thing was taking a last look at the planetary system where it had been made. It would be a natural thing for any sentient and sentimental being to do, for it was already falling toward the great dark object only a few thousand miles away.

Any ordinary planet would have been glaringly bright at that range, for Altair is an excellent illuminator and was at its best right then: Altair is not a variable star, but it rotates fast enough to flatten itself considerably, and the planet was in a part of its orbit where it got the maximum benefit from the hotter, brighter polar regions. In spite of this, the world's great bulk was visible chiefly as a fuzzy blot not very much brighter than the Milky Way, which formed a background to it. It seemed as though the white glare of Altair were being sucked in and quenched, rather than illuminating anything.

But the eyes of the machine had been designed with Tenebra's atmosphere in mind. Almost visibly the robot's attention shifted, and the whitish lump of synthetic material turned slowly. The metal skeleton framing it kept pace with the motion, and a set of stubby cylinders lined themselves up with the direction of fall. Nothing visible emerged from them, for there was still too little atmosphere to glow at the impact of the ions, but the tons of metal and plastic altered their acceleration. The boosters were fighting the already fierce tug of a world nearly three times the diameter of distant Earth, and they fought well enough so that the patchwork fabrication which held them suffered no harm when atmosphere was finally reached.

The glitter faded out of the diamond eyes as the world's great gas mantle gradually enfolded the machine. It was dropping slowly and steadily, now; the word *cautiously* might almost have been used. Altair still glowed overhead, but the stars were vanishing even to the hypersensitive pickups behind those lenses as the drop continued.

Then there was a change. Up to now, the thing might have been a rocket of unusually weird design, braking straight down to a landing on outboard jets. The fact that the jet streams were glowing ever brighter meant nothing; naturally, the air was growing denser. However, the boosters themselves should *not* have been glowing.

These were. Their exhausts brightened still further, as though they were trying harder to slow a fall that was speeding up in spite of them, and the casings themselves began to shine a dull red. That was enough for the distant controllers; a group of brilliant flashes shone out for an instant, not from the boosters themselves but from points on the metal girders that held them. The struts gave way instantly, and the machine fell unsupported.

For only a moment. There was still equipment fastened to its outer surface, and a scant half-second after the blowoff of the boosters a gigantic parachute flowered above the falling lump of plastic. In that gravity it might have been expected to tear away instantly, but its designers had known their business. It held. The incredibly thick atmosphere—even at that height several times as dense as Earth's—held stubbornly in front of the parachute's broad expanse and grimly insisted on the lion's share of every erg of potential energy given up by the descending mass. In consequence, even a gravity three times that of Earth's surface failed to damage the device when it finally struck solid ground.

For some moments after the landing, nothing seemed to happen. Then the flat-bottomed ovoid moved, separating itself from the light girders which had held the parachute, crawled on nearly invisible treads away from the tangle of metal ribbons, and stopped once more as though to look around.

It was not looking, however; for the moment, it could not see. There were adjustments to be made. Even a solid block of polymer, with no moving parts except its outer traveling and handling equipment, could not remain completely unchanged under an external pressure of some eight hundred atmospheres. The dimensions of the block, and of the circuitry embedded in it, had changed slightly. The initial pause after landing had been required for the distant controllers to find and match the slightly different frequencies now needed to operate it. The eyes, which had seen so clearly in empty space, had to adjust so that the different index of refraction between the diamond and the new external medium did not blur their pictures hopelessly. This did not take too long, as it was automatic, effected by the atmosphere itself as it filtered through minute pores into the spaces between certain of the lens elements.

Once optically adjusted, the nearly complete darkness meant nothing to those eyes, for the multipliers behind them made use of every quantum of radiation the diamond could refract. Far away, human eyes glued themselves to vision screens which carried the relayed images of what the machine saw.

It was a rolling landscape, not too unearthly at first glance. There were large hills in the distance, their outlines softened by what might have been forests. The nearby ground was completely covered with vegetation which looked more or less like grass, though the visible trail the robot had already left suggested that the stuff was far more brittle. Clumps of taller growths erupted at irregular intervals, usually on higher ground. Nothing seemed to move, not even the thinnest fronds of the plants, though an irregular crashing and booming registered almost constantly on the sound pickups built into the plastic block. Except for the sound it was a still-life landscape, without wind or animal activity.

The machine gazed thoughtfully for many minutes. Probably its distant operators were hoping that life frightened into hiding by its fall might reappear; but if this were the case they were disappointed for the moment. After a time it crawled back to the remains of its parachute harness and played a set of lights carefully over the collection of metal girders, cables, and ribbons, examining them all in great detail. Then it moved away again, this time with a purposeful air.

For the next ten hours it quartered meticulously the general area of the landing, sometimes stopping to play its light on some object like a plant, sometimes looking around for minutes on end without obvious purpose, sometimes emitting sounds of varying pitch and loudness. This last always happened when it was in a valley, or at least not on the very top of a hill; it seemed to be studying echoes for some reason.

Periodically it went back to the abandoned harness and repeated the careful examination, as though it were expecting something to happen. Naturally, in an environment having a three-hundred-seventy-degree temperature, about eight hundred atmospheres pressure, and a climate consisting of water heavily laced with oxygen and oxides of sulfur, things started to happen soon enough; and great interest was shown in the progress of the corrosion as it steadily devoured the metal. Some parts lasted longer than others; no doubt the designers had included different alloys, perhaps to check this very point. The robot remained in the general area until the last of the metal had vanished in slime.

At irregular intervals during this time, the surface of the ground shook violently. Sometimes the shaking was accompanied by the crashes which had first greeted the robot's "ears"; at other times it was relatively silent. The operators must have been bothered by this at first; then it became evident that all the hills in the neighborhood were well rounded with no steep cliffs, and that the ground itself was free of both cracks and loose stones, so there was little reason to worry about the effect of quakes on the fabulously expensive mechanism.

A far more interesting event was the appearance of animal life. Most of the creatures were small, but were none the less fascinating for that, if the robot's actions meant anything. It examined everything that appeared, as closely as it possibly could. Most of the creatures seemed to be scale-armored and eight-limbed; some appeared to live on the local vegetation, others, on each other.

With the harness finally gone, the attention of the robot's operators was exclusively occupied by the animals for a long time. The investigation was interrupted a number of times, but this was due to loss of control rather than distraction. The lack of visible surface features on Tenebra had prevented the men from getting a very precise measure of its rotation period, and on several occasions the distant ship "set" as far as the important part of the planet was concerned. Trial and error gradually narrowed down the uncertainties in the length of Tenebra's day, however, and the interruptions in control finally vanished.

The project of studying a planet three times the diameter of Earth looked rather ridiculous when attempted with a single exploring machine. Had that been the actual plan, of course it *would* have been ridiculous; but the men had something else in mind. One machine is not much; a machine with a crew of assistants, particularly if the crew is part of a more or less world-wide culture, is something very different. The operators very definitely hoped to find local help—in spite of the rather extreme environment into which their machine had fallen. They were experienced men, and knew something of the ways of life in the universe.

However, weeks went by, and then months, with no sign of a creature possessing more than the rudiments of a nervous system. Had the men understood the operation of the lensless, many-spined "eyes" of the local animals they might have been more hopeful; but as it was most of them grew resigned to facing a job of several lifetimes. It was sheer chance that when a thinking creature finally did turn up it was discovered by the robot. Had it been the other way around—if the native had discovered the machine—history could easily have been very different on several planets.

The creature, when they did see it, was big. It towered fully nine feet in height, and on that planet must have weighed well over a ton. It conformed to the local custom as regarded scales and number of limbs, but it walked erect on two of the appendages, seemed not to be using the next two, and used the upper four for prehension. That was the fact that betrayed its intelligence: two long and two shorter spears, each with a carefully chipped stone head, were being carried in obvious readiness for instant use.

Perhaps the stone disappointed the human watchers, or perhaps they remembered what happened to metals on this planet and refrained from jumping to conclusions about the culture level suggested by the material. In any case, they watched the native carefully.

This was easier than it might have been; the present neighborhood, many miles from the original landing point, was a good deal rougher in its contours. The vegetation was both higher and somewhat less brittle, though it was still virtually impossible to avoid leaving a trail where the robot crawled. The men guessed at first that the higher plants had prevented the native from seeing the relatively small machine; then it became apparent that the creature's attention was fully occupied by something else.

It was traveling slowly and apparently trying to leave as little trail as possible. It was also making allowance for the fact that to leave *no* trail was not practicable; periodically it stopped and built a peculiar arrangement consisting of branches from some of the rarer, springy plants and the sharp stone blades which it took in seemingly endless supply from a large leather sack slung about its scaly body.

The nature of these arrangements was clear, after the native had gotten far enough ahead to permit a close inspection. They were booby traps, designed to drive a stone point into the body of anything attempting to follow in the creature's footsteps. They must have been intended against animals rather than other natives, since they could easily be avoided merely by paralleling the trail instead of following it.

The fact that the precaution was being taken at all, however, made the whole situation extremely interesting, and the robot was made to follow with all possible caution. The native traveled five or six miles in this fashion, and during this time set about forty of the traps. The robot avoided these without trouble, but several times tripped others which had apparently been set earlier. The blades did no harm to the machine; some of them actually broke against the plastic. It began to look as though the whole neighborhood had been "mined," however.

Eventually the trail led to a rounded hill. The native climbed this quickly, and paused at a narrow gully opening near the top. It seemed to be looking around for followers, though no organs of vision had yet been identified by the human watchers. Apparently satisfied, it drew an ellipsoidal object from its sack, examined it carefully with delicate fingers, and then disappeared into the gully

In two or three minutes it was back, this time without its grapefruit-sized burden. Heading down the hill once more, it avoided with care both its own traps and the others, and set off in a direction different from that of its approach.

The robot's operators had to think fast. Should they follow the native or find out what it had been doing up the hill? The former might seem more logical, since the native was leaving, and the hill presumably was not, but the second alternative was the one they chose. After all, it was impossible for the thing to travel without leaving some sort of trail; besides, night was approaching, so it wouldn't get far. It seemed safe to assume that it shared the characteristic of Tenebra's other animal life, of collapsing into helplessness a few hours after nightfall.

Besides, looking at the hilltop shouldn't take too long. The robot waited until the native was well out of sight, and then moved up the hill toward the gully. This, it turned out, led into a shallow crater, though the hill bore no resemblance to a volcano; on the crater floor lay perhaps a hundred ellipsoids similar to that which the native had just left there. They were arranged with great care in a single line, and except for that fact were the closest things to loose stones that the men had yet seen on Tenebra. Their actual nature seemed so obvious that no effort was made to dissect one.

At this point there must have been a lengthy and lively discussion. The robot did nothing for quite a long time. Then it left the crater and went down the hill, picked its way carefully out through the "mine field" on the trail of the native, and settled down to travel.

This was not quite as easy as it would have been in the day time, since it was starting to rain and visibility was frequently obstructed by the drops. The men had not yet really decided whether it was better, in traveling at night, to follow valleys and remain submerged or stick to ridges and hilltops so as to see occasionally; but in this case the problem was irrelevant. The native had apparently ignored the question, and settled for something as close to a straight line as it could manage. The trail ran for some ten miles, and ended at a clearing before a cave-studded cliff.

Details could not be seen well. Not only was the rain still falling, but the darkness was virtually absolute even to the pickups of the robot. More discussion must have resulted from this; it was two or three minutes after the machine's arrival at the clearing that its lights went on and played briefly over the rock.

Natives could be seen standing inside the cave mouths, but they made no response to the light. They were either asleep, in more or less human fashion, or had succumbed to the usual night-torpor of Tenebra's animal life.

No sign of anything above a stone-age culture level could be seen anywhere about, and after a few minutes of examination the robot cut off most of its lights and headed back toward the hill and the crater.

It moved steadily and purposefully. Once at the hilltop, several openings appeared in its sides, and from some of these armlike structures were extended. Ten of the ellipsoids were picked carefully from one end of the line—leaving no betraying gaps—and stowed in the robot's hull. Then the machine went back down the hill and began a deliberate search for booby traps. From these it removed the stone blades, and such of these as seemed in good condition—many were badly corroded, and some even crumbled when handled—disappeared into other openings in the lump of plastic. Each of these holes was then covered by a lid of the same incredibly stable polymer which formed the body of the machine, so that no one could have told from outside that the storage places were there.

With this task completed, the robot headed away, at the highest speed it could maintain. By the time Altair rose and began turning the lower atmosphere back into gas, the machine, the stolen weapons, and the "kidnapped" eggs were far from the crater and still farther from the cave village.

# I. Exploration; Expectation; Altercation

Nick pushed through the tall plants into the open, stopped, and used several words of the sort Fagin had always refused to translate. He was neither surprised nor bothered to find water ahead of him—it was still early in the morning—it was annoying, however, to find it on each side as well. Sheer bad luck, apparently, had led him straight out along a peninsula, and this was no time for anyone to retrace his steps.

To be really precise, he didn't *know* that he was being followed, of course; but it simply hadn't occurred to him to doubt that he was. He had spent two days, since his escape, in making as confused and misleading a trail as possible, swinging far to the west before turning back toward home, and he was no more willing than a human being would have been to admit that it might have been wasted effort. True, he had seen not the slightest sign of pursuers. He had been delayed by the usual encounters with impassable ground and wild animals, and none of his captors had caught up; the floating animals and plants which it was never safe to ignore completely had shown no sign of interest in anything behind him; his captors during the time he was with them had shown themselves to be hunters and trackers of superlative skill. Taking all these facts into account, he might have been excused for supposing that the fact of his continued freedom meant they weren't following. He was tempted, but couldn't bring himself to believe it. They had wanted so badly to make him lead them to Fagin!

He came to himself with a start, and brought his mind back to the present. Theorizing was useless just now; he must decide whether to retrace his steps along the peninsula, and risk running into his ex-captors, or wait until the lake dried up and chance their catching him. It was hard to decide which was the smaller risk, but there was the one check he could make.

He walked to the water's edge, looked at the liquid carefully, then slapped it vigorously. The slow ripples which spread up the edge of the lake and out over its more or less level surface did not interest him; the drops which detached themselves did. He watched as they drifted toward him, settling slowly, and noted with satisfaction that even the largest of them faded out without getting back to the surface. Evidently the lake did not have long to go; he settled down to wait.

The breeze was picking up slowly as the plants awoke to the new day. He could smell it. He watched eagerly for its effect on the lake—not waves, but the turbulent hollows in the surface which would mark slightly warmer bodies of air passing over it. That would be the sign; from then on, the surface would probably drop faster down the lake bed than he could travel. The breeze should keep the air breathable, as long as he didn't follow the water too closely—yes, it couldn't be long now; the very point where he was standing was below the surface level of some parts of the lake. It was drying up.

The difference increased as he waited, the edge of the water slipping back in ghostly fashion. He followed it with caution until a wall of water towered on either side. It began to look as though the peninsula were really a ridge across the lake; if so, so much the better.

Actually, it didn't quite reach. He had to wait for a quarter of an hour at the ridge's end while the rest of the lake turned back to air. He was impatient enough to risk breathing the stuff almost too quickly after the change, but managed to get away with it. A few minutes more brought him up the slope to the tall vegetation on the east side of the erstwhile lake. Before plunging among the plants, where he would be able to see nothing but the floaters overhead, he paused a moment to look back across the dry bottom to the point where he had first seen the water—still no pursuers. Another floater or two were drifting his way; he felt for his knives, and slightly regretted the spears he had lost. Still, there was little likelihood of danger from a floater behind him as long as he traveled at a decent speed—and that's what he'd better be doing. He plunged into the brush.

Travel was not too difficult; the stuff was flexible enough to be pushed out of the way most of the time. Occasionally he had to cut his way, which was annoying less because of the effort involved than because it meant exposing a knife to the air. Knives were getting somewhat scarce, and Fagin was rather tight with those remaining.

The morning wore on, still without sight of pursuers. He made unusually good speed much of the time, because of a remarkable lack of wild animals—par for a forty-mile walk being four or five fights, while he had only one. However, he more than lost the time gained when he ran into an area rougher than any he had ever seen. The hills were sharp and jagged instead of rounded; there were occasional loose rocks, and from time to time these were sent rolling and tumbling by unusually sharp quakes. In places he had to climb steep cliffs, either up or down; in others, he threaded his way through frighteningly narrow cracks—with no assurance that there was an opening at the other end. Several times there wasn't, and he had to go back.

Even here he left a trail, the local plant life being what it was; but with that area behind him he found it even harder to justify the feeling that he was being pursued. If his ex-captors really followed through that, they deserved to catch him! But still, however often he let his attention cover his rear, no sign of them appeared.

The hours passed, Nick traveling at the highest speed he could maintain. The one fight he had scarcely delayed him at all; it was a floater that saw him from ahead and dropped nearly to ground level in time to intercept him. It was a small one, so small that his arms outreached its tentacles; and a quick slash of one of his knives opened enough of its gas-bladders to leave it floundering helplessly behind him. He sheathed the weapon and raced on with scarcely diminished speed, rubbing an arm which had been touched lightly by the thing's poison.

The limb had ceased to sting, and Altair was high in the sky, when he finally found himself in familiar surroundings. He had hunted before this far from the home valley; rapid as changes were, the area was still recognizable. He shifted course a trifle and put on a final burst of speed. For the first time, he felt sure of being able to deliver a report of his capture, and also for the first time he realized that he had not tried to organize one. Just telling what had happened to him, item by item, might take too long; it was important that Fagin and the rest get away quickly. On the other hand, it would take a pretty complete explanation of the state of affairs to convince the teacher of that fact. Nick unconsciously slowed down as he pondered this problem. He was dragged from this reverie only by the sound of his own name.

"Nick! Is that really you? Where have you been? We thought you'd slept out once too often!"

At the first sound, Nick had reached for his knives; but he checked the movement as he recognized the voice.

"Johnny! It's good to hear proper talk again. What are you doing this far out? Have the sheep eaten everything closer to home?"

"No, I'm hunting, not herding." John Doolittle pushed through the undergrowth into clear view. "But where have you been? It's been weeks since you went out, and since we stopped looking for you."

"You looked for me? That's bad. Still, I guess it didn't make any difference, or I'd have known it sooner."

"What do you mean? I don't understand what you're talking about. And what did you mean about it's being good to hear 'proper talk'? What other kind of talk is there? Let's hear the story."

"It's a long one, and I'll have to tell everyone as quickly as possible anyway. Come along home; there's no point telling it twice." He headed toward the valley they both called "home" without waiting to hear any answer. John "trailed" his spears and followed. Even without Nick's implication of trouble ahead, he would not willingly have missed the report. Fresh as he was, though, he had difficulty keeping up with the returned explorer; Nick seemed to be in a hurry.

They met two more of the group on the way, Alice and Tom, who were herding. At Nick's urgent but hasty words they followed toward the village as fast as their charges would permit.

Five more of the group were actually in the village, and Fagin was at his usual station in the center of the ring of houses. Nick called the teacher by name as he came in sight.

"Fagin! We're in trouble! What do we have for weapons that you haven't shown us yet?"

As usual, there was a pause of a couple of seconds before an answer came back.

"Why, it's Nick. We had about given you up. What's all this about weapons? Do you expect to have to fight someone?"

"I'm afraid so."

"Who?"

"Well, they seem to be people just like us; but they don't keep animals, and they don't use fire, and they use different words for things than we do."

"Where did you run into these people, and why should we have to fight them?"

"It's a long story, I'm afraid. It will be better if I start at the beginning, I suppose; but we shouldn't waste any more time than we can help."

"I agree; a complete report will make the most sense to all of us. Go ahead." Nick settled his weight back on his standing legs and obeyed.

"I started south as we decided and went slowly, mapping as I went. Nothing much had changed seriously out to the edge of the region we usually cover in farming and grazing; after that, of course, it was hard to tell whether anything had changed at all recently, or in what way.

"The best landmark I saw by the end of the first day was a mountain, of quite regular conical shape and much higher than any I had ever seen before. I was tempted to climb it, but decided that detail mapping could be accomplished better later on; after all, my trip was to find new areas, not evaluate them.

"I passed to the east of the mountain shortly after sunrise the second day. The wind was remarkably strong in that region and seemed always to blow toward the mountain; I called it Storm Hill on the map. Judging by the wind, there ought to be a lot of night-growing plants there; any exploration should be planned to get off the hill before dark.

"As far as travel goes, everything was about as usual. I killed enough in self-defense to keep me in food, but none of the animals were at all unusual that day.

"The third morning, though, with the mountain out of sight, I got involved with something that lived in a hole in the ground and reached out an arm to catch things going by. It caught me around the legs, and it didn't seem to mind my spears very much. I don't think I'd have gotten away if I hadn't had help."

"Help?" The startled question came without the pause characteristic of the teacher's remarks; it was Jim who asked it. "How could you have gotten help? None of us was down that way."

"So it wasn't one of us—at least, not exactly. He *looked* just like us, and used spears like ours; but when we finally managed to kill the thing in the hole and tried to talk to each other, his words were all different; in fact, it was quite a while before I realized that he was talking. He used the same sort of noises we do for words, but mixed them with a lot of others that we never learned from you.

"After a while I realized that the noises must be talk, and then I wondered why I hadn't thought of such a thing before—after all, if this person wasn't brought up by you, he'd have had to think up his own words for things, and it would be silly to expect them to be the same as ours. I decided to go with him and learn more; after all, this seemed a lot more important than just mapping. If I could learn his talk, he might know a lot more than we could find in months of exploring.

"He didn't seem to mind my trailing along, and as we went I began to catch on to some of his words. It wasn't easy, because he put them together in very strange ways; it wasn't just a matter of learning the noise he used for each object. We hunted together, though, and all the time we were learning to talk together. We didn't travel in a straight line, but I kept pretty good track of our path and can put his village on the map when I get the chance."

"Village?" It was Jim once more who interrupted; Fagin had said nothing.

"That's the only word I know for it. It wasn't at all like ours; it was a place at the foot of a steep cliff, and there were holes all over the face of the stone. Some of them were very small, like the solution holes you can see in any rock; others were very much larger, and there were people living in them. The one I was with was one of them.

"They were very surprised to see me, and tried to ask me a lot of questions; but I couldn't understand them well enough to give any answers. The one I had traveled with talked to them, and I suppose told how he had met me; but they stayed interested, and a lot of them were always watching me, whatever I did.

"It was getting fairly late in the afternoon when we got to the cliff, and I was starting to wonder about camping for the night. I didn't realize just at first that these people lived in the holes in the rock, and when I finally caught on I wasn't very happy about it. There are even more quakes down that way than around here, I noticed, and that cliff seemed an awfully unhealthy neighborhood. When the sun was almost down, I decided to leave them and camp a little way out on a hilltop I'd found, and then I discovered that they didn't want me to go. They were actually prepared to get rough in order to keep me around. I had learned a few more of their words by that time, though, and I finally convinced them that I wasn't trying to get away completely, and just wanted to spend the night by myself. There was a surprising amount of firewood around, and I was able to collect enough for the night without much trouble—in fact, some of the little ones helped me, when they saw what I wanted."

"Little ones? Weren't they all the same size?" Dorothy asked.

"No. That was one of the funny things I haven't had time to mention. Some of them weren't more than a foot and a half high, and some of them were nearly twice as tall as we are—nine feet or more. They all had the same shape as ours, though. I never found out the reason for that. One of the biggest ones seemed to be telling the others what to do most of the time, and I found that the little ones were usually the easiest to get along with.

"But that's getting off the story. When I built my fires a lot of them watched, but couldn't seem to make anything of it; when I lighted them, there was the biggest crowd of astonished people you ever saw. They didn't know anything about fire; that's why there was so much firewood near the cliff, I guess.

"Of course, it had started to rain by the time I lighted up, and it was funny to watch them; they seemed terribly afraid of being outside their holes in the rain, and still didn't want to miss watching the fires. They kept dithering back and forth, but gradually disappeared into their holes. After a while they were all gone, even though some of them stayed long enough to see what the fires did to the rain.

"I didn't see any more of them for the rest of the night. The water didn't get too deep along the face of the cliff, and they were out in the morning as soon as it had dried up.

"I could make a long story out of the rest of the time, but that will have to wait. I learned to talk to them pretty well—the way they put their words together makes a lot of sense once you catch on to it—and got to know them pretty well. The main thing is that they were interested in whatever things *I* knew that *they* didn't, like fire and keeping herds of animals and raising plants for food; and they wanted to know how I'd learned all these things. I told them about you, Fagin; and maybe that was a mistake. A few days ago their teacher, or leader, or whatever you can call him, came to me and said that he wanted me to come back here and bring you down to the cliff so you could teach all the things you know to his people.

"Now, that seemed all right to me. I judged that the more people you knew who could help in the things you want us to do, the better everything will be." He paused, to give Fagin a chance to answer.

"That's true enough," the voice from the robot agreed after the usual interval. "What went wrong?"

"My answer wasn't worded just right, it seems. I interpreted the proposition as a request, and answered that I would gladly come back home and ask you whether you would come to help the cave people. The leader—his name means Swift, in their words; all their names mean something—became angry indeed. Apparently he expects people to do as he says without any question or hesitation. I had noticed that but had been a little slow in applying my knowledge, I fear. Anyway, I didn't see how he could expect *you* to obey his orders.

"Unfortunately, he does; and he decided from my answer that you and the other people of our village would probably refuse. When that happens, his first thought is the use of force; and from the moment I made my answer he began to plan an attack on our village, to carry you away with him whether you wanted to go or not.

"He ordered me to tell him how to find our village, and when I refused he became angry again. The body of a dead goat that someone had brought in for food was lying nearby, and he picked it up and began to do terrible things to it with his knives. After a while he spoke to me again.

"You see what my knives are doing," he said. "If the goat were alive, it would not be killed by them; but it would not be happy. The same shall be done to you with the start of the new day, unless you guide my fighters to your village and its Teacher. It is too close to darkness now for you to escape; you have the night to think over what I have said. We start toward your village in the morning—or you will wish we had." He made two of his biggest fighters stay with me until the rain started. Even after all the time I'd been there no one ever stayed out of the caves after rainfall, so they left me alone when I lighted my fires.

"It took me a long time to decide what to do. If they killed me, they'd still find you sooner or later and you wouldn't be warned in time; if I went with them it might have been all right, but I didn't like some of the things Swift had been saying. He seemed to feel things would be better if there were none of your own people left around after he captured you. That seemed to mean that no matter what I did I was going to be killed, but if I kept quiet I might be the only one. That was when I thought of traveling at night; I was just as likely to be killed, but at least I'd die in my sleep—and there *was* a little chance of getting away with it. After all, a lot of animals that don't have caves or fire and don't wake up as early as some of the meat-eaters still manage to live.

"Then I got another idea; I thought of carrying fire with me. After all, we often carry a stick with one end burning for short distances when we're lighting the night fires; why couldn't I carry a supply of long sticks, and keep one burning all the time? Maybe the fire wouldn't be big enough to be a real protection, but it was worth trying. Anyway, what could I lose?

"I picked out as many of the longest sticks around as I could carry, piled them up, and waited until two of my three fires were drowned by raindrops. Then I picked up my sticks, lighted the end of one of them at the remaining fire, and started off as fast as I could.

"I was never sure whether those people stayed awake in their caves or not—as I said, water doesn't get up to them—but now I guess they don't. Anyway, no one seemed to notice me as I left.

"You know, traveling at night isn't nearly as bad as we always thought it would be. It's not too hard to dodge raindrops if you have enough light to see them coming, and you can carry enough wood to keep you in light for a long time. I must have made a good twenty miles, and I'd have gone farther if I hadn't made a very silly mistake. I didn't think to replenish my wood supply until I was burning my last stick, and then there wasn't anything long enough for my needs in the neighborhood. I didn't know the country at all; I'd started west instead of north to fool any of the cave people who saw me go. As a result I got smothered in a raindrop within a minute after my last light went out; and it was late enough by then for the stuff to be unbreathable. I'd kept to high ground all the time, though, so I woke up in the morning before anything had made breakfast of me."

Nick paused, and like the other listeners—except Fagin—shifted himself to a more comfortable position on his resting legs as the ground shook underfoot. "I made a good, wide sweep around to the west, then circled north and east again to get back here. I was expecting to be caught every minute; those people are marvelous hunters and trackers. I traveled for several hours after dark each night, but stopped in time to find wood and build permanent fires before my sticks went out, after the first time. I didn't get caught by rain again, and they never caught up with me. They'll still find the village here sooner or later, though, and I think we ought to move out as quickly as possible."

For a moment there was silence after Nick finished his report; then the villagers began chattering, each putting forth his own ideas without paying much attention to those of his neighbor. They had picked up quite a few human characteristics. This noise continued for some minutes, with Nick alone waiting silently for Fagin to make some comment.

At last the robot spoke.

"You are certainly right about the cave-dwellers finding the village here; they probably know where it is already. They would have been fools to catch up with you as long as they had reason to suppose you were going home. I see nothing to be gained, however, by leaving; they could follow us anywhere we might go. Now that they know of our existence, we're going to meet them in very short order.

"I don't want you people fighting them. I'm rather fond of you all, and have spent quite a long time bringing you up, and would rather not see you butchered. You've never done any fighting—it's one thing I'm not qualified to teach you—and you wouldn't stand a chance against that tribe.

"Therefore, Nick, I want you and one other to go to meet them. They'll be coming along your trail, so you'll have no trouble finding them. When you meet Swift, tell him that we'll gladly move to his village or let him move to ours, and that I'll teach him and his people all he wants. If you make clear that I don't know his language and that he'll need you to talk to me, he'll probably be smart enough not to hurt any of us."

"When shall we start? Right away?"

"That would be best, but you've just had a long trip and deserve some rest. Anyway, a lot of the day is gone, and there probably won't be much lost by letting you get a night's sleep before you start. Go tomorrow morning."

"All right, Teacher." Nick gave no evidence of the uneasiness he felt at the prospect of meeting Swift again. He had known that savage for several weeks; Fagin had never met him. Still, the Teacher knew a lot; he had taught Nick virtually all he knew, and for a whole lifetime—at least, Nick's whole lifetime—had been the final authority in the village. Probably everything would come out as Fagin predicted.

It might have, too, had not the men behind the robot grossly underestimated the tracking ability of the cave-dwellers. Nick had not even had time to get to sleep beside his watch-fire after lighting up at rainfall when a surprised yell, in Nancy's voice, sounded from a point four fires to his left; and a split second later he saw Swift himself, flanked by a line of his biggest fighters which disappeared around the hill on either side, sweeping silently up the slope toward him.

## II. Explanation; Concatenation; Recrimination

"What do you do now?"

Raeker ignored the question; important as he knew the speaker to be, he had no time for casual conversation. He had to act. Fagin's television screens lined the wall around him, and every one showed the swarming forms of the fir-cone-shaped beings who were attacking the village. There was a microphone before his face, with its switch spring-loaded in the open position so that casual talk in the control room would not reach the robot's associates; his finger was hovering over the switch, but he did not touch it. He didn't quite know what to say.

Everything he had told Nick through the robot was perfectly true; there was nothing to be gained by trying to fight. Unfortunately, the fight had already started. Even had Raeker been qualified to give advice on the defense of the village, it was too late; it was no longer even possible for a human being to distinguish the attackers from the defenders. Spears were sailing through the air with blinding speed—nothing merely tossed gets very far in a three-gravity field—and axes and knives flashed in the firelight.

"It's a good show, anyway." The same shrill voice that had asked the question a minute earlier made itself heard once more. "That firelight seems to be brighter than daylight, down there." The casual tone infuriated Raeker, who was not taking the predicament of his friends at all casually; but it was not consideration of the identity or importance of the speaker that kept him from losing his temper and saying something unfortunate. Quite unintentionally the onlooker had given him an idea. His finger stabbed at the microphone button.

"Nick! Can you hear me?"

"Yes, Teacher." Nick's voice showed no sign of the terrific physical effort he was exerting; his voice machinery was not as closely tied in with his breathing apparatus as is that of a human being.

"All right. Fight your way into the nearest hut as quickly as possible, all of you. *Get out of sight of me.* If you can't reach a hut, get behind a woodpile or something like that—below the curve of the hill, if nothing better is possible. Let me know as soon as you've all managed this."

"We'll try." Nick had no time to say more; those in the control room could only watch, though Raeker's fingers were hovering over another set of switches on the complex panel before him.

"One of them's making it." It was the high voice again, and this time Raeker had to answer.

"I've known these people for sixteen years, but I can't tell them from the attackers now. How can you identify them?" He let his glance shift briefly from the screens to the two non humans towering behind him.

"The attackers have no axes, only knives and spears," pointed out the speaker calmly. The man hastily turned back to the screens. He could not be sure that the other was right; only three or four axes could be seen, and their wielders were not very clearly visible in the swirling press. He had not noticed any lack of axes in the hands of the attackers as they came up the hill, in the brief moments after they became visible to the robot and before battle was joined; but there was no reason to doubt that someone else might have. He wished he knew Dromm and its people better. He made no answer to the slender giant's comment, but from then on watched the axes which flashed in the firelight. These really did seem to be working their way toward the huts which rimmed the top of the hill. Some failed to make it; more than one of the tools which had so suddenly become weapons ceased to swing as the robot's eyes watched.

But some did get there. For half a minute a four-armed, scaly figure stood at one of the hut doors, facing outward and smashing the crests of all attackers who approached too close. Three others, all apparently injured, crawled toward him and under the sweep of the powerful arms to take shelter in the building; one of these remained in the doorway, crouching with two spears and guarding the axeman from low thrusts.

Then another defender battered his way to the side of the first, and the two retreated together inside the hut. None of the cave-dwellers seemed eager to follow.

"Are you all inside, Nick?" Raeker asked.

"Five of us are here. I don't know about the others. I'm pretty sure Alice and Tom are dead, though; they were near me at the beginning, and I haven't seen them for some time."

"Give a call to those who aren't with you. I'll have to do something very soon, and I don't want any of you hurt by it."

"They must either be safe or dead. The fighting has stopped; it's a lot easier to hear you than it was. You'd better do whatever it is without worrying about us; I think Swift's people are all heading toward you. Only a couple are outside the door here; the others are forming a big ring around where I saw you last. You haven't moved, have you?"

"No," admitted Raeker, "and you're right about the ring. One of the biggest of them is walking right up to me. Make sure you are all under cover—preferably somewhere where light won't reach you. I'll give ten seconds."

"All right," Nick answered. "We're getting under tables."

Raeker counted a slow ten, watching the approaching creatures in the screens as he did so. At the last number his fingers tripped a gang bar which closed twenty switches simultaneously; and as Nick described it later, "the world took fire."

It was only the robot's spotlights, unused now for years but still serviceable. It seemed quite impossible to the human watchers that any optical organs sensitive enough to work on the few quanta of light which reach the bottom of Tenebra's atmosphere could possibly stand any such radiance; the lights themselves had been designed with the possibility in mind that they might have to pierce dust or smoke—they were far more powerful than were really needed by the receptors of the robot itself.

The attackers should have been blinded instantly, according to Raeker's figuring. The sad fact slowly emerged that they were not.

They were certainly surprised. They stopped their advance for a moment, and chattered noisily among themselves; then the giant who was in front of the others strode right up to the robot, bent over, and appeared to examine one of the lights in detail. The men had long ago learned that the Tenebran vision organs were involved in some way with the spiny crests on their heads, and it was this part that the being who Raeker suspected must be Swift brought close to one of the tiny ports from which the flood of light was escaping.

The man sighed and shut off the lights.

"Nick," he called, "I'm afraid my idea didn't work. Can you get in touch with this Swift fellow, and try to get the language problem across to him? He may be trying to talk to me now, for all I can tell."

"I'll try." Nick's voice came faintly through the robot's instruments; then there was nothing but an incomprehensible chattering that ran fantastically up and down the scale. There was no way to tell who was talking, much less what was being said, and Raeker settled back uneasily in his seat.

"Couldn't the handling equipment of that robot be used for fighting?" The shrill voice of the Drommian interrupted his worries.

"Conceivably, under other circumstances," Raeker replied. "As it happens, we're too far away. You must have noticed the delays between questions and answers when I was talking to Nick. We're orbiting Tenebra far enough out to keep us over the same longitude; its day is about four Earth ones, and that puts us over a hundred and sixty thousand miles away. Nearly two seconds delay in reflex would make the robot a pretty poor fighter."

"Of course. I should have realized. I must apologize for wasting your time and interrupting on what must be a very bothersome occasion."

Raeker, with an effort, tore his mind from the scene so far below, and turned to the Drommians.

"I'm afraid the apology must be mine," he said. "I knew you were coming, and why; I should at least have appointed someone to do the honors of the place, if I couldn't manage it myself. My only excuse is the emergency you see. Please let me make up for it by helping you now. I suppose you would like to see the *Vindemiatrix*."

"By no means. I would not dream of taking you from this room just now. Anyway, the ship itself is of no interest compared to your fascinating project on the planet, and you can explain that to us as well here, while you are waiting for your agent's answer, as anywhere else. I understand that your robot has been on the planet a long time; perhaps you could tell me more about how you recruited your agents on the planet. Probably my son would like to be shown the ship, if someone else could be spared from other duties."

"Certainly. I did not realize he was your son; the message telling us of your visit did not mention him, and I assumed he was an assistant."

"That is perfectly all right. Son, this is Dr. Helven Raeker; Dr. Raeker, this is Aminadorneldo."

"I am delighted to meet you, sir," piped the younger Drommian.

"The pleasure is mine. If you wait a moment, a man is coming to show you over the *Vindemiatrix*—unless you would rather stay here and join conversation with your father and me."

"Thank you, I would rather see the ship."

Raeker nodded, and waited in silence for a moment or two. He had already pressed the call button which would bring a crewman to the observing room. He wondered a little why the younger being was with his father; presumably he was serving some purpose. It would be easier to talk without him, though, since the two were virtually indistinguishable to Raeker and it would be rather embarrassing to get them mixed up. Both were giants from the human point of view; standing on their hind legs—a highly unnatural attitude for them—they would have towered nearly ten feet tall. Their general build was that of a weasel—or better, an otter, since the slender digits which terminated their five pairs of limbs were webbed. The limbs themselves were short and powerful, and the webs on the first two pairs reduced to fringes of membrane along the fingers—a perfectly normal evolutionary development for intelligent amphibious beings living on a planet with a surface gravity nearly four times that of the Earth. Both were wearing harnesses supporting sets of small gas tanks, with tubing running inconspicuously to the corners of their mouths; they were used to an oxygen partial pressure about a third greater than human normal. They were hairless, but something about their skins reflected a sheen similar to that of wet sealskin.

They were stretched in an indescribably relaxed attitude on the floor, with their heads high enough to see the screens clearly. When the door slid open and the crewman entered, one of them came to his feet with a flowing motion and, introductions completed, followed the man out of the compartment. Raeker noticed that he walked on all ten limbs, even those whose webs were modified to permit prehension, though the *Vindemiatrix'* centrifugal "gravity" could hardly have made it necessary. Well, most men use both legs on the moon, for that matter, though hopping on one is perfectly possible. Raeker dismissed the matter from his mind, and turned to the remaining Drommian—though he always reserved some of his attention for the screens.

"You wanted to know about our local agents," he began. "There's not very much to tell, in one way. The big difficulty was getting contact with the surface at all. The robot down there now represents a tremendous achievement of engineering; the environment is close to the critical temperature of water, with an atmospheric pressure near eight hundred times that of Earth. Since even quartz dissolves fairly readily under those conditions, it took quite a while to design machines which could hold up. We finally did it; that one has been down a little over sixteen of our years. I'm a biologist and can't help you much with the technical details; if you happen to care, there are people here who can.

"We sent the machine down, spent nearly a year exploring, and finally found some apparently intelligent natives. They turned out to be egg-layers, and we managed to get hold of some of the eggs. Our agents down there are the ones who hatched; we've been educating them ever since. Now, just as we start doing some real exploring with them, this has to happen." He gestured toward the screen, where the huge Swift had paused in his examination of the robot and seemed to be listening; perhaps Nick was having some luck in his selling job.

"If you could make a machine last so long in that environment, I should think you could build something which would let you go down in person," said the Drommian.

Raeker smiled wryly. "You're quite right, and that's what makes the present situation even more annoying. We have such a machine just about ready to go down; in a few days we expected to be able to cooperate directly with our people below."

"Really? I should think that would have taken a long time to design and build."

"It has. The big problem was not getting down; we managed that all right with parachutes for the robot. The trouble is getting away again."

"Why should that be particularly difficult? The surface gravity, as I understand it, is less than that of my own world, and even the potential gradient ought to be somewhat smaller. Any booster unit ought to clear you nicely."

"It would if it worked. Unfortunately, the booster that will unload its exhaust against eight hundred atmospheres hasn't been built yet. They melt down—they don't blow up because the pressure's too high."

The Drommian looked a trifle startled for a moment, then nodded in a remarkably human manner.

"Of course. I should have thought. I remember how much more effective rockets are on your own planet than ours. But how have you solved this? Some radically new type of reactor?"

"Nothing new; everything in the device is centuries old. Basically, it's a ship used long ago for deep-ocean exploration on my own world—a bathyscaphe, we called it. For practical purposes, it's a dirigible balloon. I could describe it, but you'd do better to—"

"Teacher!" A voice which even Aminadabarlee of Dromm could recognize as Nick's erupted from the speaker. Raeker whirled back to his panel and closed the microphone switch.

"Yes, Nick? What does Swift say?"

"In effect, *no*. He wants nothing to do with anything in this village but you."

"Didn't you explain the language problem to him?"

"Yes, but he says that if I was able to learn his words you, who are my teacher, should be able to learn them more quickly. Then he will not have to depend on people he doesn't trust to tell him what you're saying. I hope he's right. He's willing to leave the rest of us here, but you have to go with him."

"I see. You'd better agree, for now; it will at least keep those of you who are alive out of further trouble. It may be that we'll be able to arrange a little surprise for Swift in the near future. You tell him that I'll do what he says; I'll go along with him to the caves—I suppose he'll be starting back there tomorrow, though if he wants to stay longer don't discourage him. When they go, you stay where you are; find everyone who's still alive and get them back in shape—I suppose most of you are injured—and then wait until I get in touch with you. It may be some days, but leave it to me."

Nick was a fairly fast thinker, and remembered at once that Fagin could travel at night without the aid of fire—rain did not suffocate him. He thought he saw what the teacher planned to do; it was not his fault that he was wrong. The word "bathyscaphe" had never been used in his hearing.

"Teacher!" he called, after a moment's thought. "Wouldn't it be better if we moved as soon as we could, and arranged some other place to meet you after you escape? He'll come right back here sure as rainfall."

"Don't worry about that. Just stay here, and get things back to normal as soon as possible. I'll be seeing you."

"All right, Teacher." Raeker leaned back in his seat once more, nodding his head slowly.

The Drommian must have spent a good deal of time on Earth; he was able to interpret the man's attitude. "You seem a great deal happier than you were a few minutes ago," he remarked. "I take it you have seen your way out of the situation."

"I think so," replied Raeker. "I had forgotten the bathyscaphe until I mentioned it to you; when I did recall it, I realized that once it got down there our troubles would be over. The trouble with that robot is that it has to crawl, and can be tracked and followed; the bathyscaphe, from the point of view of the natives down there, can fly. It has outside handling equipment, and when the crew goes down they can simply pick up the robot some night and fly it away from the cliff. I defy Swift to do any constructive tracking."

"Then isn't Nick right? Won't Swift head straight for the village? I should think you'd have done better to follow Nick's suggestion."

"There'll be time to move after we get the robot. If they leave the village before, we'll have a lot of trouble finding them, no matter how carefully we arrange a meeting beforehand. The area is not very well mapped, and what there is doesn't stay mapped very well."

"Why not? That sounds rather strange."

"Tenebra is a rather strange planet. Diastrophism is like Earth's weather; the question is not whether it will rain tomorrow but whether your pasture will start to grow into a hill. There's a team of geophysicists champing at the proverbial bit, waiting for the bathyscaphe to go down so they can set up a really close working connection with Nick's group. The general cause we know—the atmosphere is mostly water near its critical temperature, and silicate rocks dissolve fairly rapidly under those circumstances. The place cools off just enough each night to let a little of the atmosphere turn liquid, so for the best part of two Earth days you have the crust washing down to the oceans like the Big Rock Candy Mountain. With three Earth gravities trying to make themselves felt, it's hardly surprising that the crust is readjusting all the time.

"Anyway, I think we're set up now. It won't be morning down there for a couple of days, and I don't see how much can happen until then. My relief will be here soon; when he arrives, perhaps you would like to see the bathyscaphe with me."

"I should be most interested." Raeker was getting the impression that either the Drommians were a very polite race or Aminadabarlee had been selected for his diplomatic post for that quality. He didn't keep it long.

Unfortunately, there was a delay in visiting the bathyscaphe. When Raeker and the Drommian reached the bay where the small shuttle of the *Vindemiatrix* was normally kept, they found it empty. A check with the watch officer—ship's watch, not the one kept on the robot; the organizations were not connected—revealed that it had been taken out by the crewman whom Raeker had asked to show Aminadorneldo around.

"The Drommian wanted to see the bathyscaphe, Doctor, and so did young Easy Rich."

"Who?"

"That daughter Councillor Rich has tagging along. Begging the pardon of the gentleman with you, political inspection teams are all right as long as they inspect; but when they make the trip an outing for their off-spring—"

"I have my son along," Aminadabarlee remarked.

"I know. There's a difference between someone old enough to take care of himself and an infant whose fingers have to be kept off hot contacts . . ." The officer let his voice trail off, and shook his head. He was an engineer; Raeker suspected that the party had descended on the power room in the near past, but didn't ask.

"Have you any idea when the shuttle will be back?" he asked.

The engineer shrugged. "None. Flanagan was letting the kid lead *him* around. He'll be back when she's tired, I suppose. You could call him, of course."

"Good idea." Raeker led the way to the signal room of the *Vindemiatrix*, seated himself at a plate, and punched the combination of the tender's set. The screen lighted up within a few seconds, and showed the face of Crystal Mechanic Second Class Flanagan, who nodded when he saw the biologist.

"Hello, Doctor. Can I help you?"

"We were wondering when you'd be back. Councillor Aminadabarlee would like to see the bathyscaphe, too." The nearly two-second pause while light made the round trip from *Vindemiatrix* to tender and back was scarcely noticed by Raeker, who was used to it; the Drommian was rather less patient.

"I can come back and pick you up whenever you want; my customers are fully occupied in the 'scaphe." Raeker was a trifle surprised.

"Who's with them?"

"I was, but I don't really know much about the thing, and they promised not to touch anything."

"That doesn't sound very safe to me. How old is the Rich girl? About twelve, isn't she?"

"I'd say so. I wouldn't have left her there alone, but the Drommian was with her, and said he'd take care of things."

"I still think—" Raeker got no further. Four sets of long, webbed, wire-hard fingers tightened on his shoulders and upper arm, and the sleek head of Aminadabarlee moved into the pickup area beside his own. A pair of yellow-green eyes stared at the image in the plate, and a deeper voice than Raeker had yet heard from Drommian vocal cords cut across the silence.

"It is possible that I am less well acquainted with your language than I had believed," were his words. "Do I understand that you have left two children unsupervised in a ship in space?"

"Not exactly children, sir," protested Flanagan. "The human girl is old enough to have a good deal of sense, and your own son is hardly a child; he's as big as you."

"We attain our full physical growth within a year of birth," snapped the Drommian. "My son is four years old, about the social equivalent of a human being of seven. I was under the impression that human beings were a fairly admirable race, but to give responsibility to an individual as stupid as you appear to be suggests a set of social standards so low as to be indistinguishable from savagery. If anything happens to my boy—" He stopped; Flanagan's face had disappeared from the screen, and he must have missed the last couple of sentences of Aminadabarlee's castigation; but the Drommian was not through. He turned to Raeker, whose face had gone even paler than usual, and resumed. "It makes me sick to think that at times I have left my son in charge of human caretakers during my years on Earth. I had assumed your race to be civilized. If this piece of stupidity achieves its most likely result, Earth will pay the full price; not a human-driven ship will land again on any planet of the galaxy that values Drommian feelings. The story of your idiocy will cross the light-years, and no human ship will live to enter Drommian skies. Mankind will have the richly earned contempt of every civilized race in—"

He was cut off, but not by words. A rending crash sounded from the speaker, and a number of loose objects visible on the screen jerked abruptly toward a near wall. They struck it loudly and rebounded, but without obeying the laws of reflection. They all bounced the same way—in the direction which Raeker recognized with a sinking feeling as that of the tender's air lock. A book flew past the pickup area in the same direction, and struck a metal instrument traveling more slowly.

But this collision went unheard. No more sound came from the speaker; the tender was silent, with the silence of airlessness.

# III. CEREBRATION; TRANSPORTATION; EMIGRATION

Nick Chopper stood in the doorway of his hut and thought furiously. Behind him the seven other survivors of the raid lay in various stages of disrepair. Nick himself was not entirely unscathed, but he was still able to walk—and, if necessary, fight, he told himself grimly. All of the others except Jim and Nancy would be out of useful action for several days at least.

He supposed that Fagin had been right in yielding to Swift as he had; at least, the savage had kept his word about letting Nick collect and care for his wounded friends. Every time Nick thought of the attack, however, or even of Swift, he felt like resuming the war. It would have given him intense pleasure to remove Swift's scales one by one and use them to shingle a hut in full view of their owner.

He was not merely brooding, however; he was really thinking. For the first time in a good many years, he was questioning seriously a decision of Fagin's. It seemed ridiculous that the Teacher could get away from the cave village without help; he hadn't been able to fight Swift's people during the attack, and if he had any powers Nick didn't know about that was certainly the time to use them. Getting away at night didn't count; he'd be tracked and caught first thing in the morning.

But wait a minute. What could the cave-dwellers actually *do* to Fagin? The hard white stuff the Teacher was covered with—or made out of, for all Nick knew—might be proof against knives and spears; the point had never occurred to Nick or any of his friends. Maybe that was why Fagin was being so meek now, when his people could be hurt; maybe he planned to act more constructively when he was alone.

It would be nice to be able to talk it over with the Teacher without Swift's interference. Of course, the chief couldn't eavesdrop very effectively, since he couldn't understand English, but he would know that a

conference was going on, and would be in a pretty good position to block
any activity planned therein. If it were practical to get Swift out of hearing—but if that were possible, the whole thing would be solved anyway.
The meat of the problem was the fact that Swift *couldn't* be handled.

Of course, it was night, and therefore raining. The invaders were being
protected by the village fires, at the moment; however, Nick reflected, no
one was protecting the fires themselves. He glanced upward at the thirty-
to-fifty-foot raindrops drifting endlessly out of the black sky, following
one of them down to a point perhaps three hundred yards above his head.
There it vanished, fading out in ghostly fashion as it encountered the
updraft from the village fires. It was not the drops straight overhead which
were troublesome—not to Fagin's village.

Another, larger drop beyond the glowing protective double ring accomplished more. It settled to the ground fifty yards beyond one of the
outer fires. The ground had been cooled enough by its predecessors to let
it remain liquid, so for a short time it was visible as it drifted toward the
blaze under the impulse of the fires' own convection currents. Then radiated heat made it fade out; but Nick knew it was still there. It had been
crystal clear, free of suspended oxygen bubbles; it was now pure steam,
equally free of combustion's prime necessity. Nick would have nodded in
satisfaction, had his head been capable of free movement, when the fire
in the path of the invisible cloud suddenly began to cool and within a
few seconds faded from visibility.

If any of the attackers noticed the incident, they certainly did nothing. None of them moved, and the fire remained out. Five seconds later
Nick had his plan worked out.

He emerged fully from the hut and walked over to the main fuel
magazine. Here he loaded himself with as much as he could carry, and
took it back to the building where the wounded were lying. None of
the raiders stopped or questioned him; none had spoken to him since
the truce had been concluded. Inside the hut, he quickly built and
lighted a fire. When it had come to an even glow he lighted a torch
from it and walked back to the woodpile. Casually he stuck the cold
end of the torch into the pile, as though to illuminate his work; then
he made several more trips carrying fuel to the hut, leaving the torch
where he had placed it. Eventually the building could hold no more
wood, so he ceased his labor.

But he left the torch.

Tenebran wood glows like punk; it does not flame. It took some time
for the stick to burn down to its base, and still longer before the increase
in brilliancy of the region around the village showed that the main stack
had properly caught. Even then, there was no reaction from the invaders.

These had gathered into a tight group surrounding the robot, which had remained in its usual position at the center of the village.

By this time, more than half of the peripheral fires were out, most of them in the outer ring. One or two of the inner ring had also been smothered, and Nick began to get an impression of uneasiness from the clustered cave dwellers. When the last of the outer fires died, a mutter began to grow from their ranks, and Nick chuckled to himself. Swift just *might* have a little trouble handling his men as their protection from the rain vanished, and no caves were available. If the muttering continued, the chief would certainly have to take some action; and all he could do, as far as Nick could see, would be to ask Nick himself for help. That should put quite a dent in his authority.

But Nick had underestimated the big fellow. From the vicinity of the robot his voice suddenly rapped out a series of orders; and obediently a dozen of his men ran from the outskirts of the group toward one of the fires which was still burning. There, to Nick's disgust, they seized sticks from the small woodpile at its side, lighted their ends, carried the torches to the dead fires, and rekindled these without the slightest difficulty. Evidently the cave-dwellers didn't sleep *all* night in their holes; someone had watched his fire-technique long enough to get at least some of the idea. If they also knew about replenishing . . . They did. More wood was being put on all the fires. Nick noted with satisfaction, however, that it was far too much wood; he wouldn't have to wait too long before the small woodpiles beside each fire were extinguished. The cave-dwellers seemed to have taken the now fiercely glowing main pile as another bonfire; Swift was going to have to do some fast thinking when the reserves disappeared.

This he proved able to do. It was fortunate that Nick had been able to keep awake, for Swift's men did not announce their coming. They simply came.

They were unarmed, rather to Nick's surprise, but they approached the hut door without hesitation, almost as though they expected him to stand aside for them. When he didn't, they stopped, the foremost half a spear's length away. He may have intended to say something, but Nick spoke first.

"What do you want? My friends are all wounded and can't help you. There is no room in the hut. Go to the others, if you want shelter."

"Swift sent us for wood." It was a calm statement, with no "or else" concealed in it, as far as Nick could tell by the tone.

"I have only enough to keep my own fire going for the night. You will have to use the other piles."

"They are used up."

"That isn't my fault. You know that wood burns up in a fire; you shouldn't have put so much on."

"You didn't tell us that. Swift says that you should therefore give us your own wood, which we saw you taking, and tell us how much to use."

It was evident that the chief had seen through at least part of Nick's scheme, but there was nothing to do now but carry it through.

"As I said, I have only enough for this fire," he said. "I shall not give it up; I need it for myself and my friends."

Very much to his surprise, the fellow retreated without further words. Apparently he had gone as far as his orders extended, and was going back for more. Initiative did not flourish under Swift's rule.

Nick watched the group as it rejoined the main crowd and began to push its way through to the chief. Then he turned and nudged Jim.

"Better get up, you and Nancy," he whispered. "Swift can't let this go. I'll fight as well as I can; you keep me in ammunition."

"What do you mean?" Nancy's thoughts were less swift than usual.

"I can't fight them with axes; they'd be through in two minutes. I'm tired and slow. I'm going to use torches—remember what it feels like to be burned? They don't; I warned them about it when I was at their village, and they were always very careful, so none of them has any real experience. They're going to get it now!"

The other two were on their feet by this time. "All right," agreed Jim. "We'll light torches and pass them to you whenever you call. Are you going to poke with the things, or throw them? I never thought of fighting that way."

"Neither did I, until now. I'll try poking first, so give me long ones. If I decide to throw, I'll call for really short ones—we don't want them throwing the things back at us, and they will if there's enough to hold on to. They're not too stupid for that—not by a long day's journey!"

Jim and Nancy gestured agreement and understanding, and turned to the piles of firewood that almost covered the floor. The fire was burning quite close to the doorway; Nick took his stand once more in the opening, and the other two on either side of the blaze, where they could hand torches to him as rapidly as he might need. Everything was ready when the party returned to the hut.

It was a little larger this time; Swift himself had joined it. They approached to within half a dozen yards, and spoke briefly and to the point.

"If you don't let us in to get the wood, my knives will take care of you. You have seen what I mean."

"I have seen," acknowledged Nick. "That's why I want nothing to do with you. If you come any closer, it is at your own risk."

He had never before seen Swift hesitant or uncertain, but for just a moment now the chief seemed to be running over the implications of Nick's words. Then he was himself again.

"Very well," he said, and swept forward with four spears couched along his forearms.

Nick's battle plan had to be scrapped at the beginning; the spears were longer than his torches. He did succeed in striking their points aside before they touched him, but he could not reach Swift even with the spears out of the way. His hatred of the chief paralyzed his judgment for an instant, and he hurled both his left-hand torches at the giant's chest.

Swift ducked, barely in time. Those behind him were a close-packed wedge whose central members were unable to dodge quickly enough, and howls of pain arose in several voices as the torches struck and scattered burning coals in all directions. The chief ducked backward to just beyond spear's length, resuming his attack stance.

"Half circle!" he snapped. The warriors obeyed with speed and precision, forming a thin line centered on Nick. "Now, all at once—get him!" The semicircle contracted, and the spear points came toward the door.

Nick was not too alarmed. None of the attackers was in a position to deliver the upward thrust which would get under scales; stone points were more likely to push him back than to penetrate. If he were pushed back against anything solid, of course, it would be a different story; the real danger at the moment, though, was that several of the fighters would get within knife range at once, and so occupy him that a spearsman could get close enough for long enough to strike from below. For just an instant he hesitated, wondering whether he should throw or strike; then he made up his mind.

"Short ones!" he ordered to the helpers behind him.

Nancy already had several foot-long sticks with their ends in the fire; she had them in his hands instantly, and was lighting others. For perhaps ten seconds Nick did his best to emulate a machine gun. More than half his projectiles missed, but a good many didn't; and after the first three or four seconds another factor complicated the fight. Still burning torches and fragments of glowing wood were being more and more thickly scattered before the doorway, and the attackers were getting involved with these. Feet were even more sensitive to the fire than were scales, and the effect was distracting, to put it mildly. Swift, to do him justice, stayed with his men and fought as hard as any; but at length even he had had enough and withdrew a few yards, limping slightly. Nick laughed aloud as he went.

"Better get your own firewood, Swift, my friend! Of course you won't find any within an hour's walk of the village; we've used it up long ago. Even if you know where the best places to get it are, you won't be able to get there and back through the rain. You needn't worry, though; we'll take care of you when you go to sleep. I wouldn't want anything to eat you, friend Swift!"

It was almost funny to watch Swift's fury. His hands tightened on the spear shafts, and he rose to full height on his walking legs, shaking all over with rage. For several seconds it seemed an even bet whether he would hurl the spears or charge the door across the scattered coals. Nick was perfectly ready for either, but was hoping for the latter; the mental picture of Swift with burned feet was a very attractive one.

But the chief did neither. In the midst of his fury he suddenly relaxed, and the spear points dropped as though he had forgotten them for a moment. Then he shifted the weapons backward until he was holding them near their centers of gravity, in "carry" position, and turned away from the hut. Then, seemingly as an afterthought, he turned back and spoke to Nick.

"Thanks, Chopper. I didn't expect that much help. I'd better say good-bye, now; and so had you—to your Teacher."

"But—you can't travel at night."

"Why not? You did."

"But how about Fagin? How do you know he can?"

"You told me he could do anything you could. You also said he'd agree to do what we said. If he forgets that, or changes his mind, we can thank you for showing us what to do. Do you suppose he'll like the touch of fire any better than we do?" Swift chuckled and strode swiftly back to the main group, bawling orders as he went. Nick began shouting at least as loudly.

"Fagin! Did you hear that? Fagin! Teacher!" In his anxiety he forgot the time it always took the Teacher to answer, and drowned the robot out for a moment. Then its answer became audible.

"What's the matter, Nick?" It was not possible to tell from the voice that Raeker was not at the other end; Nick's people had been given a general idea of the "Teacher" situation, but not all the details, and they thought inevitably of the robot as an individual. This was virtually the first time it had made any difference; the man on watch knew the general picture, of course, having been briefed by Raeker when the latter had gone off duty, but he had not actually been present during Swift's initial attack or the subsequent truce. Consequently, Nick's words did not mean all they might have to him.

"Swift is going to start back for the caves right away; he says he'll use fire on you if you don't go with him. Can you stand that?"

There was a little more than the usual hesitation. No one had ever measured the temperature of a Tenebran fire, and the man on watch was not enough of a physicist to hazard a guess from its radiation output. The main consideration in his mind was the cost of the robot.

"No," he answered. "I'll go along with him."

"What shall we do?"

Raeker's order for the villagers to stay put was one thing he had not mentioned to his relief; he had expected to be back on duty long before the start of the journey. The relief did the best he could under the circumstances.

"Use your own judgment. They won't hurt me; I'll get in touch with you again later."

"All right." Nick carefully refrained from reminding the Teacher of his earlier command; he liked the new one much better. He watched in silence as the invaders, under Swift's orders, collected what torches they could from the nearly spent fires. Then they clustered around the Teacher, leaving an opening in the crowd on the side they wished him to go. It was all done without words, but the meaning was plain enough. The robot swung around on its treads and headed south, the cave dwellers swarming after it.

Nick spent only a few moments wondering whether they'd find more torch wood before using up what they had. He had turned his mind to other matters even before the cavalcade was out of sight.

He had been given a free hand. Very well, he still felt that leaving the village was best; they would do so as soon as possible. Of course, it wouldn't be possible for a few days, until everyone was able to travel again, but the time could be spent in planning. There was certainly the question of where to go, and the corollary one of how to get there—Nick began to realize with a shock just what leaving the village, with its lifetime accumulation of property and equipment, would mean—and how to get back in touch with Fagin when the move was accomplished. It was easy to tell oneself that the Teacher could always find them wherever they went; but Nick was mature enough to doubt the omniscience of anyone, including the robot. That meant, then, three problems to solve. Since Nick had no desire to resemble Swift in any way, he postponed solving them until the others would be awake and able to help in the discussion.

The fire lasted until morning, but only just, and only by virtue of Nick's running around the hut rapidly on a number of occasions to stir oxygen into an oncoming mass of dead steam. He got very little sleep after the last of the outer fires went, and that was pretty early in the night.

Morning brought no relief. The first task normally accomplished was to put a guard on the village herd, which was penned in a hollow near the village. The depression remained full of water a little later than the surrounding country, so the "cattle" were normally safe from predators until the guards could arrive; but at the moment there simply weren't enough people in condition to guard both herd and village. They suffered several losses that morning as a result, until Nick could round up the reviving creatures by himself and herd them into the village. Then there was the problem of firewood for the next night; he had told the absolute truth to Swift in that respect. Someone had to get it. There was no choice but for the still battered Jim and Nancy to do the job together, dragging as best they could the cart on which they piled their fuel. They had never succeeded in training their cattle to pull the conveyance; the creatures stubbornly refused to budge under any sort of load.

By the second day, most of the others were on their feet if not at full efficiency, and matters were considerably easier. A consultation was held that morning, in which Nick proposed and defended vigorously the notion that they move to the viciously rough country he had crossed during his flight from the cave village. His chief point was the presence of so many spots which could only be approached from a single, narrow point, like a canyon or ridge, and could therefore be defended effectively by a small force. It was Nancy who answered the suggestion.

"I'm not sure that's a very good plan," she said. "In the first place, we don't know that any of the places you describe will still be that way when we get there." A quake lent emphasis and support to her words.

"What if they aren't?" retorted Nick. "There will always be others. I wasn't suggesting any of the specific spots I described, only the general area."

"But how is Fagin to find us? Supposing one of us does get to the cave village and get a message to him, how are we to describe the way to him? We'd have to guide him directly, which would probably interfere with his own plans—you judged, and I think rightly, that he is planning to take advantage of his ability to travel at night without fire."

Nick felt a very human surge of annoyance at this opposition, but remembered Swift in time to keep from yielding to it. He didn't want to be compared with that savage in anyone's mind, he told himself; besides, there was something to what Nancy was saying, now that he really gave his mind to it.

"What sort of place would you suggest?" he asked. "You're right about getting back in touch with Fagin, but I certainly can't think of any place which we will ever defend as easily as those canyons in the west."

"It seems to me that Fagin was right when he said it was foolish to fight Swift's people at all," returned Nancy quietly. "I was not thinking of defense; if we have to defend ourselves, we're already out of luck, I fear. What I had in mind was the sea."

"What?"

"You know. You helped map it. Off to the east there's a body of water that isn't water—at least, it doesn't dry up entirely during the daytime. I don't remember just what Fagin called it when we reported it to him—"

"He said he supposed it was mostly sulfuric acid, whatever that is, but he didn't know how to make sure," interjected the still crippled Dorothy.

"—Whatever it is, it stays there, and if we're on the edge of it Fagin can't help finding us if he simply travels along its border. Probably he can travel *in* it for a distance, too, so the cave people can't track him." A hum of approving surprise greeted this notion, and after a few moments of thought Nick gestured agreement.

"All right," he said. "If no one has other ideas, well move to the edge of the sea; we can settle on the exact spot after we get there and have looked around. It's a year or two since we mapped the place, and I don't suppose we could trust information that old.

"The next problem is getting there. We'll have to decide how much we can take from the village here, and how we can carry it. I suppose we can start with the wood cart, but I'll bet there are places we won't be able to move it across. No matter how we figure it, there's a lot we'll have to leave behind.

"Then, finally, there's the matter of getting a message to Fagin. That we can leave until we're settled; there's no point telling him where we are before we know.

"I hope we can travel by tomorrow; in the meantime, the second question is the one to work on. Anyone who has more ideas, let's hear them at any time." They dispersed, each to the tasks of which he was capable.

Jim and Nancy were practically whole again, and were now looking after the cattle. There had been no further losses since they had been able to take over the job. Dorothy was at the wagon, with all the articles they hoped to take stacked around her, arranging and rearranging them in the vehicle. No matter how she packed them, there was more outside than in, and nearly constant discussion and even argument was going on between her and the other members of the group. Each wanted his own belongings to go, and it took a good deal of talk to convince some of them that since everything couldn't be taken the losses should be shared.

The argument was still going on, to a certain extent, when the journey started. Nick was beginning to feel a certain sympathy for Swift by that time; he had discovered that at times it was necessary for a group to have a leader, and that it was not always possible for the leader to reason his followers into the desired action. Nick had had to give his first arbitrary orders, and was troubled by the thought that half his friends must by now be comparing him with Swift. The fact that he had been obeyed should have clarified him on this point, but it didn't.

The cart was perilously overloaded, and everyone except those actually herding had to pull with all his strength. When fighting was necessary, hauling had to be stopped while weapons were snatched up and used. Actually, of course, there wasn't too much fighting; the average Tenebran carnivore wasn't very brainy, but most of them steered clear of such a large group. The chief exception, was formed by the floaters, which were more vegetable than animal anyway. These creatures could be downed fairly safely by anyone having a spear longer than their tentacles; but even after their gas bladders were punctured, they were dangerous to anyone coming within reach of the poisonous appendages. Several animals of the herd were lost when one of the monsters fell almost into it, and two of the party were painfully poisoned on the same occasion. It was some hours before they could walk unaided.

Contrary to Nick's pessimistic forecast, it proved possible to get the wagon all the way to the sea. Late in the second day of travel they reached it, after some hours of threading their way among ever larger pools of quiet, oily liquid.

They had seen such pools before, of course; they formed in hollows in their own valley toward the end of the day—hollows which were lakes of water at sunrise, but only tiny pools of oleum when the day reached its height. These were larger, filling a much bigger fraction of their beds.

The ground was different, too; vegetation was as thick as ever, but underfoot among the stems the ground was studded with quartz crystals. The cattle didn't seem to mind, but the feet of their owners were not quite so tough, and progress became decidedly difficult. Such masses of crystals did occur elsewhere, but usually in isolated patches which could be avoided.

The search for a stopping place was therefore briefer, and perhaps less careful, than it might otherwise have been. They agreed very quickly on a peninsula whose main body was a hill thirty or forty feet above the sea, joined to the mainland by a crystal—studded tombolo a dozen yards in width. Nick was not the only one of the party who was still considering the problem of physical defense; and in addition to its advantages in this respect, the peninsula was roomy enough for the herd. They guided and trundled their belongings down to the sea and up the hill, and immediately settled down to the standard business of hunting for firewood. This was plentiful enough, and by dark a very satisfactory supply had been laid in. The watch fires were built, one of the herd animals slaughtered and eaten, and the group settled down for the night. It was not until the drops had appeared and the fires had been lighted that anyone thought to wonder what happened to the sea level during the nightly rain.

# IV. Communication; Penetration; Isolation

Aminadabarlee fell silent, his eyes fixed on the vision screen; and, nasty as the creature had been, Raeker felt sympathetic. He himself would have been at least as unsociable under similar circumstances. There was no time for pity, however, while there was still hope; too much had to be done.

"Wellenbach! What's the combination of the bathyscaphe?" he snapped.

The communication watch officer reached over his shoulder. "I'll get her for you, Doctor."

Raeker pushed his hand aside. "Wait a minute. Is it a regular set at the other end? An ordinary phone, I mean, or something jury-rigged into the panels?"

"Perfectly ordinary. Why?"

"Because if it weren't and you punched its combination, those kids might open their air lock or something like that in trying to answer. If it's standard in design and appearance, the girl will be able to answer safely."

"I see. She won't have any trouble; I've seen her use the punch-combination sets here."

"All right. Call them." Raeker tried not to show the uncertainty he felt as the officer punched the buttons. It was not possible to tell yet just what had happened above Tenebra's atmosphere; *something* had evidently breached the air lock of the tender, but that might or might not have affected the bathyscaphe. If it had, the children were probably dead— though their guide might have had them in space suits, of course. One could hope.

Behind him, Aminadabarlee might have been a giant statue of an otter, cast in oiled gray steel. Raeker spent no time wondering at his own fate if bad news came back through the set and that statue returned to life; all his attention was concentrated on the fate of the youngsters. A dozen different speculations chased themselves through his mind in the few seconds before the screen lighted up. Then it did, and the worst of them vanished.

A human face was looking at them out of it; thin, very pale, topped by a mop of hair which looked black on the screen but which Raeker knew was red; a face covered by an expression which suggested terror just barely held under control, but—a living face. That was the important fact.

At almost the same instant a figure came hurtling through the door of the communications room and skidded to a halt beside the motionless figure of the Drommian.

"Easy! Are you all right?" Raeker didn't need the words to identify Councillor Rich. Neither did Aminadabarlee, and neither did the child in the screen. After the two-second pause for return contact, the terror vanished from the thin face, and she relaxed visibly.

"Yes, Dad. I was pretty scared for a minute, but it's all right now. Are you coming?"

For a moment there was some confusion at the set as Rich, Raeker, and the Drommian all tried to speak at once; then Aminadabarlee's physical superiority made itself felt, and he thrust his sleek head at the screen.

"Where is the other one—my son?" he shrilled.

She replied promptly, "He's here; he's all right."

"Let me talk to him." The girl left the pickup area for a moment, and, they heard her voice but not her words as she addressed someone else. Then she reappeared, with her dark hair badly disheveled and a bleeding scratch on one cheek.

"He's in a comer, and doesn't want to come out. I'll turn up the volume so you can talk to him there." She made no reference to her injury, and, to Raeker's surprise, neither did her father. Aminadabarlee seemed not to notice it. He shifted into his own shrill language, which seemed to make sense to no one else in the room but Rich, and held forth for several minutes, pausing now and then for answers.

At first he received none; then, as he grew more persuasive, a feeble piping came back through the set. Hearing this restored the Drommian's composure, and he talked more slowly; and after a minute or so of this Aminadorneldo's head appeared beside Easy's. Raeker wondered whether he looked ashamed of himself; Drommian facial expressions were a closed book to him. Apparently one of the family had a conscience, anyway, for after a few moments' more talk from the elder one the child turned to Easy and shifted to English.

"I'm sorry I hurt you, Miss Rich. I was afraid, and thought you'd made the noise, and were trying to make me come out of the corner. My father says you are older than I, and that I am to do whatever you say until I am with him again."

The girl seemed to understand the situation. "It's all right, 'Mina," she said gently. "You didn't really hurt me. I'll take care of you, and we'll get back to your father—after a while." She glanced at the pickup as she added the last words, and Raeker grew tense again. A glance at Councillor Rich confirmed his suspicion; the girl was trying to get something across, presumably without alarming her companion. Gently but firmly Raeker took the Drommian's place in the pickup field. Easy nodded in recognition; she had met him briefly on her own tour through the *Vindemiatrix* some time earlier.

"Miss Rich," he began, "we're still a little in the dark about just what happened down there. Can you tell us? Or is your guide there, to give a report?"

She shook her head negatively at the latter question. "I don't know where Mr. Flanagan is. He stayed in the tender to have a smoke, I suppose; he told us to be sure not to touch any controls—he must think we're pretty stupid. We stayed away from the board, of course—in fact, after the first look, we stayed out of the control compartment altogether, and looked through the other rooms. They're all observation or bunkrooms, except for the galley, and we were just going to suit up to go back to the tender when a call came from Mr. Flanagan on the set he'd left tuned to suit radio frequency. He said he was at the outer lock, and would open it as soon as he closed the one on the tender—the two ships were so close together we could touch them both at once when we came across—and that we were to stay absolutely still and not do a thing until he came. 'Mina had just opened his mouth to answer when the jolt came; we were flung against the wall, and I was held there by what felt like three or four G's of acceleration. 'Mina could move around all right, and tried to call Mr. Flanagan on the set, but there was no answer, and I wouldn't let him touch anything else. The acceleration lasted half a minute or so, I guess; you can tell better than we can. It stopped just before you called us."

By this time the communication room was packed with men. Several of them began to work slide rules, and Raeker, turning from the set, watched one of these until he had finished; then he asked, "Any ideas, Saki?"

"I think so," the engineer replied. "The kid's report isn't exact, of course, but judging from her estimate of acceleration and time, and the mass of the bathyscaphe, one full ring of the solid-fuel boosters was touched off somehow. That should give just over four G's for forty seconds—about a mile a second total velocity change. There's no way to tell where the ship is, though, until we get there and home on it; we can't compute, since we don't know the direction of acceleration. I wish the 'scaphe weren't so close to the planet, though."

Raeker knew better than to ask the reason for this, but Aminadabarlee didn't.

"Why?"

The engineer glanced at him, then at the image of the other Drommian in the screen, and then apparently decided not to pull punches.

"Because a one-mile-a-second change—in any of a good many directions could put it in an orbit which would enter atmosphere," he said bluntly.

"How long to entry?" cut in Rich.

"Not my pigeon. We'll get it computed while we're under way. My guess would be hours at the outside, though."

"Then why are we standing here talking?" shrilled Aminadabarlee. "Why aren't preparations for rescue being made?"

"They are," returned the engineer calmly. "Only one shuttle was in regular use, but there are others here. One of them is being made ready, and will leave in less than ten minutes. Dr. Raeker, do you want to come?"

"I'd just add mass without being useful," Raeker replied.

"I suppose the same could be said for me," said Rich, "but I'd like to come if there's room. I certainly don't want to hamper the work, though."

"It will be better if you don't," admitted Sakiiro. "We'll keep in touch with this ship and the 'scaphe, though, so you'll know what's happening." He ran from the room.

Aminadabarlee had quite obviously meant to insist upon going; after Rich's words, however, he could hardly do that. He relieved his feelings by remarking, "No one but a fool human being would have had takeoff boosters attached to an uncompleted ship."

"The bathyscaphe is complete, except for final circuit checks and connections," another engineer replied calmly, "and the boosters were for landing as well as takeoff. As a matter of fact, they were not supposed to be connected until the last moment, and it will not be possible to tell what actually fired them until we salvage the ship. Until then, assigning blame is very much a waste of time." He stared coldly at the Drommian, and Rich stepped into the breach. Raeker had to admit the fellow was good at his job; it had seemed a virtual certainty that the big weasel was going to clean the human beings out of the room, but Rich had him calmed down below boiling point in four or five minutes.

Raeker would have liked to hear the details, but he was occupied with the radio. The children on the bathyscaphe had heard, without understanding completely, most of the engineers' statements; and Raeker found himself doing his best to keep up their morale. They were, perfectly reasonably, frightened half to death. It wasn't as hard as he'd thought it might be, though; he hadn't talked long before he realized that the girl was doing exactly the same thing. He couldn't decide whether it was for the benefit of her father or her nonhuman companion, but his respect for the youngster went even higher.

The rescue ship was well on the way by this time, and as the minutes clicked by the hopes of everyone on all three vessels began to mount. If the 'scaphe were in an orbit that did not touch Tenebra's atmosphere, of course, there was no danger; food and air equipment were aboard and had been operating for some time. On a straight chance basis, it seemed to Raeker that the probabilities were at least three to one that this was the case, though he was no ballistician. The computer on the rescue boat was kept busy grinding out possible orbits; the worst seemed to call for atmospheric contact within three-quarters of an hour of the accident; and if this didn't occur within a little over two hours, it wouldn't.

There were view ports in the 'scaphe, and Easy was able to recognize some stars; but while this told them roughly which side of the planet she was on, the lack of precision measurements at her command made the information useless. At that time, there was only one side she *could* be on.

It was sixty-seven minutes after the accident that Easy reported acceleration. By that time, even Aminadabarlee knew all the implications of the fact. The rescue boat was "there," in the sense that it was within half a diameter of Tenebra and nearly motionless with respect to the planet—perfectly useless, as far as the trapped children were concerned. The engineers could get a fix on the 'scaphe's transmitter and locate it within a few miles; but they couldn't compute an interception orbit inside Tenebra's atmosphere. No one knew enough about the atmosphere. The certain thing was that no interception whatever could be accomplished before the 'scaphe was so low that rockets could not be used— atmospheric pressure would be too high for them. Sakiiro reported this to the *Vindemiatrix* within a minute of Easy's information; then, before Aminadabarlee could start to speak, he turned to the set which he had on the depth-boat's frequency.

"Miss Rich. Please listen carefully. Your acceleration is going to get much worse, over the next few minutes; I want you to strap yourself in the seat before the control panel, and do what you can about your companion."

"None of the seats fit him," the girl answered.

"His normal weight is four G's," Rich cut in from the *Vindemiatrix*.

"He'll be taking more than that; but he'll probably be able to stand it, in that case. Just tell him to lie down. Now, Miss Rich—"

"Call me Easy; it'll save time."

"Tell me what you recognize on the board in front of you."

"Not much. Light switches are labeled over on the left. The communicators are top center; air-lock controls under a guard near the light switches; about two square feet of off-on relay buttons, labeled with letters, that don't mean anything to me—?" She let her voice trail off, and Saki nodded.

"All right. Now, near the top of the board, to the right of the communicators, you'll see an area about six inches square marked 'Hunt.' Have you found it?"

"Yes; I see it."

"Make sure the master toggle at its lower left corner says 'Off.' Then put the three in the group labeled 'Aero' in the 'On' position. Then make sure that the big one marked 'D.I.' is off. Do you have that?"

"Yes, sir."

"Now be sure you're strapped in. What you've been doing is to tie in a homing radio which is tuned to the transmission of the robot on the ground to the aerodynamic controls of the 'scaphe. I don't dare have you use any power, but with luck the autopilot will glide you down somewhere in the general vicinity of that robot. You don't have to worry about burning up in the atmosphere; the ship is designed for a power-off entry. It's a big planet, and if we can narrow down your landing area to even a five-hundred-mile radius it will be a big help in picking you up. Do you understand?"

"Yes. I'm strapped in the seat, and 'Mina is lying down."

"All right. Now reach up to the 'Hunt' region you've just been setting, and snap on the master switch. I hope you're not prone to motion sickness; it will be rough at first, I expect."

Sakiiro from the rescue boat and the group in the message room of the *Vindemiatrix* watched tensely as the girl's hand went up and out of the pickup field. They could not see her actually close the switch, and to the surprise of the engineers they could not detect very easily the results of the act. They had expected the girl to be jammed into her seat by an abrupt acceleration change; but things proved not nearly so bad.

"I can feel it," Easy reported. "The ship is rolling—now the planet is on our left side—and I'm a little heavier in my seat—now we're leveling out again, and 'Down' is forward, if this panel is at the front of the room."

"It is," replied the engineer. "You should now be headed toward the robot, and will be slowing down until you're doing about five hundred miles an hour with respect to the air around you. The braking will be jerky; the ship had throw-away speed brakes to take it down through the heat barrier. Stay strapped in."

"All right. How long will it take?"

"A couple of hours. You can stand it all right."

Rich cut in at this point.

"Suppose the machine passes over your robot's location before getting rid of its speed, Mr. Sakiiro? What will the autopilot do? Try to dive in at that point?"

"Certainly not. This is a vehicle, not a missile. It will circle the point at a distance which doesn't demand more than an extra half-G to hold it in the turn. If necessary, it will try to land the ship; but we should be able to avoid that."

"How? You don't expect Easy to fly it, do you?"

"Not in the usual sense. However, when she's down to what we can call 'flying,' speed, the main buoyancy tanks of the 'scaphe should be full of the local atmosphere. Then I'll tell her how to start the electrolyzers; that will fill them with hydrogen, and the ship should float, when they're full, at an altitude where boosters can be used. Then she and her young friend can trim the ship so that she's hanging nose up, and fire the rest of the boosters. We can be waiting overhead."

"I thought you said the boosters weren't connected to the control panel yet!"

Sakiiro was silent for a moment.

"You're right; I'd forgotten that. That complicates the problem."

"You mean my kid is marooned down there?"

"Not necessarily. It's going to call for some tight maneuvering; but I should think we could rig boosters on this boat so as to be able to reach the 'scaphe when it's floating at its highest. The whole design object, remember, was for the thing to float high enough for hydroferron boosters to work; and if they'll work on one frame, they'll certainly work on another."

"Then you can rescue her." The statement was more than half a question. Sakiiro was an honest man, but he had difficulty in making an answer. He did, however, after a moment's hesitation, staring into the face of the middle-aged man whose agonized expression showed so clearly on his screen.

"We should be able to save them both. I will not conceal from you that it will be difficult and dangerous; transferring an engineer to the outside of the 'scaphe to finish up wiring, while the whole thing is floating like a balloon, from a rocket hanging on booster blasts, will present difficulties."

"Why can't you transfer the kids to the rescue ship?"

"Because I'm pretty sure their space suits won't stand the pressure at the 'scaphe's floating height," replied Sakiiro. "I don't know about Drommian designs, but I do know our own."

"Mr. Sakiiro." Easy's voice cut back into the conversation.

"Yes, Easy."

"Is there anything more I can do? Just sitting here doesn't seem right, and—it scares me a little."

Rich looked appealingly at the engineer. As a diplomat, he was an accomplished psychologist, and he knew his daughter. She was not hysterical by nature, but few twelve-year-olds had ever been put under this sort of stress. He himself was not qualified to suggest any reasonable occupation to hold her attention; but fortunately Sakiiro saw the need, too.

"There are pressure gauges to your left," he said. "If you can give us a running report on their readings, while your friend tells us when he can first detect signs of dimming in the stars, it will be of some help. Keep it up unless you get too heavy to be able to watch easily; that may not be too long."

Rich looked his thanks; if Aminadabarlee was doing the same, no one was able to detect the fact. For long minutes the silence was broken only by the voices of the children, reading off numbers and describing the stars.

Then Easy reported that the ship was banking again.

"All right," said Sakiiro. "That means you're over the robot. From now until your speed is killed, you're going to have to take better than three and a half gravities. Your seat folds back on its springs automatically to put you in the best position to stand it, but you're not going to be comfortable. Your friend can undoubtedly take it all right, but warn him against moving around. The ship's traveling fast in an atmosphere, and going from one air current to another at a few thousand miles can give quite a jolt."

"All right."

"The stars are getting hazy." It was Aminadorneldo.

"Thanks. Can you give me another pressure reading?"

The girl obliged, with detectable strain in her voice. Until the last turn had started, the 'scaphe was in relatively free fall; but with its rudimentary wings biting what little there was of the atmosphere in an effort to keep it in a turn the situation was distinctly different. Why the vehicle didn't go into a frame-shattering series of stalls, none of the engineers could see; the turn had started at a much higher speed than had been anticipated by the designers of the machine. As it happened, the whole process was almost incredibly smooth—for a while.

Sakiiro, with no really objective data to go on, had about concluded that the vessel was down to gliding speed and was going to describe the location of the electrolysis controls to Easy when the motion changed. A series of shuddering jars shook the ship. The girl's body was held in the seat by the straps, but her head and limbs flapped like those of a scarecrow in a high wind; the young Drommian for the first time failed to stay put. The jolting continued, the thuds punctuated by the girl's sobs and an almost inaudibly high-pitched whine from Aminadorneldo. The elder Drommian rose once more to his feet and looked anxiously at the screen.

The engineers were baffled; the diplomats were too terrified for their children to have had constructive ideas even had they been qualified otherwise; but Raeker thought he knew the answer.

"They're hitting raindrops!" he yelled.

He must have been right, it was decided afterward; but the information did not really help. The bathyscaphe jerked and bucked. The autopilot did its best to hold a smooth flight path, but aerodynamic controls were miserably inadequate for the task. At least twice the vessel somersaulted completely, as nearly as Raeker could tell from the way the Drommian was catapulted around the room. Sheer luck kept him out of contact with the control switches. For a time the controls were useless because their efforts were overridden—a rudder trying to force a left turn will not get far if the right wing encounters a fifty-foot sphere of water, even though the water isn't much denser than the air. Then they were useless because they lacked enough grip on the atmosphere; the ship had given up enough kinetic energy to the raindrops to fall well below its stalling speed—low as that was, in an atmosphere seven or eight hundred times as dense as Earth's at sea level. By that time, of course, the ship was falling, in the oldest and simplest sense of the word. The motion was still irregular, for it was still hitting the drops; but the violence was gone, for it wasn't hitting them very hard.

The rate of fall was surprisingly small, for a three-G field. The reason was simple enough—even with the outside atmosphere filling most of its volume, the ship had a very low density. It was a two-hundred-foot-long, cigar-like shell, and the only really heavy part was the forty-foot sphere in the center which held the habitable portion. It is quite possible that it would have escaped serious mechanical damage even had it landed on solid ground; and as it happened, the fall ended on liquid.

Real liquid; not the borderline stuff that made up most of Tenebra's atmosphere.

It landed upside down, but the wings had been shed like the speed brakes and its center of gravity was low enough to bring it to a more comfortable attitude. The floor finally stopped rocking, or at least the Drommian did—with the vision set fastened to the ship, the floor had always seemed motionless to the distant watchers. They saw the otterlike giant get cautiously to his feet, then walk slowly over to the girl's chair and touch her lightly on the shoulder. She stirred and tried to sit up.

"Are you all right?" Both parents fairly shrieked the question. Aminadorneldo, his father's orders in mind, waited for Easy to answer.

"I guess so," she said after a moment. "I'm sorry I bawled, Dad; I was scared. I didn't mean to scare 'Mina, though."

"It's all right, kid. I'm sure no one can blame you, and I don't suppose your reaction had much to do with your friend's. The main thing is that you're in one piece, and the hull's intact—I suppose you'd be dead by now if it weren't."

"That's true enough," seconded Sakiiro.

"You've had a rough ride, then, but it should be over now. Since you're there, you might take a look through the windows—you're the first nonnatives ever to do that directly. When you've seen all you can or want to, tell Mr. Sakiiro and he'll tell you how to get upstairs again. All right?"

"All right, Dad." Easy brushed a forearm across her tear-stained face, unfastened the seat straps, and finally struggled to her feet.

"Golly, when are they going to cut the power? I don't like all these G's," she remarked.

"You're stuck with them until we get you away from there," her father replied.

"I know it. I was just kidding. Hmm. It seems to be night outside; I can't see a thing."

"It is, if you're anywhere near the robot," Raeker replied, "but it wouldn't make any difference to your eyes if it were high noon. Even Altair can't push enough light for human eyes through that atmosphere. You'll have to use the lights."

"All right." The girl looked at the board where she had already located the light switches; then, to the surprised approval of the engineers, she made sure from Sakiiro that these *were* the ones she wanted. Saki admitted later that his hopes of rescuing the pair soared several hundred per cent at that moment.

With the lights on, both children went over to the windows.

"There isn't much to see," called Easy. "We seem to have splashed into a lake or ocean. It's as smooth as glass; not a ripple. I'd think it was solid if the ship weren't partly under it. There are big foggy globes drifting down, yards and yards across, but they sort of fade out just before they touch the surface. That's every bit I can see."

"It's raining," Raeker said simply. "The lake is probably sulfuric acid, I suppose fairly dilute by this time of night, and is enough warmer than the air so the water evaporates before it strikes. There wouldn't be any waves; there's no wind. Three knots is a wild hurricane on Tenebra."

"With all that heat energy running around?" Rich was startled.

"Yes. There's nothing for it to *work* on—I use the word in its physical sense. There isn't enough change in volume when the atmosphere changes temperature, or even changes state, to create the pressure differences you need for high winds. Tenebra is about the calmest place you'll find inside any atmosphere in the galaxy."

"Does that jibe with your remarks about earthquakes a while ago?" It was a measure of Aminadabarlee's revived confidence that he could talk of something besides the stupidity of human beings.

"No, it doesn't," admitted Raeker, "and I'll have to admit, Easy, that there is a possibility that you *will* encounter some waves if you float there long enough. However, you won't be able to call them weather, and they won't carry you to any more interesting places. I'm afraid you've seen about all you can expect to, young lady; you may as well come up and be properly rescued."

"All right. Only I'd like to know just what's going to make this thing float, and whether the trip up will be as rough as the one down was."

"It won't. You'll go up vertically, and much more slowly. You're going to ride a balloon. The atmosphere there is mostly water, with enough ions loose to make it a decent conductor. The largest part of your hull is divided into cells, and each cell further divided in two by a flexible membrane. Right now, those membranes are squeezed flat against one wall of each cell by atmospheric pressure. When you start the electrolysis units, some of the water will be decomposed; the oxygen will be piped outside the hull, but the hydrogen will be released on the other side of the membranes and gradually drive the air out of the cells. The old bathyscaphe used the same idea, only it didn't need the membranes to keep the two fluids from diffusing into each other."

"I see. How long will it take to make enough gas to lift us?"

"I can't tell; we don't know the conductivity of the atmosphere. Once you start things going, there's a bank of ammeters above the switches for each individual cell; if you'll give me their reading after things start, I'll try to calculate it for you."

"All right. Where are the— Oh, here; you labeled them decently. Upper right, a bank of twelve toggles, with a gang bar and a master?"

"That's it. You can see the meters above them. Close the lot, hit the master, and give the readings."

"All right." The thin arm reached up and out of the field of vision, and everyone could hear the switches click. Easy pulled her hand back to her lap, settled back into the chair under her three hundred pounds of weight, eyed the dials one after another, and said, "The readings are all zero. What do I do now?"

# V. PEREGRINATION; CONSIDERATION; ESTIVATION

Nick had chosen a fire on the landward side of the hill, so he was the first to have to consider the sea-level problem. In the home valley, of course, the water at night had never gotten more than thirty or forty feet deep; slow as the runoff was, enough always escaped at the valley foot to keep the village itself dry. He knew, from Fagin's lectures, that the water which flowed away must eventually reach something like a sea or lake; but not even Fagin had stopped to think of what would happen then—naturally enough; the surface of Earth's oceans compared to the volume of an average day's rainfall doesn't correspond to much of a sea-level rise, to put it mildly.

On Tenebra, the situation is a trifle different. There is no single giant sea basin, only the very moderate-sized lake beds, which are even less permanent than those of Earth. What this difference could mean in terms of "sea" level might possibly have been calculated in advance, but not by any of Nick's people.

At first, there was nothing to worry about. The great, cloudy drops drifted into sight from far above, settled downward, and faded out as the radiation from the fires warmed them a trifle. Then they came lower, and lower, until they were actually below the level of the hilltop on all sides.

Once a sharp quake struck and lasted for half a minute or more, but when Nick saw that the spit of land joining the hill to the shore was still there, he put this from his mind. Something much more unusual was starting to happen. At home, raindrops which touched the ground after the latter had been cooled down for the night flattened into great, foggy half-globes and drifted around until a fire obliterated them; here they behaved differently. Drops striking the surface of the sea vanished instantly and by Nick's standards, violently. The difference in pressure and temperature made the reaction between oleum and water much less notice-

427

able than it would be in an Earthly laboratory, but it was still quite appreciable.

After each such encounter, it could be seen that further raindrops falling on the same area faded out a little higher than usual for a few minutes; Nick judged correctly that some heat was being released by the reaction.

He had been watching this phenomenon for some time, interrupted twice by the need to relight his fire when a particularly close drop smothered it, when he noticed that the hill was now an island. This startled him a trifle and he turned all his attention to the matter. The quake hadn't done it; he particularly recalled seeing the tombolo intact after the shaking was done. It didn't take him too long to conclude that if the land wasn't sinking, the sea must be rising; and a few minutes' close watch of the shore line proved that something of that sort was happening. He called the others, to tell them of what he had seen, and after a few minutes they agreed that the same thing was happening on all sides of the hill.

"How far will it come, Nick?" Betsey's voice was understandably anxious.

"I don't see how it can get this high," Nick answered. "After all, it hasn't risen as much as the water in our own valley would have by this time of night, and this hill is nearly as high as the village. We're safe enough."

It got a little harder to stick to this belief as the hours passed and the sea grew higher. They could see the pools on shore swell and overflow into the main body; as time went on, more than one great river formed, carrying runoff from no one knew what drainage area. Some of the rivers were frightening, their centers as high or higher than the hill itself before they spread out and merged with the sea. By this time the violence of water-meeting-acid had subsided; the sea, at least near the shore, was pretty dilute.

Of course, "near the shore" might be too casual a statement. No one on the hilltop could tell for certain just where the shore was now. The route they had followed was deep under the acid sea, and the only evidence that dry land existed was the rivers which still came into view above sea level.

The island that had been a hill shrank steadily. The cattle seemed unperturbed, but were driven inside the ring of fires. Then this had to be drawn in—or rather, others had to be built closer to the hilltop; and at last people and animals huddled together behind a single ring of glowing heat, while the sea bulged upward at their feeble protection. The raindrops were clear now; they had fallen from high enough levels to lose their suspended oxygen, and inevitably the last fires succumbed. Their heat had for many minutes past been maintaining a hollow in the surface of the sea; and as they cooled, the ocean reclaimed its own. Seconds after the last spark died, every living being on the hilltop was unconscious, and a minute later only a turbulent dimple in the surface of the sea showed where the slightly warmer hilltop was covered. Nick's last thought was to the effect that at least they were safe from animals; they would be uncovered long before anything could get at them.

Apparently he wasn't quite right. When they woke up the next morning and brushed the thin frost of quartz crystals from their scales, all the people were there, but the herd seemed to have diminished. A count confirmed this; ten cattle were gone, with only a few scales left behind. It was fortunate that the animals were of a species whose scale armor was quite frail, and which depended more on its breeding powers to survive; otherwise the meat-eaters who had come in the night might have made a different choice. The realization that things lived in the sea came as a distinct shock to the entire party. They knew just about enough physical science to wonder where any such creature got its oxygen.

But the new situation called for new plans.

"There seems to be a catch in the idea of telling Fagin just to hunt along the seashore until he finds us," Nick commented after breakfast. "The seashore doesn't stay put too well. Also, we can't afford to stay near it, if we're going to lose eight or ten per cent of our animals every night."

"What we'll have to do is some more mapping," commented Jim. "It would be nice to find a place protected by sea but which *doesn't* get submerged every night."

"You know," remarked Nancy in a thoughtful tone, "one could find a rather useful employment for this place right here, if the proper people could be persuaded to visit it." Everyone pondered this thought for a time, and the tone of the meeting gradually brightened. This *did* sound promising. Idea after idea was proposed, discussed, rejected, or modified; and two hours later a definite—really definite—course of action had been planned.

None of it could be carried out, of course, until it was possible to get off the island, and this was not for a dozen hours after sunrise. Once the tombolo appeared, however, everyone went into furious activity.

The herd—what was left of it—was driven ashore and on inland by Betsey and Oliver. Nick, making sure he had his axe and fire-making equipment, started inland as well, but in a more southerly direction. The other five fanned out from the base of the peninsula and began mapping the countryside for all they were worth. They were to determine as closely as possible how much of the area was submerged by the sea at its highest and make their report no later than the second night following. The group was then to pick a more suitable campsite to the north of the previous night's unfortunate choice. They were to settle at this point, and send a pair of people each morning to the base of the peninsula until either Nick returned or ten days had passed; in the latter event, they were to think of something else.

Nick himself had the task of contacting Fagin. He alone of the group was just a trifle unclear on how he was to accomplish his job. Tentatively, he planned to approach the cave village at night, and play by ear thereafter. If Swift's people had gotten into the habit of moving around at night with torches, things would be difficult. If not, it might be easy—except that his own approach would then be very noticeable. Well, he'd have to see.

The journey was normal, with enough fights to keep him in food, and he approached the cliff on the evening of the second day. He had circled far around to the west in order to come on the place from the cliff top; but even so he halted at a safe distance until almost dark. There was no telling where hunting parties might be encountered, since there was a path up the cliffs in nearly constant use by them.

As darkness fell, however, Nick felt safe in assuming that all such groups would be back at their caves; and checking his fire-lighting equipment once more, he cautiously approached the cliff top. He listened at the edge for some time before venturing to push his crest over, but no informative sounds filtered up and he finally took the chance. The cliff was some three hundred fifty feet high at that point, as he well knew; and he realized that even a single spine would be quite visible from below by daylight. It might be somewhat safer now, since no fires appeared to have been lighted yet.

When he finally did look, there was nothing to see. There *were* no fires, and it was much too dark for him to see anything without them.

He drew back again to think. He was sure the village and its inhabitants lay below, and was morally certain that Fagin was with them. Why they had no fires going was hard to understand, but facts were facts. Perhaps it would be safe to try to sneak up to the village in the dark—but the rain would come soon, and that would be that.

Then he had another idea, found some small wood, and went to work with his fire-making tools, a drill and spindle made from tough wood. He rather expected some response from below when he got a small blaze going, since it lighted up the sky more effectively than daylight; but nothing happened until he executed the next portion of the idea, by tossing a burning stick over the edge of the cliff. Then everything happened at once.

The light showed Fagin, standing motionless fifty yards from the foot of the cliff. It showed an otherwise empty expanse of rock and vegetation; the people were in their caves, as usual. That, however, was only temporary.

With the arrival of the fire, a rattle of voices erupted from the caves. Evidently, if they ever slept, they weren't doing it yet. After a moment Swift's tones made themselves heard above the others.

"Get it! Get wood to it! Don't just stand there as if you were wet already!" A crowd of figures emerged from the rock and converged on the glowing twig; then they spread out again, as though they had all realized at once that no one had any wood and it would be necessary to find some. Plants were wrenched up from the ground by a hundred different hands and carried, or sometimes thrown, toward the spark. Nick was far more amused than surprised when it went out without anyone's succeeding in lighting anything from it, and was only academically curious as to whether it had burned out of its own or been smothered by its would-be rescuers. His attention was not allowed to dwell on the problem for long; Swift's voice rose again over the disappointed babble.

"There's a glow on top of the cliff, and that's where the fire came from! Someone up there still has some; come and get it!" As usual, obedience was prompt and unquestioning, and the crowd headed toward the trail up the cliff. Nick was a trifle surprised; it was close to rainfall time and the cave-dwellers were carrying no fire. Something drastic must have happened, for them to overcome their lifelong habit of keeping to the caves at night. However, it was hardly the time to speculate on that subject; the cave men were seeking fire, and Nick happened to have all that there was around at the moment.

It took him about five seconds to dream up the rest of his idea. He lighted a stick at his small blaze and started toward the head of the trail from below, lighting all the plants he could reach as he went. When he reached the trail he tossed aside the nearly spent torch he had been using, made himself another which he hoped was small enough to shield with his body, and headed on along the cliff top. If the cave men were satisfied to take some fire, well enough; if they wanted him too, perhaps they'd look along the fire trail he had laid, which would lead them in the wrong direction. He wasn't really hopeful about this, knowing their skill at tracking, but anything seemed worth trying once.

He kept on along the cliff top, toward a point some two miles away where the cliff broke gradually away to the lower level. He was out of direct view from the head of the trail when Swift reached it, but did not let that fact slow him down. Once at the broken-rock region he picked his way carefully down, dodging boulders loosened by a sharp quake, and started back, hiding his little torch as well as he could from anyone overhead. Fifteen minutes after the disturbance had started he was beside Fagin, apparently unnoticed by any of Swift's people.

"Teacher! Do you hear me? It's Nick."

"I hear you, all right. What are you doing here? Did you start this fuss? What's going on, anyway?"

"I threw the fire down the cliff, yes; I had to make sure you were here. The rest was a by-product. I'm here because we've found a way to get you out of Swift's hands without having to worry about his getting hold of you again afterward."

"That's encouraging. I thought I had a way, too, but troubles have arisen in that direction. I need badly and quickly all the help I can get, and I can't see Swift being very helpful for some time. Let's hear your idea."

Nick described the doings of his people since Fagin had been kidnapped, and dwelt particularly on the geography of the spot where they had spent their first night at the sea.

"We assume," he said, "that you can live under the sea the way you can in rain; so we thought if you fled to this hill, and Swift followed you, he'd be trapped there at night; and while he was asleep you could take away all the weapons of his people—which would be a help anyway, since we're getting so short—and if we couldn't figure out anything else to do with him, just shove him downhill to a point which stays submerged all day."

"Would he last long in such a place?"

"Probably not, as there are animals in that sea that ate some of our cattle; but who cares? He didn't mind killing Tom and Alice, and would have done the same to the rest of us if he'd felt it necessary."

"How about the rest of his people?"

"They helped him. I don't care what happens to them."

"Well, I see your point, but I don't entirely share your view. There are reasons which might make you feel differently, but I can't go into them yet.

"Your plan, if it really rates the name yet, has some good points, but it also has some weak ones. If this place of yours is a day and a half's journey from here even for you, I'm not at all clear how I can keep ahead of Swift long enough to let me reach it; remember, you can travel faster than I. Also, now that you've brought them back the fire they'd lost, I'll be very surprised if it's as easy to get away at night as it would have been before."

"What do you mean? They brought fire with them from our village."

"They brought it, but didn't know how to make one fire except from another. They let what they had go out during the day after we arrived, and have been fireless ever since. They've been doing their best to teach me their language so I could show them how to make more, but I'm having a lot of trouble—for one thing, I can't make some of their shriller noises. Swift's been remarkably patient, though, I must say. Now he'll be even easier to get along with, I should imagine; but he certainly won't be easier to get away from."

"Then maybe I shouldn't have come, Teacher. I'm sorry."

"I'm not. My original plan for getting in touch with you again has already failed, so if you hadn't come we'd be in even worse shape. All I meant was that we have some heavy planning to do before we're out of this mess. You'd probably better get away for a few hours at least, while I think; there's no point in having you caught by Swift, too."

"But how will I get back again? They have fire, now—for that matter, as soon as they come back they'll know I've been here, and probably start tracking me. I'd probably still be in sight, even if I started now; it's beginning to rain, and I can't travel without a torch, and that will be visible for miles. I was expecting you to come with me right away."

"I see your trouble, but don't quite know what to do about it. It's hard to believe that Swift won't be back here in the next few minutes." Fagin paused, as though in thought; Nick of course did not know that such pauses really meant a tense conference among several men a hundred and sixty thousand miles away. "Look, Nick. There's a good deal of burnable material around, right?"

"Yes."

"And there is only one path from the cliff top, and that a narrow cleft?"

"Yes, not counting the way around—a good four miles."

"Hmph. I could wish it were longer. Do you think you can build a fire big enough to block the foot of that path for a while, so as to delay them while we get going? You'll have to work fast; they must be coming back by now, I should think, unless they're still looking for you on top."

"I'll try." Nick could see that this was no time for theorizing. "Someone's probably looked over the edge and seen me by now, but there's nothing to lose. If I don't catch up to you, head east-northeast until you reach the sea, then follow along its daytime shoreline until you meet the others. I'll do what I can to interfere with Swift's trackers; you'd better get going now."

Nick didn't wait for a reply; he was already racing toward the foot of the cliff trail, gathering fuel as he went. His torch was nearly gone, but he started a rough heap of wood a few yards inside the cleft, and managed to get it burning. Then he hunted around madly, tossing every bit of combustible matter he could find into the four-yard-wide crack.

A raindrop came squeezing its way down the gully and vanished as it neared the fire, but it was early enough in the evening for there still to be a good deal of oxygen in it. Nick was pleased; evidently no torch-bearing cave-dwellers were yet on the path, or the drop would have been destroyed much sooner. That gave so much more time.

With the pile big enough to satisfy him, he set off along Fagin's trail. Even Nick could follow it, a five-foot-wide track of flattened and crumbled vegetation, except where it led through hollows already filling with liquid water. He could have gone through these with his torch, since the liquid was still fairly safe to breathe, but he chose to detour around. Even so, he caught up with Fagin within a mile.

"Keep going," he said. "I'm going to do a little trail erasing." He applied his torch to a bush beside the trail, and to the crushed, brittle material on the track itself; then he started in a wide arc to the north, setting fire to every bush he passed. Eventually, a glowing belt of radiance extended from Fagin's trail almost east of the cave village around to the track down which the robot had been brought from the north. Nick thought he could hear excited voices from the caves, but wasn't sure. He raced northward at the top of his speed for another mile, and started another series of fires there. They should be visible from the cliff, too; and perhaps the cave-dwellers would come out and search along the route to the old village rather than start tracking right away.

Then he raced back to intercept Fagin's trail, shielding his torch with his body in the hope that its glow would not be seen from the cliff. He found the trail with little trouble, though Fagin was sensibly keeping to the valleys as much as possible, and finally caught up with the Teacher. Fagin heard his report, and approved.

"It's probably the best you could have done," he said. "I'll be surprised if we get through the night without having company, though."

"So will I," admitted Nick.

In spite of this pessimism, the hours passed without any sign of pursuit. Nick's higher speed allowed him to keep up with the robot, even though he had to detour puddles which the machine took in its stride. The raindrops grew clear, and correspondingly dangerous; puddles and lakes larger, deeper, and harder to avoid as the bottom of Tenebra's atmosphere gradually underwent its nightly change in phase.

"Even with your staying on dry land and leaving such an open trail, they must be having trouble following by now," remarked Fagin during one of the brief spells when they were together. "A lot of the places where you went must be well under water by now, and they can't be boiling them off with torches at this hour; the water's too clear to let them get away with it. I'm starting to feel a little happier about the whole situation."

"I'm not," said Nick.

"Why not?"

"The pools are getting very big, and some of the valleys ahead are long and deep. I remember the night before last there were some pretty big rivers emptying into the sea. If we meet one of those, and I don't see how we can help it, we're stuck."

"On the contrary, that seems to me the best thing that could happen. Swift can't follow through a river."

"Neither can I."

"Not under your own power. I can carry you, and it's pretty safe; we haven't met any creatures in sixteen years capable of living, or at least being active, in clear water—though I must admit I've always been expecting it."

"There were some in the ocean."

"That isn't water, for the most part, except late at night. Anyway, I think we needn't worry about ocean life. You've made me happier than I've been for some time; let's look for one of these rivers."

"All right. I hope you're right." Nick was accustomed enough to being knocked out by oxygen-free water, but somehow didn't like the idea of being carted around like a sack in that state. If Fagin thought it was all right, though. . .

It looked for a while as though he needn't have worried. With the common perversity of the inanimate, once a river was wanted, none could be found. They kept on their original course, knowing the futility of zigzagging over unknown ground, and got closer and closer to the sea; but they actually reached it, not too many hours before day, without finding a river.

They had reached the "shore" far south of the region where the others awaited them; Nick had selected their course so that there would be no question of which way to turn when they reached the coast. He had mapped enough to know what measuring uncertainties could mean.

Without hesitation, therefore, he directed Fagin to follow the "shore" to the left. They were, of course, far inland from the hill which Nick had planned to use to trap Swift, but that was the least of their troubles at the moment. The chief annoyance was the lack of a river; a second one, which made itself apparent an hour or so after they reached the sea, was the appearance behind them of a distinct glow of light. There was no question what it was; the sun just didn't get that distinct, or even that bright.

"They're gaining on us. I wonder how long my fires delayed them?" muttered Nick when the glow caught his eye. Fagin had not seen it yet, apparently, and Nick saw nothing to be gained in calling his attention to it. He just looked that much more intensely for a river ahead.

The robot finally spotted the light as well, and understood its meaning as clearly as had Nick.

"If they get too close before we find a river, you'd better go on ahead at your best speed; you can probably outrun them."

"What will you do?"

"Go into the ocean."

"Why not take me with you? Won't that be as good as a river?"

"Not according to your own statement. I don't want you eaten right out of my arms, and I'm not very well suited to fighting things off if they attack."

"That's true. I guess your idea is best, then."

As it turned out, though, they didn't have to use it. By the time the glow of Swift's torches had resolved itself into separate points of light, and it could be seen that the cave-dwellers were overhauling Fagin and his pupil at a rate that promised a scant hour of further freedom, a bulge had appeared on the landscape ahead; and in another minute or two this had taken on the shape of a low, rounded ridge snaking across the countryside. It had the dark hue of clear water; and well before they reached it there was no doubt that it was a river. Since it reached above Nick's crest, there was no way of telling its width; but it must certainly be wide enough to drown any torches Swift's people might be carrying.

Straight to its edge Fagin and Nick went. Ordinarily such a mass of clear water would be a frightening sight as it oozed slowly by toward the sea; but tonight neither of them felt afraid of it. Nick tossed his torch into it with a carefree gesture, noted with actual glee the way the glow died abruptly from its end, made sure his weapons and fire-drill were securely attached to his harness, and turned to the Teacher.

"All right, I'm ready."

The white bulk of the robot slid toward him, and four appendages extended from openings in its smooth carapace. Gripping devices on the ends of these clamped firmly, but not painfully, onto two of Nick's arms and his walking legs, picked him up, and draped him over the machine's back.

"All right, Nick," said Fagin. "Relax. I'll get to high ground as quickly as I can on the other side and dodge raindrops, so you shouldn't be out long. Just relax." Nick obeyed the injunction as well as he could as the machine slid into the river.

His body heat boiled a considerable volume of the liquid into gas as they entered; but the gas was oxygen-free and its physical state made no difference to Nick. He lost consciousness within half a minute.

Swift's warriors reached the spot where the trail entered the river fifteen minutes later. The chief was not philosophical enough to put the incident down to experience.

# VI. INFORMATION; NAVIGATION; OBSERVATION

"How much of a lead will that give you, Doctor?"

Raeker answered without taking his eyes from the robot's screens. "Presumably the rest of the night, and a trifle more—however long it takes that river to dry up after sunrise. It's twenty hours or so to sunrise."

"Maybe the plants will grow enough to hide the robot's trail in that time; will they?"

"I'm afraid I have no idea."

"After observing the life of this planet for sixteen years? Really, Doctor, I should have supposed you'd know something in that time.'"

"In all sixteen of those years I never had occasion to note just what kind of vegetation is on the north bank of this river," Raeker retorted a trifle impatiently, "and all I know from Nick about Swift is that he's a good tracker; I have no quantitative information as to just how good. Really, Councillor, I know you have been living in Hell the last three weeks; but if you can give only destructive criticism I can say that you won't be helping her much. You're getting to sound like Aminadabarlee."

"I'm glad you mentioned that." Rich did not sound at all offended. "I know, Doctor, that it is difficult for you to bear up under Drommian mannerisms; they are a rather impulsive race, and while they are very courteous by their standards, those standards are not quite identical to ours. Aminadabarlee is an unusually restrained member of his race; that is why he holds the position he does; but I must suggest very strongly that you check your natural impulse to answer sharply when he gets insulting, as he occasionally does. There is no point in straining his capacity for tolerance. I assure you most solemnly that if he loses his self-control sufficiently to make an emotional report to Dromm, every word he has said about the results to Earth would be literally fulfilled. There wouldn't be a war, of course, but the result of a ninety per cent—or even a fifty per cent—cut in

Earth's interstellar trade would be fully as disastrous as any war. You must remember that to most of the races we know, Earthmen and Drommians are equally alien; they are both 'creatures from the stars,' and what one race says about the other would have quite a ring of authority to most of them. This may sound a trifle exaggerated to you, but this little situation is potentially the most ticklish political and diplomatic affair that has occurred in my lifetime."

That actually took Raeker's eyes from the screen for a moment.

"I didn't realize that," he said. "Also, I'm afraid I must admit that it will make no difference in my efforts to rescue Easy and 'Mina; I was doing my best already."

"I believe that, and I'm grateful; but I had to tell you about the other matter. If Aminadabarlee weren't here it wouldn't have been necessary; but since you can't in decency avoid seeing him, it's very necessary that you understand him. Whatever he says, however intolerant or impatient or downright insulting he may be, you must keep your own control. I assure you he won't take your calmness as a sign of fear; his people don't think that way. He'll respect you the more for it—and so will I."

"I'll do my best," promised Raeker, "but right now I'll be just as glad if he doesn't come in for a few hours. I'm busy juggling Nick across the river, and if you want to regard Nick as *my* child you won't be too far wrong. I don't mind talking as long as everything is going all right, but if I stop in the middle of a sentence don't be surprised. Have you been talking to the kids?"

"Yes. They're bearing up pretty well. It's lucky that Drommian is there; I'm afraid Easy would have let go all over the place if she didn't feel responsible for her 'Mina. He seems to feel that she's keeping everything in hand, so for the moment there's no morale problem. Did I tell you that Mr. Sakiiro found that some of the inspection ports had been left open on the bathyscaphe, so that the electrolysis leads were undoubtedly corroded by outside atmosphere? He has some idea of getting your people down there to do a repair job."

"I know. That's all I can think of at the moment, too; but to do that means I have to find *them,* and *they* have to find the 'scaphe. It's some comfort that the kids can stay alive almost indefinitely down there; the machine will keep them in food, water, and air."

"That's true; but Easy won't last forever under three gravities."

Raeker frowned. "I hadn't thought of that. Have you any medical information on how long she's likely to hold out?"

"None at all. The problem has never come up for such a young person. Adults have stood it for a good many months, I know."

"I see. Well, I should think you'd have a good excuse to be nastier than Aminadabarlee, at that rate. The gravity won't bother his youngster."

"No, but something else will. The synthesizers in the bathyscaphe produce human food."

"So what? Isn't Drommian metabolism like ours? They breathe oxygen, and I've seen them eat our food here on the *Vindemiatrix*."

"In general, yes; in detail, no. Their vitamin requirements are different, though they do use fats, carbohydrates, and proteins as we do. 'Mina will almost certainly start suffering from vitamin deficiency diseases if he stays there long enough; and like me, his father has no exact medical information."

Raeker whistled, and the frown stayed on his face. Rich thought for a moment that something had occurred on Tenebra to worry him, but the screens still showed nothing but river bed. The stream must have been fully a mile wide, judging by the time it was taking to cross it. The diplomat remained silent, and watched while the robot forged ahead and, finally, out on the far side of the great watercourse.

It was still raining, of course, and without Nick's torch it was necessary to use a spotlight to locate descending raindrops. After about ten minutes in normal air, Nick began to revive; and when he was once again himself, and had found and kindled a torch, the journey went on as before, except for the lack of anxiety over Swift's whereabouts.

Shortly after this, the relief operator appeared. Raeker didn't want to leave the controls, since the situation below was still rather ticklish, but he knew there was really no choice. The human being didn't live who could maintain decent alertness through a whole Tenebran night. He brought the other man up to date and, with several backward glances, left the observation room.

"I don't think I can sleep for a while," he remarked to Rich. "Let's go back to communications and see how Easy's making out."

"She was asleep a couple of hours ago," replied the girl's father. "That's why I came to see what you were up to. No harm in checking, though." He added after a moment's silence, "I like to be there when she wakes up." Raeker made no comment.

Nothing further had happened, according to the communication watch officer, but the two settled down in view of the bathyscaphe screen. No one had much to say.

Raeker was more than half asleep when Easy's voice came from the set.

"Dad! Are you there?" Rich might have been as drowsy as Raeker, but he answered instantly.

"Yes, dear. What is it?"

"We're moving. 'Mina's still asleep, and I didn't want to wake him, but I thought I'd better tell you."

"Tell everything you can to Dr. Raeker; he's here, and knows Tenebra better than anyone else."

"All right. You remember the first night we landed I thought we were on solid ground and the lake was getting deeper, don't you?"

"Yes, Easy. We decided that the rain was diluting the acid in which you had fallen, so its density was going down and you weren't floating so high."

"That's right. After a while the side windows were covered so we couldn't even see the rain, and each night before morning the top one is covered too; we're entirely under water."

"That's using the word a bit loosely, but I see what you mean. In that case you can't see out at all, I should think; how do you know you're moving tonight?"

"We can see, with the lights on; we're at the bottom of the lake or ocean or whatever it is, and the lights show the rocks and some funny things I suppose are plants. We're going by them slowly, sort of bouncing, and the ship is rocking a little from time to time. I can hear the scrapes and bumps whenever we touch."

"All right. I can't see that it's anything in particular to worry about, though I'd like to know why the change from the last five nights. When daylight comes the extra water will evaporate and you'll float again as usual, assuming you're still in the lake or sea. If, as seems rather likely, you're being carried down a river, you may find yourselves stranded on dry land somewhere when it dries up. At least you'll have a more interesting landscape to watch tomorrow, if that's the case."

"The only problem we have here is locating you. If you're going to start drifting around every night, directing our people to you is going to be hard, to say the least. You'll have to give us every bit of information you can on your surroundings, so we can pass it on to Nick and his friends. You were very smart to call us just now, the moment you discovered you were moving."

"Thanks, Doctor. We'll keep our eyes open. I want to meet your friend Nick."

"We're doing our best to see that you do. If, as we hope, you landed within a few dozen miles of the robot, the chances are you're being washed toward the same ocean that gave him trouble a couple of nights ago; we have reason to suspect that oceans don't get very large on Tenebra, at least by Earthly standards, so getting you together may not take too long."

"Maybe I'd better stay awake for a while, so as to report to you if anything special happens, and then let 'Mina take a watch while I sleep."

"That sounds perfect. We'll always have someone listening up here." Raeker opened the mike switch and turned to Rich. The diplomat was eyeing him intently.

"How much of that was for Easy's morale, and how much for mine?" he asked.

"I made it sound as good as possible," admitted Raeker, "mostly for the kids. However, I didn't lie. I'm reasonably sure I can get my crew to the 'scaphe before too long; I admit I'm less sure what they can do after they find it. We really haven't the slightest idea of the conditions on the outside of that machine, remember; we'll have to wait for Nick's report before we decide what instructions to give him."

Rich stared hard at the biologist for a moment, then relaxed slightly. "That sounds reasonable," he said. If he had planned to say any more, he wasn't given the chance.

"It doesn't sound reasonable to me!" The shrill voice needed no identification. "Every human being in this place is dithering a lot of nonsense about teaching a bunch of savages to rewire a machine two thousand years ahead of their culture, and then risk not only a human but a Drommian life on their having done it properly. It's the sheerest nonsense I ever heard. It's hard to believe that anyone over three years old would fail to realize that nothing but another bathyscaphe has the slightest chance of making the rescue, but I haven't heard a single word about such an activity. I suppose men put the expense before the lives involved."

"I haven't heard of any messages proposing such an activity going to Dromm, either," snapped Raeker. "I've heard that it has an industrial capacity at least equal to Earth's, and it's not a parsec farther from Altair. I suppose Drommians don't bother to repair situations that they feel are someone else's fault, whether lives are involved or not."

None of the human beings present could tell just how Aminadabarlee reacted to this; Rich gave him no time to say anything.

"Dr. Raeker, you're forgetting yourself," he said sharply. "If Councillor Aminadabarlee will come with me, I will discuss with him any points of value which may have been hidden in your words, as well as the very valuable suggestion he made himself. If you have any more courteous thoughts to add, get them to me. Please come, sir." The diplomats stalked out, and the watch officer glanced uneasily at Raeker.

"You don't talk to Drommians like that," he ventured at last.

"I know," replied Raeker. "Rich was telling me, a little while ago. I didn't like to do it, but it seemed to me that Rich needed something to take his attention off his kid."

"You're taking a chance. That fellow could easily turn his whole race so anti-Earth that every human trader outside the solar system would be forced out of business."

"So everyone seems to feel," replied the biologist a trifle uneasily. "I couldn't really believe that things were that critical. Maybe I was a little hasty. Anyway, Rich will be busy for a while, and so will the Drommian; let's concentrate on getting those kids out of trouble. I'll keep my nose out of interracial diplomacy after this."

"Frankly, that relieves me. How about that suggestion—building a new 'scaphe?"

"I'm no engineer," retorted Raeker, "but even I have a pretty good idea how long that would take, even with the experience from the first one to help. I *am* a biologist, and my considered opinion is that both those youngsters would be dead before another bathyscaphe could be made ready. If Rich and the Drommian want to try it, I wouldn't discourage them; the new machine will be useful, and I might even be wrong about the time factors. However, I believe seriously that we will have to run this rescue along the lines already planned."

"And the Drommian was right about those?"

"You mean, that we plan to get Nick's people to make the repairs? Yes. It's not as ridiculous as Aminadabarlee makes it sound. I've been bringing those people up for nearly sixteen years; they're as intelligent as human beings, judging by their learning rate, and they could certainly splice a few wires."

The officer looked doubtful.

"As long as they splice the *right* wires," he muttered. "What will they use for insulation?"

"There's a glue they make—I showed them how, after some experiment—from animal scales. We'll have to make sure it's a nonconductor, but I'm not greatly worried about that."

"Even though you think there's sulfuric acid in their body fluids?"

"I said, not *greatly* worried," admitted Raeker. "The main problem right now is bringing the parties together. You're sure you can't get me a closer fix on the robot and the 'scaphe?"

"Quite sure. They're putting out different wave lengths, and I have no means of finding the dispersion factor of the planet's atmosphere in that part of the spectrum, let alone getting the precise depth of the atmosphere itself or cutting down the inherent uncertainty of radio directional measurements. The chances, as I told you, are about fifty-fifty that the two are within forty miles of each other, and about nine out of ten that they're not over a hundred miles apart. Better than that I can't do, without radiations neither machine is equipped to transmit."

"All right. I'll just have to get information from Easy, and try to match it in with Nick's maps. At least, they don't have to get too close under our guidance; Nick will be able to see the 'scaphe's lights for miles." The officer nodded, and the two fell silent, watching the live screen. Nothing could be seen in it; if Easy was awake, as she had said she would be, she was not in the control room. Occasionally the men could hear a faint bumping or scraping sound; presumably the ship was still being carried with a current, but no landmark had attracted the girl's attention as being worth reporting.

Raeker finally went to sleep in his chair. The officer stayed awake, but the only message he received was to the effect that Easy was going to sleep and Aminadorneldo was taking over the watch. Nothing excited him, either, it seemed; the speaker remained silent after the human girl signed off.

For hour after hour the bathyscaphe bumped merrily on its way. Sometimes it stopped for a moment, sometimes for minutes on end; always the journey resumed, as vagaries in the current dislodged it from whatever barred its path. Easy woke up again, and attended to the problem of breakfast. Later she prepared a rather unappetizing dinner—so she said, anyway. Aminadorneldo was polite about it, blaming the deficiencies on the synthesizers. There's not too much one can do with amino acids, fats, and dextrose, even if vitamin powders are available for seasoning. Tenebra's long night wore on; Raeker served another watch in the robot's control room, bringing Nick and Fagin to a point which he believed was fairly close to the rest of the party from the village. A single night on a planet which takes nearly a hundred hours to rotate can become rather boring—though it doesn't have to be, Raeker thought wryly, as he recalled the one when Swift had made his raid.

Things looked up after sunrise—unfortunately, since he was getting sleepy again. Nick definitely recognized the ground over which they were passing, and stated flatly that they would meet his friends in another two hours; Raeker's relief arrived, and had to be given an extremely detailed briefing; and a message came from the communications room that the bathyscaphe seemed to have stopped.

"Will you please ask Lieutenant Wellenbach if he can have visual communication rigged up between his office and this room?" Raeker asked the messenger who brought this information. "It begins to look as though I'll have to be talking to the bathyscaphe and my pupils at the same time in the near future.'"

"Certainly, sir," replied the messenger. "There'll be no particular difficulty about that, I'm sure."

"All right. I'm going up to the comm room now to hear Easy's report; I'll come back here when the set is rigged."

"But shouldn't you get some sleep, Doctor?" asked his relief.

"I should, but I can't afford to for a while. You stay on duty after I come back, and stop me if I start to do anything really silly."

"All right." The graduate student shrugged his shoulders. Raeker knew he was not being very sensible, but he couldn't bring himself to leave the scenes of action at the moment. He headed for the communication chamber at top speed.

Rich and Aminadabarlee were there. The human diplomat had apparently calmed his Drommian colleague down, at least for the time being, since Raeker's entry produced no fireworks. Easy was speaking as the biologist came in, and he said nothing until she had finished.

". . . minutes since we last moved. It's no lighter outside, but we're not being rocked so hard; I think the current is weaker. It's after sunrise, if I've been keeping track of time properly, so I guess the water's boiling away." She paused, and Raeker made his presence known.

"I take it, Easy, that neither you nor 'Mina saw any living creatures in the water while you were drifting."

"Nothing but plants, or what I guess were plants."

"How about right now?"

"Still nothing."

"Then my guess is you haven't yet reached the ocean. There were definitely animals there, according to Nick—of course, I suppose they might be frightened by your lights. Would you be willing to put them out for five minutes or so, then turn them on suddenly to catch anything which might have approached?"

"All right, as long as you don't mind the control room lights on. There aren't any windows here, so they shouldn't matter. I'd be afraid to turn them out; I might hit the wrong switch in the dark when it was time to turn them on again."

"You're quite right. I never thought of that."

"I've thought of a lot of things the last three weeks, down here."

For an instant the light-hearted mask she had been holding for the benefit of her young companion slipped a trifle, and all the men saw a miserable, terrified twelve-year-old whose self-control was near its limit. Rich bit his lip and clenched his fists; the other human beings avoided his eyes. Aminadabarlee showed no emotion; Raeker wondered whether he felt any. Then the mask was back in place, and the merry-hearted youngster they had all known before the accident turned to the Drommian child.

"'Mina, will you go to the window in the big lab? Call when you're there, and I'll turn off the outside lights."

"All right, Easy." The long body crossed the men's field of view and vanished again. Then his piping voice came from the other room, and the girl's fingers flicked the light switches.

"Is it dark outside now, 'Mina?"

"Yes, Easy. I can't see anything."

"All right. Tell me if you do; well keep it dark for a while. Dr. Raeker, is 'Mina's father there?"

"Yes, Miss Rich." Aminadabarlee answered for himself.

"Perhaps you'd better tell me and Dr. Raeker how long it takes your people's eyes to get used to the dark." Not for the first time, Raeker wondered what combination of heredity and upbringing had given Rich such an amazing child. He had known students ten years her senior whose minds would have been lagging far behind—she was thinking of important points sooner than Raeker himself, and he didn't have her worries. . .

He brought his mind back to the present when she called his name.

"Dr. Raeker, 'Mina couldn't see anything. Maybe five minutes wasn't enough for your sea animals to get over their scare, of course."

"Maybe," admitted Raeker. "Maybe they're just not interested in the bathyscaphe, for that matter. However, I think we'll assume for the present that you haven't reached the sea yet. It will be interesting to see whether you're in a lake or stranded high and dry when the rain evaporates this morning. In either case, get us as complete a description of the country around as you possibly can."

"I know. We'll do our best."

"We're rigging up an arrangement that will let you talk more or less directly to Nick, when you're in a position to give him directions, so you won't have to trust my relaying of your reports. It should be ready soon."

"That's good. I've wanted to talk to him myself ever since I saw you in the robot control room. It looked like fun. But can't I talk to him without going through you, if he finds me? Doesn't this ship have outside mikes and speakers?"

"Oh, yes. Mr. Sakiiro will tell you how to turn them on. This is for the time before he finds you."

"All right. We'll call you again as soon as the water's gone. 'Mina's hungry, and so am I." Raeker sat back and dozed for a few minutes; then he realized that he, too, was hungry, and took care of the situation. By this time he really wanted to sleep; but a call on the intraship system informed him that the communication equipment he had requested was ready for use. Sleepy or not, he had to try it out, so he went back to the robot control room. It was a good many hours before he left it again.

Nick and Fagin had just rejoined their friends at the new camping spot, and Nick was bringing the others up to date on events. Naturally, Raeker had to listen carefully; there was always the chance that Nick had seen things in a different light from the human observer. It had been known to happen; a human education had not given the Tenebrites human minds.

This time Nick's report showed no signs of such difference, but Raeker had still to learn what the others had done. Since this, as Nick had planned, involved a great deal of mapping, some hours were spent hearing the various reports. It was customary for the maps to be shown to the robot for photographing in the *Vindemiatrix;* then each was explained in detail by the one who had drawn it, since not all the information could be crowded onto the paperlike leaves or summarized in conventional mapping symbols. These verbal accounts were recorded as spoken, and as a rule immediately pre-empted by the geological crew. Since the present area was very peculiar in that it lay close to the sea and was largely submerged each night, a great deal of time was spent in bringing the men's maps and charts up to date.

Too much time, in fact.

Raeker's relief had not received, perhaps, a really clear idea of the current danger from Swift; and Raeker himself had not given the matter a thought since his return to the observation room. Neither had thought to advise Nick to have anyone on the lookout for danger, and it was sheer chance that the danger was spotted in time.

Jane was telling her tale, and everyone else was listening and comparing her map with his own, when Betsey caught sight of something. It was just for an instant, and some distance away, showing among the shrubs on a hilltop. She knew the Teacher could not have seen it; she was aware that her own vision equipment had superior resolving powers to his, though she didn't know the terminology. Her first impulse was to shout a warning, but fortunately before she yielded to it she got a better glimpse of the thing on the hill. That was enough for identification. It was a creature just like herself; and since all of Fagin's community was standing around the teacher, that meant it must be one of Swift's warriors. How he had gotten there so soon after things dried up she couldn't guess at the moment.

Speaking softly so as not to interrupt Jane, she called to Nick and John, who were closest.

"Don't make any move that would let him know you see him, but one of the cave men is watching us from the hill three quarters of a mile west-north-west. What should we do about it?"

Nick thought tensely for a moment.

"Just one is all I see. How about you?"

"Same here."

"You've been around here, and I haven't. Is it possible to go down the south or east side of this hill we're on and make a long circuit so as to get on the other side of him without being seen?" Both John and Betsey thought for several seconds, reconstructing in their minds the regions they had mapped in the last day and a half. They spoke almost together, and in almost the same words.

"Yes, from either side."

"All right, do it. Leave the group here casually—you'd both better go together; the herd is on the south side of the hill, and I would judge that some of the beasts are in his line of vision. You can go down and drive them around out of his sight, and we'll hope he thinks you're just doing an ordinary herding job. Once you and the cattle are out of his sight, get around behind him as best you can, and bring him here, preferably alive. I'd like to know how he got here so soon, and so would Fagin, I'm sure."

"Are you going to tell him, or the others?"

"Not yet. They'll act more natural if they don't know. Besides, there are still a couple of reports to be given, and Fagin never likes that to be interrupted, you know."

"I know he usually doesn't, but this seemed a sort of special case."

"Special or not, let's surprise him with your prisoner. Take axes, by the way; they seemed to impress those folks a lot, and maybe he'll give up more easily."

"All right." John and Betsey pulled up their resting legs and started casually downhill toward the herd. None of the others appeared to notice them, and Nick did his best to imitate their attitude as the two scouts disappeared from sight.

# VII. ACQUISITION; INQUISITION; INSTRUCTION

Neither Raeker nor his assistant paid any attention to the departure of John and his companion. They were much too busy operating cameras and recorders, for one reason. Easy and her companion could now watch the group on the surface indirectly, but neither of them was familiar enough with the routine activities of Fagin's pupils to notice anything out of the ordinary. Besides, they were paying very close attention to the geographical reports, in the somewhat unreasonable hope of being able to recognize part of the land described.

For the bathyscaphe was now high and dry. The river down which it had been carried had vanished with the coming day, and the ship had rolled rather uncomfortably—though, fortunately, very slowly—to the foot of a hillock which Easy had promptly named Mount Ararat. The children were having a little trouble, since they had not only had their first visual contact with natives, via the observation room of the *Vindemiatrix*, but also their first look at the solid surface of Tenebra—if one excepts the bottom of a lake and a river. They were covering both scenes as well as they could, one at the windows while the other was at the plate, but each was trying to keep the other filled in verbally on the other part, with confusing results. Their shouted words were coming through to Raeker and the others in the observation room, and were adding their little bit to the confusion there. Raeker didn't dare cut them off, partly for reasons of their own morale and partly because it was always possible that the one at the windows would have something material to report. He hoped the recording of the native reports would be intelligible to the geologists.

Jane finished her account, was asked a question or two by Raeker on points he had not fully taken in, and then settled back to let Oliver show his map. Raeker's assistant photographed it, Raeker himself made sure that the recording tape was still feeding properly, and the two relaxed once more—or came as close to relaxation as the local confusion permitted. Raeker was almost ready to decide that he needn't stay, and to catch up on his overdue sleep.

He had not actually said anything about it, though, when the cave scout caught sight of John. Within three seconds after that, the biologist lost all intention of leaving.

The scout reacted practically instantaneously. He had been crouching as low in the vegetation as his anatomy permitted; now he leaped to his walking legs and started traveling. John was south and west of him, Fagin and the rest south and east; he headed north. Immediately Betsey rose into view in that direction, and he stopped in momentary confusion. Nick, who had never lost sight of the fellow's crest since Betsey had first pointed him out, interpreted the situation correctly even though he could not see John and Betsey. He sprang to his walking legs, interrupting Oliver unceremoniously, and began issuing orders. The others were surprised, but reacted with relatively little confusion; and within a few seconds the whole group was streaming down the hillside toward the point where the cave-dweller had vanished, leaving the human observers to shout futile questions through the speakers of their robot. Seeing that words were useless, Raeker started the robot in the same direction as his pupils, and used language which made Easy raise his eyebrows as the machine was steadily left further and further behind. Nick and his friends disappeared over the hilltop where the scout had been hiding, and not even their shouts could be heard over Raeker's voice in the control room.

It was Easy who turned his words into more constructive channels, less because she was shocked than because she was curious.

"Dr. Raeker? Did I hear one of them say that there was a cave-dweller to catch? How did one get there so soon? I thought you said you'd left them behind at that river." Her question was so exactly the one Raeker had been asking himself that he had nothing to say in reply for a moment; but at least he stopped talking, and had the grace to turn slightly red.

"That's what it sounded like to me, Easy. I don't know the way they found us any more than you do; I have always supposed this was a long way outside their home grounds, so I don't see how they could have known a short cut around the river—for that matter, I don't see how there could be such a thing; that river was over a mile wide. We'll have to wait until Nick and the others come back; maybe they'll have a prisoner we can question. I suppose that's his idea; I think he said 'catch,' not 'kill.' "

"That's right; he did. Well, we'll be able to see them in a minute or two, when the robot gets up this hill, unless they've gone over another one in the meantime."

It turned out that they hadn't; the human watchers had a very good view of the chase, not that it was much to see. The valley into which the cave scout had fled was almost entirely ringed with the low, rounded hills so typical of much of Tenebra; John and Betsey had managed to get to the tops of two of these before being seen, so that they had a considerable advantage on the cave-dweller when it came to running. He had made one or two attempts to race out through the wide gaps between Betsey and John and between them and the main group, but had seen after only a few moments on each dash that he was being headed off. When the robot came in sight he was standing near the center of the valley while Fagin's people closed in slowly around him. He was rather obviously getting ready for a final dash through any gap that might present itself, after his pursuers were close enough to have sacrificed their advantage of elevation. He might also be planning to fight; he was two feet taller than Nick and his friends, and had two efficient-looking short spears.

Nick seemed to have picked up a smattering of military tactics, not to mention diplomacy, however. He halted his people a good fifty yards from the big cave-dweller, and spread them out into an evenly spaced circle. With this completed to his satisfaction, he shifted to Swift's language.

"Do you think you can get away from us?"

"I don't know, but some of you will be sorry you tried to stop me," was the answer.

"What good will that do you, if you are killed?" The scout seemed unable to find an answer to this; in fact, the very question seemed to startle him. The matter had seemed so obvious that he had never faced the task of putting it into words. He was still trying when Nick went on, "You know that Fagin said he was willing to teach Swift whatever he wanted to know. He doesn't want fighting. If you'll put your spears down and come to talk with him, you won't be hurt."

"If your Teacher is so willing to help, why did he run away?" the other shot back. Nick had his answer ready.

"Because you had taken him away from us, and we want him to teach us too. When I came to your caves to get him, he came with me to help me get away. He carried me through the river, where I could not have gone alone. When you first attacked our village, he wanted us to talk to you instead of fighting; but you gave us no chance." He fell silent, judging that his antagonist would need time to think. However, another question came at once.

"Will you do anything your Teacher tells you?"

"Yes." Nick didn't mention the times he had hesitated about obeying Fagin's commands; quite honestly, he didn't think of them at that moment.

"Then let me hear him tell you not to harm me. He is coming now. I will wait here, but I will keep my weapons, until I am sure I won't need them."

"But you don't know his language; you won't know what he's telling us."

"He learned a few of our words while he was with us, though he couldn't say them very well. I think I can ask him if he is going to hurt me, and I'll know if he says yes or no." The scout fell silent and stood watching the approach of the robot, still keeping a firm grip on his spears with two hands each. He was ready to stab, not throw.

Even Raeker could see that readiness as the robot glided into the circle, and felt a little uneasy; he would be a good two seconds slow in reacting to anything that happened. Not for the first time, he wished that the *Vindemiatrix* were orbiting just outside Tenebra's atmosphere, with three or four relay stations to take care of horizon troubles.

"What's happened, Nick? Is he going to fight?"

"Not if you can convince him it isn't necessary," replied Nick. He went on to give a precis of the scout's recent statements. "I don't quite know what to do with him myself, now that we have him," he finished.

"I wouldn't say you really had him, yet," was Raeker's dry rejoinder, "but I see the problem. If we let him go, Swift will be on us in a matter of hours, or in a day or so at the outside. If we don't, we'll have to keep a continuous watch on him, which would be a nuisance, and he might get away anyway. Killing him would of course be inexcusable."

"Even after what happened to Alice and Tom?"

"Even then, Nick. I think we're going to have to put this fellow to a use, and face the fact that Swift will know where we are. Let me think." The robot fell silent, though the men controlling it did not; plans were being proposed, discussed, and rejected at a great rate while the natives waited. Easy had not been cut off, but she offered no advice. Even the diplomats, able to hear from the communication room which they still haunted, kept quiet for once.

The cave-dweller, of course had been unable to follow the conversation between Nick and the Teacher, and after the first minute or so of silence he asked for a translation. Somehow he managed to make the request in such a way that Nick felt he was repairing an omission rather than granting a favor when he provided the requested information.

"Fagin is deciding what is best to do. He says that we must not kill you."

"Have him tell me that himself. I will understand him."

"One does not interrupt the Teacher when he is thinking," replied Nick. The cave-dweller seemed impressed; at least, he said nothing more until the robot came back on the air.

"Nick." Raeker's voice boomed into the dense atmosphere, "I want you to translate very carefully what I have to say to this fellow. Make it word for word, as nearly as the language difference will allow; and think it over yourself, because there will be some information I haven't had time to give you yet."

"All right, Teacher." Everyone in the circle switched attention to the robot; but if the scout in the center realized this, he at least made no effort to take advantage of the fact. He, too, listened, as intently as though he were trying to make sense out of the human speech as well as Nick's translation. Raeker started slowly, with plenty of pauses for Nick to do his job.

"You know," he began, "that Swift wanted me at his place so that I could teach him and his people to make fires, and keep herds, and the other things I have already taught my own people. I was willing to do that, but Swift thought, from something Nick said, that my people would object, so he came fighting when it wasn't necessary.

"That's not really important, now, except for the fact that it delayed something important to Swift as well as to us. Up until now, all I've been able to give is knowledge. I was the only one of my people here, and I can never go back where I came from, so that I couldn't get more things to give.

"Now others of my people have come. They are riding in a great thing that they made; you haven't any words for it, since I never gave them to Nick's people and I don't think Swift's people have any such things. It was something we made, as you make a bucket or a spear, which is able to carry us from one place to another; for the place from which I came is so far away that no one could ever walk the distance, and is far above so that only a floater could even go in the right direction. The people who came were going to be able to come and go in this machine, so that they could bring things like better tools to all of you, taking perhaps things you were willing to give in exchange. However, the machine did not work quite properly; it was like a spear with a cracked head. It came down to where you live, but we found that it could not float back up again. My people cannot live outside it, so they aren't able to fix it. We need help from Nick's people and, if you will give it, from yours as well. If you can find this machine in which my friends are caught, and learn from me how to fix it, they will be able to go back up once more and bring things for you all; if you can't or won't, my people will die here, and there will not even be knowledge for you—for some day I will die, too, you know.

"I want you to take this message to Swift, and then, if he will let you, come back with his answer. I would like him and all his people to help hunt for the machine; and when it is found, Swift's people and Nick's can

help in fixing it. There won't need to be any more fighting. Will you do
that?"

Nick had given this talk exactly as it came, so far as his knowledge of
Swift's language permitted. The scout was silent for half a minute or so at
the end. He was still holding his spears firmly, but Raeker felt that his
attitude with them was a trifle less aggressive. It may have been wishful
thinking, of course; human beings are as prone to believe the things they
wish were true as Drommians are to believe what occurs to them first.

Then the scout began asking questions, and Raeker's estimate of his
intelligence went up several notches; he had been inclined to dismiss the
fellow as a typical savage.

"Since you know what is wrong with your friends and their machine,
you must be able to talk to them some way."

"Yes, we—I can talk to them."

"Then how is it you need to look for them? Why can't they tell you
where they are?"

"They don't know. They came down to a place they had never seen
before, and floated on a lake for five days. Last night they drifted down a
river. They were at the bottom, and couldn't see where they were going;
and anyway they didn't know the country—as I said, they never saw it
before. The river is gone now, and they can see around, but that does no
good."

"If you can hear them talk, why can't you go to them anyway? I can
find anything I can hear."

"We talk with machines, just as we travel. The machines make a sort
of noise which can only be heard by another machine, but which travels
very much farther than a voice. Their machine can talk to one in the place
where I came from, and then that one can talk to me; but it is so far away
that it can't tell exactly where either of us is. All we can do is let them tell
us what sort of country they can see; then I can tell you, and you can start
hunting."

"You don't even know how far away they are, then."

"Not exactly. We're pretty sure it's not very far—not more than two
or three days' walk, and probably less. When you start looking for them
we can have them turn on their brightest lights, like these—" the robot's
spots flamed briefly— "and you'll be able to see them from a long distance. They'll have some lights on anyway, as a matter of fact."

The cave-dweller thought for another minute or so, then shifted the
grip on his spears to "trail." "I will give your words to Swift, and if he has
words for you they will be brought. Will you stay here?"

The question made Raeker a trifle uneasy, but he saw no alternative
to answering "yes." Then another point occurred to him.

"If we did not stay here, would it take you long to find us?" he asked. "We noticed that you got to this side of the river and into sight of our group much more quickly than we had expected. Did you have some means of crossing the river before day?"

"No," the other replied with rather surprising frankness. "The river bends north not far inland from the place where you walked through it and goes in that direction for a good number of miles. A number of us were sent along it, with orders to stop at various points, cross as soon as it dried up, and walk toward the sea to find traces of you."

"Then others presumably crossed our trail—all those who were stationed farther south—and located us."

"No doubt. They may be watching now, or they may have seen you attack me and gone off to tell Swift."

"You knew about the bend in the river. Your people are familiar with the country this far from your caves?"

"We have never hunted here. Naturally, anyone can tell which way a river is going to flow and where there are likely to be hills and valleys."

"What my people call an eye for country. I see. Thank you; you had better go on and give the message to Swift before he arrives with another crowd of spears to avenge the attack on one of his men."

"All right. Will you answer one question for me first? Sometimes you say 'I' and sometimes 'we' even when you obviously don't mean yourself and these people here. Why is that? Is there more than one of you inside that thing?"

Nick did not translate this question; he answered it himself.

"The Teacher has always talked that way," he said. "We've sometimes wondered about it, too; but when we asked him, he didn't explain—just said it wasn't important yet. Maybe Swift can figure it out." Nick saw no harm in what he would have called psychology if he had known the word.

"Maybe." The scout started south without another word, and the rest of the group, who had long since broken their circle and gathered around the Teacher, watched him go.

"That sounded good, Dr. Raeker. Should we keep the spotlights on just in case, from now on?" Easy Rich's voice broke the silence.

"I wouldn't, just yet," Raeker said thoughtfully. "I wish I could be sure I wanted Swift to find you, instead of merely wanting to keep him from attacking us."

"What?" Aminadabarlee's voice was shriller, and much louder, even than usual. "Are you admitting that you are using my son as bait to keep those savages away from your little pet project down there? That you regard those ridiculously shaped natives as more important than a civilized being, simply because you've been training them for a few years? I have heard that human beings were cold-blooded, and scientists even more so than the general run, but I would never have believed this even of human beings. This is the absolute limit. Councillor Rich, I must ask your indulgence for the loan of our speedster; I am going to Dromm and start our own rescue work. I have trusted you *men* too long. I am through with that—and so is the rest of the galaxy!"

"Excuse me, sir." Raeker had come to have a slightly better grasp of the problem the Drommian represented. "Perhaps, if you do not trust me, you will at least listen to Councillor Rich, whose daughter is in the same situation as your son. He may point out to you that the 'ridiculous natives' whose safety I have in mind are the only beings in the universe in a position, or nearly in a position, to rescue those children; and he may have noticed that I did not tell the savage even the little I heard of Easy and 'Mina's description of the country around them. I am sure we will appreciate your planet's help, but do you think it will possibly come in time? Before the human girl is permanently injured by extra gravity, and your son has exceeded your race's time limit under vitamin and oxygen deficiency? I am not asking these questions to hurt you, but in an effort to get the best help you can give. If there is anything more you can do than keep your son's courage up by staying where he can see and hear you, please let us know."

Rich's face was visible behind the Drommian's in the jury-rigged vision screen, and Raeker saw the human diplomat give a nod and an instantly suppressed smile of approval. He could think of nothing to add to his speech, and wisely remained silent. Before Aminadabarlee found utterance, however, Easy came in with a plea of her own.

"Don't be angry with Dr. Raeker, please; 'Mina and I can see what he's doing, and we like Nick, too." Raeker wondered how much of this was true; he wasn't as sure himself as he would like to have been of what he was doing, and the children had not yet talked directly to Nick, though they had been listening to him and his people for a couple of hours. Easy, of course, was a diplomat's daughter. Raeker had learned by now that her mother had died when she was a year old, and she had traveled with her father ever since. She seemed to be growing into a competent diplomat in her own right. "It doesn't really matter if Swift does find us," she went on. "What can he do to hurt us, and why should he want to?"

"He threatened to use fire on the robot if it didn't come with him to the cave village," retorted the Drommian, "and if he does the same to the 'scaphe's hull when you fail to tell him something he wants to know, you'll be in some trouble."

"But he knew that Fagin didn't speak his language, and was very patiently teaching it during the three weeks or so it was in his power; why should he be less patient with us? We're perfectly willing to teach him anything we know, and we can talk to him with less trouble than Dr. Raeker could—at least, there won't be the delay."

A burst of shrill sound from Aminadorneldo followed and, presumably, supported Easy's argument; Aminadabarlee cooled visibly. Raeker wondered how long it would last. At least, things were safe politically for the moment; he turned his attention back to Tenebra and to Nick.

That worthy had started his group back toward the original meeting place, with two running ahead—the herd had been unprotected quite long enough. Nick himself was standing beside the robot, apparently waiting for comment or instructions. Raeker had none to give, and covered with a question of his own.

"How about it, Nick? Will he come back? Or more accurately, will Swift go along with us?"

"You know as well as I."

"No, I don't. You spent a long time with Swift and his people; you know him if any of us do. Was I right in playing on his desire for things we could bring him? I realize he wanted to know about things like fire, but don't you think it was for what he saw could be done with it?"

"It seems likely," admitted Nick, "but I don't see how it's possible to be sure of what anyone's thinking or what he's going to do."

"I don't either, though some of my people keep trying." The two started after the rest of the group, scarcely noticing the minor quake that snapped a few of the more brittle plants around them. Nick almost unthinkingly gathered firewood as he went, a habit of years which had developed in the old village after the more accessible fuel near the hilltop had been exhausted. He had quite a stack in his four arms by the time they rejoined the others. This was piled with the rest; the herd was checked and the strays brought back together; and then Fagin called a meeting.

"You all heard what I told Swift's man, about the machine which was stranded somewhere here with some of my people in it. If it is not found and fixed shortly, those people will die. You know as well as I that rescue of people in danger is of more importance than almost anything else; and for that reason, we are going to drop all other activities, except those needed actually to stay alive, while we look for that ship.

"I will give you a description, as completely as possible, of the place where they are. We'll check all our maps for similarity—I'll help you there; I can do it faster—and then you'll go out in pairs to check all likely spots. If we don't find them, mapping will proceed as rapidly as possible, to the exclusion of all other scientific activities.

"For the rest of today, Betsey and Nick will take care of camp and herd; search teams will be Oliver and Dorothy, John and Nancy, and Jim and Jane. I will assign an area to each of the teams as soon as the maps have been checked; in the meantime, you might all be gathering firewood for tonight." The group scattered obediently.

The geologists in the *Vindemiatrix* had for some time been matching, or trying to match, Easy's not too complete description of the bathyscaphe's environs; they had come up with four or five possible locations, none of which made them really happy. However, when a sixth possibility was finally settled on, Raeker called the exploring teams back to the robot and assigned two of the hopeful areas to each team. These were all in the general direction of the old village, naturally, since the mapping had gone on radially from that point in the two or three years the cartography project had been going. They were all on the nearer side of that region, however, since the men who had done, the matching had been influenced by the realization that the 'scaphe must have drifted seaward on the night that it moved. It seemed likely, therefore, that a day to go, a day to explore, and a day to return would suffice for this step of the plan. By that time, Swift might be back with his people, and the rate of search could be stepped up. That was why Nick had been kept behind at the camp site; he might be needed as an interpreter.

The instructions were heard, the villagers' own maps were checked, weapons were examined, and the parties set out. Nick and Betsey, standing beside the robot, watched them go; and far away, Raeker finally left the observing room to get some sleep. The diplomats stayed awake, chatting with their children as the latter described the animals which came into sight from time to time. In this relatively dull fashion the rest of the ship's day, a night, and part of another day were spent, while the search teams plodded sturdily toward their assigned areas.

This was the twenty-seventh ship's day since the accident to the bathyscaphe, the afternoon of the seventh day as far as Nick and his people were concerned. The children were understandably impatient; both fathers had to explain again and again how small were their chances of being found at the very beginning of the search. On this day, at least, human and Drommian were in remarkably close accord. In spite of this unity of effort, however, the children tended to spend more and more time at the windows as the day drew on, and from time to time even Easy brought up the subject of using the spotlights to guide the searchers who should be approaching. Her father kept reminding her that Raeker had advised against it; but eventually Raeker withdrew his objection.

"It'll make the kid feel more a part of the operation," he said in an aside to Rich, "and I can't see that there's much, if any, more chance of Swift's sighting them than of our own people's doing it at the moment. Let her play with the lights."

Easy happily made full use of the permission, and the bathyscaphe blazed far brighter than daylight—since daylight was utter darkness to human eyes—at Tenebra's surface. Rich was not too happy about the permission; it seemed to him encouraging the youngster in her unreasonable hope of an early rescue, and he feared the effects of disappointment.

"Listen to them," he growled. "Yelling to each other every time something moves within half a mile. If they could see any farther it would be still worse—thank goodness they're using their eyes instead of the photocells of the robot. That'll last until they get sleepy; then they'll start again when they wake up—"

"They should be under water by then," pointed out Raeker mildly.

"And drifting again, I suppose. That's when everything will go to pieces at once, and we'll have a couple of screaming kids who'll probably start hitting switches right and left in the hope some miracle will bring them home."

"I don't know about the Drommian, but I think you do your daughter a serious injustice," replied Raeker. "I've never known much about kids, but she strikes me as something pretty remarkable for her age. Even if you can't trust her, you'd better not let her know it."

"I realize that, and no one trusts her more than I do," was the weary answer. "Still, she *is* only a kid, and a lot of adults would have cracked before now. I can name one who's on the edge of it. Listen to them, down there."

Aminadorneldo's piercing tones were echoing from the speaker.

"There's something on this side, Easy! Come and see this one."

"All right, 'Mina. Just a minute." Easy's small form could be seen for an instant on the screen, passing through the control room from one side of the ship to the other, calling as she went, "It's probably another of those plant-eating things that are about as big as Nick's people. Remember, the ones we want stand up on end."

"This one does. Look!"

"Where?" Aminadorneldo must have been pointing; there was a moment of silence; then the girl's voice, "I still don't see anything; just a lot of bushes."

"It looked just like Nick. It stood beside that bush for a moment and looked at us, and then went away. I saw it."

"Well, if you were right, it'll come back. We'll stand here and watch for it."

Rich looked at Raeker and shook his head dismally.

"That'll—" he began, but got no further. His sentence was interrupted by a sudden shriek from the speaker, so shrill that for a moment neither of them could tell who had uttered it.

# VIII. RADIATION; EVAPORATION; ADVECTION

John and Nancy made steady progress into the west. Their journey so far had not been particularly difficult, though most of it had been made over ground not yet surveyed. They had fought with floaters and other carnivores a reasonable number of times, eaten the fruits of their victories when they felt hungry enough, and talked more or less incessantly. The talk was mostly speculation; they had learned more about the nature of their Teacher in the last few days than in the preceding sixteen years, but what they had learned seemed only to give rise to more questions. They were young enough to be surprised at this; hence the steady conversation, which was interrupted only by their reaching a region which seemed to match part of their map.

"We must have kept our direction pretty well," Nancy said after comparing the hills around them to those indicated on the sheet. "We were trying to hit the mapped region about here," she pointed, "and seem to be only a dozen miles to the north. Oliver mapped this place; it hasn't changed enough to be really doubtful. We can head south, and be sure of ourselves in a few more miles."

"All right," agreed John. "You know, even if we are still a good many miles from either of our search areas, it wouldn't actually hurt to keep our eyes open for the machine."

Nancy sent the ripple that passed for a shrug flickering down her scales. "It's hardly worth making a special effort. We'll be able to see it miles away, if it's as bright as Fagin said. I think we'd better concentrate on the map, just now, until we're sure we're where we're supposed to be."

"Fagin would have had something to say about that sentence," muttered John, "but I suppose you're right. Let's get on."

Two miles, twenty-five minutes, one brief fight, and one longish quake later they were in a position to feel sure of themselves. Uniform as the solution-molded surface of Tenebra was, and rapid as its changes were, the present region matched the maps too closely to be coincidence. They spent a few minutes deciding whether it would be better to start gathering firewood for the night which was not too many hours away or move closer to their first search area so as to waste less time in the morning, settled on the second alternative, and went on.

Nightfall was even closer when they stopped simultaneously. Neither needed to speak, since it was quite evident to both that they had seen the same thing. Far to the south and somewhat to the west a light was shining.

For several seconds they stood looking at it. What they could see was not particularly brilliant—it was just enough to be noticeable; but light other than daylight on Tenebra can be explained only in a certain very few ways. So, at least, Fagin's students supposed.

After a moment's staring, they got out the maps once more and tried to judge where the source of the light might be. This was difficult, however, because it was next to impossible to estimate the distance. The source itself was not directly visible, just the glow which fires, spotlights, and Altair itself produced in Tenebra's soupy envelope. The direction was plain enough, but it seemed likely that the actual source was either outside mapped territory altogether or in the poorly covered region Nick had done during the trip which had discovered the cave village. It seemed equally likely that they could not possibly reach the place before rainfall, but after the briefest of discussions they agreed to start out.

The going was normal at first, but it gradually got rougher. This agreed with what they remembered of Nick's report on his trip. They also recalled his mention of a life form which lived in holes and was dangerous to passers-by, but they encountered no sign of it just then. The light kept getting brighter, which was encouraging, but for several hours they failed to get any better idea of what was making it.

Then they began to get an impression that it was coming from a point above their level, and after another half hour they were both quite sure of this. The fact was hard to understand; Fagin had said that the bathyscaphe couldn't fly because it was broken, and there had been no mention of a hill—at least, not of anything unusual in that respect—in the description of the machine's environment. As a matter of fact, they recalled, it had been stated to lie at the *foot* of a hill.

Then John remembered Nick's tale of a remarkably high hill in the region, and the two got out their maps once more. It seemed possible though far from certain, after careful checking, that the light was on the hill; but if that were the case it seemed to dispose of any remaining chance that they had found the bathyscaphe. Since the only other possibility they could envision was that Swift's people were there with a fire, a slight problem developed.

It would be raining before long, and travel without torches would be impossible. If the area ahead were actually a camp of Swift's cave-dwellers, approaching it with torches would simply be asking for capture. Of course, the chief might have accepted Fagin's offer, so that they would technically be allies; but from what John and Nancy knew of Swift they didn't want to take the chance. From one point of view, there was no reason to approach at all, since they were searching for the bathyscaphe rather than scouting the cave men; but this phase of the matter didn't occur to either of them. If it had, they would probably have insisted that they weren't *sure* the light wasn't from the crippled machine. Anyway, they kept trying to plan a method of approach to the light.

It was Nancy who finally worked it out. John didn't like the plan and didn't trust it. Nancy pointed out truthfully that she knew more physics than he did, and even if he didn't know what she was talking about he ought to take her word for it. He replied, equally truthfully, that he might be a mathematician rather than a chemist but even he knew enough about rain not to accept ideas like hers uncritically. Nancy finally won her point by the simple process of starting toward the light alone, giving John the choice of coming or staying behind. He came.

Raeker would have liked to hear that argument. He had named the little creatures who had emerged from the stolen eggs quite arbitrarily, and still had no idea of the actual gender of any of them. Nancy's display of a human feminine characteristic would have been fascinating if not very conclusive.

John watched the sky uneasily as they strode onward. Inwardly he knew perfectly well that the rain was not due for a while yet; but the mere fact of Nancy's defiance of the phenomenon made him abnormally conscious of it. By the time the first drops actually appeared far above, they were close enough to the light to see that something lay between them and the actual source—it was shining from behind a barrier of some sort, presumably a hill.

"Should we go over, or around?" John asked, when this fact became evident. "If we go up, we'll run into the rain sooner."

"That's a good reason for doing it," retorted Nancy. "If it is the cave people they won't be expecting us from that direction, and you'll see all the sooner that I'm right. Besides, I've never been up a really high hill, and Nick said this one was two or three hundred feet tall—remember?"

"I remember, but I'm not as sure as you seem to be that this is the hill he was talking about."

"Look at your map!"

"All right, I know we're close to it, but his notes were pretty rough; you know that as well as I do. There never was time to make a decent map of the country he covered, after he got back. We've been fighting or moving practically ever since."

"All right, you needn't make a thesis out of it. Come on." She led the way without waiting for an answer.

For some time there was no appreciable rise in the general ground level, though the number of ordinary hillocks remained about as usual. The first implication that Nancy might be right about the nature of the hill was a change in the nature of the ground underfoot. Instead of the usual feldspar-rich granitic rock, heavily pitted with solution cavities, a darker, much smoother material became predominant. Neither of them had ever seen fresh lava, since Nick had brought back no specimens, and it took time for their feet to get used to it.

The rain was getting very close to the surface now. There was no difficulty in dodging drops, since there was more light coming from ahead than Altair gave at high noon; the trouble was that Nancy was not bothering to dodge them. Theoretically she was right enough; they were still cloudy with oxygen bubbles, and her body heat turned them into perfectly breathable air, but it took a while for John to follow her example. Habits are as hard to break for Tenebrites as for human beings.

Gradually the slope of the dark rock began to increase. They *were* on a hill, and the light was close ahead, now. Rocks were silhouetted sharply against it, not more than a mile in front. Nancy stopped, not because of the rain but to take a final look around; and it was then that they both noticed something else.

In the first place, the raindrops were not falling straight; they were drifting horizontally as they descended, drifting in the same direction as the two were traveling. That was reasonable when one stopped to think; they had known about convection and advection currents almost as long as they could remember. It was the speed that was remarkable; the drops were heading toward the fire at a good two miles an hour. The air current that impelled them could actually be *felt*—and that was a major hurricane, for Tenebra. If the thing ahead was a fire, it was a bigger fire than Fagin's pupils had ever lighted or ever seen.

"If Swift lighted that, he must have touched off a whole map section," remarked John.

Nancy turned to him abruptly. "Johnny! Remember what happened last night, when Nick got the Teacher away from the caves? He *did* light fires over a good part of a section! Do you suppose they could still be burning, and have spread like this?"

"I don't know." John stood still and thought for a moment or two. Then he referred to the map, easily legible in the brilliant light. "I don't see how it could be," he said at length. "We're a lot closer to the caves than we were this morning, but not that close. Besides, the clear rain late at night should have put any fire out if there was no one to tend it."

"But if it were big enough, maybe it would stir up the air so there was always enough oxygen for it—feel this wind on our backs. Have you ever known anything like it?"

"No. Maybe you're right. We can go on and see, though; I still think it's more likely to be Swift. Are you still going to try that idea of yours?"

"Of course. It's all the better, with the wind carrying the drops as fast as this."

"I hope you're as right as you are reasonable." The two went on, somewhat more slowly since it was necessary to follow a rather tortuous path to keep their goal in sight among the drops. These were now reaching the surface in great numbers and remaining liquid, except for those parts most closely exposed to the body heat of the two travelers. It took a little longer than might have been expected, therefore, to get within two hundred yards of the rocks ahead, which from the absence of anything but light beyond them appeared to mark the top of the hill. At this point, Nancy decided that stealth was in order; so she brought the scary part of her plan into operation.

Finding an exceptionally large and still cloudy raindrop drifting downward at no great distance, she deliberately placed herself so as to be enveloped by it as it landed. Naturally, the bottom portion of the fifty-foot spheroid was obliterated at once by her body heat; but further descent of the drop finally hid her from view. The great, foggy blot of liquid began to follow the general pattern of activity of the others, moving slowly toward the light; and Nancy did her best to follow. This was not as easy as it might have been, even though the gas around her was perfectly breathable, since with no view of her surroundings it was nearly impossible to judge the rate of drift of the raindrop. The wind was some help, but not enough, and several times John could see her outline, as she came too close to the edge of the volume of fog. He stayed where he was, not considering it cowardly to see how the experiment turned out before he tried it himself.

In one sense, the trial was a perfect success; that is, Nancy remained conscious as long as the drop lasted. In another, however, there was something lacking. This lay in the failure of the drop to last long enough. Suffering the assault of heat radiation from both Nancy within and the fire ahead, the thing abruptly faded out in a final surge of turbulence, leaving her in full view.

This turned out to be less of a catastrophe than it might have been. For three or four seconds after the vanishing of her concealment Nancy stood perfectly still; then she called out, making no effort to direct her voice away from the light ahead, "Johnny! Here, quick!"

Her companion leaped forward, taking a little but not much less care to dodge raindrops, and came to a halt at her side.

She had stopped perhaps five yards from the edge of a nearly vertical-sided pit, fully two miles across. Her first few seconds of silence had been spent in telling herself how lucky she was that her shelter had not lasted a few seconds longer; then the blast of radiant heat coming from the floor of the crater, a scant hundred feet below, forced her to admit the matter was hardly one of luck. It could be seen from this vantage point that no raindrops at all approached the area except those which drifted up the slope of the hill from outside. The floor glowed visibly all over, and numerous patches were of almost dazzling brilliance. These last looked suspiciously like liquid, though the liquid possessed a remarkably sharp and well-defined surface.

Raeker, or even Easy, would have recognized a volcano at once; but the phenomenon was completely outside the experience and education of Fagin's pupils. Raeker had noted, in passing, Nick's earlier reference to the conical shape of the high hill he had reported; the geologists had also paid some attention to it, and even placed it on the list of things to be investigated more fully; but that was as far as matters had gone. Nick had said nothing to suggest that the thing was active—or rather, nothing the men had recognized as such evidence; he *had* mentioned wind. As a matter of fact, it had not been nearly so violent when he had passed, some three terrestrial months before. Only its size and shape had been worthy of note.

"You know," John remarked after some minutes of silence, "this would be a wonderful place for a village. We wouldn't need to keep fires going."

"How about food?" countered Nancy. "The plants growing on this dark rock are different from the ones we're used to; maybe the cattle wouldn't eat them."

"That would be easy enough to find out—"

"Anyway, that's not the assignment just now. This light obviously isn't what we're looking for, though I admit it's interesting. We'd better get on with the job."

"It's raining," John pointed out, "and there was no suggestion that we should search through the night as well as by day. This would seem a perfect place to sleep, at least."

"That's true enough—" Nancy's agreement was interrupted suddenly. Some three hundred yards to their left, a segment of the pit's edge about fifty yards long and ten or fifteen deep cracked loose with a deafening roar and plunged downward. In that gravity even Tenebra's atmosphere was an ineffective brake, and a good ten or fifteen thousand tons of well-cemented volcanic detritus made its way effortlessly through the red-hot crust of nearly solid lava at the foot of the ledge. The results left no doubt about the liquid state of the hotter material—or would have left none had the two explorers still been watching. They weren't; they were on their way downhill in the direction from which they had come before the mass of rock was completely detached. Even as he ran, John had time to feel lucky that the incident had waited to happen until Nancy had agreed with him about what a good camping spot the place was. Needless to say, he did not mention this aloud. Even John was not bothering to dodge raindrops at the moment, much less talk on irrelevant subjects.

They covered nearly a mile down the slope before stopping. The light was still quite ample to permit reading the maps, and it took only a few minutes to convince them both that this was indeed the tall, conical hill which Nick had reported. With this settled, however, neither could quite decide what to do about it The natural urge was to return to the camp to report the phenomenon to Fagin; against this, however, lay the fact that they had another assignment to complete, which involved life and death.

"This can wait a day," John pointed out. "We can perfectly well camp right here, search our areas tomorrow, and then go back as was planned. We can't drop everything for one new discovery."

"I suppose not," agreed Nancy with some slight reluctance, "but we certainly can't camp here. There isn't enough fuel for a dozen hours on this black stone, to say nothing of the rest of the night; and the raindrops are starting to get clear."

"That I had noticed," replied John. "We'd better get going, then. Just a minute; there's enough here to make a torch. Let's get one started; we may be a little pressed for time later."

Nancy agreed with this observation, and ten minutes later they were on their way once more with John carrying a glowing torch and Nancy the material for two more, all that the vegetation within convenient reach afforded. They headed toward a region which their maps showed as having slightly higher hills than usual, so as to avoid finding themselves in a lake bed before morning. Both were becoming a trifle uneasy, in spite of Nick's earlier success at all-night travel; but they were distracted once more before getting really worried.

Again a light showed ahead of them. It was harder to perceive, since the brilliance from behind was still great, but there was no doubt that a fire of some sort was on one of the hilltops ahead of them.

"Are you going to sneak up on this one the way you did on the other?" queried John.

Nancy glanced at the now dangerously clear raindrops and did not condescend to answer. Her companion had expected none, and after a moment asked a more sensible question.

"What about this torch? If we can see that fire, anyone near it can see us. Do you want to put it out?"

Nancy glanced upward—or rather, shifted her attention in that direction by a subtle alteration in the positions of her visual spines, which acted rather like a radio interferometer system, except that they were sensitive to much shorter wavelengths. "We'd better," she said. "There's plenty of light to dodge the drops."

John shrugged mentally and tossed the glowing piece of wood under a settling raindrop. The two slipped up toward the distant light.

It was an ordinary fire this time, they could see as they approached. Unfortunately, there was no one visible near it, and the vegetation was not dense enough to hide anyone of ordinary size unless he were deliberately seeking to use it for the purpose. This suggested possible trouble, and the two explorers circled the hill on which the blaze stood with the most extreme caution, looking for traces of whoever had been there in the past few hours. Not having the tracking skill of the cave-dwellers, they found no signs of people. After two full circuits and some low-voiced discussion, they were forced to conclude that either whoever made the fire was still on the hill but remarkably well hidden, or else the fire itself had been started by something a trifle unusual. The latter hypothesis would probably not have occurred to them had it not been for their recent experience with the volcano. There seemed no way, however, to decide between the possibilities by reason alone. Closer investigation was in order and, with a constant expectation of hearing the sharp voice of Swift echoing about them, they set to it. Very carefully, examining every bush, they went up the slope.

The climb bore some resemblance to a scientific experiment, in that its completion eliminated both of the hypotheses and left them completely without ideas for a moment. It was only for a moment, however; as the two loomed up beside the small fire, which had quite obviously been laid by intelligent hands, a shout sounded from the next hilltop, three hundred yards away.

"John! Nancy! Where did you come from?" The startled investigators recognized simultaneously the voice of Oliver and the fact that they had been a little hasty in eliminating possibilities; obviously they had missed a trail, since neither Oliver nor Dorothy could fly. Neither said anything about it aloud; each decided in private that the different vegetation of the area was responsible.

When Oliver and his companion came back to the fire from the separate hilltops to which they had taken on sighting John's torch, it quickly transpired that they, too, had seen the light of the volcano and had come to investigate it. Their adventures had been very similar to those of John and Nancy, except that neither of them had tried hiding in raindrops. Oliver and Dorothy had been an hour or so ahead of the others, and had found a good supply of fuel, so they were well set for the night.

"I'll bet Jim and Jane will be with us before the night's over," remarked Nancy when both parties had completed their exchange of information. "Their search areas were even closer to this place than yours, Oliver, and unless they went 'way off course coming across country they must have seen the big light, too."

"Maybe they thought it was better to stick to their assigned job," remarked John.

"Isn't investigating bright lights part of the job?" retorted his partner. "As for me, if they're not here in an hour or two I'm going to start worrying about them. This fire-hill couldn't possibly be missed or ignored, and you know it."

No one had a suitable answer for this, but no one was really impressed by the reasoning, since they had all spent some time in discussion before coming to check the mountain. At any rate, the hours passed without the predicted appearance. If Nancy was worrying, she failed to show it; certainly none of the others were. It was a very quiet night, and there was nothing to worry about. The hours were passing, but that was normal; the light was getting brighter, but there was the peculiar hill to account for that; the rain was decreasing, but the hill might account for that, too. The fire was using up its fuel with unusual speed, but there was plenty of fuel. Doubtless the wind was responsible—none of them had ever experienced such a wind, and an air current one could actually *feel* would no doubt do many queer things. The four explorers stood by their fire and dozed, while the wind grew fiercer.

# IX. Deduction; Education; Experimentation

"Daddy! Dr. Raeker! 'Mina's right; it's Nick!" Easy's voice was close to hysteria. The men glanced at each other, worried frowns on their faces. Rich gestured that Raeker should do the answering, but his expression pleaded eloquently for care. Raeker nodded, and closed his own microphone switch.

"Are you sure it's actually Nick, Easy?" he asked in as matter-of-fact a voice as he could manage. "He's supposed to have stayed at the camp, you know. There are six others actually searching, supposedly in pairs; do you see two of them, there?"

"No," replied Easy in a much calmer voice. Her father sank back in his chair with a thankful expression on his face. "There was only one, and I saw him just for a second. Wait—there he is again." Raeker wished he could see the girl's face, but she was shouting her messages from one of the observing chambers and was well out of pickup range of the vision transmitter. "I can still see only one of them, and he's mostly hidden in the bushes—just his head and shoulders, if you can call them that, sticking up. He's coming closer now. He must see the 'scaphe, though I can't tell where he's looking, or what he's looking with. I'm not sure whether he's the same size, but he certainly is the same shape. I don't see how you'd ever tell them apart."

"It isn't easy," replied Raeker. "After a few years, you find there are differences in their scale and spine arrangements something like the differences in human faces. Maybe you can tell me what this one is wearing and carrying; that should be a lot easier to describe."

"All right. He has a sort of haversack slung over what would be his right hip if he had any hips; it's held by a strap running up around the other side of his body, over the arms on the left. The front of the sack has a knife hanging from it, and I think there's another on a sort of complex strap arrangement on the other side, but he's been working toward us at an angle and we haven't had a look at that side. He's carrying four spears that look just like the ones Nick and his people had, and the more I see of him the more he looks like them."

"Does he have an axe, or anything looking like one?" asked Raeker.

"If he has, it's hanging from his straps at the left rear, where we can't see it."

"Then I'm afraid you're going to have to make good on your claim that you can get on all right with Swift's people. Mine carry only two spears, and the search teams took their axes with them. If that were one of our searchers he'd have an axe in one of his left hands, almost certainly. That means we'll have to change our plans a bit; we were hoping our folks would find you first. That's just luck; I suppose this is some hunter of Swift's. They'd hardly have had time to get an organized search going, even if he decided to run one on his own."

"Isn't it going to be a long time before any of your search teams get back to the camp?" asked Easy after some seconds of thought.

"I'm afraid so; over a week of our time. Swift's answer should be back to Nick before then, though."

"I wish the time didn't stretch out so on this darned four-days-for-one world. Didn't I hear you say you'd learned a little of Swift's language during the time he had the robot at his caves?"

"We did. Not very much, though; it's extremely hard for a human being to pronounce. We recorded a lot of it; we can give you the sounds, and as much as we could get of the meaning, if you think it will be any help. It'll help time to pass, anyway."

Easy's face appeared in the screen, wearing an impish expression.

"I'm sure it will be very helpful. Won't it, Daddy?"

Even Rich was grinning. "It will, Daughter. She'll learn any language she can pronounce nearly as fast as you can give it to her, Doctor."

"Really? I've never heard her talk anything but English to her young friend there."

"What human being can pronounce Drommian? She understands it as well as I do, though."

"Well, I wouldn't bet very much that she could pronounce Tenebran, either. It's got some sort of pitch-inflected grammar, and a lot of the pitch is above human vocal range. Of course, she's young and female, but I'll bet she confines herself to understanding."

"You may be right. Hadn't we better get back to the matter in hand? What's that native doing now, Daughter?"

"He's walking around, thirty or forty yards from the 'scaphe, looking it over, I suppose. If he's seen us through the ports he hasn't shown any sign of it. He's still alone—I guess you're right, Dr. Raeker; I remember you sent your people out in pairs, and if anything had happened to one of a pair the other would surely report back to camp before going on with the search."

"I'm not sure you're right there, but I *am* certain it's one of Swift's people," replied Raeker. "Tell us when and if he does anything new."

"He is now. He's going out of sight the way he came. He definitely doesn't carry an axe; we've seen all sides of him now. He's getting hard to see; there's less of him visible above the bushes, and he's getting out of range of our lights. Now he's gone."

Raeker glanced at a clock, and did some rapid mental arithmetic. "It's about four hours to rainfall. Easy, did you say whether he was carrying a lighted torch, or fire in any form?"

"He definitely wasn't. He could have had matches, or flint and steel, or some such fire-making apparatus in his pouch, of course."

"Swift's people don't know about them. Nick's group makes fire by friction, with a bow-drill, but I'm sure the others haven't learned the trick yet. They certainly hadn't yesterday—that is, three or four ship's days ago. Anyway, the point I'm trying to get at is that if the one you saw had no fire, he was presumably within about four hours' march, or not too much more, of Swift's main group; and they'd almost have to be either at their caves or near the line between those caves and the point where Nick and the robot took to the river last night. He may be even closer, of course; you'd better keep your eyes open, and let us know immediately if the main body shows up. That would give us a still closer estimate."

"I understand. We'll look out for them," replied Easy. "While we're watching, how about getting out those language tapes you have? The sooner we start listening to them, the more good they'll probably do us."

Raeker agreed to this, and the next few hours passed without any particular incident. Nightfall, and then rainfall, arrived without any further sign of natives; and when the drops grew clear the children stopped expecting them. They ate, and slept, and spent most of their waking hours trying to absorb what little Raeker had gleaned of Swift's language. Easy did very well at this, though she was not quite the marvel her father had claimed.

A complication which no one had foreseen, though they certainly should have, manifested itself later in the evening. The bathyscaphe began to move again, as the river formed around it and increased in depth. The children were quite unable even to guess at the rate of motion, though they could see plants and other bits of landscape moving by in the glare of their lights; the speed was far too irregular. Even if they could have reported anything more precise than "sometimes a fast walk, sometimes a creep, and sometimes not at all," they were not even sure when the motion had started. They had had their attention drawn to it by an unusually hard bump, and when they had looked outside the few features visible were already unfamiliar. They might have been drifting a minute or half an hour.

Raeker took some comfort from the event, though Easy had been slightly disposed to tears at first.

"This gives us one more chance of getting our own people to you ahead of Swift's," he pointed out. "The cave men will have the job of hunting for you all over again, while we are getting you more closely located all the time."

"How is that?" asked Easy in a rather unsteady voice. "You didn't know where we were before we started moving, we don't know which way we're moving, how fast, or when we started. I'd say we know less than we did last night, except you can't know less than nothing."

"We don't *know*," granted Raeker, "but we can make a pretty intelligent guess. We judged that you were within a few hours' walk—say twenty-five or thirty miles—of the line between Swift's caves and our people's camp. We are about as sure as we can be without having actually mapped the entire area that this region is in the watershed of the ocean Nick's people found. Therefore, you are being carried toward that sea, and I'll be greatly surprised if you don't wind up floating on it, if not tonight at least in the next night or two. That means that Nick will only have to search along the coast on land if you don't reach the ocean tonight, or look offshore for lights if you do. I shouldn't think you'd go far out to sea; the river will lose its push very quickly after getting there, and there's no wind to speak of on Tenebra."

Easy had brightened visibly as he spoke. Aminadorneldo, also visible on the screen, had not made any change of expression detectable to the human watchers, but the girl had cast a glance or two his way and seemed to be satisfied with the effect of Raeker's words on him. Then a thought seemed to strike her, and she asked a rather pointed question.

"If we do get carried out on the sea, what do Nick's people or anyone else do about it?" she asked. "We'll be out of his reach, and out of Swift's reach, and you say there aren't any winds on this planet, though I don't see why."

"The pressure's so high that the atmosphere doesn't even come close to obeying the classical gas laws," replied Raeker—he was no physicist, but had had to answer the question quite a few times in the last decade and a half—"and the small percentage changes in temperature that do occur result in even smaller changes in volume, and therefore in density, and therefore in pressure. Little pressure difference means little wind. Even changing phase, from gas to liquid, makes so little change in density that the big raindrops just drift down like bubbles, in spite of the gravity."

"Thanks, I'll remember to make sense of that when I get back to school," said Easy. "You're probably right, but you haven't answered my question about how Nick was going to reach us if we went out to sea. Forgive me if I'm spoiling an attempt to change the subject."

Raeker laughed aloud, for the first time in some weeks.

"Good kid. No, I wasn't trying to change the subject; you just asked a question that every visitor for sixteen years has put to me, and I answer it without even thinking. You pushed a button. As far as your question goes, leave it to me. I'm going to talk to Nick first thing in the morning—he couldn't do anything right now."

"All right," said Easy. "If you're that sure, I won't worry. Now how will we be able to tell when we reach the sea?"

"You'll float, the way you did in the lake, at least when some of the water boils off in the morning. I shouldn't be surprised if you were carried off the bottom even at night when the river reaches the sea, but I'm not certain of it. I don't know how completely or how far down the water dilutes the acid. Keep an eye on the landscape, and if you start to drift up from it let us know."

"All right. That'll be easy."

But they were still on the bottom when the 'scaphe stopped moving. The human beings at both ends of the communication line had slept in the meantime, but there were still some hours before local daylight was due. Something had slowed the current so that it was no longer able to push the big shell along, and Raeker suspected that the children had reached the ocean, but he admitted there was no way to be certain until day. The intervening time was used up with language work again; there was nothing else to do.

Then the ship began to rise gently off the bottom. The motion was so gradual that it was a minute or two before either of the youngsters was positive it was taking place, and more than three hours passed before the bottom could no longer be seen. Even then they had not reached the surface, or the surface had not reached them, depending on one's viewpoint. It was definitely day by this time, however, and Raeker had lost practically all his doubt about the ship's location. The river had dried up much more quickly, the day before. He told Easy what he was going to do, suggested that she listen in, and then called Nick.

There was no immediate answer, and a glance around the screens showed that both Nick and Betsey were with the herd, half a mile away.

He sent the robot rolling toward them, meanwhile repeating his call in more penetrating tones. Both herders waved spears in token of understanding, and Nick began to trot toward the approaching machine. Raeker kept it coming, since he saw part of what he wanted at the foot of the hill.

Nick met him just before he reached it, and asked what had happened.

"I'll tell you in a few moments, Nick," he replied. "Could you go to the wagon and get a bucket, and then meet me at the pool down here?"

"Sure." Nick loped back up the hill. Raeker had not had the robot bring the bucket because of a long-established habit of not using the machine's moving parts, such as the handling equipment, more than could conveniently be helped.

The pool he had mentioned lay in the bottom of a circular hollow, as was usually the case. Also as usual, it filled only a small part of the hollow, representing all that was left when the nightly lake which did cover the spot boiled almost dry by day. He had assumed for years, on rather inadequate data but without any contradicting evidence so far, that the stuff was oleum—principally sulfuric acid with a heavy lacing of metal ions from the surrounding rocks which had been dissolved in the nightly rain, and an equilibrium amount of the atmospheric gases. He ran the robot through it to make sure of its depth—the slope of the rock sometimes changed rather abruptly at the "acid line," so judging by eye was insufficient—and then waited until Nick returned with the bucket.

"Is that thing tight, Nick? Will it hold liquid without leaking?" In reply, Nick pushed the leather container beneath the surface of the pool, drew it up brimming, and waited for the fluid on the outer surface to drain away. This happened quickly, since the "leather" was not wet by the oleum, and in a few seconds only a dozen or so hazily defined drops were clinging to the outer surface. Nick held the container up at the end of one arm for another minute or so, but nothing more fell.

"I guess it's tight, all right," he said at length. "Why is it important? We'll never have to carry this stuff very far; there are pools of it everywhere."

"I'm not interested in keeping it *in* the bucket, Nick. Empty it again." The student obeyed. "Now set the bucket right side up in the pool, and let go of it—no, don't fill it." The transmission delay made this warning a trifle late; Nick emptied what had gotten into the container and started over. "That's right—*on top* of the pool. Now let go of it." Nick obeyed. The weight of the strap that served as a handle promptly tipped it over, and three or four gallons of oleum poured in. This weighted the bottom sufficiently to bring the edge to the pool's surface, and there the bucket remained. Nick was startled; he had taken for granted that the thing would plummet to the bottom.

"I'm afraid I've been a trifle negligent with your education," remarked Raeker, "though I suppose the rather ambiguous nature of most of this planet's liquid gives me some sort of excuse for leaving out Archimedes' Principle. Try it again, Nick, and this time put a couple of stones in the bucket first."

As might have been expected anywhere on Tenebra except the actively orogenic regions, there were no loose stones in the neighborhood; but by packing the bottom third of the container with broken-off shrubbery, Nick contrived to achieve the spirit of the Teacher's order. This time the bucket floated almost upright, and with a good deal of freeboard.

"See how much more you can put in it before it sinks," said Raeker. Nick obeyed, without asking for the meaning of the new verb; it was clear enough from context. To his unconcealed astonishment, it proved possible to fill the bucket with the brittle growths without actually forcing it under, though a ripple half an inch high would have accomplished this end—a fact Raeker at once proceeded to demonstrate. At his order, Nick splashed vigorously in the pool with his feet; waves curled over the edge of the bucket, and it sank almost at once.

"Do you think it would be possible to make something on that general line, capable of keeping several people from sinking?" asked Raeker.

Nick wasn't sure. "Just on the face of things, I'd say yes," he replied, "but I don't really see why that works at all. If I knew, I could answer more sensibly. What use would it be if we had such a thing?"

Raeker took this opportunity to give a rapid explanation of Archimedes' Principle, plus an account of Easy's reports, mentioning the brief appearance of the cave scout and concluding with the probability that the bathyscaphe had reached the sea. Nick could see the rest of the situation for himself, and, characteristically, went a trifle overboard in his enthusiasm.

"I see!" he exclaimed. "The ship is in the ocean where no one can get at it, so you've showed us how to travel on the ocean itself. We could get out to the ship with this big bucket you want us to make, and pull the ship along with us to the other side, where Swift wouldn't bother us. It's a good idea. We'll start making the bucket as soon as the others come back—in fact, we can start collecting leather for it right now—"

"Hold up a minute, Nick. Crossing oceans, even oceans as small as Tenebra probably has, isn't something you do quite that casually. Also, there's another point to be considered. What if you were out in this— this bucket at night?"

Nick thought briefly. "Why couldn't we carry firewood and torches?"

"You could; but that's not the point. What happens to the ocean at night?"

"It comes up; but wouldn't the bucket go up with it?"

"I'm afraid not. In going up, the ocean decreases enormously in density, and I'm afraid that rather early in the evening you'd find it oozing over the side of your bucket—and you saw what happened just now when the same thing occurred here in front of us."

"Yes," admitted Nick thoughtfully. He was silent for a time. Then he became enthusiastic again. "Wait a minute. The bucket sinks because liquid gets into it, and it is no longer lighter than the liquid it displaces—right?"

"That's right."

"Suppose, then, that instead of a bucket we have a closed bag of air? If it's tied shut the sea can't get in, no matter how much it rises."

"But if the sea becomes no more dense than the air?"

"At least when the water boils out of the sea in the morning the bag will float once more."

"All that is true only if your bag doesn't leak at all. I'd rather you didn't risk your lives by staying at sea during the night, though your idea of bags rather than buckets is a good one. It would be smart to make a ship of many bags tied together, so that if some of them do leak you will still float."

"That's plain enough. But why shouldn't we stay out at night? What if night falls before we get the ship across the ocean?"

"You won't cross the ocean. You'll work on it during the daytime, and come ashore again at night."

"But how about Swift?"

"I'll take care of him. Don't you plan to keep the agreement we offered to make with him?"

Nick thought for a moment. "I suppose so, if he really agrees. If that was one of his scouts who found the ship last night, maybe he just decided to find it for himself."

"I still think that find was sheer chance. If it should turn out that you're right, we'll solve that one when we face it. Easy is willing to face Swift, she says. Right, young lady?"

"Certainly."

"Do you *like* Swift?" Nick asked her in some surprise. "I can't forget that he killed two of my friends."

"I've never met him," Easy pointed out. "I admit it was bad for him to attack your village that way, but probably he couldn't think of any other way to get what he wanted. If you're smart, Nick, I'll bet you could have him doing just what *you* want—and make him think it's his own idea all the time."

"I never heard of such a thing!" exclaimed Nick.

"Well, listen in if Swift finds us again," replied the girl, with a confident tone that surprised even her father. "You'll learn something."

Rich signed to Raeker to cut off his transmitter for a moment, and made a comment. "I hope that young squirt isn't getting too cocky. I admit she's giving Nick just what I've given her on and off all her life; I just hope she's up to it if the occasion arises. That Swift isn't human, or Drommian either!"

Raeker shrugged. "I'm hoping she won't have to try. In the meantime, I'd much rather have her confident than scared senseless."

"I suppose you're right." Rich looked at the screen, where his daughter's confident expression glowed as she enlarged on her theme to the surprised and still doubtful Nick. Raeker listened with amusement for a while, but finally suggested tactfully that she tell him something about boat-building; Nick knew even less about that than he did about diplomacy, and was more likely to need the information. Easy was perfectly willing to change the subject as long as she could keep talking.

Presently 'Mina, who had kept faithfully to his watchman's duties at one of the windows, called to her with the information that he thought he could see the surface. Easy broke off and left the control room hastily, calling back after a moment that her young friend seemed to be right. It was not until the upper observation windows of the bathyscaphe had actually emerged into the "air" that Raeker remembered something; he had missed an opportunity to check on the mysterious sea life originally reported by Nick. Aminadorneldo had made no mention of any such creatures during his last period of watch, but Raeker didn't know the young Drommian well enough to feel sure he'd have reported them without special instructions. This was obviously not the time to ask; Easy's eager tongue was busy with more up-to-date reports.

"We're farther out to sea than you thought we would be, Dr. Raeker," she called. "I can just barely see the shore, at the very limit of our hottest lights. I can't make out any details, really; but I think maybe there are some points, or maybe islands, sticking out our way."

"Can 'Mina see anything more?"

"He says not," came Easy's answer after a brief pause. "He doesn't seem to see quite as well as I do, anyway, I've noticed."

"I see. I suppose you can't tell whether you're moving or not."

"The ocean is perfectly smooth, and there aren't any waves around us. There's nothing to tell by. The only things to see are those big jellyfish things floating in the air. They're moving slowly in different directions, more of them toward shore than away from it, I think. Let me watch them for a minute." It was considerably more than a minute before she could make up her mind that the first impression had been right. Even then she admitted willingly enough that this was not evidence of the bathyscaphe's motion.

"All right," said Raeker when this had been settled. "Just keep an occasional eye on the ocean to make sure nothing happens, and give advice to Nick as long as he'll listen to you. He'll do what he and Betsey can about it, but that won't be much before the others get back. They'll probably be gone until tomorrow night, Tenebra time—between five and six days on your clock."

"All right, Doctor. We'll be fine. It's rather fun watching those flying jellyfish." Raeker opened his mike switch and settled back thoughtfully, and with some satisfaction. Everything seemed to be progressing properly; perhaps somewhat more slowly than he would have liked, but as rapidly as could reasonably be hoped. This feeling must have showed on his face, for his thoughts were read quite accurately.

"Pleased with yourself, I take it, Man!" The speaker did not need to introduce himself. Raeker endeavored to control both his features and his feelings, with questionable success.

"Not exactly, Councillor—"

"Why *not exactly?*" shrilled Aminadabarlee. "Why should you feel any remote sense of satisfaction? Have you accomplished anything at all?"

"I think so," Raeker answered in some surprise. "We know very nearly where your boy is, and we should have a rescue team out there in a week or ten days—"

"A week or ten days! And then you'll have to give the team members degrees in electrical engineering, and then hope the wiring of that ridiculous craft hasn't corroded beyond repair in the interval. How long do you think the actual *rescue* will take?"

"I'm afraid I couldn't hazard a guess," Raeker answered as mildly as he could. "As you point out so clearly, we don't know how much damage may have been done to wiring exposed by the inspection ports. I realize that it is hard to wait, but they've been getting on all right for a month now—"

"How stupid can even a human being get?" asked the Drommian of the world at large. "You were talking to the ground just now, and heard as clearly as I did the human child's remark that my son didn't see as well as she did."

"I heard it, but I'm afraid the significance escaped me," admitted the man.

"Drommian eyesight is as good and acute as that of human beings, if not better, and my son's has always been normal for his age. If he can't see as well as the human with him, something's wrong; and my guess is that the low oxygen concentration is affecting him. I gather your engineers made no particular provision for altering that factor of the vessel's environment."

"They probably didn't, since the crew was to be human," admitted Raeker. "I did not recognize the emergency, I must admit, Councillor;

I'll try to find means of speeding up the operation—for example, I can probably get pictures of the wiring exposed by the ports from the engineers, and have Nick briefed on what to look for while he's waiting for the others. My relief is due in half an hour; as a matter of fact, he'd probably be willing to come now if I called him. Have you been able to get medical advice from Dromm yet? I understand a human doctor arrived a few hours ago, and has been finding out what he can about the diet available on the bathyscaphe."

"Eta Cassiopeia is half a parsec farther from here, and I did not get a message off quite so quickly," admitted the Drommian. "One should be here shortly, however."

Raeker felt that he had made a smart move in forcing the nonhuman to make such an admission; unfortunately, admitting mistakes under pressure does not improve the temper of the average human being, and Aminadabarlee's race was quite human in this respect. He could not be insultingly superior for the moment; even his standards prevented that; but the required repression of choler was a good deal more dangerous to peace than his usual superciliousness. He retired to his own room—which the "incompetent" human engineers had at least set up with a decent atmosphere—and brooded darkly. There were many more message torpedoes.

With the Drommian gone, Raeker decided not to bring his relief on too early; but as soon as the fellow did show up, he made his way to the engineering section and outlined the proposal he had made on the spur of the moment to Aminadabarlee. Sakiiro and his colleagues agreed that it was worth trying, and they all settled down with their blueprints to decide what would be the best things to tell Nick and the easiest way to get the information across.

They spent some hours at this. Then Raeker went to eat, and back to his own room to sleep for a few hours. When he reappeared in the observation room, his relief rose gladly.

"Easy has something to report," he said, "but she wants to tell you personally." Raeker raised his eyebrows, dived into his station, and energized the microphone.

"I'm here, Easy," he said. "What's happened?"

"I thought I'd better tell you, since you're the one who said we'd stay put," the girl responded at once. "We've been drifting closer to shore for five or six hours now."

Raeker smiled. "Are you sure the shore isn't just getting closer to you?" he asked. "Remember, the sea level had a long way to go down even after you got to the surface."

"I'm quite sure. We've been able to keep our eyes on one piece of shore, and the sea has stayed right by it while we got closer. It has a feature which makes it easy to recognize, though we weren't able to make out very clearly just what the feature was until now."

"What is it?" asked Raeker, seeing that he was expected to.

Easy looked at him with the expression children reserve for adults who have made a bad mistake.

"It's a crowd of about fifty natives," she said.

# X. COMPREHENSION; CONSTRUCTION; INUNDATION

Nick, for the hundredth time, looked toward the ocean and fumed. He couldn't see it, of course; to be out of its reach by night the camp had had to be placed well out of its sight by day, but he knew it was there. He wanted to see it, though; not only to see it but to ride on it. To explore it. To map it. That last idea presented a problem which occupied his mind for some time before he dropped it. Fagin would know the answer; in the meantime there was a boat to be built. That was the real annoyance. Nothing, really, could be done about that until the search teams got back. While it didn't actually take all of his and Betsey's time to watch the herd and gather firewood, neither could do any very effective hunting with those jobs in the background; and the boat was very obviously going to take a lot of skins.

Nick wasn't sure just how many, and to his surprise Fagin had refused to offer even a guess. This was actually reasonable, since Raeker, who was not a physicist, was ignorant of the precise densities of Tenebra's oceans and atmosphere, the volume of the average leather sack which might be used in the proposed boat, and even the weight of his pupils. He had told Nick to find out for himself, a remark which he had made quite frequently during the process of educating his agents.

Even this, however, called for a little hunting, since it seemed a poor idea to sacrifice one of the herd to the experiment. Betsey was now scouring the surrounding valleys in the hope of finding something big enough to serve—the floaters of the vicinity had already learned to leave herd and herders alone, and those killed or grounded in the process had long since been disposed of by scavengers. Besides, their skins were much too frail to make good leather.

There was no serious doubt that Betsey would find a skin, of course, but Nick wished she'd be quicker about it. Patience was not one of his strong points, as even Easy had already noticed.

483

He was a little mollified when she came; she had brought not only the kill, but the skin already removed and scaled—a job which Nick didn't mind doing himself, but it was at least that much less time spent before the actual experiment. Betsey had kept in mind the purpose to which the skin was to be put, and had removed it with a minimum of cutting; but some work was still needed to make a reasonably liquid-tight sack. It took a while to prepare the glue, though not so long for it to dry—strictly speaking, the stuff didn't dry at all, but formed at once a reasonably tenacious bond between layers of materials such as leaves or skin. Eventually the thing was completed to their satisfaction and carried down to the pool where the bucket had floated a few hours before.

Nick tossed it in and was not in the least surprised to see that it, too, floated; that was not the point of the experiment. For that, he waded in himself and tried to climb onto the half-submerged sack.

The results didn't strike either Nick or Betsey as exactly funny, but when Raeker heard the story later he regretted deeply not having watched the experiment. Nick had a naturally good sense of balance, having spent his life on a high-gravity world where the ground underfoot was frequently quite unstable; but in matching reflexes with the bobbing sack of air he was badly outclassed. The thing refused to stay under him, no matter what ingenious patterns he devised for his eight limbs to enable them to control it. Time and again he splashed helplessly into the pool, which fortunately came only up to his middle. A ten-year-old trying to sit on a floating beach ball would have gone through similar antics.

It was some time before anything constructive came of the experiment, since each time Nick fell into the pool he became that much more annoyed and determined to succeed in the balancing act. Only after many tries did he pause and devote some really constructive thought to the problem. Then, since he was not particularly stupid and did have some understanding of the forces involved—Raeker felt he had not been a complete failure as a teacher—he finally developed a solution. At his instruction, Betsey waded into the pool to the other side of the sack and reached across it to hold hands with him. Then, carefully acting simultaneously, they eased the weight from their feet. They managed to keep close enough together to get all the members concerned off the bottom of the pool for a moment, but this unfortunately demonstrated rather clearly that the sack was not able to support both of them.

Getting their crests back into the air, they waded ashore, Nick bringing the bag with him. "I still don't know how many of these we're going to need, but it's obviously a lot," he remarked. "I suppose six of us will go, and two stay with the herd, the way the Teacher arranged it this time.

I guess the best we can do until the others get back is hunt and make more of these things."

"There's another problem," Betsey pointed out. "We're going to have quite a time doing whatever job it is Fagin wants done while trying to stand on one or more of these sacks. We'd better pay some attention to stability as well as support."

"That's true enough," Nick said. "Maybe now that we've done some experimenting, the Teacher will be willing to give us a little more information. If he doesn't, there's that other person whose voice he sends us— the one he says is in this ship we're to look for— By the way, Bets, I've had an idea. You know, he's been explaining lately about the way voices can be sent from one place to another by machines. Maybe Fagin isn't really with us at all; maybe that's just a machine that brings his voice to us. What do you think of that?"

"Interesting, and I suppose possible; but what difference does it make?"

"It's information; and Fagin himself always says that the more you know the better off you are. I suppose we don't really know this, but it's something worth keeping in mind until evidence comes in."

"Now that you've thought of it, maybe he'll tell us if we ask him," Betsey pointed out. "He usually answers questions, except when he thinks it's for the good of our education to work out the answers ourselves; and how could we check on this one experimentally—except by taking the Teacher apart?"

"That's a point. Right now, though, the really important thing is to get this boat designed and built. Let's stick to that question for a while; we can sneak the other one in when there's less chance of getting a lecture about letting our minds wander."

"All right." This conversation had brought them to the top of the hill where the robot was standing, among the belongings of the village. Here they reported in detail the results of their experiment. Fagin heard them through in silence.

"Good work," he said at the end. "You've learned something, if not everything. Your question about stability is a good one. I would suggest that you build a wooden frame—oh, about the size and structure of one wall of a hut, but lying on the ground. Then the sacks can be fastened to the corners; any time one corner gets lower than the others, the buoyant force on it will increase, so the whole thing ought to be fairly stable."

"But wood sinks. How can you make a boat out of it?"

"Just count it as part of the weight the sacks—let's call those floats, by the way—have to carry. You'll need even more floats, but don't let it worry you. I'd suggest that the two of you start the frame now; you might be able to finish it by yourselves, since there's plenty of wood. Then you can start fastening floats to it whenever you can get hold of any; you make a few kills defending the herd every day, so you should make some progress.

"While you're doing that, you might lend your minds to another problem. The bathyscaphe is not staying at sea, but is drifting toward the shore."

"But that's no problem; it *solves* our problems. We'll just have to travel south along the shore until we find it. You had already decided it must be south of us, you said."

"Quite true. The problem is the fact that Swift, with most of his tribe, seems to be standing on the shore waiting for it. Strictly speaking, Easy hasn't recognized Swift, partly because she can't tell one of you from another yet and partly because they aren't close enough, but it's hard to imagine who else it could be. This raises the question of whether Swift is accepting our offer, or proposes to keep the bathyscaphe and those in it for his own purposes. I suppose it's a little early to expect an answer from him; but if we don't get one some time today, I think we'll have to assume we're on our own and act accordingly."

"How?"

"That is the problem I suggest you attack right now. I suspect that whatever solution you reach, you'll find the boat will figure in it; so go ahead with it, as far as you can."

The Teacher fell silent, and his students fell to work. As Fagin had said, there was plenty of wood around, since the camp had not been there very long. Much of it, of course, was unsuitable for any sort of construction, having the brittleness of so many Tenebran plants; but a few varieties had branches or stems both long and reasonably springy, and the two were able to locate in an hour what they hoped would be enough of these. The actual cutting of them with their stone blades took rather longer, and binding them into a framework whose strength satisfied all concerned took longest of all. When completed, it was a rectangle of some fifteen by twenty feet, made of about three dozen rods of wood which an Earthman would probably have described as saplings, lashed at right angles to each other to form a reasonably solid grillwork. Thinking of it as a floor, neither Nick nor Betsey was particularly happy; the spaces were quite large enough to let their feet through, and the said feet were even less prehensile than those of a human being. They decided, however, that this was an inconvenience rather than a serious weakness, and shifted their attention to the problem of getting floats.

All this was reported to the Teacher, who approved. The approval was more casual than the two realized, for at the moment Raeker's attention was otherwise occupied. The bathyscaphe had now drifted within fifty yards of the shore and had there run aground, according to Easy. She had offered neither observation nor opinion as to the cause of the drift, and none of the scientists who had taken so many reels of data about the planet had been able to do any better. Easy herself did not seem bothered; she was now engaged in language practice across the narrow span of liquid that kept the bathyscaphe out of Swift's reach. Raeker lacked even the minor comfort of being able to hear the conversation. The microphones of the outside speakers were, somewhat sensibly, located by the observation ports, so that the girl had taken up her station where she would have to shout to be heard in the *Vindemiatrix*. She did not bother to shout; most of the time she didn't even think of Raeker or, to be embarrassingly frank, of her father. She had not been interested in the biology, geology, or the virtually nonexistent climatology of Tenebra; her interest in the rescue operation, while profound and personal, had reached the point where she could only wait for information which was always the same; but here were people, and people she could talk, to—at least, after a fashion. Therefore, she talked, and only occasionally could anyone above get her attention long enough to learn anything.

She did find out that Swift was one of those present on the nearby shore, and Raeker duly relayed this information to Nick; but when questions were asked such as whether Swift planned to follow the suggestion he must by now have received via Nick's ex-prisoner, or how he had been able to find the bathyscaphe so quickly, no satisfactory answer was forthcoming. Raeker couldn't decide whether the trouble was Easy's incomplete mastery of the language, her lack of interest in the questions themselves, or a deliberate vagueness on Swift's part. The whole situation was irritating to a man who had exercised fairly adequate control over affairs on Tenebra for some years past; at the moment a majority of his agents were out of contact, what might be called the forces of rebellion were operating freely, and the only human being on the planet was neglecting work for gossip. Of course, his viewpoint may have been slightly narrow.

Things looked up toward the middle of the Tenebran afternoon. Jim and Jane returned, long before they had been expected, to increase the strength of the shipbuilding crew. They reported unusually easy travel and high speed, so they had reached their first search area on the initial day's travel, examined it, and been able to cover the other and return in something like half the expected time. They had found nothing in their own areas. They had seen a light to the south, but judged that John and Nancy would cover it, and had decided to stick to their own itinerary and get the desired report in. It was quite impossible, of course, for them to read any expression from the robot, and Raeker managed to keep his feelings out of his voice, so they never suspected that their report was in any way unsatisfactory. For a short time, Raeker toyed with the thought of sending them out again to check the light; but then he reflected that in the first place John and Nancy would, as Jim said, have done so, and in the second place the 'scaphe had effectively been located, and he decided the pair were of more use getting leather. The lack of initiative they had displayed tended to support this conclusion. He spoke accordingly, and the two promptly took their spears up again and went hunting.

"One point may have struck you, Nick," Raeker said after they had gone.

"What is that, Teacher?"

"They saw the light to the south of their search area. That suggests strongly that the shore of this sea bends westward as it is followed south; and since the caves of Swift lie in the same direction, it is fairly likely that they are closer to the shore than we realized. This may account for Swift's finding the ship so quickly."

"It may," admitted Nick.

"You sound dubious. Where is the hole in the reasoning?"

"It's just that I hunted with Swift's people for a good many days, and covered a lot of territory around his caves in the process, without either encountering the sea myself or hearing it mentioned by any of his people. It seems hard to believe that the lights of your missing ship could be seen a hundred miles, and something like that would be necessary to reconcile both sets of facts."

"Hmph. That's a point I should have considered. That light may call for more investigation, after all. Well, we'll know more when John and Nancy come in."

"We should," agreed Nick. "Whether we actually will remains to be seen. I'm going to get back to fastening this float we've just glued onto the frame. I'm a lot surer that something constructive will come from that." He went off to do as he had said, and Raeker devoted himself to listening. Thinking seemed unprofitable at the moment.

With two more hunters, the raft progressed more rapidly than anyone had expected. The region of the new camp was not, of course, as badly hunted out as had been the neighborhood of the old village, and skins came in about as fast as they could be processed. Float after float was fastened in place, each corner being supplied in turn to keep the balance—Nick and Betsey were very careful about that. By the late afternoon so many had been attached that it was less a matter of keeping track of which corner came next than of finding a spot not already occupied—the frame was virtually paved with the things. No one attempted to calculate the result of its stability. If anyone thought of such a problem, he undoubtedly postponed it as something more easily determined empirically.

The work was not, of course, completely uninterrupted. People had to eat, there was the need to gather firewood for the night, and the herd to be guarded. This last, of course, frequently helped in the "shipyard" by providing leather without the need of hunting, but sometimes the fighting involved was less profitable. Several times the creatures attacking the herd were floaters, to everyone's surprise.

These creatures were reasonably intelligent, or at least learned rapidly as a rule to avoid dangerous situations. They were also rather slow-flying things—resembling, as Easy had said, the medusae of her home world in their manner of motion—so that after a fairly short time in any one spot, when a reasonable number of them had been killed, the survivors learned to leave the herd alone. Nick and his friends had believed this end accomplished for the present camp; but in the late afternoon no less than four of the creatures had to be faced by the herders in not much over an hour. The situation was both unusual and quite painful: while a competent spearsman could count surely enough on grounding such a creature, it was nearly impossible to do so without suffering from its tentacles, whose length and poisonous nature went far to offset their owner's slow flight.

The attention of all four members of the group was naturally drawn to this peculiar state of affairs, and even the work on the raft was suspended while the problem was discussed. It was natural enough that an occasional floater should drift into the area from elsewhere, but four in an hour was stretching coincidence. The group's crests scanned the heavens in an effort to find an explanation, but the gentle air current toward the southwest was still too feeble at this distance from the volcano even to be felt, much less seen. The sky of Tenebra during the daytime is much too featureless to permit easy detection of something like a slow, general movement of the floaters; and the individual movement of the creatures didn't help. Consequently, the existence of the wind was not discovered until rainfall.

By this time, the raft seemed to be done, in that it was hard to see where any more floats could be attached. No one knew, of course, how many people it would support; it was planned to carry it to the ocean when the others returned, and determine this by experiment.

When the evening fires were lighted, however, it was quickly seen that the rain was not coming straight down. It was the same phenomenon that John and Nancy had observed the night before, complicated by the lack of an obvious cause. After some discussion, Nick decided to light three extra fires on the northeast side of the usual defenses, compensating for the extra fuel consumption by letting an equal number on the opposite side of the outer ring burn out. A little later he let go even more on the southwest, since no drops at all came from that direction even after the convection currents of the camp were well established. He reported the matter to Fagin.

"I know," replied the Teacher. "The same thing is happening where the ship is down, according to Easy. The drops are slanting very noticeably inland. I wish she had some means of telling direction; we could find out whether the coast is actually sloping east where she is, or the rain actually moving in a slightly different direction. Either fact, if we know it, could be useful."

"I suppose she can't feel any wind?" asked Nick.

"Not inside the ship. Can you?"

"A little, now that the motion of the drops proves there must be some. I felt more around those fires I lighted when we getting away from the caves, but that's the only time. I think it's getting stronger, too."

"Let me know if you become more certain of that," replied Raeker. "We'll keep you informed of anything from the other end which may have a bearing on the phenomenon." Raeker's use of "we" was apt; the observation and communication rooms were filling with geologists, engineers, and other scientists. The news that Tenebra was putting on its first really mysterious act in a decade and a half had spread rapidly through the big ship, and hypotheses were flying thick and fast.

Easy was giving a fascinating, and fascinated, description of events around the bathyscaphe; for while she and her companion had by now seen plenty of the nightly rainfall, they were for the first time at a place where they could actually observe its effect on sea level. The shore was in sight, and the way the sea bulged up away from it as water joined the oleum was like nothing either child had ever seen. Looking downhill at the nearby shore was rather disconcerting; and it continued, for as the bathyscaphe rose with the rising sea level it was borne easily inland with the bulging surface. This continued until the density of the sea fell too low to float the ship; and even then an occasional bump intimated that its motion had not stopped entirely.

"I can't see anything more, Dad," Easy called at last. "We might as well stop reporting. I'm getting sleepy, anyway. You can wake us up if you need to."

"All right, Easy." Rich made the answer for Raeker and the other listeners. "There's nothing much going on at Nick's camp right now except the wind, and that seems more surprising than critical." The girl appeared briefly on the screen, smiled good night at them, and vanished; Aminadorneldo's narrow face followed, and that station had signed off for the night.

Attention naturally shifted to the observation room, where the surface of Tenebra could actually be seen. Nothing much was happening, however. The robot was standing as usual in the middle of the rather unbalanced fire circle, with the four natives spaced around it—not evenly, tonight; three of them were rather close together on the northeast side and the fourth paced a beat that covered the remaining three-quarters of the circle. It was easy to see the reason with a few minutes' observation; for every fire snuffed out on the single man's beat, a full dozen went on the northeast. Someone was continually having to lope forward with a torch to relight one or two of the outer guard flames on that side. Occasionally even an inner fire would be caught, as a second drop blew too soon through the space left unguarded by the effect of a first. There seemed no actual danger, however; none of the natives themselves had been overcome, and their manner betrayed no particular excitement.

While Raeker had been eating, his assistant had had one of the pupils pace off a course which he compared with the robot's length, and then by timing the passage of a raindrop along it clocked the wind at nearly two miles an hour, which as far as anyone knew was a record; the information was spread among the scientists, but none of them could either explain the phenomenon or venture a prediction of its likely effects. It was an off-duty crewman, relaxing for a few minutes at the door of the observation chamber, who asked a question on the latter subject.

"How far from the sea is that camp?" he queried.

"About two miles from the daytime coast line."

"How about the night one?"

"The sea reaches the valley just below that hill."

"Is that margin enough?"

"Certainly. The amount of rainfall doesn't vary from one year to the next. The ground moves, of course, but not without letting you know."

"Granting all that, what will this wind do to the shore line? With the sea not much denser than the air, the way it is late at night, I should think even this measly two-mile hurricane might make quite a difference." Raeker looked startled for a moment; then he glanced around at the others in the room. Their faces showed that this thought had not occurred to any of them, but that most—the ones, he noted, most entitled to opinions—felt there was something to it. So did Raeker himself, and the more he thought of it the more worried he became. His expression was perfectly plain to Rich, who had lost none of his acuteness in the last month of worry.

"Think you'd better move them back while there's time, Doctor?" he asked.

"I'm not sure. It isn't possible to move the whole camp with just the four of them, and I hate to leave any of their stuff to be washed away.

After all, they're fifty feet higher on that hill than the sea came before."

"Is fifty feet much, to that sea?"

"I don't know. I can't decide." The expression on Rich's face was hard to interpret; after all, he had spent his life in a profession where decisions were made whenever they had to be, with the consequences accepted as might be necessary.

"You'll have to do something, I should think," he said. "You'll lose everything if the sea gets them while they're there."

"Yes, but—"

"But nothing! Look there!" It was the same crewman who had raised the wind question who cut into the exchange. His eyes were fixed on the screen which looked seaward, and both Raeker and Rich knew what he had seen in the split second before they were looking for themselves. They were quite right.

Hours before they were normally due, the oily tongues of the sea were creeping into sight around the bases of the eastern hills. For perhaps a second no words were uttered; then Raeker proceeded to destroy the image the diplomat had been forming of him—that of a slow-thinking, rather impractical, indecisive "typical scientist." With the safety of project and pupils in obvious and immediate danger, he planned and spoke rapidly enough.

"Nick! All of you! Take one second to look east, then get to work. Make sure that all the written material, maps especially, is wrapped securely and fastened to the raft. Make them firm, but leave enough rope to fasten yourselves to it as well. You and the maps are top priority, and *don't forget it*. With those as safe as possible, do the best you can at securing your weapons to yourselves or the raft. Hop to it!"

A question floated back from Nick; the transmission lag made it uncertain whether or not he had availed himself of the proffered observation time.

"How about the cattle? Without them—" Raeker cut in without waiting for the end.

"Never mind the cattle! There's a big difference between what's nice to do and what's possible to do! Don't even think about anything else until you've taken care of yourselves, the maps, and your weapons!"

Nick's three companions had started to work without argument; the urgency in the Teacher's voice drove Nick himself to follow suit in silence, and a tense period of waiting ensued in the observation room. The distant watchers sat breathless as the work and the ocean raced each other—a race more deadly than any of them had ever seen run on an Earthly track.

Raeker noticed that the streams of oleum were much higher in the center than at the edges, rather like greatly magnified trickles of water on waxed paper, even though they still showed a fairly distinct surface; evidently the sea had already been heavily diluted by the rain. That meant there was no point in expecting the raft to float. Its air-filled sacks were nearly half as dense as the straight acid; with this diluted stuff their buoyancy would be negligible.

He was almost wrong, as it turned out. The sea oozed up around the hill, snuffing the fires almost at a single blow, and for an instant blurred the picture transmitted from the robot's eyes as it covered the camp. Then the screens cleared, and showed the limp figures of the four natives on a structure that just barely scraped what had now become the bottom of the ocean. It moved, but only a few inches at a time; and Raeker gloomily sent the robot following along.

# XI. Organization; Revelation; Declaration

Nights—Tenebran nights, that is—were hard on the Drommian, Aminadabarlee. They were even harder on any men who had dealings with him while they lasted. Seeing people engaged in work that had no direct bearing on the rescue of his son, and watching them for two Earthly days at a stretch, was hard for him to bear, even though he knew perfectly well that nothing could be done while the agents on the ground were immobilized or actually unconscious. This made no difference to his emotions; somebody, or everybody, should be doing *something*, his glands told him. He was rapidly, and quite unavoidably, coming to regard human beings as the most cold-blooded and uncooperative race in the galaxy. This was in spite of the skilled efforts of Rich, who had plenty to keep him professionally busy.

So far the great nonhuman had not descended to physical violence, but more than one man was carefully keeping out of his way. These were the ones least familiar with Drommians—so far. Raeker had noted that the number was increasing.

Raeker himself wasn't worrying; he wasn't the sort. Besides, he was occupied enough to keep his mind off Dromm and its impulsive natives. The robot, fortunately, had had no fighting to do, since nothing in the form of animal life had approached the raft and its helpless passengers, or had even been sighted by the carefully watching robot. This was a relief in one way, though Raeker was professionally disappointed. He had wanted to learn something of the creatures who were responsible for the loss of his students' herd a few nights before, and who could apparently live in a remarkably small oxygen concentration. Still, the four tied to the raft were fairly safe, though no one dared let them drift far from the robot; a constant watch was necessary.

As the night wore on, the vagrant currents which had been shifting raft and occupants became fewer, and so much weaker that they were no longer able to move the assembly, whose effective weight must have been only a few pounds. The man in control of the robot found it possible to leave the machine motionless for longer and longer periods; in fact, at one point Raeker almost went to sleep in the control chair. He was aroused from a doze by the shrill voice of the Drommian, however— "And Earthmen expect people to work with them!" in what even a man could recognize as a contemptuous tone—and did not repeat the slip. It didn't matter; the raft's passengers were drifting unharmed when day arrived. This period was the hardest, as far as standing guard was concerned; as the water began to boil back out of the sea, the latter's density increased, and the raft began to float. It was extremely fortunate that there were by then no currents at all; raft and passengers went straight up. Unfortunately, but somewhat naturally, it turned upside down as it went, so that for a couple of hours the robot operator had the annoyance of seeing the natives hanging from the underside of the floating platform while they very gradually led the surface of the ocean back toward the ground. They had drifted away from the hilltop during the night, and eventually wound up floating in a relatively small pool in one of the nearby hollows. When it finally became evident that the pool would shrink no farther, the robot had to take action.

Fortunately, the oleum was shallow—so shallow that the raft was supported more by the bodies under it than by its own buoyancy. Raeker guided the machine through the liquid, pushing the four unconscious natives ahead of it to the other side. The raft naturally came along, but eventually the rather untidy heap was dripping at the edge of the oleum pool, with the foundation members struggling gradually back to consciousness.

By this time the bathyscaphe was also out of the sea. Like the raft, it had wound up in a pool at the bottom of a valley; unlike it, there was no question of its floating. The pool was too shallow. As a result, Easy and her friend found themselves in their pressure-tight castle fully equipped with a moat, which effectively prevented Swift and his crew from reaching them.

For Swift was there. He turned up within an hour of the time the pool had finished shrinking, in spite of the considerable distance the bathyscaphe must have drifted during the night. It was out of sight of the sea, Easy reported; the wind that had been moving everything else inland had brought the ship along. It didn't bother her; she said that they were getting along splendidly with Swift, and didn't seem too worried when told about Nick's reverses of the night. Rich lost his temper for the first time when he learned that Raeker had carelessly told the child about the destruction of the camp, and didn't regain it until the girl's voice made it perfectly clear that the story hadn't affected her morale.

Raeker himself was thinking less about her than about his rescue operation, at the moment; that was why he had been so careless with his words. Nick and Betsey, Jim and Jane were all safe; the maps had remained attached to the raft, and so had most of the weapons. However, it was going to take a little while to find just where they were, short as the distance they had drifted probably was; and when they did find the camp site, it seemed rather unlikely that they would find much else. The herd would be gone, or nearly so; the wagon—who could tell? A similar period under an Earthly ocean would write it off completely, even in the off chance that it could be found. Here, there was no saying, but Raeker was not optimistic.

Finding the site of last night's fire proved easier than expected. The wind proved to be a clue, when it finally occurred to someone—Jim, rather to Raeker's surprise. He and Jane, of course, had bucked it all the way back from their search areas, though they had not attached any meaning to it at the time; now it served to restore the "sense of direction" which for Tenebrans as for humans was a compound of memory and the understanding of elementary natural phenomena. Once they knew the direction of the sea, there was no more trouble; there was no question that they had drifted pretty straight inland. The wagon and the remains of the watch fires were found in an hour. Raeker was really startled to find it and its contents intact; the mere fact that the two-mile hurricane had changed from gas to scarcely denser liquid had made no difference to most of the solid objects in its path.

"I think we can save a little time," he said at length, when the status of the group's belongings had been determined. "We can go back to the sea now, carrying the boat with us. We'll leave the cart, with a written message for the others; they can either follow us or start moving camp, depending on what seems best at the time they get back. We'll test out the boat, and search as far south along the coast as time permits today."

"What do you mean by that?" asked Nick. "Do we search until dark, or until there's only enough time to get back here before dark?"

"Until nearly dark," Raeker replied promptly. "We'll go south until we decide it's far enough, and then go straight inland from wherever we are so as to get away from the ocean in time."

"Then the others had better move camp no matter what time they get back, and head south with the cart. We're going to have a food problem, and so are they, with the herd gone."

"Gone? I thought I saw quite a few, with Jim and Jane rounding them up."

"That's true, they're not all gone; but they're down to where we can't afford to eat any until a few more hatch. We couldn't even find scales of the others, this time."

"You couldn't? And I didn't see any creatures traveling around while you were in the sea, either. It seems to me that your missing cattle are more likely to have strayed than been stolen."

"That may be, but they're gone in any case, as far as we're concerned. If all four of us are heading for the sea right away to test this boat, we won't be able to look for them."

Raeker thought rapidly. Loss of the herd would be a serious blow to his community; remote-control education cannot, by itself, transform a group of people from nomadic hunters into a settled and organized culture with leisure time for intellectual activity. Without the herd Raeker's pupils would have to spend virtually all their time finding food. Still, they would live; and unless Easy and her companion were collected pretty soon *they* probably wouldn't. The question really, then, was not whether any could be spared from the cattle-hunt but whether one or two or all would be more useful in testing the boat and, if the test were successful, subsequently searching for the bathyscaphe from it.

Certainly two people were less likely to sink the thing than four. On the other hand, four could presumably drive it faster—Raeker suddenly recalled that neither he nor Nick had given any thought to the method of propulsion the raft was to have. He supposed paddles or something of that nature would be about the only possible means; the thought of trying to teach Nick the art of sailing on a world where the winds were usually nonexistent and the nearest qualified teacher sixteen light years away seemed impractical. With muscle power as the drive agent, though, the more muscles the better.

"All of you will come to the sea. We'll consider the herd problem later. If the boat won't carry all of you, the extra ones can come back and hunt for cattle. This search is important."

"All right." Nick sounded more casual than he actually felt; all his life, as a result of Raeker's own teaching, he had felt that the safety of the herd was one of the most important considerations of all. If this search were still more so, it must really mean something to the Teacher; he wished he could feel that it meant as much to him. He didn't argue, but he wondered and worried.

The four of them were able to carry the boat easily enough, though bucking the wind made matters a little awkward—the wind was even stronger today, Nick decided. In a way, that was good; a last backward glance at the deserted remnants of the herd showed that a huge floater was being swept past them by the savage current and, in spite of all its efforts, could not beat its way back to the relatively helpless creatures. Nick pointed this out to his companions, and they all felt a little better.

The two miles to the sea were covered fairly rapidly, and no formalities were wasted in testing the boat. It was carried out into waist-deep oleum and set down, and the four promptly climbed aboard.

It supported them—just. The floats were completely submerged, and the framework virtually so. The difficulty was not one of keeping on the surface, but of keeping more or less level. The four were all of almost the same age, but they did differ slightly in weight. One side of the raft persisted in settling deeper whenever they stopped moving; each time this happened they all, naturally, made a scramble for the rising portion, and each time they inevitably overcontrolled so that the raft rocked and tipped precariously first one way and then the other. It took several minutes and much misdirected action and speech before they learned the trick; then they took longer still to learn the use of the paddles Fagin had told them how to make. The robot itself was not too much use; if it stayed ashore its operators couldn't see things on the raft very clearly, and it it crawled into the sea to any point near the vessel it couldn't make itself heard—the boundary between oleum and air was sharp enough to reflect sound waves pretty completely.

"Why do you have them looking at all?" Aminadabarlee asked acidly at this point. "The robot can travel along the shore as fast as they can paddle that ridiculous craft, and the bathyscaphe isn't at sea anyway. If you think those pupils are going to be of any use, why not have them *walk* with the machine?"

"Because, while all you say is true, the kids are inaccessible to the natives unless a boat is present. It doesn't seem likely that we'd save time by having Nick and his friends search on foot, and then have to go all the way back for the boat when they found the 'scaphe."

"I see," said the Drommian. Raeker cast a quick glance at him. The fellow was being unusually agreeable, all things considered; but the man had no time to ponder possible reasons. Nick and his companions were still too much in need of watching. He spoke over his shoulder, however, remembering Rich's injunction about being as courteous as possible to the big weasel. "There's one thing that might help a great deal, though. You've been talking to your son all along, just as Councilor Rich and I have been talking to Easy; do you suppose he'd be the better for something constructive to do down there?"

"What?"

"Well, if he's as good at picking up languages as Easy was supposed to be, maybe he'd do a better job than she at finding something out from the cave-dwellers. Swift quite obviously knows where both our camp and the bathyscaphe are; it would be most helpful if someone could worm a set of directions out of him for getting from the one to the other."

The Drommian's face was unreadable to Raeker, but his voice suggested what from him was high approval.

"That's the first sensible remark I've heard from a human being in the last five weeks," he said. "I'll explain to Aminadorneldo what to do. There's no point in expecting the human girl to do it herself, or to help him." The diplomat must be credited with what for him was the ultimate in tact, courtesy, and self-control—he had restrained himself from remarking that no human being could be expected to be helpful in a situation calling for intelligence.

He decided to go to the communication room in person, instead of working from Raeker's station—the relay system was efficient, but located in a corner which was rather inconvenient to him for anatomical reasons. Unfortunately, when he reached the other compartment it was even worse; the place was crowded with human beings. Rearing the front half of his long body upward he was able to see over them without any trouble, and discovered that the screen of the set tied in with the bathyscaphe was imaging the face of the human child. His own son was also visible, very much in the background, but only the human voice was audible—as usual, he reflected. The men were listening intently to her, and Aminadabarlee quite unthinkingly stopped to do the same before ordering the interfering creatures out of the way.

"No matter how we ask the question, we always get the same answer," she was saying. "At first, he seemed surprised that we didn't know; he's gotten over that now, but still says that Nick and Fagin told him where we were."

"No matter how often you say that, it sounds silly to me," retorted one of the scientists. "Are you sure it's not language trouble?"

"Perfectly sure." Easy showed no indignation, if she felt any at the question. "You wanted to know how he found us so easily, and that's what I asked him. He claims he was given the information he needed by Nick, who had it from the robot, and that's what I told you. I don't remember exactly what was said to that prisoner when Nick's people had him; but you'd better play back the transcript and see what you can get out of it. Either the prisoner himself was able to figure it out from what Nick said to him, or Swift was able to do it from the prisoner's repetition. The first seems to make more sense, to me."

There were few flies on Easy Rich. Aminadabarlee wouldn't have agreed with that, of course; her admission that she couldn't remember exactly what had been said in a conversation she had overheard lowered her considerably in his estimation. However, even he couldn't understand, any better than the listening scientists, what the cave-dwellers had been able to learn from a brief description of country they had admittedly never seen. Then an idea occurred to him, and he dropped back to the horizontal position for a few moments to think. This might really do some good; he almost felt guilty at the thought that he'd left all the serious planning in this matter to the human beings. If they'd only keep quiet for a minute or two and let him get his idea straight— But they didn't. They kept on calling excited remarks and questions to the child so far away.

"Wait a minute!" It was a geophysicist who suddenly came up with a point, Aminadabarlee thought, but he didn't pay enough attention to be really sure. "This may be a little far-fetched; but a lot of fairly primitive peoples on Earth and other places get pretty darned good climate predictors—our ancestors knew when spring was coming, you know, and built places like Stonehenge."

"What's the connection?" Several voices asked this question, though not all in the same words.

"This planet has no weather, in our sense of the word; but its geomorphology goes on at a time-rate which almost puts it in the climate class. I just remembered that Nick's prisoner was told that the bathyscaphe stayed on one lake, motionless, for several days, and only then started to drift down a river to the sea. If were right about Tenebran weather, *that must have been a brand-new river!* That information was enough for any native—at least for any one who hadn't been cut off from the history or folklore or whatever the Tenebran equivalent may be of his race. They may never have been right on the scene of that river, but it was close enough to their regular stamping grounds so they could tell where it must lie."

"I'm going to check the lab alcohol," commented one listener. The remark put the proponent of the new idea on his mettle.

"Easy!" he called. "You heard what I just suggested. Ask Swift if it's not true that he knows when things like new rivers and rising hills are going to happen. Ask him how he dares to live in caves in a cliff—which as far as any of us can see is apt to be knocked down by a quake any day!"

"All right," the girl said calmly. Her face vanished from the screen. Aminadabarlee was too furious to notice that she had gone. How dare these little monsters take his very own ideas right out of his mind, and claim them for their own? He hadn't quite worked out the details of his notion, but it was going to be the same as the one the human scientist had broached; he was sure of that. Of course, maybe it was a bit far-fetched—of course it was, now that he thought of it a little more carefully. The whole idea was the sheerest speculation, and it was a pity that the girl had been sent to waste time on it. He'd go in and show its weaknesses to his son, and suggest a more fruitful modification, as soon as he worked out its details—only then did he notice that Aminadorneldo had also disappeared from the view screen; he must have gone with the human girl. Well, that was all right; there was a little more thinking to be done, anyway. He kept at it for fifteen or twenty minutes, scarcely noticing the human conversation around him, until the children reappeared. They reported without preamble and without apparent excitement.

"You seem to be right," Easy said. "They seem surprised that anyone wouldn't know when a place was going to become active in quakes, or when a lake was going to spill, and in what direction. They know it so well themselves that they have a good deal of trouble telling me what they use for signs." The geophysicist and his colleagues looked at each other almost prayerfully.

"Don't let them stop trying!" the first one said earnestly. "Get down everything they say and relay it to us, whether you understand it or not. And we were going to use Raeker's students to learn the crustal dynamics of this planet!"

This irrelevance was the last straw, as far as Aminadabarlee was concerned. Without regard to rules of courtesy, either human or Drommian, he plowed into the communications room, his streamlined form dividing the human occupants as a ship divides water. He brought up in front of the screen and, looking past Easy's imaged face as though the girl were not there, he burst into an ear-hurting babble of his own language, directed at his son. None of the men interrupted; the creature's size and the ten-clawed limbs would have, given most of them ideas of caution even if they had known nothing of Drommians. As it was, Councillor Rich had spread some very impressive bits of information through the complement of the *Vindemiatrix,* so ideas weren't necessary.

The shrill sounds were punctuated by others from the speaker; apparently the son was trying to get an occasional word into the conversation. He failed, however; the older being's speech only stopped when he appeared to have run out of words to say. Then it was not Aminadorneldo who answered. It was Easy, and she answered in her own language, since even her vocal cords couldn't handle Drommian speech.

"We've already told him, sir. Dr. Raeker asked me to let you know when you showed up; you had just left his room when we got the information to him, and I didn't see you until just now. He's told Nick, and the boat should be as close as they can bring it on the sea well before night. They'll start to bring it inland then; Swift says they should be able to see our lights from the sea, so the robot has started back to the camp to meet the others and start them on the way here."

The Drommian seemed stunned, but remembered enough of his manners to shift languages.

"You had already asked Swift to tell the way from the camp to where you are?" he asked rather lamely.

"Oh, yes. 'Mina thought of it some time ago. I should have told Dr. Raeker or one of you sooner." The news that it had been his son's idea calmed Aminadabarlee considerably; privately, most of the men in the room wondered how much truth the girl was speaking. They knew the effective age of the young Drommian, and they were coming to know Easy.

"How long will it take to get to you—for Nick, that is?" asked Aminadabarlee.

"Swift thinks by mid-afternoon, on foot; he doesn't know how fast the boat goes, though."

"Did you tell him about the boat?"

"Of course. He was wondering how he could get over closer to the ship here; this pool we're in the middle of is too deep for his people to wade, and they don't seem to swim. I suggested floating over on a raft made of wood, but the wood on this crazy planet sinks, we found out."

"You seem to be getting in a lot of talk with those people. Are you really good at their language?"

"Pretty good, but we're still very slow. If there's anything you want to ask Swift, though, let's have it."

"No—nothing right now," said the Drommian hastily. "You didn't suggest that your friend Swift make a raft of the sort Nick has?"

"I did, but he can't do it. His people can get all the skins they'd need, of course, but they can't make tight enough—I was going to say air-tight—bags out of them. They don't know how to make the glue Nick used, and neither do I. He's waiting until Nick gets here with the boat."

"And then will take it away from him, of course."

"Oh, no. He has nothing against Nick. I've told him who Nick is—how the robot stole the eggs from the place where Swift's people leave them to hatch. I think he may be a little mad at the robot, but that's all right. I've said I'd teach him anything he wanted to know, and that Nick had learned a lot and would help. We're getting along very well." The Drommian was startled, and showed it

"Did Dr. Raeker suggest all this to you?"

"Oh, no; I thought of it myself—or rather, 'Mina and I did. It seemed smartest to be friends with these cave people; they *might* not be able to hurt the ship if they got mad at us, but we couldn't be sure."

"I see." Aminadabarlee was a trifle dazed. He ended the conversation casually and courteously—he had never used toward Easy the mannerisms which were so natural with him when he talked to other human beings—and started to make his way back to Raeker's observation room. The scientists were questioning the girl once more before he was out of the room.

He seemed to be fated to choose bad times to move, that day. He had been in the corridors when Easy had given the bathyscaphe's location to Raeker and Nick; he was in them when the four explorers who had discovered the volcano returned and made their report to their teacher. He had stopped to eat, as a matter of fact, and didn't get back to the observation room until the report was finished. By that time the four natives and the robot were heading south with the cart in tow, answering a ceaseless flood of questions from the scientists, some of whom had been content to use the relay system while others had come down to the observation room. The bewildered Drommian found the latter compartment almost as crowded as the communication room had been a while earlier, and it took him some time to get up to date from the questions and comments flying around.

"Maybe we could get the distance by triangulation. The wind at camp and 'scaphe must be blowing right toward it."

"But we don't know absolute directions at either place. Besides, the wind might be deflected by Coriolis action."

"Not much, on a world like Tenebra. You have it backward, though; the mountain is already on the maps. With a little more data we could use the wind direction to pin down the 'scaphe— That was what the Drommian heard as he came in; it confused him badly. A little later, when he had deduced the existence of the volcano, it made a little more sense; he could see how such a source of heat could set up currents even in Tenebra's brutally compressed envelope. By then it was another question that was perturbing him.

"How strong do you suppose the wind will get? If it brings the sea farther inland each night, and the sea carries the bathyscaphe with it, how close will those kids be carried to the volcano?"

"I don't think we need worry for quite a while. Wind or no wind, the sea that far inland will be mostly water, and won't float them very far. I'll bet if that thing keeps on, too, there won't even be liquid water within miles of it, by night or day."

"Liquid or gas, it might still move the ship. The difference in density isn't worth mentioning."

"The difference in viscosity is." Aminadabarlee heard no more of that one, either; it had given him something to worry about, and he was good at worrying. He started back to the communicating room at top speed, which for him was high; he didn't want anything else to happen while he was out of touch. He managed to reach his goal without hurting anyone, though there was a narrow escape or two as his long form flashed along the corridors.

The scientists had left Easy for the new attraction, and the bathyscaphe screen was blank for the moment. Aminadabarlee didn't pause to wonder whether the children were asleep or just talking to the cave-dwellers; also, he didn't stop to wonder whether the question he had in mind should be mentioned in their hearing or not. He would have berated Raeker soundly for such a thing; but this, of course, was different.

"Miss Rich! 'Mina!" he shrilled unceremoniously into the microphone. For a minute or so there was no answer, and he repeated the call with what another member of his race would have recognized as overtones of impatience. Few human beings would have caught any difference from his normal tones. This time Easy appeared on the screen rubbing sleep out of her eyes, a gesture which either meant nothing to him or which he chose to ignore.

"Where's my son?" he asked.

"Asleep." Easy would not normally have been so short.

"Well, you'll probably do. Did you hear that they've found out what caused the wind?"

"Yes; I gather it's a volcano. I went to sleep just after that. Has anyone come up with more news?"

"Not exactly news. It's occurred to some of those human fortune tellers that your ship may be blown a little closer to the volcano each night, until you're in serious trouble. What does your friend Swift think about that? He's supposed to be able to predict what his planet is going to do, and he seems to have been able to find you each morning so far."

"Well, we certainly can't get there for several days; we can't see the light from the volcano from here."

"You mean *you* can't; it's what the natives can see, and what they think, that counts. Have you asked Swift?"

"No. I didn't know about this until just now. Anyway, I am not worried; if they'd seen the light they'd have mentioned it—they'd have thought it was the robot. We can't possibly reach the volcano for several of Tenebra's days—certainly not by tomorrow."

"Who cares about just tomorrow? How you human beings ever achieved even the civilization you have is a mystery to me. Intelligent people plan ahead."

"Intelligent people don't usually jump to conclusions, either," snapped the girl, in the first display of temper she had shown since the accident. "I'm not worried beyond tomorrow, because by the end of that day we'll be away from here. Please tell Mr. Sakiiro to have the shuttle ready to meet us." She turned her back and walked—stalked, rather—out of the field of view; and Aminadabarlee was too startled even to resent the discourtesy.

# XII. CAPITULATION; OPERATION; ELEVATION

Easy was awake again by the time Nick reached the bathyscaphe. He had had no trouble finding it; the glow from its lights was quite visible from the coast. The wind was blowing straight toward the light, but Nick and his friends knew nothing of the volcano at the time and didn't have to worry about whether they were heading for the light. They came ashore, shouldered the raft, and headed for their beacon.

Fagin and the other four pupils had arrived before them; travel on foot was a good deal faster, even for the robot, than by the decidedly clumsy raft. Swift seemed to be in a very tolerant mood. He didn't actually greet the newcomers effusively, but he was talkative enough. He took for granted that they were *his* people—people who had gone a trifle astray, and didn't always know just how to behave, but who might be expected to grow up properly if given time. As long as they treated him as chief, it seemed likely that there would be no trouble.

Within a few minutes of the arrival of John, Nancy, Oliver, Dorothy, and the robot, he had demanded to be shown how to make a fire. Easy, with her two-second advantage in reaction time, told John to go ahead before Raeker even knew the order had been given. John, knowing that the person in the bathyscaphe was one of his teacher's race, obeyed without question. He took out his friction gear and had a blaze going in two or three minutes.

Swift then demanded to be shown how to work the device himself; and by the time Nick, Betsy, Jim, and Jane arrived with the raft the chief had succeeded in lighting his own fire and was in the highest of spirits.

This was more than could be said for anyone on the *Vindemiatrix*. Aminadabarlee was more than ever convinced that human beings were an ugly-tempered, uncooperative lot; and just now he had more than the usual reason for his opinion. Every human being in the ship was furious with the Drommian, taking their lead from Easy Rich. A night's sleep had not restored her usual sunny temper; she was indignant at the alien's insults of the evening before, and not only refused to explain to Aminadabarlee her justification for saying she would escape within a Tenebran day, but would say nothing more about it to anyone for fear he would hear. It was a childish reaction, of course; but then, Easy was a child, for all her adult speech and mannerisms. Her father had been asked to persuade her to talk; he had stared at her imaged face in the screen for a moment, but no word was spoken. Something must have passed between them, though, for after a moment he turned away and said, "Please have Mr. Sakiiro get the shuttle ready to meet the bathyscaphe. I understand it takes some time to install and adjust outside boosters." He promptly left the room, ignoring the questions hurled at him, and disappeared into his own quarters.

"What do we do?" The question was not in the least rhetorical; the geophysicist who put it was a close friend of the Rich family.

"What he says, I should think," answered another scientist. "Rich seems to be sure the kid knows what she's talking about."

"I know he's sure; but does *she?* He's her father; she's all the family he's had for ten years, and he's done a marvelous job of bringing her up, but he sometimes overestimates her. She convinced him, just then, that everything is all right; but I don't—*we* don't know. What do we do?"

"We do just what he asked," pointed out another. "Even if the kid's wrong, there's no harm in having the shuttle ready. Why is everything so shaken up?"

"Because we know what will happen to Easy and her father if she's wrong," replied the geophysicist. "If she's been speaking from her own knowledge, fine; but if that ten-legged weasel made her lose her temper and shoot her mouth off so as to justify her actions—" He shook his head grimly. "She believes her own words *now,* all right, and so does her father. If they're disappointed—well, the kids have stayed alive down there so far because of the self-control of the Rich family." He ended the discussion by cutting in another phone circuit and transmitting Rich's request to the engineers.

Raeker had been eating and, occasionally, sleeping in the observation room; he'd forgotten by now how long he had been there. The robot was rather out of things, but he could still watch. His pupils seemed to have been re-absorbed into Swift's tribe, and were being told what to do alternately by the chief himself and by Easy in the bathyscaphe. Nobody was asking Fagin what to do or how to do it, but in spite of this things were happening almost too fast for Raeker to keep track of them. He knew that Easy had had an argument with Aminadabarlee, though he wasn't clear as to the details; he had been told about her promise to be off the ground the next day, but had no more idea than anyone else how she expected to do it. He had had his share of Aminadabarlee's temper, for the Drommian had not by any means been silenced by Easy's flare-up, and had spent some time pointing out to Raeker the foolishness of separating his pupils from their own culture, and how much more would have been learned about Tenebra if contact had been made with Swift's people in the first place. Raeker had not actually been rude, but his answers had been rendered vague by his preoccupation with events on the ground, and he had thereby managed to offend the lutroid more than ever. He knew it, but couldn't bring himself to worry seriously about the prospect of severed relations between Sol and Dromm.

He knew in a general way what people were doing on the ground, but he couldn't understand all of it, and no one bothered to tell him. It never occurred to Raeker that this might have been at Easy's request; that she might be going to extremes to make sure that nothing like useful information got back to the *Vindemiatrix* and the being who had angered her so. He could only watch, photograph, record what conversation he could hear, and try to interpret what went on.

The raft was launched, and Nick and Betsey took Swift out on the surface of the pool to a point just outside one of the bathyscaphe's observation ports. Raeker could see the meeting between Tenebrans and the ship's two occupants, but could not hear their conversation—Easy was, of course, using the outside speakers, and the robot was too far away to hear these directly. The talk was long, and quite animated, for the gestures of all parties concerned could be seen—the port was large enough to let Raeker see fairly well into the 'scaphe even from the robot's vantage point. He tried to interpret the motions, but had no luck. Conversation did not end until nearly night; then the raft returned to the shore, and everyone began to pack up. A dozen cave-dwellers helped carry the raft, others helped pull the cart. For the first time, Swift paid attention to the robot; he ordered it to come along, using Nick as an interpreter. Raeker agreed briefly; the journey was obviously to escape the sea, which would presumably come at least as far inland tonight as it had before.

"Where will the big ship go tonight?" he asked, more to secure a demonstration of the cave people's abilities than because the answer made any difference to him. He rather expected Swift would not bother to answer, but the chief was in a very good humor—everything had been going just as he wanted it all day. Once the group was under way, he walked beside the robot and talked quite cheerfully. Nick relayed his words, and he described in great detail the country which they were approaching and the point to which he expected the bathyscaphe to be washed. He also explained his reasons for this opinion, and the geophysicists listened, took notes, and watched with motherly care the recorders which were storing the conversation. For the first hour or two of that night there was more general happiness than the region of Altair had experienced for decades. About the only people not sharing in it were Aminadabarlee and Raeker.

Swift stopped his cavalcade after a scant two hours of rather slow travel. Night had fallen, and the rain was starting to do likewise; he set everyone to work gathering firewood, and ordered Nick to place the guard fires for a camp. Nick and his fellows obeyed without argument; Raeker suspected that they were human enough to enjoy the chance to show off their knowledge. Cave-dwellers were at each of the fire sites practicing with friction drills, and one by one the piles of fuel began to glow.

For sixteen years, the lighting of the evening fires had been a signal for a forty-eight-hour period of relaxation on the *Vindemiatrix,* since nothing but rain ever happened at night on Tenebra. Now that was changed; discussion, sometimes verging on argument, went on full tilt. The engineers were busy festooning the outside of the shuttle with hydroferron boosters and their control lines. The diplomats wouldn't have been speaking to each other if they had followed their personal inclinations, but professional pride kept them outwardly courteous. People who knew them, however, listened to their talk very uneasily, and thought of jammed reactor control rods.

A few enthusiasts kept watch through the robot's eyes, partly in the hope that something would happen and partly to keep Raeker company. The biologist refused to leave the observation room; he felt sure that matters were building to some sort of climax, but couldn't guess just what sort. Even during the night this feeling grew worse—particularly at such times as he happened to see or hear one of the diplomats. Actually, Raeker was suffering badly from a sudden lack of self-confidence; he was wondering how he could possibly teach his students to make the necessary repairs on the bathyscaphe, even if they chose to listen to him. If they wouldn't, or couldn't he didn't want to see or hear of Rich or Aminadabarlee again; he had convinced himself, quite unjustly, that his own arguments had caused them to pin their faith in him and not undertake any other steps toward a rescue.

In spite of the anxiety which let him sleep only for moments at a time, he managed to get through the night. The departure of the shuttle distracted him. for a few minutes—at one point he almost convinced himself that he should go along with it, but common sense prevailed. Several times incidents occurred at the camp, and were pictured on the robot's screen, which would have made him laugh under different circumstances.

The cave-dwellers were not at all used to fires yet, and had some odd ideas of their properties, uses, and limitations. Several times Nick or one of the other human-educated natives had to make a rescue as someone ran blithely into the dead-air zone of a boiled-away raindrop to relight a fire. when they finally realized that a newly destroyed raindrop was like a newly boiled lake in the early morning, some of them took to waiting a long time before venturing near the extinguished fires, so that the fuel cooled too far to let the blaze spring back to life at the mere touch of a torch. Several of them grew worried about the fuel supply, which the experienced group had pronounced sufficient, and kept trying to persuade Swift to organize wood-collecting parties. Raeker could not, of course, understand these requests, but he heard a couple of his own people commenting on them with something like contempt in their voices. This made him feel somewhat better; if his pupils felt that way about the cave-dwellers, perhaps they still had some attachment for their teacher.

Morning finally came without any serious incident in camp or at the bathyscaphe; and once the hill on which the camp was located ceased to be an island—it had been surrounded by the usual rainfall, but not by ocean, as far as anyone could tell—the group headed for the spot where the bathyscaphe was expected to be. This meant a walk nearly as long as that of the previous night, since Swift and his people had expected little motion on the part of the stranded machine. Raeker didn't know whether Easy had reported any drifting; he hadn't heard her voice very often during the last forty-eight hours.

Raeker himself wasn't sure how far to believe the predictions of the natives, and wasn't sure how far he wanted to believe them. If they proved right, of course, it would mean a lot to the geophysicists; but it might also mean that Easy had some grounding for her optimism about the day's events. That was good only if it was *solid* grounding; and Raeker could not for the life of him imagine how the girl expected the machine to be either flown, blown, or carried up to a point where the shuttle could meet it. On the few occasions that he had dozed, his sleep had been troubled by wild nightmares involving volcanoes, floaters, and forms of sea life whose shapes never became quite clear.

There was no question of how the geophysicists felt when the predicted spot was reached and the bathyscaphe found to be absent. They buzzed like a swarm of bees, hurling hypotheses at each other with scarcely time to listen to their neighbors. Aminadabarlee fainted, and constituted an absorbing first aid problem for several minutes until he revived by himself, none of the men having the slightest idea of what to do for him. Fortunately, the ship turned up after a quarter of an hour's search exactly where it had been left the night before, which made things easier on the fathers but left many human beings and quite a few Tenebrites rather at a loss for an explanation. The sea had certainly been there; Easy had reported as much. Apparently its transporting power had been lower than expected. Some of the scientists pointed out that this was obvious; this much farther from its natural bed, the sea would be correspondingly more diluted with water. It satisfied him and some of his friends, but Raeker wondered how a slightly greater dilution of something which must already have been pretty pure $H_2O$, as pure water went on Tenebra, could make that much difference. He wondered what excuse Swift was using, but couldn't find out.

Nor could he find, except by guesswork, the nature of the plan that was being executed before the robot's eyes.

Hunting parties—judging from their armament—were sent out in great numbers, each one accompanied by one of Fagin's pupils with his axe. The raft made trips to the bathyscaphe, and Swift and several others examined its surface with great care; Easy seemed to be talking to them while this went on, but Raeker and his companions couldn't hear what she said. The natives were greatly interested in the hot area at the top of the vessel, where its refrigerators pumped back overboard the calories they had drawn from the living quarters; they started to climb up the hull, by means of the numerous handholds, to examine this more closely. This act, since the craft was circular in cross section and just barely not floating, started the whole vessel rolling toward the raft; the climbers dropped back hastily. One of them fell into the lake, lost consciousness before he could grasp the paddles thrust down to him, and had to be shoved clumsily into shallow oleum by his fellows lying on the raft above him. This brought the raft itself closer to the robot, and Raeker was able to hear Nick remark to Betsey, "This will save a lot of time. If the teachers inside don't mind, we can *roll* that thing over here where we can work on it."

"We may do it whether they mind or not, if Swift gets the idea," was the reply. "We'd better ask in English first."

"Right. Let's get back out there." The two slid the raft back into the pool and paddled back toward the stranded vessel. This time Raeker knew what the conversation was about even though he couldn't hear it, and he knew how it came out—he could see Easy nod her head in assent. It was several seconds before a frightening thought struck him, and made him call the engineering department.

"Will turning that bathyscaphe over do any harm?" he asked without preamble. "The natives are planning to roll it out of that pool."

The men at the other end exchanged glances, and then shrugged at each other.

"Not as far as I can think at the moment," one of them said. "The ship was designed to fly, and it was assumed that inverted flight might be necessary. The kids may be bumped around a bit, and anything they've left loose will tumble, but nothing vital should suffer."

"Thank goodness for that," Raeker said feelingly, and turned back to his screens. The raft was on its way back to shore, and Nick was calling something to Swift. Raeker could catch only a word or two, since the native language was being used, but he could tell easily enough what was being discussed. Swift got aboard as soon as the raft reached wading depth, loading it to capacity. Back at the bathyscaphe, he and Betsey seized the handholds on the hull and began carefully to climb, Nick staying on the raft to keep it out of the way. Raeker expected some more accidents, but the climbers showed surprising skill and coordination, keeping just above the liquid surface as the ship slowly rocked toward them. It was lucky that the handholds extended all over the hull; Raeker was sure they hadn't checked this point before starting their stunt.

A quarter turn brought the hot "exhaust area" into contact with the pool, and set the oleum bubbling furiously—or as close to bubbling as anything could come under Tenebra's atmospheric pressure. There was enough disturbance to attract the attention of the natives on the ship, but not to be visible from shore.

Two full rolls brought her to wading depth, and robbed her of enough buoyancy to make another climber necessary. Three turns brought her right side up at the shore line. A slight complication arose when the climbers dropped off and she started to roll back, and for the first time Raeker was able to make himself heard and listened to; he gave some rapid advice about placing chocks, which Nick heeded. With the hull stable and the children staring out at the robot a few yards away, Raeker thought he might learn what was going on, and he used the machine's speaker.

"Hello, Easy. We're finally together."

"Hello, Doctor. Yes, your people are here. I thought we'd be able to do without them, but they've been a big help. Are you staying to watch the rest?"

The question startled the biologist, to put it mildly.

"Staying? We're just starting to work. I'll call the engineers and have them listen in while I explain the electrolysis circuits to Nick and the others; they'd be here now, only I didn't expect the ship to be available quite so quickly. We'll find whatever wires are corroded or disconnected, and—" Easy must have started talking before he got that far, but the transmission lag delayed his hearing her interruption.

"I'm sorry, Doctor, but I'd rather not have Nick fooling with the ship's wiring. I don't understand it myself, and I don't see how he possibly can keep from making mistakes. We're going up shortly, anyway, so please don't let him get into any of those inspection ports, if they're really open." The girl spoke as pleasantly as ever, but there was a note of firmness which no human being who heard her could mistake. Raeker was surprised, and then indignant.

"What do you mean, you'd 'rather not' have Nick work? Who else can? If you think he's ignorant of electricity, what good will it do for you to take over—or Swift? This plan has been under way for weeks, and you can't—"

"I don't care how long it's been organized, and I can," replied the girl, still politely. "Swift will do what I ask, and Nick will do what Swift orders. We're going to try Swift's idea first; I'm sure it will work, but if it doesn't perhaps we'll think about yours again."

Raeker looked around helplessly; the kid was right. There was no way in the universe for him to enforce his will. Maybe her father—no; Rich was listening in the communication room, and the relay screen showed something like an expression of satisfaction on his face. The biologist surrendered.

"All right, Easy. Will you tell me what this plan of Swift's is? And how, if you don't trust me and Nick, you can possibly consider an ignorant savage like one of these cave-dwellers worth listening to?"

"Your scientific friends do," Easy replied pointedly. "If I tell you, 'Mina's father will hear, and he'll start thinking of things wrong with it, and that'll get Dad worried. You just watch; it won't be long now."

"How does your young friend feel about not telling his father?"

"He doesn't mind, do you, 'Mina?"

"No," piped the young Drommian. "Dad told me to do what Easy said, and besides, he was rude to her. We'll show him!"

Raeker raised his eyebrows at this, and somehow felt a little happier about the whole matter. If someone was going to make a fool of Aminadabarlee. . .

And then Swift's plan became perfectly obvious. A group of hunters reappeared, towing among them the helpless form of a floater. The dangerous tentacles of the creature had been removed—it was obvious now why an axeman had accompanied each group—and enough of its gas cells punctured so that it could be held down; but some were still intact, and their intended use could easily be seen.

The hydrogen cells of the bathyscaphe possessed, naturally, pressure-equalizing vents on the lower side of the hull. While these vents opened into the cells on the wrong side of the plastic membrane designed to prevent hydrogen and air from mixing, the other side also had a plastic tube extending down to the same vent, for relief if too much electrolytic hydrogen was run into the cell. This tube was normally held shut, or rather flat, by outside pressure; but it was perfectly possible to push another tube into it from outside, and run gas or liquid into the compartment. This the natives proceeded to do; Raeker wasn't sure of the nature of the tube, but there was nothing surprising in their being able to improvise one. There must have been a good deal of gas wasted in the transfer process, but this didn't seem to bother anyone. There were, after all, plenty of floaters.

"I see," he said through the robot after a few minutes. "But I think I see a catch."

"What?" Easy snapped the question with a speed which suggested she had some doubts of her own.

"That ship was computed around the lift of hydrogen. How do you know that stuff you're using will lift you high enough for your boosters to work, even if an engineer gets aboard to—"

"What makes you think this gas isn't hydrogen?"

"What makes you think it is?"

"What else is lighter than water, in the gas state, that's likely to be found on this planet?"

"Why, lots of things, I guess—I—I don't know; I hadn't thought of that." Realization struck him. "You've been talking to the engineers!"

"Of course. I don't mean to be rude, but where else could I learn anything useful about this ship? I'll admit you know the planet, but that wasn't enough."

"I see," said Raeker slowly. "I hadn't thought as much as I should about the machine; but I did ask the engineers about its wiring—and say! Won't you need that anyway? What are you going to do when they get enough gas into your cells to lift the ship out of their reach, but not enough to get you any higher? Hadn't you better have them tie the ship down, at least? You'd better wait until we—"

He was interrupted by laughter. It didn't come from Easy, who had looked impressed for a moment, but from the scientists in the observation chamber. Raeker realized that they were laughing at him, and for a moment was furious; then he realized he had asked for it. He put the best face he could on the matter while one of them carefully explained a little elementary physics.

And that, really, was all. Nick put to use the knowledge he had picked up in balancing on the experimental float, and made sure there were always more forward cells full than after ones. When the ship lifted, it naturally rode the wind toward the volcano; and it rose so slowly at first that the children had a good look at the terrifying sight. They dipped frighteningly toward the glowing mountain as it entered warmer air, but recovered in ample time as the hydrogen in its cells also warmed up. Gradually the glow faded out below them, and Easy and her friend waited happily to meet the shuttle.

# Epilogue: Cooperation

"I told you human beings were helpless and useless." Happy as he was, Aminadabarlee gave up his ideas with difficulty. "You spend weeks trying to rig a rescue, and then are outsmarted by a savage with less education than either of these children. You spend a decade or two training agents of your own on the planet, and learn more useful facts in a week from natives you never bothered to contact directly."

"Natives who would have tried to eat the robot if any such attempt had been made," Easy pointed out. "Remember, 'Mina and I know Swift. He respected the robot because it could talk and tell him things. He'd have ignored it or destroyed it otherwise."

Aminadabarlee's eyes sought his son, who made a gesture of agreement. "Well, anyway, the natives with their own culture are a lot more use, and I'll prove it soon enough."

"How?" asked Raeker.

"I'll have a Drommian project here in three months. We can talk to Swift as well as you, and we'll see who learns more about geophysics in general and Tenebra in particular after that."

"Wouldn't it be more profitable to run the projects jointly, and exchange information?"

"You'd certainly have to say that," sneered the nonhuman. "I've had enough of cooperation with human beings, and so has the rest of Dromm, if my opinion's good for anything. You learned Swift's language, didn't you, son?"

"Yes, Dad, but—"

"Never mind the but. I know you like Easy, and I suppose she's a little less poisonous than most human beings after the time she spent with you, but I know what I'm talking about. Here—use the robot voice—and call Swift over to it; you can say something to him for me."

"But I can't, Dad." Even the human beings could see that the youngster was uncomfortable.

"Can't? What do you mean? You just said you'd learned enough of their language—"

"Oh, I understand it well enough. I just can't speak it."

"You mean you just listened, and let that human girl do all the talking? I'm ashamed of you. You know perfectly well that no chance to learn the use of a new language should ever be missed."

"I didn't miss it, Dad." Aminadabarlee seemed to swell slightly.

"Then, in the name of both suns, tell me what you did do!" His voice came closer to a roar than anyone in the room had ever heard from him. Aminadorneldo looked a little helplessly at Easy.

"All right, 'Mina," the girl said. "We'll show him."

The two took their places before the microphone, which Easy snapped on. Then, keeping their eyes fixed on each other, they began to speak in unison. The sounds they produced were weird; sometimes both were together, sometimes the Drommian carried a high note alone, sometimes Easy took the deeper registers. A similar sound, which Raeker recognized perfectly well and understood slightly, came from the speaker; Easy started an answer, using her hands to guide her "little" companion on what words were coming next. They had apparently worked out a fairly satisfactory deaf-mute code between them; and while they spoke much more slowly than Swift, they were obviously perfectly clear to the native.

"He's here, Councillor," Easy remarked after a moment. "What did you want to say to him? This particular translating team is ready to go to work. I do hope you'll forgive 'Mina for cooperating with a human being. There really wasn't any other way, you know."

Nobody laughed.

# The New England
# Science Fiction Association (NESFA)
# and NESFA Press

## Recent books from NESFA Press:

Find details and many more books on our web page: www.nesfa.org/press

Books may be ordered by writing to:
NESFA Press
PO Box 809
Framingham, MA 01701

We accept checks, Visa, or MasterCard. Please add $2 postage and handling per order.

## The New England Science Fiction Association:

NESFA is an all-volunteer, non-profit organization of science fiction and fantasy fans. Besides publishing, our activities include running Boskone (New England's oldest SF convention) in February each year, producing a semi-monthly newsletter, holding discussion groups relating to the field, and hosting a variety of social events. If you are interested in learning more about us, we'd like to hear from you. Write to our address above!

# Acknowledgments

Suford Lewis, Deb Geisler and Lisa Hertel for consultations in selecting the dustjacket art and designing the dustjacket, and Lisa Hertel for the final design.

Rick Katze for help in scanning.

George Flynn for his usual able and quick job of proofreading. Suford Lewis for yet more proofreading.

This book was typeset in Adobe Garamond using Adobe Pagemaker and printed by BookCrafters of Ann Arbor, Michigan on acid-free paper.

— Mark Olson and Tony Lewis
December, 1998